Chariots in Antiquity

Essays in Honour of Joost Crouwel

Edited by
Peter Raulwing, Stefan Burmeister,
Gail Brownrigg, and Katheryn M. Linduff

BAR INTERNATIONAL SERIES 3159 | 2023

BAR
PUBLISHING

Published in 2023 by
BAR Publishing, Oxford, UK

BAR International Series 3159

Chariots in Antiquity

ISBN 978 1 4073 6117 8   paperback
ISBN 978 1 4073 6118 5   e-format

DOI https://doi.org/10.30861/9781407361178

A catalogue record for this book is available from the British Library

© the editors and contributors severally 2023

COVER IMAGE *'Schematic drawing of the harnessed chariot on the painted box of Tut'ankhamūn (after Mary A. Littauer and Joost H. Crouwel, Chariots and Related Equipment from the Tomb of Tut'ankhamūn. Tut'ankhamūn Tomb Series 8. Oxford: Griffith Institute, 1985, Figure 2; with permission of Joost H. Crouwel).'*

The Authors' moral rights under the 1988 UK Copyright, Designs and Patents Act are hereby expressly asserted.

All rights reserved. No part of this work may be copied, reproduced, stored, sold, distributed, scanned, saved in any form of digital format or transmitted in any form digitally, without the written permission of the Publisher.

Links to third party websites are provided by BAR Publishing in good faith and for information only. BAR Publishing disclaims any responsibility for the materials contained in any third-party website referenced in this work.

BAR titles are available from:

BAR Publishing
122 Banbury Rd, Oxford, OX2 7BP, UK
info@barpublishing.com
www.barpublishing.com

Of Related Interest

Equids and Wheeled Vehicles in the Ancient World
Essays in Memory of Mary A. Littauer
Edited by Peter Raulwing, Katheryn M. Linduff and Joost H. Crouwel
BAR International Series **2923** | 2019

Chariots in Early China
Origins, cultural interaction, and identity
Hsiao-yun Wu
BAR International Series **2457** | 2013

Iron Age Chariot Burials in Britain and the Near Continent
Networks of mobility, exchange and belief in the third and second centuries BC
Greta Anthoons
BAR British Series **666** | 2021

Die Wagenbestattungen der späten Hallstattzeit und der Latènezeit im Gebiet westlich des Rheins
Dorothea van Endert
BAR International Series **355** | 1987

Horses and Humans: The Evolution of Human-Equine Relationships
Edited by Sandra L. Olsen, Susan Grant, Alice M. Choyke, and László Bartosiewicz
BAR International Series **1560** | 2006

Die Funktion und Bedeutung der Reiter-und Pferdeführerdarstellungen auf attischen Grab- und Weihreliefs des 5. und 4. Jhs. v. Chr.
Angelos Tillios
BAR International Series **2137** | 2010

The Divine Rider in the Art of the Western Roman Empire
Marjorie Mackintosh
BAR International Series **607** | 1995

The Role of the Religious Sector in the Economy of Late Bronze Age Mycenaean Greece
Susan M. Lupack
BAR International / British Series **1858** | 2008

For more information, or to purchase these titles, please visit **www.barpublishing.com**

Joost H. Crouwel

Professor Emeritus
University of Amsterdam
Amsterdam Archaeological Centre

Contents

Part I

1. Introduction 3
   Editors

2. Joost H. Crouwel as a Teacher 11
   Tess Doorewaard

3. In Search of the Origins of the Chariot: Wrong Turns, Dead Ends, and Long and Winding Roads 15
   Stefan Burmeister and Peter Raulwing

4. Research on Chariots in Slavic Studies: A Brief Overview 47
   Elena Izbitser

Part II
Egypt, Near East, the Balkans, the Steppes, China in the 2nd millenium BCE and later developments

5. Leather: An Integral Part of Chariots 61
   André J. Veldmeijer and Salima Ikram

6. 'They Shall Henceforth Be Fed in my Presence': Observations on the Training and Treatment of Chariot Horses in Ancient Egypt 67
   Miriam A. Bibby

7. The Egyptian 'Check Rowel' – A New Interpretation of its Purpose 83
   Gail Brownrigg

8. Another Storm God 'Jumping' on his Vehicle? Remarks on the Sketch on KUB 20.76 89
   Theo van den Hout

9. Bone Cheekpieces and Spoked Wheels – Chariots in the Carpathian Region 103
   Nikolaus G. O. Boroffka

10. Archaeological Evidence for the Horse-Drawn Chariot from Inner Eurasia 125
    Igor V. Chechushkov and Andrey V. Epimakhov

11. Early Cheekpieces in Eurasia 151
    Vadim S. Bochkarev and Pavel F. Kuznetsov

12. Chariots on the Central Asian Rocks: The Dating Problem 179
    Viktor Novozhenov

13. When Chariots Were First Known in China: Early Cheekpiece Development in the Late Shang Dynasty Around 1250 BCE 199
    Hsiao-yun Wu

14. Early Chinese Chariots, Carriages, and Carts in War and Peace: Evidence from New Textual and Archaeological Sources 215
    Robin D. S. Yates

15. Majiayuan Chariots and the Lustre of Eurasia 231
    Xiaolong Wu and Katheryn M. Linduff

Part III
Chariot Findings, Chariots in Action, Their Construction, and Experimental Archaeology

16. The Ancient V-spoked Chariot Wheel: Why was It Made that Way? Some Thoughts Based on Some Observations and the Experience of Making Chariot Reconstructions 245
Robert Hurford

17. Jean Spruytte – Horseman, Scholar, Chariot Builder 255
Gail Brownrigg

18. Some Observations on Chariotry and Chariot Warfare in the Near Eastern Late Bronze Age and the Battle of Kadesh 273
Steven Weingartner

Index 313

Part I

1

Introduction

Peter Raulwing
Stefan Burmeister
Gail Brownrigg
Katheryn M. Linduff

This volume of essays has been assembled to honour our esteemed colleague Joost Crouwel, emeritus professor of Aegean Archaeology at the University of Amsterdam. Since the 1970s, Joost has been a leading expert on wheeled transport in antiquity. He has published extensively, often in collaboration with the late Mary Aiken Littauer (1912–2005), on chariots and other vehicles, riding and harnessing in the Near East, Egypt, Cyprus, Greece and Italy. He was also instigator and director of a long-term field project at Geraki in Laconia (Greece) and is an authority on Mycenaean pictorial pottery.

Having just earned a degree in classical archaeology from the University of Amsterdam and beginning his doctoral thesis on chariots and other means of land transport in Bronze Age Greece under Hector Catling (1924–2013) in Oxford, he was introduced to Mary Littauer in 1969 – a meeting which led to a fruitful collaboration lasting three decades. Not long ago Joost summarised his collaboration with her:[1]

> In 1968, at the mature age of 56, Mary published her first scholarly paper "The function of the yoke saddle in ancient harnessing", which appeared in the widely read British journal *Antiquity*.[2] I read this article and was struck by its unusual, common-sense approach and her ideas on "how things actually worked". At that time I was in Oxford, where I was writing my doctoral dissertation on early chariots in Greece. I had gone there after finishing my university studies in Classical Archaeology at the University of Amsterdam, The Netherlands. It was in Oxford in the spring of 1969 that she and I were introduced to each other. This meeting marked the beginning of our close collaboration on ancient chariots, other vehicles, riding and horse equipment, which lasted for over 30 years. Together we wrote two books: *Wheeled Vehicles and Ridden Animals in the Ancient Near East* (1979)[3] and *Chariots and Related Equipment from the Tomb of Tutʿankhamūn* (1985).[4] We also published many articles, a selection of which was prepared by Peter Raulwing for another book: *Selected Writings on Chariots and Other Early Vehicles, Riding and Harness* (2002).[5] Our last joint paper was published in 2001—Mary was then 89.[6]

Of particular note are Joost's masterly studies of chariots and other wheeled vehicles in Bronze Age Greece (his PhD thesis),[7] Iron Age Greece,[8] and Italy Before the Roman Empire.[9] Joost's friend, the late Jaap Morel, prepared the detailed line drawings which enhanced these books with great skill and patience. Joost is now embarking on a companion volume focussing on the Roman Imperial period.

Joost's interests range far more widely than the vehicles themselves to include the horses that drew them, their harness and equipment, the people who rode in them, the societies to which they belonged, even the environment in which they were used. This volume celebrates his contributions in the field of early vehicles and their equipment

---

[1] Joost H. Crouwel, "Mary Aiken Littauer and Our Study of Ancient Horse–Drawn Vehicles." In: *Equids and Wheeled Vehicles in the Ancient World. Essays in Memory of Mary A. Littauer*, edited by Peter Raulwing, Katheryn M. Linduff and Joost H. Crouwel, 3–4. BAR International Series 2923. Oxford: BAR Publishing, 2019.
[2] Mary Aiken Littauer, "The Function of the Yoke Saddle in Ancient Harnessing," Antiquity 42 (1968): 27–31, reprinted in: Mary A. Littauer and Joost H. Crouwel, *Selected Writings on Chariots and Other Early Vehicles, Riding and Harness*, edited by Peter Raulwing, 479–484. Culture and History of the Ancient Near East 6. Leiden: Brill, 2002.
[3] Mary A. Littauer and Joost H. Crouwel, *Wheeled Vehicles and Ridden Animals in the Ancient Near East*. Handbuch der Orientalistik, 7. Abteilung, I. Band, 2. Abschnitt, Lieferung 1. Leiden and Cologne: Brill, 1979. Now out of print: See e-book Brill, Leiden 2022. https://brill.com/display/title/169?language=en.
[4] Mary A. Littauer and Joost H. Crouwel, *Chariots and Related Equipment from the Tomb of Tutʿankhamūn*. Tutʿankhamūn's Tomb Series 8. Oxford: Griffith Institute, 1985.
[5] See n. 2 above. *Selected Writings on Chariots and Other Early Vehicles, Riding and Harness* also contains a full bibliography in this field up to 2002.
[6] Mary A. Littauer and Joost H. Crouwel, "The Earliest Evidence for Metal Bridle Bits," *Oxford Journal of Archaeology* 20 (2001): 329–238.
[7] Joost H. Crouwel, *Chariots and Other Means of Land Transport in Bronze Age Greece*. Allard Pierson Series 3. Amsterdam: Allard Pierson, 1981.
[8] Joost H. Crouwel, *Chariots and Other Means of Land Transport in Iron Age Greece*. Allard Pierson Series 9. Amsterdam: Allard Pierson, 1992.
[9] Joost H. Crouwel, *Chariots and Other Wheeled Vehicle in Italy Before the Roman Empire*. Oxford: Oxbow, 2012.

by including essays that reflect his inspiration on the work of others and on the field at large. The topics addressed in the chapters are as diverse as the authors themselves, representing many areas of expertise: a museum curator from Taiwan, a former student, art historians, archaeologists and university professors from Russia, Ukraine, Germany, Kazakhstan, Canada and the USA, a master wheelwright, a horse expert from the UK, the director of an archaeological visitor centre from Germany. Such a combination of essays makes an innovative and wide-ranging contribution to research across a wide spectrum of interests and areas of the world. As a result, they differ in style, content and presentation, but most are centred around the expansion and influence of the chariot – defined by Joost Crouwel and Mary Littauer as "a light, fast, usually horse-drawn vehicle with two spoked wheels, used for warfare, hunting, racing and ceremonial purposes. Its crew usually stood."[10]

After this introduction, **Part I** of this volume continues with recollections from a former student of Joost's, Tess Doorewaard (**Chapter 2**), in which she describes the careful and attentive nature of his teaching. Always willing to give help and advice and constructive criticism to others, he has always sought clarity of expression and the correct use of terminology. His enthusiasm and keen interest in the ideas of others will be evident in this volume in the development of ideas, research, and practical experiments across the field.

In **Chapter 3** Stefan Burmeister and Peter Raulwing provide "In Search of the Origins of the Chariot: Wrong Turns, Dead Ends, and Long and Winding Roads". Studies on horses and chariots in antiquity cover a wide range of topics which have established a broad, independent field of research, although recognised as a contributing part of several academic disciplines. Of special interest is so-called chariotry research, i.e., investigations into a special type of chariot defined as a light, fast, two-wheeled vehicle with two spoked wheels, usually horse-drawn, used for warfare, hunting, racing and ceremonial purposes that has been used since the early second millennium BCE and is documented in various types of sources: archaeological remains, written evidence and images. From today's perspective, chariotry research is an amalgam of several interdisciplinary research areas: including, among others, archaeological disciplines, prehistory, philological disciplines, linguistics, ancient history, comparative religious studies, Old Testament studies, the history of technology, archaeozoology, paleobotany, metallurgy and the history of scholarship. Those considered in this overview are: Near Eastern Archeology and Philology (with its specialised disciplines of Sumerology, Assyriology, Hittitology (and others), Egyptology, Historical-Comparative Linguistics (Indo-European Studies), Eurasian Archaeology, Sinology, Indology (Vedic Studies), Mycenaean Studies, Old Testament Studies, experimental archaeology and others. The focus of this contribution lies in the methodologically problematic amalgamation of speakers of Indo-European languages, their proposed "homeland" and the question of the starting point of the so-called "classic" chariot. At present, the authors advise researchers to restrict themselves to investigation of the horse-and-chariot evidence in their respective find contexts and not to overload the discussion with the question of the origin of the classical chariot. This question, as well as the contribution of speakers of individual Indo-European languages to its development and spread, cannot be answered at present.

Chapter 4 by Elena Izbitser examines "Chariots in Slavic Studies". The discovery of the remains of actual chariots in burials of the Late Bronze Age in the Trans-Ural region and the establishment of the connection of cheekpieces, long known in the Pontic–Caspian steppe, with draught horses in the 1970s have intensified the studies of chariot-related topics. Among those discussed are the geographical location of the earliest conception of the chariot – the Near East or the Ural steppes – and the problematic hypotheses of Indo–European migrations; issues of the time and place of horse domestication, and use as a draught animal; the functions of the early steppe vehicles, their military use and the social status of those buried with them. In a search for proof for the steppe origin of chariots, some scholars link the chariots with spoked wheels to the wagons with four solid wheels of the Early Bronze Age, but the cited examples make reference to the graves that were erroneously interpreted as containing vehicles with two wheels and cannot be seen as the predecessors of chariots. This article provides an overview of chariots as a topic in Slavic-speaking studies.

Part II of this *Festschrift* focuses on Egypt, the Near East, the Balkans, the Steppes, China in the second millennium BCE and later developments. In **Chapter 5** André Veldmeijer and Salima Ikram discuss "Leather: An Integral Part of Chariots". Several chariots are known from the archaeological record in Egypt, with six from the tomb of Tutankhamun being the most famous. Texts and imagery in temples and tombs provide us with a body of additional knowledge about these 'racing cars,' however, due to the perishable nature of the leather and rawhide components of chariots, the importance of these particular elements has until recently been little understood. The find of the so-called Tano chariot leatherwork has considerably increased our understanding of leather and rawhide as an integral part of chariot technology and also enabled us to recognize hitherto unidentifiable leather finds, especially from Amarna. This essay focuses on some major leather elements of chariots.

In **Chapter 6** Miriam Bibby shares her "Observations on Horse Care in Ancient Egypt". Although the introduction of horse and chariot technology into the early nation state of Egypt inevitably resulted in social, economic and military changes, Egypt was able actively to embrace the new technology and to develop it in an identifiably "Egyptian" way. The horse and chariot were also indubitably used as status objects to reinforce the authority of the elite in ways that reflected attitudes that had existed for millennia. This

---
[10] Crouwel 1981:23. The same definition was also used in Littauer and Crouwel 1979a: 4-5, and Crouwel 1992: 16.

meant that horses themselves, as living beings that also provided power to the chariot, were entangled in concepts of kingliness and authority. Bibby discusses how this complex role affected the care and management of horses in Egypt using evidence for the nature of the horse-human relationship in texts, imagery and artefacts. By applying practical knowledge of horse care and how horses learn and relate to humans, this chapter encourages further interest in the way horses were treated in ancient Egypt and the range of behaviours they exhibited. Discussion of reward and punishment of horses forms a major theme of the chapter.

In **Chapter 7** Gail Brownrigg proposes a new interpretation of the purpose of "The Egyptian 'Check Rowel'". "Check rowels" are spiked discs fitted on to decorated rods, of which a few examples survive, now recognised as part of eighteenth dynasty chariot harness. Their function is discussed, and a new suggestion for their purpose is proposed.

In **Chapter 8** Theo van den Hout discusses the motif of "Another Storm God Mounting his Vehicle? A Note on the Drawing on KUB 20,76". Although Hans Ehelolf published the Hittite cuneiform tablet KUB 20,76 in the series *Keilschrifturkunden aus Boghazköi* no. 20,[11] he did not include a rare hand-drawn copy of the cuneiform text, which dates to the thirteenth century BCE. On the preserved section of the drawing a dextroverse male wearing a pointed helmet is shown with tassels hanging down from the tip with a horn or knob on the front of the helmet. Although the face and shoulders are not preserved, the torso is presented *en face* and shows the right arm bent at the elbow and overlapping with the chest, but the left arm is gone. The right hand holds an object, and around the waist is a belt above a kilt or skirt. The right leg below the hip and the left foot are not preserved. This contribution re-evaluates previous interpretations of the drawing–based on an interpretation with other scenes in Hittite art and endorses Hans Gustav Güterbock's interpretation from 1957 that the scene most likely depicts a Hittite Storm God mounting his two-wheeled vehicle showing a cross-bar wheel.

In **Chapter 9** Nikolaus Boroffka explores "Bone Cheek-Pieces and Spoked Wheels – Chariots in the Carpathian Region". In this study, the evidence for the existence and use of chariots in the Carpatho-Danubian Region is reviewed. A brief account of the necessary preconditions shows that most requirements existed from at least the first half of the third millennium BCE: wheeled transport, the domesticated horse and, at least in some areas, suitable terrain. The light spoked wheel is documented in models and/or images, from at least some time between 2000 and 1750 BCE, while bone or antler cheekpieces as parts of horse harness may reach back to the last centuries before 2000 BCE. Overall, the archaeological evidence shows surprisingly little unequivocal evidence for chariots during the entire Bronze Age in the Carpatho-Danubian Region, even when Late Bronze Age or Early Iron Age finds are taken into account. Early documentation of horse harnessing, with cheekpiece-systems original to the Carpatho-Danubian region, indicate the necessity to control the draught animals. They are largely contemporary with those found further south or southeast in the Aegean or eastern Mediterranean, and are clearly later than those known from the southern Urals. Even then they are very rare and their function in warfare is doubtful, while the (symbolic) use of chariots in racing and/or ceremony appears likely.

In **Chapter 10** Igor Chechushkov and Andrey Epimakov provide an overview of "The Earliest Spoked-Wheeled Vehicles: Archaeological Evidence from the Eurasian Steppes". They present a comprehensive overview of the archaeological evidence for Late Bronze Age two-wheeled vehicles from the Eurasian steppes. Such finds are considered by many scholars to be evidence for the world's earliest known chariots. According to the series of radiocarbon analyses, the materials under review are dated to cal. 2000–1850 BCE. Whenever possible, the authors update the original published information with the latest available data on each site and describe related horse-control equipment – cheekpieces – which came from the same graves as two-wheeled vehicles and provide technical details on their manufacture and use-wear analysis to support the hypothesis that the vehicles were used for transportation.

In **Chapter 11** Pavel Kuznetsov and Vadim Bochkarev investigate "Early Cheekpieces in Eurasia". Their paper presents the results of study and analysis of Bronze Age cheekpieces across northern Eurasia (Volga-Urals, Don and Dnieper), the Carpathian-Danube region, Southern Greece, and Western Asia, supported by extensive illustrations. These items are an integral part of burial complexes along with chariots and weapons. A few were found in pairs *in situ* at the horse's jaw. They classify cheekpieces according to various features and consider their typological development in terms of chronology, regional and cultural links to understand borrowing and exchange across the region as well as pointing out independent local contributions.

In **Chapter 12** Viktor Novozhenov reviews the topic of "Chariots on the Central Asian Rocks: The Dating Problem". Recently, in Central Asian rock art, new multi-figure compositions including chariots, different in design and in their probable purpose, have been published. Their pictorial execution–shallow dotted carvings with polishing of the patina–made it possible to depict many significant details and features. This made it possible to highlight important typological and iconographic features that determine a more accurate dating and ethno-cultural affiliation and to clarify design features of the vehicles depicted. Early chariot petroglyphs are associated with the initial stage of the Andronovo pictorial tradition (APT) already identified in Central Asian rock art. Analysis of the chariot images enables us to distinguish two artistic layers in the petroglyphs of the Middle (the first part of second millennium BCE) and Late Bronze Age (end of the second/first half of the first millennium BCE) of Central Asia, associated re-

---

[11] Hans Ehelof, *Hethitische Festrituale*. Keilschrifturkunden aus Boghazköi 20. Berlin: Akademie-Verlag, 1927.

spectively with the Andronovo and the Karasuk (Begazy-Dandybai) archaeological cultures.

In **Chapter 13** Hsiao-yun Wu discusses "When Chariots Were First Used in China: The Development of Cheekpieces in the late Shang dynasty c. 1250 BCE" Horse drawn chariots appeared in burials at the late Shang dynastic capital of Anyang, Henan, around 1200 BCE along with splendid bronze ornaments and weapons. The large number of Shang style items and weapons indicates that chariots became accoutrements of war and marks of royal prestige soon after their introduction. Previous studies have focussed on the role of chariots as war and prestige items in Shang society and their association with the steppes, but this essay investigates harness technology by examining the earliest Shang cheekpieces found at Anyang, dating to the twelfth century BCE and argues that contemporary groups in the eastern Eurasian steppes provided sources of chariot knowledge.

In **Chapter 14** Robin D. S. Yates evaluates "Early Chinese Chariots and Carriages in War and Peace: Evidence from New Textual and Archaeological Sources". Chariots, carriages and carts played central roles in the lives of those living in Warring States, Qin and Han China, roughly fifth century BCE to the second century CE, both in war and in peace. They marked status, rank and official position; they were a main means of communication on land; they accompanied the elite into the afterlife in burials, sometimes in enormous numbers, and were later represented in murals in tombs; chariots were important machines employed on the battlefield. They feature prominently in the pits of terracotta warriors to the east of the First Emperor of China's mausoleum. Carts, pulled either by horses, oxen, or even by human beings, carried essential supplies, both in military campaigns and in peacetime. Horses were both worshipped as deities and butchered in sacrifices in ceremonies. Wheeled vehicles had symbolic, religious, and practical functions and cost their owners immense financial and other resources to build, maintain, and destroy. This essay includes discussion of some of the wide range of new textual sources, especially legal and administrative documents, pertaining to chariots, carriages and carts that have been discovered in the last fifty years within the confines of the current People's Republic of China.

In **Chapter 15** Xiaolong Wu and Katheryn M. Linduff take a closer look at "Majiayuan Chariots and the Lustre of Eurasia". This essay investigates dozens of lavishly decorated chariots recently excavated from the Majiayuan cemetery in northwestern China located in a contact zone between the Chinese dynasties and Eurasian pastoralist groups. The ongoing excavations at Majiayuan have already revealed thousands of artefacts made from a variety of materials. The tombs were dated by excavators to the third century BCE and considered to belong to one of the Rong (non-Han) groups dominated by the Qin State during the Warring States period (fifth-third centuries BCE) of the Zhou Dynasty. The extravagance of these tombs suggests to the authors that their remote and topographically circumscribed location aided in bringing them wealth and giving them a strategic role in Qin history. The authors examine the various chariot designs as well as the rich chariot ornaments and trace the hybrid and innovative features of the Majiayuan chariots and ornaments as signifiers of socio-political independence. Located at the gate to the outside world, the site and the chariots enabled the local Majiayuan elite to flaunt their economic abundance as well as affording them political advantage within the fading Zhou confederation.

Part III of this *Festschrift* is dedicated to "Chariots in Action, Their Construction and Experimental Archaeology". In **Chapter 16** Robert Hurford shares his knowledge of making wheels and building chariots in "The Ancient V-Spoked Chariot Wheel: Why Was it Made that Way? Some Thoughts Based on Observations and the Experience of Making Chariot Reconstructions". He contends that the ancient Egyptians did not make chariots themselves, but that they imported them, in parts, or sometimes perhaps as complete vehicles, and embellished and refined them. For over a thousand years the wheels of these beautifully light chariots were made using a unique design, which is explained and illustrated. The author describes how craft manufacturers in areas of the Near East making and often exporting chariot parts may have worked in economic alliance with vine-growers to produce chariots for the elite to use in display and warfare.

In **Chapter 17** Gail Brownrigg provides an overview on "Jean Spruytte – Horseman, Scholar, Chariot Builder". Jean Spruytte (1919–2007) was a French riding teacher and carriage driver who constructed first scale models and then full-sized chariots based on his study of visual evidence for vehicles and harnessing in antiquity. His practical experiments demonstrated clearly that the long-held theory that ancient harness choked the draught horses was untrue and was based on confusion between two harness systems. Bringing to bear the eye and knowledge of a horseman, he analysed the relationship between the type of harness used and the design and balance of chariots in the ancient world. He published numerous articles and two books, one of which was translated into English as *Early Harness Systems* in 1983. Jean Spruytte's studies and working reconstructions have made a substantial contribution to the history of chariots and harnessing.

In **Chapter 18** Steve Weingartner investigates "Chariotry and Chariot Warfare in the Near Eastern Late Bronze Age and the Battle of Kadesh" from the perspective of military history. His paper analyses the technological development and combat employment of chariots and chariotry in the Eastern Mediterranean lands while focussing on the Middle–Late Bronze Age from the point of view of military history. The approach is holistic insofar as it explores and scrutinises the diverse aspects of chariotry and chariot warfare individually and in relation to each other based in the following premises: The chariot was an Ground Combat Vehicle (GCV) designed and built to incorporate a trio of essential attributes (or capabilities) collectively known in contemporary military engineering as the "Iron Triangle" or "Iron Trinity," and consisting of (1) protection,

(2) firepower and (3) mobility. Like modern GCVs, it was not technically possible to maximise the performance levels of all attributes at the same time due to the natural conflict that exists between them – one attribute, per force, always takes precedence over the others. The decision as to which will be dominant arises from the complex interplay between technology and tactics and is determinative in formulating a warfighting methodology that will maximise the combat strengths of a particular chariot design while minimising its weaker aspects. Based on these principles, this paper evaluates the three principal factors that were key to determining chariotry's tactical employment, namely: machines, men, and horses, and how they interact, pursuant to presentation of how chariotry was employed based on their respective technical characteristics. The Battle of Kadesh is analysed as a paradigmatic example of a clash of chariot forces involving two technologically different types of chariots with different tactical objectives, predicated by their respective technical characteristics, governing their combat employment.

The contributors to this volume share their ideas, thoughts, observations, research and conclusions. We hope that the general reader interested in ancient cultures, as well as scholars and specialists will enjoy exploring the many facets associated with chariots – their equipment, horses and harness, cultural exchanges and affiliations – reflected in the variety of essays in this collection compiled to celebrate the 80th birthday of Joost Crouwel, who has been a mentor, a voice of authority and an inspiration to so many. The editors wish to thank the immense assistance provided by Adriana Maguiña-Ugarte who patiently and carefully not only formatted each of the individual chapters, but also meticulously entered the edits of each author. Her willingness to assist us to produce this special publication is greatly appreciated.

Peter Raulwing
Independent Scholar.
Associate at the Institute for the Study of Ancient Cultures – West Asia & North Africa, The University of Chicago, IL

Stefan Burmeister
Director, Museum und Park Kalkriese, Bramsche-Kalkriese, FRG.

Gail Brownrigg
Independent Scholar, UK.

Katheryn M. Linduff
Professor Emerita, East Asian and Eurasia Art History and Archaeology, University of Pittsburgh, Pittsburgh, PA

Joost H. Crouwel
Bibliography on Wheeled Vehicles
and Ridden Animals

1972 A Chariot Sherd from Mycenae. *The Annual of the British School at Athens* 67: 99–101.

1973 Appendix. The Parasol Krater, in: Ken A. Wardle, A Group of Late Helladic IIIB 2 Pottery from within the Citadel at Mycenae: The Causeway Deposit, *The Annual of the British School at Athens* 68: 343–347.

1976 A Note on Two Mycenaean Parasol Kraters. *The Annual of the British School at Athens* 71: 55–56.

1978 Aegean Bronze Age Chariots and Their Ancient Background. *Bulletin of the Institute of Classical Studies* 25: 174–175.

1981 *Chariots and Other Means of Land Transport in Bronze Age Greece*. Allard Pierson Series 3. Amsterdam: Allard Pierson.

1985 Carts in Iron Age Cyprus. *Report of the Department of Antiquity of Cyprus* 1985: 203–221. [Reprinted in Littauer and Crouwel, *Selected Writings* (2002): 211–237].

1987 Chariots in Iron Age Cyprus. *Report of the Department of Antiquity of Cyprus* 1987: 101–118. [Reprinted in Littauer and Crouwel, *Selected Writings* (2002): 141–173].

1990 A Chariot from Salamis Newly Reconstructed. *Report of the Department of Antiquity of Cyprus* 1990: 101–105.

1991a Another Mycenaean Horse-Leader? *The Annual of the British School at Athens* 86: 65–68.

1991b A Group of Terracotta Chariot Models – Cypriote or Phoenician? In: *Cypriote Terracottas. Proceedings of the First International Conference of Cypriote Studies, Brussels, Liège, Amsterdam, 29 May–1 June 1989*, edited by Frieda Vandenabeele and Robert Laffineur, 115–129. Bruxelles and Liège: A.G. Leventis Foundation. [Reprinted in Littauer and Crouwel, *Selected Writings* (2002): 190–210].

1992 *Chariots and Other Means of Land Transport in Iron Age Greece*. Allard Pierson Series 9. Amsterdam: Allard Pierson.

1995 Chariots in Homer and in Early Iron Age. In: *Homeric Questions*, edited by Jan Paul Crielaard, 309–312. Publications of the Netherlands Institute at Athens 2. Amsterdam: Gieben.

1997a Il mondo Greco. In: *Carri da guerra e principi etruschi. Catalogo della mostra*, edited by Adriana Emiliozzi Morandi. Rome: L'Erma di Bretschneider.

1997b Review of Jean Spruytte "Attelages Antiques Libyens. Archéologie saharienne expérimentale. Paris: Editions de la Maison des Sciences de l'Homme, 1996". *American Journal of Archaeology* 101: 814.

1998 Fighting on Land and Sea in Late Mycenaean Times. In: *Polemos. Le contexte guerrier en Égée à l'âge du Bronze. Actes de la 7ᵉ Rencontre Egéenne Internationale, Université de Liège, 14–17 avril 1998*, vol. 2, edited by Robert Laffineur, 455–459. Liège: Université de Liège. [Reprinted in Littauer and Crouwel, *Selected Writings* (2002): 100–105].

2001a Vervoermiddelen over land. *Hermeneus* 73: 115–121.

2001b Review of "Silvia Penner, Schliemanns Schachtgräberrund und der europäische Nordosten. Studien zur Herkunft der frühmykenischen Streitwagenausstattung. Bonn: Habelt, 1998". *American Journal of Archaeology* 105 (3): 545–546.

2004a Der alte Orient und seine Rolle in der Entwicklung von Fahrzeugen. In: *Rad und Wagen. Der Ursprung einer Innovation. Wagen im Vorderen Orient und Europa*, edited by Mamoun Fansa and Stefan Burmeister, 69–86. Beiheft der Archäologischen Mitteilungen aus Nordwestdeutschland 40. Mainz: von Zabern.

2004b Bronzezeitliche Wagen in Griechenland. In: *Rad und Wagen. Der Ursprung einer Innovation. Wagen im Vorderen Orient und Europa*, edited by Mamoun Fansa and Stefan Burmeister, 341–346. Beiheft der Archäologischen Mitteilungen aus Nordwestdeutschland 40. Mainz: von Zabern.

2005 Early Chariots in the Aegean and their Near Eastern Connections. In: *Emporia. Aegeans in the Central and Eastern Mediterranean. Proceedings of the 10th International Conference, Athens, Italian School of Archaeology, 14–18 April 2004*, vol. 1, edited by Robert Laffineur and Emanuele Greco, 39–44. Aegaeum 25. Liège: Université de Liège.

2006 Chariot depictions – from Mycenaean to Geometric Greece and Etruria. In: *Pictorial Pursuits. Figurative Painting on Mycenaean and Geometric Pottery. Papers from Two Seminars at the Swedish Institute at Athens in 1999 and 2001*, edited by Eva Rysted, 165–170. Skrifter utgivna av Svenska Institutet i Athen 53. Stockholm: Åström.

2009 Unharnessed chariots in Attic Black- and Red-Figured Vase-Painting. In: *Shapes and Images. Studies on Attic Black Figure and Related Topics in Honour of Herman A. G. Brijder*, edited by Eric M. Moormann, 135–152. Babesch, Supplement 14. Leuven: Peeters.

2010 The Chariots. In: *Il tempio arcaico di Caprifico di Torrecchia (Cisterna di Latina). I materiali e il contest*, edited by Domenico Palombi, 123–131. Rome: Edizione Quasar.

2011 Bronzen riemophanger uit de Romeinse tijd. In: *Kennis en Passie. Geralda 33 Jaar Conservator!* edited by René van Beek, Ben van den Bercken and Laurien de Gelder, 145–149. Leiden: Sidestone Press.

2012a *Chariots and Other Wheeled Vehicle in Italy Before the Roman Empire.* Oxford: Oxbow.

2012b Metal Wheel Tyres from the Ancient Near East and Central Asia. *Iraq* 74: 89–95.

2013 Studying the Six Chariots from the Tomb of Tutankhamun – An Update. In: *Chasing Chariots. Proceedings of the International Chariot Conference, Cairo 2012*, edited by André J. Veldmeijer and Salima Ikram, 73–93. Leiden: Sidestone Press.

2019a Mary Aiken Littauer and Our Study of Ancient Horse-Drawn Vehicles. In: *Equids and Wheeled Vehicles in the Ancient World. Essays in Memory of Mary A. Littauer*, edited by Peter Raulwing, Katheryn M. Linduff and Joost H. Crouwel, 3–4. BAR International Series 2923. Oxford: BAR Publishing.

2019b Wheeled Vehicles and their Draught Animals in the Ancient Near East – An Update. In: *Equids and Wheeled Vehicles in the Ancient World. Essays in Memory of Mary A. Littauer*, edited by Peter Raulwing, Katheryn M. Linduff and Joost H. Crouwel, 29–48. BAR International Series 2923. Oxford: BAR Publishing.

Mary A. Litauer and Joost H. Crouwel

1973a The Vulture Stela and an Early Type of Two-Wheeled Vehicle. *Journal of Near Eastern Studies* 32: 324–329. [Reprinted in Littauer and Crouwel, *Selected Writings* (2002): 38–44].

1973b Early Metal Models of Wagons from the Levant. *Levant* 5: 102–126. [Reprinted in Littauer and Crouwel, *Selected Writings* (2002): 336–379].

1973c The Dating of a Chariot Ivory from Nimrud Considered Once Again. *Bulletin of the American Schools of Oriental Research* 209: 27–33.

1973d Evidence for Horse Bits from Shaft Grave IV at Mycenae? *Prähistorische Zeitschrift* 48: 207–213.

1974 Terracotta Models as Evidence for Wheeled Vehicles with Tilts in the Ancient Near East. *Proceedings of the Prehistoric Society* 40: 20–36. [Reprinted in Littauer and Crouwel, *Selected Writings* (2002): 380–402].

1977a The Origin and Diffusion of the Cross-Bar Wheel? *Antiquity* 51: 95–105. [Reprinted in Littauer and Crouwel, *Selected Writings* (2002): 272–288].

1977b Chariots with Y-Poles in the Ancient Near East. *Archäologischer Anzeiger* 1977: 1–8. [Reprinted in Littauer and Crouwel, *Selected Writings* (2002): 238–245].

1977c Appendix I. Terracotta Chariot Model. In: *Two Cypriote Sanctuaries of the End of the Cypro-Archaic Period*, edited by Vassos Karageorghis, 67–73. Serie Archeologica 22 Pubblicazioni del Centro di Studio per la Civiltà Fenicia e Punica 17. Rome: Consiglio Nazionale delle Richerche.

1979a *Wheeled Vehicles and Ridden Animals in the Ancient Near East.* Handbuch der Orientalistik, 7. Abteilung, I. Band, 2. Abschnitt, Lieferung 1. Leiden and Köln: Brill. Now out of print: See e-book Brill, Leiden 2022. https://brill.com/display/title/169?language=en.

1979b An Egyptian Wheel in Brooklyn. *Journal of Egyptian Archaeology* 65: 107–120. [Reprinted in Littauer and Crouwel, *Selected Writings* (2002): 296–313].

1980 Kampfwagen (Streitwagen) B. Archäologisch. *Reallexikon der Assyriologie und vorderasiatischen Archäologie* 5: 344–351. [Reprinted in Littauer and Crouwel, *Selected Writings* (2002): 26–37].

1982a Chariots and Harness in Mycenaean Vase Painting. In: *Mycenaean Pictorial Vase Painting*, edited by Emily Vermeule and Vassos Karageorghis, 181–187. Cambridge, MA: Harvard University Press.

1982b A Bridle Bit of the Second Millennium B.C. in Jerusalem. *Levant* 14: 178.

1983 Chariots in Late Bronze Age Greece. *Antiquity* 57: 187–192. [Reprinted in Littauer and Crouwel, *Selected Writings* (2002): 53–61].

1984 Ancient Iranian Horse Helmets? *Iranica Antiqua* 19: 41–51. [Reprinted in Littauer and Crouwel, *Selected Writings* (2002): 534–544].

1985 *Chariots and Related Equipment from the Tomb of Tut'ankhamūn.* Tut'ankhamūn's Tomb Series 8. Oxford: Griffith Institute.

1986a The Earliest Known Three-Dimensional Evidence for Spoked Wheels. *American Journal of Archaeology* 90: 395–398. [Reprinted in Littauer and Crouwel, *Selected Writings* (2002): 289–295].

1986b A Near Eastern Bridle Bit of the Second Millennium B.C. in New York. *Levant* 18: 163–167. [Reprinted in Littauer and Crouwel, *Selected Writings* (2002): 505–514].

1987 Unrecognized Linch Pins from the Tombs of Tut'ankhamūn and Amenophis II: A Reply. *Göttinger*

Miszellen. Beiträge zur ägyptologischen Diskussion 100: 57–61.

1988a New Light on Priam's Wagon? *Journal of Hellenic Studies* 108: 194–196. [Reprinted in Littauer and Crouwel, *Selected Writings* (2002): 545–549].

1988b New Type of Bit from Iran. *Iranica Antiqua* 23: 323–327.

1988c A Pair of Horse Bits of the Second Millennium B.C. from Iraq. *Iraq* 50: 169–171. [Reprinted in Littauer and Crouwel, *Selected Writings* (2002): 515–518].

1989 Metal Wheel Tyres from the Ancient Near East. In: *Archaeologia Iranica et orientalis. Miscellanea in honorem Louis Vanden Berghe*, vol. I, edited by Leon de Meyer and Ernie Haerinck, 111–121. Gent: Peeters. [Reprinted in Littauer and Crouwel, *Selected Writings* (2002): 261–271].

1990a A Terracotta Wagon Model from Syria in Oxford. *Levant* 22: 160–162. [Reprinted in Littauer and Crouwel, *Selected Writings* (2002): 403–407].

1990b Ceremonial Threshing in the Ancient Near East. I. Archaeological Evidence. *Iraq* 52: 15–19. [Reprinted in Littauer and Crouwel, *Selected Writings* (2002): 329–335].

1991a 'The Trundholm Horse's Trappings: A Chamfrein?' Reasons for Doubting. *Antiquity* 65: 199–122. [Reprinted in Littauer and Crouwel, *Selected Writings* (2002): 530–533].

1991b Assyrian Trigas and Russian Dvoikas. *Iraq* 53: 97–99. [Reprinted in Littauer and Crouwel, *Selected Writings* (2002): 258–260].

1992 Chariot. In: *The Anchor Bible Dictionary*, vol. 1, edited by David Noel Freedman, 888–892. New York: Doubleday.

1996a The Origin of the True Chariot. *Antiquity* 70: 934–939. [Reprinted in Littauer and Crouwel, *Selected Writings* (2002): 45–52].

1996b Robert Drews and the Role of Chariotry in Bronze Age Greece. *Oxford Journal of Archaeology* 15: 297–305. [Reprinted in Littauer and Crouwel, *Selected Writings* (2002): 66–74].

1996c Chariot. In: *The Dictionary of Art*, vol. 6, edited by Jane Turner, 477–482. New York: Grove.

1997a Antefatti nell'Oriente mediterraneo. Vicino Oriente, Egitto e Cipro. In: *Carri da guerra e principi etruschi. Catalogo della mostra*, edited by Adriana Emiliozzi Morandi, 5–10. Rome: L'Erma di Bretschneider.

1997b Chariots and Early Horse Equipment. In: *Furusiyya. The Horse in the Art of the Near East*, vol. I, edited by David Alexander, 17–21. Riyadh: King Abdulaziz Public Library.

1997c Chariots. In: Th*e Oxford Encyclopedia of Archaeology of the Near East*, vol. 1, edited by Eric M. Meyers, 485–487. New York and Oxford: Oxford University Press.

1997d Wheel. In: *The Oxford Encyclopedia of Archaeology of the Near East*, vol. 5, edited by Eric M. Meyers, 72–74. New York and Oxford: Oxford University Press.

2001 The Earliest Evidence for Metal Bridle Bits. *Oxford Journal of Archaeology* 20 (4): 329–238.

2002 *Selected Writings on Chariots and other Early Vehicles, Riding and Harness*, edited by Peter Raulwing. Culture and History of the Ancient Near East 6. Leiden and Boston: Brill.

Dominique Collon, Joost H. Crouwel, and Mary A. Littauer

1976 A Bronze Age Chariot Group from the Levant in Paris. *Levant* 8: 71–79. (Dominique Collon: The Figures, 79–81). [Reprinted in Littauer and Crouwel, *Selected Writings* (2002): 174–189].

Joost H. Crouwel and Gail Brownrigg

2017 Developments in Harnessing and Draught in the Roman World. *Oxford Journal of Archaeology* 36: 197–220.

Joost H. Crouwel and Veronica Tatton Brown

1988 Ridden Horses in Iron Age Cyprus. *Report of the Department of Antiquities Cyprus* 1988: 77–87. [Reprinted in Littauer and Crouwel, *Selected Writings* (2002): 411–429].

1989 A Horseback-Rider and his Companion. *Report of the Department of Antiquities Cyprus* 1989: 109–110.

1992 A Terracotta Horse and Rider in Brussels. In: Αφιέρωμα στο Βάσο Καραγιώργη / *Studies in Honour of Vassos Karageorghis*, edited by Georgios K. Ioannides, 291–295. Εταιρείας Κυπριακών Σπουδών 54–55. Nicosia: Anastasios G. Leventis Foundation. [Reprinted in Littauer and Crouwel, *Selected Writings* (2002): 430–438].

Mary A. Littauer, Joost H. Crouwel, and Harald Hauptmann

1976 Ein spätbronzezeitliches Speichenrad vom Lidar Höyük in der Südost-Türkei. *Archäologischer Anzeiger* 1991: 349–358. [Reprinted in Littauer and Crouwel, *Selected Writings* (2002): 314–326].

Peter Raulwing, Katheryn M. Linduff, and Joost H. Crouwel

2019 (eds.). *Equids and Wheeled Vehicles in the Ancient World. Essays in Memory of Mary A. Littauer*. BAR International Series 2923. Oxford: BAR Publishing.

Gail Brownrigg, Joost H. Crouwel, and Katheryn M. Linduff

2023 Developments in Equid Harnessing and Draught in the Roman Empire and Han China: Independent or Interconnected? *Oxford Journal of Archaeology* 42(2): 166–182.

Joost H. Crouwel and Robert Hurford

2022 New Light on Chinese Chariots. *Eurasia Antiqua* 24: 57–66.

Joost H. Crouwel, Gail Brownrigg, and Katheryn Linduff

Forthcoming From Chariot to Carriage: Wheeled Vehicles and Developments in Draught and Harnessing in Ancient China. *Sino-Platonic Papers*.

2

Joost H. Crouwel as a Teacher

Tess Doorewaard

As a young student in my early twenties I went to the University of Amsterdam studying to become an archaeologist. There I met Joost Crouwel, professor by special appointment heading the teaching of Aegean Prehistory. From an early age I was fascinated by Greek mythology. I therefore, unsurprisingly, tended more towards the archaeology of Greece than towards Roman archaeology. The subjects of both my first year's essay and my final thesis dealt with Minoan culture. Joost supervised both studies. He lectured on the history of theoretical approaches in archaeological research and, of course, being the resident professor in the field, on the archaeology of prehistoric Greece. I loved every minute of those lectures. Two years previously I had been on a tour to mainland Greece. In the way he spoke about the architectural remains, the finds, the ancient Aegean people, and about the history of the excavations, Joost brought to life all the sites I had visited and the people who had inhabited them.

Joost's room at the university was packed with bookcases. A huge map of Greece covered the wall above his desk. In a prominent place below the map was a cartoon of himself, in which he is intently looking at something in his hands, undoubtedly something remarkable found at the acropolis of Geraki (South-East Laconia, Greece). The *Geraki Project*, with its aim to research the history and occupation of the ancient acropolis of Geraki in prehistoric and historic times, took up a huge part of his time, alongside his obligations as a teacher. He initiated the project and was its general director for many years, until his former PhD student and field director Mieke Prent took over.

That Joost was not just focused on Aegean archaeology became clear to me when he accompanied our group of students on our educational tour to Etruria in 1995. There I learned about his passion for ancient vehicles. He took some of us on a walk along Etruscan tumuli in search of wheel tracks. Had I known my future path in archaeology at the time, I might have paid more attention. As it was, I was more interested in the tumuli themselves and the fragrant herbs lining the paths.

After my Master's degree, it was Joost, especially, who steered me towards Roman Archaeology by suggesting I took up PhD research on the construction of carts and wagons and harnessing systems from the Roman provinces. Over the years he had already undertaken research, alone and together with respected scholars, into the subject of vehicles and draught animals of the Ancient Near East, Egypt, Bronze Age and Iron Age Greece, and Cyprus, which had resulted in numerous notable publications[1]. He was working on a book on vehicles and the harnessing of draught animals in Italy before the Roman Empire[2] and was planning a similar research project dealing with finds from Italy in Roman times. Since then he has cast his eye on Chinese vehicles and harnessing.[3]

I immediately saw the potential of the subject. I would be able to get inside the minds of the people who built, used and/or owned a vehicle, and of those who chose to have a vehicle depicted on their (or their loved ones') gravestones or who were even buried with a vehicle. This research was not exclusively limited to the upper classes, as opposed to other research options he mentioned, even though much archaeological evidence derives from the finds from elite vehicle burials. Vehicles came in many forms, practical and ceremonial, simply and slightly less basically built. They were part of daily life and in certain regions they were also part of funerary practices. This subject was brimming with possibilities, and at that moment I first understood his fascination with ancient vehicles.

Although it was a subject I knew little about when I started, I soon realised that starting with a clean slate on the subject could work in my advantage. It meant I was not hindered by any preconceptions or *idées fixes* on how vehicles were supposed to be constructed and on how the draught animals were thought to be harnessed to the vehicles. Joost taught me the basics, offered me books to read with a critical eye – never to take anything for granted. He introduced me to Gail Brownrigg to get a better understanding of the harnessing systems. He told me how he had learned from working together with Mary Littauer. I was collecting images of carts, wagons and draught animals from the Roman provinces and was getting to grips with archaeological remains from vehicles found mainly

---

[1] See bibliography, Ch. 1, this volume.
[2] Crouwel 2012.
[3] Brownrigg, Crouwel and Linduff 2023.

in burials. Gradually I was able to make sense of the details depicted on these contemporary pictures.

Joost first and foremost taught me the importance of clear expression, which also included the very important differences between the terms 'cart', 'wagon' and 'chariot'. The first one, of course, is a two-wheeled vehicle, the second one is a four-wheeled vehicle, and the third could be either two- or four-wheeled, depending on its construction or use. But generally, most people further away from vehicle related research, even professional archaeologists, are ignorant of the differences in terminology, or simply do not see the relevance of accurately naming these different types of vehicles. In our discussions during my PhD research Joost took on the role of teacher as well as the role of 'interested reader'. The 'interested reader' should be able to understand anything that is written, without having expert knowledge. 'Take the reader by the hand' is what he used to say, 'don't let him have to guess what you mean'. At the same time, an expert reader on the subject should not be bored by the text. In hindsight I did not always recognise which role he took on at any given time. Now I know it was all part of the learning process he was putting me through: learning from experience. A typical PhD student, I did not always appreciate his comments immediately, but ultimately each remark he made resulted in a better written manuscript on my part.

Joost introduced me to numerous wonderful books on vehicles and related subjects, many of which now take pride of place on my bookshelves. Only recently I acquired the English translation by Mary Littauer of Jean Spruytte's *Early Harness Systems*[4] from a second hand bookshop, after having been searching for a copy of my own ever since starting my research in 1998. When I opened the cover, I was looking at a dedication which reads: 'Best wishes, Mary Littauer'. It felt like an encouragement from my teacher's teacher not to give up on researching ancient vehicles. Shortly afterwards Joost phoned me and I told him about my treasure.

Joost and I kept in touch and I always enjoy our conversations. We talk about whatever keeps us busy (football, archery, (grand-) children, archaeology, books, writing). He frequently asks whether I am still doing anything vehicle related. For a long time I thought academic research would be forever out of my reach, due to my non-academic employment after finishing my thesis. In July 2018 though, a remarkable elite burial from the Iron Age was uncovered at Heumen in the Netherlands[5]. As it was the result of an illegal excavation, the discovery had to be kept secret for nearly two years, in order not to interfere with the following legal procedures. What has been so cruelly pulled out of the ground is an Early La Tène elite cremation burial with among its goods the remnants of a two-wheeled vehicle, horse gear, a situla, a drinking vessel, and weapons. Luckily the finds could be saved before being lost forever and they have been handed over to the province of Gelderland. The exact location of the burial has been determined, and even the deposition of the finds in the burial pit could to some extent be reconstructed. At the time of writing the finds are being expertly preserved and restored. Most importantly, preparations by the VU (Vrije Universiteit Amsterdam) and the RCE (Dutch Cultural Heritage Agency), among other partners, are well under way for a thorough research project into the burial, its finds, and the relevance of this grave to our understanding of Middle Iron Age society in this part of Europe. A vehicle, found very near my home town – yes, Joost, I am and will be doing something vehicle related in the near future.

Dear Joost, thank you for tutoring me and taking me by the hand into the world of ancient vehicles and their draught animals. After all these years I still treasure and profit from all you taught me.

Joost Crouwel successfully supervised five PhD theses at the University of Amsterdam, two of which were awarded the qualification *cum Laude* (see below). Four of these research projects are related to Greek archaeology and one is concerned with vehicles in Roman times. Apart from these, Joost supervised numerous Bachelor's and Master's theses during his time as a teacher, including one on the construction of Roman vehicles by Martijn van Leusen and one from Miriam Nieuwe Weme on the development of harnessing systems for equids.

Tess Doorewaard
Archaeological Archivist, Province of Gelderland, Nijmegen, Netherlands.

---

[4] Spruytte 1983. See also Brownrigg, this volume.

[5] Roymans, Swinkels, Theunissen and Van der Vaart-Verschoof (forthcoming).

PhD Theses Supervised by Professor Joost H. Crouwel:

1996: Jan Paul Crielaard, *The Euboeans Overseas. Long-distance Contacts and Colonization as Status Activities in Early Iron Age Greece*. PhD thesis, University of Amsterdam (*cum Laude*).

1999: Gert Jan van Wijngaarden, *Use and Appreciation of Mycenaean Pottery outside Greece Contexts of LHI–LHIIIB finds in the Levant, Cyprus and Italy*. PhD thesis, University of Amsterdam.

2004: Mieke Prent, *Sanctuaries and cults in Crete from the late Minoan IIIC to the Archaic period: continuity and change*. PhD thesis, University of Amsterdam (*cum Laude*).

2010: Tess Doorewaard, *Karren en wagens: constructie en gebruik van voertuigen in Gallia en de Romeinse Rijn-Donauprovincies*. PhD thesis, University of Amsterdam.

2011: Jan Velsink, *Minoïsche en Myceense stenen mallen voor reliëfornamenten en cultusvoorwerpen*. PhD thesis, University of Amsterdam.

Vehicle Related Bachelor's and Master's Theses Supervised by Professor Joost H. Crouwel

1989: Martijn van Leusen, *Roman Vehicles. Construction, draught and use* (Master's thesis, University of Amsterdam).

2003: Miriam Nieuwe Weme, *Van halsjuk tot gareeltuig. De ontwikkeling van treksystemen voor paarden in de periode 500–1000 n. Chr.* (Bachelor's thesis, University of Amsterdam).

Bibliography

Brownrigg, Gail, Joost Crouwel, and Katheryn Linduff. 2023. Developments in harnessing and draught in the Roman Empire and Han China: Independent or interconnected? *Oxford Journal of Archaeology* 42 (2):1–17.

Crouwel, Joost H. 2012. *Chariots and Other Wheeled Vehicle in Italy Before the Roman Empire*. Oxford: Oxbow Books.

Roymans, N., L. Swinkels, L. Theunissen and S. van der Vaart-Verschoof (eds.). Forthcoming. *Chariots on fire. Early La Tène elite burials from the Lower Rhein Meuse region in context*.

Spruytte, Jean. 1983. *Early Harness Systems. Experimental Studies. Contribution to the History of the Horse*. London: Allen [Translation by M. A. Littauer of Spruytte, Jean. 1977. *Études expérimentales sur l'attelage: Contribution à l'histoire du cheval*. Paris: Crépin-Leblond].

3

In Search of the Origins of the Chariot:
Wrong Turns, Dead Ends, and Long and Winding Roads

Stefan Burmeister and Peter Raulwing

The introduction of horses and chariots has been repeatedly attributed to speakers of Proto–Indo–European, Indo–European and Indo–Aryan in the Ancient Near East without any new evidence or verifiable arguments based on written or archaeological sources. Since a couple of decades, a new phase of studies in contemporary chariot research can be identified, which has attracted great interest due to the impressive finds from the Urals and Kazakhstan, and the perspective of the Eurasian steppes. In this debate on purely prehistoric finds, however, a connection between chariots and speakers of Proto–Indo–European, Indo–European and Indo–Aryan has emerged. Where does this connection and narrative originate? What characterised these chariot warriors? In order to answer these questions, it is necessary to take another close look at the sources, methodology and history of research. Our overview provides brief methodological observations on the history and development of chariotry research with a focus on the history of the connection of speakers of Proto–Indo–Europeans, Indo–Europeans and the so–called Indo–Aryan in the Ancient Near East.

Introduction and Goal of this Study

Since the second half of the 19th century, two main hypotheses have been put forward in research on the origin of the light, horse–drawn chariot.[1] Based on the written evidence and archaeological monuments in Mesopotamia – Egypt and descriptions of chariots in the Bible were also included – it was initially thought to be an invention by the cultures of the Ancient Near East.[2] However, the discovery and research on Indo–European languages, which also began in the 19th century, focus was not only on linguistic problems but also on questions of cultural history.[3] For example, the domestication of the horse and the use of wheeled vehicles in connection with the question of the homeland of the Proto–Indo–Europeans, are still controversial issues today.[4] However, this research was not initially at the forefront of the question of the origin of horses and chariots in the Ancient Near East. This only occurred after the well–known ancient historian Eduard Meyer (1855–1930),[5] at the beginning of the 20th century, first attributed the introduction of horses and chariots to the Indo–Aryans as documented in cuneiform texts of the Ancient Near East from the middle of the 2nd millennium BCE[6] and assigned them very specific characteristics.[7] In his article on peoples in Asia Minor and the first Indo–Europeans in connection with their migrations, Meyer, again, summarised in 1925 the main reasons for an Indo–Aryan[8] introduction of horses and chariots into the Ancient Near

---

[1] See Littauer and Crouwel 1979: 4–5 for a definition.
[2] Raulwing 1998: 523–524 with a brief overview.
[3] See Mayrhofer 1994; Morpurgo Davies 1998; Meier–Brügger 2003: 9–7; Clackson 2011; Klein, Joseph and Fritz 2017: Chapter 16; see also Trask 2000.
[4] Raulwing 2000 with a brief overview.
[5] For our context important is Mayrhofer 1994; see also Raulwing, forthcoming.

[6] On the history of the term 'Aryan': Siegert 1941–42 and Wiesehöfer 1990; see also the overviews of Schmitt 1987 and Teufer 2012: 272 ff.
[7] Meyer 1908; 1909a; 1909b.
[8] With Mayrhofer 1974: 12 and note 6 defined as a Dialect group of Aryan (Indo–Iranian), to which the Aryan dialects of India also belong. The Indo–Aryan of Mitanni neither came from India nor was it introduced to India from Mitanni; it is the dialect of a group of Indo–Aryans who diverted to the Near East and probably died out early on. In contrast to the designations 'Indo–European' and 'Indo–Europeans', the term 'Aryan': (…) (OInd. *ā́rya–*, Ir. **arya–* (…) in Old Pers. *ariya–*, Av. *airiia–*etc.) is the self designation of the peoples of Ancient India and Ancient Iran who spoke Aryan languages, in contrast to the 'non–Aryan' peoples of those 'Aryan' countries (cf. OInd. *an–ā́rya–*, Av. *an–airiia–*, etc.), and lives on in ethnic names like *Alan* (Lat. *Alani*, NPers. *Īrān*, Oss. *Ir* and *Iron*. 'Aryan' is thus basically a linguistic concept, denoting the closely related Indo–Aryan and Iranian languages (including Nūrestānī), which together form the Indo–Iranian or Aryan branch of the Indo–European language family, sharing a linguistic and cultural development separate from the other IE. tribes. The use of the name 'Aryan,' in vogue especially in the 19th century, as a designation of the entire Indo–European language family was based on the erroneous assumption that Sanskrit was the oldest IE. language, and the untenable view (primarily propagated by Adolphe Pictet) that the names of Ireland and the Irishmen were etymologically related to 'Aryan.' (Quote: Schmitt 1987); see also Bailey 1987. As an approach to the difficult subject of the reception of 'Aryans' (not to be confused with the Indo–Aryans in the Ancient Near East), the studies by Beate Pachler (1998), Birgit Pernsteiner (1998) and Thomas Summerer (1998) can be mentioned continuing the tradition of still on the basis of groundbreaking book *The Aryan Myth: A History of Racist and Nationalistic Ideas In Europe* by the French Historian Léon Poliakov (1910–1997); see Poliakov 1996 and also Wiedemann 2018.

East as part of a second wave of migration; Meyer also considered the Kikkuli Text:[9]

> It had long been assumed that these Indo–Europeans probably introduced the horse and chariot to Babylonia, where the horse is known as the 'ass of the mountains', since the nineteenth century from the Kassite mountains, and then to Syria[10] and to the desert tribes of Arabia, and further to Egypt; it is well known that the way of conducting warfare in the Near East was completely reorganised, thus giving it a knightly chivalric character,[11] which also profoundly influenced the social organization of those states. This assumption has been fully confirmed by a comprehensive text from the Boghazkiöi archive, which deals with horse breeding and chariot racing.[12] Composed by a man of Mitani,[13] named Kikkuli,[14] in Hittite; however, the *termini technici* for 'rounds'[15] are, as P. Jensen recognised,[16] genuinely Vedic, so especially the numerals. This matches with the Indian gods of the Mitani and the designation '*mar[y]anni*' = Ved. '*marja*' for 'men' (…).[17]

Subsequently, it was the attributes of 'chivalry' and a specific 'appreciation' ('Wertschätzung') of horses and chariots that were applied to the Proto–Indo–Europeans, on the one hand, and to the Indo–European languages, on the other, with recourse to the relationships described in the Rigveda.[18] However, with the exception of the cited article from 1925, Meyer did not comment further on this topic. However, his research on horses, chariots and Indo–Aryans fell on fertile ground, especially in National Socialist Germany. From 1933 onwards, attempts were made to explain certain historical and sociological phenomena in the context of horses and chariots with the help of racial ideological theorems.[19] In research, 'knightly' chariot fighters now became 'blond', 'Nordic',[20] Indo–European warriors who, as members of 'Männerbünde' (brotherhoods),[21] conquered the Ancient Near East, Egypt, Minoan and Mycenaean Greece and other areas with 'Streitwagengeschwadern' ('chariot squadrons') and thus spread this 'chariot weapon' ('Streitwagenwaffe') throughout the ancient world. This argument was supported in particular by the interpretation of the hippological Indo–Aryan *termini technici*, including the profession title *maryanni*, which is documented in several archives. In the 1930s and 1940s in particular, it was Joseph Wiesner (1913 1975),[22] Fritz Schachermeyr (1895–1987),[23] and others,[24] who created the image of the 'chivalrous Aryan chariot warrior' ('ritterlicher arischer Streitwagenkrieger') racial ideological content. This has recently been emphasised once again by Joseph Maran in his important study on 'The Introduction of the Horse–Drawn Light Chariot' (2020), connecting the described Indo–Aryan topoi to the chariot research of Wiesner and Schachermeyr.[25]

While Wiesner no longer published these views in studies on horses and chariots after 1945, Schachermeyr continued to propagate his hypotheses on the introduction of the chariot, albeit with appropriately adapted post Third Reich terminology that dispensed with the Nazi jargon that had prevailed in his earlier studies. It was only after the Second World War that studies on the origin of chariots first became established, which located the Ancient Near East as

---

[9] Potratz 1938; his translation has been replaced by the edition of Kammenhuber 1961: 53–147. See Raulwing and Meyer 2004 for a hippological interpretation a training manual for chariot horses.

[10] Meyer adds in fn. 2 that the horse could have been introduced by the 'Indo–European Hittites'.

[11] 'Ritterlicher Charakter'.

[12] It was first Ferdinand Sommer (1875–1962) who pointed out in his review of Potratz 1938 that the Kikkuli Text is neither a manual for horse breeding nor for chariot racing, but the training of chariot horses (Sommer 1939).

[13] In modern research different renderings of the name Mittani can be found (Mitanni, Mittanni, etc.). 'For linguistic reasons Mittani seems to be preferable' as Cancik-Kirschbaum, Brisch and Eidem (eds.) 2014: 2 fn. 1 pointed out. On the cuneiform sources see Wilhelm 1994. See also Wilhelm 1995 and von Dassow 2022 for a recent historical overview.

[14] Kammenhuber 1961: 55 ('Thus speaks Kikkuli the horse trainer from the land of Mittani). See next section.

[15] "Rundläufe'. See next section.

[16] Jensen 1919; Forrer 1922.

[17] Meyer 1925: 252–254. Our translation. *maryanni*: Vedic *márya–* + Hurrian suffix *–nni*; *maryannu*: Vedic *márya–* + Akkadian suffix (AHw 2: 611; CAD/M(1): 281–282; EWAia II: 329–330: Vedic *márya* 'man, young man, young warrior'); Wilhelm 1987–90: 419–420. From a morphological point of view, however, the suffix *–nni* still awaits a convincing Hurrian interpretation; Wegner 2000: 49; 51. *márya* 'man, young man, young warrior'. Hurrian is a language (related to Urartian) documented in cuneiform tablets in the Ancient Near East from ca. 2300 BCE onward and had mostly vanished by 1000 BCE. Interestingly, the connection between the *maryanni* class, horses and chariots in the Hittite, Ancient Near Eastern and Egyptian textual evidence – in contrast to the group known in Hurrian Nuzi (i.e., in Nuzi, Arrapḫa and Kurruḫanni) as lú.mešrākib gišGIGIR (Dosch 1993: 15), which according to Wilhelm belong to the highest order of rank and are therefore comparable to the *maryanni* – is not documented in the terminology itself. What has not yet been sufficiently researched in this context is that the military forces in Arrapḫa can be divided into two groups: firstly, local units themselves – reserve units, which were also used for guard duties – and secondly, chariot contingents from the allied Ḫanigalbat, i.e. the Mittani heartland itself, which Timothy Kendall, who has edited the texts with military content from Nuzi, classifies them as elite troops, as professional soldiers with front-line experience, and which he puts at around 200 in the cities of Arwa and Arnapuwa (Kendall 1975). This fact is worth mentioning here because we would not have expected the Semitic–Sumerian term Terminus lú.mešrākib gišGIGIR, but rather the Indo–Aryan–Hurrian *maryanni*. A proposed connection between the *maryannu* class and the Ummān Manda groups attested since Akkadian times and speakers of Aryan had already been supported by Forrer 1922: 247 ff. Also Friedrich Cornelius should be mentioned here, who as late as the 1960s equated the Ummān Manda with 'Aryan warriors' and 'mercenaries' ('Reisige'), whereby he attempted to establish an etymological connection to a basic linguistic etymon *mandos 'chariot horse' and ERIN–manda = 'traveling[ ] troops – mandus is the Indo–European word for chariot'. Cornelius also claims that 'ERIN–*manda* [were] precisely the Marianni (…) that is, the horse–breeding (…) chariot–fighting immediate followers of the Hurrian rulers' (Cornelius 1964: 56). Such conclusions are, however, not supported by the sources.

[18] See below.

[19] See below.

[20] On both terms Raulwing 2013: 262–264 with notes 79 and 80 and further bibliography.

[21] See Burmeister 2023 with further bibliography.

[22] On Wiesner see Raulwing, forthcoming and below in more detail.

[23] On Schachermeyr see Pesditschek 2007 and 2009 with archival sources and comprehensive bibliography and below in more detail.

[24] See Mayrhofer 1966: Register p. 137 sub '*marjannu*' and p. 151 sub 'Streitwagen'.

[25] Maran 2020; see also Raulwing 2004: 521–527 and below.

the most probable area of origin: on the one hand, because a partly fragmentary but generally continuous chariot tradition is documented in the Ancient Near East, and on the other, because the Indo–Aryans in that area are highly unlikely the inventors and mediators for relative chronological reasons. Nevertheless, the introduction of horses and chariots has been repeatedly, albeit sporadically, attributed to the Indo–Aryans in the Ancient Near East in the second half of the 20th century BCE without any new evidence or verifiable arguments based on written or archaeological sources.[26] Finally, since the early 1990s at the latest, a new phase of studies in contemporary chariot research can be identified, which has attracted great interest due to the impressive finds from the Urals and Kazakhstan, and the perspective of the Eurasian steppes.[27] In this debate on purely prehistoric finds, however, a connection between chariots and speakers of Proto–Indo–European, Indo–European and Indo–Aryan has emerged. Where does this connection originate? What characterised these chariot warriors? In order to answer these questions in the spirit of our title 'In Search of the Origins of the Chariot: Wrong Turns, Dead Ends and Long and Winding Roads', it is necessary to take another close look at the sources, methodology and history of research. The following chapters first provide a brief overview of the aspects of chariot research described above and place the research of Eduard Meyer, Joseph Wiesner and Fritz Schachermeyr in the historical context of research. This is followed by methodological comments on the sources and their interpretation. The study concludes with a critical look at the vehicles from the Steppes.

A Brief Outline of Chariotry Research, Speakers of Indo–European and Indo–Aryan

In addition to the so–called 'Florence Chariot', a chariot with four–spoked wheels from New Kingdom Egypt found 1928/29 in a tomb in Thebes,[28] and the depictions of chariots from New Kingdom Egypt,[29] the wall reliefs of the Assyrian kings such as in Nineveh, Nimrud and Khorsabad displaying chariots[30] still fascinate a wide audience. Over the course of the 19th century, the superb representations of chariots from New Kingdom Egypt and and the Ancient Near East led scholars to believe that the horse–drawn chariot with two spoked wheels emerged in the eastern Mediterranean world.[31] This phase in chariotry research reaches its peak before World War I with the studies by Otto Schrader (1855–1919)[32] and the articles and monographs of the so–called 'Leipzig School' of the classical archaeologist Franz Studniczka (1860–1929)[33] and his disciples: the so–called 'Leipzig School' of Studniczka[34] – Oskar Nuoffer (*1867),[35] Hans Nachod (1885–1958)[36] and Eugen von Mercklin (1884–1969).[37]

And this is where Hugo Winckler's (1853–1914) discovery of the archive of the Hittite kings in Ḫattuša[38] in 1905/06 and the eminent ancient historian Eduard Meyer come into play. The cuneiform tablets in the archive of the Hittite rulers not only revealed a complete spectrum of Hittite literature[39] – the language was definitively classified as Indo–European in 1915[40] – but the texts also contained, completely unexpected terms which represent a slightly older stage than Old Indian, the language of the Rigveda. As no specific term for the language and its speakers from which these *termini technici* originate has survived, the artificially created terms 'Indo–Aryans' and 'Indo–Aryan' have become established in the research. The Indo–Aryan language corpus contains:[41]

- Names for the gods *Mitrá–*, *Váruṇa–*, *Índra–* and the *Nā́satyā* twins;[42] known, until then, only from the Rigveda itself.[43]

- Specific vocabulary from the Kikkuli text, named after the 'horse trainer' (ᴸᵁ*aššuššanni*)[44] from the land of Mittani.[45] Among those terms are *aika–wartanna*, *tēra–wartanna*, *panza–wartanna*, *šatta–wartanna*, and *na–wartanna* for 'one round', 'three rounds', 'five rounds', 'seven rounds', and 'nine rounds'.[46]

---

[26] See next section.
[27] See, e.g., Gening, Zdanovich and Gening 1992; Anthony and Vinogradow 1995, Epimachov and Korjakowa 2004; Anthony 2007; Kuzmina 2007; Chechushkov and Epimakhov 2018; Lindner 2020; 2021; and the articles by Izbitser and Chechushkov and Epimachov in this *Festschrift* with further bibliography.
[28] Littauer and Crouwel 1985: 105–108 ('Appendix. The Florence Chariot') based on a report of an examination of the original chariot in Florence by Jean Spruytte; on Spruytte see the contribution by Gail Brownrigg in this volume. The 'Florence chariot' has been published by Del Francia 2002. See also Raulwing 2019 for an overview on the Egyptian chariots (on the 'Florence chariot', p. 25). See also Herold 2006: 263 on the correct reconstruction.
[29] Textor de Ravisi 1878; Wilkinson 1837.
[30] Compiled, e.g., in Nuoffer 1904.
[31] See also Raulwing 1998, 523–524.
[32] Schrader 1901.
[33] Studniczka 1907.
[34] See also Schrader 1901: 839–840 ('Streitwagen'); 929–932 ('Wagen').
[35] Nuoffer 1904.
[36] Nachod 1907.
[37] von Mercklin 1909.
[38] Alaura 2006; 2022.
[39] van den Hout 2020.
[40] Hrozný 1915.
[41] Mayrhofer 1959 ff.; 1966; 1974; 1982; 2006; Fortson 2010: 186–187. See also Table 1 in Raulwing 2004.
[42] Mayrhofer 1966: Register s.v.; see also Gotō 2009.
[43] Paul Thieme (1905–2001) has shown that the combination of the gods *Mitrá–*, *Váruṇa–*, *Índra–* and the *Nā́satyā* to reaffirm treaties in which they are attested (CTH 51) represent a specifically Indo–Aryan development, which was not part of the common Indo–Iranian past (Thieme 1960). See also Fournet 2010.
[44] See Raulwing and Schmitt 1998 with an etymology first suggested by Mayrhofer 1959: ᴸᵁ*āššuššanni* < Old Indo–Aryan *aśva–* 'horse' + Old Indo–Aryan root *śam*¹ 'zur Ruhe kommen, ermatten' ('to come to rest, to tire') (Bailey 1957: 62 ff.; Mayrhofer 1959b) < early Indo–Aryan **aśva–śā–ḫ* (Lipp 2009 vol. 1, 270–271 fn. 17 and *passim*) translated as: 'der das Pferd (scil.: im Training bzw. Rennen) zur Aufbietung der letzten Reserven treibt, d.h. zur Ermattung bringt' ('who drives the horses (scil.: in training or racing) to mobilise their last reserves, i.e. to exhaustion'). The term is also documented in a Middle Assyrian training manual as *susani*, as well as later in Neo–Assyrian *susānu*, Neo–Babylonian *šušānu* and Syriac *šušbnāe* (Ebeling 1951; Mayrhofer 1966: Register s.v.).
[45] Kammenhuber 1961: 55.
[46] Cf. the Vedic numerals *éka–* 'one', *trí–* 'three', *páñza–* 'five', *sápta–* 'seven', *náva–* 'nine' (the Indo–Aryan form *na–* has been shortened from *náva–*) and the Vedic term *vartaní–* 'way, path, course etc.' Over the

- As far as the Indo–Aryan profession titles are concerned, it was the Iranist Friedrich Carl Andreas (1846–1930), who first associated the term Indo–Aryan–Hurrian *maryanni,* found in the archives in Ḫattuša, with the Vedic term *márya* 'man, young man, young warrior'.[47]

- It is also evident from other cuneiform sources that the Hurrians in the Ancient Near East were led for a certain time by rulers with Indo–Aryan royal names such as Tušratta, which has been compared with the Vedic *Tveṣáratha–, rátha–tveṣá.*[48]

As mentioned, emphasis on the introduction of horses and chariots is closely associated with the ancient historian Eduard Meyer. At the same time, the Indo–Aryans were (and still are) also connected with the introduction of certain cultural achievements in the Ancient Near East, which can be divided into two groups for the purposes of our topic: First, non–hippological, i.e. in the broadest sense technical innovations and inventions as well as social, political and religious phenomena/innovations, which will not be discussed in detail here.[49] The second level of alleged Indo–Aryan influence is a hippological component which can be described as an extraordinary Indo–Aryan 'appreciation' and 'esteem' of horses and chariot,[50] is based on a particular interpretation of the Indo–Aryan linguistic and archaeological remains in the Near East:

- The numerous hippological *termini technici* in proportion to the total number of Indo–Aryan *termini technici* attested in Anatolia, the Ancient Near East and Egypt.

- The written evidence for the term *maryannu/maryanni.*

- The equation of the Near Eastern Indo–Aryan sources for horses and chariots with the descriptions of rituals, chariot races, raids and other warlike activities as described in the Rigveda[51] and the Avesta[52] and their methodologically unsound transfer to the Indo–Aryans in the Ancient Near East.

- A number of Iranian and Indo–Aryan personal names with the compositional elements 'horse'[53] and 'chariot':[54] Some examples from Avestan and Old Indic (as well as Greek) may suffice here: Avestan **Aštaspa* 'der acht Rosse hat',[55] Young Avestan *Agraē.raϑa–* 'Mit schnellen Rossen';[56] 'An der Spitze den Streitwagen habend'[57] and Vedic **Ariyaraϑa* > Greek *Ariarathēs.*[58]

Favoured by the political developments in Europe, especially since 1933 with the beginning of Nazi Germany, the hypothesis of an Indo–Aryan introduction of horses and chariots into the Ancient Near East practically became *communis opinio*;[59] corresponding newly added racial ideological content is easily recognisable in these works (see below). With regard to the question of the origin of the chariot, several phases can be distinguished:

The first phase begins with the aforementioned Eduard Meyer and is characterised by the introduction of horses and chariots attributed to the Indo–Aryans in the Ancient Orient. It extends beyond the end of the Second World War. Typical representatives of this phase are Joseph Wiesner,[60] Fritz Schachermeyr,[61] Wolfram von Soden (1908–1996),[62] Jakob Wilhelm Hauer (1881–1962)[63] and others,[64] who crafted this image of blond, Nordic, Indo–Germanic chariot warriors with racial ideological content. In addition, in the case of the transfer of the 'cult of blondness' ('Blondheitskults') for Germanic tribes,[65] the term *Ḫurri*, which was erro-

---

course of the 20th century a handful of additional *termini technici* could be added to the Indo–Aryan lexicon in the Ancient Near East: *p/babru–nnu* compared to Vedic *babhrú–* 'reddish brown, brown,' *p/binkara–nnu* compared to Vedic *piṅgalá–* 'reddish brown, reddish, reddish yellow, greenish yellow' and *p/baritta–*nnu compared to Vedic *palitá–* 'grey,' which most probably refers to the colours of horses. These terms do not only belong to a hippological semantic field, but also follow the same morphological pattern in word formation such as Indo–Aryan *maryanni/–nnu* and Indo–Aryan *aššu–šša–nni*. This word pattern is also documented for other technical terms outside a hippological context: Indo–Aryan *mišta–nnu* 'bounty' compared to Vedic *mīḍhá–* 'booty, price for fight', Indo–Aryan *wadura–nni* 'bride price' compared to Vedic *vadhū–* 'bride, young woman' and the hapax legomenon from Nuzi *martianni* with Vedic *mártiya–* 'man, person, warrior.' Indo–Aryan–Hurrian *mak/ga–nni* and Vedic *maghá–* 'present, gift', *maninnu* 'necklace' compared to Vedic *maṇí–* 'jewelry.' A letter listing inventory gifts from the Mittani king Tušratta, a contemporary of Amenhotep III and Akhenaten, furthermore, confirms that *mani–nnu* also denoted a 'necklace [as part of the harness (decoration) for chariot horses]'. See Raulwing 2013: 257–259 with further bibliography. See also García Ramón 2017 and Gentile 2019.

[47] EWAia II, s.v.
[48] 'Having rushing or brilliant chariots'; see Mayrhofer 1966: Register sub 'Tušratta'.
[49] See Raulwing 2004: 522.
[50] Mayrhofer 1966: 150 s.v. 'Pferd'; 151 s.v. 'Streitwagen' etc.; 1974: 88 s.v. 'Pferd und Wagen'; 89 s.v. 'Streitwagen'. See eg. Kammenhuber 1968: 19–20; Edzard 1971: 313; Nagel 1987: 171; Decker 1994: 265.
[51] Rau 1983; Sparreboom 1985; Elizarenkova 1985; 1992.
[52] Oettinger 1994; Malandra 1991.
[53] Vedic /áśva/, Avestan /aspa/.
[54] Vedic /rátha/, Avestan /raϑa/.
[55] IPNB I: 25 s.v. 53.
[56] Yašt 13: 121; IPNB I: 38–39 s.v. 117.
[57] Yašt 9: 8; 13: 131; IPNB I: 17 s.v. 4.
[58] Hinz 1975: 40. See also Sparreboom 1985: 138–139 with a list of over 140 components with the element /rátha/ 'chariot'.
[59] See the index entries in Mayrhofer 1966 and 1974.
[60] Wiesner 1939.
[61] Schachermeyr 1939a ff.; esp. Schachermeyr 1944.
[62] von Soden 1937; 1939.
[63] Hauer 1936: 201 fn. 1: '(…) daß ich die arische Herrscherschicht der Mitanni […] als einen Zweig der Arier ansehe, die nicht mit nach Indien gezogen waren, sondern nach der Trennung der Indo–Arier von den Iraniern über den Kaukasus in Vorderasien eindrangen (…)'. See also Dierks 1986: 480 on an unpublished manuscript from the Bundesarchiv. Papers of Jakob Wilhelm Hauer = no. 262: 'Die Arbeit umfaßt etwa 200 S. Maschinenschrift mit handschriftlichen Ergänzungen und 7 S. handschriftliche Schlußbemerkung. Im Literaturverzeichnis sind über 200 Titel in deutscher und englischer Sprache genannt (bis zum Erscheinungsjahr 1937/38), auch wird der Nachweis von 100 Abbildungen geführt aus Standardwerken zu den Themenkreisen Pferd, Pferd und Reiter, Wagen, Pferd und Wagen, Trensen. Die Literatur, die Ergebnisse der Vor– und Frühgeschichtsforschung werden im Text allseitig erörtert und die Ergebnisse aus der Fülle des Materials unter Berücksichtigung der Kulturkreis–, der Rassen– und Wanderungsthesen dargestellt und überprüft.'
[64] See the index entries in Mayrhofer 1966 and 1974.
[65] Biehahn 1964.

neously read as Ḫarri for the Hurrians, was equated with Ari and believed to be Aryans.[66]

The second phase begins with the epoch–making study on the horse in prehistoric times by Franz Hančar (1893–1968)[67] – interestingly, this phase does start not with the lexical study on Sumerian and Akkadian texts by Armas Salonen[68] (1915–1981) as one would have expected based on the topic of these publications. In this phase, it is primarily the Ancient Near Eastern evidence that is analysed, which is pre–Indo–Aryan, i.e., evidence for horses and chariots that can certainly be dated before the middle of the 2nd millennium. A priori, this makes, as mentioned above, an Indo–Aryan introduction unlikely for chronological reasons.[69] The publications of Annelies Kammenhuber[70] (1922–1995), Wolfram Nagel[71] (1923–2019), Manfred Mayrhofer and Franz Hančar,[72] and especially Mary A. Littauer (1912–2005) and Joost H. Crouwel[73] are representatives of this direction; it is also mentioned here that Joseph Wiesner joined this opinion in 1968 and 1970.[74]

The third phase is characterised by several directions which have in common that in all studies Hančar's *terminus ante quem* of Ancient Near Eastern sources for horses and chariots before ca. 1500 BCE[75] has received little or no attention. This means that in these studies, as in the second phase, the introduction of horses and chariots is still associated with the Near Eastern Indo–Aryans. The sources presented by Hančar also remain unrefuted. Within this third phase, several directions can be distinguished:

Firstly, a series of rather scattered works in which Proto–Indo–Europeans[76] or Indo–Aryans[77] are credited with the introduction of the chariot. Fritz Schachermeyr's post-war so–called 'Hurrian–Aryan symbiosis' should also be mentioned here, which assumes that the Indo–Aryans brought all hippological expertise, including horses, with them to the Ancient Near East, while the Hurrians, as skilful 'master craftsmen' ('Werkmeister'), provided the necessary 'hardware' such as the chariot.[78] In addition, works by Piggott[79] (1983; 1992) and Roger Moorey[80] should be mentioned, in which the wheel and chariot development described by Littauer and Crouwel in particular is partly 'outsourced' to the Eurasian steppes and, in the case of Moorey, certain 'skills' within a distinct (but not defined by him) social system are attributed to the hypothetical precursors of the *maryannu* class, which enabled them to have given new impulses to Ancient Near Eastern chariotry.[81]

In the second half of the 20th century, it was above all Fritz Schachermeyr, Wolfgang Helck (1914–1993), Wolfram Nagel (1923–2019), Jürgen von Beckerath (1920–2016), Wolfgang Decker (1941–2020) and others who put forward the hypothesis of a 'chariot warrior ethos' ('Wagenkrieger–Ethos'), the assumption of a 'chariot warrior caste' ('Wagenkriegerkaste') and a 'knightly nobility' ('Ritteradels') of the Near Eastern and Egyptian chariot drivers and charioteers.[82] On the basis of his interpretation of a 'chariot warrior ethos' ('Wagenkrieger–Ethos') – which is based on speculation –, Helck came to the conclusion that 'a new 'feudalistic' society in Egypt at that time with the introduction of chariots had to arise 'naturally''.[83] Helck's characteristics of the supposed 'chariot warrior ethos' in new Kingdom Egypt were based on the following elements:[84]

- personal courage and commitment,
- experience of speed,
- the special position of the chariot fighter requires new forms of coexistence: 'knightly nobility', 'feudalistic' structures),[85]
- in contrast, the bureaucratic class as an 'opponent', growing up with traditional values.[86]

This context also includes a certain direction of interpretation of the ancient source evidence, which – on the basis of the etymological comparison of Indo–European *$h_1ék'uo$– and Indo–Aryan *áśva– 'horse with the adjectives Proto–Indo–European *$Heh_3k'ú$ and Indo–Aryan āśú– 'fast',[87] which has not yet been convincingly explained linguistically – can be specified as a concept of sport and speed.[88] This can be seen, e.g., in the Jaiminīya–Brāhmaṇa: The chariot

---

[66] Mayrhofer 1966: sub Ḫarri, 'Blondheit', 'Rassemerkmale'.
[67] Hančar 1955.
[68] Salonen 1951; Salonen 1955.
[69] See, however, Parpola 2004–2005: 2 who dated Proto–Indo–Aryans in the Ancient Near East at the beginning of the second millennium BCE: 'It is argued that Mitra and Varuṇa are 'abstract' deities created by Proto–Indo–Aryans under Assyrian influence c.1900 BCE and that they replaced the Nāsatyas in the royal function.' A discussion of this topic is outside the scope of our article.
[70] Kammenhuber 1961; 1968.
[71] Nagel 1966.
[72] Hančar and Mayrhofer 1967.
[73] Littauer and Crouwel 1979.
[74] Wiesner 1968: F 79–80.
[75] Hančar 1955: 525 ff.
[76] Nagel 1987; Messerschmidt 1988; Nagel and Eder 1992; Koch 1992; 1995; 2003; Jacobs 1995; Eder and Nagel 2006; Nagel, Eder and Strommenger 2017.
[77] Koch 1992; 1995; 2003; see Raulwing 1994: 78 f. fn. 26 with further bibliography.
[78] See the publications of Schachermeyr 1951 ff.

[79] Piggott 1983; 1992.
[80] Moorey 1986.
[81] Moorey 1989.
[82] Schachermeyr 1951 ff.; Helck 1954 ff.; Nagel 1987 ff.; von Beckerath 1964; Decker 1989; 1994.
[83] Helck 1971: 585; 1978: 338 ('eine neue 'feudalistische' Gesellschaft in Ägypten damals [durch die] Einführung der Streitwagen 'naturnotwendig' entstehen mußte').
[84] A study which includes all available interdisciplinary sources is still pending.
[85] Helck 1978: 338.
[86] Helck 1963: 71: 'ritterlich' versus 'bürokratisch'; critically Hofmann 1989: 296 ff.
[87] Sparreboom 1985: 15.
[88] Raulwing and Schmitt 1998: 676–679; 'Sport– und Schnelligkeitsgedanke'.

'race is indeed the highest glory', which Norbert Oettinger pointed out.[89]

In addition, scholars hypothesised that the Ancient Near Eastern names for the horse, such as Ugaritic *ssw*, Hebrew *sūs*, ancient Aramaic sus and Egyptian *śśm.t*, also derived from Indo–Aryan *aśva–*.[90] This is also supported by the interpretation that the horse could not have played a major role in the Ancient Near East itself until the arrival of speakers of Indo–Aryan in the middle of the 2nd millennium BCE: In this context both the Sumerogram ANŠE.KUR.RA for 'ass of the [foreign] land' (= 'horse')[91] and the famous ancient Babylonian collection of laws of the Codex Ḫammurapi, in which horses are completely absent in the paragraphs, but would be expected there.[92]

Another line of argument put forward in this context is as follows: Indo–Aryan hippological technical terms in a training manual for Hittite chariot horses, could be understood as nothing other than a centuries–old association of the Indo–Aryans with horses and chariots:[93]

- Indo–European Hittites in the 15th century BCE collaborated with 'Hurrian teachers [for] horse breeding',[94] for whom Indo–Aryan was no longer a spoken language.
- They were brought from Mittani to the royal court in Ḫattuša to collaborate with the Hittites scribes, so their training instruction could be archived.[95]
- The above mentioned horse trainer 'Kikkuli from the land of Mittani' proudly provided his profession title as *aššuššanni*.[96]
- The horse trainers from Mittani in their grammatically often incorrect Hurrian nevertheless 'reverently handed down' the Indo–Aryan *termini technici* 'as fossils'.[97]

Comparing the reception of the Indo–Aryans and Hittites in chariotry research against the background described here, the Hittites clearly take a back seat compared to the speakers of Indo–Aryan with regard to questions about the origin of the true chariot. This also includes other Indo–Aryan 'innovations' as well as the 'esteem' being interpreted as 'typically Indo–Aryan'. According to these studies, they always prove to be 'learned students of the Indo–Aryans'[98] for the following reasons: Hittite personal names – in contrast to Indo–Iranian ones – are not formed with the elements /horse/ or /chariot/;[99] Norbert Oettinger's assessment also goes in this direction, as he summarises:

> Even in the Old Hittite Empire, despite the military significance of the chariot (...),[100] the 'nobility' does not seem to have constituted their identity from it. (...) In this context it could also be significant that the etymologizable names among the Old Hittite proper names, the earliest form of which can be found in the Old Assyrian Kültepe tablets,[101] do not refer to horses, chariot competitions or chariots.[102]

Further evidence for an Indo–Aryan 'esteem' of horses and chariots has been presented by the Assyriologist Ernst Weidner (1891–1967), who argued that the use of white chariot horses in Assyria from the second quarter of the second millennium BCE onwards could possibly be interpreted as an imitation of Indo–European rites through the direct mediation of the 'knightly nobility of the Mittanni people' against the background of a large number of references in the classical sources (above all to the Persians).[103]

According to other publications, contemporary Indo–Aryan influences on eastern and south–eastern Mediterranean cultures can also be identified. This refers, for example, to loan words in Egyptian of the New Kingdom, i.e., *termini technici*, which were adopted by the Egyptians into their vocabulary, such as the technical terms *śśm.t* 'horse' and *mrkbt* 'chariot', whose etymology has been undisputed since the second half of the 19th century.[104] In 1992, Wolfram Nagel and Christian Eder claimed that the Egyptian chariot term *wrrjj.t* should be derived from an unattested (but rather to be presumed) Indo–Aryan noun *$*w\underline{r}ta$–* with the same meaning.[105] At the same time the Indo–Aryans in the Ancient Near East should also be dated to 'around 2000 BC' as Nagel hypothesised. However, this postulate, which was already advocated by researchers such as Nikolaj D. Mironov (1880–1936) and Friedrich Cornelius (1893–1976), who did not apply a methodologically sound approach to etymology, was unanimously rejected by colleagues.[106]

---

[89] Oettinger 1994: 73.
[90] Raulwing 2000: 107–108 sub 1.3.2.1 with further bibliography; Raulwing and Clutton–Brock 2009: 78 ff.
[91] Zarins 1978; 1986; 2014; Postgate 1986.
[92] Codex Ḫammurapi §§ 7–8 and §§ 224–225 (Oelsner 2022); see Meyer 1909a: 22–24; 231. On this topic Raulwing, forthcoming.
[93] On possible earlier training instructions from the time see Raulwing 2005: 69.
[94] Helck 1986: 43: 'hurritische Instrukteure [for] Pferdezucht'.
[95] On the possible collaboration between the Hittite scribes and the horse trainers from Mittani see Raulwing and Schmitt 1998: 679 ff. On the Hittite horse text in the context of archival practice in Ḫattuša see van den Hout 2002: 869 ff.
[96] Kammenhuber 1961: 55.
[97] Kammenhuber 1968: 18; 206.
[98] Schachermeyr 1944: 55: 'die gelehrigsten Schüler der Arier waren aber, dank der nordisch–indogermanischen Artverwandtschaft, die Hethiter (...).'
[99] Kammenhuber 1968: 21.
[100] Schrakamp 2015; van den Hout 2016.
[101] Kloekhorst 2019.
[102] Oettinger 1994: 73 ('Auch im althethitischen Reich scheint, bei aller militärischen Bedeutung des Streitwagens (...), der 'Adel' seine Identität nicht über ihn bezogen zu haben. (...) In diesem Zusammenhang könnte auch von Bedeutung sein, daß die etymologisierbaren unter den althethitischen Eigennamen, deren früheste Form uns in den altassyrischen Kültepe–Tafeln greifbar wird, sich nicht auf Pferd, Wettkampf oder Wagenfahrt beziehen').
[103] Weidner 1952: 159.
[104] On the Egyptian terms see Hofmann 1989; Hoch 1994; Schneider 2008. See also Dietrich and Loretz 1983.
[105] Nagel and Eder 1992: 67–81.
[106] Mayrhofer 1966: 77–78 sub 1932 I. Raulwing 1994 with comparative–linguistic and methodological criticism of Nagel's overall concept and his postulates, Schneider 1999 with a Hittite derivation, Groddek 2000 with criticism of the Hittite evidence of Schneider and Zeidler 2000 with a Hamito–Semitic proposal.

The above–mentioned terms *maryannu* / *maryanni*, which are attested in Ancient Near Eastern, Hittite and Egyptian sources used to designate social groups for which, according to the vast majority of research contributions, 'a mastery of the light chariot was associated'.[107] These terms and derivatives are documented in historical treaties, so–called 'census lists', letters, charters, historical inscriptions and diplomatic correspondence.[108] A monograph on the *maryannu* class is still a *desideratum* of research. As mentioned above, the *maryannu* class – despite a few sceptical voices – can be explained from Indo–Aryan *marya– 'young man, young warrior' + Hurrian suffix –*nni* as the abstract of a composite to characterise socially and legally associated groups.[109] The 'hurritological objections' raised by Annelies Kammenhuber and Igor M. Diakonov (1915–1999) between 1968 and 1972 in particular against an Indo–Aryan derivation of *maryannu*,[110] could (among other concerns) be refuted by Gernot Wilhelm:

> A derivation of m.[aryannu] from Old Indo–Aryan *márya*– is therefore not opposed by any weighty hurritological objections. However, with the current state of the development of the Hurrian language studies, a strict proof to the contrary cannot be provided.[111]

Finally, as mentioned above – and also represented in this volume – a new phase in contemporary chariot research can be identified since the early 1990s at the latest with the aforementioned studies, which have attracted great interest due to the impressive finds from the Urals and Kazakhstan in the Eurasian Steppes. With recourse to the results obtained so far, the connection between chariots and speakers of Proto–Indo–European, Indo–European and Indo–Aryan postulated in these studies will be discussed in more detail below from the perspective of the history of scholarship.

The Chariotry Research of Eduard Meyer, Joseph Wiesner and Fritz Schachermeyr

To better understand the following chapters of our study, it is also worth taking a brief look at the research on horses and chariots by Eduard Meyer, Joseph Wiesner and Fritz Schachermeyr – not least in view of the passage by Joseph Maran (2020) quoted above[112] – as their work not only manifests the attributes of Indo–European and Indo–Aryan charioteers and chariot warriors described above, but is also handed down to this day. It is important to emphasise that the Nazi racial ideology, or rather its assumptions, had a decisive influence on Wiesner's and Schachermeyr's research by creating a link to the present, i.e., Hitler's Germany. Wiesner worked for the *Forschungsgemeinschaft Deutsches Ahnenerbe e.V.*[113] of the 'Reichsführer–SS' Heinrich Himmler (1900–1945). Schachermeyr's research did not shy away from an almost panegyric admiration for Hitler until 1945.[114]

Eduard Meyer (1908 to 1925)

In 1994 Manfred Mayrhofer (1926–2011)[115] published an article on Meyer in which he put the three above mentioned studies of Meyer, which cover the short time–span between 1908 and 1909,[116] showing that Meyer clearly distinguished the written evidence for Indo–Iranian and the Indo–Aryan in the Ancient Near East.[117] However, Meyer's publications are not only important for studies of Indo–Aryans in the Ancient Near East, but also for the history of chariot research. In an article 'Die ältesten datierten Zeugnisse der iranischen Sprache und der zoroastrischen Religion' (1909),[118] Meyer considered an Iranian introduction of the horse as a riding animal while, as he concluded, 'the Babylonians' transformed its use to that of a draught animal harnessed to chariots.[119] Meyer's article from 1909

---

[107] EWAia II: 330 (with whom 'eine Meisterung des leichten Streitwagens verbunden war').
[108] Until 1974 cf. Mayhofer 1966 and 1974 s.v.; Helck 1980; Hofmann 1989: 296 ff.; Pereyra di Fidanza 1992; 1993; Takács 2008: 417–419; Wilhelm 1987–90.
[109] Rainey 1965: 206.
[110] Diakonoff 1972: 114 vigorously disputed the alleged 'noble status' ascribed to the *maryannu* class; see also Diakonov 1981 ff.
[111] Wilhelm 1987–90: 419 ('Einer Ableitung von *m.[aryannu]* aus altind. [isch] *márya*– stehen demnach keine gewichtigen hurritologischen Bedenken entgegen. Ein strikter Gegenbeweis kann allerdings beim gegenwärtigen Stand der Erschließung der hurr.[itischen] Sprache nicht erbracht werden').
[112] Maran 2020: 507–509.
[113] Also *SS Ahnenerbe*, see Kater 2006. See also section on Fritz Schachermeyr below.
[114] See Schachermeyr 1940: 'Das gilt von der griechischen Geschichte mit ihrem Peisistratos, ihrem Kimon, Perikles und Philipp, von der römischen Historie mit den Gracchen, Sulla und Augustus und von einer erlauchten Reihe abendländischer Staatsführer germanischen Blutes von Arminius bis Adolf Hitler' (p. 73) – 'Trotzdem hat gerade die neueste Zeit den einwandfreien Nachweis geführt, daß die Zeugungskraft des nordischen Blutes noch keineswegs erlahmt ist. Allerdings war die Kraftprobe schwer genug und konnte von dem deutschen Volke nur durch die Retterschaft Adolf Hitlers geleistet werden' (p. 128). – 'Dank der führerhaften Tat Adolf Hitlers, den Leistungen seiner engeren Gefolgschaft und der Einsatzbereitschaft der weiteren Gemeinschaft ließ sich ein so ganzheitgemäßes und organisches Ineinandergreifen aller politischen Kräfte erzielen, wie es in einem Großstaat bisher noch niemals auch nur annähernd erreicht worden war' (p. 162). – 'So dankten denn in der Tat die altgriechischen Dichter und Sänger ihre Intuition den Göttern, läßt [the composer] Hans Pfitzner [1869–1949]) seinem Palestrina die Messe von Engeln vorgesungen werden, widmete Anton Bruckner eine seiner herrlichsten Symphonien in Dankbarkeit dem lieben Gott und wandte sich Adolf Hitler in schicksalsschweren Stunden – z.B. am 7. März 1936 als Fürsprecher seines Volkes an den Allmächtigen' (p. 202–203); this date undoubtedly refers to Hitler's occupation of the Rhineland and thus the breach of the Locarno Treaty (October 1925). Cf. also Pesditschek 2009: 1064 'Personen– und Verlagsindex', sub 'Hitler, Adolf': 194; 199; 218; 222; 228–229; 236; 261; 273; 276; 280; 284; 299–302; 306; 308; 310; 351; 358; 370; 390; 399; 410; 412–413; 424; 429; 456; 493–494; 497; 524; 585; 587; 648; 689. See also Dobesch 1996 and 1988: 54 fn. 68: 'Übrigens habe ich von anderer Seite erst jüngst zufällig gehört, daß noch ein anderes, mit persönlicher Ehrung Hitlers verbundenes althistorisches Buch aus dem Jahre 1944 existieren soll. Für mich ist es völlig verschollen, so daß ich darüber überhaupt nichts zu sagen vermag.'
[115] Mayrhofer 1994; with this study Mayrhofer filled part of a gap for the Ancient Near East within the research on Meyer. From the pool of studies on Meyer see Christ 1972: 286–333; Calder and Demandt 1990 and Lehmann 1994: 309–311.
[116] Meyer 1908; 1909a; 1909b.
[117] For an overview see Mayrhofer 1966; 1974.
[118] Meyer 1909b.
[119] Meyer 1909a: 22–24. This article is quoted first as the first section is dated from March 1907 (see below).

tried to pinpoint possible traces of a further effect of this Iranian invasion:[120]

- It is well known that the horse is not indigenous to the Near East; in Egypt and in Babylonia it is represented in all older texts of the Bible by the donkey.
- The Codex Ḫammurapi likewise does not yet mention the horse.
- The horse appears in Babylonia since the time of the Kassite period[121] (beginning in 1760 BCE), in Egypt since the beginning of the New Kingdom (ca. 1600 BCE), exclusively as a war–horse harnessed to a chariot, but not as a riding or pack animal.
- In the same manner the horse was introduced apparently from Egypt to Crete and further to Greece, where the Mycenaean and Minoan monuments as well as the Homeric epics confirm its use as a chariot-horse.
- This specific use confirms that the horse must have been regarded as a rare and precious animal imported from abroad.
- It is generally acknowledged that its origin is in the East and should be located in the Turanian steppe, from whose inhabitants it appears inseparable.
- This observation is also indicated by the term *sisû* 'horse' meaning 'ass of the mountain country [of the east]' written in its logographic form ANŠE.KUR.RA.[122]
- It is also known that the horse was familiar to the speakers of Proto–Indo–European since ancient times. How specifically close the horse was to speakers of the Iranian branch is shown by the countless Iranian personal names formed with element /aspa/.
- The introduction of the horse into Babylonia and the Western world occurred at the same time as the Iranian invasion. Therefore, a connection seems very likely, leading to the conclusion that the horse was introduced by the ancient Iranian tribes to the Near East and adjacent areas.
- To resolve the discrepancy between the use of the horse as a riding animal among Iranian tribes and being used as to draw a chariot, Meyer concludes that chariot warfare originated in the ancient East where the Babylonians modified the use of the horse to that of draught animals to pull chariots.

In 1909 Meyer published his revised 2nd edition of his *Geschichte des Altertums. Die ältesten geschichtlichen Völker und Kulturen bis zum sechzehnten Jahrhundert*. In 1907 – the date of the main text in Meyer's 'Die ältesten datierten Zeugnisse der iranischen Sprache und der zoroastrischen Religion'[123] – he also hinted at an alleged Vedic origin of the Indo–Aryan name Tušratta,[124] known since the late 19th century from the Amarna Tablets.[125] In the revised 2nd edition of his *Geschichte des Altertums* Meyer, for the first time, concluded that Indo–Aryan tribes actually introduced the horse and chariot from their homeland: In § 577, titled 'Nomadische und sesshafte Stämme. Die Kultur der Arier', horses and chariots including references to Avestian and Vedic sources are included in Meyer's concept of world history ('Universalgeschichte'[126]):

> Part of the belongings, which the Indo–Aryans brought with them, was also the horse, which was not only ridden but also harnessed to the chariot. Certainly, the Aryan migrations were accompanied by numerous chariots, and the chieftains and other distinguished warriors had already driven into battle in the most ancient times; in the culture of the Vedic Indians as well as in the Avesta, chariot races were of great importance. The martial spirit is emphasised;[127] during the migration foreign peoples were attacked, plundered, destroyed, or subjugated.

Meyer used the section immediately following to associate the introduction of horses and chariots into the Near East and adjacent areas with the Indo–Aryans:

> Due to great carelessness, I have left aside, in § 455 above, the common use of the horse–drawn chariot among the Aryans; this fact explains the occurrence of the horse in exclusive connection with the chariot in the Near East much more easily, and its Aryan origin is further confirmed

In 1914, one year before Bedřich Hrozný's (1893–1951) groundbreaking study on the 'decipherment' of the Hittite cuneiform texts and its classification as an Indo–European language,[128] Meyer published his often quoted book on the Hittites (1914), in which he identified the equids on a seal from Kültepe as horses.[129] However, looking more closely at Meyer's work,[130] it can be summarised that he did not publish on this topic either before or after World War I, with the brief exception of the quotation mentioned in our first section: his article on peoples in Asia Minor and the first Indo–Europeans in connection with their migrations and alleged race which was published in 1925.

---

[120] Here translated into English. All following translations in the section on Meyer are ours.
[121] Meyer used the term 'Kossaer' referring to Delitzsch 1884.
[122] Meyer read *imer–kur–ra* at the time.
[123] Meyer 1909a sub 4: *Du–uš–rat–ta* (also *Tu–uš–rata* etc.). Brother of the previous [*Ar–ta–aš–šu.ma–ra*]: 'ein Name, der einen ganz indischen Klang hat.' ('a name with a very Indian sound.')
[124] Mayrhofer 1966: Index, s.v.
[125] Meyer 1909a: 25; Mayrhofer 1966: Index s.v.
[126] World History. See the title of Calder III and Demandt 1990.
[127] 'Der kriegerische Geist tritt stark hervor'.
[128] Hrozný 1915.
[129] Meyer 1914: 54, fig. 43 (photograph) and fig. 44 (drawing) = Littauer and Crouwel 1979: fig. 24; p. 54–55: 'denn während das Pferd nach Babylonien erst nach 2000 v. Chr. und nach Ägypten noch beträchtlich später gekommen ist, scheint es hier in Kleinasien schon beträchtlich früher bekannt und genutzt zu sein.'
[130] Marohl 1941.

Joseph Wiesner (1930s to 1970s)

Boosted by the political developments in Germany, especially in the 'Third Reich,' the postulated introduction of horses and chariots into the Ancient Near East by the Indo–Aryans was practically considered as a *communis opinio* across the various disciplines. Indo–European, Indo–Aryan and the so–called 'Nordic Race' were, at that time, used as synonyms.[131] And in this context the background of Wiesner's studies on horses and chariots offers some fascinating insights into the amalgamation of academic research and National socialist ideology.

In chariotry research Wiesner is widely known for his already mentioned interdisciplinary overview on *Fahren und Reiten in Alteuropa und im Alten Orient* (1939) and his dispute with Hanns A. Potratz (1906–post 1992) on the earliest historical evidence for driving and riding.[132] Wiesner associated Indo–Aryans with the introduction of the horse, chariots, a new elite of 'Streitwagenherren' (chariot masters) and their new combat technique:

> The Indo–Aryans 'introduced the chariot to the ancient Orient together with the knightly nobility and the motif of chariot warfare in [Ancient Near Eastern] art.[133]

The Hittites, on the other hand, as Wiesner concluded, 'knew' horses and wheeled vehicles, when migrating to Anatolia. However, the textual and archaeological evidence do not allow to draw a conclusion regarding a military use as Wiesner stated;[134] the Hittites only used horses and chariots in a 'peaceful' context.[135] In addition, the Indo–Aryan *termini technici* for 'rounds' in the Kikkuli Text prove, as Wiesner summarised, the 'unfamiliarity of the autochthonous population [in Anatolia], including the Hittites, regarding horse–breeding and chariot racing, in which the entirely new thinking and feeling rooted in the Aryan elite and their esteem of horses and chariots, revealed itself'.[136] Wiesner's booklet from 1939 was well received at the time.[137]

While the national conservative Eduard Meyer, one of the great scholars in the heyday of studies of the Ancient Near East in Berlin passed away in 1930, a little less than two and a half years before Adolf Hitler was made *Reichs Chancellor*, being a 'child' of the German Empire under Kaiser Wilhelm II (1859–1951),[138] Joseph Wiesner on the other hand engaged with the 'new Germany' under Hitler. Less well known in Ancient Near Eastern studies or studies in chariotry research is that Wiesner collaborated closely with 'SS–Standartenführer' and General Secretary of the 'Forschungsgemeinschaft Deutsches Ahnenerbe e.V.', Wolfram Sievers (1902–1948), who was hung after the Nuremberg Trials for crimes against humanity. Furthermore, Wiesner also collaborated with 'SS–Standartenführer,' Curator of the AE, 'Rektor' of the Ludwig–Maximilians–Universität in Munich and professor of 'Arische Kultur und Sprachwissenschaft' Walther Wüst (1901–1993).[139] In the few studies on Wiesner this collaboration is not mentioned.[140]

Wiesner was appointed to the so–called (second) 'Sonderkommando Jankuhn' in July 1943—a special unit of the 'SS Ahnenerbe' inaugurated by the Prehistorian Herbert Jankuhn (1905–1990)[141] under the 5th 'SS–Panzer–Division Wiking'. Wiesner took on the mission to 'secure important collections' in southern Russia,[142] tasked 'with the deployment to the Crimean Peninsula to take over the archaeological evaluation of the cities of Greek colonies in the Crimea and to give a corresponding report (...)'.[143] The files of the 'Forschungsgemeinschaft Deutsches Ahnenerbe e.V.' in the Bundesarchiv Berlin–Lichterfelde contains an ID card[144] stating that on the order of the 'Stabsabteilung der Waffen–SS beim Persönlichen Stab Reichsführer–SS,' the 'SS–Sturmmann' lecturer Dr. Joseph Wiesner had to secure particularly important scholarly evidence, which ultimately failed. Wiesner did not join the 'Sonderkommando Jankuhn' as he was ill at the time. However, the looted art from the Crimea was shipped to him in Königsberg, where Wiesner lived and taught at the university, intended to be transported to the headquarters of the *SS*

---

[131] See Mayrhofer 1966: Index sub 'Pferd,' 'Rasse,' 'Streitwagen,' etc. See also Raulwing 2013: 262–264.

[132] Wiesner 1939b; Potratz 1939–40; Steuer 1994.

[133] Wiesner 1939a: 34: 'Sie [the Indo–Aryans] haben dem alten Orient den Streitwagen mit dem ritterlichen Herrentum gebracht und seiner Kunst das Motiv des Wagenkampfes'.

[134] Wiesner 1939a: 24.

[135] Wiesner 1939a: 9: 'Sie kennen die Schirrung des Pferdes am Wagen jedoch nur in friedlichem Gebrauch'. See also Wiesner 1939a: 23–24.

[136] Wiesner 1939a: 34: 'Sie beweisen die Fremdheit der alten Bevölkerung, aber auch der Hethiter gegenüber Pferdezucht und Pferderennen, in dem sich das im arischen Herrentum wurzelnde völlig neue Denken und Empfinden offenbart.'

[137] As an example, see von Soden 1939. Although incomplete, see Souček and Siegelova 1995, vol. III: 97.3. sub no. 10, p. 369; furthermore, *Indogermanisches Jahrbuch* 25 ['Jahrgang 1941 (Bibliographie des Jahres 1939)'], Berlin: de Gruyter, 1942: 102 sub no. 32 and *Indogermanisches Jahrbuch* 26 ['Jahrgang 1942 (Bibliographie des Jahres 1940)'], Berlin: de Gruyter, 1942: 149 sub no. 882. A critical review was written by Potratz 1939–40.

[138] Calder and Demandt 1990.

[139] On Sievers and Wüst see Kater 2006; in addition, on Wüst specifically, see Schreiber 2008.

[140] Eckstein 1976; Schiering 1988; Wirbelauer 2006.

[141] Steuer 2001; 2004; Mahsarski 2011.

[142] 'Special Command Jankuhn'. 'Sonderkommando zur Sicherstellung und Erforschung vorgeschichtlicher Sammlungen in Südrussland'; Kater 2006: 155–58; Hufen 1998: 493–94; Steuer 2004: 464–69 ('Ahnenerbe'); 484–502. The first 'Special Command Jankuhn' was ordered by Himmler to southern Russia in July 1942; Steuer 2004: 489–93. Previous 'Sonderkommandos Jankuhn' was ordered by the *SS Ahnenerbe* to Prague (Dec. 1941), Kiev (Jan. 1942), Belgrade (Jul. 1942), southern Russia and Ukraine (1942 and 1943).

[143] 'Dr. Wiesner mit Einsatz auf der Krim im Rahmen des SD–Einsatzkommandos. Wiesner soll die archäologische Bearbeitung der griechischen Kolonialstädte auf der Krim übernehmen und einen analogen Bericht geben (...)'; Steuer 2004: 493–98 ; see also, e.g., letter Sievers to Wiesner Berlin–Dahlem, 3 Mai 1943, 1 page; Bundesrachiv: BArch NS/21 2688 with reference to the 'Sonderkommando Jankuhn' and the appointment of Wiesner as leader of a research section ('Fachführer') proposed by Jankuhn.

[144] BArch NS/15 244, ID, s.l. [Waischenfeld], February 1, 1945, 1 page (by or on behalf of Wolfram Sievers).

Ahnenerbe in Waischenfeld near Bayreuth (in Bavaria). However, the boxes disappeared.[145]

But, already his *Habilitationsschrift* from 1939 (*Fahren und Reiten in Alteuropa und im alten Orient*) can be connected to the 'SS Ahnenerbe'. In a letter to 'Reichsgeschäftsführer' of the 'SS Ahnenerbe' Sievers, dated July 21, 1939, Wiesner wrote that he has sent three copies of *Fahren und Reiten* to the Ahnenerbe (two to Berlin, one to Munich to Wüst) pointing out that the book could not have been completed without the help of the 'SS Ahnenerbe'.[146]

After the collapse of the Third Reich there were problems in continuing his career in the newly founded Federal Republic of Germany, and it is not surprising that Wiesner shifted his focus away from Indo–Aryans and chariots to the Classical World.[147] Not even Hančar's monumental study in 1956, in which he presented pre–Indo–Aryan evidence for horses and chariots in the Ancient Near East, could tempt him: Wiesner's review suddenly ends before having to comment on these questions.[148] Wiesner did, in the end, follow Hančar, Kammenhuber and Nagel and their prioritisation of the Ancient Near East in terms of the origin of the chariot.[149]

Fritz Schachermeyr (1930s to 1980s)

For several decades Fritz Schachermeyr advocated in his academic and historical–philosophical publications various hypotheses on the introduction of chariots into the Ancient Near East, including Asia Minor and Late Bronze Age Greece.[150] These publications were characterised by racial ideology and cultural morphology ('Kulturmorphologie').

Schachermeyr's Hypotheses on Indo–Aryans and the Introduction of the Chariot to the Ancient Near East

As in most German–language studies on the origin of the chariot in the 1930s and 1940s, Schachermeyr also postulated the thesis that Indo–Aryan chariots were introduced into the Ancient Near East[151] based on studies by Eduard Meyer[152] but with minor criticism by Joseph Wiesner.[153]

Schachermeyr's hypotheses and historical reconstructions were integrated into a racially ideological world view ('rassenideologisches Weltbild'[154]) and an educational pro-

---

[145] Schreiber 2006: 216–20; on Wüst and Till see Schreiber 2008 (Index p. 398 s.v.).
[146] BArch NS/21 2688. Letter Wiesner to Sievers, Königsberg, July 1, 1939, 1 page: 'Ich darf in der Anlage zwei Exemplare des 'Alten Orient 38, 1939' beifügen 'Fahren und Reiten in Alteuropa und im Alten Orient', dessen Entstehung weitgehend des 'Ahnenerbes' verdankt wird. Dem Kurator [W. Wüst] ging ein weiteres Exemplar zu.'
[147] Wiesner 1953.
[148] Wiesner 1959.
[149] Wiesner 1968: 78F–79F; 1970.
[150] According to Näf 1994: 86 fn. 14 the term 'Kulturmorphologie' is first documented in Schachermeyr 1944: 59 fn. 51. See also Schachermeyr's *Griechische Geschichte. Mit besonderer Berücksichtigung der geistesgeschichtlichen und kulturmorphologischen Zusammenhänge* (1969: 56–57) and the chapter 'Streitwagengeschwader erobern den Orient' ('Chariot squadrons conquer the Near East); Schachermeyr 1981: 11–14 and 1984a: 247–253 (Chapter 'Der Weg zur Tragik der Vollendung'); see also the 'Geleitwort' by the then Federal Minister of Science and Research, Univ.–Prof. Dr. Heinz Fischer: 'Darüber hinaus hat er [Schachermeyr] mit seiner kulturmorphologischen Schau der antiken und europäischen Geschichte auch in der philosophischen Forschung große Anerkennung gefunden;' where exactly is not said.

[151] See e.g., Schachermeyr 1936: 239–240; see also Schachermeyr 1950: 55 fn. 6 and Mayrhofer 1966: Register s.v. *Pferd* (p. 150) und *Streitwagen* (p. 151).
[152] Meyer 1908; 1909a; 1909b; 1925.
[153] Schachermeyr 1940b: 138 ('Eine sehr reife und beachtenswerte Veröffentlichung erblicken wir in Joseph Wiesner 'Fahren und Reiten in Alteuropa und im Alten Orient'. Wiesner scheidet m. E. mit Recht zwischen den Streitaxtleuten im Bereich wie Umkreis der Schnurkeramik und der südöstlich davon beheimateten Streitwagenbevölkerung, welche er im wesentlichen mit den Arien gleichsetzt. Er verfolgt die Vorstöße dieser Streitwagenarier im vorderen Orient und stellt im Anschluß daran, auch für die Herren von Mykenai die zwar gewagte, aber beachtenswerte Hypothese auf, daß sie zu Beginn der mykenischen Zeit aus den nordöstlichen Weiten gekommen wären und den Streitwagen von dort mitgebracht hätten. Das wenige, was Wiesner zur Stützung seiner Annahme anführt, reicht zum Beweis nicht aus. Dagegen spricht, daß uns im heroischen Namensschatz des nach vorderasiatischer Analogie zu erwartenden, arische Sprachgut fehlt und daß der archäologische Befund einer Bevölkerungsumschichtung an der vielfach so gleitenden Wende von M. Hell und S. Hell nicht gerade günstig ist. Auch hat Wiesner die andere Möglichkeit, der nachbarlichen Beeinflussung allzu sehr aus dem Auge verloren. Unter artverwandten Völkern genügt ja oft schon ein überspringender Funke, um den Brand zu entfachen und Übernahmen herbeizuführen, welche in Wahrheit zugleich Erweckung des korrespondierenden Erbgutes sind. Immerhin bleibt Wiesners These als Möglichkeit bestehen, nur müßten es dann ganz wenige Streitwagengeschlechter gewesen sein, die sich in Griechenland zu Herren aufgeworfen hätten, so wenig, daß ihr Eindringen archäologisch nicht leicht gefaßt werden kann und daß sie bald in der übrigen frühgriechisch–achäischen Bevölkerung aufgegangen sind').
[154] See e.g. Schachermeyr 1940: *Lebensgesetzlichkeit in der Geschichte. Versuch einer Einführung in das geschichtsbiologische Denken* ('The Laws of Life in History. An Attempt at an Introduction to Historical–Biological Thinking'). See also the index in Schachermeyr 1944: 621–635 with entries such as: 'Armenoide Rasse, armenoide Elemente: gleich vorderasiatische Rasse, arteigene Sprache, schwache Rasse (…), Handelstypus (…), im Semitentum (…), entzieht sich der Ausmerzung (…),' (p. 623), 'Entartung', 'Entnordung' (p. 625), 'Juden: Rassische Art (…), Geisteshaltung (…), Nutznießer des römischen Imperiums (…), Weltherrschaftsidee (…), Propaganda' (p. 628), 'Machtgedanke, wüstenländischer' (p. 629), 'Nordische Rasse (…), starke Rasse (…), Vermischung mit anderen Rassen (…), Antinordische Gegensteuerung (…), Ausmerzung infolge höherer Wehrentschlossenheit (…), Anlagedesaktivierung durch Allmacht (…), Kulturverhalten (…), Veranlagungsreichtum (…), Meisterwerk und Spitzenleistung (…), geniale Persönlichkeit (…), Schutz des geistigen Eigentums (…), Adel und Auslese (…), Zuchtidee (…), monumentales Bauen (…), Schlichtheit (…), Forschungsdrang (…), Gleichgewichtsgedanke (…), Hegemonie und Vorrang' (p. 630–631), 'Orient als für sich stehende Kultursphäre (…), Behäbigkeit und Entwicklungsträgheit' (p. 630), 'Regenerationsidee bei den Hellenen' (p. 632), 'Semiten, Semitentum; Zweirassenprinzip (…), Verschiebung des rassischen Schwergewichts bei den (p. 633), händlerische und organisatorische Fähigkeiten (…), Semitisch als arteigenes Idiom der Wüstenländischen (p. 633), 'Subversion im allgemeinen (…), der Semiten und Orientalen in Vorderasien' (p. 634), 'Übervölkerung' (p. 635)', 'Weltbürgerliche Haltung: als Folge der nordisch–westischen Mischung' (p. 635), 'Weltherrschaftsgedanke: bei den Wüstenländischen (…), abgelehnt von Hethitern und Medern' (p. 635), 'Westische Rasse (…), Vermischung mit nordischem Blut (…), geistige Haltung (…), Schöpfer der abendländischen Urbanität (…), Chauvinismus (…), Ekstase' (p. 635), 'Wüstenländische Rasse (…), Ausmerzung durch Kampf (…), Rückdämmung (…), händlerische und organisatorische Fähigkeiten (…), Kulturstarre (…), Andachtsinnigkeit (…), Astraldeterminismus' (p. 635).

gramme ('Bildungsprogram'[155]). As Martina Pesditschek summarises: Fritz Schachermeyr has

> 'represented the National Socialist racial doctrine in research and teaching during the Nazi era more consistently than any other ancient historian' and, as she repeatedly tried to show, [Schachermeyr] was convinced of the correctness of [H. F. K.] Günther's[156] purely biologistic racial theories in particular until the end of his life.[157]

Schachermeyr, according to his own statements, a 'co–founder of the national–social fighting ring of the German–Austrians in the Reich (at times [1933–1934] Gauführer in the Gau Thuringia)', 'culturally and politically active in the sense of the national social movement through lectures and publications',[158] wrote in his book *Indogermanen und Orient. Ihre machtpolitische Auseinandersetzung im Altertum* (1944):[159]

> die Arier; sie nämlich sind es, welche die den Gedanken des adligen Rittertums zu geschichtlichem Leben erwecken. (…) Die nach Vorderasien einwandernden 'Arier waren es bereits gewöhnt, sich des Pferdes als Zugtier zu bedienen. Bald verstanden sie sich auch auf die Zucht edler Rosse, und schließlich schufen sie etwas noch nie dagewesenes: Sie erfanden den Typus des zweirädrigen, leichten Rennwagens (…). Der Gedanke des Schnelligkeitssportes tritt damit das erstemal in die Welt, er ist eine Erfindung der arischen Gruppe der Indogermanen. Doch man begnügt sich nicht allein mit friedlichen Wettkämpfen. Man fährt mit Rennwagengeschwadern auch in die Schlacht und wirft den Feind in blitzschnellen Angriffen. Es war eine kriegstechnische Erfindung umwälzender Art, der Einführung der modernen Panzerwaffe vergleichbar. Streitwagenkampf, Rennsport und Rossezucht leiteten aber auch noch ein Weiteres ein: die Überführung ihrer bereits von Natur aus adligen Eigenart in einem mehr ritterliche Lebensform und Gesinnungsweise. Ein derartiger Wandel steht grundsätzlich allen Nordischen als erbangelegte Möglichkeit offen, muß aber nicht eintreten. Es kommt den Ariern zu, diese Möglichkeit als erste entdeckt und alsbald in weiterem Maße ausgenutzt zu haben. (…) Ob die Führung [of the Hyksos] von arischen Adligen ausgeübt wurde oder nicht, ist umstritten. Obgleich sich zwingende Beweise nach keiner Richtung führen lassen, bleibt eine gewisse innere Wahrscheinlichkeit, daß auch bei diesem Einbruch der Anstoß durch arische Kräfte erfolgt sei. Ging er doch von dem damals unter arischer Herrschaft stehenden Vorderasien aus, brachte er doch den Streitwagen, die Hochschätzung des Rennpferdes und so manche Züge ritterlicher Art nach bis dahin ganz anders gearteten Ägypten.[160]

It should be noted for the subject of our study that Schachermeyr here (1944), as in other contributions, made a clear reference to the political situation and Hitler's wars.

Schachermeyrs Hurrian–Indo–Aryan–'Symbiosis'

From the early 1950s to the mid–1980s,[161] Schachermeyr's reflections on Indo–Aryans and the introduction of chariots into the Ancient Near East were characterised by a view that can be outlined under the heading Hurrian–Indo–Aryan–'Symbiosis'.[162] Schachermeyr thus described a three–stage model of an Indo–Aryan migration to the Near East based on his cultural morphological framework of ideas, which he advocated practically unchanged, almost formulaically, since his essay on 'Streitwagen und

---

[155] This already goes back to Schachermeyr's article in the *Völkischer Beobachter* (Berlin edition of 13 April 1933, 2nd supplement ['Beiblatt']) with the title 'Die nordische Führerpersönlichkeit im Altertum' ('The Nordic leader personality in antiquity') and the subtitle 'Baustein zur Weltanschauung des Nationalsozialismus' ('Building block on the world view of National Socialism'; cf. Losemann 1977: 47; 206 fn. 5 with bibliographical references). At the same time, Schachermeyr was working on a comprehensive 'Versuch, zur Grundlegung der nationalsozialistischen Weltanschauung aus dem Geiste der Historie' ('Attempt to lay the foundations of the National Socialist world view from the spirit of history'; Schachermeyr 1933a: 361 and Losemann 1977: 47; 206 fn. 7), which alluded to Nietzsche in its title, in order to 'shake up the still somewhat sleepy readership of the *Neue Wege*' ('um den z.T. noch etwas schläfrigen Leserkreis der 'Neuen Wege' wachzurütteln'). Cf. also Losemann 1977: 98 on Schachermeyr's lectures in assessments by other colleagues at a conference organised by the 'NSD–Dozentenbund' ('Nationalsozialistischer Deutscher Dozentenbund', 'The National Socialist German Lecturers League') in Würzburg in January 1941, where Schachermeyr gave a keynote speech on the subject of 'Rassenkunde und Altertumsforschung' ('racial studies and studies of antiquity'), in which he 'as in 1933' emphasised 'his fundamental willingness to make the decision on the evaluation of antiquity dependent on the findings of racial studies' ('wie schon 1933 seine grundsätzliche Bereitschaft [herausstellte], die Entscheidung über die Bewertung der Antike von den Erkenntnissen der Rassenkunde abhängig zu machen').

[156] A critical analysis of Schachermeyr's racial theorems (e.g., Schachermeyr 1940) and racial positions in Hitler Germany, including the reception of the publications of the writer and advocate for racial racism Hans Friedrich Karl Günther (1891–1961), Schachermeyr's colleague in the Chair of Social Anthropology in Jena from 1930–1935, who was also widely received by him until 1945, is still a *desideratum* of research (see Pesditschek 2009: Chapter 'Professor in Jena', pp. 179 ff.).

[157] Pesditschek 2020: 192 ('Der prominente österreichische Althistoriker Fritz Schachermeyr [1895–1987] hat, wie die Autorin selbst immer wieder betont hat, 'während der NS–Zeit so konsequent wie kein anderer Altertumswissenschaftler die nationalsozialistische Rassenlehre in Forschung und Lehre vertreten' und ist, wie die Autorin selbst immer wieder zu zeigen versucht hat, bis an sein Lebensende von der Richtigkeit speziell der rein biologistischen Rassentheorien Günthers überzeugt gewesen'). See fn. 63–64 in Pesditschek 2020 with references to her PhD thesis 2009.

[158] Losemann 1977: 231 fn. 165 with documentation ('Mitbegründer des nat.soz. Kampfringes der Deutschösterreicher im Reich (zeitweise [1933–1934] Gauführer im Gau Thüringen' and 'Kulturpolitisch im Sinne der nat.soz. Bewegung durch Vorträge und Veröffentlichungen tätig').

[159] The title might be rendered as: *Indo–Europeans and Orient. Their Power–Political Conflict in Antiquity*.

[160] Schachermeyr 1944: 51–54. On the strategic and tactical use of chariots see the article of Steven Weingartner in this volume.

[161] See Schachermeyr 1986: 361.

[162] The reception of the term 'symbiosis', which originated in biology and has sometimes been used since the mid–1930s in connection with Hurrians and Indo–Aryans and to which Schachermeyr ascribes central importance with regard to the 'invention' of the chariot, cannot be discussed in detail here. Cf. the index entry 'symbiosis' in Mayrhofer 1966: Register sub R14.

Streitwagenbild im Alten Orient und den mykenischen Griechen' (1951).¹⁶³ Schachermeyr summarises:

> Eine Revolutionierung der Kriegskunst bedeutete (...) erst die Einführung des leichten und damit schnellen zweirädrigen Streit- und Rennwagens (...). Das geschah in der ersten Hälfte des zweiten Jahrtausends. In der Regel wird diese Neuerung von der Forschung den Ariern zugeschrieben, welche damals von den eurasischen Weiten am Schwarzen Meer kommend [end of the first stage], aus der Gebirgszone in Vorderasien eindrangen. Ich stimme dem mit folgender Einschränkung zu: Vor ihrem Einbruch in Mesopotamien waren die Arier in den nördlichen Gebirgsbereichen (etwa Armenien oder Kaukasus?) eine Symbiose eingegangen mit den dort bodenständigen und äußerst gewerbetüchtigen Churritern. Da es sich beim leichten Streitwagen um eine handwerkliche Meisterleistung ersten Ranges handelt, möchte ich seine Konstruktion lieber solchen churritischen Elementen zuschreiben. Dagegen mag die Zucht von Rennrossen in höherem Masse in arischen Händen gelegen haben. Die Arier, welche in der erwähnten Symbiose zugleich die politische Führung innehatten, werteten den Streitwagen dann in sportlicher wie kriegstechnischer Hinsicht aus [second stage] und nützten ihn zu Eroberungen größten Stils [third stage].¹⁶⁴

In terms of the history of scholarship, it should first be noted that with Meyer (1909a and other studies), Bruno Meissner (1968-1947),¹⁶⁵ August Köster (1873-1935)¹⁶⁶ and Arthur Ungnad (1879-1945),¹⁶⁷ the *argumentum e silentio* of the unfamiliarity during the time of Ḫammurapi of Babylon¹⁶⁸ with the horse, as Eduard Meyer called it,¹⁶⁹ continues to resonate. Schachermeyr (1951) is now forced to explain the pre-Indo-Aryan mentions of the lively horse trade of Chagar Bazar and other evidence of disputes in the Mari letters,¹⁷⁰ which were made known to a wide audience by Franz Hančar (1955):

> Das hätte zur Voraussetzung, daß damals bereits auch der leichte Streitwagen von Norden her gelegentlich bis nach Mesopotamien importiert wurde. Hiermit warf dann die Arierinvasion gleichsam ihre Schatten voraus. Offenbar gab es zur Hammurabizeit im Gebirgsbereich bereits arische Herrschaften.

However, this interpretation 'puts the cart before the horse' due to its circular reasoning.

In the context of the history of chariot research, Schachermeyr's reception of Wiesner 1939, both of whom were known to have spoken in favour of an Indo-Aryan introduction of chariots, should first be noted. The idea of an 'Hurrian-Aryan-symbiosis' in Caucasia or Armenia, which Schachermeyr attempts to periodise as a 'second stage', is henceforth passed on in all his contributions with reference to the chariot article published in 1951.¹⁷¹

These statements on the 'Hurrian-Aryan-symbiosis', which can be regarded as obsolete in most respects, are left aside here, not least because of the lack of written and archaeological evidence. Thus Schachermeyr summarises in 1984:

> Die Mehrzahl der übrigen Wanderlustigen dürfte aber wieder aus Hurritern bestanden haben. Dieser arisch-hurritischen Symbiose ist nun die Zucht edler Rosse wie die Erfindung des Streitwagens und der Rennfahrt zuzuschreiben. Beim Streitwagen handelt es sich nun um ein Gefährt von ganz besonderer Art. (...) Demgegenüber bedeutete es nun eine richtige Revolution, in der Kriegskunst, als die Konstruktion eines ganz leichten und damit schnellen zweirädrigen Rennwagens gelang, der von zwei hochgezüchteten Rennpferden gezogen werden sollte. (...) Gewöhnlich schreibt man diese Erfindung einfach den Ariern zu. Meiner Meinung nach war sie dagegen einer arisch-hurritischen Symbiose zu verdanken. Da es sich beim leichten Streitwagen um eine wahre Meisterleistung handelte, in der ganz verschiedene Holzarten je nach ihrer Festigkeit und Leichtigkeit verwendet wurden, glaube ich, daß eine so ausgetüftelte Konstruktion und Anfertigung eher hurritischen Werkmeistern zuzuschreiben sei als den stolzen arischen Herren, die dann auf solchen Wagen kutschierten. Dagegen mag die Zucht von Rennrossen in höherem Maße in den Händen der Arier gelegen haben. Also waren diejenigen Elemente, welche die politische Führung innehatten (wohl eine Mischung, in der Arisches immer mehr in Hurritischem aufging), die eigentlichen Nutznießer. Sie werteten den Streitwagen in sportlicher wie in kriegstechnischer Hinsicht aus und verwendeten ihn schließlich zu Eroberungen größten Stils.¹⁷²

The sporting component emphasised by Schachermeyr is particularly important against the background of the well-known Indo-Aryan chariot races, raids and other warlike activities as described in the Rigveda¹⁷³ and Avesta,¹⁷⁴

---

¹⁶³ 'Chariots and Chariot Image in the Ancient Near East and the Mycenaean Greeks'.
¹⁶⁴ Schachermeyr 1951: 751–752.
¹⁶⁵ Meissner 1913.
¹⁶⁶ Köster 1923.
¹⁶⁷ Ungnad 1923.
¹⁶⁸ First half of the 18th century BCE (Middle Chronology).
¹⁶⁹ Meyer 1909a: 23 fn. 1.
¹⁷⁰ van Koppen 2002.

¹⁷¹ In selection: Schachermeyr 1964: 23–24; 316; Schachermeyr 1967: 60; Schachermeyr 1984b: 56–57.
¹⁷² Schachermeyr 1984b: 129.
¹⁷³ On the *Aśvamedha* ritual see e.g., Sparreboom 1985: 51–55 ('The Chariot Drive in the Aśvamedha'); Oberlies 1998: 286 ff., especially 290–292 (p. 290 fn. 677 with bibliography). See also Sparreboom 1985: 13–27 ('The Imagery of the Chariot'), 28 ff. on the to the chariot race in the Vājapeya sacrifice etc. (esp. pp. 45 ff.; 55 ff.; 60 ff.).
¹⁷⁴ Cf., e.g., Hauschild 1959 on the legendary chariot race of Kavi Haosravah; also Raulwing 2005: 68–69, and the overviews by Oettinger 1994 and Zimmer 1998 as well as Raulwing 1999: 360–361.

as the idea of sport and speed ('Sport– und Schnelligkeitsgedanke'), and its unreflected transfer to the Near Eastern Indo–Aryans as well as the comparison of Iranian personal names with the compositional elements 'horse' (/áśva/, /aspa/ and 'chariot' (/rátha/, /raϑa/).[175]

In his last monograph, *Mykene und das Hethiterreich* (1986),[176] Schachermeyr calls out to us regarding the Indo–Aryans, as his legacy, so to speak:

> Nachher kamen – vermischt mit den Hurritern – Schwärme von Ariern gleichfalls aus dem Nordosten, strebten mit den von ihnen erfundenen Streitwagen, die von edlen Rossen gezogen wurden, aber nach den Ebenen Mesopotamiens und Syriens. Die Indo–Europäer, welche uns hier entgegentreten, ließen sich von der Sportbegeisterung der Arier anstecken. (…) Zu der Rolle der Indo–Arier im Auftreten der Streitwagenkämpfer im Vorderasien der Mitanni–Zeit fanden geschulte Historiker wie etwa Eduard Meyer sogleich eine Parallele, ja gleichsam ein Modell im Auftreten der Normannischen Fürstennamen in Rußland, in der Normandie und von dort aus in Sizilien wie in England. Auch da habe es sich ja um kampfesstarke Elemente gehandelt, die zwar überall siegten, aber ihre Siege oft genug an der Spitze von Volkselementen mit anderen Sprachen wie Kulturen erreichten, deren Sprachen (…) und auch deren Kultur übernahmen. Daher hinterließen sie für Ausgräber und Archäologen auch nichts Normannisches, für die Sprachforscher aber nur normannische Eigennamen und vor allem Fürstennamen. Dieser Typus stellt sich nun allem Anschein nach auch bei den Indo–Ariern im damaligen Vorderasien ein, denn wir haben da nur indo–arische Eigennamen und vor allem Fürstennamen, auch Götternamen, und außerdem noch Spezialbezeichnungen für ein Training von schnellen Rossen. Wie sollten denn die in anderer Weise nach Vorderasien gekommen sein??? Der Streitwagenkampf verlangt aber trainierte Rosse, und gerade da haben sich die indo–arischen Fachausdrücke ja in Keilschrifttexten erhalten. Auch Wagen verschiedener Art hat es in Vorderasien wohl stets gegeben, aber der Streitwagen von Florenz erweist uns, mit welcher Fachkunst an Holzauswahl die Leichtigkeit dieser Rennwagen ausgestattet wurde. Das wird man am ehesten den Hurritern zutrauen, die in holz– und waldreichen Bergen beheimatet waren. Diese Parallelen waren einem Historiker stets geläufig und wurden auch von den Sprachvergleichern mit historischem Weitblick vertreten. Archäologen und Nur Ausgräber der modernen Zeit finden aber – z.B. bei den Hyksos – natürlich kaum etwas Indo–Arisches. Darum wollen solche Leute von Indo–Ariern nicht viel wissen. Aber die Normannen können sie nicht abschaffen. (p. 361)

Schachermeyr's Hypotheses on the Introduction of the Chariot into Bronze Age Greece

Beginning with his contribution to the emergence of Mycenaean culture in the Hrozný *Festschrift* (1949), Schachermayr developed a hypothesis after the Second World War,[177] according to which the Mycenaeans, after the destruction of the palace in Knossos (i.e. at the beginning of Late Minoan IA, at the beginning of the 16th century BCE),[178] utilised this natural disaster and the resulting power vacuum to conquer Crete on the one hand and to intervene in the 'freedom struggle of the Egyptians against the Hyksos (ca. 1570)' ('Freiheitskampf der Ägypter gegen die Hyksos') on the other.[179] These ideas on the introduction of chariots to Greece, which had already been put forward by the Swedish archaeologist Axel W. Persson (1888–1951),[180] were also taken up by Schachermeyr in his monograph *Poseidon und die Entstehung des griechischen Götterglaubens*[181] and, just a little later, in his much–cited *Anthropos* essay of 1951 mentioned above, he attempted to substantiate them in detail.[182]

> Auf Kreta wie auch in Mykenai tritt nun, gleichsam schlagartig, der Streitwagen und der den Streitwagen ziehende Renner in Erscheinung. Für Kreta brachte das keine Änderung in der allgemeinen, vom Stil der Paläste bestimmten Lebensweise. Für die Achäer Mykenais bedeutete Streitwagenfahrt und Rossezucht aber zugleich den Ausdruck einer damit engstens verbundenen neuen ritterlichen Haltung. Waren die Griechen bisher vorwiegend Landvolk gewesen, so hob sich aus ihrem Kreis nun ein Ritterstand heraus, der sich Burgen erbaute und in diesen ein dem Kampf wie der Jagd geltendes herrisches Dasein führte. (…) Nichts ist charakteristischer für die hohe Einschätzung, welche der neueingeführte Renn– und Streitwagen wie zugleich auch das Pferd nunmehr gewinnt, als der Befund jener frühmykenischen Fürstengrüfte [Shaft Graves] (…). Neu war freilich die Schulung des Pferdes zum Ziehen des Rennwagens. So wie dieser – wohl über Ägypten – von den damals im Orient tonangebenden arischen Mitanni–Leuten übernommen wurde, könnte man von dort man von

---

[175] Schachermeyr 1944: 52.
[176] *Mycenae and the Hittite Empire*.
[177] His forced retirement in 1945 as well as the denazification process and his stay in Saalfelden took place during this time. Cf. Pesditschek 2009: 371 ff.
[178] See *Der Neue Pauly* vol. 8 (2000): 224 s.v. *Minoische Kultur* and p. 580 s.v. *Mykenische Kultur*.
[179] Schachermeyr 1950: 705.
[180] Persson 1942: 178–196. This is explicitly pointed out by Drews 1988: 173–174 and note 46; there also rightly criticising Schachermeyr's interpretation of the stelae of the shaft tombs in Mycenae and their significance for the introduction of chariots to Greece. Reference can only be made here to the more recent discussion: for criticism of Penner 1998, see Maran 2020: 508–509.
[181] 'Poseidon and the Origin of the Greek Belief in the Gods'. Schachermayr 1950: 54–55. There also on the Cretan chariot. Emphasis in the original. Cf. also the 3rd chapter with the heading 'Rossehaltung, Wagenfahrt und ritterlicher Poseidon in der mykenischen Epoche' ('Horse husbandry, chariot travel and knightly Poseidon in the Mycenaean era'), pp. 50 ff.
[182] Schachermeyr 1950: 705–706; 714 ff. (esp. 717 ff.); 740; 742.

dort vielleicht auch einige geschulte Rennrosse importiert haben.

According to this model for the introduction of chariots into Late Bronze Age Greece, the Mycenaean princes not only adopted horses and chariots as a material and cultural asset, but also the 'chariot image' (i.e. the pictorial motif, the 'Streitwagenbild') from Egypt.[183] Schachermeyr also explained 'the appearance of knighthood' in Mycenae at the same time as the chariot ('das mit dem Streitwagen gleichzeitige Auftreten von Ritterschaft') with direct Mycenaean–Indo–Aryan contacts in Egypt[184] – the Mycenaeans as 'allies of the XVIIIth Dynasty' ('Bundesgenossen der XVIII. Dynastie'),[185] so to speak: This 'knighthood' ('Ritterschaft') would have brought 'precisely the Aryans to the Ancient Near East, where their knightly nobility referred to themselves as mariannu'; more precisely: as the 'chivalrous Mariannus'[!] (the 'ritterliche Mariannus').[186] And if 'the Aryans were led to knighthood through chariot warfare,[187] Schachermeyr speculated further in 1950,

> konnte das gleiche auch bei den mykenischen Griechen geschehen. Hatten diese einmal den Streitwagen übernommen und sich der neuen Kampfesweise ganz hingegeben, so bildeten sich ganz von selbst für die Streitwagenkämpfer die nämlichen Bedingungen und Erfordernisse heraus wie für den arischen *mariannu*. Sie führen über eine gewaltige waffentechnische Überlegenheit zu einer wirtschaftlichen wie sozialen (bzw. oft auch asozialen) Auswertung der neuen Stellung im Sinne der Kastenbildung, einer engeren Kastenethik und einer kastenmäßigen Arroganz wie Brutalität[!].[188]

These clichés,[189] which are also unsupported by the textual evidence, were passed on by Schachermeyr in this form almost unchanged until the mid–1980s, i.e. until the end of his academic career.[190] Although we will not go into this any further here, it seems remarkable, at least in terms of the history of scholarship, that the main features of Schachermeyr's line of argument had already been worked out before 1945, in particular taking into account his 'historical–biological' and racial science and ideological framework, which was merely omitted terminologically in the post–war studies:[191] In the context of these outlines regarding chariotry research in Schachermeyr's academic works, it is therefore not surprising that he again modified his opinion on the origin of horses and chariots in Late Bronze Age Greece in the 1980s, nor that this new model began to emerge in his writing several decades earlier. In his interpretation of the origin of the Mycenaean chariot, Schachermeyr still presumed in the presence of 'knights with chariot skills, whether scattered Hyksos princes, or from the Mitanni region in the Near East or from eastern Anatolia' – i.e. Indo–Aryans![192]

The Indo–European *termini technici* for Horses and Chariots

The term for horse that is undoubtedly most frequently treated from the reconstructable basic Indo–European

---

[183] Schachermeyr 1951: 729 ff. summarises: 'Wenn Mykenai aber schon sein ältestes Streitwagenbild aus Ägypten bezog, so bleibt es doch bei weitem das wahrscheinlichste, daß es auch den Streitwagen selber (den man zu genau der gleichen Zeit wie das Bild übernahm!) von dort und nirgends anders her hatte.' (p. 740). Critically Nagel 1966: 47 f. Cf. also Mayrhofer 1966: Sachindex s.v. *Streitwagenbild* (p. 151).
[184] Schachermeyr 1950: 740–742. Quote p. 740; emphasis in the original.
[185] Schachermeyr 1979b: 1508.
[186] Schachermeyr 1986: 351.
[187] 'die Arier durch den Wagenkampf zur Ritterschaft geführt wurden'.
[188] Schachermeyr 1950: 741. Such an interpretation is of course untenable due to Schachermeyr's failure to analyse the sources.
[189] Cf. also the justified criticism by Nagel 1966: 47–48; Hayen 1986: 63 with a brief presentation of the research opinions, without favouring one of the hypotheses.
[190] Schachermeyr 1968: 304–306; Schachermeyr 1954: 1491–1492: 'daß die mykenische Kultur aus der m.hell. [Middle Helladic] Gesittung durch Übernahme des Streitwagens, Rittertums und minoischer Kulturelemente entstanden ist. [referring to Schachermeyr 1949]. Der Streitwagen stammte letztendes zwar von den damals in Vorderasien eingebrochenen Ariern, kam nach Mykenai aber über Ägypten [Hinweis auf Schachermeyr 1951]. Er kann also mit der Einwanderung der Griechen ebensowenig zu tun gehabt haben wie die gleichzeitig von Kreta her wirkende mykenische Kultur. Die Einführung der Ritterschaft ergab sich aber zwangsläufig einfach aus der Verwendung der Streitwagenwaffe (die ihrerseits den Typus des Streitwagenkämpfers formte). (…) Wenn wir nun aus den Tongefäßen der extramuralen Schachtgräber [in Mycenae]

erkennen, daß ihre Anlage größtenteils noch in die Zeit vor 1580 fällt, so stimmt das bestens mit unserer Annahme überein, daß erst von diesem Zeitpunkt an von Ägypten der Streitwagen eingeführt und durch die Beutezüge nach Kreta die dortigen Schätze wie Werkmeister nach Mykenai überführt wurden (…)'; see also Schachermeyr 1979b: 1508.
[191] Schachermeyr 1939: 269–270 on the 'achäisches' 'Rittertum': 'Ritterlichkeit (…) [this term has its own entry in the Lexikon der Ägyptologie; see Kaplony 1986] auf dem Festland (…) im Gegensatz zur minoischen Kultur (…) als artgemäße Reaktion der Indogermanen auf die höfische Idee' ausbildete und '[d]er festländische Achäer [somit] zwar die Idee der Hofhaltung übernehmen [konnte], doch (…) die ihm artfremde, darbietungsmäßige Ausdeutung ab[lehnte] und (…) erstere mit einem neuen, ihm artgemäßen Geist des Rittertums' erfüllte'. According to an assessment published forty years later by Schachermeyr (1979a: 326), in which the racial and ideological connotations seem to have given way to a romanticised evaluation, the Minoans (in contrast to the Mycenacans) were 'keine Ritter, sie schätzten weder das Militärische noch die Jagd allzusehr, verwendeten Waffen, um damit zu prunken, und den Streitwagen zur eleganten Spazierfahrt. Wohl begeisterten sie sich für sportliche Wettkämpfe, wirken aber auf den Abbildungen als gefallsüchtige Dandys und Stutzer. (…). Eine große Rolle spielte in der min.[oischen] Gesellschaft gegenüber dem Grandseigneur die Dame.' See also his reference to the 'weltgeschichtliche Bedeutung der arischen Ritterschaft' ('world–historical significance of the Aryan knighthood'; Schachermeyr 1944: 55–58; 66 ff.): because of their 'Fernwirkung' ('long distance effect'; p. 56–57; emphasis in the original). We can state that Schachermeyr's publications from 1949 onward are characterised by the omission of his racial and ideological diction used between 1933 and 1945 while continuing his chariotry research.
[192] 'streitwagenkundige Rittern, sei es versprengte Hyksosfürsten, sei es aus dem Mitanni–Bereich in Vorderasien oder aus dem östlichen Anatolien.' See already Schachermeyr 1950: 175–176 ('M. E. traten damals einzelne achäische Streitwagenherren in Lykien und Karien als eine Art von fahrendem Ritter auf und heirateten gelegentlich auch in die Familien des einheimischen Adels ein. Offenbar wurden sie als Spezialisten der neuen Waffentechnik von den Kleinasiaten nicht minder geschätzt als von den Königen der Levante, welche ja gleichfalls achäische Recken anwarben'). Schachermeyr refers here to his monographs *Hethiter und Achäer* (1935: 94 ff.; 141 ff.) and goes so far (1950: 175–176) to interpret a four–spoked chariot captured by the Egyptians and depicted in a relief from Medinet Habu as a 'piece of booty' ('Beutestück') of 'Achaean knights' ('achäischer Ritter').

vocabulary is *h₁éḱu̯o–.¹⁹³ This reconstruction, in which, among other things, both the asterisk and the initial laryngal *h₁éḱu̯o– a consonantal phoneme reconstructed for the basic Indo–European language¹⁹⁴ – point to the developed (and not documented in writing) character of the word, is established by phonetic developments in the individual Indo–European languages and is based on evidence such as Old Indian aśva–, Avestic aspa–, Mycenaean i–qo / ikku̯o/, Greek híppos, Latin equus (in the older phonetic state, the basic linguistic –o is still preserved in the form equos), Gallic epo, Old Irish ech, Old English eoh and others.¹⁹⁵

For the four–wheeled wagon and its constructional components, the *termini technici* for 'yoke', 'pole', 'axle' and 'hub' can be reconstructed.¹⁹⁶ On the other hand, a distribution of technical terms in Indo–European languages for 'wheel' and 'wagon' (partly as *pars pro toto* terms) to a number of so–called verbal roots can be observed, which semantically can be assigned to the actions 'to turn', 'to roll', 'to pull', 'to join', etc.¹⁹⁷ Furthermore, it is revealing that neither basic linguistic terms for spoke, rim, wheel rim and bit can be reconstructed nor a common pre–singular term for the wagon itself.¹⁹⁸

Methodological Boundaries of Historical–Comparative Linguistics

From the point of view of Indo–European studies as a discipline in which linguistic reconstructions are created with the help of linguistic methodology, only the *termini technici* for horses and chariots can be the focus of the considerations and interpretations for the questions addressed here. The historical comparative–linguistic and etymological method is abandoned as soon as the reconstructions for the basic linguistic Proto–Indo–European lexicon are based on archaeological, prehistorical or anthropological – *ergo* non–linguistic – evidence. As soon as these reconstructions are used for prehistoric, archaeological, archaeozoological or cultural–historical interpretations, they are the subject of Proto–Indo–European archaeology and linguistic palaeontology.¹⁹⁹ The latter is based on the premise that both the real–world environment and the so–called intellectual culture of the speakers of Proto–Indo–European can be inferred by means of reconstructions from Indo–European vocabulary attested in written sources: the assumption is that certain plants, animals, techniques, institutions, ideas, concepts must therefore have existed at the time when Proto–Indo–European was spoken.

However, as Indo–Europeanists have repeatedly pointed out, linguistic palaeontology quickly leaves its methodologically well–defined limits, and therefore all reconstructions are without the cultural–historical value that has been attributed to the linguistic approaches since the middle of the 19th century.²⁰⁰ What the historical comparative linguist Bernfried Schlerath (1924–2003) formulated for the possibilities of reconstructing the intangible culture of the Proto–Indo–European period also applies to the reconstruction of material culture:

> As such, Proto–Indo–European vocabulary offers no possibility of reconstructing the intellectual culture of Proto–Indo–European speakers, because with the reconstructed *termini*, components of the Proto–Indo–European language are also vindicated, which can only be eliminated at the price of non–specific blandness. The result is therefore an unjustified and apparent accumulation' and 'One must warn that the long–running discussion of Proto–Indo–European social structure, which deals with mere possibilities, may in the course of time give rise to the feeling among all concerned that it is a matter of proven results. As linguists, we know the object–constituting power of language.'²⁰¹

It cannot be emphasised enough, especially against the interdisciplinary background of our topic, that the terms 'Proto-Indo–European'/'Proto-Indo–Europeans', 'Indo–European'/'Indo–Europeans', and 'Indo–Aryan'/'Indo–Aryans', as well as their equivalents in other modern languages should be used correctly and exclusively in restricting them to their purely linguistic definition. Therefore, in no case can, ethnically, prehistorically, anthropologically – i.e. non–linguistically – defined groups be equated with speakers of Proto–Indo–European.²⁰²

Conclusions and Results for a Technical and Typological Interpretation of the Proto–Indo–European *termini technici* for Horses and Chariots

Applying the methodological principles laid out above to our topic, only the following result can be stated: A historical comparative linguistic analysis of the *termini technici* for horses and chariots allows us to make the general statement that the speakers of Proto–Indo–European were familiar with the so–called 'axle–wheel principle', i.e., the

---

¹⁹³ See, among others, Meid 1994: 54–57; Raulwing 2000: 101–109; Gaitzsch 2011.
¹⁹⁴ Lindemann 1987 and Bammesberger 1988.
¹⁹⁵ On Anatolian see Oettinger 1994: 74–75; Gaitzsch 2011.
¹⁹⁶ See 'yoke': *i̯ugó– EWAia II: 412–413; 418; 'pole' *h₂iHs–éh₂–: EWAia I: 208; 'axle' *h₂eḱ's: EWAia I: 41; 'nave' * h₃nebʰ–/*h₁nobʰ–/*h₃nbʰ–: EWAia II: 13–14.
¹⁹⁷ Rix 2001: s.v.
¹⁹⁸ Meid 1994: 63 and Raulwing 2000: 82 fn. 167.
¹⁹⁹ Schmitt 2000; Häusler 2000; see also Hajnal 2008.

²⁰⁰ See Untermann 1986; Schlerath 1987; 1995; 1996; Meid 1989 and Zimmer 1990.
²⁰¹ Schlerath 1995: 13 ('Der idg. Wortschatz bietet als solcher keine Möglichkeit, die geistige Kultur der Indogermanen zu rekonstruieren, weil mit dem rekonstruierten Wortkörper auch Inhalte der Grundsprache vindiziert werden, die man nur um den Preis der unverbindlichen Blässe eliminieren kann. Es entsteht also eine ungerechtfertigte und scheinbare Akkumulation') and Schlerath 1987: 263 ('Man muß davor warnen, daß die lang geführte Diskussion über die idg. Sozialstruktur, die sich mit bloßen Möglichkeiten beschäftigt, im Laufe der Zeit bei allen Beteiligten das Gefühl aufkommen läßt, daß es sich um gesicherte Ergebnisse handelt. Wir kennen als Linguisten die gegenstandskonstituierende Kraft der Sprache').
²⁰² Raulwing 2000; see also Pereltsvaig and Lewis 2015.

locomotion of a wheeled vehicle by means of harnessed draught animals. The basis for this result is reconstructed *termini technici* such as 'axle', 'wheel' and 'hub', to which must be added the technical terms for 'yoke' and 'pole'. However, the pole can also be characteristic of the plough. In this regard Schlerath's colleague Jürgen Untermann (1928–2013) made the sobering observation that the

> Prehistorian who observes fine differences in form and technique in his pottery, in weapons, graves and buildings, (...) can do little with it if the linguist tells him that the speakers of the language, he has reconstructed had something which they called wagon, wool or grain. And there is no prehistoric culture in Europe between the Neolithic and the Iron Age in which there is no such thing as what could have been designated by the reconstructed names (...).[203]

What this means in concrete terms for the questions raised here is illustrated by the fact that we cannot make reliable statements about basic constructional details such as the number of wheels (and thus also the axles), wheel construction (disc wheel, cross–bar wheel, spoked wheel), chariot bodies and the type of draught animals (bovids, equids) and their harness, although the hypothesis that chariots were known in Proto–Indo–European times cannot be ruled out in principle by recourse to comparative linguistic methodology due to the possible lack of relevant *termini technici* (*argumentum e silentio*). Nevertheless, it is precisely the lack of common basic linguistic reconstructions for terms such as 'spoke', 'felloe', 'bit', which must be regarded as of paramount importance for the definition of the chariot.[204] Therefore, Rüdiger Schmitt (2000: § 2) came to the conclusion in his article 'Indogermanische Altertumskunde' in the *Reallexikon für Germanische Altertumskunde* that complex reconstructions, such as the assumption of speakers of Proto–Indo–Europeans riding in chariots, 'cannot be proven from the linguistic evidence'.

If we apply the methodological criteria developed within historical–comparative linguistics and the results derived from them to the question of the origin, development and distribution of the chariot from the standpoint of Indo–European studies,[205] it is necessary – under the premise put forward by Hans–Georg Hüttel,[206] among others – to consider that 'the material possession of the Bronze Age horses and chariots is heterogeneous' and consequently that 'for each individual component a separate origin must be proven'.

This is part of the aim of Proto–Indo–European studies within chariotry research which can be outlined as follows, based on the current interdisciplinary evidence: Proto–Indo–European studies should take the initiative in no longer nourishing the futile hope in neighbouring disciplines within chariot research that a Proto–Indo–European chariot can be proven with the help of linguistic methodology and reconstructions of *termini technici*. However, this negative finding in no way leads to the conclusion that the contribution of historical–comparative Indo–European linguistics within chariot research should therefore be regarded as negligeable. Rather, the written evidence on horses and chariots from the 2nd and 1st millennia BCE must be described as precisely as possible in their respective historical, archaeological and cultural contexts.

Interim Results

If we summarise our brief overview on the history of scholarship of the speakers of Proto–Indo–European and Indo–Aryan in the Ancient Near East, they have been – and are – not only credited with the introduction of horses to the Fertile Crescent and adjacent areas, especially in the context of their association with the projection of chivalry already documented in Renaissance literature[207] and handed down through Romanticism to the present day, but also with the introduction of the true chariot,[208] including technical innovations such as the yoke saddle,[209] the introduction of a 'new chariot strategy'[210] or a new motif of chariot warfare in Ancient Near Eastern art.[211] In relation to the Levant and Egypt, it was therefore long thought that an 'Indo–Aryan wave' of 'aristocratic' Indo–Aryans who, as the 'ruling class' of the Hyksos, brought knowledge of the chariot to the eastern Mediterranean region.[212] However, such a view of cultural history does justice neither to the historical circumstances nor to the philological evidence and is therefore futile. Following the problems, questions and research priorities outlined in the previous sections, only a new investigation of all available sources, including the history of scholarship of Proto–Indo–European, Indo–European and Indo–Aryan (in the Ancient Near East), taking into account all aspects of the written evidence, promises to provide a well–founded answer to the question of their cultural–historical role with regard to horses and chariots.

A Critical Examination of Prehistoric Sources

The archaeological discussion on the early chariot necessarily focused on the Ancient Near Eastern region due to the number and quality of evidence in the early civilizations of the Fertile Crescent, Egypt and adjacent areas,

---

[203] Untermann 1986: 149 ('Der Prähistoriker, der feine Form– und Technikunterschiede bei seiner Keramik, bei Waffen, Gräbern und Gebäuden beobachtet, (...) wenig damit anfangen können [wird], wenn der Sprachwissenschaftler ihm sagt, dass die Sprecher der von ihm erschlossenen Sprache etwas gehabt haben, was sie Wagen, Wolle oder Korn genannt haben. Und es gibt zwischen Neolithikum und Eisenzeit in Europa keine prähistorische Kultur, in der es so etwas nicht gibt, was durch die rekonstruierten Namen bezeichnet worden sein könnte (...)').
[204] Specht 1944: 103.
[205] Raulwing 1998; 2000: 14–36; 98–100.
[206] Hüttel 1994: 204.
[207] Graf 2002; Bumke 1986; Paravicini 2011.
[208] Cf. Raulwing 1994: 76 and Raulwing 2000: 29 fn. 35.
[209] Koch 1992.
[210] Börker–Klähn 1988: 217.
[211] Moortgat 1930.
[212] 'eine bis Palästina geschlagen[e]' 'indoarische Welle' 'aristokratische[r]' Indo–Aryans als 'Führungsschicht' of the Hyksos'. This has been viewed critically by Mayrhofer 1974: 18.

which had long prevailed over other cultures. As we have seen, the discovery of textual Indo–Aryan evidence in the Ancient Near Eastern texts broadened the discussion in the course of the first half of the 20th century[213] and was – to a good degree – focused on hippological terminology and a special 'connection' of the Indo–Aryans to horses and chariots, to the extent that linguistic arguments were forwarded in favour of the introduction of the chariot into the Near East by incoming Indo–Aryans. As there was a lack of at least contemporaneous, if not older, archaeological evidence for the knowledge and use of chariots outside the cultures of the Ancient Near East, which would have located the origin of chariot geographically.

Since the 1990s, however, the tide has turned. With the opening of the Iron Curtain, the graves with the remains of chariots that had been excavated since the 1970s in the south–eastern Urals and northern Kazakhstan were also perceived in the West. These finds gave new impetus to the discussion about the genesis and spread of the chariot. We are confronted with a group of monuments that not only prove the use of a type of vehicle that is commonly understood as a chariot, but which may also have chronological priority over the Ancient Near East. The search for the origins was now channelled in a new geographical direction.

The question of the origin and distribution of the chariot is more than just an interesting aspect of the history of technology and innovation research. As we have seen, the chariot is said to have given rise to a new class of warriors that had a far–reaching influence on the history of Eurasia and the Ancient Near East,[214] not least due to its new fighting tactics. The far–reaching derivations of an Indo–Aryan horse–and–chariot–ideology from the linguistic evidence are transferred into a comprehensive cultural and historical model, the implications of which will not be considered here, but which should once again be a reason to take a closer look at the archaeological evidence. The focus here is on the early evidence of chariot use with regard to the 'question of origin' and on the technical characteristics of these chariots, insofar as they can be deduced from the archaeological record.

The chariots of the so–called Sintashta culture in the south–eastern Ural area and the Petrovka culture in northern Kazakhstan carry the most weight in the discussion. As the only remains of real chariots from the beginning of the second millennium BCE that have been discovered to date, they are the point of reference for the current discussion. So far, chariot remains have been discovered from 29 graves, with the majority of the evidence coming from the eponymous site Sintashta.[215] In all cases, these are burial chambers into which a two–wheeled chariot had been placed, which stood in the chamber; the wheels had been set about 30 cm into the chamber floor. The chariots must have been made entirely of organic materials, which, however, have decayed over time. Only the wheel sections embedded in the chamber floor were recorded as discolorations in the archaeological findings. Recognizable here are two–wheeled spoked wheel chariots with a gauge in average of 120–150 cm; the wheels had a diameter of 0.9–1.2 m, 8–12 spokes (with a mostly rectangular cross–section of $3 \times 3{,}5 – 3{,}5 \times 4{,}5$ cm) and a rim width of around 4 cm.[216] In Krivoe Ozero, Kazakhstan, remains of a hub, the axle and the floor frame could also be observed.[217] With a track width of 120 cm, this wagon was significantly narrower than the other wagons in this group. The nave had a length of approx. 20 cm; the position of the wheels on the chamber wall means that a corresponding hub length can also be inferred for other sites.

Since the archaeological inventory of the material evidence consists for the most part only of the negatives of the lower third of the wheels, it is hardly possible to make any statements about the vehicle construction that go beyond the key data taken from the wheels (number of spokes, wheel diameter, rim width, nave length, gauge). The detailed reconstruction of the driver's box of the Krivoe Ozero chariot, as proposed by Christian Eder and Wolfram Nagel (2006), cannot be inferred from the findings. The authors assume a rear–mounted axle, which would have given the chariot special driving characteristics.[218] However, neither the description of the find nor the drawing of the original by David Anthony and Nikolai Vinogradov (1995) suggest this; the position of the timbers of the floor frame behind the axle suggest a central axle.[219]

As will be shown below, the gauge is of critical importance. The position of the wheels in the burial chamber may give an indication of the gauge, but it must be borne in mind that in most cases it is not certain whether a complete chariot – at least the wheels in conjunction with the axle – was really deposited in the grave or whether we are not confronted with a deposit of wheels on the chamber wall as a *pars pro toto* grave good representing a chariot. In the latter case, the wheel remains cannot provide any information of the gauge.[220]

In some of the burial chambers, one or two horses lay in front of the chariot; in the burials of the Petrovka culture, the horse skeletons were located outside the burial chamber. However, entire horse skeletons were rare, usually only individual body parts (skulls, front and hind legs)

---

[213] Mayrhofer 1966; 1974; 1982; 2006.
[214] See e.g. Anthony 2007: 412 ff.; Kristiansen 2004; Penner 1998: 213–215.
[215] See Chechushkov and Epimakhov this volume; see also Cherlenok 2006: Table 1.
[216] After Chechushkov and Epimakhov this volume: Tab. 1; see also Epimakhov and Korjakova 2004: 222–224; Kuzmina 2001: 12–13.
[217] Anthony and Vinogradov 1995.
[218] Littauer and Crouwel 1979: 53; Sandor 2004: 160.
[219] Anthony and Vinogradov 1995: Figure on p. 39.
[220] At least for Sintashta grave 16 (SMG16) and Vetlyanka IV cemetery, Kurgan 14, grave 6 (VIVK14G6) this seems reasonable. Both depositions have an outstanding reconstructed gauge of 65 resp. 200 cm. In both cases the wheels stood next to the chamber walls, which might give evidence, that these wheels were placed without the axle in the burial chamber. In all other cases the wheels were placed with enough space to at least one of the chamber walls (see Chechushkov and Epimakhov this volume: Tab. 1).

were deposited.²²¹ The layout of Sintashta SM, grave 30 shows the burial as a selective arrangement:²²² the three(!) cheekpieces were not in a functional position, but lying together next to one of the horse skulls; only the skulls and front extremities of two horses were deposited; at least the pole of the chariot would not have been placed in the chamber, which was too small for it. This lends further weight to the previously expressed idea of a *pars pro toto* representation.

Based on the horse depositions, we can assume that these vehicles were drawn by horses. This would be the first evidence of horse–drawn chariots in the Eurasian region. This observation is supported by an increasing number of finds of cheekpieces.²²³ The pieces, which mostly appear as disc shaped cheekpieces, are considered to be part of the harness of draught horses (see below). However, most of the cheekpiece finds come from graves that did not contain chariots, some also from settlements.²²⁴ They are interpreted as indirect evidence for the use of horse–drawn vehicles, whereby their wider distribution and more frequent occurrence – compared to the finds of chariots or chariot parts – gives them great significance.

Based on calibrated 14C data, the group of Sintashta and Petrovka chariots have been dated to the period 1950–1750 BCE.²²⁵ This means that they are definitely older than the chariots that have been known at so far. Nevertheless, the dating range is too wide to give the Trans–Uralic finds any real primacy in the genesis of chariot technology. Although with archaeological typology a two–phase cultural sequence can be identified, the calibrated 14C dates have a too large dating range so that the phases overlap in absolute chronological terms and therefore cannot be separated at all. For several graves from kurgans from the Kamennyi Ambar 5 cemetery, Stephan Lindner was able to achieve a more precise dating using a Bayesian approach. The dating could be narrowed down further, particularly on the basis of the ceramic typology: the blurred time interval of the calibrated samples of 1970–1770 cal BC (at 95.4 %) is now narrowed down to 1950–1880 cal BC (at 95.4 %) in a Bayesian model. This means that the appearance of the first chariots in this region can be dated to the 20th century BCE.²²⁶ Stanislav Grigoriev recently rejected Lindner's application of the ceramic typology, as it does not have the assumed chronological selectivity and therefore cannot provide the basis for the statistical analysis.²²⁷ This criticism must be taken seriously and requires a critical revision of the 14C data.

Provided the data are correct, the 14C data justify the special significance of the Trans–Uralian and North Kazakh chariots: they are the oldest horse–drawn chariots to date and the oldest chariots with spoked wheels. However, the origins of this group are unknown. Since no precursor of the Sintashta culture has yet been identified,²²⁸ the horse–drawn chariot comes out of a sudden and its origin remains enigmatic. Repeated attempts have been made to draw a connection to the long vehicle tradition of the northern Pontic Yamnaya and Catacomb Culture. However, it should be borne in mind that the vehicles of the third millennium were heavy four–wheeled wagons with disk wheels pulled by teams of cattle – there is also no evidence of bridle harnesses. Elena Izbitser has repeatedly rejected the reconstruction of two–wheeled carts with source–critical arguments; although two–wheeled vehicles appear in the Catacomb Culture, they are an exception here and also point to Caucasian connections.²²⁹ The Trans–Uralic chariots cannot be derived technologically from the North Pontic vehicles, and the great geographical distance between the North Pontic and Trans–Uralic steppes and the hitherto barely tangible cultural connection between these areas make them appear more as a novelty than as an expression of a long chariot–making tradition.²³⁰

The Carpathian region is another area of archaeological evidence that has so far been insufficiently considered in the discussion.²³¹ Actual chariot finds from an early period are still unknown. However, there are numerous spoked wheel models from the Middle Bronze Age from settlement contexts, although these belong to four–wheeled wagons. A recently published wagon model found in a burial from Encs in Hungary has four spoked wheels. By 14C the burial is dated to 1960 to 1740 cal BC.²³² This clearly demonstrates the early knowledge of spoked wheels in the Carpathian Basin, but also that these were not restricted to chariots. Individual clay wheel models can be identified as spoked wheels; however, their date is unlikely to be at the beginning of the second millennium BCE.²³³ The models show in all cases four spokes per wheel, which distinguishes them from the wheels of the Sintashta culture with their 8–12 spokes.

We get an indication of possible chariots from numerous cheekpieces. These are also mostly settlement finds. Disc shaped cheekpieces, as they are known from the Eurasian steppe region, are also represented here in individual specimens; however, the majority of the finds are so–called rod shaped cheekpieces.²³⁴ There is no evidence from this region that these were accessories for horse harnesses; only more recent pictorial representations of chariot teams with rod shaped cheekpieces from the Aegean region and the Near East establish this connection.

The first rod shaped cheekpieces finds in Romania come from layers of the Monteoru Ic3 and Ic2 phases. For many of the finds, it is not possible to clearly determine which

---

²²¹ Epimachov and Korjakowa 2004: 224.
²²² Epimachov and Korjakowa 2004: 225, fig. 4.
²²³ See Bochkarev and Kuznetsov this volume; earlier reviews Teufer 1999; Epimakhov and Korjakova 2004.
²²⁴ See Bochkarev and Kuznetsov this volume.
²²⁵ Kuznetsov 2006: 643.
²²⁶ Lindner 2020; 2021: 91–110.
²²⁷ Grigoriev 2023: 19 fn. 137.

²²⁸ Parzinger 2006: 246.
²²⁹ Her name rendered in the bibliography as Izbicer (2009).
²³⁰ Kaiser 2010.
²³¹ See Boroffka this volume.
²³² Mengyán et al. 2023.
²³³ Boroffka 2004.
²³⁴ See Boroffka this volume; Boroffka 1998, Lindner 2021, 51–53.

layer they belong to; reliable 14C dates have hardly been published. One 14C date gives an indication of a settlement layer of the Monteoru Ic3 phase: 2279–1915 cal BC.[235] According to the new evidence, Monteoru Ic2 should already begin in the late third millennium BCE.[236] So, the cheekpieces in Romania would be at least as old as those from the Trans–Uralic region. Though both regions were in contact, the difference in the disc shaped and rod shaped cheekpieces make it plausible that both follow different traditions and are not technical offsprings from each other – also the different number of spokes per wheel hint in this direction. This leads to suggestions of independent development or different paths of external influence. Boroffka now considers that the early cheekpieces in the Carpathian basin were not for chariot use but for riding.[237]

The rich evidence of artefacts, images and texts from the Near East and Egypt has long shaped our understanding of early chariot technology and use. Until the discovery of the chariots from Sintashta, the chariot from Thebes (now in Florence) and the eight known Egyptian chariots of the 18th Dynasty were considered the oldest real evidence for this type of vehicle.[238] From a technical point of view the chariots could have easily derived from regional predecessors.[239] Despite an overall high number of records, the evidence regarding the early chariot does show some gaps. The most relevant sources for us are a series of pictorial representations from the first half of the second millennium BCE. These are mostly seal imprints from settlement contexts. The limited representational possibilities of the seal cutters – as well as their artistic skills and technical expertise with regard to the depicted objects – make it difficult to interpret these pictorial works and deduct technological and typological conclusions in regard to chariots. Sometimes it is not possible to distinguish between spoked wheels and cross–bar wheels, and the species of draft animals – although they are undoubtedly equines – and their harness often remain unrecognizable. The oldest depiction to date of a two–wheeled chariot with cross–bar wheels or spoked wheels comes from Tepe Hissar (IIIb) in northern Iran and dates to the second half of the third millennium BCE.[240] Further evidence of the use of spoked wheels is given by a small number of models and depictions from eastern Iran, Turkmenistan, Afghanistan and Pakistan that date back to late third millennium BCE,[241] though it is not always above doubt that it is really spoked wheels that are shown. A two–wheeled platform car with spoked wheels is clearly depicted on a vessel from eastern Iran. Unfortunately, it is from the art market and has no clear find context. Typologically the vessel can be linked to similar vessels that date at the end of the third millennium BCE.[242] Seal images from Kültepe in central Anatolia can certainly be referred to as spoked wheels;[243] these wheels appear on both four– and two–wheeled vehicles; the seal impressions date to the late twentieth and early nineteenth century BCE.[244] The two–wheeled vehicles are light chariots pulled by equids, which are reminiscent of early forms of the later chariots.

A bit harness–system in the eastern Mediterranean region is not documented until the seventeenth century BCE with the discovery of a metal bridle from Tel Haror, Israel;[245] the *in situ* find shows that it was used to harness a donkey(!). Some of the early seal impression suggest nostril rings, but this is highly unlikely in the case of horses;[246] here we have to assume that the depiction is factually incorrect or artistically inaccurate. It could also be that the artist simply applied nostril rings known for bovids to equid–drawn vehicles. Without reliable evidence of a bridle, one could also assume that the harness was a *Kappzaum*, which gave the driver sufficient control over the team of horses. In general, however, it should be borne in mind that real evidence of bridles only began with the use of metal forms; bridles made of organic materials – which were also widespread outside the Ancient Near East – may well have been used but are unlikely to have survived in the ground.

To summarize, some aspects of the synoptic view of the sources should be critically assessed. On the basis of archaeological finds, it should be noted that around 2000 BCE – shortly before, shortly after – the chariot came into use in the three regions: in the Trans–Uralic steppes, in the Ancient Near East with Iran and in the Carpathian Basin. If one considers the dating ranges of the chronological approaches in each of these regions, it must be stated that the oldest archaeological evidence from the individual regions can be considered simultaneous. The evidence of the Trans–Uralic steppes is much denser, the evidence of real chariots is clearer in their significance, and the now numerous 14C dates are more concrete; the evidence in the other regions is clearly inferior. However, Nikolaus Boroffka rightly warns against a one–sided 'Sintashta fascination'.[247] It would be wrong to be too impressed by the Russian and Kazakh evidence and to give this region chronological priority over the other regions on the basis of the available finds and dating. Though the evidence is less concise, it is significant enough that the Ancient Near East extending at least to the eastern Iran and the Carpathian Basin are to be taken into account in the further discussion of the chariot's origins.[248]

The archaeological record and its specific selective filters have to be taken into consideration. In the Trans–Uralic

---

[235] After Motzoi–Chicideanu 1995: 224, fn. 2.
[236] Motzoi–Chicideanu and Șandor–Chicideanu 2015; Constantinescu 2020: 149–157 – we thank Nick Boroffka for this welcome information.
[237] Boroffka this volume.
[238] Littauer and Crouwel 1985; Crouwel 2019; Veldmeijer and Ikram 2013; 2018; Raulwing 2019.
[239] See Littauer and Crouwel 1979: especially 68–69; rejecting this Eder and Nagel 2006: especially 61–62.
[240] Littauer and Crouwel 1979: fig. 21; the 14C date for the settlement layer of Tepe Hissar IIIB is 2400–2170 cal BC (Voigt and Dyson 1992: 173–174).
[241] Teufer 2012: 293–299.

[242] Teufer 2012: 296; 299; 300 fig. 18,1.
[243] Littauer and Crouwel 1979: figs. 28–29.
[244] Littauer and Crouwel 1979: fig. 24; 25; 28; 29.
[245] Littauer and Crouwel 2001; Crouwel 2004: 80.
[246] Horn 1995: 52.
[247] Boroffka 1998: 117 fn. 81.
[248] In the same sense Teufer 2012; Maran 2020; Grigoriev 2023.

steppes, these are primarily burials with real chariots; in the Ancient Near East they are pictorial representations; in the Carpathian region they are mainly single settlement finds. In the steppes they are an expression of the intentional selection as part of a burial practice, in the Ancient Near East of the intentional choice of images as specific ruling practice and status representation, and in the Carpathian region they are due to the coincidence of loss and soil preservation – under conditions that generally prevent the preservation of entire chariots, or parts of them. In each case the record represents very specific sections of their culture, which cannot be easily paralleled. From this perspective, a mere comparison of chronological data does not lead very far. The discussion about the chronological priority of the very close dates in absolute terms, which are still based on statistically uncertain data, overstretches the archaeological evidence – and not only ignores the archaeological context, but also processes of innovation, adoption and adaptation.

Which way to go?

The question of the definition of the chariot has been deliberately omitted so far. In the presentation of the archaeological evidence, we have consistently referred to the chariots discussed as 'chariots' or 'true chariots', without making a clear distinction between chariots and other possible technological and typological variations of chariot types. A chariot is generally understood to be a light and fast two–wheeled vehicle that is used for military purposes as well as for hunting or chariot racing.[249] Its great ritual significance is evidenced by numerous texts. Chariots have spoked wheels and are usually pulled by a team of horses (camels are also documented as draught animals in Central Asia) – spoked wheels and teams of horses are an important prerequisite for achieving the speed required by definition. The crew – chariot driver and charioteer – stood in the chariot's box. These are vague characterizations, yet they are sufficiently precise to identify a specific type of construction and its use. Ultimately, these are generalized derivations of the chariots that are well documented from the Ancient Near East and Egypt from the middle of the second millennium BCE. If these are referred to as 'true chariots', the earlier chariots are sometimes labeled as 'proto–chariots'.[250]

The characteristic features and functions of the chariot have some implications for the driving characteristics of these vehicles – they were supposed to be stable and manoeuverable also at high speeds. This was denied to the Trans–Uralian vehicles due to their sometimes very small gauge and short nave length.[251] They would therefore not have been able to meet the requirements of military use or chariot racing. Christian Eder und Wolfram Nagel argue that the – narrow – chariot from Krivoe Ozero corresponds in its proportions to those of Egyptian chariots.[252] They compare a series of dimensional ratios that lead them to the conclusion that the principle of the true chariot was already mastered in this Kazakh chariot, which ultimately enabled it to perform all the manoeuvres known to have been carried out with chariots.[253] However, the technical figures they use for their comparison are of secondary importance for the question of driving characteristics. The relationship between the center of gravity and gauge is decisive for the turning ability at high speed. The vehicle is considered to be at risk of tipping over if the center of gravity height exceeds half the track width. And although we can only speculate about the height of the Krivoe Ozero chariot, it is clear that it would easily tip over with a track width of 112 cm. This is of secondary importance for the question of the origin and genesis of the chariot, but not for the cultural–historical interpretations derived from the use of these chariots.[254]

According to Eder and Nagel

> the political and military upper class of the *mariyaninu*, which is well attested in the written sources in the 15th–13th century BCE deserves special attention. It defined itself through the possession and use of the light chariot. This elite probably originally comprised the early Indo–Aryan groups that migrated to the Near East. However, this 'chariot nobility' was certainly formed before the invasion of the Near East, and it is tempting to recognize the burials of members of this aristocratic class in the chariot tombs of the Sintashta–Petrovka culture, in which the chariot and its team take center stage, as it were.[255]

Under this premise, however, all persons in the Eurasian steppes buried with horse and chariot could be seen as members of the *maryanni* class. This view leads to a dead end insofar as the technical term *maryanni* is an Indo–Aryan–Hurrian compound that cannot have originated before the Indo–Aryans met the Hurrians;[256] unless one were to assume that *marya– was identical in content to the compound *maryanni* attested in the Ancient Near East before the middle of the second millennium BCE. However, this is more than unlikely. Both the socio–historical content of ai. *márya–* 'young man, young warrior [etc.])', Younger Avestan *mairiia–* (pejorative) 'scoundrel' (and the like) – Indo–Iranian *máryās*, which is understood by some

---

[249] Littauer and Crouwel 1979: 4–5; 2002: XVII.
[250] See Littauer and Crouwel 2002b.
[251] Littauer and Crouwel 2002b: 51–52.
[252] Eder and Nagel 2006: 58–59.
[253] Raulwing 2000: 51–58.
[254] See, e.g., Anthony 2007: 397–405.
[255] Eder and Nagel 2006: 69: ((...)verdient 'die im 15.–13. Jahrhundert v.Chr in den Schriftquellen gut bezeugte politische und militärische Oberschicht der *mariyaninu* (...) [besondere Beachtung]. Sie definierte sich über den Besitz und Gebrauch des leichten Streitwagens. In dieser Elite sind ursprünglich wohl jene frühindoarischen Gruppen zu erkennen, die nach Vorderasien einwanderten. Eine Formierung dieses 'Streitwagenadels' erfolgte aber sicher vor der Invasion nach Vorderasien, und es ist verlockend, in den Wagengräbern der Sintašta-Petrovka-Kultur, in denen der Streitwagen und sein Gespann gleichsam im Mittelpunkt stehen, schon die Bestattungen von Angehörigen dieser Adelsschicht zu erkennen.')
[256] von Dassow 2008: 77 ff.; 268 ff.

scholars as being part of a 'Männerbund' (brotherhood)[257] – still needs to be proven. In addition, the Indo–Aryan–Hurrian prehistory is also not as clear as we would like the sources to be. However, from the third millennium onwards, the Hurrians are to be placed in the immediate vicinity of the Ancient Near East,[258] not in the steppes. Eder's and Nagel's suggestion that warriors buried with horses and chariot are members of an ancient Near Eastern *maryanni* class ends, methodologically, in a cul–de–saq.

We currently have to assume three larger regions of origin for the chariot. The Carpathian Basin should definitely be included and placed alongside the previous controversial focus on the 'steppes vs. the Ancient Near East'. In all three areas, it can be assumed that both the necessary chariot technology and sufficient experience in handling domesticated horses were available.[259] Based purely on the archaeological evidence, no answer to the question of origin can be expected at present. This also applies to the comparative linguistic evidence. Therefore, it cannot be the task of historical–comparative linguistics to confirm to neighbouring disciplines that a 'Proto–Indo–European chariot' can be proven with the help of linguistic methodology and reconstructions and located in a geographically (and thus culturally) determinable 'original homeland'. Moreover, it should not be forgotten that we are only operating with mere possibilities, which in the course of time and by repeating their hypotheses give those involved the feeling that they are dealing with confirmed results.

In the medium term, attention should therefore be focused less on the search for the supposedly oldest evidence for the chariot – this applies in particular to associated attempts to determine the 'Proto–Indo–European Homeland' – and more on understanding the basis of our evidence, including the written sources. One example of archaeological evidence should be mentioned briefly. In the absence of real chariot finds, cheekpieces are regarded as the main indicator of the use of a horse–drawn chariot and as key evidence of the spread of this type of chariot. The main argument is that the cheekpiece is a necessary means of communication for the chariot driver to control the horses even at high speed. This aid is not absolutely necessary for the rider.[260] However, numerous examples show that cheekpieces were quite common in the military use of riding horses.[261] The bridle is therefore not compelling evidence for the use of the chariot,[262] just as the use of a team of horses can do without the bridle.[263] What evidential value does a bridle find have for the use of the chariot? This question naturally arises in connection with the Carpathian region, which has provided neither real chariot finds nor pictorial evidence for the chariot. But of course, it also arises in connection with the spread of the disk shaped cheekpiece between Southern and Eastern Europe and Central Asia and the spread of the chariot derived from this. Ute Dietz assumes that the snaffle was transferred from the draught horse to the riding horse due to new demands on the mount and rider.[264] But when did this happen and why?

In the search for the oldest, the origin and the spread that started from it, a critical evaluation of the underlying cultural–historical processes is pushed into the background. Chariot warriors swarm out across Europe and Asia and replace the regional upper classes – according to common historical images. How should we imagine this process? The Vedic texts that support the hypothesis of the swarming predecessors of the Aryans later attested on the Indian subcontinent depict the chariot as extremely susceptible to damage;[265] they also describe that the chariots were only assembled immediately before their use (as racing chariots).[266] The possibly inadequate manoeuvrability of the Trans–Uralic chariots has already been pointed out above. How should we imagine the chariot as a penetrating weapon in action? Did the Indo–Aryans or their predecessors set off with the chariot from their homes – which cannot be located with the desired certainty – in order to overrun and subjugate other cultures? The grave from Zardča Khalifa, Tadžikistan, contained several cheekpieces of Uralic type[267] – it is interpreted as the burial of a steppe dweller who migrated with his chariot, presumably from the cultural Sintashta region.[268] However, the accompanying grave goods belong to the regional Bactrian–Margian archaeological complex; the grave is richly furnished. Why are the cheekpieces evidence of a chariot–driving immigrant or conqueror? Why was the chariot itself not adopted by a representative of the regional elite? Similar questions need to be asked about the disc shaped cheekpieces from Mycenae, which Silvia Penner interprets as evidence of a steppe invasion and the exchange of the local upper class.[269] Why is this numerically very small group of objects the key evidence here, when the finds from the Mycenaean shaft tombs reflect a multitude of diverse supra–regional cultural influences?[270]

The discussion of the chariot as a means of transportation and assertion for a migrating group must be expanded to include the concept of 'prestige technology'.[271] The chariot was an attractive medium of social representation and distinction for local elites. This can also be seen as a reason for the rapid spread of this cultural asset. The early phase of the establishment and spread of the automobile around 1900 provides a possibly very appropriate analogy. Although it is undisputed that the technical development of the automobile had its starting point in Germany, the triumphant advance of the automobile began in France. The new mo-

---

[257] EWAIa II: 329–330.
[258] Wilhelm 1995.
[259] Becker 1994: 159 f.; Benecke 2004: 460 f.; Guimares et al. 2020.
[260] Brownrigg and Dietz 2004; Dietz 1992: 18 f.; Hüttel 1994: 198 f.
[261] See e.g. Junkelmann 1992: 11–34.
[262] Hüttel 1994: 198.
[263] Littauer 2002: 492.
[264] Dietz 1998: 10–11.
[265] Sparreboom 1983: 19–20.
[266] Sparreboom 1983: 31; compare also Elizarenkova 1992: 131 ff. (ai. *rátha–*).
[267] Bobomulloev 1997: 127.
[268] Anthony 2007: 431; Kuzmina 2001: 25.
[269] Penner 1998: 215.
[270] Maran 2020.
[271] Piggot 1992; Feldman and Sauvage 2010.

torized vehicles were enthusiastically received there, and the conditions for the social integration of this innovation were also created there. It was above all the well–to–do middle class in France who turned to the new technology: it was ideally suited to social differentiation; the car corresponded perfectly to their attitude to life of exclusivity, prestige and modernity as well as their needs for individual mobility. In France, the first car races were held, the first motor shows opened, and the first automobile clubs were founded – since this time, the tire manufacturer Michelin has been the taster for the exclusive gourmet.[272] Since this time, the automotive vocabulary has also been predominantly French, e.g. *automobile, limousine, convertible, chauffeur, chassis, coupé, fond, garage, pneu,* etc. This does not reflect the language of the technical developers, but that of those consumers who had adopted the new technology on a broader basis. Linguistically, the origins – the 'original home' – of the automobile at the end of the nineteenth century CE cannot be traced – and archaeologically, too, one would quickly reach the limits of what is possible. For methodological reasons alone, we do not see any solid starting points for archaeology and linguistics – alone or in combination – to make tenable statements about a (Proto–) Indo–European chariot and its origins given the state of the sources, which has not changed for hundred years (if we take the classification of Hittite as an Indo–European language as a milestone).[273] Based on the premise mentioned by Hans Georg Hüttel that 'the material possession of the Bronze Age horse–and–chariot complexes is heterogeneous' and consequently 'separate proof of origin must be provided for each individual component',[274] it is therefore advisable to restrict ourselves to a thorough investigation of the horse–and–chariot evidence in their respective find contexts and not to overload the discussion with the question of the origin of the classical chariot.

This question, as well as the contribution of speakers of individual Indo–European languages to its development and spread, cannot be answered at present. In conclusion, we can state that the discussion about the chariot is characterised by the narrative of the (Proto–)Indo–European chariot warrior. This narrative stems from a world view of the the first half of the 20th century CE and is not covered by the evidence of original linguistic records. The roots of this narrative can be clearly identified today, including the strong ideological charge it was given during the Nazi era. As there has been a lack of critical debate on the subject to date, chariotry research has still not rid itself of this baggage. In numerous cultural-historical syntheses, one can almost attest to an obsession with Indo–European stormtroopers who conquered the centres of civilisation of the ancient world from the steppe. In companion with these chariot warriors, we certainly do not come to a valid conclusion. It is time to take a new comprehensive look at all relevant sources and their genesis, as well as the processes of innovation, expansion and adoption of the chariot and its social embedding and function.

Stefan Burmeister
Director, Museum und Park Kalkriese, Bramsche-Kalkriese, FRG.

Peter Raulwing
Independent Scholar.
Associate at the Institute for the Study of Ancient Cultures – West Asia & North Africa, The University of Chicago, IL

We would like like to thank Katheryn M. Linduff and Gail Brownrigg for their careful proofreading. Of course all remaining mistakes are ours.

---

[272] Merki 2002: 49–65.
[273] Hrozný 1915.
[274] Hüttel 1994: 204.

Bibliography

AHw. *Akkadisches Handwörterbuch. Unter Benutzung des lexikalischen Nachlasses von Bruno Meissner (1868–1947)*, vol. 1–3, edited by Wolfram von Soden 1965–1981. Wiesbaden: Harrassowitz.

Alaura, Silvia. 2006. *'Nach Boghasköi'. Zur Vorgeschichte der Ausgrabungen in Boğazköy–Ḫattuša und zu den archäologischen Forschungen bis zum Ersten Weltkrieg. Darstellung und Dokumente*. Sendschrift der Deutschen Orient–Gesellschaft 13. Berlin: Deutsche Orient–Gesellschaft.

Alaura, Silvia. 2022. Rediscovery and Reception of the Hittites: An Overview. In: *Handbook Hittite Empire. Power Structures*, edited by Stefano de Martino, 693–780. Empires Through the Ages in Global Perspective 1. Berlin and Boston: De Gruyter Oldenbourg.

Anthony, David W. 2007. *The Horse, the Wheel and Language. How Bronze–Age Riders from the Eurasian Steppes shaped the Modern World*. Princeton: Princeton University Press.

Anthony, David. W. and Nikolai B. Vinogradov. 1995. Birth of the Chariot. *Archaeology* 1995 (March–April): 36–41.

Arntz, Helmut (ed.). 1936. *Germanen und Indogermanen. Volkstum, Sprache, Heimat, Kultur. Festschrift für Herman Hirt*, 2 vols. Indogermanische Bibliothek. Abteilung 3, Untersuchungen 15. Heidelberg: Winter.

Bailey, Harold W. 1957. A problem of the Indo–Iranian vocabulary. *Rocznik Orientalistyczny* 21: 59–69.

Bailey, Harold W. 1987. Arya. In: *Encyclopædia Iranica* 2: 684–687.

Bammesberger, Alfred (ed.). 1988. *Die Laryngaltheorie und die Rekonstruktion des indogermanischen Laut– und Formensystems*. Heidelberg: Winter.

Becker, Cornelia. 1994. Zur Problematik früher Pferdenachweise im östlichen Mittelmeergebiet. In: Hänsel and Zimmer 1994: 145–177.

Benecke, Norbert. 2004. Die Domestikation der Zugtiere. In: Fansa and Burmeister 2004: 455–466.

Biehahn, Erich. 1964. Blondheit und Blondheitskult in der deutschen Literatur. *Archiv für Kulturgeschichte* 46: 309–333

Börker–Klähn, Jutta. 1988. Die archäologische Problematik der Hurriterfrage und eine mögliche Lösung. In: *Hurriter und Hurritisch*, edited by Volkert Haas, 211–289. Konstanz: Universitätsverlag.

Boroffka, Nikolaus. 1998. Bronze– und früheisenzeitliche Geweihtrensenknebel aus Rumänien und ihre Beziehungen. Alte Funde aus dem Museum für Geschichte Aiud, Teil II. *Eurasia Antiqua* 4: 81–135.

Boroffka, Nikolaus. 2004. Bronzezeitliche Wagenmodelle im Karpatenbecken. In Fansa and Burmeister 2004: 347–354.

Brownrigg, Gail and Dietz, Ute L. 2004 Schirrung und Zäumung des Streitwagenpferdes: Funktion und Rekonstruktion. In: Fansa and Burmeister 2004: 481–490.

Bumke, Joachim. 1986. *Höfische Kultur. Literatur und Gesellschaft im hohen Mittelalter*, vols. 1–2. Munich: Deutscher Taschenbuch–Verlag.

Burmeister, Stefan. 2023. Indogermanische Männerbünde – für Frauen kein schöner Land. In: *What Does This Have to Do with Archaeology? Essays on the Occasion of the 65th Birthday of Reinhard Bernbeck*, edited by Editorial Collective / Herausgeber*Innenkollektiv, 51–63. Leiden: Sidestone Press.

CAD. *The Assyrian dictionary of the Oriental Institute of the University of Chicago University of Chicago*, edited by Martha T. Roth et al. 1956–2010. Chicago: The Oriental Institute.

Calder III, William M. and Alexander Demandt (eds.). 1990. *Eduard Meyer. Leben und Leistung eines Universalhistorikers*. Leiden: Brill.

Cancik-Kirschbaum, Eva Christiane, Nicole Brisch and Jesper Eidem. 2014. *Constituent, Confederate and Conquered Space. The Emergence of the Mittani State*. Berlin and Boston: de Gruyter.

Chechushkov, Igor V. and Alexander V. Epimakhov. 2018. Eurasian Steppe Chariots and Social Complexity During the Bronze Age. *Journal of World Prehistory* 31: 435–483.

Cherlenok, Evgeny A. 2006. The Chariot in Bronze Age: Funerary Rites of the Eurasian Steppes. In: *Horses and Humans. The Evolution of Human–Equine Relationship*, edited by Sandra L. Olsen, 173–179. BAR International Series 1560. Oxford: BAR Publishing.

Christ, Karl. 1972. *Von Gibbon zu Rostovtzeff. Leben und Werk führender Althistoriker der Neuzeit*. Darmstadt: Wissenschaftliche Buchgesellschaft.

Clackson, James. 2011. *Indo–European Linguistics. An Introduction*. 2nd edition, Cambridge: Cambridge University Press.

Constantinescu, Mihai. 2020. *Începuturile culturii Monteoru. Aşezarea de la Năeni–Zănoaga Cetatea* 2. Biblioteca Mousaios 15. Cluj–Napoca: Mega.

Cornelius, Friedrich. 1964. Synchronismus Idrimi–Telepinus? *Compte–Rendu de l'onzième rencontre assyriologique internationale, organisée à Leiden du 23 au 29 Juin 1962*, 55–58. Leiden: Nederlands Instituut voor Het Nabije Oosten.

Crouwel, Joost H. 2019. Wheeled Vehicles and their Draught Animals in the Ancient Near East – An Update. In: *Equids and Wheeled Vehicles in the Ancient World. Essays in Memory of Mary A. Littauer*, edited by Peter Raulwing, Katheryn M. Linduff and Joost H. Crouwel, 29–48. BAR International Series 2923. Oxford: BAR Publishing.

Decker, Wolfgang. 1989. Review of Hofmann 1989. *Nikephoros. Zeitschrift für Sport und Kultur im Altertum* 2: 250–256.

Decker, Wolfgang. 1994. Pferd und Wagen im Alten Ägypten. In Hänsel and Zimmer 1994: 259–270.

Del Francia, Pier Roberto. 2002. Il carro di Firenze. In: *Il carro e le armi di Museo Egizio di Firenze*, edited by Maria Cristina Guidotti, 16–37. Firenze: Ministero per i Beni e le Attività Culturali.

Delitzsch, Friedrich. 1884. *Die Sprache der Kossäer*. Leipzig: Hinrichs.

Diakonoff, Igor M. 1972. Die Arier im Vorderen Orient. Ende eines Mythos. Zur Methodik der Erforschung verschollener Sprachen. *Orientalia* N.S. 41: 91–121.

Diakonoff, Igor M. 1981. Evidence on the Ethnic Division of the Hurrians. In: *Studies on the Civilization and Culture of Nuzi and the Hurrians. In Honor of Ernest R. Lacheman, on his Seventy–Fifth Birthday, April 29, 1981*, edited by Martha A. Morrison and David J. Owen, 77–79. Studies on the Civilization and Culture of Nuzi and the Hurrians 1. Winona Lake: Eisenbrauns.

Diakonoff, Igor M. 1990. Language Contacts in the Caucasus and the Near East. In: *When Worlds Collide. The Indo–Europeans and Pre–Indo–Europeans. The Rockefeller*

Foundation's Bellagio Study and Conference Centre, Lake Como, Italy, February 8–13, edited by Thomas L. Markey and John A. C. Greppin, 53–65. Ann Arbor, MI: Karoma.

Diakonoff, Igor M. 1993. On Some Supposed Indo–Iranian Glosses in Cuneiform Languages. *Bulletin of the Asia Institute* 7: 47–49.

Diakonoff, Igor M. 1995. Two Recent Studies of Indo–Iranian Origins. *Journal of the American Oriental Society* 11: 473–477.

Dierks, Margarete. 1986. *Jakob Wilhelm Hauer, 1881–1962. Leben, Werk, Wirkung. Mit einer Personalbibliographie*. Heidelberg: Schneider.

Dietrich, Manfried und Oswald Loretz. 1983. Ug. *ssw/ssw* 'Pferd', *sswt* 'Stute' und akk. **sisitu*? 'Stute'. *Ugarit–Forschungen* 15: 301–302.

Dietz, Ute L. 1992. Zur Frage vorbronzezeitlicher Trensenbelege in Europa. *Germania* 70: 17–36.

Dietz, Ute L. 1998. *Spätbronze– und früheisenzeitliche Trensen im Nordschwarzmeergebiet und im Nordkaukasus*. Stuttgart: Steiner.

Dobesch, Gerhard. 1988. Fritz Schachermeyr. *Anzeiger der Österreichischen Akademie der Wissenschaften* 138: 419–436.

Dobesch, Gerhard. 1996. Allgemeine Würdigung. *American Journal of Ancient History* 13 (1): 11–55.

Drews, Robert. 1988. *The Coming of the Greeks. Indo–European Conquests in the Aegean and the Ancient Near East*. Princeton, NJ: Princeton University Press.

Dosch, Gudrun. 1993. *Zur Struktur der Gesellschaft des Königreichs Arraphe*. Heidelberger Studien zum Alten Orient 5. Heidelberg: Heidelberger Orientverlag.

Ebeling, Erich. 1951. *Bruchstücke einer mittelassyrischen Vorschriftensammlung für die Akklimatisierung und Trainierung von Wagenpferden*. Institut für Orientforschung: Veröffentlichung 7. Berlin: Akademie–Verlag.

Eckstein, Felix. 1976. Joseph Wiesner. *Freiburger Universitätsblätter* 51: 9–10.

Eder, Christian and Wolfram Nagel. 2006. Grundzüge der Streitwagenbewegung zwischen Tiefeurasien, Südwestiran und Ägäis. *Altorientalische Forschungen* 33: 42–93.

Edzard, Dietz–Otto. 1971. Review of Kammenhuber 1968. *Zeitschrift der Deutschen Morgenländischen Gesellschaft* 120: 310–314.

Elizarenkova, Tatyana Y. 1987. Notes on the Contests in the Ṛgveda. *Annals of the Bhandarkar Oriental Research Institute* 68: 99–109.

Elizarenkova, Tatyana Y. 1992. 'Wörter und Sachen'. How Much Can the Language of the Ṛgveda be Used to Reconstruct the Word of Things? In: *Ritual, State and History in South Asia. Essays in Honour of J. C. Heesterman*, edited by Albert W. van den Hoek, D. H. A. Kolff and M. S. Oort, 128–14. Leiden: Brill.

Epimachov, Andrej und Ludmila Korjakowa. 2004. Streitwagen der eurasischen Steppe in der Bronzezeit: Das Wolga–Uralgebiet und Kasachstan. In Fansa and Burmeister 2004: 221–236.

EWAia. *Etymologisches Wörterbuch des Altindoarischen*, vols. 1–2, edited by Manfred Mayrhofer. Heidelberg: Winter.

Fansa, Mamoun and Stefan Burmeister (eds.). 2004. *Rad und Wagen. Der Ursprung einer Innovation. Wagen im Vorderen Orient und Europa*. Archäologische Mitteilungen aus Nordwestdeutschland, Beiheft 40. Mainz: Zabern.

Feldman, Marian H. and Caroline Sauvage. 2010. Objects of Prestige? Chariots in the Late Bronze Age Eastern Mediterranean and Near East. *Ägypten und Levante* 20: 67–181.

Forrer, Emil O. 1922. Die Inschriften und Sprachen des Ḫatti–Reiches. *Zeitschrift der Deutschen Morgenländischen Gesellschaft* 76: 74–269.

Fortson IV, Benjamin W. 2010. *Indo–European Language and Culture. An Introduction*. Blackwell Textbooks in Linguistics 19. Oxford: Blackwell.

Fournet, Arnaud. 2010. About the Mitanni–Aryan Gods. *The Journal of Indo–European Studies* 38: 26–40.

Gaitzsch, Torsten. 2011. *Das Pferd bei den Indogermanen. Sprachliche, kulturelle und archäologische Aspekte*. Berlin and Münster: Lit.

García Ramón, José Luis. 2017. Old Indo-Aryan Lexicon in the Ancient Near East: Proto-Indo-European, Anatolian and Core Indo-European. *Atti del Sodalizio Glottologico Milanese* 10: 17–33.

Gening, V. F., G. B. Zdanovich and V. V. Gening. 1992. *Sintashta. Archaeological Sites of Aryan Tribes of the Ural–Kazakh Steppes* [Russian with parallel English title]. Chelyabinsk: Južno–Ural'skoe Knižnoe Izd.

Gentile, Simone. 2019. Indo–Iranian Personal Names in Mitanni: A Source for Cultural Reconstruction. *Onoma* 54: 137–159.

Gotō, Toshifumi. 2009. Aśvín– and Nā́satya– in the Ṛgveda and Their Prehistoric Background. In: *Linguistics, archaeology and human past in South Asia*, edited by Toshiki Osada, 199–226. Delhi: Manohar.

Graf, Klaus. 2002. *Ritterromantik. Renaissance und Kontinuität des Rittertums im Spiegel des literarischen Lebens im 15. Jahrhundert*. Veröffentlichungen der Kommission für Saarländische Landesgeschichte und Volksforschung 34. St. Ingbert: Röhrig: 517–532.

Grigoriev, Stanislav. 2023. Horse and Chariot. Critical Reflections on One Theory. *Archaeologia Austriaca* 107: 1–32.

Groddek, Detlev. 2000. Ist das Etymon von *wrry.t* 'Wagen' gefunden? *Göttinger Miszellen* 175: 109–111.

Häusler, Alexander. 2000. Indogermanische Altertumskunde II. Archäologisches. *Reallexikon der Germanischen Altertumskunde* 15: 403–408.

Hänsel, Bernhard and Stefan Zimmer (eds.). 1994. *Die Indogermanen und das Pferd. Akten des Internationalen Interdisziplinären Kolloquiums Freie Universität Berlin, 1.–3. Juli 1992*. Archaeolingua 4. Budapest: Archaeolingua Alapítvány.

Hajnal, Ivo. 2008. Indogermanische Dichtersprache und die Grenzen der Rekonstruktion. In: *Chomolangma, Demawend und Kasbek. Festschrift für Roland Bielmeier*, edited by Brigitte Huber, vol. 2, 457–481. Beiträge zur Zentralasienforschung 12, 1–2. Halle (Saale): International Institute for Tibetan and Buddhist Studies / VGH Wissenschaftsverlag.

Hančar, Franz. 1955. *Das Pferd in prähistorischer und früher historischer Zeit*. Munich and Vienna: Herold.

Hančar, Franz and Manfred Mayrhofer. 1967. Zum Stand der Streitwagenforschung [= Review of Nagel 1966]. *Berliner Jahrbuch für Vor– und Frühgeschichte* 7: 257–268 [Hančar] and 269–271 [Mayrhofer].

Hauer, Jakob Wilhelm. 1936. Die vergleichende Religionsgeschichte und das Indogermanenproblem. In Arntz 1936: 177–202.

Hayen, Hajo. 1986. Der Wagen im altgriechischen Kulturbereich. In: *Achse, Rad und Wagen. Fünftausend Jahre Kultur– und Technikgeschichte*, edited by Wilhelm Treue, 60–79; 401–402. Göttingen: Vandenhoeck and Ruprecht.

Helck, Wolfgang. 1954. *Untersuchungen zu den Beamtentiteln des ägyptischen Alten Reiches*. Glückstadt: Augustin.

Helck, Wolfgang. 1963. Entwicklung der Verwaltung als Spiegelbild historischer und soziologischer Faktoren. *Studii Semitici* 7: 59–80.

Helck, Wolfgang. 1971. *Die Beziehungen Ägyptens zu Vorderasien im 3. und 2. Jahrtausend v.Chr.* Wiesbaden: Harrassowitz.

Helck, Wolfgang. 1977. *Die Seevölker in den ägyptischen Quellen*. Jahresbericht des Instituts für Vorgeschichte der Universität Frankfurt am Main 1976. München: Beck.

Helck, Wolfgang. 1978. Ein indirekter Beleg für die Nutzung des leichten Streitwagens zu Ende der 13. Dynastie. *Journal of Near Eastern Studies* 37: 337–340.

Helck, Wolfgang. 1980. marijannu, *Lexikon der Ägyptologie* 3: 1190–1191.

Helck, Wolfgang. 1986. *Politische Gegensätze im alten Ägypten. Ein Versuch*. Hildesheim: Gerstenberg.

Herold, Anja. 2006. *Streitwagentechnologie in der Ramses–Stadt. Knäufe, Knöpfe und Scheiben aus Stein*. Die Grabungen des Pelizaeus–Museums Hildesheim in Qantir–Piramesse 3. Mainz: Zabern.

Hinz, Walther. 1975. *Altiranisches Sprachgut der Nebenüberlieferungen*. Wiesbaden: Harrassowitz.

Hoch, James E. 1994. *Semitic Words in Egyptian Texts of the New Kingdom and Third Intermediate Period*. Princeton: Princeton University Press.

Hofmann, Ulrich. 1989. *Fuhrwesen und Pferdehaltung im Alten Ägypten*. PhD Thesis. Bonn: Selbstverlag.

Horn, Valentin. 1995. *Das Pferd im Alten Orient. Das Streitwagenpferd der Frühzeit in seiner Umwelt, im Training und im Vergleich zum neuzeitlichen Distanz–, Reit– und Fahrpferd*. Documenta hippologica. Hildesheim: Olms.

Hrozný, Friedrich. 1915. Die Lösung des hethitischen Problems. *Mitteilungen der Deutschen Orient–Gesellschaft zu Berlin* 56: 17–50.

Hüttel, Hans–Georg. 1994. Zur archäologischen Evidenz der Pferdenutzung in der Kupfer– und Bronzezeit. In Hänsel and Zimmer 1994: 197–215.

Hufen, Christian. 1998. Gotenforschung und Denkmalpflege. Herbert Jankuhn und die Kommandounternehmen des 'Ahnenerbes' der SS. In: *'Betreff Sicherstellung'. NS–Kunstraub in der Sowjetunion*, edited by Wolfgang Eschwede and Ulrike Hartung, 75–95. Bremen: Edition Temmen.

IPNB. *Iranisches Personennamenbuch*, vol. 1, edited by Manfred Mayrhofer and Rüdiger Schmitt 1977. Vienna: Verlag der Österreichischen Akademie der Wissenschaften.

Izbicer, E. Elena V. 2009. Povozka iz pogrebenija 32 Bol'šogo Ipatovskogo kurgana i odnoosnye stepnye povozki epochi srednej bronzy [A Wheeled Vehicle from Grave 32 of the Big Ipatovo Kurgan and One–Oxled Steppe Wagons of the Middle Bronze Age]. *Materialy po izučeniju istoriko–kul'turnogo nasledija Severnogo Kavkaza* 9: 125–130.

Jacobs, Bruno. 1995. Als die Welt ins Rollen kam. Die Erfindung von Rad und Wagen in der europäischen Frühzeit und im Altertum. *die waage. Zeitschrift der Grünenthal GmbH, Aachen* 34 (1): 2–9.

Jensen, Peter. 1919. Indische Zahlwörter in keilschrifthittitischen Texten. *Sitzungsberichte der Akademie der Wissenschaften [Berlin], phil.–hist. Klasse 1919*: 367–372.

Junkelmann, Marcus. 1992. *Die Reiter Roms*. Vol. 3. *Zubehör, Reitweise, Bewaffnung*. Mainz: Zabern.

Kaiser, Elke. 2000. Review of Penner 1998. *Prähistorische Zeitschrift* 75 (2): 239–241.

Kammenhuber, Annelies. 1961. *Hippologia hethitica*. Wiesbaden: Harrassowitz.

Kammenhuber, Annelies. 1968. *Die Arier im Vorderen Orient*. Heidelberg: Winter.

Kaplony, Peter. 1986. Ritterlichkeit. In: *Lexikon der Ägyptologie*, edited by Wolfgang Helck, vol. 5, 270–271. Wiesbaden: Harrassowitz.

Kater, Michael H. 2006. *Das 'Ahnenerbe' der SS 1935–1945. Ein Beitrag zur Kulturpolitik des Dritten Reiches*. 4th edition, München: Oldenbourg.

Kendall, Timothy B. 1975. *Warfare and Military Matters in the Nuzi Tablets*. Ann Arbor, MI: University Microfilms.

Klein, Jared S., Brian D. Joseph and Matthias Fritz (eds.). 2017. *Handbook of Comparative and Historical Indo–European Linguistics. An International Handbook*. Berlin and Boston: De Gruyter / De Gruyter Mouton.

Kloekhorst, Alwin. 2019. *Kanišite Hittite. The Earliest Attested Record of Indo–European*. Leiden: Brill.

Koch, Anke. 1992. Die indogermanische Jochgabel. *Acta Praehistorica et Archaeologica* 24: 65–75.

Koch, Anke. 1995. Zur Technik des Streitwagens in Ostiran. *Achse, Rad und Wagen. Beiträge zur Geschichte der Landfahrzeuge* 3: 3–9.

Koch, Anke. 2003. Die Rekonstruktion des Streitwagens bei den Indoariern im Zeitalter des Rigveda (ca. 1500–1000 v.Chr.). In: *Altertumswissenschaften im Dialog. Festschrift für Wolfram Nagel zur Vollendung seines 80. Lebensjahres*, edited by Reinhard Dittmann, Christian Eder and Bruno Jacobs, 345–368. Münster: Ugarit–Verlag.

Köster, August. 1921. *Die Herkunft des Pferdes in Babylonien. Festschrift zu C. F. Lehmann–Haupts 60. Geburtstag*, edited by Kurt Regling and Hermann Reich, 158–167. Janus 1. Vienna and Leipzig: Braumüller.

Kristiansen, Kristian. 2004. Kontakte und Reisen im 2. Jahrtausend v. Chr. In Fansa and Burmeister 2004: 443–454.

Kuzmina, Elena E. 2001. The First Migration Wave of Indo–Iranians to the South. *The Journal of Indo–European Studies* 29 (1–2): 1–40.

Kuzmina, Elena E. 2007. *The Origin of the Indo–Iranians*. Leiden and Boston: Brill.

Kuznetsov, Pavel F. 2006. The Emergence of Bronze Age Chariots in Eastern Europe. *Antiquity* 80 (309): 638–645.

Lehmann, Gustav Adolf. 1994. Eduard Meyer. *Neue Deutsche Biographie* 17: 309–311.

Lindeman, Fredrik Otto. 1987. *Introduction to the Laryngeal Theory*. Oslo and Oxford: Norwegian University Press and Oxford University Press.

Lindner, Stephan. 2020. Chariots in the Eurasian Steppe: A Bayesian Approach to the Emergence of Horse–Drawn Transport in the Early Second Millennium BC. *Antiquity* 94 (374): 361–380.

Lindner, Stephan. 2021. *Die technische und symbolische Bedeutung eurasischer Streitwagen für Europa und die Nachbarräume im 2. Jahrtausend v. Chr.* Berliner archäologische Forschungen 20. Rahden/Westf.: Leidorf.

Lipp, Reiner. 2009. *Die indogermanischen und einzelsprachlichen Palatale im Indoiranischen. Neurekonstruktion, Nuristan–Sprachen, Genese der indoarischen Retroflexe. Indoarisch von Mitanni*, vol. 1; *Thorn–Problem, indoiranische Laryngalvokalisation*, vol. 2. Heidelberg: Winter.

Littauer, Mary A. and Joost H. Crouwel. 1979. *Wheeled Vehicles and Ridden Animals in the Ancient Near East*. Handbuch der Orientalistik Abt. 7, Kunst und Archäologie, vol. 1, Der alte Vordere Orient, Abschnitt 2, Die Denkmäler, B Vorderasien, Lief. 1. Leiden: Brill.

Littauer, Mary A. and Crouwel, Joost H. 1985. *Chariots and Related Equipment from the Tomb of Tut'ankhamūn*. Oxford: Griffith Institute, Ashmolean Museum.

Littauer, Mary A. and Crouwel, Joost H. 2002a. *Selected Writings on Chariots and other Early Vehicles, Riding and Harness. Mary Aiken Littauer and Joost H. Crouwel*, edited by Raulwing. Culture and History of the Ancient Near East 6. Leiden: Brill.

Littauer, Mary A. and Crouwel, Joost H. 2002b. A Note on the Origin of the True Chariot. In: Littauer and Crouwel 2002a: 45–52. [Reprinted from *Antiquity* 70 (270), 1996: 934–939].

Losemann, Volker. 1977. *Nationalsozialismus und Antike. Studien zur Entwicklung des Faches Alte Geschichte 1933–1945*. Hamburg: Hoffmann & Campe.

Mahsarski, Dirk. 2011. *Herbert Jankuhn (1905–1990). Ein deutscher Prähistoriker zwischen nationalsozialistischer Ideologie und wissenschaftlicher Objektivität*. Rahden/Westf.: Leidorf.

Malandra, William W. 1991. Chariot. *Encyclopædia Iranica* 5: 377–380.

Maran, Joseph. 2020. The Introduction of the Horse–Drawn Light Chariot – Divergent Responses to a Technological Innovation in Societies between the Carpathian Basin and the East Mediterranean. In: *Objects, Ideas and Travelers. Contacts between the Balkans, the Aegean and Western Anatolia During the Bronze and Early Iron Age. Volume to the Memory of Alexandru Vulpe. Proceedings of the Conference in Tulcea, 10–13 November 2017*, edited by Joseph Maran, Radu Băjenaru, Sorin–Cristian Ailincăi, Anca–Diana Popescu and Svend Hansen, 505–528. Universitätsforschungen zur prähistorischen Archäologie 350. Bonn: Habelt.

Marohl, Heinrich. 1941. *Eduard Meyer. Bibliographie. Mit einer autobiographischen Skizze Eduard Meyers und der Gedächtnisrede von Ulrich Wilcken*. Stuttgart: Cotta.

Mayrhofer, Manfred. 1959a. Zu den arischen Sprachresten in Vorderasien. *Die Sprache* 5: 77–95.

Mayrhofer, Manfred. 1959b. Über einige arische Wörter mit hurritischem Suffix. *Annali dell'Istituto orientale di Napoli, sezione linguistica* 1: 1–11.

Mayrhofer, Manfred. 1960. Indo–iranisches Sprachgut aus Alalaḫ. *Indo–Iranian Journal* 4: 136–149.

Mayrhofer, Manfred. 1961. Der heutige Forschungsstand zu den indoiranischen Sprachresten in Vorderasien. *Zeitschrift der Deutschen Morgenländischen Gesellschaft* 111: 451–458.

Mayrhofer, Manfred. 1965a. Ein arisch–ḫurritischer Rechtsausdruck in Alalaḫ? *Orientalia* N. S. 34: 336–337.

Mayrhofer, Manfred. 1965b. Zu den Zahlwortkomposita des Kikkuli–Textes. *Indogermanische Forschungen* 70: 11–13.

Mayrhofer, Manfred. 1965c. Zur kritischen Sichtung vorderasiatisch–arischer Personennamen. *Indogermanische Forschungen* 70: 146–163.

Mayrhofer, Manfred. 1965d. Hethitisches und arisches Lexikon. *Indogermanische Forschungen* 70: 245–257.

Mayrhofer, Manfred. 1966. *Die Indo–Arier im Alten Vorderasien. Mit einer analytischen Bibliographie*. Wiesbaden: Harrassowitz.

Mayrhofer, Manfred. 1969. Die vorderasiatischen Arier. *Asiatische Studien* 23: 139–154.

Mayrhofer, Manfred. 1974. *Die Arier im Vorderen Orient – Ein Mythos? Mit einem bibliographischen Supplement*. Sitzungsberichte. Österreichische Akademie der Wissenschaften, Philosophisch–Historische Klasse 294 (3). Vienna: Verlag der Österreichischen Akademie der Wissenschaften.

Mayrhofer, Manfred. 1982. Welches Material aus dem Indo–Arischen von Mitanni verbleibt für eine selektive Darstellung? In: *Investigationes philologicae et comparativae. Gedenkschrift für Heinz Kronasser*, edited by Erich Neu, 72–90. Wiesbaden: Harrassowitz.

Mayrhofer, Manfred. 1994. Eduard Meyer und die älteste indo–iranische Onomastik. *Die Sprache* 36: 175–180.

Mayrhofer, Manfred. 1996. Ein indo–arischer Rechtsterminus im Mittanni–Brief? *Historische Sprachforschung* 109: 161–162.

Mayrhofer, Manfred. 2006. Eine Nachlese zu den indo–arischen Sprachresten des Mittanni–Bereichs. *Anzeiger der philosophisch–historischen Klasse* 141 (2): 83–101.

Meid, Wolfgang. 1989. *Archäologie und Sprachwissenschaft. Kritisches zu neueren Hypothesen der Ausbreitung der Indogermanen*. Innsbrucker Beiträge zur Sprachwissenschaft / Vorträge und kleinere Schriften 43. Innsbruck: Institut für Sprachwissenschaft.

Meid, Wolfgang. 1994. Die Terminologie von Pferd und Wagen im Indogermanischen. In Hänsel and Zimmer 1994: 53–65.

Meier–Brügger, Michael. 2003. *Indo–European Linguistics*. Berlin: de Gruyter.

Meissner, Bruno. 1913. Das Pferd in Babylonien. Assyriologische Studien VI. *Mitteilungen der Vorderasiatischen Gesellschaft* 18: 1–10.

Mengyán, Ákos, Anett Gémes, Tamás Szeniczey and Tamás Hajdu. 2023. Two Bronze Age Miniature Wagon and Wheel Burials in Encs (North–Eastern Hungary). *Oxford Journal of Archaeology* 42 (3): 199–220.

Merki, Christoph Maria. 2002. *Der holprige Siegeszug des Automobils 1895–1930. Zur Motorisierung des Straßenverkehrs in Frankreich, Deutschland und der Schweiz*. Vienna: Böhlau.

Messerschmidt, Wolfgang. 1988. Der ägäische Streitwagen und seine Beziehungen zum Nordeurasisch–vorderasiatischen Raum. *Acta Praehistorica et Archaeologica* 20: 31–44.

Meyer, Eduard. 1908. Das erste Auftreten der Arier in der Geschichte. *Sitzungsberichte der Berliner Akademie der Wissenschaften. Phil.–hist. Klasse 1908*: 14–19.

Meyer, Eduard. 1909a. *Geschichte des Altertums*, vol. 1–2. *Die ältesten geschichtlichen Völker und Kulturen bis zum sechzehnten Jahrhundert*. 2nd edition, Stuttgart and Berlin: Cotta.

Meyer, Eduard. 1909b. Die ersten Zeugnisse der iranischen Sprache und der zoroastrischen Religion. *Zeitschrift für Vergleichende Sprachforschung auf dem Gebiete der indogermanischen Sprachen* 42: 1–27.

Meyer, Eduard. 1914. *Reich und Kultur der Chetiter*. Kunst und Altertum. Alte Kulturen im Lichte neuer Forschung 1. Berlin: Curtius.

Meyer, Eduard. 1925. Die Volksstämme Kleinasiens, das erste Auftreten der Indogermanen in der Geschichte und die Probleme ihrer Ausbreitung. *Sitzungsberichte der Preußischen Akademie der Wissenschaften 1925*: 244–260.

Moorey, P. R. S. 1986. The Emergence of the Light, Horse–Drawn Chariot in the Near East c.2000–1500 B.C. *World Archaeology* 18: 196–215.

Moorey, P. R. S. 1989. The Hurrians, the Mitanni and Technological Innovation. In: *Archaeologia Iranica et Orientalis. Miscellanea in Honorem Louis Vanden Berghe*, edited by Léon de Meyer and Ernie Haerinck, 273–286. Gent: Peeters.

Moortgat, Anton. 1930. Der Kampf zu Wagen in der Kunst des Alten Orients. Zur Herkunft des Bildgedankens. *Orientalistische Literaturzeitung* 33: 841–854.

Morpurgo Davies, Anna. 1998. *Nineteenth–Century Linguistics*. History of Linguistics 4. London: Longman.

Motzoi–Chicideanu, Ion I. 1995. Fremdgüter im Monteoru–Kulturraum. In: *Handel, Tausch und Verkehr im bronze– und früheisenzeitlichen Südosteuropa*, edited by Bernhard Hänsel, 219–242. Munich and Berlin: Südosteuropa–Gesellschaft and Seminar für Ur– und Frühgeschichte der Freien Universität zu Berlin.

Motzoi–Chicideanu, Ion and Monica Şandor–Chicideanu. 2015. Câteva date noi privind cronologia culturii Monteoru. *Mousaios* 20: 9–53.

Nachod, Hans. 1907. *Der Rennwagen bei den Italikern und ihren Nachbarn*. PhD. University Leipzig. Leipzig: Radelli & Hille.

Näf, Beat. 1994. Der Althistoriker Fritz Schachermeyr und seine Geschichtsauffassung im wissenschaftsgeschichtlichen Rückblick. *Storia della Storiografia* 26: 83–100.

Nagel, Wolfram. 1966. *Der mesopotamische Streitwagen und seine Entwicklung im ostmediterranen Bereich*. Berliner Beiträge zur Vor– und Frühgeschichte 10. Berlin: Hessling.

Nagel, Wolfram. 1986. Die Entwicklung des Wagens im frühen Vorderasien. In: *Achse, Rad und Wagen. Fünftausend Jahre Kultur– und Technikgeschichte*, edited by Wilhelm Treue, 9–34; 361. Göttingen: Vandenhoeck and Ruprecht.

Nagel, Wolfram. 1987. Indogermanen und Alter Orient. Rückblick und Ausblick auf den Stand des Indogermanenproblems. *Mitteilungen der Deutschen Orientgesellschaft zu Berlin* 119: 157–213.

Nagel, Wolfram and Christian Eder. 1992. Altsyrien und Altägypten. *Damaszener Mitteilungen* 6: 1–108.

Nagel, Wolfram, Christian Eder and Eva Strommenger. 2017. *Archaische Wagen in Vorderasien und Indien. Bauweise und Nutzung*. Berlin: Reimer.

Nuoffer, Oskar. 1904. *Der Rennwagen im Altertum*. Leipzig: Hallberg & Buechting.

Oberlies, Thomas. 1998. *Die Relgionen des Ṛgveda. Erster Teil – Das religiöse System des Ṛgveda*. Publications of the Nobili Reserach Library 26. Vienna: Sammlung Nobili.

Oelsner, Joachim. 2022. *Der Kodex Ḫammu–rāpi. Textkritische Ausgabe und Übersetzung*. dubsar 4. Münster: Zaphon.

Oettinger, Norbert. 1994. Pferd und Wagen im Altiranischen und Anatolischen. Zur Frage ererbter Termini. In Hänsel and Zimmer 1994: 67–76.

Pachler, Beate. 1998. *Der 'Arische Mythos'. Ein wissenschaftsgeschichtlicher Beitrag zum 'Indogermanenproblem'*. 'Diplom–Arbeit' Vienna University.

Paravicini, Wolfgang. 2011. *Die ritterlich–höfische Kultur des Mittelalters*. 3rd edition, Munich: Oldenbourg.

Parpola, Asko. 2004–2005. The Nāsatyas, the Chariot and Proto–Aryan Religion. *Journal of Indological Studies* 16/17: 1–63.

Parzinger, Hermann. 2006. *Die frühen Völker Eurasiens. Vom Neolithikum bis zum Mittelalter*. Munich: Beck.

Penner, Silvia. 1998. *Schliemanns Schachtgräberrund und der europäische Nordosten. Studien zur Herkunft der frühmykenischen Streitwagenausstattung*. Bonn: Habelt.

Pereltsvaig, Asya and Martin W. Lewis. 2015. *The Indo-European Controversy. Facts and Fallacies in Historical Linguistics*. Cambridge: Cambridge University Press.

Pernsteiner, Birgit. 1998. *Die Geschichte des 'arischen' Mythos. Von seiner geistigen Entstehung bis zum Nationalsozialismus*. 'Diplom–Arbeit' Vienna University.

Pereyra di Fidanza, Violeta. 1992. Los maryannu: su inserción socio–politica en los estados de Siria y Palestina durante el Período del Bronce Reciente. *Revista de Estudios de Egiptología* 3: 45–62.

Pereyra di Fidanza, Violeta. 1993. Los maryannu: su inserción socio–politica en los estados de Siria y Palestina durante el Período del Bronce Reciente. II. *Revista de Estudios de Egiptología* 4: 45–62.

Pesditschek, Martina. 2007. Die Karriere des Althistorikers Fritz Schachermeyr im Dritten Reich und in der Zweiten Republik. *Mitteilungen der Österreichischen Gesellschaft für Wissenschaftsgeschichte* 25: 41–71.

Pesditschek, Martina. 2009. *Barbar, Kreter, Arier. Leben und Werk des Althistorikers Fritz Schachermeyr*, 2 vols. Saarbrücken: Südwestdeutscher Verlag für Hochschulschriften.

Pesditschek, Martina. 2020. Fritz Schachermeyr und die Indogermanenfrage. In: *Archäologie in Österreich 1938–1945. Beiträge zum internationalen Symposium vom 27. bis 29. April 2015 am Universalmuseum Joanneum in Graz*, edited by Daniel Modl and Karl Peitler, 190–201. Schild von Steier Beiheft 8; Forschungen zur geschichtlichen Landeskunde der Steiermark 79. Graz: Universalmuseum Joanneum.

Piggott, Stuart. 1983. *The Earliest Wheeled Transport. From the Atlantic Coast to the Caspian Sea*. London: Thames & Hudson.

Piggott, Stuart. 1992. *Wagon, Chariots and Carriage. Symbol and Status in the History of Transport*. London: Thames and Hudson.

Poliakov, Léon. 1996. *The Aryan Myth. A History of Racist and Nationalist Ideas in Europe*. London: Heinemann.

Postgate, J. Nicholas. 1986. The Equids of Sumer, Again. In: *Equids of the Ancient World*, edited by Richard H. Meadow and Hans–Peter Uerpmann, 194–206. Beihefte zum Tübinger Atlas des Vorderen Orients, Reihe A – Naturwissenschaften, 19/1. Wiesbaden: Reichert.

Potratz Johannes A. 1938. *Das Pferd in der Frühzeit*. Rostock: Hinstorff.

Potratz, Johannes A. 1939–1940. Fahren und Reiten nach den Ergebnissen der Bodenforschung. *Prähistorische Zeitschrift* 30/31: 385–392.

Rainey, Anson F. 1965. The Military Personnel of Ugarit. *Journal of Near Eastern Studies* 24: 17–27.

Rau, Wilhelm. 1983. *Zur vedischen Altertumskunde*. Abhandlungen der Geistes– und Sozialwissenschaftlichen Klasse/ Akademie der Wissenschaften und der Literatur 1983, 1. Mainz and Wiesbaden: Steiner.

Raulwing, Peter. 1994. Ein indoarischer Streitwagenterminus im Ägyptischen? – Kritische Bemerkungen zur Herleitung der Wagenbezeichnung wrjj.t aus einem für das indoarische Sprachcorpus erschlossenen Nomen *wr̥ta– 'Streitwagen'. *Göttinger Miszellen* 140: 71–79.

Raulwing, Peter. 1998. Pferd, Wagen und Indogermanen – Grundlagen, Probleme und Methoden der Streitwagenforschung. In: *Sprache und Kultur der Indogermanen. Akten der X. Fachtagung der Indogermanischen Gesellschaft Innsbruck, 22.–28. September 1996*, edited by Wolfgang Meid, 523– 546. Innsbruck: Institut für Sprachwissenschaft.

Raulwing, Peter. 1999. Neuere Forschungen zum Kikkuli–Text. Eine kleine Bestandsaufnahme trainingsinhaltlicher Interpretationen zu CTH 284 vier Jahrzehnte nach A. Kammenhubers *Hippologia hethitica*. In: *Festschrift für Wolfgang Meid*, edited by Erzsébet Jerem and Peter Anreiter, 351–364. Archaeolingua Main Series 10. Budapest: Archaeolingua Alapítvány.

Raulwing, Peter. 2000. *Horses, Chariots and Indo–Europeans. Foundations and Methods of Chariotry Research from the Viewpoint of Comparative Indo–European Linguistics*. With a Foreword by Joost H. Crouwel. Archaeolingua. Series Minor 13. Budapest: Archaeolingua Alapítvány.

Raulwing, Peter. 2004. Indogermanen, Indoarier und *maryannu* in der Streitwagenforschung. Eine rezeptions– und wissenschaftsgeschichtliche Spurenlese. In Fansa and Burmeister 2004, 515–531.

Raulwing, Peter. 2005. The Kikkuli Text (CTH 284). Some Interdisciplinary Remarks on Hittite Training Texts for Chariot Horses in the Second Half of the 2nd Millennium B.C. In: *Les Équidés dans le monde méditerranéen antique. Actes du colloque organisé par l'École française d'Athènes, le Centre Camille Jullian, et l'UMR 5140 du CNRS, Athènes, 26–28 Novembre 2003*, edited by Armelle Gardeisen, 61–75. Monographies d'archéologie méditerranéenne 1. Lattes: Édition de l'Association pour le développement de l'archéologie en Languedoc–Rousillon.

Raulwing, Peter. 2013. Manfred Mayrhofer's Studies on Indo–Aryan and the Indo–Aryans in the Ancient Near East. A Retrospective and Outlook on Future Research. In: *Egyptology from the First World War to the Third Reich. Ideology, Scholarship, and Individual Biographies*, edited by Thomas Schneider and Peter Raulwing, 248–285. Leiden: Brill.

Raulwing, Peter. 2019. Hommage to Mary Aiken Littauer (1912–2005). In: *Equids and Wheeled Vehicles in the Ancient World. Essays in Memory of Mary A. Littauer*, edited by Peter Raulwing, Katheryn M. Linduff and Joost H. Crouwel, 5 – 26. BAR International Series 2923. Oxford: BAR Publishing.

Raulwing, Peter. *Forthcoming*. Horses and Chariots, Hittites and Indo–Aryans in the Studies of Eduard Meyer, Joseph Wiesner and Annelies Kammenhuber: A Look Behind the Curtain of Chariotry Research. In: *Studies in Honor of Theo van den Hout*. Chicago: Institute for the Study of Ancient Cultures – West Asia & North Africa, The University of Chicago.

Raulwing, Peter and Juliet Clutton–Brock. 2009. The Buhen Horse: Fifty Years After its Discovery (1958–2008). *Journal of Egyptian History* 2 (1–2): 1–106.

Raulwing, Peter and Herbert Meyer. 2004. Der Kikkuli–Text. Hippologische und methodenkritische Überlegungen zum Training von Streitwagenpferden im Alten Orient. In Fansa and Burmeister 2004: 491–506.

Raulwing, Peter and Rüdiger Schmitt. 1998. Zur etymologischen Beurteilung der Berufsbezeichnung *aššuššanni* des Pferdetrainers Kikkuli von Mittani. In: *Man and the Animal World. Studies in Archaeozoology, Archaeology, Anthropology and Palaeolinguistics in Memoriam Sándor Bökönyi*, edited by Peter Anreiter, 675–706. Archaeolingua 8. Budapest: Archaeolingua Alapítvány

Rix, Helmut (ed.). 2001. *Lexikon der indogermanischen Verben. Die Wurzeln und ihre Primärstämme*. 2nd edition, Wiesbaden: Reichert.

Salonen, Armas. 1951. *Die Landfahrzeuge des alten Mesopotamien nach sumerisch–akkadischen Quellen (mit besonderer Berücksichtigung der 5. Tafel der Serie ḪAR–ra = ḫubullu). Eine lexikalische und kulturgeschichtliche Untersuchung*. Suomalaisen Tiedeakatemian toimituksia, Sarja B 72,3. Helsinki: Suomalaisen Tiedakatemia.

Salonen, Armas. 1955. *Hippologica Accadica*. Suomalaisen Tiedeakatemian toimituksia, Sarja B 100. Helsinki: Suomalaisen Tiedakatemia.

Sandor, Bela I. 2004. The Rise and Decline of the Tutankhamun–Class Chariot. *Oxford Journal of Archaeology* 23: 153–175.

Schachermeyr, Fritz. 1933a. Die nordische Führerpersönlichkeit im Altertum. Ein Baustein zur Weltanschauung des Nationalsozialismus. *Humanistische Bildung im nationalsozialistischen Staate. Neue Wege zur Antike* 1 (9): 36–43.

Schachermeyr, Fritz. 1933b. Die Aufgaben der Alten Geschichte im Rahmen der Nordischen Weltgeschichte. *Vergangenheit und Gegenwart. Monatsschrift für Geschichtsunterricht und politische Erziehung* 23: 589–600.

Schachermeyr, Fritz. 1936. Wanderungen und Ausbreitung der Indogermanen im Mittelmeergebiet. In Arntz 1936, vol. 1: 229–253.

Schachermeyr, Fritz. 1940a. *Lebensgesetzlichkeit in der Geschichte. Versuch einer Einführung in das geschichtsbiologische Denken*. Frankfurt am Main: Klostermann.

Schachermeyr, Fritz. 1940b. Bericht über die Neufunde und Neuerscheinungen zur ägäischen und griechischen Frühzeit. *Klio* 32: 103–140.

Schachermeyr, Fritz. 1940c. Der Begriff des Arteigenen im frühzeitlichen Kunstgewerbe. *Klio* 32: 339–357.

Schachermeyr, Fritz. 1944. *Indogermanen und Orient. Ihre machtpolitische Auseinandersetzung im Altertum*. Stuttgart: Kohlhammer.

Schachermeyr, Fritz. 1949. Welche geschichtlichen Ereignisse führten zur Entstehung der mykenischen Kultur? In: *Symbolae ad studia orientis pertinentes Frederico Hrozný dedicatae*, vol. 2, edited by Václav Čihař and Josef Klíma, 331–350. Archiv Orientální 18. Praha: Orientální Ústav.

Schachermeyr, Fritz. 1950. *Poseidon und die Entstehung des griechischen Götterglaubens.* München: Lehnen.

Schachermeyr, Fritz. 1951. Streitwagen und Streitwagenbild im alten Orient und bei den mykenischen Griechen. *Anthropos* 46: 705–753.

Schachermeyr, Fritz. 1954. Kreta und Mykenä. *Historia Mundi* 3: 42–55.

Schachermeyr, Fritz. 1955. Prähistorische Kulturen Griechenlands. *Realencyclopaedie* 22 (2): 1350–1548.

Schachermeyr, Fritz. 1964. *Die minoische Kultur des alten Kreta.* Stuttgart: Kohlhammer.

Schachermeyr, Fritz. 1967. Ägäis *und Orient. Die überseeischen Kulturbeziehungen von Kreta und Mykenai, der Levante und Kleinasien unter besonderer Berücksichtigung des 2. Jahrtausends v.Chr.* Denkschriften der Österreichischen Akademie der Wissenschaften, Phil.–hist. Klasse 93. Vienna: Böhlau.

Schachermeyr, Fritz. 1968. Zum Problem der griechischen Einwanderung. In: *Atti e Memorie del 1° Congresso Internazionale di Micenologia, Roma 27 Sett. – 3 Ott. 1967,* I, 297–312. Incunabula Graeca 25, 1. Roma: Edizioni dell'Ateneo.

Schachermeyr, Fritz. 1969. *Griechische Geschichte. Mit besonderer Berücksichtigung der geistesgeschichtlichen und kulturmorphologischen Zusammenhänge.* 2nd edition, Stuttgart: Kohlhammer.

Schachermeyr, Fritz. 1979a Die minoische Kultur des alten Kreta. 2nd edition, Stuttgart: Kohlhammer.

Schachermeyr, Fritz. 1979b. Mykenische Kultur. *Der Kleine Pauly* 3: 1506–1514.

Schachermeyr, Fritz. 1981. *Die Tragik der Vollendung. Stirb und Werde in der Vergangenheit. Europa im Würgegriff der Gegenwart.* Vienna and Berlin: Koska.

Schachermeyr, Fritz. 1984a. *Fritz Schachermeyr, Ein Leben zwischen Wissenschaft und Kunst,* edited by Hilde Schachermeyr and Gerhard Dobesch. Vienna: Böhlau.

Schachermeyr, Fritz. 1984b. *Griechische Frühgeschichte. Ein Versuch, frühe Geschichte wenigstens in Umrissen verständlich zu machen.* Österreichische Akademie der Wissenschaften Phil–hist. Klasse, Sitzungsberichte 425. Vienna: Verlag der Österreichischen Akademie der Wissenschaften.

Schachermeyr, Fritz. 1986. *Mykene und das Hethiterreich.* Veröffentlichungen der Kommission für Mykenische Forschung 11 / Österreichische Akademie der Wissenschaften, Philosophisch–Historische Klasse: Sitzungsberichte 472. Vienna: Verlag der Österreichischen Akademie der Wissenschaften.

Schiering Wolfgang. 1988. Anhang. In *Archäologenbildnisse. Porträts und Kurzbiographien von Klassischen Archäologen deutscher Sprache,* edited by Reinhard Lullies and Wolfgang Schiering, 334. Mainz: von Zabern.

Schlerath, Bernfried. 1987. Können wir die urindogermanische Sozialstruktur rekonstruieren? Methodologische Erwägungen. In: *Zum indogermanischen Wortschatz,* edited by Wolfgang Meid, 249–264. Innsbruck: Institut für Sprachwissenschaft.

Schlerath, Bernfried. 1995. Georges Dumézil und die Rekonstruktion der indogermanischen Kultur. 1. Teil, *Kratylos* 40: 1–48.

Schlerath, Bernfried. 1996. Georges Dumézil und die Rekonstruktion der indogermanischen Kultur. 2. Teil. *Kratylos* 41:1–67.

Schmitt, Rüdiger. 1987. Aryans. *Encyclopædia Iranica* 2: 684–687.

Schmitt, Rüdiger. 2000. Indogermanische Altertumskunde *Reallexikon der Germanischen Altertumskunde* 15: 384–402.

Schneider, Thomas. 1999. Zur Herkunft der ägyptischen Bezeichnung *wrry.t* 'Wagen'. Ein Indiz für den Lautwert von <r> vor Beginn des Neuen Reiches. *Göttinger Miszellen* 173: 155–158.

Schneider, Thomas. 2008. Fremdwörter in der ägyptischen Militärsprache des Neuen Reiches und ein Bravourstück des Elitesoldaten (Papyrus Anastasi I 23, 2–7). *Journal of the Society for the Study of Egyptian Antiquities* 35: 181–205.

Schrader, Otto (ed.). 1901. *Reallexikon der Indogermanischen Altertumskunde. Grundzüge einer Kultur– und Völkergeschichte Alteuropas.* Straßburg: Trübner.

Schrakamp, Ingo. 2015. Militär und Kriegführung in Vorderasien. In: *Krieg. Eine archäologische Spurensuche,* edited by Harald Meller, 213–228. Darmstadt: Theiss.

Schreiber, Maximilian. 2006. Altertumswissenschaften im Nationalsozialismus. Die Klassische Philologie an der Ludwig–Maximilians–Universität. In: *Die Universität München im Dritten Reich. Aufsätze,* Teil 1, edited by Elisabeth Kraus, 181–248. München: Utz.

Schreiber, Maximilian. 2008. *Walther Wüst. Dekan und Rektor der Universität München 1935–1945.* München: Utz.

Siegert, Hans. 1941–1942. Zur Geschichte der Begriffe 'Arier' und 'arisch'. *Wörter und Sachen. Zeitschrift für indogermanische Sprachwissenschaft, Volksforschung und Kulturgeschichte* N. F. 4: 73–99.

Sommer, Ferdinand. 1939. Review of Potratz 1938. *Orientalistische Literaturzeitung* 42: 621–634.

Souček, Vladimír and Jana Siegelová. 1995. *Systematische Bibliographie der Hethitologie 1915–1995,* 3 vols. Leiden: Brill.

Sparreboom, Marcus. 1985. *Chariots in the Veda.* Leiden: Brill.

Steuer, Heiko. 1994. Fahren und Reiten. II. Archäologisches. *Reallexikon der Germanischen Altertumskunde* 8: 153–155.

Steuer, Heiko. 2001. Herbert Jankuhn und seine Darstellungen zur Germanen– und Wikingerzeit. In: *Eine hervorragend nationale Wissenschaft. Deutsche Prähistoriker zwischen 1900 und 1995,* edited by Heiko Steuer, 417–473. Berlin: de Gruyter.

Steuer, Heiko. 2004. Herbert Jankuhn – SS–Karriere und Ur– und Frühgeschichte. In *Nationalsozialismus in den Kulturwissenschaften,* vol. 1. *Fächer – Milieus – Karrieren,* edited by Hartmut Lehmann and Otto Gerhard Oexle, 447–529. Göttingen: Vandenhoeck & Ruprecht.

Studniczka, Franz. 1907. Der Rennwagen im syrisch–phönikischen Gebiet. *Jahrbuch des Kaiserlich Deutschen Archäologischen Instituts* 22: 147–196.

Summerer, Thomas. 1998. *Der 'Arier'. Grundlagen, Ursprung, Wandel und Aktualität eines Mythos.* 'Diplom–Arbeit' Vienna University.

Takács, Gábor. 2008. *Etymological Dictionary of Egyptian,* vol. 3. Handbuch der Orientalistik: Abteilung 1, Der Nahe und Mittlere Osten 48. Leiden: Brill.

Teufer, Mike. 1999. Ein Scheibenknebel aus Džarkutan (Südusbekistan). *Archäologische Mitteilungen aus Iran und Turan* 31: 69–142.

Teufer, Mike. 2012. Der Streitwagen. Eine 'indo–iranische' Erfindung? Zum Problem der Verbindung von Sprachwissenschaft und Archäologie. *Archäologische Mitteilungen aus Iran und Turan* 44: 271–312.

Textor de Ravisi, Aanatole Arthur. 1878. Études sur les chars de guerre égyptien. In: *Congrès provençal des Orientalistes français. Compte rendu de la première session, Saint–Étienne 1875*, 439–472. St. Etienne: Maisonneuve et Cie.

Thieme, Paul. 1960. The 'Aryan' Gods of the Mitanni Treaties. *Journal of the American Oriental Society* 80: 301a–317b.

Trask, Robert L. 2000. *The Dictionary of Historical and Comparative Linguistics*. Edinburgh: Edinburgh University Press.

Ungnad, Arthur. 1923. Babylonische Sternbilder oder der Weg babylonischer Kultur nach Griechenland. *Zeitschrift der Deutschen Morgenländischen Gesellschaft* 77: 81–91.

Untermann, Jürgen. 1986. Ursprache und historische Realität. Der Beitrag der Indogermanistik zu Fragen der Ethnogenese. In: *Studien zur Ethnogenese*, edited by the Rheinisch–Westfälische Akademie der Wissenschaften, 133–163. Cologne and Opladen: Westdeutscher Verlag.

van den Hout, Theo. 2002. Another View of Hittite Literature. In: *Anatolica Antica. Studi in Memoria di Fiorella Imparati*, edited by Stefano de Martino and Franca Pecchioli Daddi, 857–879. Eothen 11. Collana di Studi sull Civiltà dell'Oriente Antico 11. Florence: LoGisma Editore.

van den Hout, Theo. 2016. Wagen B. Hethitisch. *Reallexikon für Assyriologie* 14: 622–627.

van den Hout, Theo. 2020. *A History of Hittite Literacy. Writing and Reading in Late Bronze-Age Anatolia (1650–1200 BC)*. Cambridge: Cambridge University Press.

van Koppen, Frans. 2002. Equids in Mari and Chagar Bazar. *Altorientalische Forschungen* 29: 19–30.

Veldmeijer, André and Salima Ikram (eds.). 2013. *Chasing Chariots. Proceedings of the First International Chariot Conference (Cairo 2012)*. Leiden: Sidestone Press.

Veldmeijer, André and Salima Ikram (eds.). 2018. *Chariots in ancient Egypt. The Tano Chariot. A Case Study*. Leiden: Sidestone Press.

von Beckerath, Jürgen. 1964. *Untersuchungen zur politischen Geschichte der Zweiten Zwischenzeit in Ägypten*. Ägyptologische Forschungen 23. Glückstadt: Augustin.

von Dassow, Eva. 2008. *State and Society in the Late Bronze Age: Alalaḫ under the Mittani*. Bethesda, MD: CDL Press.

von Dassow, Eva. 2022. Mittani and Its Empire. In: *The Oxford History of the Ancient Near East*, edited by Karen Radner, Nadine Moeller and Daniel T. Potts., vol. 3: *From the Hyksos to the Late Second Millennium BC*. New York: Oxford Academic online edition. https://doi.org/10.1093/oso/9780190687601.003.0029.

von Mercklin, Eugen. 1909. *Der Rennwagen in Griechenland*. Erster Teil. PhD thesis Leipzig University. Leipzig: Radelli & Hille.

von Soden, Wolfram. 1937. *Der Aufstieg des Assyrerreiches als geschichtliches Problem*. Der Alte Orient 37. Leipzig: Hinrichs.

von Soden, Wolfram. 1939. Zur Kultur des Mitannireichs. *Göttingische Gelehrte Anzeigen* 201: 437–448.

Voigt, Mary M. and Robert H. Dyson, Jr. 1992. The Damghan/Khorasan Sequence. In: *Chronologies in Old World Archaeology*, vol. 1, edited by Robert W. Ehrich, 169–174. Chicago: University of Chicago Press.

Wegner, Ilse. 2000. *Einführung in die hurritische Sprache*. Wiesbaden: Harrassowitz.

Weidner, Ernst. 1952. Weiße Pferde im Alten Orient. *Bibliotheca Orientalis* 9: 157–159.

Wiedemann, Felix. 2018. The Aryans: Ideology and Historiographical Narrative Types in the Nineteenth and Early Twentieth Centuries. In: *Brill's Companion to the Classics, Fascist Italy and Nazi Germany*, edited by Alison John and Bastiaan Willems, 31–59. Brill's Companions to Classical Reception 12. Leiden and Boston: Brill.

Wiesehöfer, Josef. 1990. Zur Geschichte der Begriffe Arier und arisch in der deutschen Sprachwissenschaft und Althistorie des 19. und der ersten Hälfte des 20. Jahrhunderts. In: *Achaemenid History V. The Roots of European Tradition. Proceedings of the 1987 Groningen Achaemenid History Workshop*, edited by Heleen Sancisi–Weerdenburg and Jan Willem Drijvers, 149–165. Leiden: Nederlands Instituut voor het Nabije Oosten.

Wiesner, Joseph. 1939a. *Fahren und Reiten in Alteuropa und im Alten Orient*. Der Alte Orient 38, 2–4. Leipzig: Hinrichs.

Wiesner, Joseph. 1939b. *Fahren und Reiten in Alteuropa und im alten Orient. Forschungen und Fortschritte* 15: 229a–231a.

Wiesner, Joseph. 1939–1940. Zum 'Fahren und Reiten' in Alteuropa und im Alten Orient. *Prähistorische Zeitschrift* 30/31: 378–385.

Wiesner, Joseph. 1941. Indogermanen in der Frühzeit des Mittelmeerraumes und des vorderen Orients. *Neue Jahrbücher für Antike und deutsche Bildung* 4: 184–207.

Wiesner, Joseph. 1942a. Der Osten als Schicksalsraum Europas und des Indogermanentums. *Germanien. Monatshefte für die Germanenkunde* N. F. 4: 208–221.

Wiesner, Joseph. 1942b. Die Bedeutung des Ostraumes für die Antike. *Neue Jahrbücher für Antike und deutsche Bildung* 5: 257–269.

Wiesner, Joseph. 1943a. Neues zur Indogermanenfrage. *Europäischer Wissenschafts–Dienst* 1942, 3 (17): 2–4.

Wiesner, Joseph. 1943b. Von den Wurzeln des ritterlichen Stils im indogermanischen Altertum. *Altpreußen: Vierteljahrschrift für Vor– und Frühgeschichte* 35: 181–187.

Wiesner, Joseph. 1953. Review of Édouard Delebecque, Le cheval dans l'Iliade [...] (Paris: Klinksieck, 1951) and Nikolaos Yalouris, Athena als Herrin der Pferde. Museum Helveticum 7 (1950) 19–101. *Gnomon* 25: 314–319.

Wiesner, Joseph. 1959. Rezension zu Franz Hančar, Das Pferd in prähistorischer und früher historischer Zeit. (Wiener Beiträge zur Kulturgeschichte und Linguistik, 11). Wien: Herold, 1956. *Gnomon* 31: 289–301.

Wiesner, Joseph. 1968. *Fahren und Reiten*. Archaeologia Homerica, Kapitel F. Göttingen: Vandenhoeck and Ruprecht.

Wiesner, Joseph. 1970. Zum Stand der Streitwagenforschung. *Acta Archaeologica et Praehistorica* 1: 191–194.

Wilhelm, Gernot. 1987–1990. Marijannu. *Reallexikon der Assyriologie* 7: 419–421.

Wilhelm, Gernot. 1994. Mittan(n)i. *Reallexikon der Assyriologie* 8: 286–296.

Wilhelm, Gernot. 1995. The Kingdom of Mitanni in Second–millennium Upper Mesopotamia. In: *Civilizations of the Ancient Near East*, edited by Jack Sasson, vol. 2, 1243–1254. New York: Scribner.

Wilkinson, John Gardner. 1837. *The Manners and Customs of the Ancient Egyptians* (…). London: Murray.

Wirbelauer, Eckhard. 2006. Das wissenschaftliche Personal der Freiburger Philosophischen Fakultät (1910–1970). In: *Die Freiburger Philosophische Fakultät 1920–1960. Mitglieder – Strukturen – Vernetzungen*, edited by Eckhardt Wirbelauer, 1020–1021. Freiburg im Breisgau and München: Alber.

Zarins, Juris. 1976. *The Domestication of Equidae in Third Millennium B.C. Mesopotamia*. 2 vols. PhD thesis University of Chicago.

Zarins, Juris. 1986. Equids Associated with Human Burials in Third Millennium B.C. Mesopotamia: Two Complementary Facets. In: *Equids of the Ancient World*, edited by Richard H. Meadow and Hans–Peter Uerpmann, 164–193. Beihefte zum Tübinger Atlas des Vorderen Orients, Reihe A – Naturwissenschaften, 19/1. Wiesbaden: Reichert.

Zarins, Juris [with the assistance of Rick Hauser]. 2014. *The Domestication of Equidae in Third Millennium B.C. Mesopotamia*. Bethesda, MD: CDL Press.

Zeidler, Jürgen. 2000. Zur Etymologie von *wrr.yt* 'Wagen'. Mit einigen Bemerkungen zur 'syllabischen' Schreibung. *Göttinger Miszellen* 178: 97–111.

Zimmer, Stefan. 1990. *Ursprache, Urvolk und Indogermanisierung. Zur Methode der Indogermanischen Altertumskunde*. Innsbruck: Institut für Sprachwissenschaft der Universität.

4

Research on Chariots in Slavic Studies: A Brief Overview

Elena Izbitser

The discovery of the remains of actual chariots in graves of the Late Bronze Age in the Trans-Ural region in the 1970s and establishing the connection of cheekpieces, long known in the Pontic-Caspian steppe, with draught horses has intensified the studies of chariot-related topics. Among those extensively discussed are the place of the origin of the chariot, the time and place of horse domestication, and its use as a draught animal. Other topics in focus include the functions of the steppe vehicles and the social status of those buried with chariots. While finds of chariots are scarce, and out of almost thirty graves presently known less than ten preserved the traces of their wooden constructions, there are over one hundred burials containing paired and single cheekpieces. This allows scholars to categorise cheekpieces and examine assemblages accompanying the deceased by this part of horse harness. Based on the remains of chariots, several reconstructions of chariots, though hypothetical, have been suggested. In the search for proof that the steppe was the area from which chariots emerged, some scholars mistakenly link the chariots with spoked wheels to wagons with four solid wheels of the Early Bronze Age, seeing them as the predecessors of chariots.

Introduction

An interest in Eurasian chariots has generated a significant number of studies. Although we cannot provide a comprehensive historiography of the related publications, this study offers a brief overview outlining the sources of our knowledge about these vehicles with two spoked wheels by highlighting the principal associated controversial challenges which have been discussed over the years.

The evidence for the existence of chariots in different areas of Bronze Age Eurasia comes from several sources: pictorial images, remains of parts of actual chariots in graves, and cheekpieces as elements of horse harness. Each of these sources has its own history of study and methodological approach to its analysis.

The majority of depictions of chariots, besides a few images on vessels and rocks known in the East European steppes, come from petroglyphs known across the mountains of Siberia and Central Asia. Studies of images of chariots can be found in both general works on petroglyphs of a certain site or region and in works dedicated specifically to chariots. Among numerous publications, most of which are primarily descriptions of petroglyphs on discovered sites where depictions of chariots have been categorised and analysed, a monograph of 1980 by Yakov Sher should be mentioned first. In this work, the author concentrated on theoretical methods of analysis of both iconographic and semantic aspects related to the petroglyphs. Based on a database of stylistic elements and with the help of computer processing, it became possible to identify persistent stylistic features and their combinations typical for a certain culture and period. In some cases, images of chariots served as the basis for dating of groups of petroglyphs. The detailed study of the vehicles and draught animals depicted allowed Sher to offer some historical and semantic reconstructions, such as the spread of chariots within the Central Asia regions, and designate scenes with mythological motifs.[1] Some of his conclusions regarding different styles of images were disputed by Elena E. Kuz'mina, who discussed chariots recorded on petroglyphs extensively in her studies of the Andronovo culture.[2] An elaborate classification of chariot images in petroglyphs was proposed by Viktor A. Novozhenov in his work on wheeled vehicles and nomadic migrations in prehistoric times. In this classification, typological variants of petroglyphs are identified according to a type of vehicle with its variants and by the species of animals that pulled a vehicle. Also considered are techniques with which petroglyphs were executed. First published in 1994, this enhanced classification was included in the author's latest monograph focusing on the role of wheeled transport in communication between different regions of the Old World.[3] The publications provide extensive lists of publications on petroglyphs with images of chariots that go back to the late 19th century. Among the most discussed are topics related to the dispersal of speakers of Indo-European languages, mythological characters reflected in images and their compositions, the link

---

[1] Sher 1980.
[2] Kuz'mina 1994: 165–171.
[3] Novozhenov 1994; 2012. Novozhenov, this volume.

of petroglyphs to a particular prehistoric culture, and technical features of the depicted chariots.

The Question of the Existence of Chariots in the Eurasian Steppes

The question regarding the existence of chariots in the Eurasian steppes was raised more than a decade before their first finds in graves. Konstantin F. Smirnov suggested that the presence of two horse skeletons in the Late Bronze Age graves in the Volga-Ural region indicates a two-horse chariot, such as on the Near Eastern reliefs or Egyptian frescoes depicting war or hunting scenes.[4] The discovery of the remains of chariots in burials of the Late Bronze Age at the Sintashta burial ground in the Trans-Ural region in the mid-1970s[5] sparked new studies of chariot-related topics and broadened the range of subjects discussed. And although Nikolay N. Cherednichenko in the 1970s pointed out that topics related to Eurasian chariots of the Late Bronze Age were undeveloped in the Soviet studies,[6] later research has filled this lacuna. Besides the Indo-European migrations, the focus of studies became the place and time of the origin of the chariot, the functions of the steppe vehicles and their construction, the use of horses as draught animals, and the social status of the deceased buried with chariots. However, the connection between wheeled transport and (Proto)Indo-Europeans, often with references to the Vedic hymns and Old Indian epics, continued to be present in many works that dealt with chariots.

The Sintashta Chariots and the Question of Origin of the "True Chariot"

In the 1970s, the Sintashta finds served as an important argument for Smirnov and Kuz'mina – despite the lack of written evidence – for the Indo-Iranian roots of the Andronovo culture. Scholars drew parallels between features of its burial rites and texts of *Mahābhārata* and *Rigveda*, suggesting a special group of warriors riding on chariots within the social structure of the Andronovo culture.[7] Kuz'mina continuously expressed in her articles and monographs, that the "archaeological realia that reflect these mythological ideas about the creation of a divine weapon and sky chariot are found only in the culture of the Eurasian steppes of the 17th–16th centuries BC."[8] The early presence of vehicles with two spoked wheels accompanied by horse skeletons in graves of the Ural region made scholars to favour the steppes as the place of the invention of the chariot, specifically the war chariot, and called into question its Near Eastern origin.

The steppe finds were designated 'light war chariots' following the discovery of imprints of the lower parts of spoked wheels at Sintashta.[9] They continue to be considered as such despite the excavations of the following years which added only a few more details of their design.[10] Several proposed reconstructions of the steppe chariot were also based on the assumption that it was a war vehicle. The military function of these chariots was not disputed until 1996 when Mary A. Littauer and the recipient of this *Festschrift*, Joost H. Crouwel, published an article titled "On the origin of the true chariot."[11] The article came as a response to the publication of David W. Anthony and Nikolay B. Vinogradov of a chariot grave at Krivoe Ozero, where the authors expressed their belief in the steppe origin of chariots and their use in warfare, though with a reservation of possible use in ritual races.[12] Taking into consideration the available parameters – the distance between the wheels and the maximum length of the naves estimated by the distance from the wheels to the grave walls, Littauer and Crouwel concluded that the steppe vehicles "would not be manoeuvrable enough for use either in warfare or in racing" and there are no grounds for the existing reconstructions of these chariots above the axle level.[13] Their arguments for the Near Eastern origin of the chariots were as follows: two-wheeled vehicles were introduced in the region long before the end of the 3rd millennium, with an indication of the proper harness dated to the 23rd–21st centuries BCE, with an example of a horse figurine from Tell es-Sweyhat in Syria.[14]

Agreeing with Littauer and Crouwel on the insufficient data for suggested reconstructions, some scholars, including Kuz'mina, did not accept their arguments against the military function of chariots, arguing that chariot burials were accompanied by new types of weapons.[15] The presence of weapons in burial assemblages of chariot graves was also among the grounds provided by David Anthony in his disagreement with Littauer and Crouwel. The others include reasonings that steppe chariots were made in many sizes in terms of a gauge and were big enough for a two-man crew; a war chariot with narrow gauge could be driven by one man armed with a javelin or a bow; the majority of chariot graves contained various types of weapons and accompanied, when sexed, male burials; together with chariots, appeared a type of antler or bone cheekpieces allowing more severe horse control for greater speed and precise manoeuvres, while the same type of metal cheekpieces appeared later in the Near East; radiocarbon dates for steppe assemblages point to approximately a hundred years difference with the oldest chariot images on the Near Eastern seals. All this led to the view that chariots were invented in the Ural steppes.[16] Counterarguments provided by Anthony are not flawless and, in some points, erroneous.

---

[4] Smirnov 1961: 46.
[5] Gening and Ashikhmina 1975: 145.
[6] Cherednichenko 1976: 144.
[7] Smirnov and Kuz'mina 1977.
[8] Quote from Kuz'mina 2007: 137; see also Kuz'mina 1994: 191.
[9] Gening and Ashikhmina 1975: 145; Gening 1977: 73. Chechushkov and Epimakhov, this volume.
[10] Novozhenov 1994: 201; Anthony and Vinogradov 1995.
[11] Littauer and Crouwel 1996: 937.
[12] Anthony and Vinogradov 1995: 40.
[13] Littauer and Crouwel 1996: 939.
[14] Littauer and Crouwel 1996: 937.
[15] Kuz'mina 2000: 6.
[16] Anthony 2007: 402–403; 2009: 61–62.

Regarding chariots made in many sizes, it should be remembered that these sizes were measured by the distance between two wheel pits, which did not always have imprints of spokes and were not always parallel. Points on the number in a chariot crew – one or two men – and the types of weapons a crew used are only hypothetical. Artefacts listed by Anthony as a warrior's armament include such items as mace-heads that are usually considered prestigious, not military objects. Before suggesting the functionality of axes and projectile points from chariot graves, the objects need to be analysed by type and material; contexts of similar finds should be compared in graves without chariots. Out of almost thirty graves attributed as chariot graves, nine contained individual burials, and only two or three skeletons were sexed as adult males.[17] The disc-shaped cheekpieces from the steppes indeed have an earlier date than the similarly shaped Near Eastern cheekpieces, but the focus on manoevrability in Littauer and Crouwel's article was based on the technical parameters of vehicles, not on a way of managing the horse. In discussing the chronological priority of the Eurasian horse-drawn chariots over the Near Eastern ones, Anthony preferred to leave out the find from Tell es-Sweyhat and avoided a discussion on the estimated length of the naves of the steppe chariots.

In addition to defining chariots as military vehicles, the presence of fortified settlements has been considered another piece of evidence of the increased warfare activities in the steppes in the early Sintashta period,[18] in accordance with a concept of the 'Country of towns' and the well-known settlement of Arkaim in it.[19] Some think that fortification systems testify to the military situation during this period, indirectly confirming the military functionality of the chariot complex.[20] There is, however, a different explanation for these fortified sites. Based on detailed analysis of their spatial orgnisation and topography, Nikolay P. Anisimov concluded that these sites were well-planned and well-stocked yards for cattle and sheep. The so-called fortifications – ditches and ramparts – were made around the areas where there were wells, to protect places from the rustling of animals and not from enemies on chariots; the disadvantageous strategic locations of settlements also speak against the military function of the fortifications.[21] Though the data for archaeological cultures following the Sintashta culture, as well as ethnographical materials on stock-raising nomads of the 18th–20th centuries from the same regions where the 'fortified' settlements of the Late Bronze are known to support the results of Anisimov's studies,[22] they are hardly mentioned by other scholars, perhaps because they do not fit the picture of military battles.

Over time, however, interpretations of remains of vehicles as war chariots and as markers of 'the caste of chariot warriors and their leaders'[23] became less unreserved. For example, Evgeny Cherlenok suggested that a chariot in a grave served as a means of conveyance for the buried individual to the Other World[24] and only stated that it symbolised the martial status of the deceased.[25] Vinogradov also assumed that the placement of two-wheeled vehicles in the grave could reflect a funerary myth about the journey of the soul of certain clan members, who were not necessarily military leaders but who held a high position in the system of metal production and in the sphere of various rituals.[26] Igor Chechushkov wrote that the connection between the chariot and single male burials is not so straightforward, and its presence in a collective grave does not allow us to assert that it was a marker of an individual's social status.[27] While considering the military use of chariots as their primary function, Chechushkov and his colleague Andrey Epimakhov do not exclude the possibility of their use as an object of ritual practice and as a marker of social status.[28] Meanwhile, discussing the Sintashta culture, Stanislav Grigoriev mentioned that graves with chariots cannot be distinguished from others in burial rites or accompanying goods; thus there are no grounds to prove the existence of a special stratum of warrior-charioteers in Sintashta society.[29] Analysing weapons of the Sintashta culture, Natalia A. Berseneva pointed to the absence of archaeological and anthropological traces of military activities with the use of weapons. She assumed that the number of men trained in military affairs and chariotry was relatively small and that this activity was not their primary occupation.[30] Calculations on the number of chariots used over the 200-year period within the Sintashta communities made by Chechushkov and Epimakhov showed that one chariot was produced every 35 years. However, adherence to the idea of the military function of chariots forces the authors to look for interpretations that would connect the low number of chariots with the military theme, assuming that chariots were used 'probably, for warfare,' as 'a means of transport to the battlefield,' and 'as a platform for shooting, and a symbol of the prestige and power of a war-leader'.[31] Pavel F. Kuznetsov voiced a similar opinion suggesting that the main aim of the chariot was the fastest possible conveying of a warrior by a driver to the battlefield and doubted the ability of a warrior to fight on the move directly from the chariot because of the rugged terrain.[32]

Several variants of graphic and artistic reconstructions of the chariot offered by different scholars also reflect the military purpose of the vehicles; all chariots are pictured with platforms open at the rear. The form and size of the chariot's body and draught pole are unknown, and

---

[17] Chechushkov 2011: 58; Chechushkov and Epimakhov 2018: 461.
[18] Anthony 2007, 393; 405; 2009: 54; 62.
[19] Zdanovich and Batanina 1995.
[20] Chechushkov 2013: 192.
[21] Anisimov 2009; 2015.
[22] Tkachev 2019.
[23] Zdanovich 1999: 43–44.
[24] Cherlenok 2001.
[25] Cherlenok 2006.
[26] Vinogradov 2011: 90–91; 2020.
[27] Chechushkov 2011: 59.
[28] Epimakhov and Chechushkov 2006: 180; Chechushkov and Epimakhov 2010: 192.
[29] Grigoriev 2002: 125; 2015: 132.
[30] Berseneva 2013.
[31] Chechushkov and Epimakhov 2018: 446; 472.
[32] Kuznetsov 2017: 43; 47.

their parameters are calculated based on the size of the inner space of graves. Chariots from the Sintashta graves are shown with the rectangular floor of the box-shaped body, the slightly bent draught pole, and wheels with ten (Figure 4.1)[33] and eleven (Figure 4.2)[34] spokes on an axle shifted to the rear.[35] Chariots on other reconstructions have oval or D-shaped floors, different designs of the body, curves of the draught pole, and wheels with a different number of spokes on the axle placed under the centre of the floor. A chariot in a picture of the Krivoe Ozero grave first published by Anthony and Vinogradov has the wicker-basket style of the oval body and twelve-spoked wheels (Figure 4.3).[36] Taking into account the data available in 2006, Chuchushkov made a schematic diagram of the wheel with twelve spokes – the maximum number of spokes estimated from imprints.[37] Later, he offered a reconstruction of the whole light steppe chariot with eight-spoked wheels, the D-shaped floor made of planks, the body formed of several posts supporting the railing, and the bent draught pole (Figure 4.4).[38] The existing reconstructions are discussed in detail by Kuznetsov. He accepted the variant proposed by Chechushkov but with some additions and modifications; the most significant one is the type of draught pole, which he considered to be of the same construction as the Mycenaean chariots depicted in Linear B script (Figure 4.5).[39] Another vision of the steppe chariot was offered by K. Altynbekov and V. Novozhenov. It is similar to the variant drawn by Chechushkov but with a different design for the body formed of two rods meeting at the centre at an acute angle (Figure 4.6).[40] Due to the limited data available, all reconstructions are based on parallels to the Egyptian, Chinese, or Celtic chariots and are largely imaginary.[41]

It should be noted that authors of these reconstructions favour the origin of chariots in the steppe, even though they are not supported by the archaeological evidence from the burials. The established number of spokes in the wheels (up to twelve)[42] indicates that while the Ural chariots are the earliest of the actual chariots presently known from the

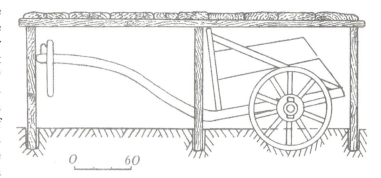

Figure 4.1. Reconstruction of the Eurasian war chariot from Sintashta, grave 19 (after Gening et al. 1992: fig. 94).

Figure 4.2. Reconstruction of the Eurasian war chariot from Sintashta, grave 28 (after Gening et al. 1992: fig. 108).

Figure 4.3. Reconstruction of the Eurasian war chariot from Krivoe Ozero, kurgan 9, grave 1 (after Anthony and Vinogradov 1995: 37).

---

[33] Gening et al. 1992: 184, fig. 94.
[34] Gening et al. 1992: 205, fig. 108.
[35] Gening et al. 1992: 165–167; 184–185; 203–206; 209–219; figs. 80; 94; 108; 116.
[36] Anthony and Vinogradov 1995: 37; Kislenko and Valiakhmetov 2018: 20.
[37] Chechushkov 2006: 127; 129.
[38] Chechushkov 2011: fig. 1; Chechushkov and Epimakhov 2018: fig. 7a.
[39] Kuznetsov 2017, 45–46: fig. 5.
[40] Novozhenov 2014: 101, fig. 68; 2019: fig. 8.
[41] The war function of the steppe chariots was not once put into question as Burmeister and Raulwing 2012: 98–106 pointed out. Also, the recent studies show a misinterpretation of militarised Aryans in the Rigveda who came to the present-day India on their horse-driven chariots (Danino 2019).
[42] Chechushkov 2011: 62; Chechushkov and Epimakhov 2018: 458.

Research on Chariots in Slavic Studies: A Brief Overview

technical point of view, they cannot be the first vehicles with spoked wheels. Despite the statement that the steppe finds make it possible to trace the evolution of vehicles,[43] there is not enough evidence to support this view.

In the search for supporting arguments for the origin of the chariot in the Eurasian steppes, scholars are looking for a link to connect two-wheeled chariots of the Late Bronze Age with vehicles of the previous period found in the graves of the earlier periods in the Pontic-Caspian steppes. For example, Kuz'mina, following Novozhenov, added a few other instances in listed burials of the Pit Grave and Catacomb cultures where, in her opinion, 'two-wheeled carts and their clay models have been found'.[44] But her list includes the graves where only wheels were preserved, not whole vehicles, and attribution of clay models as carts is just historiographic tradition. In almost 350 kurgan graves with wagons of the Early and Middle Bronze Age, excavators found wheels preserved in a wide raging number from 1 to 8. Meanwhile, the well-established schemes of the arrangement of one and two wagons allow us to assert that except for a tradition when one wheel covered an entrance to the catacomb chamber, the number of wheels other than 4 and 8 is the number of wheels left due to poor conditions for preservation of organic matter.

The Interpretation of the Vehicles from Kurgan Tyagunova Mogila and the Bolshoi Ipatovskiy kurgan in the North Caucasus

More often, two catacomb burials from different areas are cited as prototypes for the Eurasian chariots: kurgan Tyagunova Mogila, grave 27 (also referred to as Mar'evka, kurgan 11, grave 27) in the Dnieper region and grave 32 of the Bolshoi Ipatovskiy kurgan in the North Caucasus; in both cases, the wooden remains are wishfully interpreted as one-axled, two-wheeled vehicles[45] and as forerunners of classic chariots.[46]

The grave at Tyagunova Mogila, indeed, contained a poorly preserved and disassembled wheeled vehicle. Both wheels were at some distance behind the remains of a wooden construction, one leaning against the wall and the other laid on the floor. According to the excavators, these remains are interpreted as a war chariot and include the lower part of the box made of a solid piece of wood, with an oval front and straight sides that looked like a trough, rectangular planks, and a fragment of a draught pole with a curve typical for

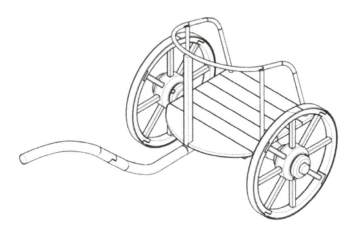

Figure 4.4. General reconstruction of the Eurasian war chariot by Igor V. Chechushkov (after Chechushkov 2011: fig. 1,1).

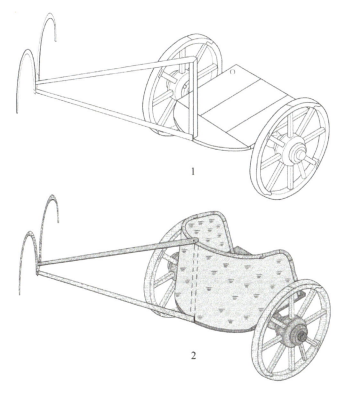

Figure 4.5. General reconstruction of the Eurasian war chariot by Pavel F. Kuznetsov (after Kuznetsov 2017: fig. 5).

Figure 4.6. General reconstruction of the Eurasian war chariot by Kyrym Altynbekov and Viktor Novozhenov (after Novozhenov 2014: fig. 68).

---

[43] Epimakhov and Chechushkov 2018: 156.
[44] Kuz'mina 2007: 132.
[45] Belinskij and Kalmykov 2004: 215–216; Korenevsky et al. 2007: 110–111; Chechushkov 2011: 58; Kuznetsov 2017: 47; Lindner 2021: 105 (about Ipavosky kurgan only).
[46] Eder and Nagel 2006: 60; 69–70, with reference to Alexander Häusler and Asko Parpola.

chariots.[47] However, it should be taken into consideration that the grave was excavated in the 1970s. At that time, only an insignificant number of kurgan burials in pits and catacombs with remains of wagons had been discovered. Interpretations of vehicles were greatly influenced by the Near Eastern and Egyptian images of war scenes and actual chariots. Now, it is well known that the bottom part of the steppe wagon is preserved as a rectangle frame, and the documented draught poles were straight, not bent. In cases when a vehicle in a grave was disturbed, as it was in Tyagunova Mogila, the number of the preserved wheels of a disassembled vehicle cannot be treated as the original number.

Grave 32 of the Bolshoi Ipatovskiy kurgan represents a different case. In describing the find, the excavators wrote that decayed wood on both sides of the vehicle could 'probably',[48] or 'most likely' be interpreted as remains of wheels, and that no nave or other parts of wheels were traced.[49] They proposed that the chariot had a rear axle and its light body hint of a prototype for the chariot.[50] Although this interpretation is not supported by the documented evidence, where not only wheels are absent but also an axle, some scholars incorrectly state remains of chariots as fact.[51]

The drawing of the chamber shows on one side of the construction a segment of a round wooden artefact that has a rim more suitable for a vessel, not for a wheel. Remains on the other side preserved several wooden fragments that are shapeless.[52] The significant number of excavated burials accompanied by wagons makes it now possible to identify the poorly preserved vehicles in those cases when no wheels were found, but other distinctive details could be clearly recognised as belonging to wheeled vehicles. Usually, these are bottom frames of the standard type and size. However, the frame of a vehicle in grave 32 was of a different design and had the A-shaped draught-pole typical for mountainous terrain but unusual for the steppes. Since the kurgan is located in the borderland of Eastern Europe and the Caucasus, this find is clear evidence of the connections between the two areas in the Middle Bronze Age. Though the vehicle from grave 32 could be a wagon of unknown steppe construction or, more likely, a kind of travois, it does not have features that could link it to the Sintashta chariots. In addition, supporters of such a link point to the presence of shallow depressions comparable with the wheel-pits of Sintashta graves in two other wagon graves from the same Bolshoi Ipatovskiy kurgan. In their opinion, this feature of the burial rite, together with the chronological priority of the Catacomb graves, indicates the Ciscaucasian origin of these features.[53]

An explanation for the wheel-pits, or slots, as purposely dug to install the wheels is widely accepted.[54] These pits, taking into account the presence/absence of traces of the chariot, are classified as: pits with impressions of spokes as evidence that a real chariot was positioned in a grave; pits that did not have the imprints of spokes and are considered as symbolic representation of a chariot; where chariots were not placed in a grave and assumed to have been installed only for the duration of the ceremony and then removed.[55]

The pits measure from 1/3 to 1/4 of the wheel diameter and are lens-shaped in cross-section, reflecting the wheel's shape.[56] However, it is precisely the shape of the cross-sections that casts doubt on the human-made origin of the pits. These wheel-pits/slots appeared as the result of the pressure of the earth which collapsed on the chariots. Similar slots were discovered during the excavations of wagon burials of the Pit Grave culture in the Kuban region. They were traced under the wheels of the standing wagon (similarly to the ones from the Ipatovo kurgan). However, when the wagon was disassembled and their wheels were placed flat, the pressure from the soil pushed the naves into the ground, leaving hollows below the surface. Thus, the symbolic explanation of the wheel-pits and the rather exotic suggestion that the chariot was removed after the burial rite was performed, are invalid. The absence of the chariots themselves, while there are pits that can be positively associated with wheels, should be attributed solely to the poor preservation of wood in a particular soil. The same rationale applies to an attempt of some scholars to connect all pits in the graves with chariots, suggesting that only wheels or wheels on an axle were placed in a grave when a burial chamber represented a chariot body.[57]

The Discussion of Horse Harnessing

While publications on chariots, besides the limited data of their presence in graves, contain primarily hypothetical lines of argument, studies on cheekpieces are based on actual artefacts. Cheekpieces come from burials and settlements over the vast territory of the Eurasian steppes, and their locations allow scholars to identify the areas of the spread of chariots. The studies of cheekpieces touch on a broad range of issues. Besides the usual brief cultural and chronological analysis given during the publication of either recently excavated pieces or finds from old collections, scholars explore the technology of their manufacturing; reconstruct ancient horse bridles; offer a classification of different types of cheekpieces; analyse rituals connected to cheekpieces in settlements.

---

[47] Cherednichenko and Pustovalov 1991: 208–209.
[48] Belinskij and Kalmykov 2004: 210.
[49] Korenevsky et al. 2007: 41.
[50] Belinskij and Kalmykov 2004: 216; Korenevsky et al. 2007: 110.
[51] Chechushkov and Epimakhov 2018: 400.
[52] Belinskij and Kalmykov 2004: fig. 209; Korenevsky et al. 2007: fig. 23.
[53] Korenevsky et al. 2007: 111.

[54] E.g., Anthony and Vinogradov 1995: 36; Kaiser 2010: 152; Chechushkov 2011: 58; Chechushkov and Epimakhov 2010: 216; 2018: 444.
[55] Chechushkov 2011: 62; Epimakhov and Novikov 2017; Chechushkov and Epimakhov 2018: 461.
[56] Chechushkov 2011: 58.
[57] Vinogradov 2003: 265; 2020: 22–24; Zdanovich and Kupriyanova 2008: 193.

Cheekpieces have served as a chronological indicator for certain complexes, archaeological cultures and their interrelations, and migrations; burials with cheekpieces in their grave goods were used in discussion about the social structure of prehistoric societies.[58] An interest in cheekpieces that increased in the last quarter of the 20th century led to the publication of a volume with a collection of papers devoted specifically to issues related to this element of horse bridles and harness of the 'chariot cultures' (*kolesnichnye kul'tury*) in the Eurasian steppe and forest steppe during the Middle and Late Bronze Age.[59] The results of a traceological examination of cheekpieces have been presented in a monograph by Anatoliy N. Usachuk whose thorough analysis allowed him to distinguish the differences in cheekpieces made in different regions of Eurasia and offer suggestions on the arrangement of different types of cheekpieces in horse bridles.[60] Substantial bibliographies on cheekpieces can also be found in this monograph, and in a series of joint articles by Viacheslav A. Podoved, Anatoliy N. Usachuk, and Vitaliy V. Tsimidanov.[61] In their recent publications, these scholars outlined the long history of studies of Eurasian cheekpieces and divided it into four stages. According to this historiographic scheme, the beginning of Stage I goes back to the 1890s when cheekpieces entered the museum collections. Until the mid-1960s, these artifacts were not correctly identified and considered either buckles, plaques, lids of vases, details of helmets, or other things. For another decade, scholars connected cheekpieces only with control of the riding horse. It was in the first half of the 1970s when cheekpieces became associated with chariot horses, that were thought to pull either military or cult vehicles. From the second half of the 1970s to the mid-1980s, during stage II, the first publications about the discovery of the remains of chariots at Sintashta were published. Then the hypothesis about the existence of a social group of chariot warriors and light military chariots in the societies of the Eurasian steppes was formed and widely accepted. It was on the next, stage III, which lasted from the second half of the 1980s to the 1990s and was designated as 'chariot euphoria,' when this hypothesis gained the most number of supporters. Graves where cheekpieces and weapons appeared together were interpreted as burials of chariot warriors, while burials with cheekpieces without weapons were described as those of horse trainers. Sometimes, chariot warriors were depicted as the creators of the processes of cultural genesis, who made distant migrations that determined the norms and style of social life. However, some sceptical opinions began to grow in the second half of the 1990s after Littauer and Crouwel concluded that the technical characteristics of the steppe chariots were unfit for military goals. The last and continuing stage IV started at the beginning of the 21st century and has been characterised by the decline of interest in sociological interpretations of burials with cheekpieces identifying them exclusively with chariot warriors.

The horse bridle, in the context of the funeral rite, is seen as a symbolic replacement for a chariot. However, based on the analysis of burial goods with cheekpieces in the assemblages, scholars suggest that cheekpieces could accompany religious or secular leaders or even craftworkers.[62] Thus, similarly to the studies of chariot graves, the latest examination of burials with cheekpieces cast doubt on the hypothesis that these artifacts indicate, primarily, the burials of chariot warriors.

The presence of cheekpieces and horse skeletons in the same burial complexes has led scholars to propose that these skeletons belonged to the horses harnessed to chariots. The process and results of the study of the bones of the 'chariot horses' are presented in a series of articles.[63] One of the conclusions of this analysis is that the earliest 'chariot horses' of the South Ural area were brought there by the bearers of the Sintashta culture, probably from the steppes of the Northern Caucasus of Lower Don.[64]

The Issue of Origins of Horse and Chariot Cultures – Once Again

Over the years, excavations revealed more graves containing evidence of chariots attributed to several archaeological cultures in the Ural-Kazakhstan region. They are often referred to as 'chariot cultures' or the 'block of chariot cultures.' This block also includes archaeological cultures distributed within the Volga-Don and Volga-Ural regions, where no traces of chariots but cheekpieces, burial goods defined as the weapons of a charioteer, and horse offerings were found.[65] Supporters of the steppe origin of the chariot consider these areas as the place of its invention. For Kuz'mina, it was the Urals, where a complete complex consisting of a chariot, two horses, and cheekpieces is known.[66] Other scholars, connecting the first appearance of the chariot with a region of the formation of the Sintashta culture, would place this happening in the Don-Volga interfluves.[67] Contrary to the supporters of the steppe origin of the chariot, S. A. Grigoriev suggests that the migrating bearers of the Sintashta culture brought the chariot to the steppes from the Near East.[68] Opponents of the Near Eastern origin of the chariot argue that it is more a tradition to connect technological and social innovations, including the chariot complex, with the centres of civilizations, linking it to the psychological attitude of the researchers. For instance, Chechushkov and Epimakhov discuss issues of the horse domestication and the chronological relation between the two regions and conclude that there is a lack of reliable data in favour of the priority of the Near East in these areas.[69]

---

[58] Podoved et al. 2010: 15–16 and passim.
[59] Psalii 2004.
[60] Usachuk 2013.
[61] Podoved et al. 2010; 2016; 2020.
[62] Podoved et al. 2016: 28–32; 2020, 279–282; 293.
[63] Kosintsev 2008; 2010; Usmanova et al. 2018; Chechushkov et al. 2020.
[64] Kosintsev 2010: 29.
[65] Kuznetsov 2017: 39.
[66] Kuz'mina 2007: 111.
[67] Vinogradov 2003: 265; Epimakhov and Chechushkov 2018: 473.
[68] Grigoriev 2020a: 76.
[69] Epimakhov and Chechushkov 2018.

Izbitser

In recent years, scholars have been trying to locate the territory of the earliest domesticated horse with the help of genomic analyses.[70] A problem of chronological relations of the steppe and the Near Eastern data lies, as it has been pointed out, in different dating systems: the radiocarbon method for the northern part of Eurasia and relative chronology for Mesopotamia.[71] At the time of excavation, the Sintashta finds were dated to the 17th–16th centuries BCE.[72] Later, radiocarbon analyses offered slightly different but close dates: 2000–1800 BCE,[73] 1950–1750 BCE,[74] 2030–1750 BCE,[75] 2100 BCE.[76] Lately, the examination of the previously received radiocarbon dates has confirmed with high probability the appearance of the chariots in the Urals close to the end of the 3rd millennium BCE,[77] which does not give a significant priority to the Eurasian chariots over the Near Eastern ones.[78] It is especially true if we consider that the comparisons use different sources of evidence – actual chariots in the steppes and chariots on seal images in the Near East.

In the spring of 2021, the Department of Archaeology of the Bronze Age at the Institute of Archaeology (the Russian Academy of Sciences, Moscow) held a two-part online seminar, *Chariots at the Crossroads*. Presented at the seminar were two papers, *The Theory of the Birth of the Chariot* by Pavel Kuznetsov and *The Origin of Chariots and Evolution of Check-pieces in Eurasia in the Light of the Indo-European problems* by Stanislav Grigoriev. The papers and extended discussions that followed the presentations touched practically all chariot-related issues, though the focus continues to be on the topic raised since the first evidence for actual chariots of the Late Bronze Age was discovered about 50 years ago at the burial ground of Sintashta: the place of invention – the Near East or the Eurasian steppes. An answer to this question could lie either in clear new evidence or in different methodological research approaches.

Elena Izbitser
Independent Scholar, USA

Bibliography

Anisimov, Nikolay P. 2009. Arkaim – strana kard: empirika prostranstva zaural'skoi sredy [Arkaim – a Country of Livestock Yards: Empiricism of Space of the Trans-Ural Environment]. *Akademicheskii vestnik UralNIIproekt RAASH* 2: 16–21.

Anisimov, Nikolay P. 2015. Arkaim, territoriia kardy, sistema rasseleniia [Arkaim, a Territory of Livestock Yards, Settlement System]. In: *Homo Eurasicus v sistemakh sotsial'nykh kommunikatsii: kollektivnaia monografiia po materialam VI vserossiiskoi konferentsii, Sankt-Peterburg, RGPU im. A. I. Gertsena, 26 oktiabria 2015 goda*, edited by E. A. Okladnikova and V. A. Popov, 67–120. Moscow and Berlin: DirectMedia.

Anthony, David W. 2007. *The Horse, the Wheel, and Language. How Bronze-Age Riders from the Eurasian Steppes Shaped the Modern World*. Princeton: Princeton University Press.

Anthony, David W. 2009. The Sintashta Genesis. The Roles of Climate Change, Warfare, and Long-Distance Trade. In: *Social Complexity in Prehistoric Eurasia. Monuments, Metals, and Mobility*, edited by Bryan K. Hanks and Katheryn M. Linduff, 47–73. Cambridge: Cambridge University Press.

Anthony, David W. and Nikolai B. Vinogradov. 1995. Birth of the Chariot. *Archaeology* 48 (2): 36–41.

Belinskij, Andrej B. and Aleksei A. Kalmykov. 2004. Neue Wagenfunde aus Gräbern der Katakombengrab-Kultur im Steppengebiet des zentralen Vorkaukasus. In: *Rad und Wagen. Der Ursprung einer Innovation. Wagen im Vorderen Orient und Europa*, edited by Mamoun Fansa and Stefan Burmeister, 201–220. Archäologische Mitteilungen aus Nordwestdeutschland, Beiheft 40. Mainz: von Zabern.

Berseneva, Natalia A. 2013. O podkhodakh k izucheniiu militarizatsii sintashtinskogo obshchestva [On Approaches to the Study of the Militarisation of Sintashta Society]. *Kratkie soobshcheniia instituta arkheologii* 231: 36–43.

Burmeister, Stefan and Peter Raulwing. 2012. Festgefahren. Die Kontroverse um den Ursprung des Streitwagens. Einige Anmerkungen zu Forschung, Quellen und Methodik. In: *Archaeological, Cultural and Linguistic Heritage. Festschrift für Erzsébet Jerem in Honour of her 70th Birthday*, edited by Peter Anreiter, Eszter Bánffy, László Bartosiewicz, Wolfgang Meid, and Carola Metzner-Nebelsick, 93–113. Budapest: Archaeolingua.

Chechushkov, Igor V. 2006. Koleso evraziiskoi stepnoi kolesnitsy epokhi bronzy [The Wheel of the Eurasian Steppe Chariot of the Bronze Age]. *Vestnik Iuzhno-Ural'skogo gosudarstvennogo universiteta* 7 (72): 127–130.

Chechushkov, Igor V. 2011. Kolesnitsy evraziiskikh stepei epokhi bronzy [Chariots of the Eurasian Steppes in the Bronze Age]. *Vestnik arkheologii, antropologii i etnografii* 2 (15): 57–65.

Chechushkov, Igor V. 2013. *Kolesnichnyi Kompleks epokhi pozdnei bronzy stepnoi i lesostepnoi Evrazii (ot Dnepra do Irtysha)* [The Chariot Complex of the Eurasian Steppes (from the Dnieper to the Irtysh Rivers)]. Unpublished PhD dissertation. Moscow: Institute of Archaeology of the RAS.

Chechushkov, Igor V, Emma R. Usmanova, and Pavel A. Kosintsev. 2020. Early Evidence for the utilization of Horses in the Eurasian Steppes and the case of the Novoil'inovskiy 2 Cemetery in Kazakhstan. *Journal of Archaeological Science; Reports* 32 (4): 102420. https://doi.org/10.1016/j.jasrep.2020.102420.

---

[70] Librado et al. 2021.
[71] Epimakhov and Chechushkov 2018: 156–157; Grigoriev 2020a; 2020b: 99, comm. 1.
[72] Gening et al. 1992: 376.
[73] Epimachov and Korjakova 2004: 231.
[74] Kuznetsov 2006: 643.
[75] Epimakhov and Chechushkov 2008: 491.
[76] Anthony 2009: 60, comment.
[77] Lindner 2020: 377.
[78] Grigoriev 2020b: 99, comm. 1.

Chechushkov, Igor V. and Andrey V. Epimakhov. 2010. Kolesnichnyi kompleks Uralo-Kazakhstanskikh stepei [The Chariot Complex of the Ural-Kazakhstan steppes]. In: *Horses, Chariots and Chariot Drivers of the Eurasian steppes*, edited by Pavel F. Kuznetsov et al., 182–229. Yekaterinburg: Rifey.

Chechushkov, Igor V. and Andrey V. Epimakhov. 2018. Eurasian Steppe Chariots and Social Complexity During the Bronze Age. *Journal of World Prehistory* 31 (4): 435–483.

Cherednichenko, Nikolay N. 1976. Kolesnitsy Evrazii epokhi pozdnei bronzy [Eurasian Chariots of the Late Bronze Age]. In: *Eneolit i bronzovyi vek Ukrainy*, edited by Sofia S. Berezanskaia et al., 135–150. Kiev: Naukova dumka.

Cherednichenko, Nikolay N. and Sergei Z. Pustovalov 1991. Boevye kolesnitsy i kolesnichie v obshchestve katakombnoi kul'tury (po materialam raskopok v Nizhnem Pridneprov'e) [War Chariots and Charioteers of the Catacomb Culture (Based on Excavations in the Lower Dnieper Region.]. *Sovetskaia arkheologiia* 4: 206–216.

Cherlenok, Evgeny A. 2001. Kolesnichnaia zapriazhka v pogrebal'nom obriade (nachalo epokhi pozdnei bronzy evraziiskikh stepei) [The Chariot in the Funeral Rite (the Beginning of the Late Bronze Age in the Eurasian Steppes)]. *Vestnik molodykh uchenykh* 1: 22–29.

Cherlenok, Evgeny A. 2006. The Chariot in Bronze Age Funerary Rites of the Eurasian Steppes. In: *Horses and Humans. The Evolution of Human-Equine Relationships*, edited by Sandra S. Olsen, Susan Grant, Alice M. Choyke et al., 173–179. BAR International Series 1560. Oxford: BAR Publications.

Danino, Michel. 2019. Demilitarizing the Rigveda: A Scrutiny of Vedic Horses, Chariots and Warfare. *Studies in Humanities and Social Sciences* 26 (1): 1–32.

Eder, Christian and Wolfram Nagel. 2006. Grundzüge der Streitwagenbewegung zwischen Tiefeurasien, Südwestasien und Ägäis. *Altorientalische Forschungen* 33: 42–93.

Epimakhov, Andrey V. and Igor Chechushkov. 2006. Evraziiskie kolesnitsy: konstruktivnye osobennosti i vozmozhnosti funktsionirovaniia [Eurasian Chariots: their construction and functioning possibilities]. In: *Arkheologiia Iuzhnogo Urala. Step' (problem kul'turogeneza)*, edited by Sergei G. Batalov, 169–183. Chelyabinsk: Rifey.

Epimakhov, Andrey V. and Igor Chechushkov. 2008. Gorizont kolesnichnykh kul'tur Severnoi Evrazii: poeticheskaia metafora i istoricheskoe soderzhanie [Horizon of chariot cultures of the Northern Eurasia: poetic metaphor and historical substance]. *Problemy istorii, filologii I kul'tury* 22: 480–500.

Epimakhov, Andrey V. and Igor V. Chechushkov 2018. "Ex oriente lux"? Genezis kolesnitsy v svete noveishikh dannykh arkheologii ["Ex oriente lux"? The Genesis of the Chariot in the Light of the Latest Archaeology Data]. *Vestnik Tomskogo gosudarstvennogo universiteta. Istoriia* 54: 155–160.

Epimakhov, Andrej and Ludmila Korjakova. 2004. Streitwagen der eurasischen Steppe in der Bronzezeit: das Wolga-Uralgebiet und Kasachstan. In: *Rad und Wagen. Der Ursprung einer Innovation. Wagen im Vorderen Orient und Europa*, edited by Mamoun Fansa and Stefan Burmeister, 221–236. Archäologische Mitteilungen aus Nordwestdeutschland, Beiheft 40. Mainz: von Zabern.

Epimakhov, A. V. and Novikov I. K. 2017. Problema interpretatsii kolesnichnoi simvoliki bronzovogo veka v lesostepnom Zaural'e (mogil'nik Ozernoe-1) [The Problem of Interpretation of Chariot Symbolism of the Bronze Age in the Forest-Steppe of the Trans-Ural (Ozernoe-1 burial ground)]. *Arkheologicheskie vesti* 23: 345–354.

Gening, Vladimir F. 1977. Mogil'nik Sintashta i problema rannikh indoiranskikh plemen [The Sintashta Cemetery and the Problem of the Early Indo-Iranian Tribes]. *Sovetskaia Archaeologiia* 4: 53–73.

Gening, Vladimir F. and Lidiia I. Ashikhmina. 1975. Mogil'nik epokhi bronzy na reke Sintashta [A Bronze Age Cemetery on the Sintashta River]. In *Arkheologicheskie otkrytiia 1974 goda*, edited by Boris Aleksandrovich Rybakov, 144–147. Moscow: Nauka.

Gening, Vladimir F., Gennadiy B. Zdanovich and Vladimir V. Gening. 1992. *Sintashta. Arkheologicheskie pamiatniki ariiskikh plemen Uralo-Kazakhstanskikh stepei [Sintashta. The Archaeological Sites of Aryans Tribes of the Ural-Kazakh Steppes]*. Chelyabinsk: Iuzhno-Ural'skoe knizhnoe izd-vo.

Grigoriev, Stanislav A. 2002. *Ancient Indo-Europeans*. Chelyabinsk: Rifei.

Grigoriev, Stanislav A. 2015. *Drevnie indoevropeitsy [Ancient Indo-Europeans]*. Chelyabinsk: Tsistero.

Grigoriev, Stanislav A. 2020a. Khronologiia sintashtinskikh i blizhnevostochnykh kolesnits [Chronology of Sintashta and Near Eastern Chariots]. *Magistra Vitae* 2: 69–80.

Grigoriev, Stanislav A. 2020b. Indoevropeiskaia problema: osnovnye tendentsii v rasprostranenii iazyka, kul'tury i genov v Evrazii [The Indo-European Problem: Main Trends in the Spreading of the Language, Culture and Genes in Eurasia]. *Stepnaia Evraziia: bronzovyi mir. Sbornik nauchnykh trudov k 80-letiiu Gennadiia Borisovicha Zdanovicha*, edited by Tatiana S. Maliutina et al., 73–109. Chelyabinsk: Izdatel'stvo Chelyabinskogo gosudarstvennogo universiteta.

Kaiser, Elke. 2010. Wurde das Rad zweimal erfunden? Zu den frühen Wagen in der eurasischen Steppe. *Prähistorische Zeitschrift* 85 (2): 137–158.

Kislenko, Aleksandr M. and Ilya A. Valiakhmetov. 2018. *Drevneishie kolesnitsy Stepnoi Evrazii [The Earliest Chariots of the Eurasian Steppe]*. Chelyabinsk: Zapovednik "Arkaim".

Korenevsky, Sergei N., Andrey B. Belinsky, and Aleksei Kalmykov. 2007. *Bol'shoy Ipatovskiy kurgan na Stavropol'e [The Big Ipatovo Kurgan in the Staropol Region]*. Moscow: Nauka.

Kosintsev, Pavel A. 2008. Proiskhozdenie "kolesnichnykh loshadei" [The Origin of "Chariot" Horses]. In: *Proiskhozhdenie i rasprostranenie kolesnichestva. Sbornik nauchnykh statei*, edited by Andrey I. Vasilenko, 113–129. Lugansk: Globus.

Kosintsev, Pavel A. 2010. Chariot horses. In: *Horses, Chariots and Chariot Drivers of Eurasian Steppes*, edited by Pavel F. Kuznetsov et al., 55–79. Yekaterinburg, Samara, and Donetsk: Rifey.

Kuz'mina, Elena E. 1994. *Otkuda prišli indoarii? Materialnaia kultura plemen andronovskoi obshchnosti i proiskhozhdenie indoirantsev [Whence came the Indo-Aryans? The Material Culture of the Andronov Tribes and the Origin of the Indo-Iranians]*. Moscow: Nauka.

Kuz'mina, Elena E. 2000. Koni i kolesnitsy Yuzhnogo Urala i indoevropeiskie mify [Horses and Chariots of the Southern Ural and Indo-European Myths]. In: *Problemy izucheniia eneolita i bronzovogo veka Iuzhnogo Urala. Sbornik nauchnykh trudo*, edited by Svetlana N. Zasedateleva et al., 3–9. Orsk: Institut Evraziiskikh issledovanii.

Kuz'mina, Elena E. 2007. *The Origin of the Indo-Iranians*. Leiden Indo-European Etymological Dictionary Series 3. Leiden and Boston: Brill.

Kuznetsov, Pavel F. 2006. The Emergence of Bronze Age Chariots in Eastern Europe. *Antiquity* 80 (309): 638–645.

Kuznetsov, Pavel F. 2017. O rekonstruktsii drevneishikh kolesnits Evrazii [On the Reconstruction of Ancient Chariots of Eurasia]. *Voiadzher: mir i chelovek* 8: 39–51.

Librado, Pablo, Naveed Khan, Antoine Fages et al. 2021. The Origins and Spread of Domestic Horses from the Western Eurasian Steppes. *Nature* 598: 634–640.

Lindner, Stephan. 2020. Chariots in the Eurasian Steppe: a Bayesian Approach to the Emergence of Horse-Drawn Transport in the Early Second Millennium BC. *Antiquity* 94 (374): 361–380.

Lindner, Stephan. 2021. *Die technische und symbolische Bedeutung eurasischer Streitwagen für Europa und die Nachbarräume im 2. Jahrtausend v. Chr.* Berliner Archäologische Forschungen 20. Rahden/Westf.: Leidorf.

Littauer, Mary A. and Joost H. Crouwel. 1996. The Origin of the True Chariot. *Antiquity* 70 (270): 934–939.

Novozhenov, Viktor A. 1994. *Naskal'nye izobrazheniia povozok Srednei i Tsentral'noi Azii (k probleme migratsii naseleniia stepnoi Evrazii v epokhu eneolita i bronzy)* [Images of Wheeled Vehicles in the Rock Art of Central and Central Asia (On the Problems of Migration of the Population of the Eurasian Steppe in the Eneolithic and Bronze Age)]. Almaty: Argumenty i fakty Kazakhstan.

Novozhenov, Viktor A. 2012. *Chudo kommunikatsii i drevneyshii kolesnyi transport Evrazii* [The Wonder of Communications and Earliest Wheeled Transport of Eurasia]. Moscow: TAUS Publishing.

Novozhenov, Viktor A. 2014. Protoindoevropeiskie innovatsii [Proto-Indo-European Innovations]. In: *Tainstvo etnicheskoi istorii drevneishikh novadov stepnoi Evrazii*, edited by Andrey V. Epimakhov, 88–109. Almaty: Ostrov Krym.

Novozhenov, Viktor A. 2019. Bronze Age Transeurasian Communications. *Otan tarikhy* 3 (87): 183–204.

Podobed, Viacheslav A., Anatoliy N. Usachuk, and Vitaliy V. Tsimidanov. 2010. Psalii, "zabytye" v ostavlennom dome (po materialam poselenii Azii i Vostochnoi Evropy epokhi bronzy) [Cheekpieces "Left" in an Abandoned House (According to Finds on the Bronze Age Settlement of Asia and Eastern Europe)]. In: *Drevnosti Sibiri i Tsentral'noi Azii* 3 (15), edited by Vasilii A. Soenov, 15–34. Gorno-Altaisk: GAGU.

Podobed, Viacheslav A., Anatoliy N. Usachuk, and Vitaliy V. Tsimidanov. 2016. Pogrebeniia s drevneishimi psaliiami stepnoi Evrazii [Burials with the Oldest Checkpieces in the Eurasian Steppe]. *Ufimskii arckheologicheskii vestnik* 16: 28–71.

Podobed, Viacheslav A., Anatoliy N. Usachuk, and Vitaliy V. Tsimidanov. 2020 "...Kolesnitsa moia pozlashchenna i koni moi tuchny...": o sotsiologicheskoi interpretatsii pogrebenii s drevneishimi psaliiami stepnoi Evrazii ["...My Chariot is Gilded and My Horses Are Fat...": On the Sociological Interpretation of Burials with the Oldest Cheekpieces of the Eurasian Steppe]. *Arkheologiia evraziiskikh stepei* 2: 278–309.

Sher, Yakov A. 1980. *Petroglify Srednei i Tsentral'noi Azii* [Petroglyphs of Central Asia]. Moscow: Nauka.

Tkachev, Vitaliy V. 2019. Gorno-metallurgicheskoe proizvodstvo v structure khoziaistvenno-kulturnykh modeleI zapadnoi periferii alakul'skoi kul'tury [Mining and Metallurgical Production in the Structure of the Economic and Cultural Model of the Western Periphery of the Alakul' Culture]. *Ural'lskii istoricheskii vestnik* 1 (62): 38–47.

Smirnov, Konstantin F. 1961. Arkheologicheskie dannye o drevnikh vsadnikakh Povolzhsko-Ural'skikh stepei [Archaeological Evidence About Ancient Riders of the Volga and Ural Steppes]. *Sovetskaia arkheologiia* 27: 46–72.

Smirnov, Konstantin F. and Elena Kuz'mina. 1977. *Proiskhozhdenie indoirantsev v svete noveishikh arkheologicheskikh otkrytii* [The Origin of Indo-Aryans in the Light of the Latest Discoveries]. Moscow: Nauka.

Usachuk, Anatoliy N. 2013. *Drevneyshiye psalii (izgotovleniye i ispol'zovaniye)* [The Earliest Cheekpieces (Production and Utilization)]. Kiev and Donetsk: Institut arkheologii NAN Ukrainy.

Usmanova, Emma, Igor V. Chechushkov, Pavel A. Kosintsev et al. 2018. Loshad' v dukhovnoi kul'ture i sotsial'nom ustroistve naseleniia Uralo-Kazakhstanskikh stepei v epokhu bronzy (po materialam mogil'nika Novoil'insky II) [The Horse in the Spiritual Culture and Social Structure of the Population of the Ural-Kazakhstan Steppes in the Bronze Age (Based on the Materials of the Novoyilinovsky Cemetery 2)]. In: *Stepnaia Evraziia v epokhu bronzy: kul'tury, idei, tekhnologii. Sbornik nauchnykh trudov k 80-letiiu Gennadiia Borisovicha Zdanovicha*, edited by Dmitriy G. Zdanovich et al., 198–215. Chelyabinsk: Izdatel'stvo Chelyabinskogo gosudastvennogo universiteta.

Vinogradov, Nikolay B. 2003. *Mogil'nik bronzovogo veka Krivoe Ozero v Iuzhnom Zaural'e* [The Cemetery of the Bronze Age Krivoe Ozeo in the southern Trans-Ural]. Chelyabinsk: Iuzhno-Ural'skoe knizhnoe izdatel'stvo.

Vinogradov, Nikolay B. 2011. *Stepi Iuzhnogo Urala i Kazakhstana v pervye veka II tys. do n.e. (pamyatniki sintashtinskogo i petrovskogo tipa)* [Steppes of Southern Urals and Kazakhstan in the First Centuries of the 2nd Millennium BC (Sites of the Sintashta and Petrovka Types)]. Chelyabinsk: Abris.

Vinogradov, Nikolay B. 2020. Mif o puteshestvii dushi i pograbal'nye pamiatniki sintashtinskogo i petrovskogo tipa bronzovogo veka v Iuzhnom Zaural'e [The Myth of the Journey of the Soul and Bronze Age Funerary Sites of the Sintashta and Petrovka Type in the Southern Trans-Urals]. *Vestnik arkheologii, antropologii i etnografii* 2 (49): 20–28.

Zdanovich, Gennadiy B. 1999. Iuzhnoe Zaural'e v epokhu srednei bronzy [Southern Trans-Urals Region in the Middle Bronze Age]. In: *Kompleksnye obshchestva Tsentral'noi Evrazii v III–I tys. do n.e.: regional'nye osobennosti v svete universal'nykh modelei. Materialy konferentsii, 25 avgusta – 2 sentiabria*, edited by Gennadiy B. Zdanovich, 43–45. Chelyabinsk: Chelyabinskii universitet.

Zdanovich, Dmitriy G. and Elena V. Kupriyanova. 2008. Parnye zhertvoprinosheniia loshadei v bronozvom veke Tsentral'noi Evrazii: arkheologiia, mifologiia i ritual [The Twin Horse Sacrifices in the Bronze Age of Central Eurasia: Archaeology, Mythology and Ritual]. In: *Proiskhozhdenie i rasprostranenie kolesnichestva. Sbornik nauchnykh statei*, edited by Andrey I. Vasilenko, 188–197. Lugansk: Globus.

Zdanovich, Gennadiy B. and Irina Batanina. 1995. "Strana gorodov" – ukreplennye poseleniia epokhi bronzy XVIII–

XVII vv. do n.e. na Iuzhnom Urale [The "Country of Towns" – Fortified Settlements of the Bronze Age, 18th–17th centuries B.C. in the Southern Ural]. In: *Arkaim: Issledovaniia. Poiski. Otkrytiia*, edited by G. B. Zdanovich. Chelyabinsk: Kamennyi poias.

Part II

Egypt, Near East, the Balkans, the Steppes, China in the 2nd millenium BCE and later developments

5

Leather: An Integral Part of Chariots

André J. Veldmeijer and Salima Ikram

Several chariots are known from Egypt's archaeological record, with the six from the tomb of Tutankhamun being the most famous. Even these, however, are incompletely preserved, with nearly all of the leather elements missing. Fortunately, texts and imagery in temples and tombs provide us with a fair body of additional knowledge about these 'racing cars' of antiquity. Sadly, though, due to the perishable nature of the leather and rawhide components of chariots, our knowledge on the importance of some of these particular elements has been little understood until recently. The find of the so-called Tano chariot leather has considerably increased our understanding of leather and rawhide as an integral part of chariot technology, and also enabled us to recognise hitherto unidentifiable leather finds, especially from the site of Amarna. This communication focuses on some of the more important leather elements of chariot design: support straps and casing and their attachments.

Introduction

The discovery of six chariots in the tomb of Tutankhamun, masterfully published by Littauer and Crouwel (Figure 5.1),[1] has greatly increased our understanding of these ancient vehicles as until then, only three (partial) chariots were known from ancient Egypt: the unprovenanced chariot in the Florence Museum,[2] the chariot from the tomb of Yuya and Tjuiu[3] and the chariot body from the tomb of Thutmose IV[4]. However, though wonderful, rare and precious objects, they survived only in partial form, mainly as wooden frameworks. The fragile organic materials that were used in their manufacture, especially animal products such as rawhide and leather, often have not been or, at best, have been only partially preserved, and in many cases when elements were preserved at the moment of recovery, subsequently they have deteriorated drastically (Figure 5.2).[5] Therefore, leather, a major component of chariots, has not been given the attention in research that it deserves, and the leather and rawhide elements of chariots that are key to their functionality, especially in terms of their strength, manoeuvrability and speed, are often neglected in experimental archaeology related to chariot construction.[6] Leather and rawhide were used extensively in chariots, and served a number of purposes. The Tano leather, so-named by the authors as it was purchased by the Egyptian Museum (Tahrir Square) from the well-established antiquities dealer, Georges Tano in 1932, is an exceptional find of the nearly-complete leather cladding of a chariot. It includes support straps, nave sleeves (see

Figure 5.1. Joost Crouwel and the present authors kneeling on the floor to have a good look at Tutankhamun's chariot CN 332 (A 5) in the Military Museum in Cairo (2013). Photograph by Erno Endenburg.

---

[1] Littauer and Crouwel 1985; see also Crouwel 2013. – Joost Crouwel is a world authority on ancient chariotry. We had the pleasure of his company and benefited greatly from his expertise when he was invited as the keynote speaker for our chariot conference, held in Cairo 30 November to 2 December 2012, where we had an opportunity to examine some of the Tutankhamun chariots together. We dedicate this small offering to him with affection and respect.
[2] Guidotti 2002.
[3] Newberry 1907: 24–33; Quibell 1908.
[4] Carter and Newberry 1904, 24–33.
[5] Even the post-excavation rawhide straps that were used in restoring some of Tutankhamun's chariots have started to deteriorate. However, fortunately, they can still be differentiated from the original and will be removed by the Museum's conservators.
[6] A good example is the NOVA TV documentary 'Building Pharaoh's Chariot' (2013; www.youtube.com/watch?v=0Loti-WBK_k&t=1851s), where a chariot was re-created after extensive research based on the work of a number of specialists. Although leather was discussed in the documentary, the focus was on the wooden frame, rather than the connections of its parts, and thus the role of leather in chariot production was not studied in any detail.

Figure 5.2. The axle tree of chariot CN 161 (A 4). The gelatinised leather running down the pole is circled. Note the substantial leather fragments, remains of the cladding of the body, still hanging at the rail as well as the leopard skin that was used as carpet over the rawhide floor. Courtesy of the Griffith Institute Oxford. Photograph by Harry Burton.

Figure 5.3. Chariot CN 333 (A 6), showing the, still partially covered, lashing securing the junction floor/axle (axle block). In the case of a separate axle block, lashing was also used to secure the axle block to the axle itself. Photograph by André J. Veldmeijer. Courtesy of the Ministry of Antiquities and Tourism.

Figure 5.6), parts of the bow-case and much of the harnessing. Since these are the only near-complete examples of such elements, this find provided a wealth of information on how wood, leather/rawhide and lashings together were integrated and helped in the overall strength of this important vehicle of the ancient world.[7]

'Mechanical' Components

Rawhide was an intrinsic material for creating, stabilising, and strengthening a chariot as it is extremely well-suited to lashing together different wooden components: upon drying, it shrinks and further tightens the bond. Even so, rawhide has some small degree of give, which allows for the motion of the chariot, regardless of the terrain. Rawhide bindings were used to secure various parts of the vehicle. The body was fastened to the axle at the junction of the floor and the axle block, which was, in the case of Tutankhamun's chariots, neatly finished with gold foil or even more elaborate coverings including inlays of semi-precious stones and glass (Figure 5.3), as well as with lashings around the axle and through the rear floor beam (Figure 5.4). Indeed, bindings were used throughout the chariot, securing its varied parts, including railings, poles and axles, and so forth. Moreover, the floor of the chariot was made from a woven web of rawhide strips that created a slightly springy surface – the equivalent of modern shock absorbers. This was usually covered with animal skin or a thick piece of textile (Figure 5.2). Such a surface required balance and core-strength from the charioteer and/or passenger, especially when wielding a weapon, but was a better surface to work from than a hard unyielding wooden floor, that could be damaged when going over inhospitable terrain.

Figure 5.4. Chariot CN 333 (A 6) showing two of the four additional rawhide lashings through the rear floor beam and around the axle. Photograph by André J. Veldmeijer. Courtesy of the Ministry of Antiquities and Tourism.

The wheels of the chariot were encircled with leather or rawhide 'tyres'. The tyres would have helped hold together and strengthen the wheels,[8] as well as providing traction. They also protected the wooden wheels from wear and damage, but had the drawback of relatively quick wear and tear. However, the tyres were easier to replace than the wheels because wheels were difficult to make, as the wood needed to be bent and assembled.[9] Thus, it would have been profitable to protect them so that they did not have to be replaced often.

Leather was sometimes used for nave hoops and was identified in Tutankhamun's chariot Carter Number [CN] 332,[10] and all of the naves were lined with leather. Two decorated leather nave sleeves, which protected the nave from grit and sand were also identified in the Tano chariot leather.

Two complete examples of support straps feature on the Tano chariot leather. Many, but not all, depictions show

---

[7] Veldmeijer and Ikram 2018.

[8] Sandor 2013: 227; 228.
[9] See Hurford this volume.
[10] A5; Littauer and Crouwel 1985: 76.

Leather: An Integral Part of Chariots

Figure 5.5. Artist's impression of the Tano chariot with photographic details and diagrams of the support straps. The extremely well-made straps of thick and, in the case of the long extensions, double layered leather are stitched through several times, pointing to their important task of strengthening the wooden frame. The ingenious construction of loops at the back of the rectangular element prevented the straps from moving. Photographs by André J. Veldmeijer/Erno Endenburg. Courtesy of the Ministry of Antiquities and Tourism. Diagram by Erno Endenburg/André J. Veldmeijer. Impression by Erno Endenburg.

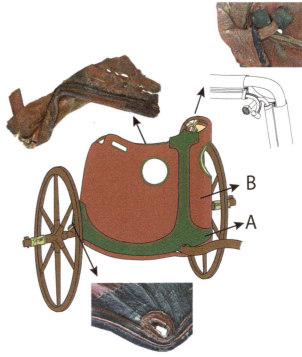

Figure 5.6. Artist's impression with the system of tubes and drawstrings that secured the casing in the Tano chariot (and toggles closure) highlighted. The green main casing is marked 'A' the red siding fill is marked 'B'. The fragment of siding fill seen above (left) the artist impression shows, besides the tube, also the original red colour of the leather where it was covered with a patch of leather, which was secured with straps through the unreinforced slits. At either side the leather is discoloured grey from handling and gripping the rail. The photograph below the impression shows an example of an original reinforced hole in the main casing to secure it at the corner. Photographs by André J. Veldmeijer/Erno Endenburg. Courtesy of the Ministry of Antiquities and Tourism. Diagram by Erno Endenburg/André J. Veldmeijer. Impression by Erno Endenburg.

such straps being tied to the upper railing and extending down to the bottom rail of the chariot body.[11] Though not always visible in depictions (in cases where an entirely enclosed chariot is shown, the straps would have been obscured by the cladding), probably all chariots had these support straps to stabilise and secure the frame. Beside this most important task, they also seem to have functioned as a reinforcement for the cladding, and probably also used to secure bow-cases and/or quivers. The straps consist of a rectangular (or with one rounded end) section with loops at the back, and one, two (usually) or even three long straps attached to it (Figure 5.5). The rectangular element is folded around the top railing, the strips are pulled through the loops at the back and secured, probably simply by tying the ends, which are rolled up lengthwise, to the bottom railing. It is also probable that the slit in the far end of the strap played a part in the fastening.[12] In pulling the leather support straps tight, the wooden construction becomes more rigid. These elements have not been found (or recognised/preserved) amongst the chariot material from the tomb of Tutankhamun, but are known from various other provenances: two from Amarna[13] and two from the tomb of Thutmose IV.[14]

Cladding and Decorative Components

Aside from state and processional chariots, such as that of Thutmose IV, chariot bodies would have had a leather casing, which could have covered it entirely or partially (in varying degree). While two of the six chariots that were recovered from the tomb of Tutankhamun were enclosed with wood and extensively decorated, the others were clad with leather (in at least one of these the leather was covered with gold sheets). The Tano leather shows that, at least for that chariot, there were two parts to the casing. Both could be used together or the so-called T-shaped 'main casing' (marked 'A'; in Figure 5.6) could be used on its own. This created a large fenestration kept the chariot light and was possibly used without the siding fill when hunting in the desert, probably for game such as gazelle, hartebeest, and

---

[11] See Veldmeijer and Ikram 2018: 30–34; 257–258; 402–415 for the Tano and other examples from the ancient Egyptian pictorial record.
[12] Perhaps with the involvement of a toggle. However, the other support strap does not have such a slit (Veldmeijer and Ikram 2018: 32).
[13] Veldmeijer 2011a: 113–116.
[14] Veldmeijer and Ikram 2018: 257–262. – Though both examples from the tomb are described in the Catalogue by Veldmeijer and Ikram (2018), the analysis and table II.1 (pp. 323–333) does not include JE 97802.

other antelope. The more complete surround, the so-called 'siding fill' (marked 'B' in Figure 5.6), provided more protection, but would have had some impact on the speed of the chariot. It is not at all clear whether leather casings were always fastened with leather only: in the chariot from the tomb of of Yuya and Tjuiu, as reported by Newberry,[15] the leather was secured with copper pins,[16] a constructional feature not noted in any of the chariots from the tomb of Tutankhamun. In the Tano chariot, the main casing as well as the siding fill were held in place by a system of tubes with drawstrings that ran along the wooden framework of the chariot and were secured using toggle closures (Figure 5.6) in combination with leather straps. These were custom made to the measurements of a specific chariot, as the tube with drawstring runs under the pole, whereas the leather of the casing itself lies above it, thus enclosing the pole. The casings were further secured with leather straps being pulled through reinforced slits and holes at various places and running over the railings. Possibly, the top of the tripartite central part of the main casing had, in addition to the tubes with drawstrings, similar fastenings to those seen with the support straps, such as loops at the back that would secure it to the wooden frame. Sets of lacings consisting of leather strips threaded through reinforced holes and slits further secured the casing to the framework of the body of the chariot (Figure 5.6). Some of these are later additions, reflecting the use-life of the chariot, since several of the slits in the leather of the siding fill are not reinforced, and the colour of the casing underneath shows fading from being exposed before these straps were added. The straps might have been secured simply by being knotted on the inner side of the chariot.

Another use of leather was to decorate the chariot; generally, though, the embellishments were not only decorative (and sometimes apotropaic), but also served a practical function, reinforcing and protecting the wood from breakage, or preventing sand, grit, and dirt from entering the joints. Thus, the axle of Yuya and Tjuiu's chariot is covered with leather. Appliquéd decoration, including leather, is still extant in some of Tutankhamun's chariots, which is rather remarkable considering the poor preservation circumstances for leather in that tomb. In addition, the bits of leather that were visible in the Burton photographs of the chariots when they were first found have since vanished (see Figure 5.2). Examples of decorated leatherwork consist of broad strips of leather with coloured appliqué, or leather that is embossed with various motifs. The Tano chariot body and leather coverings, particularly along the edges, are also enhanced by leather reinforcements made with different coloured appliquéd bands, as well as designs quilted onto the leather. The multiple layers strengthen the edges but are also incorporated into the seams in such a way that they are reinforced, and simultaneously protect the more fragile edge of the leather proper.

Accessories

Leather was the main component of accessories that were attached to chariots, such as bow-cases and quivers. These were made separately and then strapped onto the chariot, generally using individual leather straps, although they might also have made use of the support straps. If independent straps secured them, these would have further reinforced the wooden frame, surely preferable to making the support straps do double duty.

Concluding Remarks

The Tano chariot leather shows that a chariot did not derive its strength solely from the wooden framework and its lashings. Rather, the resilience of a chariot is a symbiosis of these two elements, including the support straps, the fastenings of the casings (whether only of leather, or combined with other means of securing them), and the addition of accessories that were tied to the body. The function of leather, however, exceeded this very practical goal of tying and lashing, in that it also had a protective function. First and foremost, if the chariot had an entirely closed casing, it offered better protection for the charioteer. Secondly, leather covered various parts, such as the wheels and sometimes the naves, and thus prevented rapid wear and the need to replace the complicated and difficult-to-make wheels that required heating and bending of the wood. Even leather components which would appear to be only decorative also had a reinforcing and protective function, as often seen in their appliqué edges. Thus, when looking at chariots, it should be remembered that the wooden framework is only a part of the whole, and that all the components need to be taken into account in order to understand the technology that made these amazing vehicles possible and highly successful.

André Veldmeijer
Visiting Research Scholar, American University in Cairo, Egypt.

Salima Ikram
Distinguished University Professor of Egyptology, American University, Cairo, Egypt.

---

[15] Newberry 1907: 36.
[16] This needs to be checked. The authors had the opportunity to make a cursory examination of the chariot, and no copper pins or evidence thereof were observed. However, the chariot is heavily restored and specialised equipment might be needed to see any traces of these pins. Note that it is possible that split pins, like the ones used in other chariot leather (Veldmeijer and Ikram 2018, 301–302), and footwear (Veldmeijer 2011b: 98–105; 109–121; 130–139) might have been used, in which case the leather would have been folded around the railing and the edge of the leather secured to the body of the leather rather than to the wood (cf. the rod with leather in the Metropolitan Museum of Art, though here not secured with split pins; Veldmeijer and Ikram 2018: 288–289).

Bibliography

Carter, Howard and Percy E. Newberry. 1904. Catalogue of the Antiquities found in the Tomb. In *The Tomb of Thoutmosis IV*, edited by Theodore M. Davis, 1–144. London: Constable.

Crouwel, Joost H. 2013. Studying the Six Chariots from the Tomb of Tutankhamun. – An Update. In *Chasing Chariots. Proceedings of the First International Chariot Conference (Cairo 2012)*, edited by André J. Veldmeijer and Salima Ikram, 73–93. Leiden: Sidestone Press. Available online: https://www.sidestone.com/books/chasing-chariots)

Guidotti, Maria Cristina Ed. 2002. *Il carro e le armi del museo Egizio di Firenze*. Florence: Giunti Gruppo Editoriale.

Littauer, Mary A. and Joost H. Crouwel. 1985. *Chariots and Related Equipment from the Tomb of Tutankhamun*. Oxford: Griffith Institute.

Newberry, Percy E. 1907. Description of the Objects Found in the Tomb. In *The Tomb of Iouiya and Touiyou*, edited by Theodore M. Davis, 1–48. London: Constable.

Quibell, James E. 1908. *The Tomb of Yuaa and Thuiu. Catalogue Générale des Antiquitiés Égyptiennes de Musée du Caire*. Nrs. 51001–51191. Cairo: l'Institut Français d'Archéologie Orientale.

Sandor, Bela I. 2013. Chariot's Inner Dynamics: Springs and Rotational Inertias. In: *Chasing Chariots. Proceedings of the First International Chariot Conference (Cairo 2012)*, edited by André J. Veldmeijer and Salima Ikram, 217–228. Leiden: Sidestone Press. Available online: https://www.sidestone.com/books/chasing-chariots.

Veldmeijer, André J. 2011a. *Amarna's Leatherwork. Part I. Preliminary Analysis and Catalogue*. Leiden: Sidestone Press. Available online: https://www.sidestone.com/books/amarna-s-leatherwork.

Veldmeijer, André J. 2011b. *Tutankhamun's Footwear. Studies of Ancient Egyptian Footwear*, with contributions by Alan J. Clapham, Erno Endenburg, Aude Gräzer, Fredrik Hagen, James A. Harrell, Mikko H. Kriek, Paul T. Nicholson, Jack M. Ogden and Gillian Vogelsang-Eastwood. Leiden: Sidestone Press. Available online: https://www.sidestone.com/books/tutankhamun-s-footwear.

Veldmeijer, André J. and Salima Ikram (eds.). 2018. *Chariots in Ancient Egypt: The Tano Chariot, A Case Study*, with contributions by Ole Herslund, Lisa Sabbahy and Lucy Skinner. Leiden: Sidestone Press. Available online: https://www.sidestone.com/books/chariots-in-ancient-egypt.

6

'They Shall Henceforth Be Fed in my Presence': Observations on the Training and Treatment of Chariot Horses in Ancient Egypt

Miriam A. Bibby

The introduction of horse and chariot technology into Egypt resulted in social, economic, and military changes to this early state, which is frequently viewed as a conservative society. The successful manner in which Egyptian society actively embraced the new technology and developed it in an identifiably 'Egyptian' way questions whether Egypt was really so conservative. This meant that horses, as living beings that also provided power to the chariot, were entangled in existing concepts of kingliness and authority. How did this complex role affect the care and management of horses in Egypt, and is it possible to find evidence for the nature of the horse-human relationship in texts, imagery, and artefacts? How different were the attitudes of the elite to those of the people responsible for the day-to-day care of the animals? Previous studies have tended to focus on technology and its use in warfare and hunting, as well as its potential for display. Applying practical knowledge of horse care and how horses learn and relate to humans, this chapter intends to encourage further interest in the way horses were treated in ancient Egypt and the range of behaviours they exhibited. Discussion of reward and punishment of horses forms a major theme.

Kings and their Horses: Two Literary Examples

Documentary sources can reveal much about the relationship between horses and humans, and often in unexpected and possibly unintended ways. In Act 5 Scene V of Shakespeare's play *Richard II*, the imprisoned King Richard and a groom reminisce together in the gloom of Pomfret jail. The subject of their dialogue is Richard's favourite horse, roan Barbary. Probably a creation of the playwright himself, who is said to have had a particular predilection for roans as he mentions this unusual colouring three times in his work,[1] roan Barbary tells us a certain amount about himself simply through his name. Indeed, in a sense, as in the 1960s song by the group America, he is 'a horse with no name'. He is identified through his colour and his place of origin (or breed) and 'roan' is not capitalised. He is a roan – that is, his coat is a mixture of white hairs in a base coat of either red (chestnut), bay (rich dark brown) or black. As roans have darker coloured points (legs, mane, head and tail), so too will roan Barbary, if he is a true roan. Above all, roan Barbary is an expensive horse appropriate for use by royalty and the elite, because he is a Barb, most likely originating in north west Africa.[2] He is a member of the triad of breeds that will come to be known somewhat misleadingly as 'Oriental' horses: Arabians, or Arabs; Turkomans, or Turks; and Barbs, less frequently known as Berber horses or Berbers. Thereby hangs a tale, and a tail; roan is not a colouring that is particularly associated with any of those breeds in modern form, or any of their surviving relatives, such as the Akhal-Teke in the case of the Turkoman. He may therefore be a cross between a Barb and another type of horse. Roan Barbary's true origins highlight just one of the issues in trying to engage more deeply with horses in literature and iconography.

While the interchangeability of the terms Arab, Turk and Barb in early modern Britain and Europe is an issue which still causes confusion for researchers today, one thing is clear. Roan Barbary was recognised by Richard as a valuable and valued royal favourite until the groom advised the vanquished king that the horse was commandeered by Henry Bolingbroke for his coronation and 'went so proudly under him as if he disdain'd the ground'. The horse falls immediately from favour. Richard expostulates 'So proud that Bolingbroke was on his back! That jade hath eat bread from my own hand;/This hand hath made him proud with clapping him'.[3] Then he relents: 'Forgiveness, horse! Why do I rail on thee,/Since thou, created to be aw'd by man,/ Was born to bear?' The information about roan Barbary conveyed in this brief scene is condensed, yet it nonetheless reveals some key details relating not only to the horse but also to the complex relationship between royalty and horses which has existed for centuries. It lifts a corner of the veil, but only lets us see so far. This is also the case with many ancient Egyptian references to horses.[4]

---

[1] Though Anthony Dent comments that in total in Shakespeare's works, there are also three references to bay horses, one to grey, one to dun, one to white and one to black (Dent 1987: 78). Colour was a recognised way to describe horses in various records, including stud books and popular ballads, in early modern times.
[2] The Barbs imported and bred for racing by the Gonzaga family of Mantua were well-known in Shakespeare's day, though their fame may also predate the period of Richard's reign. See Cavriani: 1909, *passim*.
[3] 'Clapping' him here most likely means patting him hard on the neck, almost slapping him. Contrary to general belief, horses dislike this, much preferring to be scratched.
[4] For an exploration of the relationship between Richard II and his horse in contemporary Renaissance contexts, see Fudge 2020.

Richard's words about his relationship with roan Barbary – and particularly the fact that the king has *fed* him – resonate across the centuries with those of Ramesses II when praising his chariot horses after the Battle of Kadesh, words which provided the inspiration for this chapter: 'They shall henceforth be fed in my presence'.[5] Why did this matter and what does it tell us about the relationship between ancient Egyptian royalty and horses? The phrase was effectively emblazoned for eternity, along with further details of the dubious success of the king at Kadesh, on his monuments. In particular, Ramesses noted that his great horse *Victory in Thebes* and yoke-mate *Beloved of Mut* were 'supporting me/When I alone fought many lands'.[6] His horses receive particular praise for being there for him when many of his soldiers and followers were not, and he felt abandoned until the god Amun came to his rescue. Thus, the horses will now receive the particular royal favour of being fed before him whenever he is in his palace.

Are Images More Revealing?
Contextualising the Relationship Through Art

The common factor in the words of Kings Richard and Ramesses relative to their horses is, of course, food, of which more shortly. In this chapter, I wish to take a novel approach to the analysis of material culture, imagery and texts relating to the horse in ancient Egypt. While what is *said* about horses, such as the words of Ramesses, is important, even more so are the visual records, which give us a better idea of how the Egyptians really felt about and related to their horses. Imagery is also of greater importance in attempting to discover the horse's eye view, since although horses, like dogs, have the capacity to understand a substantial human vocabulary, their principal means of exploration and communication are through the senses and body language, including scent and hearing. Just as Shakespeare revealed much about roan Barbary through his name and a brief conversation between king and groom, I believe that there are both obvious and more subtle clues to the treatment of horses in ancient Egypt to be found within imagery and texts, and in re-examining some of these, I hope to provoke further debate on this topic.

First of all, it is necessary to recollect the purpose of Egyptian art. It might be argued that in representing the daily experience of life, the ancient Egyptians were believers in the 'getting it right first time' principle. The art of the Old Kingdom was not intended as a prototype for further development, but a template representing the first and the best, to be adhered to for practical and magical purposes (magic being a wholly practical subject in any case). Just as on the first occasion when earth emerged from the waters with the solar disk upon it, or the bennu bird came to stand on the mound, the horse arguably needed to emerge in Egyptian art whole, complete, and fully formed on its own 'first occasion'. However, horses provide an interesting study in Egyptian art, since they were at first a novelty, and their representation does change substantially over time. This fact has been used to suggest a change in breeds or breeding programmes.[7] Egyptian art itself was not wholly static of course – and the art of the Amarna period is often viewed as a time of the most radical change –, but certain themes tend to greater variation over time than others, and this is true of the horse. This is interesting in itself as the horse came into use relatively late in Egyptian history and therefore any changes in style were occurring over a more compressed period of time.

Lonneke Delpeut and Hylke Hettema, in their interesting analysis of Egyptian horse imagery and the modern belief systems regarding horses that it has inspired, propose that the earliest artists of the horse in Egypt were drawing on their long-term experience of the closest comparable animal – the donkey. Changes in the art, therefore, represent better knowledge of the horse, its movements and behaviour as the artists had greater opportunities to observe the animals.[8]

Above all, the people who had to care for and work with the horses on a daily basis – trainers, grooms, and royalty themselves – needed to have some understanding of horse behaviour and how to obtain the results they wanted through various means. Historically, this has broadly come under the heading of 'training', a form of teaching and learning based on interaction between human and horse.

Communicating Through Training:
Learning Through Emotions

While the intellectual and rational aspect of the human mind is often stressed, particularly with regard to learning, the emotions of both animals and humans play a significant part in the learning process. Modern animal trainers and communicators have developed ideas and practices, which can also be usefully applied to humans, based on the 'quadrant of learning'. The four principles are: positive reinforcement (reward); negative reinforcement (removal of something unpleasant); negative punishment (removal of a reward); and positive punishment (application of something unpleasant). Is it valid to apply modern theories to ancient cultures? I will argue in favour of this, and my reason for doing so is two-fold. First of all, the quadrant of learning is based on long-term observation by qualified animal behaviourists of interactions within a single species (for instance, horses or dogs) and also in animal-human encounters. It is not a theoretical construct that is unique to modern times, but based on what is observable and has been observed, in some cases for millennia, and on behaviour that is repeatable and known to be repeated. Secondly, while domestication has resulted in changes in the phenotype of horses over the past 6,000 years,[9] many of their emotional responses and basic needs have not changed. In terms of wants, the horses of ancient Egypt and the

---

5 Lichtheim 1976: 70.
6 Lichtheim 1976: 70.
7 Rommelaere 1990: 31–46.
8 Delpeut and Hettema 2021: 168–182; Delpeut 2021: 17–45.
9 Librado et al. 2017.

modern horse are the same. They need appropriate nutrition, particularly access to grazing or an equivalent in fodder, free access to fresh water, the presence of members of their own kind as they are social animals living in herds, and protection from predators and extremes of weather. These basic requirements represent what horses will seek for and find for themselves when living without human intervention.

Humans can, of course, do much more for horses than this. They can improve the horse's chances of survival through management, including veterinary intervention, and enhance their comfort (or remove it). They can teach, play with, ride and drive horses. They can quite simply use them, as food, transport, for sport or for other purposes. Most people who have contact with horses today will interact with them in more than one of these ways. Some activities are appetitive to the horse – the horse enjoys them and wants to encourage them – and others are aversive – the horse wishes to avoid them. Some activities indeed are punitive, and in this case the horse may not be able to escape them however much it wishes to do so. I will cite examples throughout this chapter, but for the present time it is important to know that food of various kinds – characteristically, in the modern world, apples, carrots, and mints – are appetitive to the horse and can be used to reward desirable behaviour. King Richard, as well as King Ramesses, was clearly aware of this. The distinctly unhealthy but very appetitive sugar lump was, of course, a favoured reward for horses in times past, and this was the treat of choice for equestrians in the Spanish Riding School who wished to show approval to their horses. Indeed, Colonel Alois Podhajsky, former director of the Spanish Riding School, provides some very interesting comments and valuable insights on the use of aversives and appetitives by horse trainers.[10]

Punishment and Reward in Horse Training: The Historical Context

Podhajsky uses the terms 'punishment' and 'rewards', providing a brief overview of their use by well-known trainers such as Pluvinel, Guérinière, and de la Broue, commenting that 'anyone today reading the latter's advice on how to treat a horse that ran away would find his hair standing on end'.[11] It is clear, however, that Podhajsky believes punishment, specifically by the use of whip and spurs, is a necessary part of horse training, since he goes into detail about how, when and why to apply punishment effectively, including the fact that spurs should not draw blood.[12] Equally importantly, he comments that 'In most books on riding, punishments are discussed in much more detail than rewards'.[13] This is in fact true of his own book, which devotes five and half pages to punishment and a single page to rewards. He also notes the belief that the ending of punishment was historically viewed as a reward by writers such as Grisone.[14] While technically it is not – it is negative reinforcement – this is a belief that is still widely held today. Noting that to be effective, rewards, like punishment, must follow immediately after the performance of a particular behaviour, Podhajsky recommends the following as being all rewarding: speaking kindly and softly to the horse, patting it, 'which does not mean slapping the horse with the open hand to make as much noise as possible, which is often done to impress the onlookers',[15] giving the horse a break by letting the horse walk on a loose rein (technically negative reinforcement, not reward) and 'food or sugar [which] after a successful exercise is another way of showing appreciation, provided it is given immediately'.[16] He also notes the Greek general Xenophon's (ca. 430–355 BCE) suggestion of dismounting from the horse to reward the successful completion of a desired behaviour.[17] Again, this is technically negative reinforcement, the removal of something undesirable, not reward, which is a good reminder that human activity with horses is not always appetitive to the horse.

That horses looked to humans for relief from things that were aversive to them was known in Xenophon's time:

See to it that the colt be kind, used to the hand and fond of men when he is put out to the horse-breaker. He is generally made so at home and by the groom, if the man knows how to manage so that solitude means to the colt hunger and thirst and teasing horseflies, while food, drink, and relief from pain come from man. For if this be done, colts must not only love men, but even long for them. Then too, the horse should be stroked in the places which he most likes to have handled; that is where the hair is thickest, and where he is least able to help himself if anything hurts him.[18]

In practice, many, perhaps the majority of current horse trainers and communicators – with some exceptions which I will discuss later in this chapter –, access all areas of the quadrant of learning to one degree or another. Several schools of modern horsemanship and training use the 'pressure-release' principle. This can be explained easily – pressure, which can be exerted physically, using the hand, leg, or by an implement such as a stick or whip, is applied until the point at which the horse moves away, as the pressure is aversive to them. As soon as the horse responds, the handler, rider, or driver removes the pressure. The timing of the removal is key to the learning process. Often in moving away the horses remove the pressure themselves, and if working on the ground the handler does not follow, maintain the pressure, or increase it, but simply allows the horse to step away. Whether the horse moves away, or the trainer removes the pressure, this is known as 'release'. The aversive stimulus is removed by the horse's own

---

[10] Podhajsky 1983: 63–69.
[11] Podhajsky 1983: 63.
[12] Podhajsky 1983: 66.
[13] Podhajsky 1983: 68.
[14] Podhajsky 1983: 68.
[15] Podhajsky 1983: 68.
[16] Podhajsky 1983: 69.
[17] Podhajsky 1983: 69.
[18] Xenophon 1979: 21.

action, which results in the trainer achieving their desired aim. Various levels of pressure-release on different parts of the body can be used to create subtle movements in the horse without ever getting into the saddle. As trainer and horse work together, the cues become lighter and less and less visible to onlookers. What is more, it is possible to use psychological as well as physical pressure on the horse, since horses are remarkably good at reading human emotions through both human facial expressions and vocal tone, as well as cross-modally.[19] Humans, on the other hand, are not so good at reading horses' emotions unless they are already committed to reinforcing behaviour positively,[20] despite the fact that equine ethology has been part of the research landscape for decades.[21]

Historically, most equestrian activities have been based on some form of pressure, and one hopes, release, though this should not be taken for granted, as will shortly be shown. The use of pressure is evident from tools that have been utilised for millennia; these include bits made from various materials such as rope, bone, and metal; bridles that exert pressure on the nose or poll of the horse, and reins, some of which can be fixed to set the horse's head in a position that is desirable to the rider or driver, in which case there is no instance of release until the rein is removed. Infamously, in Victorian England use was made of the bearing rein (US check rein), of which there were several kinds. The use and abuse of bearing reins formed the basis of one of the great equine welfare debates of the nineteenth century, which was represented in the pages of Anna Sewell's novel *Black Beauty*.[22] Anti-bearing rein protestors called the system 'torture in harness'[23] and it was known that use of the fixed rein affected the whole body of the horse, not only the neck and head. It further affected the horses not just pathologically but also psychologically. A similar debate has taken place in the twenty-first century on the use of the technique known as *Rollkur*.[24]

Head Position: Why it Matters

Sometimes given as an example of a type of bearing rein, the ancient Egyptian fixed rein consisted of a fixed rod, with a spiked 'check rowel' on the outer side of each horse in a team of two. Examples still exist, and the principles of its operation have been the subject of discussion as well as experimentation over the years.[25] We are very fortunate to have the detailed analysis produced by Littauer and Crouwel after their key work on the chariots found in Tutankhamun's tomb, which has proved invaluable to researchers over the years;[26] now augmented by the work of Ikram and Veldmeijer on leatherwork.[27] We also have examples of practical experience such as the application of the system in the reconstructions of Jean Spruytte. His description of the fixed rein and check rowel is particularly good as he uses the word 'escape' several times, as well as 'obliges' indicating the horse's desire to relieve the pressure, which it therefore clearly experiences as an aversive, not an appetitive influence. Note that Spruytte terms the combination of fixed rod and check rowel, described variously elsewhere as fixed rein, bearing rein/rod, or check rein, the 'auxiliary reining system':

The auxiliary reining system, when in place, obliges the animals first of all to position themselves (that is to raise their necks) since the studs would bruise their necks or shoulders if they lowered their heads, and the rigid connection between the bits would prevent them from turning their heads or necks in order to escape the studs. The arrangement also permits an accentuation of the transfer of the weight of the neck from one shoulder to the other in both horses at once by a simple action of the left or right reins.

For example, an action of the right reins obliges the left-hand horse to exaggerate the displacement of his head and neck towards the right, as he attempts to escape the studs on the left hand side of his neck. The same effect, caused by the rigid connection between the bits, obliges his companion also to emphasise the displacement of his head and neck towards the right without any resistance on his part, since this keeps his neck away from the studs on his side.[28]

Describing it as 'rather primitively conceived',[29] Spruytte nonetheless concedes that it works. It keeps the horses in step and prevents them from freeing themselves from the yoke, which as Brownrigg notes was an observable issue with inexperienced horses.[30] Spruytte further comments that the technicians who created the auxiliary system had an understanding of the horse's natural movements and balance. Both Spruytte[31] and Littauer suggest that the fixed rod with rowel was possibly a training system for young horses. Littauer noted its similarity to the head poles in use on modern harness horses in the sport of trotting, and suggested it may have still been in a developmental stage in the Amarna period.[32] She also noted its apparent disappearance after the Ramesside period, and that it was never depicted on non-Egyptian horse teams.[33] Littauer and Crouwel's earlier work traced the development of

---

[19] Trösch et al. 2019.
[20] https://thehorse.com/191284/can-you-spot-an-unhappy-horse/?fbclid=IwAR2lhrH4DZ3hRN48Tq-jlkML_XEEqk1S7pFc1PpViPmL-fRhrRS9a02q-lxI.
[21] Goodwin 1999: 15, 19. An excellent collection of scientific articles relating to equine ethology is available at https://www.esieducation.com/articles/. I am very grateful to Dr Katherine Kanne for drawing my attention to this resource. Donnell 2003 is a foundation text on the topic.
[22] Sewell 1989. This edition includes a useful discussion on the welfare aspects of the bearing rein on pp. 60–64 and 192–201.
[23] Sewell 1989: 199.
[24] Most eloquently stated in Heuschmann 2007: *passim*.
[25] See, for instance, Spruytte 1983: 46; Brownrigg 2019: 85–96.

[26] Littauer and Crouwel 1985.
[27] Veldmeijer et al. 2013: 257–271; see also Veldmeijer and Ikram in this volume.
[28] Spruytte 1983: 46.
[29] Spruytte 1983: 47.
[30] Brownrigg 2019: 89. Brownrigg also notes the independent conclusion of Mary Littauer regarding Spruytte's experiences in relation to the positioning and use of yoke and auxiliary reining system; see Brownrigg 2019: 89; Littauer 1968.
[31] Spruytte 1983: 47.
[32] Littauer 1978: 293.
[33] Littauer 1978: 295.

The quadrants of reinforcement and punishment

	Reinforcement *Increasing the likelihood of a behaviour*	Punishment *Decreasing the likelihood of a behaviour*
Negative (Subtraction)	The removal of an adverse stimulus to reward a desired response. Example: Rein tension is applied until the horse stops and the removal of the tension rewards the correct response.	The removal of a desired stimulus to punish an undesired response. Example: The horse tries to take food from the handler but food is withheld until the behaviour ceases.
Positive (Addition)	The addition of a pleasant stimulus to reward a desired response. Example: The horse approaches when called for and receives a carrot to reward the response.	The addition of an aversive stimulus to punish an undesired response. Example: The horse bites and receives a slap on the muzzle.

Figure 6.1. The Quadrant of Learning as described by McLean and Christensen 2017.

harness systems from their original use for bovids, rather than equids, commenting in depth on the issues created for horses as a result.[34] Kathy Hansen argued that the horses driven using this mechanical system were 'in collection', but this is debatable.[35] These issues will form some of the aspects of this chapter as I explore the interaction between the technology of the fixed rein, horse-human relationships and approaches to training in ancient Egypt, as well as the intersection of ancient Egyptian belief and New Kingdom chariot technology.

The Quadrant of Learning in Egyptian Contexts: The Evidence

Figure 6.1, reproduced from McLean and Christensen, represents the Quadrant of Learning as experienced by animals, and also humans, through emotional responses.[36]

Can examples of each of the four quadrants be recognised in ancient Egyptian art or texts? Let us examine some evidence. First of all, in a beautifully executed relief from Amarna (Figure 6.2), now in the Metropolitan Museum of New York, we see a pair of chariot horses moving apparently calmly along at a walk. Interestingly, the sculptor has shown the horses exhibiting two different behaviours, one with head up and the other with head lowered. Is the horse depicted in the act of lowering its head, or is it being prevented in some way from lowering it further? This is an interesting and intriguing image of a horse displaying a natural response to pressure which it wishes to relieve. It is also possible that the horse is rubbing, or attempting to rub, its knee, either because a fly has annoyed it or as a displacement activity/response.

Most riders will be familiar with this activity in horses, who will often exhibit head movements either to request release from pressure on the bit or after pressure has been released in order to stretch and exercise the neck and back. Horses also raise and lower their heads to better observe their surroundings.[37] There does not seem to be a fixed rein in this image. The relatively loose rein on the horse on the far side suggests that light contact on the bit from the driv-

Figure 6.2. Horses from Amarna, one of which is showing signs of attempting to relax head, possibly after removal of fixed rod which may have been in place during exercise/activity (image from the Metropolitan Museum of Art, New York, in the public domain).

er's hands is intended to be shown in this scene, but not sufficiently light to allow the left-hand side horse to stretch its neck past a certain point. Looking up towards the yoke fork, which appears to be very well padded, something interesting emerges; there is tension in the lower part of the rein, but then apparently a relaxed section of rein beyond the yoke that even lies loosely on the back of the horse. It would seem that the sculptor intended to create the precise moment at which the horse was given release or reached its head down for release. The possibility that the horse cannot draw the rein beyond a certain point should also be considered. Whatever the reason, this is a remarkable piece of work that shows a movement carried out naturally by horses, frequently after intensive exercise.

This is potentially an image of negative reinforcement – the removal of something aversive. Note also the possible tail holder keeping the tail in place so that it does not get caught up in the chariot or interfere with the movement of the horse. Modern versions of the tail holder are in use in driving competitions today. This may be responsible, in part at least, for the proudly arched tails that are prominent in horses in Egyptian art and may have served an aesthetic as well as a practical purpose.

A chariot horse from the temple at Karnak (Figure 6.3), provides an excellent example of Podhajsky's horse moving on a loose rein free from pressure. The auxiliary reining system is not in evidence, the driving rein is slack, and the horse is able to exhibit natural head carriage. Whether the auxiliary reining system has been removed or was not

---

[34] Littauer and Crouwel 1979: passim.
[35] Hansen 1992: 173–179. This topic is now the focus of ongoing collaborative research between Miriam Bibby, Lonneke Delpeut, Jennifer Jobst and Katherine Kanne, with a view to future publication.
[36] McLean and Christensen 2017: 18–27.
[37] Jennifer Jobst, personal communication. See also Jobst forthcoming.

Figure 6.3. Chariot horses at Karnak on a 'loose rein' – that is without the fixed or check rein in place, and with the driving reins clearly relaxed so that there is no contact on the bit, which does not look like a linked snaffle but rather a straight bar of some kind (image by Zany Lomas, used with kind permission).

Figure 6.4. Chariot horses with check rein/rod in place, causing the heads to be drawn in and fixed close into the neck. The bit exerts greater pressure, drawing down the lower jaw, and the nosebands of the pair, possibly with spikes as indicated, press onto the nose. Since the horse cannot find release from this pressure, this classifies as positive punishment (Karnak image by Zany Lomas used with kind permission).

Figure 6.5. Close-up of noseband showing position of possible spike. Spiked nosebands are known to have been used as examples exist. Gail Brownrigg suggests alternatively that this is the squared-off end of the cheek piece where it attaches to the noseband (personal communication). However, it is not visible in all images, so this is not proven (image by Zany Lomas, used with kind permission).

in use with this chariot pair is hard to tell; however the artist has managed to convey something of the relaxed nature of the horse once pressure is removed. Note the position of the bit, which sits low down in the horse's mouth. Since the pressure of bit, reins and rod is not present – though noseband pressure may still be in place –, this classifies as negative reinforcement (compare with Figure 6.2 at Karnak). It is worth pointing out that most of the horses of ancient Egypt are shown with alert, forward-pointing ears. Susan Turner notes astutely in her thesis *The Horse in Ancient Egypt* that flattened ears, indicating fear and aggression, were used as a device by Egyptian artists to convey negative emotion in the Hittite horse teams.[38]

Figure 6.4, on the other hand, shows a pair of chariot horses with the auxiliary reining system/fixed rod in place. Their heads are tightly drawn in so far that they are shown as pressed against their necks. Lasting damage can be caused by the pressure of tight nosebands.[39] The response to the pressure is clear; the horses have opened their mouths in an attempt to escape it (Figure 6.5). Interestingly, the reconstructions used by Spruytte, based on existing examples of the bearing rein system, did not force the ponies' heads into this position. I would suggest that possibly different lengths of fixed reins were used to achieve different effects in ancient Egypt. Their use was also, I suggest, more than simply for practical purposes while driving the team. If the reins were fitted anywhere approaching this tightness, producing an effect which seems exaggerated and even impossible to the modern eye, it must have been in order to produce a type of head carriage which Egyptian rulers found attractive or impressive. Above all, it conveyed the sense of *control*, a concept which was imperative to kingly authority.

Notably, among the indices of pain identified in bitted horses are the following: 'slightly open or gaping mouth; teeth grinding, holding the bit between the teeth; tongue persistently moving or protruding from the mouth, tongue placed above the bit or retracted behind it; excessive salivation or drooling'.[40]

Multiple theses could probably be written on the topic of control of the horse's head as an actual and symbolic act. I have commented on this in ancient Egypt elsewhere.[41] As noted earlier, this would later become one of the principal issues about which nineteenth century equine welfare campaigners fought to raise awareness, arguing at that time particularly against the use of the bearing rein on carriage horses.[42] They used similarly striking images to convey their concerns. What is interesting in the British Equine Defence League sign shown in Figure 6.6 is that this is clearly a draught animal, a horse used for commercial work, rather than a carriage horse. Why, and how frequently, owners of working animals, who were often extremely knowledgeable about horses, should have chosen to use a type of rein that was particularly associated with the elite and their carriage horses is unclear. However, the work of welfare organisations frequently does focus on the

---

[38] Turner 2015: 334.
[39] Pérez-Manrique et al. 2020.
[40] Mellor 2020.
[41] Bibby 2008: 18–20.
[42] A similar issue is emerging today over the use of bits versus bitless bridles.

less wealthy, permitting injustices to continue unabated among the influential in society. The choice of words is interesting too; 'restraint and pain' versus 'freedom and power'. In ancient Egyptian examples, restraint and pain could frequently work together for kingly power.

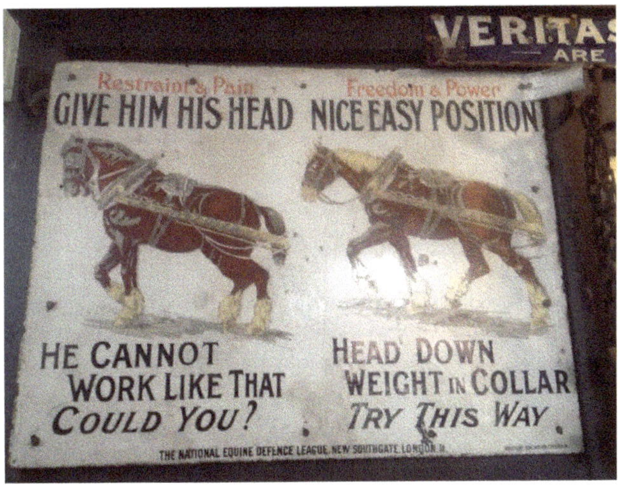

At Amarna, ancient Akhetaten, numerous examples exist to show the horse in its real and symbolic role. The Amarna royal family exploited the opportunities for display created by the use of the chariot. Indeed, the progress up and down the royal road on a daily basis was the ultimate in display, described by Barry Kemp as comparable to the modern presidential motorcade.[43] In Figure 6.7 we see once again the use of the auxiliary reining system to bring the horses' heads in towards the chest. The human figures in the scene represent adoration of and subservience to the royal family.

It is from Amarna, too, that a potential example of severe punishment can be seen, in the tomb of Meryre, the High Priest of the Aten and Fan-bearer on the Right Hand of the King, therefore a senior official of Akhetaten (Figure 6.8). Here there is a typical attendance scene, which, although very damaged, clearly shows a chariot, team and charioteer awaiting the arrival of the tomb owner Meryre. In front of the team, in contrast to the usual image of a groom or attendant holding up a hand to pacify the horses, stands a man with a heavy club or paddle-shaped instrument apparently beating, or at least threatening, the horses. It is hard to interpret the stance of this figure in any other way. Although de Garis Davies comments 'The charioteer waits beside the chariot, reins in hand, but a *saïs* also holds the horses, threatening them with a bunch of fodder (?)',[44] the image appears to be rather more aggressive than 'a bunch of fodder' would suggest. The concept of threatening horses with fodder is itself somewhat strange.

In contrast, several images from ancient Egypt show an official, or groom, in front of a pair of chariot horses apparently making a 'calming gesture' towards them. Sometimes the groom is actually holding onto the horses with one hand while lifting the other in a gesture similar to that of Meryre himself in the image of Akhenaten and Nefertiti in their chariot. The pose is somewhat similar to that which indicates adoration of a god or ruler. In some cases

Figure 6.6. An age-old issue; campaigners in the nineteenth century fought for better understanding of the need for horses to work free from discomfort and pain. Sign in Beamish Museum Town Livery Stables (photo courtesy of Max Easey of Horse Charming).

Figure 6.7. Akhenaten and Nefertiti kiss in a chariot, while one of their daughters is apparently about to poke the horses with a stick. As the horses are most likely wearing blinkers, they cannot see the stick nor respond to it in order to adopt the appropriate activity to avoid it (increase speed, presumably). This, then, is an example of positive punishment. The horses are also wearing the fixed rein (after Davies 1906: Pl. XXII; image in the public domain).

Figure 6.8. Man threatening horses with what appears to be a wooden club or paddle. From the tomb of Meryre at Amarna (after Davies 1903: Pl. IX; image in the public domain).

---
[43] Kemp 1991: 279.
[44] Davies 1903: 22.

the horses, apparently eager to be off, have lolling tongues. The ancient Egyptians were experts in the production of various scents and had numerous botanicals and flowers that they could use for medical or other purposes. I would suggest that it is possible the raised hand is more than simply a gesture and that some unguent or liquid has been placed on the palm and/or fingers that is appetitive or possibly even sedative to the horses. Some modern horse trainers make use of the horse's olfactory senses in training, and it is a key part of many horsemanship traditions, whether well-known or purportedly 'secret'. A possible reference to the use of scent occurs in a New Kingdom papyrus which references the anointing of chariot horses (iry. i s[gnn]).[45] The whole text refers to the harnessing of horses with the names *Mut is Content* and *Beloved of Amun*, the names of the horses of Ramesses at Kadesh. Leitz translates one of the lines as 'I cause an arousing of scent for (the horse) *Beloved of Amun*.'[46]

Figure 6.9 Carnelian plaque of Amenhotep II (ca. 1427–1401) showing the throned king offering an item, possibly food, to a horse in front of him. Image of BM EA4074 © The Trustees of the British Museum.

Rewards, Favours, and Kindly Treatment

What of reward, or at least kindly treatment of horses, in ancient Egypt? There are several examples from diverse places and times. One notable artefact is a carnelian plaque of Amenhotep II, which appears to show the ruler seated on his throne and offering something edible to a horse in front of him (Figure 6.9)[47].

The plaque is inscribed with the king's prenomen, with a hunting scene on the obverse which shows him hunting ibex. Since Amenhotep II has left the best documented material relating to the relationship between Egyptian rulers and their horses, it is interesting that this unusual and intimate scene between horse and king dates to his reign too.[48]

Figure 6.10. Horse wearing sun hat. Scene from the temple of Taharqa now in the Ashmolean Museum, Oxford. Possibly guided by a simple rope around the neck rather than bit and bridle (image courtesy of Prof. Joann Fletcher, who kindly provided this for my MPhil many years ago – good example of positive reinforcement in humans).

The unusual and indeed, as far as I know, unique image of a horse wearing a type of sun hat (Figure 6.10) depicted on a block from the Nubian temples is a good example to show how much the ancient Egyptians understood the needs of their horses. Horses can suffer from both sunstroke and sunburn. Horses with pink skin – usually visible on the muzzle, around the anus and sometimes around the eyes – are particularly vulnerable to high UV exposure. The cut-out holes for the ears ensure the hat fits properly. Indeed, the horse or donkey wearing a sun hat is an enduring and appealing theme which still appears on greeting cards today. This can be interpreted as an example of negative reinforcement; the horse is protected from the heat of the sun, which interestingly given the nature of Egyptian solar religion, is therefore the 'bad' element removed. The horse is unlikely to see this as a 'reward' however, though it will probably appreciate the shade. This can only be confirmed if the horse actively seeks out the hat from the human and requests to have it put in place, which is entirely consistent with the behaviour of horses trained by positive reinforcement. This image is also unusual in that the horse is ridden, and appears to be directed without bridle or bit, but by a rope around the neck which the rider holds in one hand. The scene is a processional one, and although there is an arm clearly visible below the horse's nose, there is nothing to indicate the horse is being led. Being able to ride a horse without bridle or saddle, especially with distracting activity going on in close proximity, would be taken as an indication of deep trust between horse and rider today. This rider has sometimes been interpreted as being King Taharqa himself, and if so, it is a timely reminder that

---

[45] Leitz 1999: 90.
[46] Leitz 1999: 91. For further discourse on names see Eshmawy 2007: 665–676.
[47] Hall 1913: x.
[48] Lichtheim 1976: 42. See also Bianchi and Meltzer 2023.

some of the kings of ancient Egypt and Nubia were genuinely skilled horsemen.

A possible further example of practical horse care can be seen in the various images that show horses wearing coverings of some kind, occasionally described as barding. This appears in both royal hunting and battle scenes as well as on some ceramics. Coverings, apparently of net such as the one shown in Figure 6.11, have been compared with the net 'dresses' worn by some goddesses, indicating 'the physical manifestation of a war goddess on the battlefield'.[49] This clearly is not the case in Figure 6.11, as it is not a battlefield scene. However, what will come to mind for the majority of equestrians will most likely be a traditional sweat sheet, a type of 'string vest' which allowed the horses to cool down slowly after exercise. Interestingly, in recent years, a great deal of research has been done into the equine response to rug wearing and their usefulness in horse welfare. In fact, one investigation showed that horses can indicate, by use of a symbol hanging on a fence, whether they wish to wear a rug or not in cold weather, an example of agency in horses.[50]

One very valuable piece of research has recently discovered that rugs with zebra stripes on them significantly reduce the incidence of fly attack.[51] While the symbolic and display potential of equine clothing is of course of great importance in interpreting imagery, it is also not impossible that those who cared for horses in ancient Egypt, like all horse keepers, were aware of tips and tricks to keep their animals comfortable in difficult environmental conditions. Fly strike is one of the most challenging issues that faces all horse keepers today, whether keeping animals in temperate, Mediterranean, tropical, or sub-tropical regions and a great deal of effort and skill is put into combatting biting insects. Gridded designs, or netted fabrics, may have assisted in this even in ancient times (Figure 6.12).

A possible ambivalent example of horse care occurs in the words of Piankhi (Piye) on his famous victory stela: 'His Majesty then proceeded to the stable of the horses and the quarters of the foals. When he saw [that] they were starved, he said: 'As I live, as Re loves me, as my nose is rejuvenated with life, how much more painful it is in my heart that my horses have been starved than any other crime that you have committed at your discretion.'[52] He thus berates the ruler of Hermopolis for allowing the horses of the city

Figure 6.11. A number of fine ceramics and ostraca show this interesting theme: a horse running freely wearing bridle/halter with lead rope dangling loose, interspersed with images of an animated ankh with staff of power indicating supernatural control and authority. Whether intentional or not, this is an excellent visual to express the concept of the relationship that needs to exist between horse and human. It is not about physical control using ropes, halters and whips; it can be invisible to the lay onlooker which endows it with a magical quality. Note also the possible blanket or rug (drawn by M. Bibby, from photograph of vase in Neues Museum, Berlin).

to be without food and water during a siege which Piankhi himself had laid as part of his conquest of Egypt in order to become supreme ruler of the land. Piankhi takes a proprietorial attitude to the horses, but rather than simply viewing them as royal assets that have suffered collateral damage through warfare, it has been argued that it reflects his own genuine interest in and knowledge of horses, traits which were also reflected in his institution of equine burials at el-Kurru.[53] Decker even suggested that word of Piankhy's deep affection for horses ('a fanatic ... a real fool for horses'[54]) circulated round the lands of the Libyan rulers of the Egyptian Delta so that the shrewd ones made sure they offered him fine horses when they submitted to his rule. Certainly, there is evidence to indicate that possibly even before the Theban Dynasty acquired horses, both the Nubians and Kushites were skilled in keeping horses, 'learning their natures, skilled in training them, understanding their ways'; even more so perhaps than Amenhotep II to whom this description applied.[55]

To sum up, we can find examples of the full quadrant of learning in images, texts, and artefacts from ancient Egypt, for example:

- Positive punishment (application of something unpleasant): Amarna princess poking horse with a goad; pressure of the check rowel on the neck; whips; pointed studs on bit rings pressing on the horse's mouth; beating horses, depicted in scene from Amarna and referenced in teaching texts.

- Negative punishment (taking away something pleasant): leading horses away from their own kind; keeping them intensively in stables; withholding food

---

[49] Calvert 2013: 45.
[50] Mejdella et al. 2016: 66–73. In fact, I have adopted this approach for many years, by simply holding a rug up in front of my horses and ponies. If they wish to have the rug on, they touch it with their nose. If they do not, they turn away their heads.
[51] Caro et al 2019.
[52] Schellinger 2009: 96.

[53] Schellinger 2009: 94.
[54] Decker 1993: 50.
[55] Lichtheim 1976: 42.

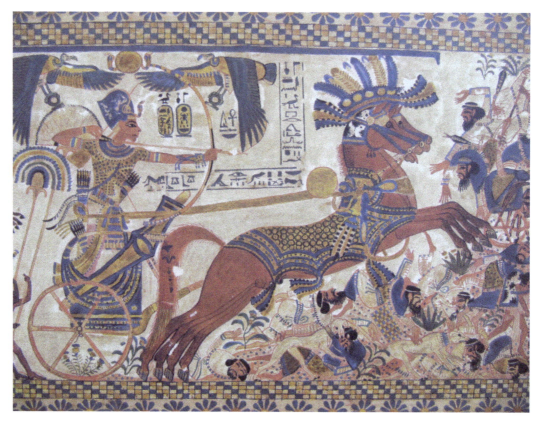

Figure 6.12. Tutankhamun in his chariot displayed on the casket discovered with his funerary goods. The gloriously ornate covering and decorative plumes of the royal pair contrast with those of his courtiers and soldiers shown elsewhere on the casket, whose horses are distinguished by their lack of ornamentation, although some apparently wear similar headpieces of spotted fur without plumes. Was there a practical aspect to body covering such as reducing the effects of fly attack? (photograph by kind permission of Patrick Houlihan).

(although as food is essential, this would quickly become punishment).

- Negative reinforcement (the removal of something unpleasant): allowing horses to relax after exercise; the removal of the fixed rod with check rowel; relief from flies; protection from the sun; relief from hunger and thirst.

- Positive reward/reinforcement (application of something pleasant): giving horses access to the company of other horses; providing them with rest and relaxation; playful activities; stroking, grooming, and even more positively, scratching horses in the way they self-groom; offering appealing scents; most important of all, food rewards! These, when applied immediately after a desired action, are extremely reinforcing and mean that action is more likely to be repeated.

While there is nothing to suggest that the ancient Egyptians understood these principles as a theory, there is every indication that they understood them on a practical level. They also understood that knowledge of the needs of horses was essential for their well-being. There are also areas that the horse would definitely have seen as punitive, while humans may have viewed them as palliative – slitting nostrils, for instance, to allow more air into the nose. Further, while the Egyptians may have understood that food could be rewarding to horses, there is little to suggest they understood it should be applied immediately after the desired action in order to reinforce it. The evidence suggests that punishment is likely to have been the principal way to elicit an immediate response.

Fight, Flight, Fear, and Rage

As Charlotte Carrington-Farmer has pointed out with regard to the eighteenth-century sugar plantations in Surinam, horses can potentially be the targets of grudges or sabotage.[56] As symbols of authoritarian regimes and the wealthy elite, they are vulnerable to attack by those who are responsible for their care, and can become by proxy the victims of revenge, a theme which has been the subject of more than one detective story and is a staple of the work of Dick Francis. This may have been another reason for kingly interest in the daily activities of the stable.

It is also worth pointing out that both Richard II and Ramesses II go through their own learning experiences during their periods of 'punishment'. Richard, incarcerated in jail, learns the true value of his groom and his horse, and exhibits forgiveness to the latter, realising his own pride in assuming that simply being fed from his royal hand should be enough to make a permanent impression on an animal. Incarceration brings him the enlightenment that horses

---

[56] Carrington-Farmer 2019: 104.

are often victims and symbols of projected human pride and desire. Ramesses learns what counts in moments of utmost danger, as well as his own vulnerability in the face of enemies. They both learn the importance of those that were there for them in times of crisis. Both also learn a lesson about what motivates others, and how it does not necessarily match their own expectations. However, only Richard appears to have acquired a depth of understanding that leads to compassion – he asks his horse to forgive him. Ramesses, on the other hand, appears to be clearly still bearing a grudge for the behaviour of his household and troops. Only his horses, Menna and his god were there for him in his moment of crisis, and he has neither forgotten nor forgiven. The emotions of fear, panic and rage have not entirely departed, and fear and rage are psychologically closely related, in both humans and animals. Not just his thoughts, but his emotions are recorded forever in the words he had inscribed in several locations.

'Fear and terror,' writes Silvan S. Tomkins, 'evoke massive defensive strategies which are as urgent as they are gross and unskilled. Further, they motivate the individual to be as concerned about the re-experience of fear or terror as he is about the activator of fear or terror. In contrast, the lower toxicity of distress permits the individual to mobilize all his resources including those which take time (e.g., thinking through a problem) to solve the problems which activate distress'.[57]

Giving horses, as well as humans, time to think and process is an important part of learning. Substantial modern research shows that positive reinforcement (reward, particularly food rewards) is the most effective way to elicit the behaviour that the trainer or communicator would like to produce in an animal. Indeed, Podhajsky confirms this: 'The rider has many different rewards at his disposal, from patting to giving sugar or other delicacies. There are many ways to gain the horse's confidence and regard in order to make him take pleasure in his work. The thinking rider will soon find out that his horse is not only grateful for any reward but will be stimulated to satisfy his rider'.[58] Given that the use of positive reinforcement as the most effective way to relate to animals has been known since ancient times and is reinforced by acknowledged experts such as Podhajsky, why resort to other means at all, as even Podhajsky in fact does?

The most obvious answer is expediency, driven by human cultural constraints, complications, and legacies. In ancient Egypt this was particularly interesting since the principles of semi-divine kingship had been established nearly 1500 years before the horse and chariot became an essential expression of the authority of the ruler.

Controlling Horse Behaviour in the Context of Ma'at

The Egyptian attitude to horses and horse training therefore reflects the individual's own embeddedness, whether high or low, in a complex hierarchical society with clearly defined roles and responsibilities. From the Old Kingdom onwards, wise teachers such as Ptahhotep had written instructions for young men to ensure their success in the world. Their words encouraged forbearance, generosity, and forgiveness, suggesting that the wise man ignore any offenses against him and accentuate the good in the other, a key factor in positive reinforcement, which encourages ignoring unwanted behaviour and rewarding desired responses: 'If you are angered by a misdeed,/Lean toward a man on account of his rightness;/ Pass it over, don't recall it,/Since he was silent to you the first day'.[59]

This, then, is the attitude of a man towards his equals. However, Ptahhotep also recommends his readers to 'Punish firmly, chastise soundly, /Then repression of crime becomes an example;/Punishment except for crime/Turns the complainer into an enemy'.[60] Punishment is a necessary part of social relations but it must be just, in keeping with the laws of *Ma'at*.

Further, with regard to those in power, one should 'Bend your back to your superior,/Your overseer from the palace;/Then your house will endure in its wealth,/Your rewards in their right place'.[61] Ptahhotep and his scribal peers throughout Egyptian history understood that their society was an orderly one, with a place for everyone and everyone in his or her place. They had roles to adopt and duties to perform. Those who kept to righteousness and order gained rewards. This was true of horses as well as people; domestic animals were expected to know their place and keep it, as if they failed to do so, they would become part of the chaotic realm or *isfat* that orderly Egyptian society governed by *ma'at* worked constantly to exclude, although they recognised it was necessary for cosmic balance. The system that kept the horses' heads in place was therefore not only practical, but also richly symbolic and a potent way of representing the ultimate authority of the king; and the grooms at Amarna literally bent their backs as they stood behind the chariots with the horses fidgeting in front as they waited for their highborn occupants to arrive. Just as a pinioned *rekhyt* bird (the lapwing) was symbolic of control over the Egyptian people, the restrained heads of the horses expressed the ultimate power of the king; the horses were out in front, but totally under his control, reflecting order, otherwise '... all the ranks, they are not in their place,/Like a herd that roams without a herdsman'.[62] Thus could the new technology of the horse and chariot reflect concepts of authority that far predated its arrival.

---

[57] Tomkins 1963: 13.
[58] Podhajsky 1983: 68.
[59] Lichtheim 1975: 71.
[60] Lichtheim 1975: 73.
[61] Lichtheim 1976: 72.
[62] Lichtheim 1975: 158.

Accessing all areas of the quadrant of learning when training horses (or people) was therefore entirely in keeping with a belief system that was founded on the innate tension and interaction between the two forces of *isfat* and *ma'at*. Both were required to keep the cosmos in balance and functioning correctly. The interface between the two was at once clearly drawn and yet highly fluid; without constant alertness on the part of the ruler, the forces of chaos would seep through and disrupt the cosmic harmony of *ma'at*. Between divinely justified eternal reward and divinely justified eternal punishment lay the liminal areas of removal or withholding of reward and punishment.

In fact, the knowledge that the horses moved against restraint, resulting in further restraint needing to be applied, reflected, in a way, the status conferred by keeping and using horses as official and personal transport. It replicated the words of the wise in understanding the principles of constraint and reward. It was also a novel way to regenerate ancient themes of power and the forces of the cosmos. One of the earliest non-royal provincial tombs to include horses was that of Paheri, an official – usually described as a 'mayor' – of Nekheb, not far from Thebes. He used his tomb to depict everyday activities such as watching over workers in the fields. Having just arrived by chariot, Paheri's driver-groom restrains the animals, telling them to keep still: 'Do not struggle, excellent team of the mayor, beloved of your master, about whom the mayor boasts to everyone'.[63] Thus the response of the horses to pressure and restraint when unable to release themselves from it became part of the age-old pattern of necessary tension between diverse cosmic forces, the ultimate control of authority, and upholding *ma'at*. Overcoming the resistance of horses was a skill to be learned by any prince who aspired to driving a chariot and pair, however much the prince claimed to understand the animals, according to Lichtheim's interpretation of the words of Amenhotep II.[64] In this sense, then, the horses that had to be dominated and controlled were a lesson in absolute kingship. However, Decker offers a somewhat different interpretation, as he suggests that Amenhotep was advised to 'calm [the horses] if they were unruly'.[65] There lies a world of philosophical difference in training between these two interpretations, dominating or calming, which deserves further exploration.

It is not surprising, therefore, that belief in the effectiveness of domination during training existed in an education system that assumed beating played a major part in successful learning outcomes. Comparisons were naturally drawn between reluctant scholars and horses that did not show total submission to their drivers or owners: 'Horses brought from the field, they forget their mothers. Yoked they go up and down on all his majesty's errands. They become like those that bore them, they stand in the stable. They do their utmost for fear of a beating... But though I beat you with every kind of stick, you do not listen. If I knew another way of doing it for you, I would do it for you, that you might listen'.[66] The student responds: 'You beat my back; your teaching entered my ear. I am like a pawing horse. Sleep does not enter my heart by day; nor is it upon me at night ... I will serve my lord just as a slave serves his master'.[67] In this, the famous 'Be a Scribe' text – also known as Papyrus Lansing –, ownership of horses is also one of the incentives for the successful scribe. The teacher dins it into his student to learn to be a scribe – and avoid all those other terrible career options – and once he has learned well, to build his teacher a house, which will of course include a stable for his horses. Indeed, in one scene in the tomb of Ipuya[68] we see young horses apparently being dragged reluctantly along to their training, gripped tightly at the top of the lead rope, reminiscent of the reluctant would-be scribe of ancient Egypt, or, indeed, Shakespeare's 'whining schoolboy...creeping like snail/ Unwillingly to school'.[69]

The instruction texts tell us that both punishment and the giving of incentives were very well understood, and the ancient Egyptians knew all about food as a reward. Piled high on altars and festival boards in the images of their 'Houses of Eternity', food and drink that lasted forever through magical means represented the ultimate delayed gratification for life's labours; nor did it always need to be delayed: 'Lo, a man is happy eating his food. Consume your goods in gladness, while there is none to hinder you. It is good for a man to eat his food. God ordains it for him whom he favors'.[70] Decker notes the response of an overseer to an anxious owner's enquiry about his horses while he is away: 'My lord's horses are well. I had their portion mixed before them, and the stable boys bring them the best grass from the papyrus thicket. I give them their daily feed and their yellow salve in order to brush them down every month. The stable master lets them go for a trot every ten days.'[71]

When Ramesses made the connection between the desirable behaviour of his horses at Kadesh and his promise they would from now on be fed in his presence, he was effectively stating that feeding the horses was a valued and rewarding activity; but for whom? Is it that *he* took pleasure in seeing that his horses were fed properly ('the sound of contented ponies munching' last thing at night being a staple in many a pony book) or is it that he understood the value of rewarding them personally, from his own hand, like Richard II? If the former, he passed by the chance to let his horses associate food rewards with him, by simply observing them being fed, rather than feeding them

---

[63] James 2003: 111.
[64] Lichtheim 1976: 42.
[65] Decker 1993: 48.
[66] Lichtheim 1976: 169.
[67] Lichtheim 1976: 172.
[68] Decker 1993: 50.
[69] Shakespeare, As You Like It, Act 2, Scene 7, 145–147. It is worth noting that the images of horses expressing the most natural equine behaviour are those of mares and foals in which the foals skip delightfully in a recognisably foalish fashion, while the mares tend to be shown as if being led in ranks like their male chariot horse counterparts.
[70] Lichtheim 1975: 157.
[71] Decker 1993: 49.

himself. This would have been a major opportunity to develop his own relationship with his animals. However, he would be exhibiting an understanding of the old phrase 'The eye of the master makes the horse grow fat' – in other words, good horsemasters oversee their horses' care personally, they do not simply leave it to others who may not have the horses' best interests in mind. That does not necessarily mean that the master fills water buckets and mixes feed, however. Perhaps that would be seen as too lowly a job for one of the supreme rulers of the ancient world. It is interesting to consider that, however dependent on a hierarchy of producers and administrators ancient kings were, their self-image showed that they believed themselves to be wrapped safely in the protective bubble of semi-divinity, closer to the gods than mortals. How aware were they of their ultimate dependency on others, human and animal? Or was their sense of privilege complete? Could the rulers see and take pleasure in the rewards enjoyed by others, whether animal or human? Here again, the texts commissioned by Ramesses may provide a clue, since they hint at his own psychology and emotional state.

The Dawn of Empathy

As long ago as 1965, Grahame Clark and Stuart Piggott were commenting on the possibility of isolation and even loneliness in the semi-divine rulers of Egypt.[72] It is also clear from texts and a few mixed human-animal interments that elite ancient Egyptians believed they were on affectionate terms with at least some of their animals. While we cannot hear the views of the animals themselves, it is possible to understand how in the loneliest moment of kingship, facing death on the battlefield, the ruler might have a sudden revelation of his dependency and that his emotions would transfer to the creatures immediately responsible for his security – the horses. In this instance, they take priority even over the charioteer, whose role was neither to be seen nor heard in kingly images and texts. In other words, the horses were the beings (as much as the god Amun on whom he called, who filled Ramesses with divine inspiration) who made the king feel less alone in his most isolated moment. It was possibly a rare moment of empathy and enlightenment for a king. The dedication to his horses that Ramesses caused to have placed on his temples enables the reader to witness this rare moment: the self-identification of a semi-divine ruler with real living individuals of another species, as distinct from the theoretical animals of traditional kingship such as the lion and the bull. In modern times, the initiates of secret trade associations such as the Horseman's Grip an' Word would be told that they and their horses must be 'one'. Only by considering the horses to be their equals, not by domination, would success as a horseman be achieved. The words of Ramesses may show him reaching towards this, if not attaining the 'oneness'.

Recognition for the Equine Contribution

A final point: the respect due to animals that have participated in and survived war, such as the chariot horses of Ramesses is a recurring theme across the globe. One of the most famous narratives is that of Comanche, the horse that was the sole survivor on the US cavalry side after the disastrous engagement known as the Battle of the Little Big Horn. He, like the horses of Ramesses, was seen as worthy of recognition. Comanche was first taken to Fort Mead by a unit of the Seventh Regiment of Cavalry where he was treated for the wounds he received. The horse was then sent to Fort Riley in Kansas, where he lived out the rest of his long life with all the status of a military hero and veteran.[73] His heroism was recognised with a general order that his kind treatment and comfort shall be a matter of special pride and solicitude on the part of every member of the Seventh Cavalry to the end that his life be preserved to the utmost limit. '(...) Further, Company I will see that a special and comfortable stable is fitted for him and he will not be ridden by any person whatsoever, under any circumstances, nor will be put to any kind of work.'[74]

The 'special and comfortable stable' subsequently took on the status of a quasi-shrine where visitors could come to contemplate the veteran animal and his deeds. Comanche's body was preserved and is still on view today. He is one of a small number of war horses to have received recognition in this way. Other examples are the horses of Gustavus of Sweden. What is more, there is a long history of preserving body parts as souvenirs, such as the hooves of Napoleon's horse, displayed in honour of the horse's contribution.

Further examples of reverential treatment can be proposed, including examples from Egypt. In fact, the only horse in Egypt discovered to have had an attempt at deliberate preservation was found near the tomb of Senenmut. It is believed to have been a mare. Another mare was found interred in the Delta, opening up the possibility of burials of revered breeding animals. It has also been suggested that mares may have been used in Egyptian chariotry.[75]

Exploring the relationship between people and horses opens up new and innovative research opportunities. Candelora's exploration of communities of practice 'united by their joint enterprise' in Second Intermediate Period Egypt highlights the value of further investigation of material culture, texts and visual records in the light of original, often anthropologically-inspired methods and methodology: '… the infantry, the chariot corps and other specialized branches of the soldiery, as well as military craftsmen, metal smiths, and even horse trainers all constitute a con-

---

[72] Clark and Piggott 1965: 215.

[73] https://www.sdpb.org/blogs/images-of-the-past/the-sole-survivor-on-the-army-side-of-custers-last-stand/.
[74] https://www.sdpb.org/blogs/images-of-the-past/the-sole-survivor-on-the-army-side-of-custers-last-stand/.
[75] Pope 1970: 56–61.

stellation of communities of practice united by their joint enterprise'.[76]

I suggest that further examination of equine remains and equine material culture, texts and imagery may in time lead to greater insights into the way the horse was treated in ancient Egypt, further insights into the horse-human relationship and possibly even the identification of different styles and approaches within these different communities to training and communicating with horses. This may in turn augment broader historical and social analyses of Egypt and its interactions with surrounding regions.

Miriam Bibby
Independent Scholar and Author; Tutor, University of Manchester, UK.

Bibliography

Bianchi, Robert Steven, and Edmund S. Meltzer. 2023. A Ring Bezel Inscribed for Pharaohs Tuthmosis III and Amenhotep II. *Cheiron: The International Journal of Equine and Equestrian History* 3(1): 7-24.

Bibby, Miriam. 2008. Egyptian Horses and Chariots: A Metaphor for Control. *Tracking-up*, Winter 2008–2009: 18–20. Open access at: https://www.academia.edu/12783840/Egyptian_horses_and_chariots_a_metaphor_for_control; accessed 09.01.2022.

Brownrigg, Gail. 2019. Harnessing the Chariot Horse. In: *Equids and Wheeled Vehicles in the Ancient World,* edited by Peter Raulwing, Katheryn M. Linduff and Joost H. Crouwel, 85–96. Oxford: BAR Publishing.

Calvert, Amy. 2012. Vehicle of the Sun: The Royal Chariot in the New Kingdom. In: *Chasing Chariots: Proceedings of the First International Chariot Conference*, edited by André J. Veldmeijer and Salima Ikram, 45–72. Leiden: Sidestone Press.

Candelora, Danielle. 2019. Hybrid Military Communities of Practice: The Integration of Immigrants as the Catalyst for Egyptian Social Transformation in the 2nd Millennium BC. In: *A Stranger in the House – the Crossroads III. Proceedings of an International Conference on Foreigners in Ancient Egyptian and Near Eastern Societies of the Bronze Age*, edited by Jana Mynářová, Marwan Kilani, and Sergio Alivernini, 25–47. Prague: Charles University.

Caro, Tim, Yvette Argueta, Emmanuelle Sophie Briolat et al. 2019. Benefits of Zebra Stripes: Behaviour of Tabanid Flies Around Zebras and Horses. *PLoS One* 14 (2): e0210831. https://doi.org/10.1371/journal.pone.0210831.

Carrington-Farmer, Charlotte. 2019. Trading Horses in Eighteenth Century Rhode Island and the Atlantic. In: *Equestrian Cultures: Horses, Human Society and the Discourse of Modernity*, edited by Katrin Guest and Monica Mattfeld, 92–109. Chicago: University of Chicago Press.

Clark, Grahame and Stuart Piggott. 1965. *Prehistoric Societies.* Harmondsworth: Penguin Books.

Davies, Norman de Garis. 1903. *The Rock Tombs of el-Amarna, Part I. The tomb of Meryra.* London: Egypt Exploration Society.

Davies, Norman de Garis. 1906. *The Rock Tombs of el-Amarna, Part IV. Tombs of Penthu, Mahu, and others.* London: Egypt Exploration Society.

Decker, Wolfgang. 1993. *Sport and Games of Ancient Egypt.* Cairo: American University in Cairo Press.

Dent, Anthony. 1987. *Horses in Shakespeare's England*. London: Allen.

Delpeut, Lonneke. 2021. What Makes a Horse a Horse? Configurational Aspects of Ancient Egyptian Equines. *Cheiron, the International Journal for Equine and Equestrian History* 1: 17–45.

Delpeut, Lonneke and Hylke Hettema. 2021. Ancient Arabian Horses? Revisiting Ancient Egyptian Equine Imagery. In: *Current Research in Egyptology 2019: Proceedings of the Twentieth Annual Symposium*, edited by Marta Arranz Cárcamo, Raúl Sánchez Casado, Albert Planelles Orozco, Sergio Alarcón Robledo, Jónatan Ortiz García, and Patricia Mora Riudavets, 168–182. Oxford: Archaeopress.

Donnell, Sue. 2003. *The Equid Ethogram: A Practical Field Guide to Horse Behaviour*. Lexington: Eclipse.

---

[76] Candelora 2019: 26.

Eshmawy, Aiman. 2007. Names of Horses in Ancient Egypt. In: *Orientalia Lovaniensia Analecta* 150, *Proceedings of the Ninth International Congress of Egyptologists*, edited by Jean-Claude Goyon and Christine Cardin, 665–676. Leuven: Uitgeverij Peeters en Departement Oosterse Studies.

Fudge, Erica. 2020. 'Forgiveness, horse': The Barbaric World of Richard II. In: *The Routledge Handbook of Shakespeare and Animals*, edited by Karen Raber and Holly Dugan, 292–306. New York: Routledge.

Goodwin, Deborah. 1999. The Importance of Ethology in Understanding the Behaviour of the Horse. *Equine Veterinary Journal* 28: 15–19.

Hansen, Kathy. 1992. Collection in Ancient Egyptian Chariot Horses. *Journal of the American Research Center in Egypt* 29: 173–179.

Heuschmann, Gerd. 2007. *Tug of War: Classical versus 'Modern' Dressage*. North Pomfret: Trafalgar Square Books.

James, Thomas G. H. 2003. *Pharaoh's People: Scenes from Life in Imperial Egypt*. London: Tauris Parke.

Jobst, Jennifer. Forthcoming. *Horse Head Position in Premodern Times: A Textual, Iconographic, and Archaeological Analysis of 'Behind the Vertical' and 'Hyperflexion'*.

Kemp, Barry. 1991. *Ancient Egypt: Anatomy of a Civilization*. London: Routledge.

Leitz, Christian. 1999. *Magical and Medical Papyri of the New Kingdom*. London: British Museum Press.

Librado, Pablo et al. 2017. Ancient Genomic Changes Associated with Domestication of the Horse. *Science* 356 (6336): 442–445. DOI: 10.1126/science.aam5298.

Lichtheim, Miriam. 1975. *The Old and Middle Kingdoms*. Ancient Egyptian Literature, Vol. 1. Berkeley: University of California Press.

Lichtheim, Miriam. 1976. *The New Kingdom*. Ancient Egyptian Literature, Vol. 2. Berkeley: University of California Press.

Littauer, Mary. 1968. The Function of the Yoke Saddle in Ancient Harnessing. *Antiquity* 42: 27–31.

Littauer, Mary. 1974. An Element of Egyptian Horse Harness. *Antiquity* 48: 293–295.

Littauer, Mary and Joost H. Crouwel. 1979. *Wheeled Vehicles and Ridden Animals in the Ancient Near East*. Leiden and Köln: Brill.

Littauer, Mary and Joost H. Crouwel. 1985. *Chariots and Related Equipment from the Tomb of Tut'ankhamūn*. Oxford: Griffith Institute.

McLean, Andrew N. and Janne Winther Christensen. 2017. The Application of Learning Theory in Horse Training. *Applied Animal Behaviour Science* 190: 18–27. DOI:10.1016/j.applanim.

Mellor, David J. 2020. Mouth Pain in Horses: Physiological Foundations, Behavioural Indices, Welfare Implications, and a Suggested Solution. *Animals* 10 (4): 572. Doi: 10.3390/ani10040572.

Mejdella, Cecilie, M., Turid Buvik, Grete H. M. Jørgensen, and Knud E. Bøe. 2016. Horses Can Learn to Use Symbols to Communicate their Preferences. *Applied Animal Behaviour Science* 184: 66–73. Doi.org/10.1016/j.applanim.

Pérez-Manrique, Lucia, Karina León-Pérez, Emmanuel Zamora-Sánchez et al. 2020. Prevalence and Distribution of Lesions in the Nasal Bones and Mandibles of a Sample of 144 Riding Horses. *Animals* 10 (9): 1061. Doi.org/10.3390/ani10091661.

Podhajsky, Alois 1983. *The Complete Training of Horse and Rider*. Harrap, London.

Pope, Marvin H. 1970. A Mare in Pharaoh's Chariotry. *Bulletin of the American Schools of Oriental Research* 200: 56–61.

Raulwing, Peter. 2019. Hommage to Mary Aiken Littauer (1912–2005). In: *Equids and Wheeled Vehicles in the Ancient World*, edited Peter Raulwing, Katheryn M. Linduff and Joost H. Crouwel, 5–26. Oxford: BAR Publishing.

Rommelaere, Catherine. 1991. *Les Chevaux du Nouvel Empire Egyptien: Origines, Races, Harnachements*. Brussels: Connaissance de l'Egypt Ancienne.

Schellinger, Sarah M. 2009. Victory Stela of Piankhi. In: *Milestone Documents in World History*, edited Brian Bonhomme and Cathleen Boivin, 91–107. Dallas: Schlager.

Sewell, Anna. 1989. *The Annotated Black Beauty*. London: Allen.

Spruytte, Jean. 1983. *Early Harness Systems*. London: Allen.

Tomkins, Silvan S. 1963. *Affect Imagery Consciousness Volume II: The Negative Affects*. New York: Springer.

Trösch, Miléna, Florent Cuzol, Céline Parias et al. 2019. Horses Categorize Human Emotions Cross-Modally Based on Facial Expression and Non-Verbal Vocalizations. *Animals* 9 (11): 862. Doi: 10.3390/ani9110862.

Turner, Susan. 2015. *The horse in New Kingdom Egypt: its introduction, nature, role and impact*. PhD thesis. Sydney: McQuarrie University.

Veldmeijer, André J., Salima Akrim, and Lucy-Anne Skinner. 2013. Charging Chariots: Progress Report on the Tano Chariot in the Egyptian Museum Cairo. In: *Chasing Chariots*, edited by André Veldmeijer and Salima Ikram, 257–271. Leiden: Sidestone Press.

Xenophon. 1979. *The Art of Horsemanship*. London: Allen.

7

The Egyptian 'Check Rowel' – A New Interpretation of its Purpose

Gail Brownrigg

Abstract

'Check rowels' are decorated rods fitted with spiked discs, of which a few examples survive, now recognised as part of eighteenth dynasty chariot harness. Their function is discussed, and a new suggestion for their purpose is proposed.

In the Ashmolean Museum, Oxford, is a decorative object inlaid with patterns made from coloured barks (Ashmolean Museum no. 1924.73). Dating to the 14th century BCE, it was found during the 1923 excavation of a private house which probably belonged to a 'steward of Akhetaten' in Tell el-Amarna on the east bank of the Nile. Consisting of a slender rod ca. 33 cm long, topped by a small disc like a spindle whorl 0.92 cm in diameter, with short bronze spikes projecting from its edges,[1] it was described as a 'mace'. Closer examination later revealed that one end of the rod had been broken off (Figure 7.1).

When ten similar objects were discovered in the tomb of Tutankhamun (now in the Grand Egyptian Museum at the foot of the pyramids in Giza), it was realised that their association with the chariots meant that they had belonged to the horses' harness (Figure 7.2). Among the seven from the Antechamber, there were three pairs, while one found in the Annexe (presumably dropped there by the thieves who had broken in soon after the burial) matched one of the two which had probably originally been placed in the Treasury.[2] They varied in length from 18.5 to 56.5 cm, the majority being 53 cm or over. The discs, which rotated on the centre of the rods, measured 0.55 to 0.85 cm in diameter (excluding their bronze spikes). Referred to by the excavators, Howard Carter and Arthur Mace in their notes as 'rowels', 'goads' or 'spurs', they were described in their final publication as 'spur-like goads'.[3] Howard Carter suggested that they were used as goads 'to prevent the horses from breaking from the line of draught'.[4]

They are first clearly depicted in Egypt in the Amarna period, resembling a lozenge on a taut second rein running from the bit to a point level with the yoke or yoke fork,

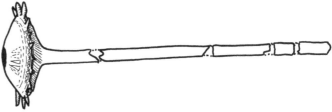

Figure 7.1. Check rowel from Amarna, Ashmolean Museum no. 1924.73. Drawing by author.

and can be seen on numerous wall paintings and bas-reliefs of the eighteenth dynasty (Figure 7.3).[5] They would have been attached to the bit by the leather thongs threaded through holes at each end and perhaps to the finials on the yoke terminals.[6] If they were tied on to the yoke fork itself, they would have been constantly pricking the horses'

---

[1] Rieth 1957: 148 ff; Littauer 1974: 293; Littauer and Crouwel 1985: 84, Pl. LXXIV.
[2] Littauer and Crouwel 1985: 98, figs. 10, 18, pl. XXXVIII.
[3] Carter and Mace 1922–1933: 59.
[4] Carter 1927: 112ff.; Littauer 1974: 293; Littauer and Crouwel 1985: 84.
[5] Littauer 1974: 295; Littauer and Crouwel 1985: 84; Hofmann 1989: 67; see also Bibby, this volume.
[6] Hofmann 1989: 67, fn. 307.

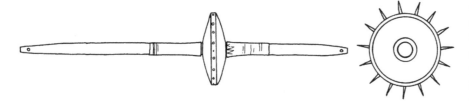

Figure 7.2. Check rowel from the tomb of Tutankhamun, object no. 620, found in the Annexe. Adapted from Littauer and Crouwel 1985, 63.

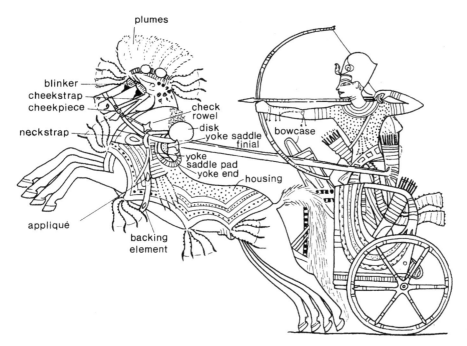

Figure 7.3. Tutankhamun in his chariot. After Littauer and Crouwel 1985, fig. 2. By permission of Joost Crouwel.

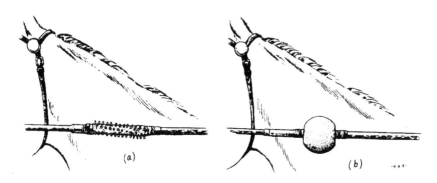

Figure 7.4. 'Burrs' and 'balls' on head poles used on the trotting track to prevent horses from bending their necks to one side. After Littauer 1974, fig. 2.

down or stop the team. She considered that the rods, fitted on the outside, would have discouraged the stallions from turning their heads inwards to try and bite one another. She compared them with 'head poles' fitted with pricking devices used on harness horses on the trotting track to prevent them from carrying their heads to one side, a fault that may spoil their gait or even affect their speed (Figure 7.4). If a horse carries head crookedly, the 'burrs' or 'balls' on the pole cause discomfort and make him straighten his neck.[8]

Jean Spruytte, who reconstructed ancient chariots and harness, experimented with such devices (without the spikes) and considered them to be an auxiliary reining system used particularly for training. Being rigid, they would prevent the animals from lowering their heads unduly. In turning, the action of the reins would cause the studs to prick the neck muscles of the outside horse and encourage him to move over quickly, thus facilitating a sharp turn and helping to keep the team both in step and in balance (Figure 7.5).[9] Working together would be less tiring on a long journey or during strenuous activity. The length of the rods would have been suitable for ponies no bigger than 12.3 hands (130 cm).

When driving a pair of ponies, one of which was a novice, harnessed to a replica of an Egyptian chariot, I had trouble keeping them under the yoke – they tended to veer outwards, away from the draught pole, so that the yoke forks slipped over to one side.

necks, and there would have been no release from their contact. They do not seem to have been used later than the Ramesside period, towards the end of the second millennium BCE, which could be due to a lack of figured documents. There is no evidence for them outside Egypt and they are not illustrated on foreign teams.

Adolf Rieth[7] also thought that they would help to spur the horses on to faster gaits, but Mary Littauer has pointed out that this would have resulted in problems trying to slow

Early harnessing was always by means a yoke attached to the front of a central draught pole. Originally designed for cattle, and placed on the forehead or the nape of the neck and bound on to the horns, or lying in front of the withers, it was adapted for horses with their higher head carriage by lashing wishbone-shaped 'yoke forks' on either side. These lay in front of the animals' shoulders and transferred the pull to the top of the scapula (Figure 7.6). A neckstrap

[7] Rieth 1957.

[8] Littauer 1974; with fig. 2.
[9] Spruytte 1983: 46–47.

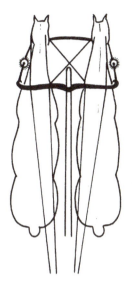 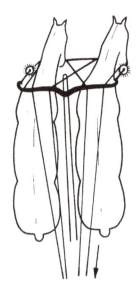

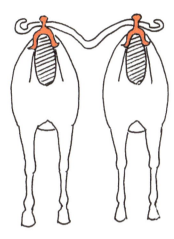

Figure 7.6. The yoke forks, lashed to the yoke, lay on the horses' necks just in front of their shoulders. Drawing by author after Spruytte 1982, 171.

Figure 7.5. Spruytte's diagram showing the action of the auxiliary reins. As the horses turn their heads, the rowel pricks the neck of the outside horse. After Spruytte 1983, 51. By permission of Alain Spruytte.

held them in place[10], and prevented the horses from backing out from under the yoke. A long strap from the outer leg of the yoke fork, running under the belly and up to the front of the pole, facilitated braking and reversing (Figure 7.3).

Clearly I had not adjusted the harness properly, and as I had decided for safety reasons to drive with modern harness using breaststraps and traces[11] in addition to the yoke which balanced the vehicle, I had rashly omitted the 'backing element' which might have prevented the yoke forks from lifting and slipping inwards off the ponies' necks (Figure 7.7). However, the experience showed that the yoke does not in itself hold the draught animals close together, and that any tendency to drift outwards away from the pole could cause problems.

A ridden horse is trained to move away from leg pressure: a tap with both heels means 'go forward', while a touch on the flank asks him to move to the side. The way to control a driven horse is by verbal commands, reinforced by a whip or goad, and by the bridle and reins. It is generally accepted that bits and/or their cheekpieces are intended to control a horse, or other animal such as a mule, donkey[12] or cattle,[13] and that they were invented to manage draught animals, especially chariot horses. A bit does not act either as a brake or a steering wheel. It does not stop a horse: it tells the horse that we wish to stop or turn. However, it can also have other effects, such as causing the horse to throw

Figure 7.7. Experimenting with a replica of an Egyptian chariot, using modern harness as well as the yoke for safety reasons, as the bay pony is a novice. The traces help to keep the ponies straight, but even though turning the stallion's head outwards helps to keep him from swinging his quarters out, it does not prevent him drifting sideways away from the draught pole. A check rowel on his neck would encourage him to stay closer to his team mate. Note that that the ponies are naturally keeping in step, despite being driven as a pair for the first time.
Photo: C. Kirk.

up its head in resistance, or to bend its neck downwards or to the side. Turning the horse's head does not *make* it go in the required direction: it can still drift sideways or simply ignore the signal. Another result of pulling on one rein is to cause the horse's rear end to pivot in the opposite direction: turning the head to the right, for example, can result in the quarters moving to the left.

If the horse is one of a pair, one or both animals can pull outwards, away from the draught pole (Figures 7.8 and 7.9). The automatic reaction of most drivers is to tighten the inside rein to bring the animals closer together. However, this can have the opposite effect, causing their back ends to swing outwards, making matters worse. In modern harness with traces, these help to keep the animals straight[14] – this

---

[10] Despite the oft-repeated claim that they tightened on the windpipe and choked the horses, Spruytte (1983) showed that traction was by the shoulders and not by the throat. See also Brownrigg 2019.
[11] Traces are long straps, ropes or chains leading from either side of the modern collar or breaststrap to the vehicle or implement, by which it is pulled.
[12] Bar Oz et al 2013: fig. 3.
[13] For a wall painting of a Nubian chariot drawn by bridled cattle, see Burmeister 2013: Abb. 1, 2.

[14] Rieth (1957: 153, fn. 11) has a note to the effect that Vienna fiacre drivers attached thick knobs to the outer traces of their horses on the level

Figure 7.8. Horses harnessed with modern collars and traces pulling outwards away from the draught pole, as their heads are turned towards each other by tight inside reins. Author's drawing after Pape 1982, 76 left.

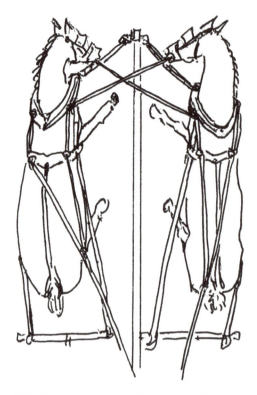

Figure 7.9. The ponies' heads are turned inwards as they pull away from the chariot pole, causing the harness to slip. Experimental reconstruction of a Celtic chariot, using a dorsal yoke combined with modern harness with traces. Photo in the public domain.

is why most reconstructions tend to use modern harnessing with which the drivers are familiar, so that the animals are more easily managed. But with yoke harnessing, there were no traces: draught and steering were by means of the central pole. The neckstraps on Egyptian harness kept the horses from moving out from under the yoke but did nothing to control their relative positions. The only means of keeping them straight would be by the reins.

In his classic work on driving and harnessing, *The Art of Driving*, Max Pape[15] advises: 'When fitting the reins it is important to make sure that the [inside] reins are not too short, otherwise they will pull the horses' heads together, and the horse cannot go straight. As a result they will hang away from the pole. It is better to have their heads pointing slightly to the outside. This will stop them from hanging away from the pole....'

Thus, one way to straighten one or both chariot horses if they are travelling crooked or too far from the pole, is to tighten the *outside* reins, which is counter-intuitive. If the charioteer is not sufficiently competent in his rein handling, this shortcoming could be compensated for by preventing the horses from bending their necks inwards by placing the 'check rowel' (in German 'Halssporn – 'neck spur') between the bit and the yoke. They will then be discouraged from turning their heads inwards and will travel with their necks bent slightly out, and the hind end consequently kept close to the pole instead of swinging away from it.[16] In turning, the outer rein is slackened, allowing the outside horse to accelerate and to bend his head in the direction of the turn, at which point the rowel will come into contact with his neck and encourage him to stay close to his team mate and turn quickly with him.

Jean Spruytte and his son Alain would have had no trouble because they were both excellent horsemen, driving well-trained ponies in a quiet environment (Figure 7.10), but perhaps the Egyptians, who had gained their knowledge of chariots and horses from the Hyksos, appreciated the extra control provided by the auxiliary rein with its prongs. There might be occasions when one or both horses might shy to the side in the heat of battle or the excitement of the chase. The Pharaoh is sometimes depicted alone in his chariot with the reins tied around his waist, wielding a weapon (Figure 7.3). With the danger of being caught up should the chariot overturn, it is unlikely that the Pharaoh would actually risk his life in this position on the battlefield, but the convention provided the artist with a way to display him in solitary glory. Mary Littauer[17] has suggested that this is a 'heroic motif' like that of the warrior king stepping over the chariot breastwork, with one foot on the pole to smite his enemy – a dashing pose probably transferred from the striding stance of the conquering Pharoah on the ground. The great ruler liked to be depicted defeating the enemy single-handed, with no charioteer in evidence, though he would undoubtedly have had a personal chauffeur. Nonetheless, to drive a chariot well was an accomplishment expected of the Pharaoh, and surely any

---

of their flanks to keep them from breaking from the line of draught (Littauer 1974: 295). See also Pape 1982, drawing on p. 77 showing a strap with a leather pad to prevent them from hanging away from the pole.
[15] Pape 1982: 9.

[16] It is noticeable that on Greek vases, the outer horses of a quadriga are shown with their heads turned outwards (Spruytte 1983: 60, fig.2; Jurriaans-Helle 2021). This may be artistic license, or a reflection of actual practice.
[17] Littauer 1968: 150, 2002: 136.

Figure 7.10. Jean Spruytte's experimental reconstruction of an Egyptian chariot. The ponies' heads are turned slightly outwards, and they are travelling straight and parallel to one another. After Spruytte 1983, fig. 7.2. By permission of Alain Spruytte.

piece of equipment that would enhance his performance and make him look good must have been welcomed.

The fact that check rowels are widely depicted and were found in Tutankhamun's tomb, indicates that they were more than just a training aid, but formed part of the standard equipment of the luxury royal chariots during the eighteenth dynasty.

Following Carter's perceptive suggestion, made a century ago when horse-drawn carriages were a familiar sight, that the 'check rowels' would 'prevent the horses from breaking from the line of draught'.[18] I would go further and propose another interpretation. Whilst I agree with Mary Littauer and Jean Spruytte that their primary purpose was to encourage or force the horses to turn their heads, I believe that an additional benefit of their use was to facilitate control by keeping both horses close to the draught pole, thus helping to keep the yoke in place just in front of the withers and the yoke forks on their shoulders, enabling them to pull with maximum effect.

Gail Brownrigg
Independent Scholar, UK

Bibliography

Bar-Oz, Guy. Pirhiya Nahshoni, Hadas Motro and Eliezer D. Oren. 2013. Symbolic Metal Bit and Saddlebag Fastenings in a Middle Bronze Age Donkey Burial. *PLoS ONE* 8, 3: e58648. DOI: 10.1371/journal.pone.0058648.

Brownrigg, Gail. 2019. Harnessing the Chariot Horse. In: *Equids and Wheeled Vehicles in the Ancient World: Essays in Memory of Mary A. Littauer,* edited by Peter Raulwing, Katheryn M. Linduff and Joost H. Crouwel, 85-96. BAR International Series 2923. Oxford: BAR Publishing.

Burmeister, Stefan. 2013. Die Sicherung der ethnischen Ordnung: Das Wandbild eines eigenartigen nubischen Streitwagens im Grab des Huy, Vizekönig von Kusch (Neues Reich). Preservation of the Ethnic Order: A Painting of a Curious Nubian Chariot in the Tomb of Huy, Viceroy of Kush (New Kingdom). *Journal of Egyptian History* 6, 131–151. doi: https://doi.org/10.1163/18741665-12340006.

Carter, Howard and Arthur C. Mace. 1922–1933. *The Tomb of Tut.ankh.Amen* (3 vols). London: Duckworth.

Carter, Howard. 1927. *The Tomb of Tut.ankh.Amen* II: The Burial Chamber. London: Duckworth.

Jurriaans-Helle, Geralda. 2021. *Composition in Athenian Black-Figure Vase-Painting: The 'Chariot in Profile' 'Type Scene'.* Babesch Supplementa 41. Leuven: Peeters. https://doi.org/10.2307/j.ctv1q26xv1

Littauer, Mary A. 1968. A 19th and 20th Dynasty Heroic Motif on Attic Black-Figure Vases. *American Journal of Archaeology* 72, 150–152. Reprinted in Littauer and Crouwel 2002, 136–140.

Littauer, Mary A. 1974. An Element of Egyptian Horse Harness. *Antiquity* 48, 293–295. Reprinted in Littauer and Crouwel 2002, 521–524.

Littauer, Mary A. and Joost H. Crouwel. 1985. *Chariots and Related Equipment from the Tomb of Tutʿankhamūn.* Tutʿankhamūn's Tomb Series 8. Oxford: Griffith Institute.

Littauer, Mary A. and Joost H. Crouwel. 2002, *Selected Writings on Chariots and Other Early Vehicles, Riding and Harness,* edited by Peter Raulwing, Culture and History of the Ancient Near East 6. Leiden and Cologne: Brill.

Pape, Max. 1982. *The Art of Driving.* London: Allen.

Rieth, Adolf. 1957. 'Halssporen' am Pferdegeschirr des Neuen Reiches, *Mitteilungen des Instituts für Orientforschung* 5, 148–154.

Spruytte, Jean. 1982. Démonstration expérimentale de biges d'après quelques oeuvres rupestres sahariennes. In: *Les Chars préhistoriques du Sahara. Archéologie et Techniques d'attelage.* Actes du Colloque de Sénanque 21-22 mars 1981, Aix-en-Provence, edited by Gabriel Camps and Marceau Gast, 163–172. Aix-en-Provence: Laboratoire d'Anthropologie et Préhistoire et d'Ethnologie des Pays de la Mediterranée Occidentale, Université de Provence.

Spruytte, Jean. 1983. *Early Harness Systems, Contribution to the History of the Horse* (translation by Mary A. Littauer of Jean Spruytte's, *Études expérimentales sur l'attelage. Contribution à l'histoire du cheval.* Paris: Crépin-Leblond, (1977). London: Allen.

---

[18] Carter 1927: 112ff.

8

Another Storm God 'Jumping' on his Vehicle?
Remarks on the Sketch on KUB 20.76

Theo van den Hout

Although Hans Ehelolf published the Hittite cuneiform tablet KUB 20.76 in the series Keilschifturkunden aus Boghazköi no. 20 (Hethitische Festrituale, Berlin: 1927), he did not include a rare drawing in the hand copy of the cuneiform text, which dates into thirteenth century BCE. The drawing itself was published separately by Ursula Moortgat-Correns in 1952. Most of the tablet's surface in that area has broken away leaving only the part near the lower edge of the tablet relatively intact. As far as preserved, the drawing shows a dextroverse male wearing a pointed helmet with tassels hanging down from the tip as if fluttering in the wind, and possibly a horn or knob on the front of the helmet. The face, originally in profile, and shoulders are not preserved. The torso, as usual represented en face, with the right arm bent at the elbow and overlapping with the chest, is clearly visible but the left arm is gone. The right hand seems to be holding some object. Around the waist a kind of belt may be indicated. Below it, we see what likely was a kilt or skirt, with the figure's left leg lifted up and bent at the knee. The right leg below the hip and the left foot are not preserved. The paleography of the text dates the drawing to roughly the thirteenth century BCE. This contribution re-evaluates previous interpretations of the drawing and – based on an interpretation with other scenes in Hittite art such as a seal impression of Urhitessub/Mursili III and reliefs from Aleppo, Malatya and Imamkulu – endorses Hans Gustav Güterbock's interpretation from 1957 that the scene on the cuneiform tablet KUB 20.76 probably depicts a Hittite Storm God mounting his two-wheeled vehicle showing a cross-bar wheel.

Introduction and Formal Analysis

In a world where clay seems to have been the default medium, to which to entrust one's statements and thoughts in writing, one might expect there to have been artistic expressions in the form of drawings as well. Yet drawings, particularly figurative ones, are extremely rare: on a corpus of roughly 30,000 fragments of clay tablets we have so far recognised only three of them, a lion (KUB 28.4), two human heads (KUB 38.3), and a full human figure to be discussed below.[1] It is possible that the workings and work ethics of the state's chancellery, that generated these records, did not appreciate artistic outpourings of any kind unless strictly necessary. But more likely perhaps, in an oral society, writing is supposed to be primarily heard, not seen. Tablets were not there to be shown with illustrations explaining what writing might not easily convey. Whenever in Hittite Anatolia words and pictures occur side by side it is the text explaining the picture by way of captions, as we see them often in Hieroglyphic Luwian inscriptions, but not the other way around, and never, it seems, in combination with cuneiform script.[2] In the following I will discuss and reject some interpretations of the sketch on the tablet fragment known as KUB 20.76 and revive one that was almost off-handedly suggested 65 years ago in a footnote. At the end, I will briefly consider a possible philological consequence of the interpretation argued for below.

It is a great pleasure to be able to dedicate this essay to Joost Crouwel. I still remember my archaeology classes as a first-year student of Classical Philology in 1973 at the University of Amsterdam, taught by Joost on the Weesperzijde. He made me write my first (very brief) paper on a topic of Minoan archaeology. I also remember how I felt that here was an instructor who was passionate and at the forefront of his field.[3] So, it is an honour to dedicate this somewhat longer paper to Joost on the occasion of his 80th birthday along with my very best wishes for continued productivity!

The drawing of a male figure (Figures 8.1, 8.2) was added to the remaining blank space following the colophon in the fourth column of the tablet fragment KUB 20.76 (Bo 2566 + Bo 7553).[4] The drawing was not included in the hand copy of the cuneiform text by Hans Ehelolf in KUB 20, which came out in Berlin in 1927, and was published only as late as 1952 (see below). Ehelolf only noted there

---

[1] See in general Waal 2015: 82–84. I would like to express my gratitude here to Peter Raulwing, Jürgen Seeher, Steven Weingartner, and Willemijn Waal for their willingness to discuss the drawing with me and for their criticisms and suggestions. Obviously, I alone am responsible for the interpretation put forward here.

[2] The only exception might be the fragmentary drawing of an augur's possible field of vision or *templum* on the tablet KUB 49.60 iv (Sakuma 2014: 38 f.; 51); interesting from the point of view of text and image are also the liver omens in the shape of an actual liver, see de Vos 2013.

[3] See also the contribution of Doorewaard in this volume.

[4] The drawing is on Bo 2566. For the text of the colophon see Waal 2015: 454.

van den Hout

Figure 8.1. Photo of sketch on KUB 20.76. Courtesy of Vorderasiatisches Museum, Berlin.

Figure 8.2. Line drawing of sketch on KUB 20.76 by the author.

was under the colophon a blank space of about seventeen lines with, in its lower part, "sketches, among them a lower arm with fist."[5] Most of the tablet's surface in that area has broken away leaving only the part near the lower edge of the tablet relatively intact. As far as preserved, the drawing shows a dextroverse male wearing a pointed helmet with tassels hanging down from the tip as if fluttering in the wind, and possibly a horn or knob on the front of the helmet.[6] The top of the helmet almost touches the left edge of the tablet. The figure's face, originally in profile, and shoulders are not preserved. Only part of the lower jaw may be there. The torso, as usual represented *en face*, with the right arm bent at the elbow and overlapping with the chest, is clearly visible but the left arm is gone. The right hand seems to be holding some, as yet unidentified, object. Around the waist a kind of belt may be indicated. Below it, we see what in all likelihood was a kilt or skirt, with the figure's left leg lifted up and bent at the knee. The right leg below the hip and the left foot are not preserved. To the right of the legs, there are a few vertical lines, and further to the right some faint traces, of which it is unclear whether they are damage to the clay surface or remains of the sketch. The paleography of the text dates the drawing to roughly the thirteenth century BCE.[7]

From the point of view of the text's writing and reading direction, the artist turned the tablet 90 degrees to the right

creating a rectangular space of ca. 7 x 8.5 cm high and long framed by the tablet's left edge now on top, the lower *Randleiste*[8] on the left, the *intercolumnium*[9] at the bottom, and the colophon on the right. According to that colophon the text composition was part of the 'Great Festival of the town of Arinna,' an important cult center of the Hittite sun-goddess near Hattusa, the Hittite capital. The preserved text describes the various movements and actions of the king and queen, and of a number of high officials such as the chief of the royal bodyguard, the chief of the palace attendants, a herald, a cupbearer, the overseer of the 'waiters' as well as lower ranking personnel like singers, cooks, bodyguards, palace attendants, and reciters. Not a single deity is mentioned, but then, only part of the tablet has been preserved. Neither do other fragments from the same festival (CTH 634) offer any material relevant to the sketch discussed here. On the other hand, thousands of such cultic texts have come down to us without any 'illustrations' like this one. So, we should not necessarily expect there to be a meaningful relationship between text and drawing.

The sketch does not stop at the lower *Randleiste*: some lines at the top behind the helmet and in the middle continuing the line of the lower arm and elbow to the left are visible beyond the *Randleiste*. Looking at how this *Leiste* bisects these lines it seems as if it has been drawn after the sketch was made. The implications of this observation are not clear. Was the scribe himself the artist who finished his writing assignment, added the sketch, and then, to mark

---

[5] Ehelolf 1927 (KUB 20): 36: "Freier Raum von etwa 17 Zz. – Auf dem unteren Teil der Kolumne Ritzzeichnungen, u.a. ein Unterarm mit Faust."
[6] As remarked by Seeher 2007: 712, such tassels are rarely depicted in Hittite art.
[7] For a brief history and the importance of paleography in dating Hittite texts see van den Hout 2009.

[8] i.e., the horizontal line usually drawn by a scribe at the bottom of a tablet's obverse, top, and reverse; see Waal 2015: 103–107.
[9] i.e., the double and parallel vertical lines usually drawn by a scribe to divide a tablet into two or more columns; see Waal 2015: 91–94.

Another Storm God 'Jumping' on his Vehicle? Remarks on the Sketch on KUB 20.76

Figure 8.3. Reconstruction by Ursula Moortgat-Correns. Drawing after Moortgat-Correns 1952, Fig. 2.

the end of his work, as a final flourish, put in the *Randleiste*? Or did he, before doing so, let the artist do his/her work?

Previous Interpretations

Over the years, a few scholars have tried to interpret the fragmentary sketch. In 1952, Ursula Moortgat-Correns, who seems to have been the first one to publish it, noted the 90 degrees turn of the tablet and resulting *Querstellung* of the drawing vis-à-vis the text and indeed assumed identity between scribe and artist.[10] In the reconstruction accompanying the article (Figure 8.3) she considered two positions for the figure: either sitting or "im Knielauf." The *Knielaufschema* or *kneeling running* is a technical term for a low running movement often but certainly not exclusively associated with archers.[11] The decisive element for Moortgat-Correns was the round line beneath the skirt that she interpreted as the bent right knee. As a consequence, the next rounded line to the immediate right would indicate the left calf, and the next straight one, the left shin bone. Rejecting a seated position, therefore, she opted for the *Knielauf* although there is no parallel for it in Hittite iconography. She also noted the two crescent-shaped additions on the lower right arm and near the buttocks and the two circles, one behind the figure's head and one below the right arm. She considered them doodles (*Kritzeleien*), probably without any relation to the depicted figure. Finally, she dated the drawing into the 14th/13th century following Heinrich Otten's paleographic criteria (p. 40): "Da jedoch Text und Zeichnung aus technischen Gründen zu gleicher Zeit entstanden sein müssen, kann die Zeichnung ebenfalls nur in das 14. bis 13. Jahrhundert gehören."

Margarete Riemschneider, in her 1954 book *Die Welt der Hethiter*, opted for a sitting deity without presenting any arguments for her choice.[12] In the proceedings of a symposium on *Narration in Ancient Art*, held at the Oriental Institute of Chicago in 1955[13], Hans Güterbock briefly referred to the drawing and Moortgat-Correns' interpretation in a footnote: "If the knee really is bent, the god may have been stepping onto his chariot (…) rather than being in 'Knielauf,' a position not befitting a great god!" For his interpretation he referred to the Iron Age relief MALATYA 8[14] (Figure 8.4, left) showing the Storm God stepping on his bull-drawn two-wheeled vehicle[15] with a curved weapon in his raised right hand.

Figure 8.4. MALATYA 8 (from Hawkins 2000, vol. 3 Plate 149). Courtesy of J. D. Hawkins.

---

[10] Moortgat-Correns 1952. Emil Forrer did mention the presence of a drawing on Bo 2566 but nothing more (Forrer 1922, 180: "auch Bo. 2566 trägt eine Zeichnung").
[11] Sapienza 2017.
[12] Riemschneider 1954: 242 with Plate 43.
[13] Güterbock 1957: 70 n. 55.
[14] See Hawkins 2000 vol. 3, Plate 149 with photo and drawing; on the date see p. 306. Güterbock refers to it as Malatya "K." In Güterbock 1993, dealing with the sea impression of Urhitessub, the Malatya 8 and Karkamish reliefs (see below), he no longer mentioned KUB 20.76.
[15] As correctly pointed out in a personal communication by Nolke Tasma (Leiden), instead of the Storm God mounting his chariot one could also see him as stepping down from it and subsequently receiving the offering. This supposes that the two gods are one and the same (thus also Güterbock 1957: 65; Hawkins 2000: 309) with the caption "DEUS.TONITRUS" placed strategically in between them. If a narrative is indeed intended here, it could, however, also be the Storm God setting out on his journey and being worshiped on arrival. According to Dietz 2019: 192, it might also be "another instance of the god and his cult statue being displayed together in one medium, which would make the god in front of the libating king the actual god and the god ascending the chariot the cult statue."

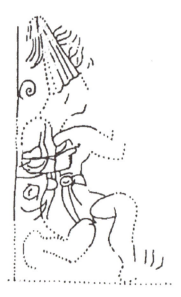

Figure 8.5. Reconstruction by Jutta Börker-Klähn. Drawing after Börker-Klähn 1999, Fig. b 1-3.

Figure 8.6. Alaca Höyük, Storm God on his throne. After Bittel 1976: 195, Fig. 221.

Without committing himself, in a 1989 article on "Drawings, Graffiti and Squiggles" on Hittite tablets, Ahmet Ünal rejected both Moortgat-Correns' and Güterbock's interpretations.[16] The former because the *Knielauf* is not attested in Hittite visual culture and the latter because nothing is left of the supposed two-wheeler ("The three vertical lines in front of the legs can hardly be the traces of a wheel"). As a further option he considers "the god might be sitting on a very simple stool."

Finally, Jutta Börker-Klähn in 1999 stressed at the outset that in a sketch not every line may be intended as final. She used this observation to explain the lines around the right elbow, which, she claimed, was at first drawn too short and then lengthened onto the lower edge. The crescent-looking shape, for instance, visible in the lower right arm would be the result of a repeated attempt to draw the elbow. She described the figure's stance as "vehemently moving" ("in heftiger Bewegung", p. 54) with the volute visible behind the figure's head possibly representing part of his hair flying in the wind. Referring to the sherd of a relief vase and to cultic texts mentioning "dancers" ($^{\text{LÚ.MEŠ}}$ḪUB.BI/ḪUB.BÍ/ḪÚB.BI/ḪÚB.BÍ) Börker-Klähn reconstructed the right leg as pulled up towards the buttocks and, since dancing deities are not attested, the figure as a dancer dressed as a god (Figure 8.5). As to the four lines to the right of the left leg in her drawing, she wondered about some object in front of the figure or "even toes seen from below."

Interpretation

Reviewing these interpretations, sitting can be ruled unlikely, as sitting figures in relief always seem to have both feet depicted one before the other, as, for instance, the Storm God on his throne at Alaca Höyük (Figure 8.6). This is the usual artist's way to render in two dimensions two feet that were next to each other in sculpture-in-the-round, as can be seen, for instance, in the small gold pendant of a goddess from the Metropolitan Museum (Figure 8.7).

Likewise, standing or walking can be ruled out because of the lifted left leg. If we take the Twelve-Gods relief at Yazılıkaya (Figure 8.8) as representing a phalanx of marching gods, it is the right heel lifted off the ground with the forefoot and the full left foot firmly on the ground, that suggests movement.

As a consequence, the other gods at Yazılıkaya can be taken as standing with both feet fully and firmly planted on the ground but clearly wider apart than seen in the sit-

Figure 8.7. Seated goddess with her two feet (in the center) next to each other, ca. fourteenth–thirteenth century BCE Gift of Norbert Schimmel Trust, 1989 Accession Number: 1989.281.12 Courtesy of Metropolitan Museum of Art, New York ("Open Access" program).

---

[16] Ünal 1989: 507 f.

Figure 8.8. Twelve gods marching. Yazılıkaya reliefs nos. 69-81. Photo by the author.

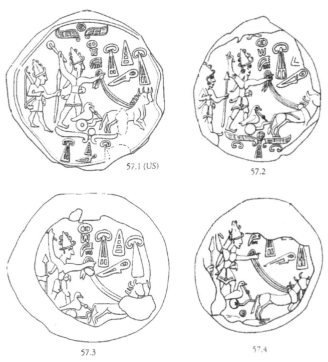

Figure 8.11. Drawings of various impressions of Urhitessub/ Mursili III seal (from Herbordt et al. 2011: no. 57). Courtesy of Suzanne Herbordt.

Figure 8.9. Relief of IMAMKULU (from Alexander 1991: 170). Drawing after D. Alvarado.

Figure 8.10. Drawing of the cylinder seal impression AO 20138 (Louvre). Drawing after Parrot 1951: 183, Fig. 2.

ting figures. Again, this is the artist's way to render in two dimensions two feet that were next to each other in a three-dimensional world. The *Knielauf* can indeed be considered unlikely for being unattested elsewhere in Late Bronze Age Anatolia. The same is true, finally, for dancing since there are no parallels for dancing gods or for cultic personnel dressed as gods.

That leaves Güterbock's suggestion of a god mounting his two-wheeler. When writing "If the knee really is bent," he may have confused the bent right knee, as Moortgat-Correns saw it and which made her opt for the *Knielauf*, with the clearly lifted and bent left knee. For Güterbock must have been talking about the left leg since the right one, when stepping on a two-wheeler in dextroverse direction, is always straight (see below). Nevertheless, he may well have been right with his suggestion. At the time of

the symposium in 1955 only three clear examples of such depictions were known: the Late Bronze Age IMAMKULU relief (Figure 8.9),[17] the closely related unprovenanced cylinder seal AO 20138 of uncertain date from the Louvre (Figure 8.10),[18] and the Iron Age MALATYA 8 (Figure 8.4). Meanwhile, three others have become known: the seal impression of Urhitessub/Mursili III (ca. 1274-1267 BCE, Figure 8.11)[19] from Boğazköy, the ALEPPO 4 relief probably dating to the 11th century BCE (Figure 8.12),[20] and from Boğazköy the fragment of a relief vase[21] (Figure 8.13).[22] A possible seventh example is the "much damaged" relief from the Water Gate at Karkamish mentioned by Guy Bunnens in his publication of the TELL AHMAR 6 stele with inscription[23] (Figure 8.14).[24] As Bunnens writes, the "chariot is no longer visible" but he assumes it "can be safely restored." He dates the relief to the 11th cen-

---

[17] See also Kohlmeyer 1983: 83 (Fig. 33). For the correct reading of the hieroglyphic caption to the right of the Storm God just over his underarm see Hawkins 2003. With his reading of the supposed TONITRUS sign as the fourth hieroglyph from the top, the suggestion by Börker-Klähn 1977: 64–65, that it might represent the thunderbolt as the Storm God's weapon should now be given up.

[18] Parrot 1951; Parrot (1951: 190) dates it around the middle of the second millennium, Güterbock 1993: 114 to the second half of the 13th century BCE.

[19] See Hawkins 2003, Herbordt et al. 2011: no. 57 and the discussion ibid. 60 f.

[20] See Kohlmeyer 2000: pls. 16 f.

[21] See Seeher 2007.

[22] I am leaving out of consideration the fragment of a relief vase, also from Boğazköy, briefly discussed in Littauer/Crouwel 1979: 56 with Ill. 27, showing one foot on a "bovid-drawn two-wheeler … [on an] entirely open platform, and mentioned also in Seeher 2007: 712.

[23] Bunnens 2006: 127.

[24] For a possible Old Assyrian example see Dietz 2019: 192–193 Fig. 4.

van den Hout

Figure 8.12 (a and b). ALEPPO 4 relief. Courtesy of Kay Kohlmeyer.

tury, whereas Güterbock prefers a pre-1200 dating on stylistic grounds.[25] Let us first address the human figures in those depictions and then the supposed bull-drawn two-wheeler.

In general, the center of a human figure is around the waist or loins, and this is true also of all Storm God figures considered here. This means that, if we assume one straight leg, our figure's base or ground line should be just above the *intercolumnium* line and the artist thus used the entire column width for his upright figure. All dextroverse figures in the parallel scenes hold their right leg straight while they lift their left leg to step onto the two-wheeler; for the sinistroverse Karkamish Stormgod and the one on AO 20138 it is his left leg. For the KUB 20.76 drawing, however, Moortgat-Correns (and Börker-Klähn following her) imagined the slight curve of the hip and buttocks continuing on and were perhaps influenced by the curving shape of the break in the tablet's surface that seems to follow. Once that assumption has been made the curved line, as indicated in Moortgat-Correns' rendering (Figure 8.3), can indeed be nothing else than the right knee. But that same slight rounding of the hip and buttocks can be seen in the Urhitessub sealing (Figure 8.11: 57.3), the ALEPPO 4 relief, and the relief vase but it is combined with a perfectly straight leg coming from under the kilt. The same can be reconstructed for the drawing on KUB 20.76. In the Moortgat-Correns and Börker-Klähn reconstructions the figure hovers somewhat awkwardly in the air, suspended as it were, from the left edge of the tablet.[26]

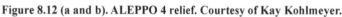

Figure 8.13. Fragment of a relief vase from Boğazköy (from Seeher 2007, Abb. 8a and b). Courtesy of Jürgen Seeher.

As to the left leg, in the Iron Age examples from ALEPPO 4 and MALATYA 8, or the right one in AO 20138 and the Karkamish relief, it is shown in its entirety whereas in the Urhitessub sealing, AO 20138, and (probably) the relief vase the foot goes hidden behind the two-wheeler box: in the first two the god is in the process of stepping, in the latter three his foot is already on the two-wheeler. The very weathered IMAMKULU and Karkamish reliefs look ambiguous in this respect. The IMAMKULU drawings by Robert Alexander and Horst Ehringhaus both show the left lower leg disappearing behind the two-wheeler box but the angle between thigh and lower leg on some photos could also be taken to suggest otherwise.[27] If one assumes that the entire left leg was visible in the drawing on KUB 20.76, the almost horizontal line below the knee could be the same one as visible also in the Urhitessub seal impression (Figure 8.11: 57.2 and 3) and represent the kneecap. According to

---

[25] Güterbock 1993: 115.
[26] Note that in her reconstruction sketch (Fig. 5) Börker-Klähn (1999) adds an imaginary ground line.

[27] Alexander 1991: 170, Ehringhaus 2005: 72 drawing different than the one in Alexander 1991). For the IMAMKULU relief see also Hazenbos 2002.

Figure 8.14. The relief from the Water Gate at Karkamish (from Woolley 1921, Plate B. 30, a).

Jürgen Seeher, the kneecap is also indicated in the relief vase.[28]

It looks as if the artist struggled with rendering the hemline of the kilt. Anatolian kilts, both in the Late Bronze Age and the Iron Age and also in the sketch under discussion, usually show a vertical or diagonal element in front, which can be either something like an embroidery or woven-in pattern, possibly on the seam, where the fabric was sewn together, or the kilt consisted of a wrap-around piece of textile with the opening worn in front. The latter would allow more freedom of movement. When a man was standing, the two overlapping ends of the cloth simply came together more or less forming a straight hemline. But when one of the legs was lifted this was no longer the case and the hemline had to be adjusted in a drawing, as can be seen in the Aleppo 4 relief and the Urhitessub seal impression. The artist of the Malatya 8 relief kept the Storm God's legs closer together and used curved hemlines (*geschwungene Säume*[29]) that we see more often both in the Late Bronze Age and Iron Age.

Turning to the presence of a bull-drawn two-wheeler, as implied in Güterbock's suggestion, the biggest problems are (a) the whereabouts of a supposed wheel and (b) what the preserved four vertical lines in front of the lifted foot are. But first of all, we need to go back to the *Querstellung* of the drawing relative to the cuneiform text (Figure 8.15).

In fact, Güterbock's interpretation is the only one that makes us understand why the artist turned the tablet 90 degrees. Supposing the text had been finished when the drawing was added and the artist planned to draw a single figure, a skilled artist would never have pushed the figure all the way up against the lower edge leaving the rest blank. He or she could have used the remaining space in 'portrait'-orientation following the colophon without turning the tablet. The artist could have centered the lone figure in the available space and made it larger. The reason he or she turned the tablet must have been to obtain a rectangular space in 'landscape'-orientation to accommodate something in front of the figure, as also shown by the four lines to the right of the lifted leg. Besides the MALATYA 8 relief,

[28] Seeher 2007: 710.
[29] For the expression see, for instance, Ehringhaus 2005: 83.

Figure 8.15. Photo of KUB 20.76 col. iv with the last lines of the colophon visible on the right. Courtesy of Daniel Schwemer, Mainzer Photoarchiv, Akademie der Wissenschaften und der Literatur.

Figure 8.16. The striated railing of the two-wheeler box on Aleppo 4. Detail from Fig. 12. Courtesy of Kay Kohlmeyer.

where the depiction of the Storm God and his two-wheeler is as high as it is long, the two-wheeler scenes on the Urhitessub sealing and the IMAMKULU and Karkamish reliefs are twenty to thirty percent longer than they are high. That same space is available in front of the figure on KUB 20.76 and I therefore think the artist used it to add a two-wheeler with a bull (or bulls). Note that in three of the five parallels where the animals are preserved, the Storm God's two-wheeler and his emblematic bull(s) are all disproportionate, that is, small in relation to the Storm God. Only in ALEPPO 4 and Karkamish do the proportions of the animal(s) seem more reasonable, esp. the head of the bull, creating something of a balance in the relief that is lacking in the other three.

The vehicle's wheel in these scenes is usually as high or somewhat smaller than the lower straight leg and partly under and partly in front of the lifted left leg. There is enough room to assume the same for KUB 20.76, in front of the lifted leg and under the four preserved lines. What can these lines indicate? On the IMAMKULU relief and the Urhitessub sealing only the general outline of the two-wheeler box is discernable, and the relief vase shows just enough of the top of the front to recognise the bird shape.

But the ALEPPO 4 relief shows its edge or rim to have been striated and curving downwards from the front, then upwards to the knee and making a sharp turn down again to disappear behind the wheel (Figure 8.16). With Seeher, we can imagine that the top of the box is a 'rudimentary' representation of the Late Bronze Age bird shape. The striations may be a continuation of the bird's plumage visible in the ALEPPO relief.

Assuming a similar edge or rim for the two-wheeler box in KUB 20.76 the four lines in question may be what remains of the artist's way of drawing it. Obviously, the drawing on the tablet may well have had the original bird shape. With that, we also still have enough room for one or two bulls in front of the two-wheeler, as shown in the reconstruction drawing in Figure 8.17. I have used here the bulls of MALATYA 8 in David Hawkins' copy as a placeholder to show the similarities with the other parallel scenes and how this design would easily have fit the available space.

Figure 8.17. Reconstruction of what the original design on KUB 20.76 might have looked like by the author.

If this reconstruction is correct, we can safely identify the figure in the drawing on KUB 20.76 as the Storm God, since in three of the parallels (IMAMKULU, Urhitessub-sealing, MALATYA 8) the figure mounting his vehicle is explicitly identified as such by a hieroglyphic caption. If our sketch here once had a caption is unknown. Although the DEUS MATTEA ("mace god")[30] of the ALEPPO 4 relief is not marked as a Storm God his weapon, the club or mace, is the same as the Storm Gods wield in the other three. The Aleppo Storm God is also the only one who holds his right arm bent to his chest, which then leads to the question:

What Does the God of KUB 20.76 Hold in his Hand?

The Storm Gods of IMAMKULU, the Urhitessub sealing, and the MALATYA 8 relief, all have their right arms raised as in the "classical" smiting god pose. In the Karkamish relief it is the god's left arm; on AO 20138 the god holds both arms outstretched, each grasping a rein, but he also has a stick- or staff-like object ("bâton")[31] in his right hand. Only the ALEPPO 4 god holds his arm to his side, bent at the elbow while clutching a mace in his right hand. The mace is repeated—although with a slightly heavier mace head—in the hieroglyphic caption that identifies him as the "mace god." Only on the relief vase is the weapon broken away. Given all these parallels, the god of KUB 20.76 probably also holds a club or mace.[32] The weapon that the two Storm Gods on MALATYA 8 are swinging shows a boomerang-like curve and the same may be true of the god on IMAMKULU. The weapon held by the gods on the Karkamish and ALEPPO reliefs is a more 'classical' mace, that is, a shaft with a probably rounded (?) head at the top. The most substantial mace head is the one seen on the Urhitessub sealing (Figure 8.10: 57.1), showing a full circle. This could be taken as an argument to interpret the circle visible just to the left of the pointed helmet as such a mace head but ultimately this has to remain uncertain. The biggest problem is that in the sketch on KUB 20.76 the right hand does not grasp the shaft of the alleged mace, which is drawn behind the wrist instead of the hand. To the right of the shaft there seems to be indicated some kind of extension(?) that the hand is actually grasping. The only other possibility is to look at the texts below under 5. describing a Storm God jumping on his vehicle as either "thundering" (*tetḫešnanza*, KUB 33.106 + i 8) or "with (his) thunder" (*tetḫešnaza*, ibid. iv 21): could the lines somehow have been intended to depict thunderbolts?[33]

---

[30] Hawkins 2011: 40: "(a) DEUS.MATTEA Divine Mace (b) (DEUS) CERVUS2-ti (Ku)runtiya. (…) DEUS.MATTEA ('God Mace') is an unparalleled writing and curious as the epigraph to this icon. The link has been made to the 'weapon' (GIŠTUKUL) of the Storm-God of Aleppo, which itself possessed cultic status (Kohlmeyer 2000: 31–32 […]). The epigraph might refer specifically to the mace on the god's shoulder, and in this way it would avoid clashing with the other epigraph, ALEPPO 5, identifying the older figure of the Storm-God of Aleppo placed in the middle of the east wall in the Hittite Empire phase of the temple lay-out."
[31] Parrot 1951: 183.

[32] Deities standing with their arm bent at the elbow can be seen holding various weapons or objects: axes, spears, bows, clubs or maces, sickle swords, throwing sticks, or *litui* but all the parallels point to a mace.
[33] This admittedly somewhat far-fetched interpretation draws its inspiration from Börker-Klähn's idea (see above fn. 16) that the second TONITRUS sign on the IMAMKULU relief might be the Storm God's weapon, which has to be abandoned now, however.

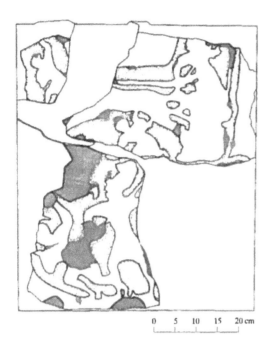

Figure 8.18. Old Hittite relief from Büyükkale (from Schachner 2012: 133 Abb. 1). Courtesy of Andreas Schachner.

What vehicle does the Storm God ride in the texts?

The existence of seven images (or eight if one includes the drawing on KUB 20.76), that is, four from the Late Bronze Age (Bo.-relief vase, IMAMKULU, AO 20138, Urhitessub-sealing), three from the Iron Age (MALATYA 8, ALEPPO 4, Karkamish) of a Storm God mounting a bull-drawn two-wheeler ranging from the fifteenth (the Boğazköy-relief vase) and the thirteenth centuries BCE (the Urhitessub sealing), to the tenth or ninth century BCE attests to a lasting iconographic motif. Another recurring image is the Storm God *standing on* his chariot known already from the Early Bronze Age onwards.[34] In Hittite visual culture, images of wheeled vehicles generally are quite rare.[35] Besides the Late Bronze Age examples discussed here, we have the 'Old-Hittite' relief from Büyükkale (Figure 8.18)[36] and the wagon or cart on the Hüseyindede vase A from the Çorum province. The identity of the charioteer on the Büyükkale relief is unclear, as is the exact nature of the harnessed animal(s) (bull(s) or horse(s)?; the vehicle on the Hüseyindede vase is clearly a loaded wagon (*Lastwagen*) but whether it was a two- or four-wheeled wagon is, unfortunately, difficult to determine.[37]

As far as the Late Bronze Age is concerned, because of the captions, only in the case of IMAMKULU and the Urhitessub sealing are we with certainty dealing with the Storm God but his identity seems likely also in the case of the other parallels. Of course, in real life, a war chariot would never be drawn by bulls or bovines, but in the case of the Storm God, it is no surprise that two bulls, his iconic animals, Seri and Hurri (or Tella, as one of them is called in the Ullikummi myth),[38] draw his chariot. What is interesting, is the observation that the Storm God in the mounting pose with one leg lifted while stepping onto the chariot, seems thus far attested in (Syro-)Anatolian context only.[39]

Turning to the various Hittite texts where the god is mentioned together with his vehicle, when a Sumerogram is used, it is always a ⁽ᴳᴵˢ⁾MAR.GÍD.DA(.ḪI.A). The standard interpretation is that of a four-wheeled or two-axled vehicle, a wagon.[40] The translation "wagon/*Lastwagen*" is probably based on a few occurrences with the verb *taištae*- "to load", compare:

nu ᴸᵁ́SANGA *IŠTU* NINDA.ḪI.A KAŠ[≠*ia*] ᴳᴵˢMAR.GÍD.DA.ḪI.A *ta*[*e*]*štiyazi* ... *nu* ᴳᴵˢMAR.GÍD.DA.ḪI.A *IŠTU* MUN *ta*[*e*]*š'tiyanzi*

The priest loads the ᴳᴵˢMAR.GÍD.DA.ḪI.A with bread (and) beer ... and they load the ᴳᴵˢMAR.GÍD.DA.ḪI.A with salt (IBoT 2.131 rev. 6–7, 16–17, CTH 528 – NS)

But if we combine the iconographic evidence with what we find in the texts, it is clear that the ⁽ᴳᴵˢ⁾MAR.GÍD.DA(.ḪI.A) as the vehicle used by the Storm God could also denote a two-wheeler/chariot and did not always have to refer to a (four-wheeled) vehicle or wagon.[41] For the Storm God *standing* on a two-wheeler or chariot, as often attested iconographically, see, for instance, the following Old Hittite *Bildbeschreibung*:

nu aniyattan teḫḫe MAR.GÍD.DA IM-*aš* GU₄.ḪI.A-*uš* IM-*aš šēr-a-ššan* MAR.GÍD.DA-*aš* IM-*aš* LÚ. ᵈIM-*an iyami n-aš-šan* MAR.GÍD.DA-*aš šēr arta nu išḫarwanta* ᴷᵁˢ⁷*išmeri ḫarz*[*i*]

As a ritual, I place a MAR.GÍD.DA of clay (and) bulls of clay and on the MAR.GÍD.DA of clay I shape a Man-of-the-Storm God and he stands on the MAR.GÍD.DA and he holds bloodied/blood-red reins (KBo 30.39 rev. 14–17 + KUB 35.164 iii! 11–14, CTH 752 – OS)

---

[34] For the image of a Storm God mounting an either two- or four-wheeled vehicle already in the Early Bronze Age see Boehmer 1965 Abb. 372 (two-wheeled), 373 f. (four-wheeled); see also Schwemer 2008: 31–36. For yet another chariot-related motif see Aro 2014, seemingly reserved for earthly rulers (as opposed to the Storm God) in a war context with one or even two accompanying figures standing on the chariot and sometimes trampling an enemy; see also Duru 2004: 31 Fig. 14 and Plates 39 and 41, for an example from Yesemek.

[35] van den Hout 2014–16: 625 f.

[36] See Schachner 2012: 133 Abb. 1.

[37] For a drawing see Yıldırım 2007: 850 Fig. 6.1. The reconstruction drawing shows it with only one axle. The front of the cart is broken away (as is visible on the photo) but the arch indicating the load suggests that the front is near; yet there could have been another, second axle and pair of wheels.

[38] Schwemer 2001: 483 f. For the Ullikummi myth see Güterbock 1951 and 1952 as well as Hoffner 2017.

[39] Bunnens 2006: 127.

[40] CAD s.v. *eriqqu* ("wagon, cart"), see also for Hittite HZL no. 191 ("Lastwagen"), Weeden 2011: 575 ("cart"); Yıldırım 2007: 844 f.; see also van den Hout 2014–16: 622 on further Hittite terminology for vehicles.

[41] I cannot follow Dietz 2019: 193 who claims that the vehicle on the Old Assyrian example (see above fn. 23) was a four-wheeler: again, we are dealing with the rendering of a 3D reality in a 2D medium.

The detail of the blood-stained reins suggests a war-like context. Also, since the (singular) Man-of-the-Storm God cannot stand on more than one vehicle at a time, it shows that the Hittite word behind ⁽ᴳᴵˢ⁾MAR.GÍD.DA(.ḪI.A)-*aš* (plural dative-locative) was in all likelihood a collective plural or *plurale tantum*, as is likely because it is being counted with Akkadian TAPAL and marked by the Sumerian plural morphemes MEŠ and ḪI.A.[42] The character of the vehicle as a war chariot becomes explicit in a few passages from the Ullikummi Myth. Kumarbi has created a stone monster named Ullikummi in his fight against the Storm God. After the goddess Ishtar has tried in vain to charm the creature into submission it is time for the Storm God to come into action. His bulls, Serisu and Tella, are readied and harnessed, the ᴳᴵˢMAR.GÍD.DA.ḪI.A is brought out, and finally the Storm God himself steps forth to fight (*z*)*aḫḫiyauwanzi*[iv 10):

namma=za UNUT M[È *and*]*a ēpta* ᴳᴵˢMAR.GÍD.DA.ḪI.A=*ia*[*=za*] *anda ēpta n*[*u nepi*]*šaza arḫa alpa*ᴴᴵ·ᴬ *pēda*[*š*]

Then, he held on to his ba[ttle] gear, he grabbed [his] ᴳᴵˢMAR.GÍD.DA.ḪI.A and he brought the clouds from heaven (KUB 33.106 iv 3–4 + KUB 36.14: 4–5, CTH 345 – NS)

These passages alone already make it unlikely that the Storm God, off to war, is riding a bulky transport wagon, but the images discussed above show that this was a true chariot.

As to the verb used, in the *Bildbeschreibung* quoted earlier the Man-of-the-Storm-God was "standing" on the ᴳᴵˢMAR.GÍD.DA: the verb we find is the deponent *ar*-. For the Storm God not yet in battle but mounting it, we twice find the verb *watku*-, both again in the Ullikummi Myth, once for the Storm God's first and doomed attempt to defeat Ullikummi and once when he rides out a second time after Ullikummi has probably already been felled by the primeval saw that long ago had cut heaven and earth apart. The choice of *watku*- "to jump" instead of the more calm or regular *tiya*- "to step" also contributes to the battle-like urgency of the scene.[43] In the former passage Astabi, a lesser deity,[44] rushes to help the Storm God. The text is very fragmentary:

4. ᵈ*Aštabiš=kan* [...]
5. *watkut n=aš=kan* ᴳᴵˢMAR.GÍD.D[A...]
6. ᴳᴵˢ*tiyarita nininkiš*[*kezzi*...]
7. *nu tetḫeškezzi* ᵈ*Aštabiš nu* x[...]
8. *nu=kan tetḫešnanza* ᵈ*Aštābiš a*-x[...]
9. *aruni* GAM-*anda tarnaš nu* ᴳᴵˢMAR.GÍD.DA!

wātar [...]
10. *ḫaniēr nu* ᵈ*Aštabiš* [*t*]*ittiya*[- ...]

"Astabi jumped [...] and [on?] the chariot he stands/stood? [...] He set[s] the chariot(?) in motion [...] He thunders, Astabi, and ... [...] Thundering(?) Astabi ... [...] down into the sea he let go and the chariot water [...] they scooped and Astabi ..." (KUB 33.106 + KBo 57.49 i 4–10, CTH 345 – NS)

The latter passage is the better preserved of the two:

ᵈU-*aš=kan* ᴳᴵˢ*tiyaridaš šarā gagaštiyaš mān watkut n=aš=kan tetḫešnaza katta aruni āraš n=an zaḫḫeškezzi* ᵈU-*aš* ᴺᴬ⁴*kunkunuzin*

The Storm God jumped on his chariot like a *gagaštiya*- and with (his) thunder [*tetḫešnaza*] he reached the sea below and the Storm God started to fight him, the Stone (KUB 33.106 iv 21–22, CTH 345 – NS)

Unfortunately, *gagaštiya*- is a hapax and its meaning therefore unknown. Previous editors and translators of the text have usually taken it as denoting some kind of animal.[45] Although that is certainly possible other similes (e.g., like fire, like the wind, like a storm) are equally well imaginable. Whether ᴳᴵˢMAR.GÍD.DA(.ḪI.A) and ᴳᴵˢ*tiyarid*- can be equated, as it has been suggested, remains uncertain.[46] Both words share the GIŠ determinative and the status of being *pluralia tantum*. However, ᴳᴵˢ*tiyarid*- has been interpreted in various ways and the evidence is confusing. On the basis of a lexical text from Ugarit where Hurrian *teari* is glossed as Akkadian *pilakku* "spindle"[47] Frank Starke translates the preceding passage as "Der Wettergott sprang wie Wirteln oben auf den Spindeln."[48] Volkert Haas, on the other hand, equated Hurrian *tiyari* with Hittite *zuppari*- "torch" on the basis of a text from the *hisuwa*-festival.[49] Is it possible that *tiyarid*- is a loanword from Hurrian into Luwian[50] originally denoting a pole- or stick-like object that could be "spindle" and/or "torch" in Hurrian

---

[42] Thus, already Güterbock 1993: 116, cf. Hoffner/Melchert 2008: 159 f.; see also van den Hout 2014-16: 624.
[43] For *tiya*- see KUB 20.96 iii 20 *t=aš* (i.e., the king) *=kan* ᴳᴵˢGIGIR-*ni tiyazi*.
[44] On this see Ayali-Darshan 2014.

[45] See HW² K s.v.
[46] Güterbock 1952: 41: "iii 13: In favour of the proposed equation ᴳᴵˢMAR.GÍD.DA = ᴳᴵˢ*tiiarit*(*a*-) (*Kum.* p. 76), Otten privately quoted Code § 122, where ᴳᴵˢMAR.GÍD-*it* occurs as accusative (or should one correct that into ᴳᴵˢMAR.GÍD.DA?). I have used this equation in the transcription and translation, indicating uncertainty of the reading *tiyarit*(*a*-) where the text has ᴳᴵˢMAR.GÍD.DA of the translation 'cart' where the text has *tiyarit*. As for the choice of the English word 'cart' for the vehicle used by the gods in battle, cf. Kum. p. 77; apparently the gods rode on ox-carts as depicted in Arslantepe and Imamkulu."
[47] Laroche 1977: 265 ("fuseau").
[48] Starke 1990: 218-220, followed by Rieken et al., hethiter.net/: CTH 345.I.3.1 (TX 2009-08-31, TRde 2009-08-30), and Ayali Darshan 2014: 97. The text IBoT 2.129 obv. 5–6 quoted by Starke is of very little help since it has no obvious connection to either vehicles or spinning at all and the reading rests on the emendation of the first sign to GIŠ! whereas photo and hand copy point to either TE or DU (note that HW2 A s.v. *arimpa*-¹ reads (-)*du*-). CCL 231 s.v. *tiyarit* "For discussion see Starke, StBoT 31.218ff, whose interpretation 'spindle' is possible, but the pl. tantum would be odd."
[49] Haas 2003: 170; for further lit. see Richter 2012: 156 f. s.v. *tiaru/tijari*.
[50] For this see Starke 1990: 210 f.

but in Luwian perhaps "axle", standing *pars pro toto* for a wheeled vehicle?[51]

In the end, trying to interpret and to tentatively restore the drawing is much like the text restorations that we, Hittitologists, often make: an educated guess. It is easy to reject other interpretations and restorations but proving one is difficult. In the case of texts with a damaged surface, as is the case with KUB 20.76, waiting for a join piece does not come into question. But a previous text restoration can sometimes be confirmed (or falsified) by a duplicate manuscript. Hoping for such a duplicate that has the same drawing seems very unrealistic, given the rarity of such drawings. So, in this case parallels are the only thing we can rely on and they point to another Storm God jumping on his chariot.

Theo van den Hout
Arthur and Joann Rasmussen Professor Emeritus of Hittite and Anatolian Languages, Institute for the Study of Ancient Cultures – West Asia & North Africa, and Executive Editor, Chicago Hittite Dictionary Project

Abbreviations

Bo — Boğazköy

CAD — *The Assyrian Dictionary of the Oriental Institute of the University of Chicago.* 21 vols. Chicago: Chicago University Press, 1956–2010. (https://oi.uchicago.edu/research/publications/assyrian-dictionary-oriental-institute-university-chicago-cad).

CHD — *The Hittite Dictionary of the Oriental Institute of the University of Chicago*, 1980 ff. (https://oi.uchicago.edu/research/publications/hittite-dictionary-oriental-institute-university-chicago-chd).

CTH — Emmanuel Laroche, *Catalogue des textes hittites*, 2nd ed. Paris: Klincksieck, 1971. (see also: https://www.hethport.uni-wuerzburg.de/CTH/).

HW² — Johannes Friedrich and Annelies Kammenhuber, *Hethitisches Wörterbuch*, 2nd ed. Heidelberg: Winter, 1975 ff.

HZL — Christel Rüster and Erich Neu, *Hethitisches Zeichenlexikon. Inventar und Interpretation der Keilschriftzeichen aus den Boğazköy-Texten* (Studien zu den Boğazköy-Texten, Beihefte 2). Wiesbaden: Harrassowitz, 1989.

IBoT — İstanbul Arkeoloji Müzelerinde Bulunan Boğazköy Tabletleri(nden Seç Metinler). Istanbul 1944, 1947, 1954; Ankara 1988.

KUB — Keilschrifturkunden aus Boghazköi, 60 vols. Berlin: 1921–90.

KUB 20 — See Ehelolf 1927 and Groddek 2004 for transliterations.

NS — New Script (Hittite cuneiform used ca. 1350-1200 BCE).

OS — Old Script (Hittite cuneiform used ca. 1600-1400/1350 BCE).

StBoT — Studien zu den Boğazköy-Texten. Wiesbaden: Harrassowitz, 1965 ff.

Bibliography

Alexander, Robert. 1991. Šaušga and the Hittite Ivory from Megiddo. *Journal of Near Eastern Studies* 50: 161–182.

Aro, Sanna. 2014. The Relief on the Slab NKL 2 at Karatepe-Azatiwataya: Neo-Assyrian Impact in Cilicia? In: *From Source to History. Studies on Ancient Near Eastern Worlds and Beyond Dedicated to Giovanni Battista Lanfranchi on the Occasion of His 65th Birthday on June 23, 2014*, edited by Salvatore Gaspa et al., 11–31. Münster: Ugarit-Verlag.

Ayali-Darshan, Noga. 2014. The Role of Aštabi in the *Song of Ullikummi* and the Eastern Mediterranean "Failed God" Stories. *Journal of Near Eastern Studies* 73: 95–103.

Bittel, Kurt. 1976. *Die Hethiter. Die Kunst Anatoliens vom Ende des 3. bis zum Anfang des 1. Jahrtausends vor Christus.* Universum der Kunst 24. München: Beck.

Boehmer, Rainer Michael. 1965. *Die Entwicklung der Glyptik während der Akkad-Zeit.* Berlin: de Gruyter.

Börker-Klähn, Jutta. 1977. Imamkulu gelesen und datiert? Zeitschrift für Assyriologie 67: 64–72.

---

[51] cf. "wheels" in American English? Although not a reading for ᴳᴵˢMAR.GÍD.DA, for ⁽ᴳᴵˢ⁾ḫulukanni- (a vehicle) in immediate context with ᴳᴵˢMAR.GÍD.DA see KUB 2.3 v 33–38 (ed. Singer 1984: 69); see also Taracha 2000: 121, HW² Ḫ 705–710 and van den Hout 2014–16: 622.

Börker-Klähn, Jutta. 1999. Schrift-Bilder. *Ugarit-Forschungen* 31: 51–73.

Bunnens, Guy. 2006. *A New Luwian Stele and the Cult of the Storm-God at Til Barsib-Masuwari*. Louvain [etc.]: Peeters.

de Vos, An. 2013 *Die Lebermodelle aus Boğazköy*. Studien zu den Boğazköy-Texten Beiheft 5. Wiesbaden: Harrassowitz.

Dietz, Albert. 2019. Deity or Cult Statue? The Storm-God of Aleppo in the Visual Record of the Second Millennium BCE. In: *Ancient Near Eastern Temple Inventories in the Third and Second Millennia BCE: Integrating Archaeological, Textual, and Visual Sources*, edited by Jean M. Evans, Elisa Roßberger, and Paola Paoletti, 189-206. PeWe-Verlag, Gladbeck.

Duru, Refik. 2004. *Yesemek, Eski Önasya Dünyasının En Büyük Heykel Atelyesi / The Largest Sculpture Workshop of the Ancient Near East*. Istanbul: Türsab Kültür Yayaınları.

Ehelolf, Hans. 1927. *Hethitische Festrituale*. Keilschrifturkunden aus Boghazköi 20. Berlin: Akademie-Verlag.

Ehringhaus, Horst. 2005. *Götter, Herrscher, Inschriften. Die Felsreliefs der hethitischen Großreichszeit in der Türkei*. Zaberns Bildbände zur Archäologie. Mainz: von Zabern.

Forrer, Emil. 1922. Die Inschriften und Sprachen des Ḫatti-Reiches. *Zeitschrift der Deutschen Morgenländischen Gesellschaft* 76: 174–269.

Groddek, Detlev. 2004. *Hethitische Texte in Transkription KUB 20*. Dresdner Beiträge zur Hethitologie 13. Dresden: Verlag der Technischen Universität Dresden.

Güterbock, Hans Gustav. 1951. The Song of Ullikummi. Revised Text of the Hittite Version of a Hurrian Myth. *Journal of Cuneiform Studies* 5: 135–161.

Güterbock, Hans Gustav. 1952. The Song of Ullikummi. Revised Text of the Hittite Version of a Hurrian Myth (Continued). *Journal of Cuneiform Studies* 6: 8–42.

Güterbock, Hans Gustav. 1957. Narration in Anatolian, Syrian, and Assyrian Art. *American Journal of Archaeology* 61: 62–71.

Güterbock, Hans Gustav. 1993. Gedanken über ein hethitisches Königssiegel aus Boğazköy. *Istanbuler Mitteilungen* 43: 113–116.

Haas, Volkert. 2003. *Materia Magica et Medica Hethitica. Ein Beitrag zur Heilkunde im Alten Orient*. Berlin and New York: de Gruyter.

Hawkins, J. David. 2000. *Corpus of Hieroglyphic Luwian Inscriptions*. 3 vols. Berlin and New York: de Gruyter.

Hawkins, J. David. 2003. The Storm-God Seal of Mursili III. In: *Hittite Studies in Honor of Harry A. Hoffner Jr. on the Occasion of his 65th Birthday*, edited by Gary Beckman, Richard Beal and George McMahon, 169–175. Eisenbrauns: Winona Lake, IN.

Hawkins, J. David. 2011. The Transcriptions of the Aleppo Temple. *Anatolian Studies* 61: 35–54.

Hazenbos, Joost. 2002. Zum İmamkulu-Relief. In: *Silva Anatolica. Anatolian Studies Presented to Maciej Popko on the Occasion of His 65th Birthday*, edited by Piotr Taracha, 147–161. Warsaw: Agade.

Herbordt, Suzanne et al. 2011. *Die Siegel der Großkönige und Großköniginnen auf Tonbullen aus dem Nişantepe-Archiv in Hattusa*. Boğazköy-Ḫattuša 23. Mainz: von Zabern.

Hoffner, Harry. 2017. Hittite Compositions: The Kumarbi Series Myths (4.6). The Song of Emergence (4.6A); The Song of the God LAMMA (4.6B); The Song of Silver (4.6C); The Song of Ḫedammu (4.6D); The Song of Ullikummi (CTH 345) (4.6E). In: *The Context of Scripture, Vol. 4: Supplements*, edited by Kenneth Lawson Younger Jr., 39–57. Leiden and Boston: Brill.

Kohlmeyer, Kay. 1983. Felsbilder der hethitischen Großreichszeit. *Acta Praehistorica et Archaeologica* 15: 7-154.

Kohlmeyer, Kay. 2000. *Der Tempel des Wettergottes von Aleppo*. Münster: Rhema.

Littauer, Mary A. and Joost H. Crouwel. 1979. *Wheeled Vehicles and Ridden Animals in the Ancient Near East*. Handbuch der Orientalistik, Abteilung 7, Bd. 1, Abschnitt 2. Leiden and Cologne: Brill.

Moortgat-Correns, Ursula. 1952. Ritzzeichnung auf Tontafel aus Bogazköy. *Mitteilungen der Deutschen Orient-Gesellschaft* 84: 38–40.

Parrot, André. 1951. Cylindre hittite nouvellement acquis (AO 20138). *Syria* 28: 180–190.

Richter, Thomas. 2012. *Bibliographisches Glossar des Hurritischen*. Wiesbaden: Harrassowitz.

Riemschneider, Margarete. 1954. *Die Welt der Hethiter*. Große Kulturen der Frühzeit 1 / Sammlung Kilpper. Stuttgart: Kilpper.

Sakuma, Yasuhiko. 2014. Analyse hethitischer Vogelflugorakel. In: *Divination in the Ancient Near East. A Workshop on Divination Conducted During the 54th Rencontre Assyriologique Internationale, Würzburg 2008*, edited by Jeanette Fincke, 37–51. Eisenbrauns, Winona Lake, IN.

Sapienza, Anna. 2017. Lo 'Knielauf Schema'. Analisi iconografica dei documenti numismatici e archeologici. *Antesteria* 6: 63–75.

Schwemer, Daniel. 2001. *Die Wettergottgestalten Mesopotamiens und Nordsyriens im Zeitalter der Keilschriftkulturen. Materialien und Studien nach den schriftlichen Quellen*. Harrassowitz, Wiesbaden.

Schwemer, Daniel. 2008. The Storm-Gods of the Ancient Near East: Summary, Synthesis, Recent Studies. Part II. *Journal of Ancient Near Eastern Religions* 8: 1–44.

Seeher, Jürgen. 2007. Eine Kultvase mit der Darstellung des Wettergottes von Halab aus Hattuša. In: *VITA. Belkıs Dinçol ve Ali Dinçol'a Armağan / Festschrift in Honor of Belkıs Dinçol and Ali Dinçol*, edited by Metin Alparslan, Meltem Doğan-Alparslan and Hasan Peker, 709–720. Istanbul: Ege Yayınları.

Starke, Frank. 1990. *Untersuchung zur Stammbildung des keilschriftluwischen Nomens*. Studien zu den Boğazköy-Texten 31. Wiesbaden: Harrassowitz.

Taracha, Piotr. 2000. *Ersetzen und Entsühnen. Das mittelhethitische Ersatzritual für den Großkönig Tuthalija (CTH *448.4) und verwandte Texte*. Culture and History of the Ancient Near East 5. Leiden [etc.]: Brill.

Ünal, Ahmed. 1989. Drawings, Graffiti and Squiggles on the Hittite Tablets – Art in Scribal Circles. In: *Anatolia and the Ancient Near East. Studies in Honor of Tahsin Özgüç*, edited by Kultu Emre et al., 505–513. Ankara: Türk Tarih Kurumu Basımevi.

van den Hout, Theo. 2009. A Century of Hittite Text Dating and the Origins of the Hittite Cuneiform Script. *Incontri Linguistici* 32: 11–35.

van den Hout, Theo. 2014–16. Wagen B. Hethitisch. In: *Reallexikon der Assyriologie und vorderasiatischen Archäologie* vol. 14: 622–627.

Waal, Willemijn. 2015. *Hittite Diplomatics. Studies in Ancient Document Format and Record Management*. Studien zu den Boğazköy-Texten 57. Wiesbaden: Harrassowitz.

Wäfler, Markus. 1975. Zum Felsrelief von Imamkulu. *Mitteilungen der Deutschen Orient-Gesellschaft* 107: 17–26.

Weeden, Mark. 2011. *Hittite Logograms and Hittite Scholarship*. Studien zu den Boğazköy-Texten 54. Wiesbaden: Harrassowitz.

Woolley, Leonard. 1921. *Carchemish. Report on the Excavations at Jerablus on Behalf of the British Museum* Conducted by C. Leonard Woolley with T. E. Lawrence and P. L. O. Guy. Part II, The Town Defences. London: Trustees of the British Museum.

Yıldırım, Tayfun. 2007. New Scenes on the Second Relief Vase from Hüseyindede and their Interpretation in the Light of the Hittite Representative Art. In: *VI Congresso Internazionale di Ittitologia, Roma, 5–9 settembre 2005*, edited by Alfonso Archi, 837–850. Studi Micenei ed Egeo-Anatolici 50. Rome: CNR, Istituto di Studi sulle Civiltà dell'Egeo e del Vicino Oriente.

9

Bone Cheekpieces and Spoked Wheels – Chariots in the Carpathian Region

Nikolaus G. O. Boroffka

In this study dedicated to Joost Crouwel, the evidence for the existence and use of chariots in the Carpatho-Danubian Region is reviewed. A brief account of the necessary preconditions shows that most requirements existed at least since the first half of the third millennium BCE: wheeled transport, the domesticated horse and, at least in some areas, suitable terrain. The light spoked wheel is documented in models and/or images, at least from sometime between 2000 and 1750 BCE, while bone or antler cheekpieces as parts of horse harnesses may reach back to the last centuries before 2000 BCE.

A critical review of these indications for the knowledge and use of chariots, however, needs to take into consideration other interpretations as well. Thus, spoked wheels may have been used on other vehicles than chariots and cheekpieces, even when more severe, could have been used by horse riders or for other light vehicles, rather than for chariots. Overall, the archaeological evidence shows surprisingly little unequivocal evidence for chariots during the entire Bronze Age in the Carpatho-Danubian Region, even when Late Bronze Age or Early Iron Age finds are also taken into account.

Early documentation of horse harnessing, with cheekpiece-systems original to the Carpatho-Danubian region, indicate the necessity to strictly control the draught animals. However, images and/or models of chariots do not seem to exist in the area before ca. 1650 BCE. They are thus largely contemporaneous to those further south or southeast in the Aegean or eastern Mediterranean, and clearly later than those known from the southern Urals. Even then they are very rare and their function in warfare is doubtful, while the (symbolic) use of chariots in racing and/or ceremony appears likely.

The brief explanation of what a chariot is, given by Joost Crouwel in his doctoral dissertation published in 1981, very suitably and concisely describes a specific type of vehicle: "*Chariot. A light, fast, two-wheeled, usually horse-drawn vehicle with spoked wheels; used for warfare, hunting, racing and ceremonial purposes. Its crew usually stood.*".[1] The same definition had also been used, when he discussed wheeled vehicles and ridden animals in the Near East together with Mary Littauer[2] and again roughly ten years after his dissertation when he turned to the Iron Age vehicles in Greece[3]. The definition can still be considered useful and valid up to today.

Several conditions are prerequisites for the construction and use of the chariot, whatever its use may have been: warfare, hunting, racing or ceremony. 1) Most obvious is the knowledge of wheeled transport, or more specifically the spoked wheel according to the definition of the chariot by Crouwel as cited above. 2) The specialised breeding and training of the domesticated horse is equally important, although other strong and fast animals (e.g. camels) may have been used very occasionally. Images with harnessed birds, rams, stags, or hybrid beings such as griffons or winged horses, most probably had only symbolic value, even if this may have been expressed in reality, as in the case of Scythian horses 'dressed up' as stags, ibex or griffons.[4] 3) Especially the efficient use of the chariot, in any of the scopes mentioned in the definition above, further required a suitable landscape and terrain, as Crouwel had already pointed out.[5] Roads were, in contrast, not absolutely necessary, except perhaps for racing or ceremonial display;[6] however, the use of chariots in warfare and hunting most probably took place away from roads. 4) Feldman and Sauvage,[7] studying the reception of chariots in Egypt, the Levant, the eastern Mediterranean and the Aegean, have drawn attention to a further important facet of the spread of the horse-chariot-complex, perhaps underestimated in much of the older literature. Maran followed their argumentation specifically for Greece. They all underline the role played by multiple sources of the elements of necessary technology, and especially their differing adaptation and the integration or use, in local socio-political systems.[8]

General Indications for the Preconditions of Chariot Technology and Use

1) Wheeled transport has been documented at least since the 4th millennium BCE, in the Near East, south-eastern Central Europe (i.e. the Carpathian region mainly interesting

---

[1] Crouwel 1981: 23.
[2] Littauer and Crouwel 1979: 4–5.
[3] Crouwel 1992: 16.
[4] Boroffka 2004b: 467, fig. 1–2; 2018: 12.
[5] Crouwel 1981: 29.
[6] Crouwel 1981: 29–31.
[7] Feldman and Sauvage 2010.
[8] Feldman and Sauvage 2010; Maran 2020a; 2020b.

us here), the Caucasus and the north-western Indian subcontinent, the latter perhaps slightly later. However, these early vehicles are mostly four-wheeled heavy wagons, probably drawn by bovids.[9] Two-wheeled vehicles can first be documented as early as the 4th millennium BCE from circum-alpine lake dwellings, documented examples becoming more frequent during the 3rd millennium BCE, then also in the Near East, the northern Caucasus and in the Indus culture of Pakistan and their respective immediately neighbouring areas.[10] These are described as carts with heavy disc-wheels, usually drawn by bovids and can thus not be connected directly to chariots in the sense defined by Crouwel.[11] Light spoked wheels appear later, with the earliest preserved traces of actual spoked wheels at present known from burials of the early 2nd millennium BCE in the southern Ural region.[12] It must be noted, however, that the oldest depiction of a two-wheeled vehicle with spoked wheels and equid draught animals is probably still one on a seal from Tepe Hissar (Tappeh Hesār), layer IIIb, which can be roughly dated to the third quarter of the third millennium BCE.[13]

2) New data on the question of horse domestication have been provided in the last few years, especially by studies on genetics. They have not definitely solved the problems, and various scenarios are still discussed. A central Eurasian domestication centre in the steppe regions of Kazakhstan has been well documented,[14] but a second and probably independent western centre has also been indicated in Iberia.[15] A further possibility, Anatolia (and the Near East), has also been proposed as the origin of mid-third millennnium BCE horses for Southeastern Europe.[16] Since wild horses seem to have survived in this area during the Holocene, at least in small numbers,[17] this could have been a third domestication centre, or at least an important transmission bridge for the domesticated horse between Asia and Europe.[18] The role of Przewalski's horses in the domestication and breeding process remains controversial.[19] Studies on coat colour variation have given a highly probable period of domestication around the mid-fourth millennium BCE,[20] most probably in the steppes of central Eurasia. In a recent study several areas of possible primary domestication in various parts of Eurasia are again considered. The ancestors of modern horses (termed DOM2) are not widely documented before ca. 2200 BCE, these being located in the Volga-Don steppe, and thus not far from the southern Urals, where early chariots do appear slightly later. The DOM2 horses could, chronologically, not have played any significant role in the "steppe pastoralist expansion north of the Carpathians" (popularly named Yamnaya migration), and the question of any earlier horse riding and/or transport still remains open.[21]

3) Crouwel had already pointed out the natural obstacles of Greek terrain,[22] which was more suited to travel and transport on foot or on animal back, besides the very important boats for the coastal zone. He also pointed out the great effort needed to construct and maintain roads – an additional impediment to the widespread adoption of wheeled vehicles in Greece, and even more so for the use of chariots. Well documented and convincingly dated roads in Greece are rare. However, Crouwel could also refer to the Linear-B tablets, which give evidence of large numbers of chariots, thus indirectly pointing to the existence of road networks. Especially recent evaluation of remote sensing data has been fruitful in documenting road-systems for the Near East.[23]

4) Feldman and Sauvage studied the integration of chariots in Egypt, the Levant, the eastern Mediterranean and the Aegean, especially regarding the way in which texts, actual chariots and their images were used and functioned in the various social systems.[24] According to them, Egypt has most images and archaeological remains, and is thus the best documented area. The chariot was introduced to Egypt by the Hyksos, in the second quarter of the second millennium BCE, so that mainly the 18th and 19th Dynasties are of interest here.[25] There is a change in the reception insofar as during the 18th Dynasty, chariots were deposited in royal burials, while in the private tombs of a lower elite group they were represented in images, but not by actual vehicles. The illustration of chariots in royal propaganda is also found on temple walls, and thus also has a ritual

---

[9] Hansen et al. 2017; Klimscha 2017; Maran 2020a, each with older literature.
[10] For a good overview see the contributions in Fansa and Burmeister 2004, especially those by Bakker, Belinskij and Kalmykov, Burmeister, Kenoyer, and Schlichterle, each with further literature.
[11] See Kaiser 2010 with clear arguments against an evolutionary connection between the Caucasus and the Steppe. – See also Lindner 2021.
[12] Burmeister and Raulwing 2012: especially 98–100; Chechushkov and Epimakhov 2018; Chechushkov and Epimakhov this volume. – But see the recent discussion of chronology by Grigoriev 2020 and Grigoriev 2021.
[13] Littauer and Crouwel 1979: 40, fig. 21; Burmeister and Raulwing 2012: 101 with note 23; Crouwel 2019: 36 fig. 18.
[14] Ludwig et al. 2009.
[15] E.g. Lira et al. 2010; Warmuth et al. 2011; Fages et al. 2019.
[16] Benecke 2009; 2018.
[17] Martin and Russell 2006.
[18] Koban et al. 2012.
[19] Pro: Wutke et al 2018; contra: Cai et al. 2009; Gaunitz et al. 2018.
[20] Ludwig et al. 2009; Cieslak et al. 2010; Gaunitz et al. 2018; Felkel et al. 2019.

[21] Librado et al. 2021. In actual fact, none of the horses predating DOM2 are certified archaeologically as domestic (e.g. by harnessing or documented traction complexes), so that it is still questionable whether these horses were wild, tamed or domesticated, and exploited otherwise than for food (milk and/or meat). The authors, concerning DOM2, also state that "However, the rise of such profiles in Holubice, Gordineşti II and Acemhöyük before the earliest evidence for chariots supports horseback riding fuelling the initial dispersal of DOM2 outside their core region, in line with Mesopotamian iconography during the late third and early second millennia BC. Therefore, a combination of chariots and equestrianism is likely to have spread the DOM2 diaspora in a range of social contexts from urban states to dispersed decentralized societies:" (Librado et al. 2021, 636). This statement can, in my opinion, not be accepted as such, since it incorrectly presumes that, besides possibly being ridden, horse traction could be applied only to chariots, and not to any other kind of vehicle.
[22] Crouwel 1981: 29–31; mentioned also in Crouwel 2019: 42.
[23] E.g. Ur 2003.
[24] Feldman and Sauvage 2010.
[25] Feldman and Sauvage 2010: 163; Maran 2020a: 506, each with older bibliography. See also Neumann and Lohwasser 2022 on the use and significance of horses and chariots in the Near East and Egypt.

symbolism. During the 19th Dynasty, the novelty of these vehicles appears to wane – they are no longer depicted or deposited in burials, and the images are integrated into monumental narratives of historical battles. The southern Levant appears closely linked to the situation in Egypt. In contrast, further north (especially Ugarit) a high-status group is named in the texts as the *mariyannu*, a nobility often considered as chariot warriors dependent on the king and thus not part of the highest social level. It is possibly this group who demonstrate their identity by chariot fittings (i.e. yoke saddle bosses and/or finials, as well as some bronze bits, all found mostly in domestic contexts), perhaps displayed in houses, and images of chariots on (imported) kraters found almost exclusively in burials. Cyprus, according to the study by Feldman and Sauvage, appears closely tied to Ugarit. On the mainland, the situation in Mitanni is less clear, and, at least partly, seems to be influenced by neighbouring areas, e.g. the proximity of Ugarit for Alalakh. For Hatti there is a striking difference between the numerous textual mentions of horse trading, breeding and military use and the contrasting rarity of images and the almost complete lack of artefacts. This is similar to Babylonia, where chariots were associated with the kings, were used in warfare and held a high importance, but do not seem to have been used as status or identity markers in depictions or burials. For the Aegean, the chariot may have been introduced from the Levant.[26] Fast chariot archers appear only in the early period, while in later images bows and arrows are omitted and chariots are depicted mainly in processions.[27] For Greece, Maran further focussed attention to the apparent lack of wheeled vehicles or their images in the fourth and third millennium BCE, in contrast to Eastern and Central Europe.[28] He brings forward arguments which indirectly argue for the existence of such vehicles, but observes a different social reception, which did not lead to great symbolic or religious importance being attributed to these vehicles and a corresponding lack of deposition or depiction. Treating a later period in Greece, Maran elsewhere discussed the late introduction of the chariot, most probably sometime towards the end of the 17th or the beginning of the 16th century BCE.[29] Following Hüttel,[30] he underlines the heterogeneous sources of the individual elements of the horse-chariot complex, with technological features such as the bone or antler cheekpieces (both rod-shaped and discoid) presumably being transmitted from, or at least via, the Carpathian region, while he links the Greek imagery of chariots being used in hunting, warfare or driving over fallen enemies more closely to the iconography of the Near East and/or Egypt.[31]

A general intermediate conclusion may be drawn here insofar as the Mediterranean regions discussed by Feldman and Sauvage and Maran had developed political societies by the late 17th or early 16th century BCE, in which the royalty controlled chariots and their use in images, while the actual producers, horse managers and chariot warriors were of high status, but clearly situated below the ruling elites.[32] This reception of chariots and the symbolic importance given to their display, real or in images, differed regionally, even though the significance of chariots was basically recognised in all regions.

Preconditions: Wheeled Transport, Draught Animals and Terrain in the Carpathian Region

Turning specifically to the Carpathian region (Figure 9.1) the necessary conditions for the full use of chariots are briefly presented, followed by a discussion of the actual archaeological indications for the presence, use and function of chariots.

Wheeled vehicles have been known in the Carpathian region at least since the 4th millennium BCE, although this is documented mainly by clay models and not by actual remains of vehicles or elements of harness.[33] These are, almost exclusively, four-wheeled wagons,[34] with heavy disc-wheels and which were most probably drawn by bovids, as is indicated by occasional bovid protomes on the models. Indications for the castration of male bovids, easier to train and stronger than cows, also exist since the 4th millennium BCE.[35]

The vast majority of wheel models from the Early and Middle Bronze Age in the Carpathian region are simple undecorated examples, often with a pronounced nave, which appear to represent massive disc wheels. From the Early Bronze Age of the Carpathian only one clay model, attributed to the Hatvan culture and thus dateable to the late third or early second millennium BCE, shows a composite disc wheel, apparently made from three boards (Figure 9.3,1).[36] Wagon models, in their vast majority four-wheeled, are still frequent in various Middle Bronze Age cultures (Figure 9.2).[37] Some of these wagon models, such as for example the one from Nemesnádudvar (Figure 9.2,4) dated to the Early Bronze Age or early Middle Bronze Age, show complex shapes and bear very elaborate decorations, evidently conveying symbolic meanings, which we may not always decipher today.[38] In the case of Nemesnádudvar the wagon model was found in a pit, for which the authors mention no indications of special function or sacrifice,[39] but some wagons apparently did play a role in funerary rituals across various Middle Bronze Age cultures.[40] So far only the four-wheeled wagon model from

---

[26] But see below on the indications for a contribution from the Carpatho-Danubian region.
[27] Feldman and Sauvage 2010: 163.
[28] Maran 2020b.
[29] Maran 2020a: 506.
[30] Hüttel 1981.
[31] Maran 2020a: 516.

[32] Feldman and Sauvage 2010; Maran 2020a; 2020b.
[33] See e.g. Bondár 2011; 2012; Țurcanu and Bejenaru 2015.
[34] Boroffka 2008; Bondár 2011; 2012.
[35] Țurcanu and Bejenaru 2015: 200–201 – see also Nadler 2002: 110 for southern Germany.
[36] Kalicz 1968: 127, pl. 116,4.
[37] Boroffka 2004a; Boroffka 2008; Bondár 2011; 2012.
[38] Bondár and Székely 2011: 544–545.
[39] Bondár and Székely 2011: 539.
[40] Boroffka 2004a: 352–353; 2008: 41.

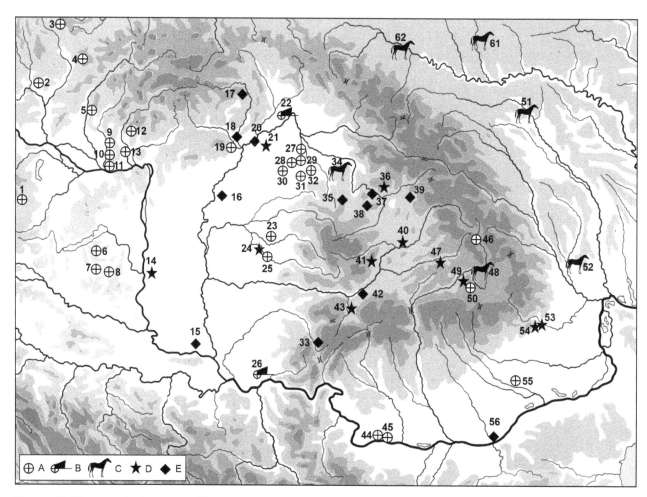

Figure 9.1. Map of spoked wheel models (A), images of chariots (B), paired horse burials (C), Middle Bronze Age (D) and Late Bronze Age/Early Iron Age (E) sites mentioned in this study. 1 Velem Szent Vid, 2 Blučina, 3 Mondschütz, 4 Bánov, 5 Veselé, 6 Kánya, 7 Szalacska, 8 Lengyel, 9 Nitriansky Hrádok, 10 Hetény, 11 Iža, 12 Malinovce, 13 Kéménd, 14 Nemesnádudvar, 15 Futog, 16 Nádudvar, 17 Obišovce, 18 Sajóvámos, 19 Emőd, 20 Tarcal, 21 Polgár, 22 Veľke Raškovce, 23 Békés, 24 Vărşand, 25 Socodor, 26 Dupljaja, 27 Tiream, 28 Sălacea, 29 Dindești, 30 Săcueni, 31 Otomani, 32 Pir, 33 Caransebeș, 34 Oarța de Sus, 35 Periceni, 36 Ciceu Corabia, 37 Gîrbău, 38 Viștea, 39 Arcalia, 40 Lechința de Mureș, 41 Cetea, 42 Orăștie, 43 Cioclovina, 44 Plosca, 45 Cârna, 46 Miercurea Ciuc, 47 Sighișoara, 48 Arcuș, 49 Cuciulata, 50 Feldioara, 51 Ripiceni, 52 Negrilești, 53 Cârlomănești, 54 Sărata Monteoru, 55 București – Tei, 56 Bujoru, 57 Füzesabony, 58 Tószeg, 59 Vatin, 60 Trușești, 61 Husiatyn, 62 Bukivna. Map produced by R. Boroffka.

Ciceu Corabia shows very sketchy animals drawn on either side of the wagon body, which could be interpreted as equids (Figure 9.2,3).[41] Models of spoked wheels, either with four modelled spokes or with decorations indicating four, very seldom more, spokes, are documented especially in the classical Middle Bronze Age cultures of the Carpathian region: Maďarovce, Gârla Mare (Žuto Brdo), Otomani (Füzesabony-Gyulavarsánd), Tei, Transdanubian Encrusted Pottery, and Wietenberg (Figure 9.3,2–15).[42] They are distributed along the Middle and Lower Danube (Slovakia, Hungary, eastern Vojvodina and eastern Serbia, Romania and Bulgaria), the Great Plain of Eastern Hungary, the south-eastern plain of Romania and in Transylvania (Figure 9.1,A)[43] and have so far not been discovered in Bulgaria[44]. In the later Bronze Age and Early Iron Age (Urnfield Period and later), clay models of spoked wheels (Figure 9.3,16), but also some full-size originals are known, which will be briefly discussed further below. Detailed dating of the Middle Bronze Age spoked-wheel models individually is difficult. Many of those from the Wietenberg culture come from sites where several phases are present and can thus not be attributed to a specific period – only two decorated spoked wheels from Feldioara can be more precisely dated to earlier phases A–B of the culture,[45] which would place them most probably between BCE 2000 and 1750, in the calibrated radiocarbon chronology for Transylvania.[46] For the wheels from the Otomani and Tei cultures the same problem is encountered, as most of them cannot be precisely connected to specific phases. However, a date similar to that for the Wietenberg culture is well within the range of possibilities. The fairly large number of spoked wheel models from Nitriansky Hrádok-Zámeček in Slovakia are attributed to the Maďarovce

---

[41] Boroffka 1994: 30 nr. 113, pl. 59.
[42] Boroffka 2004a.
[43] See also maps in Bóna 1960: 107 fig. 7; 1975: map X; Pare 1987: 29–30 fig. 6; Bondár 2011: 83 fig. 33; 2012: 88 fig. 33; Ilon 2019: 32 fig. 1.
[44] Minkov 2021. On Bronze Age models of spoked wheels in Europe further to the northwest see Precht 2002.
[45] Boroffka 1994: 255, tab. 13, pl. 78,15–16.
[46] Boroffka and Boroffka 2020: 74–78.

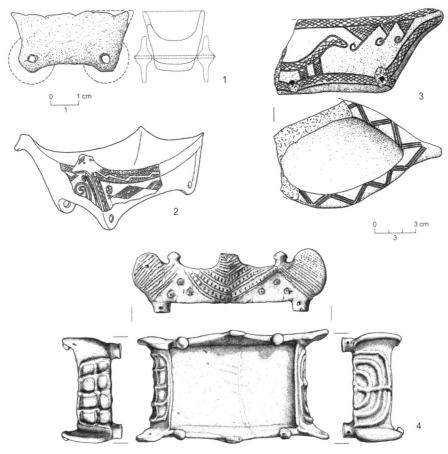

Figure 9.2. Clay models of four-wheeled wagons: 1 Cuciulata, 2 Lechința de Mureș, 3 Ciceu Corabia, 4 Nemesnádudvar. 1–3 after Boroffka 2004a, Abb. 2 and 8–9; 4 courtesy of M. Bondár (originally published Bondár 2011: Fig. 23; Bondár and Székely 2011: Fig. 3; Bondár 2012: Fig. 23).

culture,[47] while the Transdanubian Encrusted Pottery further south has yielded comparatively few examples. The two latter cultures can largely be dated approximatively to BCE 1900–1600 in the calibrated radiocarbon chronology.[48] The Gârla Mare (Žuto Brdo) culture has yielded few radiocarbon dates, but can be reasonably dated as beginning around 1650 BCE and lasting perhaps until around 1250 BCE.[49] Spoked wheels, judging by the miniature clay models, were thus known in the Carpatho-Danubian region at the latest by around 1750 BCE, and possibly some time earlier. Spoked wheels, however, although a prerequisite for chariots, do not necessarily prove the use of chariots, since they were and still are also attached to four-wheeled vehicles.

In the Carpathian region the domesticated horse has been documented in osteological collections at least since the Late Chalcolithic/Early Bronze Age in Hungary,[50] Romania (both sides of the Carpathians)[51] and in Slovakia.[52] The percentages in the osteological collections are usually low, which may indicate that they were not kept mainly for milk or meat, but rather for traction and/or transport. Apparently there is a sharp rise in numbers from the later Middle Bronze Age Tumulus culture onwards in Hungary,[53] although some other Late Bronze Age sites still yield surprisingly few horses.[54] East of the Carpathians the horse is constantly present, although in varying percentages, in Late Bronze Age faunal assemblages.[55]

The landscape and terrain of the Carpathian region is highly varied.[56] Many parts are mountainous, often cut by narrow and steep rocky gorges, or otherwise uneven and hilly. These areas are thus hardly suited for large scale use of the light chariots in warfare or hunting, while short distance racing and ceremonial display would have been possible. Especially the Great Plain in eastern Hungary and the plateaus in eastern and southern Romania are quite different, with large open spaces, only occasionally cut by river valleys or streams. Although the environment on the Great Hungarian Plain may have been wetter[57] and less suitable to chariot use, the flat open landscape as it appears today is highly convenient for all the possible uses of chariots mentioned above. This is basically also true for the plateaus

---

[47] Točik 1978; 1981.
[48] E.g. Kiss et al. 2015; Schlütz and Bittmann 2016.
[49] Șandor-Chicideanu 2003: 213; Șandor-Chicideanu and Constantinescu 2019: 65.
[50] E.g. Bartosiewicz 1996; Choyke and Bartosiewicz 1999/2000.
[51] E.g. Haimovici and Gheorghiu-Dardan 1970; Becker 1999; 2000.
[52] E.g. Oravkinová et al. 2017: 34–35, with older literature.
[53] Bartosiewicz 1996: 33 tab. 1, 35.
[54] E.g. Vörös 1996.
[55] See Diaconu et al. 2014 with older literature.
[56] Breu 1970–1989.
[57] See Gyucha et al. 2013 for a recent discussion of human-environment interaction in the region.

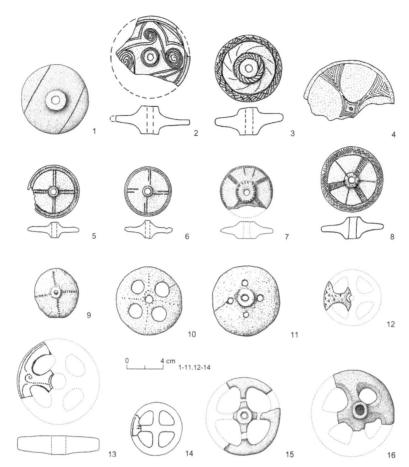

Figure 9.3. Clay models of wheels. 1 Composite wheel model attributed to the Hatvan culture, 2–9 Wheel models ornamented with four or more spokes attributed to the Maďarovce, Otomani (Gyulavarsand/Füzesabony), Tei and Wietenberg cultures, 10–16 Wheel models with four spokes, attributed to the Maďarovce, Gârla Mare, Otomani (Gyulavársand/Füzesabony), Tei, Wietenberg and Urnfield cultures. 1 Polgár, 2–3 Dindeşti, 4-6.9 Otomani, 7 Emőd, 8.11 Bucureşti – Tei, 10 Nitriansky Hrádok, 12 Miercurea Ciuc, 13 Cârna, 14 Plosca, 15 Lengyel, 16 Velem Szent Vid. 1-16 redrawn by R. Boroffka after Bader 1978, pl. XXXVI,12–13.15; Bichir 1964: Fig. 7, 1–2.4–5; Boroffka 1994: Taf. 67,11–12; Boroffka 2004a: Abb. 3–6; Fischl et al. 2011: fig. 8,6; Kalicz 1968: pl. CXVI,4; Miske 1908: Taf. LVI,15; Şandor-Chicideanu 2003: pl. 153,3; 166,8; Wosinsky 1888: Taf. IX, 38a.

Figure 9.4. Image of chariot: incrusted incision on a vessel from Veľke Raškovce, attributed to the Suciu de Sus culture. After Vizdal 1972, and Boroffka 2004a: Abb, 12.

and wide river valleys of eastern and southern Romania, where studies of the palaeoenvironment are still insufficient. Roads, or similar structures such as bridges, are, to my knowledge, not documented in the Carpathian region before the later Iron Age.[58]

Summarising the above, the general requirements for the development and use of chariots in the Carpathian region are largely present from at least the third millennium BCE, wheeled transport and the domesticated horse being documented. Suitable terrains lie in the Great Hungarian Plain, as well as in eastern and southern Romania. The spoked wheel is documented from at least around 1750 BCE onwards, if not earlier. As a further indication of the knowledge and use of chariots, Bronze Age horsegear and other archaeological data are discussed below.

Archaeological Indications for Chariots

Images of Chariots

Three clear depictions of chariots are known from the Carpathian Basin. These are the incised image of three chariots on an urn from a grave discovered at Veľke Raškovce, Slovakia, (Figure 9.4).[59] It was originally attributed to the Piliny culture of the Late Bronze Age,[60] but was later con-

---

[58] E.g. Teodor and Şadurschi 1978; 1979.

[59] Vizdal 1972.
[60] Vizdal 1972.

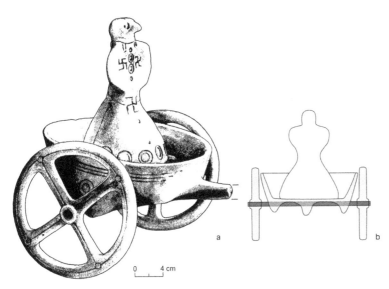

Figure 9.5. Chariot model no. 1 (fragmentary) from Dupljaja, attributed to the Gârla Mare culture. Redrawn by R. Boroffka after Garašanin 1983: pl. LXXXIV,1 and Milleker 1930: pl. 8.

stated, especially for those cheekpieces with sharpened edges or spikes, which allow better control of the horse.[67] Basically two main categories of cheekpieces, as well as some hybrid shapes, were in use during the Bronze Age of the Carpathian Basin:

Rod-shaped bone or antler cheekpieces (Figure 9.7) have long been considered characteristic for the Carpatho-Danubian region and are most likely a local invention, since the oldest examples, dated to the late third or early second millennium BCE, are found here.[68] They can be classified according to the function of the number, position and plane of large holes (presumably for attaching the bit and the reins), and the corresponding arrangement of smaller drill holes, the function of which cannot always be determined with certainty (Figure 9.8).[69] Half-finished products and possible local workshops have been described by Boroffka.[70]

vincingly placed in the context of the early Suciu de Sus culture and dated to the phase Reinecke B1,[61] thus corresponding roughly to the 17th or the 16th century BCE.[62] Among the images of Bronze Age chariots the two clay models from Dupljaja, Vojvodina, also need to be mentioned (Figures 9.5–9.6).[63] Stylistically they belong to the Gârla Mare (Žuto Brdo) culture and can thus be dated to a period similar to the urn from Veľke Raškovce (1650 BCE–1250 BCE).[64] Especially wagon model no. 2 (Figure 9.6) is of special interest, since the front part, ending in bird-heads on either side of a single wheel, could be interpreted as indicating the use of two lateral draught poles. These could have been used with a collar, much more efficient than the usually presumed yoke. However, it must be taken into consideration that the model is a stylized object, most probably of symbolic meaning, and two draught poles are otherwise not known before the 1st millennium BCE.[65] While these three depictions are the only direct indications of chariots or chariot-like vehicles in the Carpathian region, there is also indirect archaeological evidence.

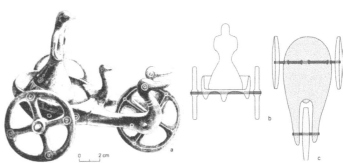

Figure 9.6. Chariot model no. 2 (complete with figurine) from Dupljaja, attributed to the Gârla Mare culture. Redrawn by R. Boroffka after Garašanin 1983: Taf. LXXXIII,1-3 and Milleker 1930: pl. 9–11.

Cheekpieces

Excavations and chance finds have provided many Bronze Age (and later) bone and antler parts of harness, mainly cheekpieces,[66] from the Carpatho-Danubian region. They can be interpreted as indirect evidence for the knowledge and use of domesticated horses in transport, probably also including chariots. This presumption has often been

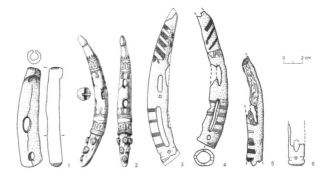

Figure 9.7. Rod-shaped cheekpieces. 1 Vărşand, 2 Cârlomăneşti, 3–6 Cioclovina. 1 after Boroffka 1998: Abb. 6,2; 2 courtesy of M. Şandor-Chicideanu (originally published: Motzoi-Chicideanu et al. 2012, pl. 11), 3–6 redrawn by R. Boroffka after Boroffka 1998: Abb. 5,10–11 and Emödi 1978: Fig. 6,1–2.

---

[61] Demeterová 1984: 43; similar dating by Kacsó 1999: 99.
[62] Gogâltan 2015. – Recently a date as late as the 14th Century has been stated without argumentation: Metzner-Nebelsick 2021: 113.
[63] Milleker 1930; Petrović 1930; Garašanin 1983; Boroffka 2004a: fig. 10–11.
[64] Şandor-Chicideanu 2003: 213; Şandor-Chicideanu and Constantinescu 2019: 65.
[65] In the Near East: Littauer and Crouwel 1979: 5; Crouwel 2019: 30.
[66] See Bochkarev and Kusnetsov, this volume.
[67] E.g. Hüttel 1981: 175–176; Maran 2020a: 514; 518, each with references.
[68] Most recently Lindner 2021: 46–53, with older references. See also critically Grigoriev 2020 and Grigoriev 2021.
[69] Boroffka 1998.
[70] Boroffka 1998: 122 list 15.

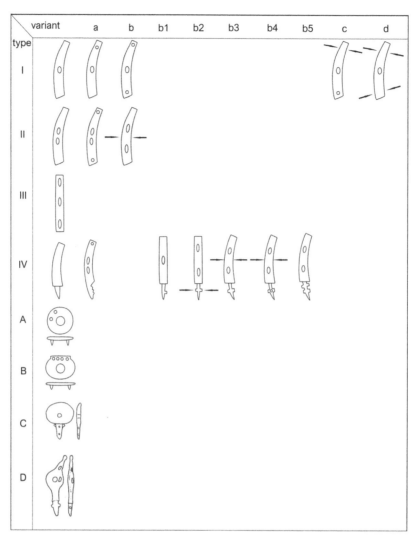

Figure 9.8. Rough classification table of bone and horn cheekpieces in the Danubian-Carpathian region. Adapted and revised by R. Boroffka from Boroffka 1998: Abb. 10.

Disc-shaped cheekpieces, usually with spikes on one side, are the second main category used in the Bronze Age Carpatho-Danubian region (Figure 9.9).[71] Due to their comparative rarity in this area and their clearly much higher frequency further east in the steppe regions roughly between the river Bug, Kazakhstan and Central Asia, with a high concentration around the southern Urals, these cheekpieces are usually described as Volga-Ural type. Very roughly they can be classified into two variants (Figure 9.8).[72] A) with a large central hole and one or two smaller lateral ones (Figure 9.9,1–2); B) with a large central hole and a row of smaller ones along one side, usually also set off by a small ledge (Figure 9.9,3). In both cases the cheekpiece may be carved from one piece of bone or the spikes may be inserted separately into suitable drilled holes. More detailed typological classifications of the disc-shaped cheekpieces have variously been proposed for the steppe areas.[73] Both basic types appear in the Carpatho-Danubian region, although not in large numbers. A little remarked bone object from Sighișoara (Wietenberg)/Dealul Turcului (Figure 9.9,4)[74] appears to be an unfinished example of a disc-shaped cheekpiece of the B type, as yet without the central hole or the smaller holes along a lateral ledge, which is already carved. Two spikes were carved as an integral part of the main bone body, while further spikes could have been inserted in appropriate drilled holes. This eponymous site of the Wietenberg culture does not have a documented Bronze Age stratigraphy and was settled during most periods of the culture's lifespan. Therefore, the object does not contribute more precise chronological information to these cheekpieces. However, as a half-finished product it documents the local production of this category generally thought to belong to the steppes further east. The oldest well datable disc-shaped cheekpieces and related objects are those from Oarța de Sus (Wietenberg culture phase II, ca. 2000–1750 BCE) and Sărata Monteoru (Monteoru culture, phase Ic3, ca. 2200–1850 BCE).[75] In spite of the fact that the cultural phases from which they originate in

---

[71] Boroffka 1998.
[72] Boroffka 1998.
[73] E.g. Teufer 1999; contributions in Chechushkov and Epimakhov 2010; Usachuk 2004; 2013; Grigoriev 2021, all with rich bibliography.

[74] Boroffka 1994: 76–77 no. 398, pl. 130,6.
[75] Boroffka and Boroffka 2020: 74–78 (Wietenberg). For the revised classification and absolute chronology of the Monteoru culture, beginning well before 2000 and ending sometime after 1600 BCE, see

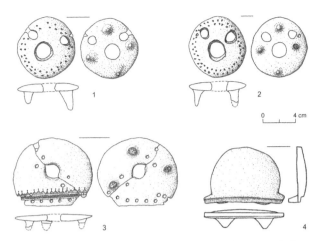

Figure 9.9. Disc shaped bone cheekpieces with spikes. 1–2 Sărata Monteoru, Burial 1926/1927, 3 Sărata Monteoru, settlement lazer of stage Ic3, 4 Sighișoara – Wietenberg, unfinished product from the settlement. 1–3 after Boroffka 1998: Abb. 1–2.4, 4 after Boroffka 1994: Taf. 130,6.

the Carpathian region partly began much earlier, and in view of their presumed eastern origin, where they are not dated to before 2000 BCE,[76] the disc-shaped cheekpieces discussed here probably also belong to the 2nd millennium BCE.

Two further types of cheekpieces were named by Hüttel as "kontamierte Scheibenknebel", differentiating between the "mitteldanubische Kontaminationsform" (Figure 9.8,D) and the "kazachische Kontaminationsform" (Figure 9.8,C).[77] The "Kontaminationssonderform Vatin" of Hüttel appears similar to the Kazakh one, even though the lateral projection (Zapfen) has a different shape and the site, of course, lies very far from Kazakhstan. The "mitteldanubische Kontaminationsform" is documented only in two examples from Tószeg. Their stratigraphic context is not given, so they can only generally be dated to the Middle Bronze Age. In fact, the two cheekpieces are not as similar as it might seem at first sight. One of the pieces (Figure 9.8,C)[78] shows the typical disc, to which, instead of a lateral hole, a ring has been added. The "Carpathian" element may be seen in the added projection with protuberances, which corresponds well to the "Spiš" group of Hüttel, or type IVb after Boroffka (Figure 9.8).[79] In contrast the second cheekpiece from Tószeg is closer to the rod-shaped "Spiš" type of Hüttel and type IVb after Boroffka (Figure 9.8,D), but with a round widened area around the main hole, into which a small lateral hole is placed – in its overall arrangement thus corresponding well to variant IVb3 or IVb4 after Boroffka (Figure 9.8).[80] The "kazachische Kontaminationsform" (Figure 9.8,C)[81] is basically a disc-shaped cheekpiece, with larger central hole, while the lateral hole is inserted from one side into the body. To this a projection with protuberances is added on one side, which again strikingly reminds of the "Spiš" group of Hüttel and type IVb after Boroffka (Figure 9.8,C). These "Kontaminationsformen" were not treated specially by Boroffka, although he does illustrate an apparent half-finished product from the Late Bronze Age Noua culture settlement of Trușești in eastern Romania.[82] This has an unfinished, partly angular, plaque with some drill holes (none penetrating the disc) and a lateral projection with two protuberances. Here again the half-finished product documents the local manufacture of such hybrid forms (combination of disc-shape with Spiš type projections), and in this case also provides a Late Bronze Age date, comparable to the chronology of the examples in Kazakhstan. Besides the half-finished product from Trușești, spatially intermediate cheekpieces, which may bridge the area between the "Kontaminationssonderform Vatin" and the "kazachische Kontaminationsform" (now usually named type Alakul) have recently been found at Sfântu Gheorghe-Arcuș.[83]

The basic shape for cheekpieces with rectangular plaques, usually with tooth- or spike-sharpened edges,[84] also described as "Grooved cheekpieces",[85] are not known in the Carpatho-Danubian region so far but distributed only in the steppes further to the east.

Especially the disc-shaped cheekpieces have usually been considered as indicating the use of chariots, mainly due to their find contexts in the eastern steppe. These are overwhelmingly burials, in which they are combined either with actual chariot remains, or indications of such in the shape of elongated pits for placing the wheels.[86] A major difference in the find contexts of bone and antler cheekpieces between the eastern steppes and the Carpatho-Danubian region are precisely these contexts. In the area treated here most cheekpieces come from settlement contexts (or chance finds), although some burials may be mentioned:

At Sărata Monteoru a pair of rod-shaped cheekpieces was found in grave 35 of burialground 2, dated to phase Monteoru Ia.[87]

Also at Sărata Monteoru, Ioan G. Andrieșescu and Ion Nestor opened a grave in 1926/1927 which contained, among others, a pair of disc-shaped cheekpieces with spikes, dated stylistically to phase Monteoru Ic2.[88]

At least one burial at Cândești of the phase Monteoru IIa–IIb contained an element of horse harness, although no illustrations were published and the type of cheekpieces

---

Motzoi-Chicideanu and Șandor-Chicideanu 2015; Constantinescu 2020: 149–157.
[76] See Chechushkov and Epimakhov 2010; Grigoriev 2021, each with further references.
[77] Hüttel 1981: 56–64, pl. 4,27–28 and 29–31.
[78] Hüttel 1981: 56–64, pl. 4,27.
[79] Boroffka 1998.
[80] Boroffka 1998.
[81] Hüttel 1981: 56–64, pl. 4,29–31.

[82] Boroffka 1998: 94 no. 28; 98 fig. 8,6.
[83] Unpublished; – I am greatly indebted to Valeriu Kavruk (Cavruc) for preliminary information.
[84] Plattenknebel: Hüttel 1981: 24–35.
[85] Grigoriev 2021: 164–166.
[86] See for example Usachuk 2004; 2013; Lindner 2021; Grigoriev 2021, all with bibliography. Chechushkov and Epimakhov, this volume.
[87] Boroffka 1998: 93 no. 24b–c; 96 fig. 6,4 only one piece illustrated.
[88] Boroffka 1998: 93 no. 24d–e; 98 fig. 8,1–2. Unpublished information from the excavation archives confirms a burial find.

is not described.[89] This very large Monteoru cemetery is, unfortunately, still largely unpublished.

The situation at Oarța de Sus appears a little unclear. The site is described as a sanctuary, consisting of one or two circular ditches (enclosures?) with pits inside it and in the surrounding area.[90] In pit no. 3 two horses were buried, side by side in a crouched position. A pair of sub-rectangular disc-shaped and spiked cheekpieces lay by the head of one horse. Besides the horses there were also smaller animals, many pottery vessels and sherds. Above all these, there were two more horse skeletons with the heads pointing downwards, stray human and animal bones, various other finds, burnt earth and charcoal. The entire context was covered by rocks, some of which showed traces of fire. The author dates the pit to the phase Wietenberg II,[91] which corresponds roughly to the period 1900–1600 BCE.[92] Unfortunately, so far only a small selection of material from this site has been published. There are no plans, sections, or photographs of this particular situation published. In the description we thus learn of four horse skeletons (two pairs), as well as human bones, besides numerous other pieces of inventory. This could also be interpreted as a (disturbed?) high-status burial with several horses, reminiscent of some of the burials at Sintashta,[93] all the more so, since the habit of including horses with disc-shaped cheekpieces in burials is considered to be typical of the southern Urals.

Besides settlement finds, where sometimes pairs of very similar cheekpieces may be considered as actually complete sets (e.g. at Coslogeni [two differing pairs], Niculițel, Otomani or Sălacea), we thus know of at least three burials from the Monteoru culture, each containing a pair of cheekpieces, and the somewhat unclear sitaution at Oarța de Sus, which can be interpreted as a high-status burial with four horses, only one of which was, however, equipped with cheekpieces. Thus, even though the settlement finds very clearly dominate, the statements of Maran[94] and Metzner-Nebelsick[95] are, at best, incomplete and thus somewhat misleading. The Late Bronze Age (Urnfield Period) hoard from Cioclovina cave needs to be added, which included fragments of four similar rod-shaped cheekpieces, thus actually representing the only case from the region discussed where two complete sets, i.e. the equipment for a pair of horses, appear to have been present (Figure 9.7,3–6).[96]

The fact that the burials mentioned contained only one pair of cheekpieces each may lead to the question whether these are indeed headsets for chariots (or other vehicles), or were rather used on a single animal for riding on horseback. It was Hüttel[97] who specifically addressed the question of horseback riding, underlining the impossibility of differentiating between driving and riding by the harness, or rather the cheekpieces. It was also Hüttel[98] who drew attention to what he named "Zweipferdereiten". However, Wiesner[99] actually interpreted the ancient texts in a somewhat different way, stating that probably a groom is meant, who selects four (not two) horses in the pasture for a quadriga or two harnessed pairs, and shows off his special skill standing and jumping from horse to horse, also in order to burden the animals equally on the way to his master. In the interpretation we therefore again return to the harnessing of horses to light vehicles, or chariots, at least when observing pairs of horses or sets of cheekpieces. This does not, of course, solve the question of single sets, or the problem of early horseback riding.

The oldest indications for the riding of equids at present appear to be depictions from the Bakun period at Tol-e Nurabad,[100] dated to the first half of the 5th millennium BCE, and the Sialk III period at Arisman,[101] dated to the second half of the 5th or first half of the 4th millennium BCE. In both of these cases from Iran the ridden animals are probably donkeys, depicted with saddle blankets. These newer finds would significantly push back the earliest dates for riding compared to the date in the later 3rd millennium BCE proposed by Littauer and Crouwel many years ago.[102] However, the widespread use of horses for riding is hardly documented before the 2nd millennium BCE in the Near East or Greece, and even later in the Carpatho-Danubian region, with mounted warfare documented only from the 1st millennium onwards.[103] Studies on pathological modifications of human skeletal material, such as those which may indicate horse riding in eastern Eurasia at the latest by the mid-2nd millennium BCE,[104] have not yet been carried out for the Carpatho-Danubian region. In conclusion, except for the rather unsure indication of (apparently) single sets of cheekpieces, the question of horseback riding in the Bronze Age Carpatho-Danubian region cannot be conclusively answered at present.

The various types of cheekpieces, their find contexts, and their combination, besides analogies from other parts of Eurasia, thus indirectly signify the use of chariots in the Carpatho-Danubian region, most probably from the early 2nd millennium BCE (20th–19th century BCE) onwards. This is roughly contemporaneous to the earliest appear-

---

[89] Boroffka 1998: 89 no. 5.
[90] Kacsó 2013.
[91] Kacsó 2013.
[92] See Boroffka and Boroffka 2020: 77.
[93] Gening, Zdanovich and Gening 1992. Chechushkov and Epimakhov, this volume
[94] Maran 2020a: 518 – only one Monteoru burial with cheekpieces mentioned.
[95] Metzner-Nebelsick 2021: 115 – "(...) all antler/bone cheekpieces in the Carpathian Basin were found in settlement context or come from ritual or unknown contexts (...)". Metzner-Nebelsick 2021: 119 later does mention one of the burials from Sărata Monteoru.
[96] Boroffka 1998: 90 no. 9 – mistakenly mentioning only two pieces and not citing the publication by Emödi 1978.

[97] Hüttel 1981: 176–177.
[98] Hüttel 1981: 177, citing Wiesner 1968.
[99] Wiesner 1968: F 110–111.
[100] Potts 2011.
[101] Boroffka, R. and Parzinger 2011: 128; 171 fig. 38,282.
[102] Littauer and Crouwel 1979: 45–46.
[103] Crouwel 1981: 45–53; see also Boroffka 2004b: 478; 476 fig. 58–60, 62–63. A late dating for mounted warfare has also been argued for northern Europe by Pauli Jensen and Kveiborg 2021.
[104] Grupe et al. 2019.

ance of chariots in the steppes to the east or in the Near East, and significantly earlier than Mycenaean Greece.

Paired Horse Burials

Although already excavated in 1980 the remarkable find from Oarța de Sus[105] mentioned above (Figure 9.1,34)[106] has not been remarked in most of the scientific literature. This is due to the unfortunate fact that the site, and specifically pit no. 3 with the horse burials, has still not been completely published. Of the two pairs of horses (one at the bottom of the pit, the other higher up) apparently buried there, only one animal from the lower pair had remains of a bridle in the form of two trapezoidal disc-shaped cheekpieces with inserted sharpened spikes, which were found near the head. I shall return to this detail below. At present this is the only published paired horse burial (two pairs) from within the Carpathian Basin[107] and being dated to Phase II (or B) of the Wietenberg culture, probably among the oldest of the wider region.

Beyond the Carpathian Mountain ring the burial of a pair of horses had already been excavated in 1931 at Bukivna (Bukówna), oblast Ivano-Frankivsk, north-western Ukraine (Figure 9.1,62). Bukówna (now Bukivna), kurgan 16 is briefly described in Bryk,[108] including the mention of a double animal burial with their feet towards each other. This site has recently been mentioned again by Przybyła,[109] who names kurgan V and erroneously cites Bryk.[110] A team around P. Makarowicz[111] restudied the site from 2010 onwards, however, no further paired horse burials are mentioned and thus do not appear to have been found. Burial mound 16 of Bryk was renumbered as "Barrow 17" and the two animal skeletons are mentioned somewhat critically.[112] The burial is attributed to the Bronze Age Komarov culture on account of pottery found in the mound.[113] No cheekpieces or other elements of horsegear are indicated.

Much more recently during the excavation of a burial mound (T. 1) at Ripiceni "La Trei Movile", jud. Botoșani, Romania (Figure 9.1,51), in 1997 a pit (no. 1) was uncovered, containing the remains of two horses, not lying in anatomical connection due to disturbances. Besides the pit with the horse burial, the mound contained a grave of the Yamnaya Culture and a burial, which can be attributed to the Middle Bronze Age Multi-Roller Ware Culture (now named Babino) or possibly the late Bronze Age Noua-

Figure 9.10. Excavation photo of the paired horse-burial from Negrilești, Galați county, Romania, 14C-dated to 1691–1409 cal BC (95,4 % - 2σ confidence). The surveyors rod indicates North. Foto by C. Ilie, courtesy of A. Bălășescu (originally published: Bălășescu et al. 2018–2019 [2020]: Fig. 5).

Sabatinovka complex or Srubnaya culture on the basis of few and not very characteristic pottery fragments.[114]

In 2015, a kurgan (no. 75 in the local register of monuments) was excavated by V. Ilchishin at Husiatyn, oblast Ternopil, north-western Ukraine (Figure 9.1,61[115]). Two horses lying on their sides with legs folded underneath and facing each other were found. Horse no. 1 had one cheekpiece not far from the head, as well as two bone discs with copper alloy rivets. Horse no. 2 had two cheekpieces near the mouth, as well as another bone disc with a copper alloy rivet. Ilchishin attributed the burial to the time of the Komarov-Trziniec culture and saw connections to the Monteoru and Noua cultures.[116] The pair of cheekpieces from horse no. 2 are similar with minor differences, while the one from horse no. 1 is slightly different. However, generally all three cheekpieces can be classified as belonging to the rod-shaped cheekpieces of the "Spiš" group after Hüttel (Zapfenknebel) and type IVb after Boroffka. No human burial is mentioned from the mound. In my opinion there are no reasonable grounds for (re-)dating the "Spiš" group after Hüttel, and thus the burial, to the beginning of the second millennium BCE,[117] which should rather belong to the second quarter or middle of that millennium.

Between 2007 and 2017 an extended site of around 12 hectares was excavated at Negrilești "Curtea Școlii", jud. Galați, Romania (Figure 9.1,52), which included contexts of the Early Neolithic (Starčevo-Criș culture), Late Bronze Age (Noua culture), the fourth century CE (Sântana de Mureș-Chernyakhov culture), the eighth to tenth centuries, and the Medieval and Modern periods.[118] Feature 22, excavated in 2015, is a rectangular pit of 2.70 x 1.6 m reaching a depth of up to 1.25 m. Two buried horses lying on their sides with legs folded underneath and facing each other were uncovered (Figure 9.10). Two unspecific

---

[105] See also the contribution of Vadim Bochkarev and Pavel Kuznetsov in this volume.
[106] Boroffka 1994: 60–61 no. 301; Kacsó 2013. Some further information on the site is provided by Kacsó 2011: 408–414 [vol. I]; 215–226 fig. 188–209 [vol. II] but there is no mention of pit no. 3, the horse burials or the cheekpieces.
[107] But see Sfântu Gheorghe-Arcuș below.
[108] Bryk 1932: 22.
[109] Przybyła 2020: 123, citing Bandrivs'kyi 2016: 12.
[110] Bryk 1934–1935: 117.
[111] Makarowicz et al. 2013; 2016, each with extensive older bibliography.
[112] Makarowicz et al 2016: 200.
[113] Makarowicz et al 2016; Bandrivs'kyi 2016: 12.

[114] El Susi and Burtănescu 2000; Burtănescu 2002.
[115] Il'chyshyn 2016.
[116] Il'chyshyn 2016: 81.
[117] Proposed by Bandrivs'kyi 2016.
[118] Bălășescu et al. 2020.

pottery fragments (near the hindlegs of horse 1) can be attributed to the Noua culture. The infill further contained one human bone and some animal bones, but their connection to the horses is not secure. In order to determine the date of this paired horse burial a bone sample (femoral diaphysis) from horse no. 2 was radiocarbon dated at the RoAMS Laboratory,[119] which fully confirms the attribution of the burial to the (early) Noua culture.[120] No objects of horse gear were found.

Discovered in 1996 and studied by preventive excavations connected to building projects in 2019 and 2020 (and ongoing) the site of Sfântu Gheorghe-Arcuș, jud. Covasna, Romania (Figure 9.1,48) has yielded important new data to the discussion of chariotry in Southeast-Europe. The multiperiod site has a size of ca. 90 hectares, of which around 10 have so far been studied.[121] Amongst others several burials of different Bronze Age cultures (probably Monteoru, Wietenberg and Noua) were discovered, both inhumation and cremation being represented. For the topic discussed here four pits with buried pairs of horses, all in anatomical cohesion, are relevant. The horses lay either on their sides or on their bellies. Several of the horses had bone/antler cheekpieces at their mouths. The cheekpieces are various, all having projections with protuberances. Rod-shaped ones are generally close to the "Spiš" group of Hüttel, or type IVb after Boroffka, while there are also disc-shaped cheekpieces, closer to the "kazachische Kontaminationsform" after Hüttel, or Alakul type.[122] The horse pairs were not always equipped with the same types of cheekpieces – in the same burial one horse could have disc-shaped cheekpieces of the Alakul type, while the other had rod-shaped ones close to "Spiš" group. In some cases, only one bone/antler cheekpiece lay by the mouth of the horse, Radiocarbon dates from the laboratories in Århus and Poznań indicate a date of around 1700–1600 BCE, confirming the cultural attributions by Valeriu Kavruk (Cavruc) mentioned above.

At present we thus know of six sites with at least 10 buried horse pairs (two pairs at Oarța de Sus, four pairs at Arcuș, one pair each at the other sites), from the region discussed here. In fact the phenomenon of horse burials is spread much wider, as examples of pairs from southern Poland show[123]. From Germany burials of complete single and paired horses are documented, mostly dating to the Late Bronze Age[124], but possibly as early as as the Aunjetitz culture[125] have been known for some time. They have hardly been taken into consideration when horseback riding (single animals) or traction (pairs) is discussed. Several of the horses from the Carpatho-Danubian region had cheekpieces near the mouth (Arcuș, Husiatyn, Oarța de Sus) and were thus bitted, probably indicating chariot teams. Both rod-shaped and disc-shaped cheekpieces were used, sometimes with differing types for one bit. They belong to various cultures of the Middle and Late Bronze Age, possibly beginning as early as 1900 BCE (Oarța de Sus), and certainly well documented by the second quarter of the 2nd millennium BCE.

Comments and Discussion

Several points touched on above merit further discussion. The models of spoked wheels from the Bronze Age Carpatho-Danubian region mentioned above practically all show four spokes. They are thus similar to earlier chariot wheels in the Near East and to those on the vast majority of Bronze Age images from Greece.[126] This is a different construction to both the actual finds from the eastern steppes and to the later development in the Near East, where 6–12 spokes are decidedly more frequent.[127] The use of only four spokes has sometimes been considered as not functional,[128] although Littauer[129] had already pointed out that this detail of construction was a matter of

---

[119] Măgurele, Romania: 3258 ± 68 BP, calibrated to 1691–1409 cal BCE at 95,4 % (2σ) confidence.
[120] Bălășescu et al. 2020.
[121] A conference discussing, among others, the finds from this site took place in December 2020: Sesiunea Științifică Anuală a Muzeului Național al Carpaților Răsăriteni, ediția a XVII-a. Muzeului Național al Carpaților Răsăriteni, Sfântu Gheorghe 9–11 decembrie 2020. No reports have been published yet, and I am greatly indebted to Valeriu Kavruk (Cavruc), director of the excavations, for some preliminary information – a first publication is planned for 2021.
[122] One is illustrated on the programme folder: https://www.mncr.ro/stiri%2b2020%2bsesiune%202020%20decembrie.html; last accessed 20 Aug. 2021.
[123] Recently collected, published and (partly) redated to the Trzciniec culture: Przybyła 2020, some also with cheekpieces at the horses' heads. Further cases from the Late Bronze and Early Iron Age were discussed by T. Węgrzynowicz, specifically named as animal burials (Węgrzynowicz 1981, 502: "Selbstständige Tierbestattungen wurden auf 15 Friedhöfen entdeckt." – it is not stated which animals were buried, but further on bovids, ovicaprids and horses are given as frequent, while pigs are rare and others only sporadically appear). It is unclear whether these cremated remains belong to complete animals or are only parts, which may have been food offerings, which also occur (Węgrzynowicz 1981, 502).
[124] In the Late Bronze Age cremation and burial in urns is the usual funerary rite, so that the identification of horses is more difficult. In spite of this, quite a remarkable number of cases have been published, some of which may be mentioned: Altdöbern (Teichert 1987: all major skeletal parts of a single cremated horse), Berlin, Am Kesselpfuhl (Metzner 1986, 115, 147 Stelle 71: most parts of a single horse, determination by W. Wolska), Kospoda (Montag 2001–2002 – cremated remains of all body parts of at least 4 horses), and most remarkably Tornow, with 40 horses (Montag 2001–2002, 20, with literature; specifically Teichert and Teichert 1976, 101–102: 17 burials with cremated remains of all major body parts of adult horses, besides several others with only parts of the animal). Although in Tornow it is not always clear whether one or more cremated horses were buried, at least one case appears to have been a pair of horses (Teichert and Teichert 1976, 104).
[125] H. Behrens (1964) collected and discussed discoveries of animal skeletons from the Neolithic to the Early Bronze Age of the Old World. Among them he lists a few Early Bronze Age examples from Germany (Gleina – Behrens 1964, 99 [single horse]; Köllme – Behrens 1964, 100 [single horse]; Seußlitz – Behrens 1964, 102 [single horse]) and Austria (Groß Höflein – Behrens 1964, 108 [two adult horses, a foal, and the skull of another horse]). Out of these the burial from Gleina stands out, since two perforated boar tusks lay near the head and have been interpreted as cheekpieces (Schulz 1932, 5–8, pl. II,1–2; Behrens 1964, 99). A remarkably early horse burial from Potyry in Poland, attributed to the Globular Amphora culture can apparently not be verified (Behrens 1964, 111).
[126] Littauer 1972: 155–156; Crouwel 1981: 81–90.
[127] Grigoriev 2021 recently underlined this difference – with extensive older literature; see also Crouwel 2019: 40 and Hurford this volume.
[128] Hänsel 1988: 63 "Ein vierspeichiges Rad ist niemals funktionstüchtig; ...", repeated in Hansen 1992: 378.
[129] Littauer 1972: 155–156.

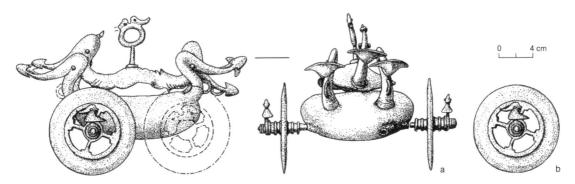

Figure 9.11. Bronze wagon model with cauldron from Bujoru with iron axles. After Moscalu and Beda 1991 and Boroffka 2004a, Abb. 14.

choice and most probably depended on the intended use of the respective chariot. From an engineering and technological point of view wheels with four spokes have further been discussed as fully functional for early chariots from Egypt, where the wheels also have only four spokes, even if this may have meant some loss of comfort.[130] The washboard effect discussed by Sandor, could significantly be reduced or even completely eliminated by the use of stiffening tyres[131] such as those clearly indicated on the four-wheeled *Kesselwagen* from Bujoru, (Figure 9.11).[132] Metal tyres were already in use on composite disc-wheels in the later third millennium BCE in the Near East and in Central Asia.[133] In the Carpatho-Danubian region (as in Greece) four-spoked wheels remain in use well into the Iron Age, as is documented by finds of complete full-sized wheels (e.g. Arcalia, Romania, Figure 9.12, and Obišovice, Slovakia, Figure 9.13). Both finds are of a pair of wheels each, which could be interpreted as representing chariots. Although especially the pair of differing wheels from Arcalia (Hungarian Arokalja) have been known for a very long time (since 1793) they have often been wrongly published as identical. Their technology and chronology have never been fully studied. Correct illustrations of both of the two differing wheels have more recently been published again.[134] For a critical research history see Soroceanu[135], whom I thank for preliminary information. A technological study of the originals kept in Budapest is being prepared by János Gábor Tarbay and their chronology will be treated by Claudia Pankau, so these topics are not discussed here. Since these two finds, Arcalia and Obišovice, each contain only one pair of wheels, they could be interpreted as indicating chariots, or at least two-wheeled vehicles. Chronologically they would in any case be dated rather late (probably not before the Urnfield Period), when the role of the chariot in warfare was waning or even already insignificant. Besides these two pairs of full-sized bronze wheels, bronze naves may be mentioned, especially the Tarcal group, which also show provisions for only four spokes (Figure 9.14).[136] They are dated between the period Bronze Age D and Hallstatt B1. Since they are mostly single pieces or fragments from hoards or isolated finds it remains even more uncertain whether they were used for two- or four-wheeled vehicles[137] than in the case of the wheel pairs from Arcalia and Obišovice.

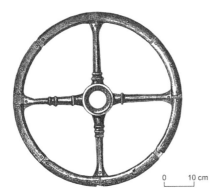

Figure 9.12. One of two full size bronze wheels from Arcalia. Adapted from Hampel 1886, pl. LIX,2.

Figure 9.13. One of two full size bronze wheels from Obišovce. Adapted from Hampel 1886, pl. LIX,1.

---

[130] Sandor 2004: 163–164.
[131] Sandor 2004: 164.
[132] Pare 1992: 181–186; Boroffka 2004a: 350–351; Boroffka 2008: 37–38.
[133] See Crouwel 2012, with further references. On the possible function of metal brackets in connection with rawhide tyres on the Sintashta-Petrovka steppe chariots recently see Lindner 2022.
[134] Jockenhövel and Verse 1999: 245 no. 126; Szabó 2015: 160–161 fig. III,10.
[135] Soroceanu 2022.
[136] Pare 1987: 36–38; 1992: 22–23; Soroceanu 1995; Tarbay and Havasi 2019, each with further literature.
[137] Pare 1987: 38; 1992: 22.

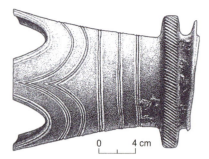

Figure 9.14. Full size bronze nave of the Tarcal type from Gîrbău. Courtesy of T. Soroceanu (originally published Soroceanu 1995: Abb. 1,9).

The probability that such four-spoked wheels were (also) used on four-wheeled vehicles is demonstrated by models with cauldrons (*Kesselwagen*). The two examples from the Carpathian Basin, Bujoru and Orăștie/Vaidei, together with one from Delphi in Greece, form a group of their own characterized by the antithetic bird protomes (Figure 9.11). Their ritual contexts (hoard and burial, birds) and symbolism have often been discussed and does not need to be repeated here.[138] Recently the identification of burnt animal fats (perhaps for use in lamps) in a related vessel with bird protomes of the Urnfield period from Slovakia has underlined the symbolic and ritual aspect once again.[139] However, I shall limit discussion here only to the fitting of such *Kesselwagen* with light four-spoked wheels as indicating the use of the latter not only for chariots (or other two-wheelers), but also on four-wheeled vehicles.

Quite a different question is raised by a specific aspect of the paired horse burials mentioned above. Some of them contained just the horse skeletons, without remains of bits or harness being mentioned (Bukivna, Negrilești, Ripiceni), while the horses in others had cheekpieces near the mouth (Arcuș, Husiatin, Oarța de Sus). Remarkably at all these latter sites there were horses with a pair of cheekpieces (i.e. a complete set), together with horses, which either had only one bone/antler cheekpiece or none at all (i.e. apparently incomplete sets). A possible explanation is offered by a burial excavated in an isolated kurgan east of the Volga river at Novo Yablonovka, oblast Saratov, Russia.[140] On the floor of the burial pit remains of two disc-shaped cheek-pieces made from wood with inserted bone/antler spikes were documented.[141] Organic parts of the bit have often been mentioned[142] and, for example, the wooden mouthpiece from Möringen[143] has long been known. Discovered more recently, a mouthpiece made from twisted fibres, combined with bronze cheekpieces and leather straps (reins?), have been preserved in the Late Bronze Age

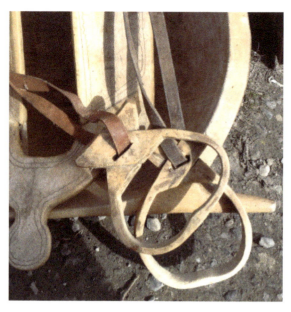

Figure 9.15. Wooden stirrups from Poiana Sibiului (Transylvania, Romania). Courtesy of Z.-K. Pinter (originally published Pinter and Luca 2018a: Fig. 9; Pinter and Luca 2018b: Photo 10).

Bækkedal hoard from Denmark, which included the harness for two horses, besides other predominantly female items.[144] Experiments have variously demonstrated the efficiency of stiff wooden mouthpieces as well as of flexible ones from rope or leather.[145] However, these mostly referred to the mouthpieces and straps (including the reins), which have usually not been preserved with the bone/antler and (later) metal cheekpieces. The idea that cheekpieces may also have been made of wood, with all caution, has been expressed variously,[146] perhaps more often in the Russian-language literature, mainly based on thoughts about finds of inset spikes without the corresponding disc-shaped cheekpieces.[147] Miniature wooden cheekpieces, together with iron mouthpieces and fly whisks, have been found in burials from the last centuries BCE or the first centuries CE at Oglakhty, in the Minusinsk Basin,[148] while older examples from China have been mentioned[149] and are discussed in detail by Hsiao-yun Wu in the present volume. Headstalls made from rope and/or leather with wooden parts have recently been proposed as explanation of the lack of archaeologically documented horse gear, in contrast to numerous images and textual references, in Early Medieval Ireland, with experimental and ethnographic examples from several regions of northern Europe.[150] From Romania even wooden stirrups, an element perhaps even more ex-

---

[138] E.g. Pare 1992: 181–186; Boroffka 2004a: 350–351; Boroffka 2008: 37–38.
[139] Ondrkál et al. 2020.
[140] Usachuk and Afrikanov 2007; Usachuk et al. 2011; Grigoriev 2021: 158 fig. 5 (mistakenly given as coming from Ureni); – I am grateful to S. Grigoriev for drawing my attention to this find.
[141] Usachuk et al. 2011: 252–254 fig. 4.
[142] E.g. Crouwel 1981: 101; Hüttel 1981: 1; Crouwel 2019: 30.
[143] Hüttel 1981: 123 no. 169, pl. 16,169, with bibliography.

[144] Sarauw 2015.
[145] See, for example, Brownrigg 2006; contributions in Usachuk 2004, as well as experiments described in Usachuk 2013.
[146] E.g. Hüttel 1981, 1; Brownrigg 2006, 166.
[147] See Usachuk and Afrikanov 2007: 204 referring to mentions, e.g. by Zdanovich, Pryakhin, Matveev, Besedin, Pyslaru/Pâslaru and the respective bibliography.
[148] Pankova and Shirobokov 2021, 68 fig. 4b; Pankova et al. 2021, 32, 46 (only mentions).
[149] Beck et al. 226.
[150] Maguire 2020. I am grateful to G. Brownrigg for also pointing out the leather and wood bridles of American Indians: Cowdrey et al. 2011.

posed to strain than cheekpieces, have recently been documented for the early 20th century (Figure 9.15).[151] The existence of Bronze Age wooden cheekpieces, and generally purely organic harnesses, makes it highly likely that the paired horse burials from the Carpatho-Danubian region do indeed represent draught teams, even when no horse gear has been preserved.

In Place of Conclusions

Overall the existence and use of chariots (or very chariot-like two-wheeled vehicles) in the Carpatho-Danubian region is very strongly indicated. Elements in this sense are a few images (including models), models of spoked wheels, cheekpieces (as representing bits) and burials of what appear to be draught teams of two horses each (with bridles). These elements are well documented at latest from the 18th century BCE onwards, with some indications that they may go back to the 19th or even 20th century BCE. The presence of chariots does not, at the present stage of research, especially on chronology, precede the development of such vehicles in the Near East,[152] or in the Eastern Steppe.[153] As far as the chronology permits, they are apparently simultaneous. However, the chariot is clearly earlier in the Carpatho-Danubian region, than in Greece. The Eastern Steppe and the Carpatho-Danubian region were probably in more or less direct contact. In contrast, connections between the Near East and either the Eurasian Steppes, or the Carpatho-Danubian region are much less documented. The rather later presence of the chariot in Greece excludes this region as transmission zone to the latter. Presuming an influence from the Near East, where the tradition of vehicles and draught animals is certainly the longest,[154] to the Eurasian Steppe[155] and perhaps from there to the Carpathians would imply an extremely rapid spread of technology. However, this idea is somewhat contradicted by the basically differing systems of bit construction (disc-shaped against rod-shaped). In any case, taking account of the complexity of chariot construction and use, I would, at present, not go so far as to claim a separate invention of such vehicles in the Carpatho-Danubian region. Possibly the very early rod-shaped bits of that area were indeed first used for riding and not for driving chariots, and that would certainly have made an adoption of the new technology much easier and quicker.

While this definitely excludes dependence of the Carpathian Basin on Mycenaean Greece, as well as vice versa, their use in a symbolic and prestigious role (as exotic and costly objects of prestige, in ritual and burials), rather than in warfare, is a common feature of both regions (possibly also valid for the Eurasian Steppe). In this respect the Carpatho-Danubian region, Greece, and perhaps the Steppe too, differ from the Near East. The general social context was probably also comparable in all these regions, to cite Hüttel on the tell settlements of the Carpathian Basin: "… *complex durchstrukturierte Herrensitze, 'Akropolen'* …".[156]

Finally, the long discussion on the relationship between Indo-Europeans or Indo-Aryans, horse and chariots has been convincingly refuted again and again by serious arguments.[157] This topic therefore does not need to be reopened again here, in spite of the regrettable fact that it still haunts some recent studies.[158]

Acknowledgements

I am very grateful to the editors for the invitation to contribute to the volume in honour of Joost Crouwel. Several colleagues contributed to this study by discussions and comments, permitting re-use of their illustrations, providing original images, indications on literature and/or further informations, for all of which I remain indebted: Adrian Bălășescu (București), Mária Bondár (Budapest), Gail Brownrigg (Okewoodhill), Stefan Burmeister (Bramsche-Kalkriese), Valeriu Cavruc/Kavruk (Sfântu Gheorghe), Mihai Constantinescu (București), Stanislav Grigoriev (Chelyabinsk), Zeno-Karl Pinter (Sibiu), Monica Șandor-Chicideanu (București) and Tudor Soroceanu (Berlin). I am especially thankful to Gail Brownrigg for editing the English language, and to my wife Rodica Boroffka for producing the illustrations. All errors and mistakes remain my own..

Nikolaus Boroffka
Senior Researcher, Deutsches Archäologisches Institut, Eurasia Department, Berlin, FRG.

---

[151] Pinter and Luca 2018a: 257 footnote 15; 258 fig. 9; 2018b: 162 footnote 15; 173 photo 10.
[152] Crouwel 2019: 35.
[153] Grigoriev 2021.
[154] Crouwel 2019.
[155] E.g. Grigoriev 2021.
[156] Hüttel 1981: 37. – A contrasting position is taken by Kienlin 2015.
[157] See Teufer 2012; Burmeister and Raulwing 2012; Crouwel 2019: 39, each with extensive bibliography.
[158] E.g. Drews 2017; Klontza-Jaklová 2020.

Bibliography

Bader, Tiberiu. 1978. *Epoca bronzului în nord-vestul Transilvaniei. Cultura pretracică și tracică*. București: Editura științifică și enciclopedică..

Bălășescu, Adrian, Costel Ilie, Adrian-Ionuț Adamescu, Tiberiu Sava, and Corina Simion. 2020. The Noua culture horse burials from Negrilești (Galați county). *Dacia N.S.* LXII–LXIII, 2018–2019 (2020): 351–368.

Bandrivs'kyi, Mykola. 2016. Pro neobkhidnist' ponyzhennia chasu datuvannia kistianykh stryzhnepodibnykh psaliiv i poshyrennia odnoos'ovykh kolisnyts' na zakhodi ukrains'kogo lisostepu (za materialamy rozkopok 2015 r. kurganu v Husiatyni na Zbruchi) [On the Necessity of Redating Rod-shaped Psalia and the Spread of One-axled Wagons in the Western Ukrainian Forest-steppe (Based on the Excavations of the Burial Mound at Husiatyn on the Zbruch in 2015]. *Arkheologichni doslidzennia L'vivs'kogo universitetu* 20: 5–18.

Bartosiewicz, László. 1996. Bronze Age Animal Keeping in northwestern Transdanubia, Hungary. *Pápai Múzeumi Értesítő* 6: 31–42.

Beck, Ulrike, Mayke Wagner, Xiao Li, Desmond Durkin-Meisterernst, and Pavel E. Tarasov. 2014. The Invention of Trousers and its Likely Affiliation with Horseback Riding and Mobility: A Case Study of Late 2nd Millennium BC Finds from Turfan in Eastern Central Asia. *Quaternary International* 348: 224–235.

Becker, Cornelia. 1999. Domesticated and Wild Animals as Evidenced in the Eneolithic-Bronze Age Cultures Coțofeni and Monteoru, Romania. In: *The Holocene History of the European Vertebrate Fauna. Modern Aspects of Research. Workshop, 6th to 9th April 1998, Berlin*, edited by Norbert Benecke, 91–105. Archäologie in Eurasien 6. Rahden/Westf.: Leidorf.

Becker, Cornelia. 2000. Subsistenzstartegien während der frühen Metallzeit im zentralkarpatischen Raum – neue archäozoologische Daten zur Coțofeni- und Monteoru-Kultur. *Prähistorische Zeitschrift* 75: 63–92.

Behrens, Hermann. 1964. *Die neolithisch-frühmetallzeitlichen Tierskelettfunde der Alten Welt. Studien zu ihrer Wesensdeutung und historischen Problematik*. Veröffentlichungen des Landesmuseums für Vorgeschichte in Halle 19. Berlin: VEB Deutscher Verlag der Wissenschaften.

Benecke, Norbert. 2009. 10 Jahre archäogenetische Forschungen zur Domestikation des Pferdes. Die Arbeiten der Jahre bis 2018. *TÜBA-AR Türkiye Bilimler Akademisi Arkeoloji Dergisi* 12: 13–24.

Benecke, Norbert. 2018. On the Beginning of Horse Husbandry in the Southern Balkan Peninsula – The Horses from Kirklareli-Kanligeçıt (Turkish Thrace). *E-Forschungsberichte des Deutschen Archäologischen Instituts* 2018, Faszikel 2: 62–70.

Bichir, Gheorghe. 1964. Autour du problème des plus anciens modèles de chariots découvertes en Roumanie. *Dacia N.S.* 8: 67–86.

Bóna, István. 1960. Clay Models of Bronze Age Wagons and Wheels in the Middle Danube Basin. *Acta Archaeologica Academiae Scientiarum Hungarica* 12, 83–111, Taf. 61–68.

Bóna, István. 1975. *Die mittlere Bronzezeit Ungarns und ihre südöstlichen Beziehungen*. Archaeologia Hungarica Series Nova 49. Budapest: Akadémiai Kiadó.

Bondár, Mária. 2011. *Agyag kocsimodellek a Kárpát-medencéből (Kr. e. 3500–1500)*. Budapest: Archaeolingua.

Bondár, Mária. 2012. *Prehistoric Wagon Models in the Carpathian Basin (3500–1500)*. Archaeolingua, Series Minor 32. Budapest: Archaeolingua Foundation.

Bondár, Mária and Györgi V. Székely. 2011. A New Early Bronze Age Wagon Model from the Carpathian Basin. *World Archaeology* 43 (4): 538–553.

Boroffka, Nikolaus. 1994. *Die Wietenberg-Kultur. Ein Beitrag zur Erforschung der Bronzezeit in Südosteuropa*. Universitätsforschungen zur Prähistorischen Archäologie 19. Bonn: Rudolf Habelt.

Boroffka, Nikolaus. 1998. Bronze- und früheisenzeitliche Geweihtrensenknebel aus Rumänien und ihre Beziehungen. Alte Funde aus dem Museum für Geschichte Aiud, Teil II. *Eurasia Antiqua* 4: 81–135.

Boroffka, Nikolaus. 2004a. Bronzezeitliche Wagenmodelle im Karpatenbecken. In: *Rad und Wagen. Der Ursprung einer Innovation. Wagen im Vorderen Orient und Europa*. edited by Mamoun Fansa and Stefan Burmeister, 347–354. Archäologische Mitteilungen aus Nordwestdeutschland, Beiheft 40. Mainz: von Zabern.

Boroffka, Nikolaus. 2004b. Nutzung der tierischen Kraft und Entwicklung der Anschirrung. In: *Rad und Wagen. Der Ursprung einer Innovation. Wagen im Vorderen Orient und Europa*. edited by Mamoun Fansa and Stefan Burmeister, 467–480. Archäologische Mitteilungen aus Nordwestdeutschland, Beiheft 40. Mainz: von Zabern.

Boroffka, Nikolaus. 2008. Glinianye modeli povozok v Karpatakh i problema proiskhozhdeniia boevykh kolesnits [Clay Wagon Models and the Problem of the Origin of War Chariots]. In: *Proiskhozhdenie i rasprostranenie kolesnichestva. Sbornik nauchnykh statei*, edited by A. I. Vasilenko, 30–46. Lugansk: Globus.

Boroffka, Nikolaus. 2018. Bronzezeitlicher Transport. Akteure, Mittel und Wege – Eine Einführung in das Thema. In: *Bronzezeitlicher Transport. Akteure, Mittel und Wege*, edited by Bianka Nessel, Daniel Neumann, and Martin Bartelheim, 9–29. RessourcenKulturen 8. Tübingen: University Press.

Boroffka, Nikolaus and Rodica Boroffka. 2020. Prähistorische Siedlungsbefunde und Bestattungen. In: Radu Harhoiu, Nikolaus Boroffka, Rodica Boroffka, Erwin Gáll, Adrian Ioniță, and Daniel Spânu, *Schäßburg-Weinberg / Sighișoara-Dealul Viilor. Archäologische Grabungen bei der Fundstelle "Gräberfeld" / "Necropolă"*, 51–83. Archaeologia Romanica 6. Târgoviște: Editura Cetatea de Scaun.

Boroffka, Rodica and Hermann Parzinger. 2011. Sialk III Pottery from Area B. Description, Classification, Typology. In: *Early Mining and Metallurgy on the Western Central Iranian Plateau. The First Five Years of Work*, edited by Abdolrasool Vatandoust, Hermann Parzinger, and Barbara Helwing, 100–195. Archäologie in Iran und Turan 9. Mainz: von Zabern.

Breu, Josef. 1970–1989. *Atlas der Donauländer*. Bundesministeriums für Wissenschaft und Forschung, Wien: Österreichisches Ost- und Südosteuropa-Institut, Deuticke.

Brownrigg, Gail. 2006. Horse Control and the Bit. In: *Horses and Humans: The Evolution of Human-equine Relationships*, edited by Sandra L. Olsen, Susan Grant, Alice M. Choyke and László Bartosiewicz, 165–171. BAR International Series 1560. Oxford: BAR Publishing.

Bryk, Jan. 1932. Tymczasowe sprawozdanie z badan archeologicznych w Bukownie, pow. tłumacki [Interim Archaeological Report on Survey in Bukowno, pow. Tłumacz]. *Sprawozdania z czynności i posiedzeń Polskiej Akademji Umiejętnośći* 37 (5): 21–22.

Bryk, Jan. 1934–1935. Badania archeologiczne w Ostapiu na Podolu [Achaeological Research in Ostap in Podolu], *Światowit* 16: 117–144.

Burmeister, Stefan and Peter Raulwing. 2012. Festgefahren. Die Kontroverse um den Ursprung des Streitwagens. Einige Anmerkungen zu Forschung, Quellen und Methodik. In: *Archaeological, Cultural and Linguistic Heritage. Festschrift für Erzsébet Jerem in Honour of her 70th Birthday*, edited by Peter Anreiter, Eszter Bánffy, László Bartosiewicz, Wolfgang Meid, and Carola Metzner-Nebelsick, 93–113. Budapest: Archaeolingua.

Burtănescu, Florentin. 2002. Un complex cu schelete de cai din epoca bronzului descoperit într-un tumul la Ripiceni (jud. Botoşani). *Forum cultural. Buletin informativ* 2 (1): 7–10.

Cai, Dawei, Zhuowei Tang, Lu Han, Camilla F. Speller, Dongya Y. Yang, Xiaolin Ma, Jian´en Cao, Hong Zhu, and Hui Zhou. 2009. Ancient DNA Provides New Insights into the Origin of the Chinese Domestic Horse. *Journal of Archaeological Science* 36: 835–842.

Chechushkov, Igor V. and Andrei V. Epimakhov. 2010. Kolesnichnyi kompleks Uralo-Kazakhstanskikh stepei [The chariot complex of the Ural-Kazakhstan steppe] In: *Horses, Chariots and Chariot's Drivers of Eurasian Steppes*, edited by Pavel F. Kuznetsov, Anatolii N. Usachuk, Pavel A. Kosintsev, 182–229. Yekaterinburg, Samara, Donetsk: Rifey.

Chechushkov, Igor V. and Andrei V. Epimakhov. 2018. Eurasian Steppe Chariots and Social Complexity During the Bronze Age. *Journal of World Prehistory* 31: 435–483.

Choyke, Alice M. and László Bartosiewicz. 1999/2000. Bronze Age Animal Exploitation on the Central Great Hungarian Plain. *Acta Archaeologica Academiae Scientiarum Hungaricae* 51: 43–70.

Cieslak, Michael, Melanie Pruvost, Norbert Benecke et al. 2010. Origin and History of Mitochondrial DNA Lineages in Domestic Horses. *PloS ONE* 5 (2): e15311. DOI: 10.1371/journal.pone.0015311.

Constantinescu, Mihai. 2020. *Începuturile culturii Monteoru Aşezarea de la Năeni-Zănoaga Cetatea 2* [The Beginnings of Monteoru Culture. The Settlement of Năeni-Zănoaga Fortress 2]. Biblioteca Mousaios 15. Cluj-Napoca: Mega.

Cowdrey, Mike, Ned Martin and Jody Martin. 2011. *Horses and Bridles of the American Indians*. Bridles of the Americas 2. Nicasio, CA: Hawk Hill Press.

Crouwel, Joost. 1981. *Chariots and Other Means of Land Transport in Bronze Age Greece*. Allard Pierson Series 3. Allard Pierson Series, Amsterdam.

Crouwel, Joost. 1992. *Chariots and Other Wheeled Vehicles in Iron Age Greece*. Allard Pierson Series 9. Amsterdam: Allard Pierson Series.

Crouwel, Joost. 2012. Metal Wheel Tyres from the Ancient Near East and Central Asia. *Iraq* 74: 89–95.

Crouwel, Joost. 2019. Wheeled Vehicles and their Draught Animals in the Ancient Near East – An Update. In: *Equids and Wheeled Vehicles in the Ancient World. Essays in memory of Mary A. Littauer*, edited by Peter Raulwing, Katheryn M. Linduff, and Joost H. Crouwel, 29–48. British Archaeological Reports, International Series 2923. Oxford: BAR Publishing.

Demeterová, Soňa. 1984. Influence de la culture de Suciu de Sus dans la plaine de la Slovaquie orientale. *Slovenská Archeológia* 32 (1): 11–74.

Diaconu, Vasile, Adrian Adamescu, and Daniela Calistru. 2014. Piese de harnaşament din Bronzul Târziu. Despre două psalii de corn din Moldova [Late Bronze Harness Pieces. About two horn Psalia from Moldova]. *Arheologia Moldovei* 37: 219–227.

Drews, Robert. 2017. *Militarism and the Indo-Europeanizing of Europe*. London and New York: Routledge.

El Susi, Georgeta and Florentin Burtănescu. 2000. Un complex cu schelete de cai din epoca bronzului descoperit intr-un tumul la Ripiceni (judeţul Botoşani) [A Complex of Bronze Age Horse Skeletons Discovered in a Burial Mound at Ripiceni (Botoşani County)]. *Thraco-Dacica* 21: 257–263.

Emödi, Ioan. 1978. Noi date privind depozitul de la Cioclovina [New Data on the Cioclovina Deposit]. *Studii şi Cercetări de Istorie Veche şi Arheologie* 29 (4): 481–495.

Fages, Antoine, Kristian Hanghøja, Naveed Khan et al. 2019. Tracking Five Millennia of Horse Management with Extensive Ancient Genome Time Series. *Cell* 177. DOI: 10.1016/j.cell.2019.03.049.

Fansa, Mamoun and Stefan Burmeister, eds. 2004. *Rad und Wagen. Der Ursprung einer Innovation. Wagen im Vorderen Orient und Europa*. Archäologische Mitteilungen aus Nordwestdeutschland, Beiheft 40. Mainz: von Zabern.

Feldman, Marian H. and Caroline Sauvage. 2010. Objects of Prestige? Chariots in the Late Bronze Age Eastern Mediterranean and Near East. *Ägypten und Levante/Egypt and the Levant* 20: 67–181.

Felkel, Sabine, Claus Vogl, Doris Rigler et al. 2019. The Horse Y Chromosome as an Informative Marker for Tracing Sire Lines. *Scientific Reports* 9: 6095. DOI: 10.1038/s41598-019-42640-w.

Fischl, Klára P., Magdolna Hellebrandt, and János Pál Rebenda. 2011. A Füzesabonyi kultúra települése Emőd-Istavánmajor (M30/36. LH.) és Emőd-Karola Szőlők területén [The Settlement of the Füzesabony culture in the Area of Emőd-Istavánmajor (M30/36. LH.) and Emőd-Karola Szőlők]. *A Herman Ottó Múzeum Évkönyve* 50: 105–129..

Garašanin, Milutin. 1983. Dubovačko-Žutobrdska grupa [The Dubovačko-Žutobrdska Goup]. In: *Praistorija Jugoslavenskih Zemalja IV. Bronzano doba*, edited by Borivoj Čović, 520–535, pl. LXXXI–LXXXIV. Sarajevo: Akademija Nauka I Umjetnosti Bosne I Hercegovine, Centar za balkanološka ispitivanja.

Gaunitz, Charleen, Antoine Fage, and Kristian Hanghøj. 2018. Ancient Genomes Revisit the Ancestry of Domestic and Przewalski´s Horses. *Science* 360: 111–114.

Gening, Vladimir F., Gennadii B. Zdanovich, and Vladimir V. Gening. 1992. *Sintashta. Arkheologicheskie pamiatniki ariiskikh plemen Uralo-Kazakhstanskikh stepei* [Sintashta. The Archaeological Sites of Aryan Tribes of the Ural-Kazakh Steppes]. Chelyabinsk: Iuzhno-Ural'skoe knizhnoe izd-vo.

Gogâltan, Florin. 2015. The Early and Middle Bronze Age Chronology on the Eastern Frontier of the Carpathian Basin. Revisited after 15 years. In: *Bronze Age Chronology in the Carpathian Basin. Proceeding of the International Colloquium from Târgu Mureș, 2–4 October 2014*, edited by Rita E. Németh and Botond Rezi, 53–95. Bibiotheca Mvsei Marisiensis, Seria Archaeologica 8. Târgu Mureș: Editura Mega.

Grigorev, Stanislav A. 2020. Khronologiia sintashtinskikh i blizhnevostochnykh kolesnits [Chronology of Sintashta and Near Eastern Chariots]. *Magistra Vitae* 2: 69–80

Grigoriev, Stanislav. 2021. The Evolution of Antler and Bone Cheekpieces from the Balkan-Carpathian Region to Central Kazakhstan: Chronology of "Chariot" Cultures and Mycenaean Greece. *Journal of Ancient History and Archaeology* 8, 2: 148–189.

Grupe, Gisela, Michael Marx, Pia-Maria Schellerer et al. 2019. Bioarchaeology of Bronze and Iron Age Skeletal Finds from a Microregion in Central Mongolia. *Anthropologischer Anzeiger. Journal of Biological and Clinical Anthropology* 76 (3): 233–243.

Gyucha, Attila, Paul R. Duffy, and William A. Parkinson. 2013. Prehistoric Human-Environmental Interactions on the Great Hungarian Plain. *L'Anthropologie* 51 (2): 157–168.

Haimovici, Sergiu and Geanina Gheorghiu-Dardan. 1970. L´élevage et la chasse à l´Âge du Bronze en Roumanie. In: *Actes du VIIme Congrès International des Sciences Anthropologiques et Ethnologiques, Moscou 3 Août – 10 Août 1964*, Vol. 5: 557–567. Moscow: Nauka.

Hänsel, Bernhard. 1988. Mykene und Europa. In: *Das mykenische Hellas. Heimat der Helden Homers*, edited by Katie Demakopoulou, 62–64. Athen: Kulturministerium Griechenlands – ICOM Sektion Griechenlands/Berlin: Freie Universität Berlin.

Hampel, József. 1886. *A bronzkor emlékei magyarhonban I rész.: Képes Atlasz* [Monuments of the Bronze Age in Hungary Part I: Illustrated Atlas]. Budapest: Az Országos Régészeti és Embertani Társulat Kiadványa.

Hansen, Svend. 1992. Depozite ca ofrandă: O contribuție la interpretarea descoperirilor de depoyzite din perioada timpurie a UFZ [Deposits as an Offering: A Contribution to the Interpretation of Early UFZ Hoard Finds]. *Studii și Cercetări de Istorie Veche și Arheologie* 43 (4): 371–392.

Hansen, Svend, Jürgen Renn, Florian Klimscha, and Jochen Büttner. 2017. Innovationen. Wie das Rad erfunden wurde. *Spektrum der Wissenschaft Spezial* 4 (2017): 50–53.

Hüttel, Hans-Georg. 1981. *Bronzezeitliche Trensen in Mittel- und Osteuropa. Grundzüge ihrer Entwicklung*. Prähistorische Bronzefunde XVI.2. München: Beck.

Il'chyshyn, Vasyl'. 2016. Pokhovannia konei epokhi bronzy v kurgani bilia Husiatina Ternopil'skoï oblasti [Burial Place of the Bronze Age Horses in the Murial Mound Near Husiatyn, Ternopil' Region]. *Visnyk Riativnoï Arkheologiï* 2: 77–90.

Ilon, Gábor. 2019. Halomsíros kocsimodell töredéke Mesterházáról (Nyugat-Magyarország, Vas megye) [A Fragment of a Fish-Banded Carriage Model from Mesterháza (West Hungary, Vas county)]. *Communicationes Archæologicæ Hungariæ* 2019 (2021): 31–38.

Jockenhövel, Albrecht and Frank Verse. 1999. Catalogue no. 126 Wheels, a Pair of. In: *Gods and Heroes of the Bronze Age. Europe at the Time of Ulysses. 25th Council of Europe Art Exhibition, National Museum of Denmark, Copenhagen, Denmark, December 19, 1998 – April 3, 1999*, edited by Katie Demakopoulous, Christiane Eluère, Jørgen Jensen et al., 245 no. 126. London: Thames and Hudson.

Kacsó, Carol. 1999. Neue Daten zur ersten Phase der Suciu de Sus-Kultur. In: *Transsilvanica. Archäologische Untersuchungen zur älteren Geschichte des südöstlichen Mitteleuropa. Gedenkschrift für Kurt Horedt*, edited by Nikolaus Boroffka and Tudor Soroceanu, 91–106. Internationale Archäologie, Studia honoraria 7. Rahden/Westf.: Leidorf.

Kacsó, Carol. 2011. *Repertoriul arheologic al județului Maramureș I–II* [Archaeological repertory of Maramureș county I–II]. Bibliotheca Marmatia 3. Baia Mare: Editura Eurotip.

Kacsó, Carol. 2013. Contribuții la cunoașterea ceramicii epocii bronzului de la Oarța de Sus – Ghiile Botii (I) [Contributions to the Knowledge of Bronze Age Pottery from Oarța de Sus – Ghiile Botii (I)]. *Terra Sebus* 5: 111–139.

Kaiser, Elke. 2010. Wurde das Rad zweimal erfunden? Zu den frühen Wagen in der eurasischen Steppe. *Prähistorische Zeitschrift* 85: 137–158.

Kalicz, Nándor. 1968. *Die Frühbronzezeit in Nordost-Ungarn*. Archaeologia Hungarica N.S. 45. Budapest: Akadémiai Kiadó.

Kienlin, Tobias L. 2015. *Bronze Age Tell Communities in Context. An Exploration into Culture, Society, and the Study of European Prehistory. Part 1: Critique. Europe and the Mediterranean*. Oxford: Archaeopress.

Kiss, Viktória, Szilvia Fábián, Tamás Hajdu et al. 2015. Contributions to the Relative and Absolute Chronology of the Early and Middle Bronze Age in Western Hungary Based on Radiocarbon Dating of Human Bones. In: *Bronze Age Chronology in the Carpathian Basin. Proceedings of the International Colloquium from Târgu Mureș, 2–4 October 2014*, edited by Rita E. Németh and Botond Rezi, 23–36. Bibliotheca Mvsei Marisiensis, Seria Archaeologica 8. Târgu Mureș: Editura Mega.

Klimscha, Florian. 2017. Transforming Technical Know-how in Time and Space. Using the Digital Atlas of Innovations to Understand the Innovation Process of Animal Traction and the Wheel. *eTopoi. Journal for Ancient Studies* 6: 16–63.

Klontza-Jaklová, Věra. 2020. Bez koně nebude slunce. Role koně v tranformačnich procesech doby bronzové [Without the Horse, There Will be No Sun. The Role of the Horse in Bronze Age Transformation Processes]. In: *Ultra velum temporis. Venovanè Jozefovi Bátorovi k 70. narodninám*, edited by Anita Kzubová, Erika Makarová, and Martin Neumann, 327–336. Slovenská Archeológia, Supplementum 1. Nitra: Archeologický ústav SAV.

Koban, Evzen, Melis Denizci, Ozgur Aslan et al 2012. High Microsatellite and Mitochondrial Diversity in Anatolian Native Horse Breeds Shows Anatolia as a Genetic Conduit between Europe and Asia. *Animal Genetics* 42 (4): 401–409.

Librado, Pablo, Naveed Khan, Antoine Fages et al. 2021. The Origins and Spread of Domestic Horses from the Western Eurasian Steppes. *Nature* 598: 634–640.

Lindner, Stephan. 2021. *Die technische und symbolische Bedeutung eurasischer Streitwagen für Europa und die Nachbarräume im 2. Jahrtausend v. Chr.* Berliner Archäologische Forschungen 20. Rahden/Westf.: Leidorf.

Lindner, Stephan. 2022. Einige Gedanken zur Verwendung gebogener Metallklammern aus den Gräbern der Sintašta-Petrovka-Kultur zwischen dem südlichen Trans-Ural und Kasachstan in der Bronzezeit. In: *Wissensschichten. Festschrift für Wolfram Schier zu seinem 65. Geburtstag*, edited by Elke Kaiser, Michael Meyer, Silviane Scharl and Stefan Suhrbier, 371-390. Internationale Archäologie, Studia honoraria 41. Rahden/Westf.: Leidorf.

Lira, Jaime, Anna Linderholm, Carmen Olaria et al. 2010. Ancient DNA Reveals Traces of Iberian Neolithic and Bronze Age Lineages in Modern Iberian Horses. *Molecular Biology* 19: 64–78.

Littauer, Mary Aitken. 1972. The Military Use of the Chariot in the Aegean in the Late Bronze Age. *American Journal of Archaeology* 76(2): 145–157.

Littauer, Mary Aiken and Joost Crouwel. 1979. *Wheeled Vehicles and Ridden Animals in the Ancient Near East*. Handbuch der Orientalistik Abt. 7, Bd. 1, Abschnitt 2, Lieferung B 1. Leiden and Cologne: Brill.

Ludwig, Arne, Melanie Pruvost, Monika Reissmann et al. 2009. Coat Color Variation at the Beginning of Horse Domestication. *Science* 324(5926): 485.

Maguire, Rena. 2020. Hard Times on Horseback. *Archaeology Ireland* 34(132): 47–49.

Makarowicz, Przemysław, Sergiej Lysenko, and Igor Kočin. 2013. Wyniki badań cmetarzyska kultury Komarowskiej w Bukivnej nad Górnym Dniestrem w 2010 roku [Results of the Study of the Komarov Culture Cemeteries in Bukivna nad Horný Dniester in 2010]. *Materiały Archeologiczne* 39: 103–123.

Makarowicz, Przemysław, Ihor Kochkin, Jakub Niebieszczański et al. 2016. *Catalogue of Komarów Culture Barrow Cemeteries in the Upper Dniester Drainage Basin (former Stanisławów province)*. Archaeologia Bimaris, Monographies 8. Poznań: Adam Mickiewicz University in Poznań, Institute of Archaeology, Department of East-Central European Prehistory.

Maran, Joseph. 2020a. The Introduction of the Horse-drawn Light Chariot – Divergent Responses to a Technological Innovation in Societies between the Carpathian Basin and the East Mediterranean. In: *Objects, Ideas and Travellers. Contacts between the Balkans, the Aegean and Western Anatolia during the Bronze and Early Iron Age. Volume to the Memory of Alexandru Vulpe. Proceedings of the Conference in Tulcea, 10–13 November 2017*, edited by Joseph Maran, Radu Băjenaru, Sorin-Cristian Ailincăi et al., 505–528. Universitätsforschungen zur Prähistorischen Archäologie 350. Bonn: Habelt.

Maran, Joseph. 2020b. Earliest Wheeled Vehicles: Power, Prestige and Symbolic Significance? The Aegean as Counterexample. In: *Repräsentationen der Macht. Beiträge des Festkolloquiums zu Ehren des 65. Geburtstags von Blagoje Govedarica*, edited by Svend Hansen, 209–220. Kolloquien zur Vor- und Frühgeschichte 25. Wiesbaden: Harrasowitz.

Martin, Louise and Nerissa Russell. 2006. The Equid Remains from Neolithic Çatalhöyük, Central Anatolia: A Preliminary Report. In: *Horses and Humans: The Evolution of Human-equine Relationships*, edited by Sandra L. Olsen, Susan Grant, Alice M. Choyke, and László Bartosiewicz, 115–126. BAR International Series 1560. Oxford: BAR Publishing.

Metzner, Carola. 1986. Das Gräberfeld Am Kesselpfuhl, Berlin-Wittenau. *Ausgrabungen in Berlin* 7: 111–148.

Metzner-Nebelsick, Carola. 2021. Chariots and Horses in the Carpathian Lands During the Bronze Age. In: *Distant Worlds and Beyond. Special Issue Dedicated to the Graduate School Distant Worlds (2012–2021)*, edited by Beatrice Baragli, Albert Dietz, Zsombor J. Földi et al., 111–131. Distant Worlds Journal Special Issue 3. Heidelberg: Propylaeum. DOI: 10.11588/propylaeum.886.c11954.

Milleker, Feliks. 1930. Praistorijska kolica iz Dupljaje [Prehistoric Wagons from Dupljaja]. *Starinar, Series 3*, vol. 5, (1928–1930): 20, pl. 8.

Minkov, Petar. 2021. Early Bronze Age Clay Models of Vehicles and Wheels: An Attempt to Identify them on Present-day Bulgarian Territories. In: *Studies in Memory of Rumen Katincharov*, edited by Diana Gergova. Izvestiia na Natsionalniia Arkheologicheski Institut 47: 203–214.

Miske, Kálmán Freiherr von. 1908. *Die prähistorische Ansiedlung von Velem St. Vid. Band I: Beschreibung der Raubbaufunde*. Wien: Konegen (Ernst Stülpnagel).

Montag, Torsten. 2001–2002. Eine Tierbrandbestattung der Osterländischen Gruppe aus Kospoda, Saale-Orla-Kreis. *Ausgrabungen und Funde im Freistaat Thüringen* 6: 17–23.

Moscalu, Emil and Corneliu Beda. 1991. Bujoru. Ein Grabhügel der Basarabi-Kultur mit Votivkesselwagen aus Rumänien. *Prähistorische Zeitschrift* 66: 197–218.

Motzoi-Chicideanu, Ion and Monica Șandor-Chicideanu. 2015. Câteva date noi privind cronologia culturii Monteoru [Some New Data on the Chronology of the Monteoru Culture]. *Mousaios* 20: 9–53.

Motzoi-Chicideanu, Ion, Sebastian Matei, and Despina Măgureanu. 2012. O piesă de harnașament din epoca bronzului descoperită la Cârlomănești, Cetățuia [A Piece of Bronze Age Harness Discovered at Cârlomănești, Cetățuia]. *Mousaios* 17: 47–63.

Nadler, Martin. 2002. Tierische Arbeitskraft im Neolithikum? – Belege von Ochsen im frühen Jungneolithikum von Marktbergel, Mittelfranken. In: *Schleife, Schlitten, Rad und Wagen. Zur Frage früher Transportmittel nördlich der Alpen. Rundgespräch Hemmenhofen 10. Oktober 2001*, edited by Joachim Köninger, Martin Mainberger, Helmut Schlichtherle et al., 109–110. Hemmenhofener Skripte 3. Freiburg im Breisgau: Landesdenkmalamt Baden-Württemberg, Archäologische Denkmalpflege, Referat 27.

Neumann, Georg and Angelika Lohwasser. 2022. Ein Luxusobjekt mit militärischem Nutzen: Pferde in Ägypten und Vorderasien. *Antike Welt* 53,4: 17–21.

Ondrkál, Filip, Jaroslav Peška, Klára Jagošova et al. 2020. The Cult-Wagon of Liptovský Hrádok: First Evidence of Using the Urnfield Cult-Wagons as Fat-Powered Lamps. *Journal of Archaeological Science: Reports* 34 A: 102579. DOI: 10.1016/j.jasrep.2020.102579.

Oravkinová, Dominika, Bibiána Hromadová, and Martin Vlačiky. 2017. Kostená a parohová industria z výšinného opevneého sídliska v Spišskom Štvrtku [Bone and Antler Industry from the Highland Fortified Settlement in Spišské Štvrtek]. *Slovenská Archeológia* 65, 1: 23–80.

Pankova, Svetlana V. and Igor G. Shirobokov. 2021. Pogrebal'naia kukla s krematsiei iz Oglakhtinskoi mogily 4 (raskopki L. R. Kyzlasova 1969 g.) [A Burial Doll with Cremation from Oglakhtinskaya Grave 4]. *Sibirskie istoricheskie issledovaniia* 3, 60–96.

Pankova, Svetlana V., Nikolay P. Makarov, St John Simpson et al. 2021. New Radiocarbon Dates and Environmental Analyses of Finds from 1903 Excavations in the Eastern Plot of the Tashtyk Cemetery of Oglakhty. *Sibirskie istoricheskie issledovaniia* 3: 24–59.

Pare, Christopher F. E. 1987. Der Zeremonialwagen der Bronze- und Urnenfelderzeit: Seine Entstehung, Form und Verbreitung. In: *Vierrädrige Wagen der Hallstattzeit. Untersuchungen zu Geschichte und Technik*, 25–67. Monographien des Römisch-Germanischen Zentralmuseums 12. Mainz: Römisch-Germanisches Zentralmuseum.

Pare, Christopher F. E. 1992. *Wagons and Wagon-graves of the Early Iron Age in Central Europe*. Oxford University Committee for Archaeology, Monograph 35. Oxford: University Committee for Archaeology.

Pauli Jensen, Xenia and Jacob Kveiborg. 2021. Bridles and Bones: Early Cavalry in Sputhern Scandinavia. In: *The Liminal Horse: Equitation and Boundaries*, edited by Rena Maguire and Anastasija Ropa, 201-233. Rewriting Equestrian History 3. Budapest: Trivent Publishing.

Petrovic, Jozo. 1930. Votivna kolitsa iz Dupljaje [Votive Wagon from Dupljaja]. *Starinar, 3 red.*, 5 (1928–1930): 21–29, pl. 9–11.

Pinter, Zeno-Karl and Sabin Adrian Luca. 2018a. Tărtăria-Gura Luncii. Fortificația medievală timpurie care taie tellul prehistoric [Tărtăria-Gura Luncii. An Early Medieval Fortification Cutting Through the Prehistoric Tell]. In: *Studii și articole de arheologie. In memoriam Ioan Andrițoiu*, edited by Nicolae Cătălin Rișcuța and Iosif Vasile Ferenc, 253–263. Cluj-Napoca: Editura Mega.

Pinter, Zeno-Karl and Sabin Adrian Luca. 2018b. Tărtăria-Gura Luncii. Die frühmittelalterliche Befestigung, die den prähistorischen Tell durchschneidet. *Forschungen zur Volks- und Landeskunde* 61: 157–173.

Potts, Daniel T. 2011. Equus Asinus in Highland Iran: Evidence Old and New. In: *Between Sand and Sea. The Archaeology and Human Ecology of Southwestern Asia. Festschrift in honor of Hans-Peter Uerpmann*, edited by Nicholas J. Conard, Philipp Drechsler, and Arturo Morales, 167–175. Tübingen: Kerns Verlag.

Precht, Jutta. 2002. Ein Hinweis auf einen jungbronzezeitlichen Miniaturwagen in Niedersachsen? Ein Urnengrab mit vier Rädern aus Daverden, Ldkr. Verden. *Die Kunde N.F.* 53: 209–226.

Przybyła, Marcin M. 2020. New Finds of Antler Cheekpieces and Horse Burials from the Trzciniec Culture in the Territory of Western Little Poland. *Analecta Archaeologica Ressoviensia* 15: 103–138.

Sandor, Bela I. 2004. The Rise and Decline of the Tutankhamun-Class Chariot. *Oxford Journal of Archaeology* 23(2): 153–175.

Șandor-Chicideanu, Monica. 2003. *Cultura Žuto Brdo-Gârla Mare. Contribuții la cunoașterea epocii bronzului la Dunărea Mijlocie și Inferioară I–II* [Žuto Brdo-Gârla Mare Culture. Contributions to the Knowledge of the Bronze Age in the Middle and Lower Danube I–II]. Cluj-Napoca: Editura Nereamia Napocae.

Șandor-Chicideanu, Monica and Mihai Constantinescu. 2019. *Necropola din epoca bronzului de la Plosca* [The Bronze Age Necropolis at Plosca]. Cluj-Napoca: Editura Mega.

Sarauw, Torben. 2015. The Late Bronze Age Hoard from Bækkedal, Denmark – New Evidence for the Use of Two-horse Teams and Bridles. *Danish Journal of Archaeology* 4(1): 3–20.

Schlütz, Frank and Felix Bittmann. 2016. Dating Archaeological Cultures by their Moats? A Case Study from the Early Bronze Age Settlement Fidvár near Vráble, SW Slovakia. *Radiocarbon* 58(2): 331–343.

Schulz, Walther. 1932. Die ältesten Trensenknebel aus Mitteldeutschland. *Jahresschrift für die Vorgeschichte der Sächsisch-Thüringischen Länder* 20: 1–18, and pl. I–II.

Soroceanu, Tudor. 1995. Der Bronzefund von Gîrbău, Kr. Cluj. In: *Bronzefunde aus Rumänien*, edited by Tudor Soroceanu, 197–211 and pl. 9. Prähistorische Archäologie in Südosteuropa 10. Berlin: Wissenschaftsverlag Volker Spiess.

Soroceanu, Tudor. 2022. Restitutiones bibliographicae et archaeologicae ad res praehistoricas pertinentes (ohne Punkt nach pertinente) IV. Arokallya/Kallesdorf/Arcalia: ein Bronzefundschicksal. *Acta Praehistorica et Archaeologica* 54: 101-187.

Szabó, V. Gábor. 2015. Bronzkor: az őskori fémművesség virágkora [The Bronze Age: The Heyday of Prehistoric Metalworking]. In: *A Kárpát-medence ősi kincsei. A kőkortól a honfoglalásig*, edited by Ádám Vágó, 104–183. Budapest: Kossuth Kiadó, Magyar Nemzeti Múzeum.

Tarbay, János Gábor and Bálint Havasi. 2019. Wheels, Vessels and Late Bronze Age fibulae – An "Elite Hoard" from Szentgyörgyvár-Felsőmánd, Site B (Hungary, Zala County). In: *"Trans Lacum Pelsonem". Prähistorische Forschungen in Südwestungarn (5500–500 v. Chr.) – Prehistoric Research in South-Western Hungary (5500–500 BC)*, edited by Eszter Bánffy and Judit P. Barna, 341–371. Castellum Pannonicum Pelsonense 7. Rahden/Westf.: Leidorf.

Teichert, Lothar. 1987. Knochenbrandreste eines Pferdes vom bronzezeitlichen Gräberfeld Altdöbern, Kr. Calau. *Veröffentlichungen des Museums für Ur- und Frühgeschichte Potsdam* 21: 173–174.

Teichert, Manfred and Lothar Teichert. 1976. Osteoarchäozoologische Untersuchung der Tierleichenbrandreste von einem Lausitzer Hügelgräberfeld bei Tornow, Kr. Calau. *Veröffentlichungen des Museums für Ur- und Frühgeschichte Potsdam* 10: 101–106.

Teodor, Silvia and Paul Șadurschi. 1978. Descoperirile arheologice de la Lozna, comuna Dersca, județul Botoșani [Archaeological discoveries from Lozna, Dersca commune, Botoșani county]. *Hierasus* 1: 121–140.

Teodor, Silvia and Paul Șadurschi. 1979. *Dépôts d'outils en fer d'époque La Tène de Lozna, Dép. de Botoșani* [Iron tool deposits of the La Tène period from Lozna, Botoșani County]. Inventaria Archaeologica, Roumanie 11 (R71a-l). București: Editura Academiei Republicii Socialiste Romania.

Teufer, Mike. 1999. Ein Scheibenknebel aus Džarkutan (Südusbekistan). *Archäologische Mitteilungen aus Iran und Turan* 31: 69–142.

Teufer, Mike. 2012. Der Streitwagen. Eine „indo-iranische" Erfindung? Zum Problem der Verbindung von Sprachwissenschaft und Archäologie. *Archäologische Mitteilungen aus Iran und Turan* 44: 271–312.

Točik, Anton. 1978. *Nitriansky Hrádok-Zámeček Bez. Nové Zámky. Bronzezeitliche befestigte Ansiedlung der Madarovce-Kultur*. Nitra: Archeologický ústav Slovenskej akadémie vied.

Točik, Anton. 1981. *Nitriansky Hrádok-Zámeček. Bronzezeitliche befestigte Ansiedlung der Madarovce-Kultur, Bd. 1 – Text Heft 1–2*. Materialia Archaeologica Slovaca 3. Nitra. Archeologický ústav Slovenskej akadémie vied.

Țurcanu, Senica and Luminița Bejenaru. 2015. Data Regarding the Usage of Animal Traction within the Cucuteni–Tripolye Cultural Complex. In *Orbis Praehistoriae. Mircea Petrescu-Dîmbovița – in memoriam*, edited by Victor Spinei, Nicolae Ursulescu, and Vasile Cotiugă, 197–241. Honoraria 11. Iași: Editura Universității "Alexandru Ioan Cuza".

Ur, Jason. 2003. CORONA Satellite Photography and Ancient Road Networks. A Northern Mesopotamian Case Study. *Antiquity* 77(295): 102–115.

Usachuk, Anatolii N. (editor). 2004. *Psalii.Elementy upriazhi i konskogo snariazheniia v drevnosti* [Psalia. Elements of Harness and Horsegear in Antiquity]. Arkheologicheskii almanakh 15. Donetsk: Donetskii oblastnoi kraevedsheskii musei.

Usachuk, Anatolii N. 2013. *Drevneishie psalii (izgotovlenie i ispol'zovanie)* [The Earliest Cheekpieces (Production and Use)]. Kiev, Donetsk: Institut arkheologii NAN Ukrainy.

Usachuk Anatolii N. and Yu. A. Afrikanov. 2007. K voprosu o shchitkovykh psaliiakh iz dereva [On the Question on the Shield-Shaped Wooden Psalia]. In: *Formirovanie i vzaimodeistvie ural'skikh narodov v izmeniaiushcheisia etnokul'turnoi srede Evrazii: problemy izucheniia i istoriografiia. Chteniia pamiati K. V. Sal'nikova (1900–1966). Materialy mezhdunarodnoi konferentsii (20–22 aprelia 2007 g., gorod Ufa*, edited by V. S. Gorbunov, V. A. Ivanov, G. T. Obydennova, 204–208. Ufa: Kitap.

Usachuk, Anatolii N., A. I. Yudin, and Yu. A. Afrikanov. 2011. Novye nakhodki shchitkovykh psaliev v Saratovskom Povolzh'e [New Finds of the Shield-Shaped Cheek-Pieces in the Volga River Basin Near Saratov]. *Stratum plus* 2: 247–264.

Vizdal, Jaroslav. 1972. Erste bildliche Darstellung eines zweirädrigen Wagens vom Ende der mittleren Bronzezeit in der Slowakei. *Slovenská Archeológia* 20(1): 223–231.

Vörös, István. 1996. Némétbánya késő bronzkori település állatcsontleletei [Animal Skeletons from the Late Bronze Age Settlement of Némétbánya]. *Pápai Múzeum Értesítő* 6: 209–218.

Warmuth, Vera, Anders Eriksson, Mim A. Bower et al. 2011. European Domestic Horses Originated in Two Holocene Refugia. *PloSONE* 6(3): e18194. DOI: 10.1371/journal.pone.0018194.

Węgrzynowicz, Teresa. 1981. Tierbestattungen und tierische Überreste als Beweise eines Kultwandels in der Bronze- und Eisenzeit Polens. In: *Studien zur Bronzezeit. Festschrift für Wilhelm Albert v. Brunn*, edited by Herbert Lorenz, 499–507. Mainz: von Zabern.

Wiesner, Joseph. 1968. *Fahren und Reiten. Archaeologia Homerica I*, Kapitel F. Göttingen: Vandenhoeck & Ruprecht.

Wosinsky, Mauritius. 1888. *Das prähistorische Schanzwerk von Lengyel. Seine Erbauer und Bewohner, Erstes Heft*. Budapest: Kilian.

Wutke, Saskia, Edson Sandoval-Castellanos, Norbert Benecke et al. 2018. Decline of genetic diversity in ancient domestic stallions in Europe. *Science Advances* 4(4): eaap9691.

Postscript

This study was finished in April 2022, so the mention of lacking studies on pathological modifications of human skeletal material in the Carpatho-Danubian region was correct at that time (p. 112 with fn. 104).

Since then a study has been published by Trautmann et al. (Trautmann, Martin, Alin Frînculeasa, Bianca Preda-Bălănică, Marta Petruneac, Marin Focșăneanu, Stefan Alexandrov, Nadeyhda Atanassova, Piotr Włodarcyak, Michał Podsiadło, János Dani, Zsolt Bereczki, Tamás Hajdu, Radu Băjenaru, Adrian Ioniță, Andrei Măgureanu, Despina Măgureanu, Anca-Diana Popescu, Dorin Sârbu, Gabriel Vasile, David Anthonz and Volker Heyd, First bioanthropological evidence for Yamnaya horsemanship. Science Advances 9. DOI: 10.1126/sciadv.ade2451), analysing pathological skeletal changes on Copper Age to Bronze Age individuals, mainly from Romania, Bulgaria and Hungary. The authors conclude "... that horseback riding was already a common activity for some Yamnaya individuals as early as ~3000 calBCE." (Trautmann et al. 2023: 7).

Earlier on the authors do mention: "Some activities other than riding, such as barrel making or basket weaving, could result in similar biomechanical stress and, thus, similar reactions of bone tissue." (Trautmann et al. 2023: 2). However, in line with the somewhat declarative use of "horsemanship" already proclaimed in the title, they do not mention intense and frequent walking/running or the riding of animals other than horses, which can produce the same pathologies.

The authors are also aware of further problems, such as the significantly later appearance of the ancestors of modern horses named DOM2 (see above; Librado et al. 2021), which even then would have been ridable only to a limited degree ("Even DOM2 horses can be highly strung and excitable animals, …" Trautmann et al. 2023: 7).

Another problem, acknowledged by the authors (Trautmann et al. 2023: 7), is the individual from Csongrád-Kettőshalom, who "… scores as high as our five Yamnaya individuals and thus meets our requirements to qualify as a rider with a sufficiently high probability. However, his Copper Age date in the second half of the fifth millennium BCE and his geographical isolation call for caution because we lack comparably assessed skeletons of this period and his special cultural context …", although the early dating and the isolation do not only call for caution – at this time horses were surely not yet domesticated in Hungary, so that evidently other activities can produce the pathologies claimed for horse riding.

Thus, although this new study is a very welcome addition to the database on equid-related transport, at the present stage of research it does not convincingly clear the question of early horse riding.

10

Archaeological Evidence for the Horse-Drawn Chariot from Inner Eurasia

Igor V. Chechushkov and Andrey V. Epimakhov

In this chapter, we present a comprehensive overview of the archaeological evidence for Late Bronze Age two-wheeled vehicles from the Eurasian Steppes. Such finds are considered by many scholars to be evidence for the world's earliest known chariots. According to the series of radiocarbon analyses, the materials under review are dated to cal. 2000–1850 BCE. First, we provide the original sources by describing each of the twenty-seven cases in a standardised manner. The description includes such features as site locations, burial contexts, human and animal remains from the same contexts, preserved material culture, and chronology. Whenever possible, we update the original published information with the latest available data on each site. Special attention is paid to the description of the preserved remains of the wheels of the vehicles and to the location of vehicles inside tombs. In a separate section, we describe related horse-control equipment – cheekpieces – which came from the same graves with two-wheeled vehicles. We provide technical details on their manufacture and use-wear analysis to support the hypothesis that the vehicles were used for transportation.

Introduction

This chapter presents a comprehensive overview of the archaeological evidence for Late Bronze Age two-wheeled vehicles from the Eurasian Steppes. Their existence is suggested by finds from 29 graves of the people associated with the Sintashta-Petrovka and Alakul' archaeological cultures (ca. 2050–1650 BCE). The evidence comes in the indirect form of imprints of spoked wheels or wheel-slots with no imprints but shaped and located similarly to those with imprints.[1] Bones of sacrificed domestic horses and cheekpieces (elements of the soft-bit bridle) were discovered in the same contexts.

The discovery of traces of spoked wheels in burials in the Late Bronze Age cemetery of Sintashta in the Trans-Ural region of Russia in the 1970s caught the attention of scholars and researchers. The cemetery consisted of 65 graves, some of which contained bronze weapons and stone projectile points, horse bones, and slots dug into the earthen floor. In four of these, the imprints of partial wheel rims and some spoke ends remained in the soil in the form of discolouration where the wood had decomposed and disintegrated (Figure 10.2, 5). The evidence for vehicles with two multi-spoked wheels was immediately interpreted as being associated with Indo-European migrations and chariot-borne warriors.[2] Further discoveries at the cemeteries of Berlik,[3] Krivoe Ozero[4] and Satan[5] also provided evidence of spoke-wheeled vehicles in the form of imprints left in the soil, including traces of their wheel hubs. Based on the publication in English of the Krivoe Overo burial,[6] Littauer and Crouwel[7] considered that they would be unsuitable for warfare or racing due to their narrow gauge which would make them unstable on tight turns, while the nave would not be long enough to prevent the wheel from wobbling on the axle. Discussions continue as to whether these vehicles would have been used simply as a means of transportation or if they should be seen as the early forerunners of the war chariots developed in the Near East and Egypt.[8] Meanwhile, other researchers suggested that they had a predominantly ritual purpose.[9]

Plaques of antler or bone with a hole in the centre and studs on the inside are interpreted as cheekpieces for bridle bits, which would have been essential for the control of pairs of harnessed horses travelling at speed. They have been the subject of much discussion and analysis, and it is now generally accepted that this was their function.[10] Around 280 examples are now known,[11] many of which were found in pairs, over a wide area from eastern Europe to central Asia and covering a centuries-long time span including finds from Mycenae some 500–600 years later than the Sintashta burials. Their typology and chronological development have been extensively studied and used as a guide for dating associated artefacts.[12]

---

[1] Gening 1977.
[2] Gening 1978.
[3] Zdanovich 1988.
[4] Vinogradov 2003.
[5] Novozhenov 1989; 2012.
[6] Anthony and Vinogradov 1995.
[7] Littauer and Crouwel 1996.
[8] Anthony and Vinogradov 1995; Anthony 2007; Chechushkov and Epimakhov 2018.
[9] Jones-Bley 2000; Vinogradov 2011.
[10] Usachuk 2004; Brownrigg 2006; Kuznetsov 2006; Usachuk 2013; Chechushkov et al. 2018.
[11] Chechushkov 2013.
[12] Hüttel 1981; Kuzmina 1994.

We describe and analyse 29 graves that yielded grooves interpreted as wheel slots. We aim to research which of these graves had probably contained such vehicles, or whether the evidence points to chariot symbolism, in which they may sometimes have been placed in the burial chamber as part of the funerary ritual and later removed. In a classic definition by Littauer and Crouwel,[13] a chariot is a light, fast, two-wheeled, usually horse-drawn vehicle with spoked wheels; used for warfare, hunting, racing, and ceremonial purposes. Its crew usually stood. Elsewhere, after Gorelik,[14] we have highlighted the difference between the "chariot complex" as a social phenomenon and an archaeological one. In a social sense, the chariot complex consists of a skilled charioteer, a horse-drawn chariot, a set of weapons, and its production and support systems. In the archaeological record, it comprises remains of an actual vehicle, accompanied by sacrificed domestic horses, cheekpieces, and long-range weapons.[15] This distinction is important for the analysis of primary archaeological sources, as it allows us to hypothesise whether the archaeological record indicates the existence of both – the technological and social phenomena – and to highlight the differences between various places and periods.

Firstly, we provide the necessary information on the study area, including its geography and climate, and a brief description of the archaeological sequence. Secondly, we explain our terminology and the way we describe our sources. Thirdly, we summarize the evidence and explain the basis for distinguishing whether the finds can be interpreted as chariot remains. In the Appendix, we provide the sources by describing each of the 29 cases in a standardised manner, organising the descriptions by the cemeteries in which they were found. We include brief descriptions of horse-control equipment – cheekpieces – from the same graves with the two-wheeled vehicles.

Geography and Archaeological Background

The majority of finds came from the steppes of the southern Trans-Urals. This area is located to the east of the Ural River and south of the Ui River (the Tobol River basin), in the peneplain of the Ural Mountains spreading east towards western Siberia (Figure 10.1). In the modern political sense, this is the area of the Chelyabinsk Region, Russia. Some finds were also made in the territory of the modern Republic of Kazakhstan, located to the south and southeast of the Chelyabinsk Region, and it is reasonable to expect more finds from this area in the future as archaeological research is developing in this huge and understudied area.[16] The steppe grassland comprises low rolling hills and river valleys, occasionally covered with areas of forest. As recent studies suggest, during the Late Bronze Age, the climate of the Trans-Urals resembled that of the present day, probably with somewhat warmer and more humid conditions.[17]

The series of radiocarbon dates obtained for Sintashta-Petrovka fall between cal. 2050 BCE and cal. 1750 BCE.[18] The material assemblage is typical for Bronze Age Eurasia with bronze and stone axes, metal spears, and stone projectile points, even though the artefact morphology differs from the approximately contemporaneous Pokrovka-Abashevo and Seimo-Turbino assemblages.[19] The terms "Sintashta" and "Petrovka" often refer to separate archaeological cultures or cultural types.[20] However, we prefer to define them as two periods of the same cultural entity as there are no significant differences in the lifestyles and ritual practices. In this scheme, the Sintashta period is the formative period, and Petrovka is the following period. After the Petrovka period, the Alakul' period follows (also referred to in the Russian literature as an archaeological culture). The Alakul' period materials differ significantly with dispersed unwalled settlements and somewhat more homogenous burial practices.

Two-wheeled vehicles and nucleated walled settlements are integral elements of the Sintashta-Petrovka archaeological phenomenon. The settlements are the most recognisable features of Sintashta-Petrovka, as some 22 of them are densely located in this area with no parallels known elsewhere in the steppes. The most studied sites are Sintashta, Arkaim, Ust'ye, and Kamennyi Ambar.[21] All are surrounded by ditches and earthen walls. The other essential feature is large (up to 220 m^2) and densely packed houses that share outer walls with neighbouring buildings. Up to 50 houses may comprise one walled settlement. The houses were homes for people and domestic animals and places of productive activities which included smelting of copper ore and bronze production, pottery, woodworking, weaving, skilled antler and bone carving, etc. No significant evidence for vertical social stratification can be found within the Sintashta-Petrovka walled settlements.[22]

The local subsistence economy was based on complex pastoralism with some degree of hunting, fishing, and harvesting of wild plant resources.[23]

The Sintashta-Petrovka burial grounds typically consist of several earthen mounds known as 'kurgans' with one, two or 15–20 graves beneath them. Such a 'grave yard' is usually surrounded by a symbolic shallow ditch, which is also covered by the kurgan mound due to taphonomic processes (the destruction of individual grave structures). Their social nature remains unclear: a recent DNA study revealed a small number of related individuals within the

---

[13] Littauer and Crouwel 2002: xvii.
[14] Gorelik 1985.
[15] Chechushkov and Epimakhov 2018: Tab. 1.
[16] Kukushkin and Dmitriev 2019.
[17] Stobbe et al. 2016; Chechushkov et al. 2021.
[18] Hanks et al. 2007; Molodin et al. 2014.
[19] Koryakova and Epimakhov 2007; Kohl 2007.
[20] Vinogradov 2011.
[21] Gening et al. 1992; Zdanovich and Batanina 2007; Vinogradov 2013; Krause and Koryakova 2013.
[22] Chechushkov 2018.
[23] Krause and Koryakova 2013.

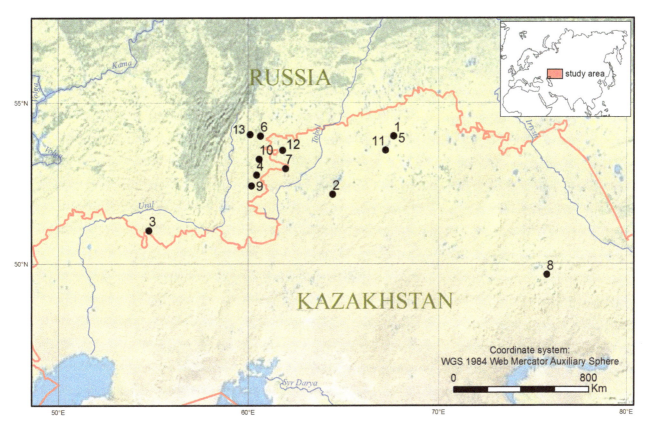

Figure 10.1. Map of the distribution of chariot burials in Inner Eurasia (cal. 2050–1750 BCE). Source of the geographic map: National Geographic Society, i-cubed, 2013; redrawn after Chechushkov and Epimakhov 2018. 1 – Berlik II Cemetery; 2 – Bestamak Cemetery; 3 – Vetlyanka IV Cemetery; 4 – Kamennyi Ambar 5 Cemetery; 5 – Kenes Cemetery; 6 – Krivoe Ozero Cemetery; 7 – Nikolayevka II Cemetery; 8 – Satan Cemetery; 9 – Sintashta Cemetery; 10 – Solntse II Cemetery; 11 – Ulubai Cemetery; 12 – Ozernoye-1 Cemetery; 13 – Stepnoye Cemetery.

buried population.[24] The number of people interred within a single cemetery is obviously smaller than the population of a single settlement. For example, a completely excavated cemetery of Kamennyi Ambar-5 contained 129 individuals while the settlement of Kamennyi Ambar would be home to some 300–600 people during a period of less than a century. The analysis of funerary practices has revealed some degree of differentiation within the buried population, related to the sex-age structure.[25]

A typical Sintashta-Petrovka grave is a rectangular pit with a wooden chamber with a ceiling, placed inside the pit. Typically, one or several people (up to 8 or 10) were buried at the bottom of the chamber. Funerary offerings, including the inventory (ceramic vessels, stone and metal artefacts, including knives, adzes, arrowheads, spearheads, mace heads, etc.) and sacrificial animals, were located inside the chamber or on top of the chamber ceiling. Thus, the sacrificed animals and offerings may be located outside the burial chamber but within the grave, as the ceiling was below the upper limit of the pit.[26]

In the 29 graves of special interest, two-wheeled vehicles may have been either actually or symbolically placed inside the tombs. In the earliest publications, the evidence was interpreted as remains of actual chariots, as the imprints of spoked wheels were recorded in several graves at the Sintashta Cemetery (Figure 10.2).[27] In such cases, the soil differed in tone from the surrounding filling, representing decayed parts of the rim and spokes of the wheel. A pair of slots was usually dug into the floor of the grave with their narrow sides adjacent to one of the shortest walls of the grave, parallel to the long walls. A common view is that during the burial process, the wheels of the two-wheeled vehicle were placed upright into semi-circular or segment-shaped slots dug into the floor of the grave which became sealed with clay or soil. During the process of decomposition, wooden parts of wheels were replaced with soil from the filling of the grave. Their location also suggests that the rest of the space inside the grave was reserved for some other element. As the vehicle would have been pulled by animals, it needed a draught pole, which would occupy the empty space in front of the wheel slots, aligned with the long walls. An additional argument was that in the graves of the Sintashta Cemetery with wheel imprints, posts supporting the ceilings of the wooden chambers had always been moved closer to one of the long walls, leaving the space in the centre empty.[28] If it was installed at all, the body of the vehicle was located in the hollow space inside the burial chamber (Figure 10.3).

---

[24] Narasimhan et al. 2019.
[25] Epimakhov and Berseneva 2012.
[26] See Koryakova and Epimakhov 2007: 75–81.
[27] Gening 1977; 1978.
[28] Gening et al. 1992: 162; 180.

Figure 10.2. A horse cranium (stallion) with two antler cheekpieces next to it (left) and a wheel imprint (right) from the Sintashta Cemetery (SM), Grave 30 (photos by Nikolay B. Vinogradov).

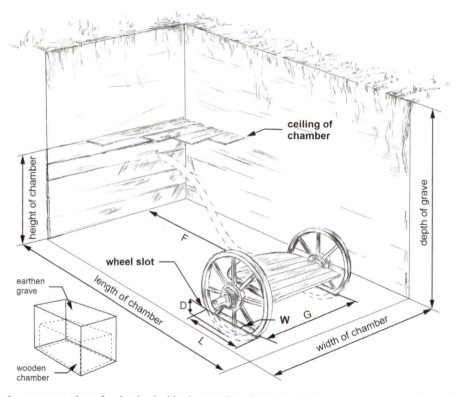

Figure 10.3. Artistic representation of a chariot inside the wooden chamber within a grave (based on the Sintashta Cemetery, Grave 12). Note that all superstructure is hypothetical and provided as a broad reference (original drawing by Daria Chechushkova and Igor Chechushkov).

Since the graves with the wooden chambers inside in effect functioned as sealed crypts, oxygen and post-depositional wood and soil replacement prevented the preservation of the wooden parts of the vehicles, as well as other organic materials. There are only two cases – the Krivoe Ozero and Satan 1 cemeteries – in which the naves and central axles were also imprinted into the floors of the graves. Such rare cases support the interpretation of the wheel-slots as evidence for two-wheeled vehicles (Figures 10.4–10.6).

There are a number of sources for detailed analysis of the chronology of the Eurasian steppe chariot complex and the related material culture of the Late Bronze Age.[29]

Horses and Cheekpieces

Represented by whole or part skeletons, head and leg bones, in pairs and in groups, horses were clearly an important element of the funerary ritual. These were domestic horses and have recently been confirmed by DNA analysis as belonging to the domestic lineage (DOM2).[30] In the Sintashta-Petrovka period, more than 115 sacrificed horses occur in funerary contexts in the Ural-Kazakhstan region. Typically, sacrificial complexes contain full skeletons or skulls with distal sections of the limbs (so-called 'head and hoof burials'). The position in a burial varied: in the space

---

[29] Epimachov and Korjakova 2004; Cherlenok 2006; Kosintsev 2006; Kuznetsov 2006; Koryakova and Epimakhov 2007; Kohl 2007; Chechushkov and Epimakhov 2018; Chechushkov et al. 2018.

[30] Librado et al. 2017; Gaunitz et al. 2018; Fages et al. 2019; Librado et al. 2021.

Archaeological Evidence for the Horse-Drawn Chariot from Inner Eurasia

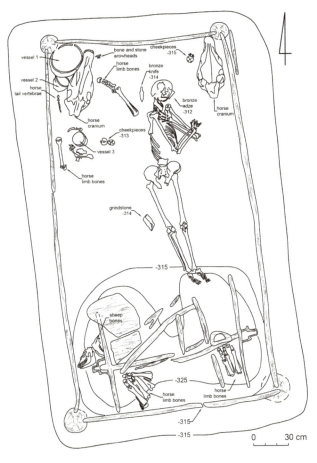

Figure 10.4. The bottom of the chariot burial, Krivoe Ozero (MKO), Kurgan 9, Grave 1. Negative numbers on the drawing denote depths from the upper outline of the grave (digitised by Igor Chechushkov from original field drawings).

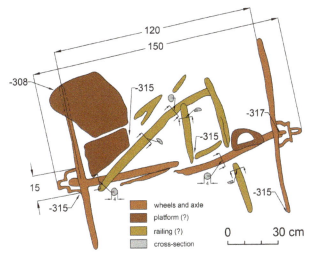

Figure 10.5. Chariot remains from Krivoe Ozero (MKO), Kurgan 9, Grave 1. The remaining parts of a platform and railing bars are visible and coloured (digitised by Igor Chechushkov from original field drawings).

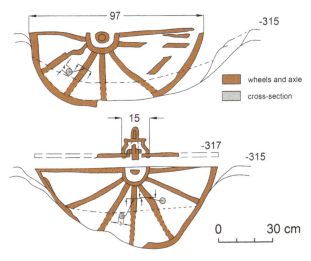

Figure 10.6. Cross-sections of chariot wheels from Krivoe Ozero (MKO), Kurgan 9, Grave 1 (digitised by Igor Chechushkov from original field drawings).

between graves, on the bottom and along the side of the grave, or in a separate burial pit. Of particular interest are examples of sacrificed horses in the Petrovka burial complexes. At ground level under the Petrovka kurgans, pairs of sacrificed horses are located outside the graves (probably symbolising vehicles). There are several cases of two horses buried in conjunction with four cheekpieces within a single grave.[31]

From bone measurements, Kosintsev[32] concluded that the horses in the Sintashta, Petrovka and Potapovka burials and settlements were of medium build and marginally more slender than wild Przewalski horses, typically reaching a height of 136–144 cm at the shoulder, within a range from 120 to 152 cm. The data in the age patterns of the slaughtered horses[33] suggest that 43 % of horses from Sintashta-Petrovka settlements were killed for consumption at the young age of one to five years, another 55 % lived until the age of 5–12 years. Some individuals, like those from the Novoil'inovskiy 2 Cemetery in Kazakhstan lived until 18–20 years of age and were probably utilised for transportation.[34]

Many of the graves studied contained cheekpieces, some of them in pairs (see Appendix). In addition, a large number have been found in graves with no evidence for actual vehicles, and in settlements. Around 280 Late Bronze Age cheekpieces from the Eurasian steppes are currently known. They were made of wood, antler, or bone. They are the external elements of a snaffle bit, used to apply additional pressure on the horse's cheeks and lips and to connect the straps of the bridle (Figure 10.7). The main element of a cheekpiece is a platform or a plaque (often referred as a "shield") that bears and organises other functional elements of the cheekpiece such as studs, an upper tab (an outset) and perforations. In the centre of the plaque, there is a hole through which the organic mouthpiece passes. The reins are connected to the two ends of the mouthpiece by a knot or link positioned just outside the hole. The inner surface often has integral or inserted studs, either ridged or cone-shaped. If only one rein is pulled, the mouthpiece presses on the jaw and tongue, while the

---

[31] Chechushkov and Epimakhov 2018.
[32] Kosintsev 2010.
[33] Kosintsev 2006.
[34] Chechushkov et al. 2020.

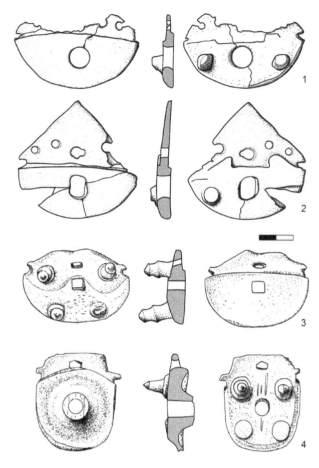

Figure 10.7. Cheekpieces from chariot burials. 1–2 – Berlik II, Kurgan 10, Grave 1; 3 – Kamennyi Ambar-5, Kurgan 4, Grave 9; 4 – Solntse II, Kurgan 4, Grave 1 (original drawings by the authors).

cheekpiece on the opposite side is pulled against the lips and cheek, applying additional pressure from the pointed studs. In other words, as cheekpieces are needed to reinforce the action of soft bits, their most likely function is to control and guide driven horses. While not essential for riding or for slow-moving carts led by a man on foot, a bit with cheekpieces is an important element for the control of the driven horse, especially, at speed.[35] The functionality of the cheekpieces as parts of bridles for driving horses has been tested experimentally, and the results support this interpretation.[36] During our experimental work with a horse being both ridden and driven, we produced use-wear on our experimental replicas that corresponded closely with the original artefacts.[37]

Technical Details and Vehicle-Related Terminology

In the Appendix, we provide detailed descriptions of all 29 graves with wheel slots. In describing a grave, we refer to its horizontal dimensions recorded at the upper level and/or at the bottom of the grave (if not otherwise specified). The depth is measured from the upper outline of the

[35] Littauer 1969: 489; Dietz 1992; Brownrigg 2004: 285; 2019: 85.
[36] Brownrigg 2006; Chechushkov et al. 2018.
[37] Chechushkov et al. 2018.

grave as it was first recorded during the excavation (usually at the sterile level, which is somewhat deeper than the ground surface during the construction of the grave). The height of the chamber ceiling, if present, is measured from the bottom of the grave (Figure 10.3).

When we describe the wheel-pits or slots, we provide their dimensions, which are: W is width (the short axis in the horizontal plane) and L is length (the long axis in the horizontal plane), both measured in cross-section whenever possible; and D is the maximum depth from the upper outline of the pit to its bottom. The shape of the wheel-pits is typically rectangular in the horizontal plane and shaped as a minor segment of a circle in the vertical plane, and we note whether there are any deviations from this standard (Figure 10.3).

The rim is the outer edge of a wheel that makes up its circumference. The spoke is one of several rods radiating from the nave in the centre of the wheel to the rim. The nave is the central part of the wheel, independently rotating on the axle and allowing the vehicle to move. The existence of rotating wheel technology in the Bronze Age is suggested by numerous finds of wagons with wheels rotating on their axles in tombs of the related Catacomb culture[38] and by the construction of the nave of the chariot from Krivoe Ozero (see Appendix). The axle is an integral part of a vehicle, joining the wheels and connecting them to the draught pole. The latter transmits the pull of the draught animals to the axle and the wheels. The platform is the main body of a vehicle, located above the axle and the draught pole, and serves to carry the crew and cargo. However, in most cases, none of these has been preserved or recorded, but the dimensions of the wheel-pits and their location inside the burial chambers allow for the putative reconstruction of the invisible parts of the vehicle in the grave.

The shape of the wheel-pits is typically rectangular in the horizontal plane and shaped as a minor segment of a circle in the vertical plane. Thus, the length of the slot (L) and its depth (D) can be used to estimate the approximate (maximum) diameter of the wheel with the formula for calculating the radius if a chord and a height of a segment are known. The formula is the following:

$$R = \frac{D}{2} + \frac{L + L}{8D},$$

where R is the estimated maximum radius of the wheel; D is the depth of the slot from its upper outline at the grave's floor; L is length of the slot. The diameter is twice the radius.

If there are no imprints present, the results of the calculation are reported as the estimated diameter, i.e., the maximum size of the wheel that would fit into the slot. We cannot assume that the estimation corresponds precisely with the actual diameter of the wheel but while it is always

[38] See Gej 2004; Shishlina et al. 2014.

somewhat larger than the actual diameter, it should allow the wheel to fit inside the slot. Next, the estimated diameter can be compared to the height of the ceiling to ensure that the upright wheel would fit into the chamber. Other than the remains of wooden bars on the chariot from Krivoe Ozero (Figure 10.5), we do not have information on the superstructure above the axle, but it can reasonably be assumed that it consisted of a flat platform, perhaps with upright sides. The sides should also fit inside the chamber, though Late Bronze Age petroglyphs allow us to assume that they were less than the half the height of the wheel.[39]

The distance between the short front edges of the wheel pits and the opposite wall of the burial chamber helps us to estimate the average length of the draught pole and check whether it was present. The length of the pole would be relative to the size of the draught animals. The typical length of the body of the Sintashta-Petrovka horses with an average height at the withers of 136–144 cm[40] would be some 140–160 cm. The pole would thus need to measure a minimum of 1.6 m from the front of the box. If the vehicles were buried intact, and not dismantled or removed after the funeral ceremony, there would need to be enough space for them to fit into the wooden chamber.

The length of the outer part of the nave can be assumed to be somewhat shorter than the distance between the chamber walls and the centres of the wheel pits, allowing for the axle to project sufficiently to enable a linchpin to be inserted.

Summary of the Chariot Burials

In our catalogue (below), we provide detailed descriptions of the graves that have been interpreted as chariot burials. Here, we summarise the archaeological evidence to consider the question of whether they are consistent with the existence of a 'chariot complex' as a technical phenomenon, leaving aside the discussion on its social meaning.[41] First, it is crucial to establish whether an actual vehicle had been located inside the tomb by reconstructing the burial rites. Second, we examine whether the evidence suggests the symbolic representation of a chariot, rather than the deposition of an actual vehicle. Finally, the evidence could have been misinterpreted, and there may have been no chariot symbolism present in a particular grave, which is important to diagnose.

The observations that suggest the presence of an actual vehicle are the following:

1) There are imprints of wheels with rims, spokes, or naves.

2) The height of the ceiling is 90 cm from the bottom of the grave. The empty space inside the chamber has to permit a vehicle to fit. The wheel diameter varies from 74 cm to 122 cm according to the cases with imprints, and the mean wheel diameter calculated from all cases with imprints is 102 ± 8 cm at 95 % confidence. The depth of the slot varied from 20 % to 50 % of the wheel diameter, so the space needed for an average wheel to fit would vary from 47 cm (a small wheel sunk by 50 %) to 88 cm (a large wheel sunk by 20 %). In other words, a 90 cm wheel would fit under a lower ceiling if the wheel were sunk into a slot 20 cm deep.

3) The distance between the slots and the opposite wall of the chamber is 160 cm or more to permit a draught pole to fit inside the chamber.

Elsewhere, we have suggested that the vehicle could have been placed in the grave only temporarily and then removed after the funeral; or it could be symbolised in various ways.[42] Chariot symbolism rather than an actual chariot burial can be diagnosed in the following way:

1) There are two slots, segment-shaped in their cross-section, but with no imprints, adjoining a shorter wall of a grave, parallel to the longer walls.

2) There are cheekpieces in the burial inventory and sacrificed horses in related funeral contexts (inside the chamber, on the ceiling, or outside the grave, but spatially related).

3) The height of the ceiling is less than 90 cm, but the other criteria are met.

Finally, a case of a mistaken interpretation is characterised by the absence of paired slots or their form is not segmental in cross-section; the ceiling of the burial chamber is below 90 cm; and there are no offerings of cheekpieces and horses.

Table 10.1 provides a summary of the finds against the selected criteria. This summary allows grouping of all cases into three categories: 1) actual vehicles, 2) symbolic representations, and 3) cases of misinterpretation (Figure 10.8).

As is evident from Table 10.1, among 29 finds that have been interpreted as chariot burials, only 11 meet the criteria for actual vehicles to have been present in the grave. In the two cases of Krivoe Ozero and Satan 1, the remains of rims, spokes, naves and possible platforms were also recorded, clearly demonstrating that the excavators encountered actual two-wheeled vehicles deposited inside the graves. The case of Krivoe Ozero is well known following the publication by Anthony and Vinogradov,[43] but some additional details can be gathered from the field drawings. Thus, there are plausible details to suggest a reconstruction of the superstructure of the chariot. The floor was possibly constructed with wooden planks as there are imprints of two boards that overlay the left wheel. The long piece of wood across the body could be remains of a railing, as it is long, located diagonally to the floor and it has a segment shape in cross-section (Figure 10.5).

---

[39] Novozhenov 2012: 37–42.
[40] Kosintsev 2010: 62.
[41] See Jones-Bley 2000; Kuznetsov et al. 2010; Kupriyanova et al. 2017.
[42] Chechushkov and Epimakhov 2018.
[43] Anthony and Vinogradov 1995.

Table 10.1. Summary of presumed "chariot burials".

Grave[1]	No. of slots	Imprints	Ceiling height (m)	Left wheel diameter[2]	Right wheel diameter	Gauge[3]	Distance to opposite wall (m)	Cheek-pieces	Horses (MNI)	Category
BIIK2G1	2	present	1	100 / 90	121 / 90	130	1.9	0	2	actual
BIIK10G1	2	absent	1.4	121	121	140	1.95	3	2	actual
KenK5G1	2	absent	1	71	71	145	2.3	0	0	symbolic (?)
BSG140	2	absent	0.95	83	–	115	2.3	0	2	actual
KA5K2G6	1	absent	0.3	60	–	–	2.12	1	2	symbolic
KA5K2G8	2	absent	0.35	106	90	120	2.2	3	2	symbolic
KA5K4G9	2	absent	0.76	100	–	140	2.45	0	1	symbolic
MKOK2G1	2	absent	0.5 / 1.3	92	94	150	2.7	1	1	symbolic (?)
MKOK9G1	2	present	0.95	98 / 100	101 / 100	120	2	4	3	actual
NIIK1G1	2	absent	0.9	121 / 81	81 / 81	130	2.2	0	0	actual
O1K7G8	2	absent	1.05	109	100	115	2.3	0	0	symbolic (?)
S1K1G1	2	present	1.1–1.2	74	74	150	~2.50	0	0	actual
SMG4	2	absent	0.3	78	85	140	2.3	0	4	symbolic
SMG5	2	absent	0.5	42	38	130	1.8	4	9	symbolic
SMG12	2	present	1.9	117 / 93	101 / 93	120	1.9	2	4	actual
SMG16	2	absent	1.1	125	125	65	1.16	0	> 2	misinterpreted
SMG19	2	present	1.1	90 / 80	90 / 80	130	2.3	0	4	actual
SMG28	2	present	1.2	113 / 90	122 / 90	150	1.9	0	0	actual
SMG30	2	present	1	103	100	125	1.9	2	2	actual
SIIIG1	2	absent	0.5	51	69	110	2.12	0	1	misinterpreted
SIIK4G1	2	absent	0.7	97	106	140	2.43	1	4	symbolic
SIIK5G2	2	absent	0.4	86	81	133	2.4	0	0	symbolic
SIIK11G2	2	absent	0.3	236	187	130	2.4	0	1	symbolic
Step1K1G1	2	absent	1.1	50	44	145	2.8	4	2	symbolic
StepVIIC2G5	2	absent	1.3	133	133	120	2.6	2	0	actual
StepVIIC2G18	4	absent	1.3	116 and 191	140 and 80	135 and 140	–	3	0	symbolic
UK1G1	2	absent	0.3	158	171	120	2.1	0	2	symbolic
UK4G1	2	absent	0.5	145	100	140	2	0	1	symbolic
VIVK14G6	2	absent	0.5	43	43	200	2	0	1	symbolic

[1] – for abbreviations see Appendix

[2] – the wheel diameter is estimated from the dimensions of the slot, and is thus the maximum possible. Where a second number is given, it reflects the wheel size as estimated from imprints

[3] – The gauge can be measured in cases where imprints are present. For the rest of the cases, we calculated the distance between the centres of the wheel slots, which is a rough approximation of the gauge

Moreover, among these 11 graves, cheekpieces accompanied burials five times. Grave 1 from Kurgan 9 of Krivoe Ozero yielded two pairs of cheekpieces, and two of them show work-related use-wear that matches the patterns produced by experimental horse driving.[44] Complete horse skeletons or crania associated with limb bones were also recorded in 8 out of 11 actual cases, suggesting a strong correlation. The cheekpieces and horses, in conjunction with the Late Bronze Age petroglyphs depicting standing persons using chariots drawn by pairs of horses,[45] allow us to interpret these 11 cases as evidence for actual chariots. Perhaps, they had been offered as part of funerary rituals, symbolising the journey of high-ranking individuals to the Other World after death.[46]

Sixteen out of 29 cases do not entirely meet the criteria for the presence of actual vehicles in the tomb. Perhaps, at least 13 or 14 cases (the case of Step1K1G1 is problematic[47]) could be explained as the use of vehicles in funerary rituals with their subsequent withdrawal from the graves or a symbolic representation of the chariot by its parts. In these cases, the slots closely resemble those with actual wheels (they are parallel, segment-shaped, and located next to the one of the short walls). Sacrificed horses and cheekpieces also accompany the burials. Such an arrangement could represent the *pars pro toto* principle, when essential elements signify the whole phenomenon. For instance, only a single slot, shaped as a wheel-pit, but with no imprints, and a single antler cheekpiece were recorded in Grave 6, Kurgan 2 of the Kamennyi Ambar-5 cemetery. The ceiling of the chamber in this grave had a height of

---

[44] Chechushkov et al. 2018: Supp. Fig. 2.
[45] Novozhenov 2014.
[46] Jones-Bley 2000.
[47] Kupriyanova et al. 2017: 47.

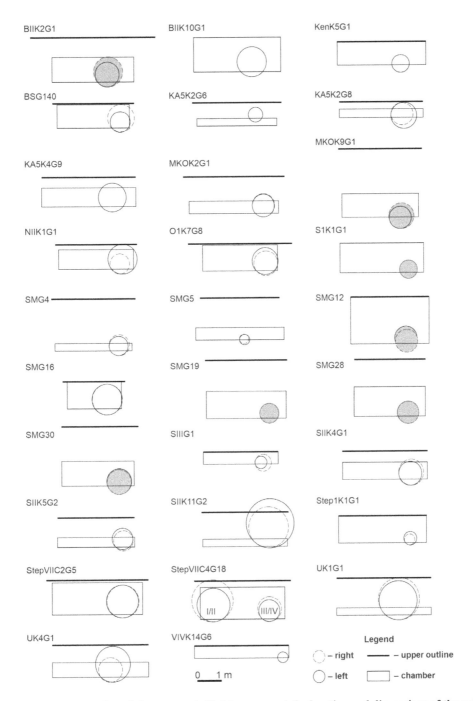

Figure 10.8. Schematic representation of the graves studied to represent the location and dimensions of the principal elements. The grave is depicted in cross-section from the left side of the presumed chariot. Rectangular shapes represent dimensions (the length and the height) of the wooden burial chamber; bold lines represent upper outlines of graves inside which those chambers where located. White circles represent the estimated maximum wheel diameter that would fit in the wheel slots. Grey-shaded circles represent actual wheel imprints with diameters calculated from them.

20–30 cm above the floor. So, while symbolism is present, it is clear that no vehicle had been placed into the grave.

There are two graves (SM Grave 16 and SIII) which do not meet any criteria. The case of Grave 16 of the Sintashta cemetery is an interesting example of an artistic reconstruction which does not correspond well with the archaeological observations.[48] First, the holes, which have been interpreted as wheel slots, did not yield imprints, and they are somewhat rectangular rather than segment-shaped in cross-sections. Second, the burial chamber would not allow for the location of a draught pole inside, as it is too short (1.16 m from the edges of the pits to the opposite wall of the burial chamber). There are no cheekpieces, and a few horse mandibles were mixed with other animal bones, unlike in other cases when horses would be placed separately. In the original Russian text, the authors suggest that the grave could contain 'an elevated platform, a cart, a chariot or some other structure' where human bones were located. They do not insist on the presence of the actual chariot. Finally, the burial was not accompanied by sacrificed horses nor cheekpieces, to meet the *pars pro toto*

[48] Gening 1978: 43–44; Gening et al. 1992: 154, Fig. 72.

principle. Contrary to these facts, the well-known image shows a two-wheeled vehicle with solid wheels and a short pole, which became almost a text-book case.[49] Nonetheless, no evidence would support this reconstruction.

It is also unlikely that an actual vehicle was placed into Grave 1 of Sintashta III, as the slots do not resemble wheel-pits; they contained rocks and no decayed wood. The burial symbolism is rather related to the sphere of production (i.e., metallurgy) than to a chariot complex.

A total of 30 cheekpieces came from the graves studied, or about 8 % of all known Bronze Age cheekpieces from the Eurasian steppes (30/277). Only 12 graves with chariot symbolism yielded cheekpieces. However, cheekpieces accompany many Bronze Age burials across the steppes which do not possess any other features of chariot graves. In the morphological sense, these cheekpieces belong to the shield-like group (Figure 10.7). Many artefacts show use-wear, and some of them are intensively abraded, which suggests their use for the control of driven horses, and many of them could have been used for dozens of hours.[50] At least three are made of animal bone, and the rest are probably made of antler (the four SM cheekpieces are unidentified). It is also worth noting that the photo of the cheekpieces located on the horse cranium from Grave 11 of the Sintashta Cemetery[51] is erroneous, as the artefacts were placed in that position by the excavator Nikolay B. Vinogradov to demonstrate their function. However, there are actual cheekpieces located on horse crania in the Maitan and Tabyldy cemeteries in Kazakhstan, Khripunovskyi cemetery in western Siberia, and in Kurgan 5 of the Komarovka cemetery.[52] As the correlation is not too strong, we assume that, along with horse sacrifices, cheekpieces in graves could symbolise the transportation of a deceased person to the Other World on a chariot.

Concluding Remarks

Excavations of the graves described in this paper, providing evidence for multi-spoked wheels, together with finds of weapons, bridle bits, and horse skeletons, have led to international interest and many discussions among archaeologists and researchers from different disciplines. Whether the remains of vehicles (or evidence for them in the form of wheel-pits) are interpreted as chariots, carts, or symbolic representations, they demonstrate the earliest known examples of the technology needed to construct spoked wheels. Drawn by pairs of horses controlled by bridle bits with cheekpieces, they predate the classic chariots which spread throughout the Near East during the second millennium BCE and were the forerunners of the prized chariots introduced into China under the Shang dynasty in the 13th century BCE.[53] The importance of these burial sites from the Sintashta-Petrovka and Alakul' sites, securely dated from the end of the third to the early second millennium BCE, cannot be under-estimated.

Acknowledgments

On behalf of the South Ural State University, the author A. V. Epimakhov thanks the Ministry of Culture and Science of the Russian Federation for financial support (A. V. Epimakhov, the governmental assignment # FENU 2020-0021). Nikolay Vinogradov kindly allowed us to provide the illustrations of the Krivoe Ozero Cemetery. Daria Stulova is an artist who helped us to prepare the illustrations. Gail Brownrigg helped to express our ideas in the clearest possible way. Any mistakes are the sole responsibility of the authors.

Igor Chechushkov
Senior researcher, Institute of History and Archaeology, Ural Branch of the Russian Academy of Sciences
Ekaterinburg, RF.

Andrey Epimakhov
Professor, South Ural State University, Chelyabinsk, RF.
Leading researcher, Institute of History and Archaeology, Ural Branch of the Russian Academy of Sciences, Ekaterinburg, RF.

---

[49] Parpola and Carpelan 2005.
[50] Usachuk 2013.
[51] Gening et al. 1992: 155–158.
[52] Kukushkin and Dmitriev 2019.
[53] Wu 2013; Rawson et al. 2020.

Bibliography

Anthony, David W. 2007. *The Horse, the Wheel, and Language: How Bronze-Age Riders from the Eurasian Steppes Shaped the Modern World*. Princeton, NJ: Princeton University Press.

Anthony, David W. and Nikolay B. Vinogradov. 1995. Birth of the Chariot. *Archaeology* 48 (2): 36–41.

Brownrigg, Gail 2004. Schirrung und Zäumung des Streitwagenpferdes. In: *Rad und Wagen. Der Ursprung einer Innovation. Wagen im Vorderen Orient und Europa*, edited by Mamoun Fansa and Stefan Burmeister, 481–490. Beiheft der Archäologischen Mitteilungen aus Nordwestdeutschland 40. Mainz: von Zabern.

Brownrigg, Gail. 2006. Horse Control and the Bit. In: *Horses and Humans: The Evolution of Human-Equine Relationships*, edited by Sandra. L. Olsen, Susan Grant, Alice M. Choyke, and László. Bartosiewicz, 165–171. BAR International Series 1560. Oxford: BAR Publishing.

Brownrigg, Gail. 2019. Harnessing the Chariot Horse. In: *Equids and Wheeled Vehicles in the Ancient World: Essays in Memory of Mary A. Littauer*, Peter Raulwing, Katheryn M. Linduff, and Joost H. Crouwel, 85–96. BAR International Series 2923. Oxford: BAR Publishing.

Chechushkov, Igor V. 2013. *Kolesnichnyy kompleks epokhi pozdney bronzy stepnoy i lesostepnoy yevrazii (ot Dnepra do Irtysha)* [The Chariot Complex of the Eurasian Steppes (from the Dnieper to the Irtysh Rivers)]. Unpublished PhD dissertation. Moscow: Institute of Archaeology of the RAS.

Chechushkov, Igor V. 2018. *Bronze Age Human Communities in the Southern Ural Steppes: Sintashta-Petrovka Social and Subsistence Organization.* Unpublished PhD dissertation. University of Pittsburgh, Pittsburgh.

Chechushkov, Igor V. and Andrey V. Epimakhov. 2018. Eurasian Steppe Chariots and Social Complexity During the Bronze Age. *Journal of World Prehistory* 31 (4): 435–483.

Chechushkov, Igor V., Andrey V. Epimakhov, and Andrey G. Bersenev. 2018. Early Horse Bridle with Cheekpieces as a Marker of Social Change: An Experimental and Statistical Study. *Journal of Archaeological Science* 97: 125–136.

Chechushkov, Igor V., Emma R. Usmanova, and Pavel A. Kosintsev. 2020. Early evidence for horse utilization in the Eurasian steppes and the case of the Novoil'inovskiy 2 Cemetery in Kazakhstan. *Journal of Archaeological Science, Reports* 32: 102420.

Chechushkov, Igor V., Iliya A. Valiakhmetov, and William W. Fitzhugh. 2021. From Adaptation to Niche Construction: Weather as a Winter Site Selection Factor in Northern Mongolia, the Quebec Lower North Shore, and the Southern Urals. *Journal of Anthropological Archaeology* 61: 101258.

Cherlenok, Evgeniy A. 2006. The Chariot in Bronze Age Funerary Rites of the Eurasian Steppes. In: *Horses and Humans: The Evolution of Human-Equine Relationships*, edited by Sandra L. Olsen, Susan Grant, Alice M. Choyke, and László Bartosiewicz, 173–179. BAR International Series 1560. Oxford: BAR Publishing.

Dietz, Ute. 1992. Zur Frage vorbronzezeitlicher Trensenbelege in Europa. *Germania* 70: 17–36.

Epimakhov, Andrey. V. 1996. Kurgannyi mogil'nik Solntse II – nekropol' ukreplennogo poseleniia Ust'e epokhi srednei bronzy [The Cemetery of Solntse II – the Necropolis of the Settlement Ust'e of the Middle Bronze Age]. In: *Materialy po arkheologii i etnografii Yuzhnogo Urala: Trudy muzeia-zapovednika Arkaim*, edited by N. O. Ivanova, 22–42. Chelyabinsk: Spetsializirovannyi prirodno-landshaftnyi i istoriko-arkheologicheskii tsentr Arkaim, Chelyabinskii Gosudarstvennyi Universitet.

Epimakhov, Andrey V. 2004. K voprosu o "degradatsii" kolesnichnogo kompleksa v period pozdnei bronzy v Yuzhnom Zaural'e (po materialam mogil'nika Nikolayevka II) [On the question of "Degradation" of the Chariot Complex During the Late Bronze Age in the Southern Urals (from the Materials from the Nykolaevka II Cemetery)]. *Vestnik ChGPU* 1 (2): 105–111.

Epimakhov, Andrey V. 2005. *Rannie kompleksnye obshchestva severa Tsentral'noi Evrazii: po materialam mogil'nika Kamennyi Ambar-5* [Early Complex Societies of the North of Central Eurasia: from the Materials from the Cemetery of Kamennyi Ambar-5]. Chelyabinsk: Chelyabinskii Dom Pechati.

Epimakhov Andrey V. and Natalia A. Berseneva. 2012. Variativnost' pogrebal'oi praktiki sintashtinskogo naseleniia (poisk ob"iasnitel'nykh modelei) [Variability of the Burial Practice of the Sintashta population (Search for Explanatory Models)]. V*estnik Novosibirskogo gosudarstvennogo universiteta. Seriia: Istoriia, Filologiia* 11 (3): 148–170.

Epimakhov, Andrey and Ludmila Korjakova. 2004. Streitwagen der Eurasischen Steppe in der Bronzezeit: Das Wolga-Uralgebirge und Kasachstan. In: R*ad und Wagen: Der Ursprung einer Innovation Wagen im Vorderen Orient und Europa*, edited by Mamoun Fansa and Stefan Burmeister, 221–236. Beiheft der Archäologischen Mitteilungen aus Nordwestdeutschland 40. Mainz: von Zabern.

Epimakhov, Andrey V. and Igor K. Novikov. 2017. Problema interpretatsii kolesnichnoi simvoliki bronzovogo veka v lesostepnom Zaural'e (mogil'nik Ozernoe-1) [The Problem of Interpretation of Chariot Symbolism of the Bronze Age in the Forest-Steppe of the Trans-Urals (the Ozernoe-1 cemetery)]. *Arkheologicheskie Vesti* 23: 345–354.

Evdokimov, Valerii V. 1981. Raboty Karagandinskogo otryada (The Fieldwork near Karaganda). *Arckheologicheskie Otkrytyia 1980 goda,* 434. Moscow: Nauka.

Fages, Antoine, Kristian Hanghøj, Naveed Khan et al. 2019. Tracking five Millennia of Horse Management with Extensive Ancient Genome Time Series. *Cell* 177. DOI: 10.1016/j.cell.2019.03.049.

Gaunitz, Charleen, Antoine Fages, Kristian Hanghøj et al. 2018. Ancient Genomes Revisit the Ancestry of Domestic and Przewalski´s Horses. *Science* 360: 111–114.

Gej, Alexander N. 2004. Die Wagen der Novotitarovskaja-Kultur. In: *Rad und Wagen: Der Ursprung einer Innovation Wagen im Vorderen Orient und Europa*, edited by Mamoun Fansa and Stefan Burmeister, 177–190. Beiheft der Archäologischen Mitteilungen aus Nordwestdeutschland 40. Mainz: von Zabern.

Gening, Vladimir F. 1977. Mogilnik Sintashta i Problema Rannikh Indoiranskikh Plemyen [The Sintashta Cemetery and the Problem of Migrations of the Early Indo-Iranians]. *Soviet Archaeology* 4: 53–73.

Gening, Vladimir F. 1978. The Sintashta Burial Ground and the Problem of Early Indo-Iranian Tribes. *Soviet Anthropology and Archeology* 17 (2): 34–66.

Gening, Vladimir F., Gennadiy B. Zdanovich, and Vladimir V. Gening. 1992. *Sintashta: arkheologicheskie pamiatniki ariiskikh plemen Uralo-Kazakhstanskikh stepei* [Sintashta: The Archaeological Evidence for Aryans in the Ural-

Kazakhstan Steppes]. Chelyabinsk: Uzhno-Ural'skoe knizhnoe izd-vo.

Gorbunov, Vladimir S., Igor V. Denisov, and Ramil B. Ismagilov. 1990. *Novyye materialy po epokhe bronzy Yuzhnogo Priural'ya* [New Materials on the Bronze Age of the Southern Urals]. Ufa: Izd-vo BashGPI.

Gorelik, Mikhail V. 1985. Boevye kolesnitsy Perednego Vostoka III–II tysyacheletii do n.e [The Battle Chariots of the Near East in 3–2 millennium BC]. In: *Drevnyaya Anatolia* [*Ancient Anatolia*], edited by B. B. Piotrovsky et al., 183–202. Moscow: Nauka, Glavnaia redaktsiia vostochnoi literatury.

Hanks, Bryan K., Andrey V. Epimakhov, and A. Colin Renfrew. 2007. Towards a Refined Chronology for the Bronze Age of the Southern Urals, Russia. *Antiquity* 81 (312): 352–367.

Hüttel, Hans-Georg. 1981. *Bronzezeitliche Trensen in Mittel- und Osteuropa. Grundzüge ihrer Entwicklung*. Prähistorische Bronzefunde XVI.2. München: Beck.

Jones-Bley, Karlene. 2000. The Sintashta "Chariots". In: *Kurgans, Ritual Sites, and Settlements: Eurasian Bronze and Iron Age*, edited by Jeannine Davis-Kimball, Eileen M. Murphy, Ludmila Koryakova et al., 135–140. BAR International Series 890. Oxford: BAR Publishing.

Kohl, Philip L. 2007. *The Making of Bronze Age Eurasia*. Cambridge: Cambridge University Press.

Koryakova, Ludmila N. and Andrey V. Epimakhov. 2007. *The Urals and Western Siberia in the Bronze and Iron Ages*. Cambridge: Cambridge University Press.

Kosintsev, Pavel A. 2006. The Human-Horse Relationship on the European-Asian Border in the Neolithic and Early Iron Age. In: *Horses and Humans: The Evolution of Human-Equine Relationships*, edited by Sandra L. Olsen, Susan Grant, Alice M. Choyke et al., 127–136. BAR International Series 1560. Oxford: BAR Publishing.

Kosintsev, Pavel A. 2010. Chariot horses. In: *Horses, chariots and chariot's drivers of Eurasian steppes*, edited by Pavel F. Kuznetsov et al., 55–79. Yekaterinburg-Samara-Donetsk: Rifey.

Krause, Rüdiger and Ludmila N. Koryakova (eds.). 2013. *Multidisciplinary Investigations of the Bronze Age Settlements in the Southern Trans-Urals (Russia)*. Frankfurter Archäologische Schriften 23. Bonn: Habelt.

Kukushkin, Igor A. and Evgenii A. Dmitriev. 2019. Burial with a Chariot at the Tabyldy Cemetery, Central Kazakhstan. *Archaeology, ethnography and anthropology of Eurasia* 47 (4): 43–52.

Kupriyanova, Elena, Andrey Epimakhov, Natalia Berseneva, and Andrey Bersenev. 2017. Bronze Age Charioteers of the Eurasian Steppe: a Part-Time Occupation for Select Men? *Prähistorische Zeitschrift* 92: 40–65.

Kuz'mina, Elena E. 1994. *Otkuda prishli indoarii? Materialnaya kultura plemen andronovskoy obsshosti i proishozhdenie indoirancev* [Where did the Indo-Aryans come From?: Material Culture of the Andronovo Community and the Origin of the Indo-Iranians]. Moscow: Nauka.

Kuznetsov, Pavel F. 2006. The Emergence of Bronze Age Chariots in Eastern Europe. *Antiquity* 80 (309): 638–645.

Kuznetsov, Pavel F., Anatolii N. Usachuk, Pavel A. Kosintsev et al (eds.). 2010. *Koni, kolesnicy i kolesničie stepej evrazii* [*Horses, Chariots and Chariot's Drivers of Eurasian Steppes*]. Yekaterinburg-Samara-Donetsk: Rifey.

Librado, Pablo, Cristina Gamba, Charleen Gaunitz et al. 2017. Ancient Genomic Changes Associated with Domestication of the Horse. *Science* 356 (6336): 442–445.

Librado, Pablo, Naveed Khan, Antoine Fages et al. 2021. The Origins and Spread of Domestic Horses from the Western Eurasian Steppes. *Nature* 598: 634–640.

Littauer, Mary A. 1969. Bits and Pieces. *Antiquity* 43: 289–300. (Reprinted in Littauer and Crouwel 2002: 487–504).

Littauer, Mary A. and Joost H. Crouwel. 1996. The Origin of the True Chariot. *Antiquity* 70 (270): 934–939. (Reprinted in Littauer and Crouwel 2002, 45–52).

Littauer, Mary A. and Joost H. Crouwel. 2002. *Selected Writings on Chariots and Other Early Vehicles, Riding and Harness*, edited by Peter Raulwing. Culture and History of the Ancient Near East 6. Leiden: Brill.

Logvin, Vladimir N. and Irina V. Shevnina. 2008. Elitnoe pogrebenie sintashtinsko-petrovskogo vremeni s mogil'nika Bestamak [An Elite Burial of the Sintashta-Petrovka Period from the Bestamak Cemetery]. In: *VII istoricheskiye chteniya pamyati Mikhaila Petrovicha Gryaznova: sbornik nauchnykh trudov*, edited by S. F. Tataurov and I. V. Tolpeko, 190–197. Omsk: Izd-vo Omskogo gos. un-ta.

Molodin, Vyacheslav I., Andrey V. Epimakhov, and Zhanna V. Marchenko. 2014.

Molodin, Vyacheslav I., Andrey V. Epimakhov, and Zhanna V. Marchenko. 2014. Radiouglerodnaia khronologiia kul'tur epokhi bronzy Urala i yuga Zapadnoi Sibiri: printsipy i podkhody, dostizheniia i problemy [Radiocarbon chronology of the South Urals and the south of the Western Siberia cultures (2000–2013-years investigations): principles and approaches, achievements and problems]. *Vestnik Novosibirskogo gosudarstvennogo universiteta, Seriia: Istoriia, Filologiia* 13 (3): 136–167.

Narasimhan, Vagheesh M. et al. 2019. The Formation of Human Populations in South and Central Asia. *Science* 365(6457): eaat7487.

Novozhenov, Viktor A. 1989. Kolesnyy transport epokhi bronzy Uralo-Kazakhstanskikh stepei [Wheeled Transport of the Bronze Age of the Ural-Kazakhstan Steppes]. In: *Voprosy arkheologii Tsentral'nogo i Severnogo Kazakhstana: sbornik nauchnykh trudov*, edited by V. V. Evdokimov, 110–122. Karaganda: Izd-vo KarGU.

Novozhenov, Viktor A. 2012. *Chudo kommunikatsii i drevneyshiy kolesnyy transport Yevrazii* [Communications and Earliest Wheeled Transport of Eurasia]. Moscow: Taus Publishing.

Novozhenov, Viktor. A. 2014. Glava 3. Izobrazitel'nyye kommunikatsii [Chapter 3. Graphic communications]. In: *Tainstvo etnicheskoi istorii drevneishikh nomadov stepnoi Evrazii*, edited by A. V. Epimakhov and V. A. Novozhenov, 206–249. Almaty: "Ostrov Krym".

Parpola, Asko and Christian Carpelan. 2005. The Cultural Counterparts to Proto-Indo-European, Proto-Uralic and Proto-Aryan: Matching the Dispersal and Contact Patterns in the Linguistic and Archaeological Record. In: *The Indo-Aryan controversy: Evidence and Inference in Indian History*, edited by Edwin F. Bryant and Laurie L. Patton, 107–141. Oxford: Routledge.

Rawson, Jessica, Konstantin Chugunov, Yegor Grebnev et al. 2020. Chariotry and Prone Burials: Reassessing Late Shang China's Relationship with its Northern Neighbours. *Journal of World Prehistory* 33 (2): 135–168.

Shishlina, Natalia I., Denis S. Kovalev, and Elena R. Ibragimova. 2014. Catacomb Culture Wagons of the Eurasian Steppes. *Antiquity* 88 (340): 378–394.

Stefanov, Vladimir I. and Andrey V. Epimakhov. 2006. Sintashtinskii III [malyi] kurgan: nekotorye podrobnosti i novye siuzhety [The Sintashta III (Small) Mound: New Details and New Plots]. In: *Voprosy arkheologii Povolzh'ya* 4: 263–271. Samara: Izd-vo "Nauchno-tekhnicheskiy tsentr".

Stobbe, Astrid, Maren Gumnior, Lisa Rühl, and Heike Schneider 2016. Bronze Age Human–Landscape Interactions in the Southern Transural Steppe, Russia – Evidence from High-Resolution Palaeobotanical Studies. *The Holocene* 26(10): 1692–1710.

Usachuk, Anatoliy N. (ed.) 2004. *Psalii.Elementy upriazhi i konskogo snariazheniia v drevnosti* [Psalia. Elements of Harness and Horse Gear in Antiquity]. *Arkheologicheskii almanakh* 15. Donetsk: Donetskii oblastnoi kraevedsheskii musei.

Usachuk, Anatoliy N. 2013. *Drevneyshiye psalii (izgotovleniye i ispol'zovaniye)* [The Earliest Cheekpieces (Production and Use)]. Kiev-Donetsk: Institut arkheologii NAN Ukrainy.

Vinogradov, Nikolay B. 2003. *Mogil'nik bronzovogo veka Krivoye Ozero v Yuzhnom Zaural'ye* [The Bronze Age Cemetery of Krivoe Ozero in the Southern Urals]. Chelyabinsk: Yuzhno-Ural'skoye kn. izd-vo.

Vinogradov, Nikolay B. 2011. *Stepi Yuzhnogo Urala i Kazakhstana v pervyye veka II tys. do n.e. [pamyatniki sintashtinskogo i petrovskogo tipa]* (Steppes of the Southern Urals and Kazakhstan in the First Centuries of the 2nd Millennium BC. [Sites of the Sintashta and Petrovka Types]). Chelyabinsk: Abris.

Vinogradov, Nikolay B. (ed.). 2013. *Drevneye Ust'e: ukreplennoe poseleniye bronzovogo veka v Yuzhnom Zaural'e: Kollektivnaia monografiia* [Ancient Ust'e: Fortified Settlement of the Bronze Age in the Southern Trans-Urals. A Collective Monograph]. Chelyabinsk: Abris.

Zdanovich, Gennadiy B. 1978. *Otchet ob arkheologicheskikh issledovaniyakh UKAE v 1977 godu* [A Field Report on the Archaeological Investigations of the UKAE in 1977]. Retrieved from the Archive of the Chelyabinsk State University.

Zdanovich, Gennadiy B. 1988. *Bronzovyi vek Uralo-Kazakhstanskikh stepei* [The Bronze Age of the Ural-Kazakhstan steppes]. Sverdlovsk: Izd-vo Ural'skogo un-ta.

Zdanovich, Gennadiy B. and I. M. Batanina. 2007. *Arkaim – strana gorodov. Prostranstvo i obrazy* (Arkaim and the Country of Towns. Spatial Dimension and Images). Chelyabinsk: Krokus.

Wu, Hsiao-yun. 2013. *Chariots in Early China: Origins, Cultural Interaction, and Identity*. BAR International Series 2457. Oxford: BAR Publishing.

Appendix
Catalogue of Late Bronze Age chariot burials from the Eurasian Steppes (Figure 10.1)

We provide a standardised description of the chariot burials, including offerings and information on the human remains. We use G to signify the gauge, or distance between the wheels (the wheel track), measured between the centres of the long axes of the wheel pits. E is the distance from the external edges of the wheel pits to the nearest wall. F is the distance from their front edges to the opposite wall. When describing the wheel slots, W is width (the short axis in the horizontal plane); L is length (the long axis in the horizontal plane); and D is the maximum depth from the upper outline of the pit to its bottom (Figure 10.3).

*Indicates graves with imprints of wheels and parts of a vehicle or traces of wood.

1. Berlik Cemeteries, Northern Kazakhstan

The Cemeteries near the Village of Berlik, consisting of the Berlik II, Kenes and Aksayman sites, are located at 54°0' N and 67°37' E on the left bank of the Ishim River. They are attributed to the Petrovka period. Kurgans 2 and 10 of Berlik II cemetery were associated with the "chariot complex", while in Kurgan 1, the complete skeletons of two horses were located under the burial mound next to the looted grave, which contained the cranium of a third horse. Seven cheekpieces were found in Aksayman and Berlik II. Four cheekpieces from Aksayman are made of tubular bone and belong to the plate-shaped type, and three from Berlik II are made from flattened bone and belong to the shield type.[54]

*Berlik II, Kurgan 2, Grave 1 (BIIK2G1)

The irregularly shaped grave measured 4.1 m x 5.2 m in its upper outline and had a depth of 1.8 m. At a depth of 0.8 m, the grave took a rectangular shape with dimensions of 3.4 m x 2.5 m. There was no burial chamber with a ceiling inside the grave. Two complete horse skeletons were located under the mound, adjacent to the grave on its north and south sides.

In the eastern part of the grave, adjoining a short wall, were two slots for spoked wheels – right slot: W = 15 cm, L = 80 cm, D = 20 cm, left slot: W = 20 cm, L = 90 cm, D = 20 cm. In the vertical sections, the imprints of rims and three spokes of each wheel were recorded. The spokes measured 3.5 cm x 3.5–4 cm and were described as rectangular in cross-section. The estimated diameters are 100 cm and 120 cm, respectively, but the actual wheel diameter was somewhat smaller as the weight of the filling soil had distorted the wheels. It had perhaps been about 90 cm. The slots were aligned parallel to each other in a WNW–ESE direction.

G = 130 cm.

E = 20 cm on the left and 25 cm on the right.

F = 190 cm.

No human remains were reported. The artefact assemblage consisted of a metal awl, a metal brace, and sherds from 16 ceramic vessels. In the upper filling were the skeletons of two dogs and several incisors, fish gill covers, and various horse bones. Moreover, horse ribs and teeth were found on

---
[54] Zdanovich 1988: 71–86.

a ledge near the northern wall, and a horse cranium had been placed in the north-eastern corner of the grave.[55]

This find is a clear example of a two-wheeled vehicle which was placed into the grave during the funerary ritual and remained there.

*Berlik II, Kurgan 10, Grave 1 (BIIK10G1)

Kurgan 10 contained a single grave, measuring 3.6 m x 2.7 m x 1.4 m deep, with its long walls aligned WNW–ESE. There was no burial chamber with a ceiling inside the grave. A skeleton of a horse and a cranium from another horse were found under the burial mound lying outside the grave.

In the east-south-eastern part of the grave, adjoining a short wall, were two slots filled with clay. Both slots measured W = 30 cm, L = 90 cm, D = 20 cm. The estimated wheel diameter is 100 cm for each slot. Inside the right wheel-pit, decayed wood was recorded. The slots were aligned parallel to each other in a W–NW direction.

G = 140 cm.

E = 20 cm on the left and 25 cm on the right.

F = 195 cm.

No human remains were reported. The artefact assemblage consists of five stone arrowheads, a bronze awl, fragments of four ceramic vessels, and three cheekpieces.[56] The cheekpieces are made of bone and each of the two better-preserved examples had a pair (?) of small studs (Figure 10.7, 1–2). There is evidence of wear in the lower areas around their bit-holes, which is suggestive of moderate use. The dimensions of the chamber and the presence of cheekpieces allow us to conclude that the actual vehicle was originally placed in this tomb.

Kenes, Kurgan 5, Grave 1 (KenK5G1)

The looted grave measured 3.7 m x 2.2 m x 1 m deep and was aligned in a SSE–NNW direction. Both slots measured W = 30 cm, L = 70 cm, D = 30 cm. The reconstructed diameter of a wheel that would fit into the slot is about 70 cm. The slots were aligned parallel to each other along to the long axis of the grave.

G = 145 cm.

E = 20 cm.

F = 230 cm.

No human remains or funeral offerings were reported.[57]

As the evidence is scanty, it is hard to conclude whether a vehicle had originally remained in the grave or if it was displaced or removed when the burial was looted.

2. Bestamak Cemetery, Grave 140, Northern Kazakhstan (BSG140)

The Bestamak burial ground and settlement are located on the right bank of the Buruktal River, a left tributary of the Ubagan River of the Ishim basin in Northern Kazakhstan at 52°13' N, 64°26' E. The cemetery consists of over 150 graves of the Sintashta, Petrovka and Alakul' periods. A total of eight antler and bone cheekpieces were found in various graves of the cemetery.

The Sintashta period grave 140 measured 3.6 m x 2.5 m x 1 m deep and was aligned in an E–W direction. The wooden chamber measured 3 m x 1.75 m with the ceiling located 0.95 m above the floor. Above the ceiling, two horses were placed along the long walls of the grave. The southern horse was laid on its left side, and the northern horse was probably laid on its right side, but the remains were disturbed by a later intrusion.

In the southeast corner of the grave, parallel to a long wall, was found an apparent pit for a left wheel. The second (right) slot had been severely disturbed by the ditch of a later burial ground. The slots were easily visible in the yellow sandy bottom as they were filled with greyish-brown and grey soil. The left slot measured: W = 20 cm, L = 67 cm, D = 17 cm, and that on the right was W = 20 cm, L = 76 (?) cm, D = 15 cm. The estimated wheel diameter corresponding to the left slot is 83 cm.

G = 115 cm.

E = 25 cm on the left and ~15 cm on the right.

F = 230 cm.

The slots were aligned parallel to each other in a W–E direction. The height of the ceiling, the dimensions and location of the slots suggest that a two-wheeled vehicle had been present in the burial.

The remains of a 50–55-year-old male were found in the grave. The inventory consisted of five ceramic vessels, twelve long arrowheads, a stone mace, three pestles, three grinding stones, flat pebbles, two pieces of azurite, a battle axe, a bronze plaque-pendant, a bronze knife, a bronze hook, a transverse blade axe, a chisel, and two bronze sickles.[58]

3. Kamennyi Ambar-5 Cemetery, Southern Ural, Russia

The Kamennyi Ambar-5 cemetery (KA5) is located at 52°49'37" N and 60°28'6" E, on the right bank of the Karagaily-Ayat River, a left tributary of the Tobol River. The three graves of Kurgan 2 and Kurgan 4 yielded Sintashta-like wheel-pits, while 12 cheekpieces were found in various contexts within the kurgans. 17 AMS radiocarbon dates from various contexts provide chronological information.

---

[55] Zdanovich 1988: 74–75.
[56] Zdanovich 1988: 76–77.
[57] Zdanovich 1988: 71–74.
[58] Logvin and Shevnina 2008.

Kamennyi Ambar-5 Cemetery, Kurgan 2, Grave 6 (KA5K2G6)

The rectangular grave measured 3.7 m x 2.1 m x 0.95 m deep, and was aligned in a north-south direction with an inclination of 8° east. A wooden box was placed inside the grave creating the inner space of the burial chamber. Its internal dimensions were 3.3 m x 1.8 m, with a ceiling demarcated by wooden planking of about 0.2–0.3 m above the floor of the grave. The crania and leg bones of two horses were found above the ceiling in the west-southwest corner.

The grave belongs to the list of chariot burials with a great deal of convention, as it yielded a single wheel slot. The groove was located parallel to the long walls of the grave adjoining the north wall. It had an elongated oval contour, was oriented along the SW–NNE axis, and was segment-shaped in cross-section. Its dimensions are W = 110 cm, L = 60 cm, D = 30 cm.

Eight individuals were buried in the grave: two genetically and skeletally male individuals 30–35 and 13–16 years old, two adolescents of 8–12 and 9–13 years old, and four children of various ages from 0 to 10. The grave had been looted: parts of human skeletons were detached and chaotically scattered on the floor. The deceased were accompanied by a metal knife, a metal adze, a metal plaque (an ornament?), five flint arrowheads, a bone spindle whorl, a jasper grinding stone, a hammer of porphyrite, five ceramic vessels, and an antler cheekpiece.[59] The use-wear analysis of the cheekpiece revealed slightly polished areas on the main platform and all four studs. The upper tab is reshaped, which could be due to long-term wear from a strap.[60]

The radiocarbon age of a bone belonging to Individual 2 is 3572 ± 29 BP (OxA-12530), and of a bone from Individual 8 is 3550 ± 25 BP (PSUAMS-1954). The dates do not differ statistically ($\chi^2 = 0.3$, $p = 0.05$, $df = 1$) and agree well with the larger dataset of Sintashta culture radiocarbon dates.

Kamennyi Ambar-5 Cemetery, Kurgan 2, Grave 8 (KA5K2G8)

The rectangular grave measured 3.5 m x 2.2 m x 0.65 m deep, with its long walls aligned on an NW–SE axis. The wood plank ceiling was located 0.35 m above the floor of the grave. Two post-holes along the long axis of the grave mark the supporting posts of the ceiling.

In the southern part of the grave, adjoining a short wall, were found two wheel slots – left slot: W = 25 cm, L = 100 cm, D = 35 cm; right slot: W = 30 cm, L = 85 cm, D = 30 cm. They were not parallel to each other: the right slot deflected 20° west from the central axis of the grave. The estimated wheel diameters corresponding to the slots are about 90–100 cm.

G = 120 cm.

E = 40 cm on the left and 35 cm on the right.

F = 220 cm.

The crania of two horses lay next to the north ends of the slots, with a bovid cranium and leg bones placed near them.

Four individuals were buried in the grave. A 22–26-year-old genetically male Individual I and an 8–12-year-old genetically female Individual II faced and embraced each other. A genetically male Individual III of 3–7 years of age lay next to Individual II. Individual IV was a genetically male neonate. The genetic relatedness analysis did not reveal any family ties between the individuals.

The burial inventory is represented by two stone mace heads, a metal knife and a chisel, a stone arrowhead, numerous ornaments, four ceramic vessels, three antler cheekpieces, and an artefact possibly imitating a cheekpiece.[61]

A pair of cheekpieces have no evidence of use but demonstrate how cheekpieces could be attached to the bridle, as little pins were inserted into the holes of their tabs. These pins were probably used to fix sinew thongs inside the holes. Another cheekpiece from Grave 8 is a unique southern-Urals example of a decorated artefact, resembling in form counterparts from the Volga–Don region. The artefact is intensively worn: use-wear is located around the mouthpiece hole, on the studs, and the tab, suggesting 115 ± 32 hours of work.[62] The fourth artefact is not a cheekpiece, but it is interpreted as a ritual replacement for a missing specimen. It resembles a cheekpiece in general shape with a thin circular platform and two pointed studs.

As no evidence for the presence of wood was recorded inside the slots, and the height of the ceiling is only 0.3 m, it is reasonable to assume that a chariot was not present inside the tomb when it was sealed. Rather, a chariot may have been symbolically represented by the horses, the cheekpieces and the wheel-pits.

Kamennyi Ambar-5 Cemetery, Kurgan 4, Grave 9 (KA5K4G9)

The rectangular grave measured 3.25 m x 4 m x 1.2 m, with its long walls aligned with a NE–SW axis. The remains of a wooden ceiling were recorded approximately 0.76 m above the bottom. The wooden burial chamber of Grave 9 had been set on fire after the funeral rituals, and the pit was disturbed by animal burrows. Two accumulations of animal bones were located near the bottom, perhaps, due to the collapse of the ceiling because of the fire.

---

[59] Epimakhov 2005: 28–32; Narasimhan et al. 2019.
[60] Epimakhov 2005: 181; analysis by A. Usachuk.
[61] Epimakhov 2005: 32–39; Narasimhan et al. 2019.
[62] Chechushkov et al. 2018: 132.

Among the bones are a few horse and caprid bones and parts of a wolf skeleton.

In the eastern part of the grave, adjoining a short wall, two wheel-pits were found, but the burrowing partially destroyed the right slot. The dimensions of the left slot were W = 25 cm, L = 91 cm, D = 22 cm, and the preserved parts of the right slot were measured as W = 28 cm and D = 25 cm. The calculated diameter of the left wheel is 116 cm. The slots were aligned parallel to each other in a SW direction.

G = 137 cm.

E = 55 cm on both sides.

F = 249 cm.

A pit from a supporting pillar was located near the centre of the floor, slightly offset from the central axis. Given that the wheel would not fit into the chamber, it is reasonable to assume that the grave represents chariot symbolism.

At least two adult individuals were buried in the grave: a genetically male individual of 9–15 years of age and a genetically female individual of 12–18 years old. Among the items are a sickle-shaped bronze tool, a pestle, fragments of a silver pendant, and fragments of three ceramic vessels.[63]

4. Krivoe Ozero Cemetery, Southern Ural, Russia

The Krivoe Ozero cemetery (MKO) is located at 54°0'31" N and 60°40'12" E, on the right bank of the Ui River, a left tributary of the Tobol River. The two burial mounds (Kurgan 2 and Kurgan 9) yielded evidence for two two-wheeled vehicles as well as cheekpieces. One of the chariot graves (Kurgan 9, Grave 1) was directly dated by the AMS radiocarbon method. A total of 11 cheekpieces were found in three excavated kurgans.[64]

Krivoe Ozero Cemetery, Kurgan 2, Grave 1 (MKOK2G1)

The rectangular grave measured 4.1 m x 2.8 m x 1.5 m deep, with its long walls aligned in a W–E axis. The wooden burial chamber was 3.7 m x 2.4 m, with the reconstructed height of the ceiling at about 1.3 m from the floor, though there could have been another layer of the ceiling about 0.5 m above the floor.

In the western part of the grave, next to a short wall and oriented towards the east, two slots filled with mixed soil and some wood decay were found – right slot: W = 40 cm, L = 69 (decay) / 100 (slot itself) cm, D = 15 cm; left slot: W = 30 cm, L = 68/100 cm, D = 15 cm. The calculated diameter is 94 cm for the right wheel and 92 cm for the left wheel.

G = 150 cm.

E = 45 cm on the left and 12 cm on the right.

F = 270 cm.

The remains of a 50–55-years-old male and a few horse and caprid bones were found within the filling at various depths. In the space between the slots were located an inverted ceramic vessel and a bronze spearhead 25 cm long. Some horse bones were discovered in the grave filling. A well-preserved antler cheekpiece was found in the western part of the grave.[65] The artefact is a typical shield-like cheekpiece with four integral studs, a trapezoid-shaped upper tab with three additional holes, and two notches. As the manufacturing traces are very well visible, it is likely that the cheekpiece had only been lightly used or not used at all.[66]

As the ceiling is only at 50 cm above the floor, it is likely that the grave represents chariot symbolism, rather than having a real vehicle located inside.

*Krivoe Ozero Cemetery, Kurgan 9, Grave 1 (MKOK9G1)

The rectangular grave measured 3.7 m x 2.3 m x 2.65 m, and was aligned in an approximately N–S direction. An animal sacrificial complex was located next to the grave and included a horse and a bovine cranium and corresponding bones of eight legs underneath. Caprid, bovid, and horse bones lay in a heap, with complete skeletons of a dog and a newborn calf above them, laid to the west. At various depths inside the grave, there were three sheep leg bones and an animal rib. Inside, was placed a wooden box, forming an inner space of the burial chamber with internal dimensions of 3.2 m x 1.6 m, with a ceiling about 0.95 m above the floor. Four circular patches of decayed wood 10–15 cm in diameter were recorded in each corner of the pit. The remnants of wooden planking intersected the circular patches, suggesting the fastening points for the plank walls (Figure 10.4).

In the southern part of the grave, adjoining its short wall, large patches of wood decay were recorded. They varied significantly in colour from the remains of the chamber and covered one-third of the area. At a level of the floor, was an oval outline of wood decay measuring 1.7 m x 1.2 m. On excavation, parts of the body and the two wheels of the chariot were recorded. Organic decay the colour of wood covered the southern part of the grave. As it became clear that a chariot had been buried in the grave, the remains were recorded in detail. However, organic decay should not be considered as a "photograph" of the chariot, but rather as a poorly preserved imprint that the excavators have tried to record as well as they could using simple drawing paper and a pencil without more precise recording technique. Thus, not every detail can be accurately meas-

---

[63] Epimakhov 2005: 116–120; Narasimhan et al. 2019.
[64] Vinogradov 2003.
[65] Vinogradov 2003: 65–67
[66] Vinogradov 2003; analysis by A. Usachuk.

ured and explained, and the preservation should not be considered as perfect.

Above the wheels, decay from wooden bars and possible planking from a platform were recorded. The bars could be remains of the superstructure of the chariot as they are rounded and located above the axle and at right angles to it. The wooden planks overlaid the left wheel and the axle, and thus could be remains of the floor (Figure 10.5). The wheels resembled two parallel strips of wood decay, measuring 2–4 cm across and 90 cm (the western, left), and 100 cm (the eastern, right) long (Figure 10.6). The distance between their central axes is 120 cm. Decayed remains from the axle ran between the wheels at a right angle to them with a break in the centre, so that the two parts of the axle do not meet precisely. The decay of the axle intersected the wheels in their centres, and the outlines of the two naves were recorded on either side. The entire length of the axle is about 150 cm, and its diameter is about 5 cm. The gauge (G) is 120 cm. According to the field drawings, the outer diameters of the naves are 14 cm on the left and 10 cm on the right. The wheel-pits were cross-sectioned from their outer sides, which enabled the lower halves of both wheels to be revealed and their characteristics recorded. As found, the diameter of the left wheel is 97 cm, and the diameter of the right wheel is 102 cm. Since both wheels were deformed during post-depositional soil movements, a diameter of 100 cm seems to be a reasonable assumption. The cross-section also revealed seven spokes in each pit, about 3–4 cm in diameter. The chariot was oriented towards NNW with space for a draught pole of at least 200 cm. As the ceiling was located 0.95 m from the bottom of the grave, and the vehicle body was slightly sunk into the ground, it is plausible that any front could have reached 90–100 cm in height.

A complete human skeleton was located to the north of the chariot (no analyses of the sex and age of the individual have been performed), lying on its left side, with the head towards the north and the legs extended. The left arm was bent at the elbow, with the wrist placed on the chest, while the right wrist was next to the left elbow. The fingers of the right hand were clenched into a fist, probably, holding the handle of a bronze adze, the wedge of which was in front of the face of the deceased. A bronze knife with the remains of a fur-covered sheath was located behind the head. Near the right femur was a stone tool, while stone and bone arrowheads were located closer to the northern wall of the chamber, beside three ceramic vessels.

The crania of two horses were placed in both north corners of the grave, also facing north. In addition, horse limb bones (distal forelegs trimmed at the knee and distal hind legs trimmed at the hock) and tail vertebrae lay beneath each skull. In the southern part of the burial chamber, two groups of horse leg bones were found near the wheels. The bones of three legs were laid near the right wheel with the fourth leg in the north-west corner of the pit, while four additional limbs were found next to the left wheel. Two pairs of antler cheekpieces were located next to the corresponding horse crania.[67]

All four cheekpieces are poorly preserved, which limits the possibility of use-wear analysis. Still, it can be confidently said that they formed two distinguishable pairs as the two pairs differ in appearance. At the same time, all four artefacts share typological traits (platforms with four integral studs and upper tabs with additional holes), which would allow their simultaneous use with a team of horses. At least some evidence for use-wear is found on the better-preserved pair with polishing on the studs and around their mouthpiece holes, suggesting some degree of use.[68]

The four radiocarbon dates are 3580 ± 50 BP (AA-9874a), 3740 ± 50 BP (AA-9874b), 3700 ± 60 BP (AA-9875a), and 3525 ± 50 BP (AA-9875b).[69] There is an apparent conflict between the dates, as there were four samples from the two horse crania, and pairs of dates are statistically different ($\chi^2 = 5.12$, $p = 0.05$, $df = 1$ for the AA-9874 pair; and $\chi^2 = 5.02$, $p = 0.05$, $df = 1$ the for AA-9875 pair). The two dates corresponding with the majority of the Sintashta dates are 3580 ± 50 BP and 3525 ± 50 BP (Molodin et al. 2014). Their weighted mean age is 3552 ± 35 BP ($\chi^2 = 2.84$, $p = 0.05$, $df = 1$).

5. *Nikolayevka II (NIIK1G1), Southern Ural, Russia

The Nikolayevka II cemetery lies at 53°1'4" N and 61°58'19" E, on the left bank of the Ayat River. Under the Alakul' period mound of Kurgan 1, a rectangular grave 1 was excavated. It was aligned in a W–E direction. The looted grave measured 2.05 m x 3.1 m x 1 m. The wooden ceiling was 0.8–0.9 m above the floor.

In the western part of the grave, adjoining a short wall, two oval slots were found, oriented with their long axes towards the west – left slot: W = 25 cm, L = 90 cm, D = 20 cm; right slot: W = 25 cm, L = 70 cm, D = 20 cm. The calculated maximum wheel diameters are 81 cm on the right and 121 cm on the left. In the slots, were found some decayed wood and a metal (bronze?) nail. Because the shape of the left slot is not segmental but somewhat triangular, the actual diameter of the wheels is most likely represented by the right groove.

G = 130 cm.

E = 40 cm on the left and 35 cm on the right.

F = 220 cm.

As the size of the chamber permits it, and additional evidence in the form of decayed wood and a metal nail were recorded, we can assume that a real vehicle had been present inside the grave.

---

[67] Vinogradov 2003: 82–88.
[68] Chechushkov et al. 2018; analysis by A. Bersenev.
[69] Anthony and Vinogradov 1995.

No human remains were reported. The artefact assemblage consisted of three bone arrowheads, a needle, two dog canines, fragments of at least two ceramic vessels, a piece of metallurgical slag, three beads, and the nail. The burial had been disturbed by robbers.[70]

6. Ozernoye-1, Kurgan 7, Grave 8 (O1K7G8), Western Siberia, Russia

The cemetery of Ozernoye-1 is dated to the Petrovka/Alakul' period. The site is at 54°26'17" N and 64°39'58" E on the left bank of the Tobol River. The various elements representing a chariot complex came from two excavated kurgans. A bone cheekpiece was found under Kurgan 5, and wheel-pits were studied in Kurgan 7.

Aligned ENE–WSW, the central Grave No. 8 was rectangular and at the bottom level measured 3.6 m x 2.3 m x 1.1 m. Inside was placed a box made of wooden logs, organising the inner space of the chamber with internal dimensions of 3.1 m x 1.6 m. The ceiling was demarcated by wooden planking at 1.05 m above the floor. The chamber was constructed of 30 cm wide logs, abutting at their ends.

In the south-eastern part of the chamber, adjoining a short wall, were found wheel slots No. 1 and No. 2. Both slots were filled with dark grey humus sandy loam mixed with sterile sand. The right slot No.1 measured: W = 20 cm, L = 80 cm, D = 20 cm, the left slot No.2: W = 30 cm, L = 75 cm, D = 15 cm. The calculated maximum wheel diameters are 100 cm on the right and 109 cm on the left. The slots were aligned parallel to each other in a north-south direction.

$G = 115$ cm.

$E = 10$ cm on the left and 5 cm on the right.

$F = 230$ cm.

There were two additional small pits in the floor in front of the slots along the long axis of the grave, spaced 1.2 m apart. Pit No. 3 measured 10 cm x 5 cm x 7 cm, Pit No. 4 measured 10 cm x 5 cm x 7 cm.

The size of the chamber would allow enough room for a vehicle (but not enough room for the outer parts of the axle), but the other pieces of evidence are too scanty for any conclusion as to whether one had been present or not.

No human remains were reported, and two ceramic vessels were the only artefacts.[71]

7. Satan 1 Cemetery, Kurgan 1, Grave 1 (S1K1G1), Central Kazakhstan

The Petrovka/Alakul' period site is located at approximately 49°6' N and 75°51' E on the left bank of the Taldy River, 5 km north of the modern village of Auul Kasym Amanzholov in the Karaganda District of Kazakhstan. The grave under kurgan 1 yielded remains of a wooden vehicle, and a cheekpiece was found in kurgan 3.[72]

The rectangular grave measured approximately 3.9 m x 2.5 m x 1.2 m deep, and was aligned in a NW–SW direction. Inside, the wooden chamber was constructed of logs. The grave was looted (perhaps, during the post-burial ritual [?]), and the wooden construction was burned, which helped to preserve parts of the chariot. This lay in the north-western part of the grave, next to the short side of the pit. The rectangular platform measuring 106 cm in width and 60 cm in length was made of wooden planks. Beneath the platform were two subrectangular parallel slots. Lens-shaped in cross section, these wheel-pits measured approximately: W = 13 cm, L = 69–73 cm, D = 25 cm. Both pits contained traces of wooden wheels, including decay from rims and cylindrical naves with a round spoke slot preserved in one of them. According to the excavators, the length of the naves was about 10–20 cm, and their diameter was about 14 cm.[73] In a later publication, Novozhenov[74] confirmed that the previous statement giving the length of the naves as about 10–20 cm was incorrect, and the actual length was at least 30 cm. The traces of both decayed rims measured about 5 cm in cross section. Under the rim in one of the slots were a small piece of red rawhide and four cone-shaped bone nails, 8 to 17 mm long. Apparently, these nails fastened a leather tyre to the wooden rim. The dimensions of the slots correspond with an estimated a wheel diameter of 73–75 cm, though Novozhenov[75] estimates it as much as 100 cm.

$G = 150$ cm.

E = [unknown due to the discrepancy between the published plan of the grave and its description].

$F = 250$ cm.[76]

The radiocarbon age of a sample of wood is 3420 ± 160 BP (LOIA-2320).[77] Despite the large standard deviation, the date agrees well with the rest of the Petrovka period measurements.[78]

8. Sintashta Complex, Southern Urals, Russia

The Sintashta complex of sites is located at 52°28'57" N and 60°12'1" E, on the left bank of the Sintashta river, a left tributary of the Tobol River. It includes a walled settlement and a cemetery containing no less than four complexes with 65 graves. A preliminary journal publication of the cemetery material enabled the principal investigator to highlight the site's unusual nature among other Bronze

---

[70] Epimakhov 2004.
[71] Epimakhov and Novikov 2017.
[72] Evdokimov 1981: 434.
[73] Novozhenov 1989: 111.
[74] Novozhenov 2012: 201.
[75] Novozhenov 1989: 111.
[76] Novozhenov 2012: 197–200.
[77] Novozhenov 1989.
[78] Molodin et al. 2014.

Age cemeteries of the Eurasian steppes.[79] The eight graves of Sintashta Cemetery (SM) and the Sintashta Small Kurgan (SIII) yielded evidence for what the investigators believed to be the remains of chariots, as imprints of spokes and rims of two-wheeled vehicles were discovered, while horse sacrifices and cheekpieces accompanied the burials. In some other graves, only cheekpieces were found, 16 specimens in total. Moreover, the site had a striking assemblage of animal and material offerings, including the entire bodies of many horses, weapons, and ornaments.[80] Four radiocarbon dates were obtained from the chariot burials using the liquid scintillation counting method. Finally, at least three horses from the cemetery were sampled for a DNA study, enabling them to be traced as the earliest of those sequenced to belong to the DOM2 line of domesticated horses.[81]

Sintashta Cemetery, Grave 4 (SMG4)

The rectangular grave measured 3.5 m x 2.1 m, with a depth of 2.1 m, with its long walls oriented north–south. The walls were lined with wooden boarding, leaving the inner space of the burial chamber with internal dimensions of 3.2 m x 1.8 m. The height of the ceiling was approximately 0.3 m, as the ceiling is recorded at -1.8 m, while the floor is at -2.1 m.

Above the chamber, the bones of four horses were recorded. Part of a spine and ribs were found along the long wall, leg bones in the south-eastern part, and the skulls of two horses (I, IV) in the north-western and south-eastern corners. There were two other horse skulls (II, III) in the southern part of the pit, apparently laid separately. Along with horse bones, sheep/goat bones were found, mostly disarrayed and broken.

Two segment-shaped slots filled with mixed soil were found adjacent to the short northern wall in the bottom of the burial pit – right slot (No. 2): W = 15 cm, L = 72 cm, D= 20 cm; left slot (No. 3): W = 21 cm, L = 68 cm, D = 20 cm. The reconstructed wheel diameter is about 80 cm (78 cm on the left and 85 cm on the right). The slots were aligned parallel to each other in a north-south direction.

G = 140 cm.

E = 5 cm on the left and 22 cm on the right.

F = 230 cm.

A square hole (No.1) was recorded in the centre of the floor slightly inclined to the west from the long axis of the grave. In it was some decayed wood mixed with soil, suggesting that it had contained a post for ceiling support.

The grave contained the burial of at least two individuals: an adult and a child, but only the crania and a femur and tibia of the adult are preserved, as the grave was looted and severely disturbed by the looters. The remaining inventory consisted of 12 flint arrowheads, a metal knife, a polishing stone, a grinding stone, two awls, and a piece of a copper/bronze wire.[82]

The fact that the support post for the wooden ceiling is not central might suggest that space had been left for a draught pole. As the ceiling was only 30 cm high, and no decayed wood or imprints were recorded, it is reasonable to assume only the symbolic presence of a chariot.

Sintashta Cemetery, Grave 5 (SMG5)

The rectangular grave measured 3.6 m x 3.2 m, with a depth of 1.7 m, aligned in an approximately north–south direction with an inclination of 12° west. Inside was placed a box of wooden planks, organising the inner space of the burial chamber with internal dimensions of 3.65 m x 3.1 m, with a ceiling of about 0.5 m above the floor (-200 cm and -250 cm below the surface, respectively).

The skeletons of six horses and a skull were laid on top of the ceiling. Two (I and II) lay on their left sides in the south-western half of the pit, with their heads towards the south. Two other skeletons (IV and V) were in the north-western part, also on their left sides, with their heads towards the north. The first two animals lay partially on top of the skeletons of horses IV, and V. Two more horses (VI and VII) were located in the north-eastern part of the pit, squeezed into the remaining space with their heads bent back and perpendicular to the other horses. Horse cranium III was next to horses I and II.

Inside the chamber, two segment-shaped pits were found in the north-eastern part of the floor, aligned in a NE–SW direction. Their location is not typical as they were not adjacent to a short wall but placed almost in the middle of the huge rectangular grave. The pits measured: W = 9 cm, L = 37 cm, D = 15 cm (No.5); W = 12 cm, L = 42 cm, D = 20 cm (No.6). The observed dimensions represent a wheel diameter of only about 40 cm. In pit No.5, some wood dust was recorded.

G = 130 cm.

E = 32 cm on the left and 143 cm on the right.

F = 180 cm.

In the south-eastern corner of the grave lay the cranium of horse VIII, facing east. Two cheekpieces lay next to it, one on each side. The lower jawbone, belonging to horse IX, was found 60 cm west of the first skull, lying parallel to the wall and facing west. The tibia, the pelvic bones, and several other horse bones lay in conjunction with a jawbone. Another two pairs of cheekpieces were found between the jawbone and the wall.

The tomb contained the remains of at least five adult individuals. The investigators define them as three males and

---

[79] Gening 1977.
[80] Gening et al. 1992.
[81] Fages et al. 2019.

[82] Gening et al. 1992: 123–126.

two females based on the assemblage composition, but no anthropological assessment of sex and age was made. The accompanying inventory consisted of six ceramic vessels, 20 arrowheads, two bronze knives, an awl, two boar tusk pendants, an amulet made from a horse tail vertebra, an astralagus, threads of beads, and a bone shaft. Two of four poorly preserved cheekpieces have the typical features of the shield-like type, including the four integral studs and additional perforations. No use-wear analysis has been undertaken.[83]

As the ceiling is only 50 cm high and the calculated wheel diameter is only 40 cm, it is unlikely that a real vehicle was present, but rather the burial ritual represented the symbolic representation of a chariot.

The radiocarbon date of the wood sample is 3360 ± 70 BP (Ki-862), and is thus a late outlier in comparison to the majority of the Sintashta dates.[84]

*Sintashta Cemetery, Grave 12 (SMG12)

The rectangular grave measured 3.6 m x 2.1 m x 3.3 m deep, with its long walls aligned ENE–WSW. The wooden burial chamber was 3.3 m x 1.9 m, with a height of 1.9 m. Three posts marked by round holes in the floor supported the ceiling. The burial chamber was empty until the ceiling collapsed, and the inner space was filled with soil.

The skeletons of four horses had been laid initially on top of the ceiling but were displaced after the ceiling collapsed. Horse I lay on its right side with its legs bent, along the west part of the northern wall, facing east. Horse II lay on its left side by the east part of the same wall, with its legs stretched, facing west. Apparently, the skeleton of horse I had moved from its original position, in which the body would lie next to the body of horse II. The remains of horses III and IV, probably, lay in similar poses next to the southern wall of the grave, but due to the collapse of the chamber' ceiling, the bones were displaced and poorly preserved. The displaced crania of these animals were recorded next to the southern wall, one on top of the other.

In the western part of the chamber were found two wheel-pits aligned in a W–E direction. The pit for the right wheel (No.2) with dimensions of W = 40 cm, D = 96 cm, L = 35 cm was filled with small rocks. The decayed remains of the wooden rim of a wheel, four spokes, and the nave were recorded within it. The approximate dimensions of the rim were 4 cm x 4 cm. Dimensions and characteristics of the spokes and the nave remained unspecified by the excavators. The left wheel-pit (No. 3) measured: W = 30 cm, L = 95 cm, D = 25 cm had decayed wood from the rim and two spokes. The maximum wheel sizes calculated from the shape of the slots are 101 and 117 cm, respectively, but the excavators reconstructed the wheel diameter as 92–93 cm based on the traces of the rims.

G = 120–125 cm.

E = 28 cm on the left and 40 cm on the right.

F = 190 cm.

In the eastern part of the chamber were found two other slots with no imprints (Nos. 6 and 7) and an additional groove with no imprints (No. 8) in the centre of the floor next to the south wall. They were filled with small rocks and presumably had been left empty during the funeral.

An adult individual was buried in the grave. The poorly preserved human bones were located above the wheel-pits and some above the floor. This fact led the investigators to suggest that the deceased had been buried in the chariot. The individual was accompanied by a pair of cheekpieces, two ceramic vessels, six stone and two bone arrowheads, a wooden item, a bronze and a bone harpoon, and a fishhook. The cheekpieces are poorly preserved and no use-wear analysis was made. Typologically, they belong to the shield-like type with integral studs and perforated tabs and could have been used as a pair.[85]

Sintashta Cemetery, Grave 16 (SMG16)

The rectangular grave measured 2.7 m x 1.85 m x 3.13/2.9 m deep and contained two burial chambers, one above the other (a later Grave 10 overlaying an earlier Grave 16). The pit was oriented west–east. The wooden burial chamber of Grave 16 measured 2.6 m x 1.65 m x 1.1 m, sharing the same ceiling. Inside that chamber, another was constructed, measuring 2.25 m x 1.5 m. The western half contained oval depressions, measuring W = 60 cm, L = 100 cm, D = 25 cm (No.1) and W = 80 cm, L = 100 cm, D = 25 cm (No.2). The estimated diameter of wheels that would fit within them is 125 cm.

G = 65 cm.

E = 10 on the left and 6 on the right.

F = 116 cm.

The oval depressions were originally interpreted as evidence for a vehicle due to the location of human remains. The investigators believed that human bones were cleaned of soft tissue and placed inside a chariot, above the floor of the grave, as they were not in anatomical order. Human bones were presumed to have fallen chaotically from this elevated platform and then been further pushed by soil moving inside the grave to the east.

The inventory consisted of a bronze ring and fragments of another ring, a harpoon, three arrowheads (two of them made of bone and one of flint), a bone spatula, a mortar, a pestle, a bronze knife, three ceramic vessels, fragments of a worked antler. In the narrow space between the inner and outer chambers at their eastern ends were parts of sacrificed animals, including a cranium and several mandibles

---

[83] Gening et al. 1992: 126–137.
[84] Molodin et al. 2014.

[85] Gening et al. 1992: 162–168.

of horses, parts of a cranium and legs of sheep and goat, and parts of the carcasses of a calf and a dog.[86]

Despite the conclusions of the original excavator, the finds in Grave 16 do not meet our criteria for denoting an actual vehicle, and the present evidence does not directly suggest chariot symbolism in this burial.

*Sintashta Cemetery, Grave 19 (SMG19)

The grave measured 3.4 m x 1.9 m x 2.35 m deep, with its long walls oriented in a NNW–SSE direction. The burial chamber was constructed of wooden boards and measured 3.3 m x 1.8 m, with the ceiling at approximately 1.1–1.25 m above the floor. In the oval-shaped hole No. 1, in the centre of the floor with some inclination to the east, had been a ceiling support post.

Above the burial chamber, the bones of four horses were recorded at various depths as they had been displaced during the post-depositional process. Two skeletons lay parallel to the long walls in the southern part of the grave, and two other skeletons in the northern part lay across the long axis of the pit. Horse I was laid next to the east wall on its left side, facing south. Horse II was laid in the opposite corner, on its right side. Horses III and IV were facing east, with their heads next to each other. They were placed ventrally with their legs bent. Among the horse bones was found a human cranium, indicating that the grave had been disturbed.

In the northern part of the grave, adjoining a short wall, were wheel-pits No. 5 and No. 6 – right slot (No.5): W = 30 cm, L = 75 cm, D = 20 cm; left slot (No.6): W = 27 cm, L = 75 cm, D = 20 cm. The calculated wheel diameters are in both slots 90 cm, respectively, though the excavators reconstructed the diameter as being about 80 cm. The imprints of rims and spokes (three on the right and two on the left) were recorded in the vertical sections. The spokes measured 3–3.5 cm x 3–3.5 cm in cross-section. The slots were aligned parallel to each other in a north-south direction with a slight western inclination.

G = 130 cm.

E = 20 cm on the left and 30 cm on the right.

F = 230 cm.

In the space between the slots were three more holes with remains of wooden posts. Pit No.2 measured 40 cm x 40 cm x 2–3 cm deep and had imprints of a wooden post, measuring 19 cm x 16 cm. Hole No.3 measured 20 cm x 15 cm x 16 cm deep. It was in the centre and contained the imprint of a 9 x 6 cm wooden post. Finally, Hole No.4 had a conical shape and measured 21 cm x 15 cm x 15 cm deep.

The remains of an adult individual were found inside the chamber and the cranium of another at the level of the ceiling. The burial was accompanied by four ceramic vessels located on the ceiling of the chamber.[87]

The radiocarbon ages yielded by two wood samples are 3560 ± 180 BP (Ki-864) and 3620 ± 60 BP (unknown code). The dates do not differ statistically ($\chi^2 = 0.1$, $p = 0.05$, $df = 1$) from one another, and the weighted mean age of 3614 ± 57 BP agrees with the larger dataset of the Sintashta culture radiocarbon dates.

*Sintashta Cemetery, Grave 28 (SMG28)

The rectangular grave measured 3 m x 1.97 m x 2.3 m deep, with its long walls aligned NE–SW. The grave was looted, and above the bottom contained a mix of detached animal bones, predominantly those of horses, ceramic sherds, and metal artefacts. The burial chamber was constructed of vertically installed wooden boards, preserved 35–65 cm high from the bottom. The chamber measured 2.9 m x 1.9 m. The height of the chamber is unknown, even though the excavators provide the figure of 1.2–1.8 m, leaving it unexplained.

In the northern part of the grave, adjoining a short wall, were found wheel-pits No. 5 and No. 6 – right slot (No. 5): W = 11 cm, L = 100 cm, D = 30 cm; left slot (No. 6): W = 13 cm, L = 105 cm, D = 30 cm. The imprints of rims and spokes (four on the right and three on the left) were recorded in the cross-sections. The spokes measured 3.5–4 cm x 4–4.5 cm in cross section. The slots were aligned parallel to each other in a SW–NE direction. The calculated wheel diameter is 113–122 cm, but the excavators note that the soil pressure during the decomposition process probably deformed the wheels and reconstruct the diameter as about 90 cm.

G = 150 cm.

E = 23 cm on the left and 18 cm on the right.

F = 190 cm.

Two individuals were placed with their heads towards the southwest in the southern part of the grave. The eastern skeleton was better preserved, but the arm bones and the skull are missing. One was lying on their back with the legs bent at the knees. Only the ribcage and the metatarsal bones were preserved from the second, who lay parallel to the first. The burial was accompanied by three ceramic vessels, a grinding stone, a metal nail, and unidentified metal objects in small pieces.

The radiocarbon age of a wood sample is 3760 ± 120 BP (Ki-657) and is an outlier compared to the majority of the Sintashta dates, though the younger end of the 68.2 % error range intersects with them.[88]

---

[86] Gening et al. 1992: 149–155.

[87] Gening et al. 1992: 178–185.

[88] Molodin et al. 2014.

*Sintashta Cemetery, Grave 30 (SMG30)

The rectangular grave measured 3.2 m x 2 m x 2.4 m deep, with its long walls aligned NW–SE. The wooden burial chamber measured 3 m x 1.8 m, with the reconstructed height of the ceiling at about 1–1.1 m from the floor. Three post holes along the long axis of the grave mark the posts that were installed to support the ceiling (Nos. 2, 4, 5).

In the north-eastern part of the grave, adjoining a short wall, were found wheel-pits No. 6 and No. 7. After the wheels were installed in an upright position, the pits were filled with clay, allowing preservation. The right slot (No. 6) measured: W = 25 cm, L = 95 cm, D = 34 cm; the left slot (No. 7): W = 25 cm, L = 97 cm, D = 34 cm. The calculated diameters are 100 cm and 103 cm, respectively, but the wheel diameter reconstructed by the excavators is about 90–92 cm. In the vertical sections, the imprints of rims and three spokes on each wheel were recorded. The spokes measured 4 cm x 4 cm in cross section. The wheels were dug in for approximately one-third of their height. The slots were aligned parallel to each other in a SW direction.

G = 125 cm.

E = 25 cm on the left and 35 cm on the right.

F = 190 cm.

The remains of an adult individual were found in a heap in the south-western part of the grave. The bones had been separated from each other during the burial ritual. All the bones were intact, but the pelvic bones were detached from the sacrum, and the lower jaw was separated from the cranium. Next to the human remains, in the corners of the grave, were two horse skulls and the bones of the forelegs of two horses, cut off above the tibia. Next to the eastern horse skull, were found a pair of cheekpieces, a bone plaque, and a round bone object. A bronze knife and a ceramic vessel were located next to the human cranium, and 11 flint and two bone arrowheads lay on the leg bones of a horse near the southern wall. Under the horse bones near the south-eastern wall, was pit No. 1, which turned out to be a cache covered with clay. At the bottom was found a bronze spearhead.[89]

A pair of cheekpieces belongs to the shield-like group and demonstrates clear evidence of repair. As the studs had been broken in one of them, holes were drilled in the same spots to insert replacements. While no use-wear analysis has been done, the repair indicates the intensive use of the cheekpieces.

Sintashta Small Kurgan, Grave 1(SIIIG1)

The Sintashta III Small Kurgan (SIII) was excavated in 1972, but it was first published only 20 years later by Gening et al.[90] Stefanov and Epimakhov[91] republished the complex, correcting the inaccuracies of the initial publication and providing new details. Before excavation, the mound was 15–16 m in diameter, and measured 0.4 m in height. The single rectangular grave was located beneath it. This measured 4 m x 3.1 m x 3 m deep, with its long walls aligned NW–SE. The burial chamber was constructed of thin wooden boards preserved near the bottom and measuring 3.1 m x 1.76 m. The ceiling was 0.5–1 m above the bottom of the grave, and was constructed with planks and tree branches. The floor of the grave comprised of a horizontal layer of marlstone, in which two slots were dug.

In the northern part of the grave, adjoining a short wall, two slots were found. The dimensions of the eastern slot (No. I, right) are W = 25 cm, L = 50 cm, D = 15-20 cm. The western slot (No. II, left) had an elongated-oval shape and measured: W = 20-30 cm, L = 68 cm, D = 30 cm. The estimated diameters are 69 cm on the right and 51 cm on the left. In cross-section, the slots looked rectangular and not segment-shaped. The filling was extremely dense, packed with rocks and artefacts.

G = 108–110 cm.

E = 20 cm on the left and 30 cm on the right.

F = 220 cm.

The authors of the 1992 publication interpreted these slots as evidence for a chariot, while the republished data does not provide the same degree of confidence. Though chariot symbolism may be present in the grave, it remains rather unclear.

At the bottom, poorly preserved crania and the scattered bones of five adult individuals were found. Four were near the northern wall, along with long bones, phalanges, and pelvic bones. The fifth individual's cranium, arm bones bent at the elbows, phalanges, and a femur were found in the south-eastern corner of the chamber.

A horse cranium lay near the southern wall, and the jawbones of another large animal (a horse or a cow) were found under stones in the south-western corner. The burial inventory consisted of eight vessels, stone, bronze and clay artefacts (a stone mace-head; two clay nozzles; a bronze knife, an awl, scrap metal, and three talc slabs, which are interpreted as blanks for casting moulds). A significant part of the finds was concentrated in the area near the slots or within them.[92]

9. Solntse II Cemetery, Southern Ural, Russia

The Solntse II cemetery (SII) is located at 53°18'36" N and 60°35'38" E, on the left bank of the Nizhniy Toguzak River, a left tributary of the Toguzak of the Tobol basin.

---

[89] Gening et al. 1992: 207–219.
[90] Gening et al. 1992: 333–341.
[91] Stefanov and Epimakhov 2006.
[92] Stefanov and Epimakhov 2006.

The three graves from three separate kurgan mounds yielded wheel-pits and a cheekpiece.

Solntse II, Kurgan 4, Grave 1 (SIIK4G1)

The kurgan had three pits: the largest is Grave 1, and two smaller pits that contained ritual offerings. The rectangular pit of Grave 1 was looted. Upon excavation, it measured 3.6 m x 2.5 m, with a depth of 1.15 m, and was aligned in an approximately north–south direction with an inclination of 10° west. Inside, was placed a wooden box, organising the burial chamber with internal dimensions of 3.57 m x 2.17 m, with a ceiling of about 0.7–0.8 m above the floor. In the northern part of the pit above the ceiling, the crania of two horses, two tail vertebrae, and the lower legs were located. In the centre of the floor was a 10 cm deep circular hole.

Inside the chamber, there were two segment-shaped slots in the southern part of the floor, aligned NNW–SSE: The left slot (A) measured: W = 22 cm, L = 85 cm, D = 25 cm; the right slot (B): W = 30 cm, L = 90 cm, D = 25 cm. The dimensions given correspond with a wheel diameter of about 100 cm.

G = 140 cm.

E = 13 cm on the left and 34 cm on the right.

F = 243 cm.

As the ceiling was relatively low and no imprints were recorded, it is likely that a chariot was not left in the grave when it was sealed.

The bones of one deceased person were scattered within the filling of the pit indicating that the grave had been looted. Another relatively complete skeleton was discovered in the centre of the grave, lying 1 m above the floor, possibly, at the level of the ceiling. The inventory includes stone and bone arrowheads, a piece of copper ore, an awl, and an antler cheekpiece. The cheekpiece has four integral studs, its mouthpiece hole is reinforced with a rim. No use-wear analysis has been undertaken. In offering pit No. 2 were the crania and leg bones of four horses.[93]

Solntse II, Kurgan 5, Grave 2 (SIIK5G2)

Under the kurgan were three graves, with wheel slots recorded in Grave 2. This rectangular grave measured 3.2 m x 2.3 m x 1.2 m, with its long walls aligned NW–SE. The ceiling is reconstructed at 0.4 m from the bottom of the pit. The grave was looted. This is suggested by a mix of detached bones, a ceramic piece, and an amulet made from the canine tooth of a wolf found above the floor.

In the southern part of the grave, adjoining a short wall, two slots were found – right slot: W = 30 cm, L = 63 cm, D = 15 cm; left slot: W = 15 cm, L = 55 cm, D = 10 cm. The slots were aligned parallel to each other in a NW-SE direction.[94] The estimated diameters are 86 cm and 81 cm, respectively.

G = 133 cm.

E = 30 cm on the left and 25 cm on the right.

F = 240 cm.

The size of the chamber did not permit the location of an actual vehicle inside.

Solntse II, Kurgan 11, Grave 2 (SIIK11G2)

Kurgan 11 contained two looted graves, with wheel slots recorded in Grave 2. The rectangular grave measured 3.6 m x 2.7 m x 1.4 m deep, with its long walls aligned NW–SE. The wooden chamber measured 2 m x 3.5 m, with the ceiling at approximately 0.30 cm from the floor of the grave (judging from the construction of the pit, as the ceiling lay on the step that was located 30 cm above the floor). Parts of ritually offered animals had once been located in the niches between the planking of the chamber and the walls of the grave but then were scattered inside the grave.

Two poorly preserved slots were recorded in the southern part of the grave, aligned NW-SE – right slot: W = 25-40 cm, L = 71 cm, D = 7 cm; left slot: W = 25 cm, L = 68 cm, D = 5 cm. The estimated diameters are obvious overestimations at 187 cm and 236 cm, respectively.

G = 130 cm.

E = 20 cm on the left and 22 cm on the right.

F = 240 cm.

As the ceiling was only 30 cm above the floor, it is unlikely that a chariot had been left in the grave after the burial ritual.

A horse skull was in the western corner of the grave, and detached caprid bones were scattered around. The artefact assemblage consisted of a polished quartzite tile, a marble tile, an abrasive stone, an antler pestle, and a bone awl.[95]

10. Stepnoye Cemetery, Southern Ural, Russia

The Petrovka and Alakul' periods Stepnoye cemetery lies at 54°6'47" N and 60°20'42" E on the left bank of the Ui River. The site yielded the largest collection of cheekpieces originating from the same place (23 specimens), ritual offerings of horses, and three possible cases of wheel-pits. The principal investigators published the detailed description of the complex in English.[96]

---

[93] Epimakhov 1996: 25–27.
[94] Epimakhov 1996: 29.
[95] Epimakhov 1996: 33–34.
[96] Kupriyanova et al. 2017.

Stepnoye I, Kurgan 1, Grave 2 (Step1K1G2)

The Petrovka period kurgan 1 had three graves. Grave 2 measured 3.75 m x 2.35 m at the bottom, with a depth of 1.9 m. The ceiling of the chamber was 1.1 m above the floor. The bones of two horses were located above the ceiling (crania, extremities and vertebrae). There were slots on the western side of the grave near the short wall – left slot (No. I): W = 15 cm, L = 40 cm, D = 10 cm; right slot (No. II): W = 15 cm, L = 37 cm, D = 10 cm. The calculated diameters are 50 cm and 44 cm, respectively.

G = 145 cm.

E = 52 cm on the left and 20 cm on the right.

F = 280 cm.

Three individuals were buried in the grave: a 15–17-year-old female, a 14–15-year-old of unidentified sex, and an infant of 1.5 years of age The female individual lay between the slots, where the body of a vehicle would have been located. In addition, four antler cheekpieces were found in the grave. They belong to the shield type with integral studs. At least two of them had been used, and the other two could have been votive items.

The size of the chamber and the dimensions of the finding do not permit the conclusion that an actual chariot was present in the grave.

*Stepnoye VII, Complex 2, Grave 5 (SVIIC2G5)

The Alakul' period grave measured 3.75 m x 2.35 m x 1.4 m deep with the ceiling at 1.3 m above the floor. The slots were on the eastern side of the pit near its short wall, parallel to each other, and aligned in W–E direction. The wheel pits both measured W = 12-15 cm, L = 79 cm, D = 12-13 cm. The calculated wheel diameters are about 133 cm.

G = 120 cm.

E = 40 cm on the left and 76 cm on the right.

F = 260 cm.

A 30–40-year-old male was buried in the grave, accompanied by a stone arrowhead, a pair of cheekpieces, and two ceramic vessels. The bone cheekpieces belong to the category of shield type cheekpieces, but their morphology differs from the typical Sintashta specimens. One of them has only two small integral studs, and the other has no studs.

The size of the chamber, the dimensions of the wheel-pits and the presence of cheekpieces allow us to assume the presence of an actual chariot in the grave.

Stepnoye VII, Complex 4, Grave 18 (SVIIC4G18)

The Petrovka period grave measured 3.5 m x 2.1 m x 1.2 m deep with the ceiling at 1.2 m above the floor. The grave had been looted at least twice in antiquity and is severely disturbed. Oval-shaped slots aligned with the grave's long sides were encountered in all four corners. Two slots aligned west have dimensions of W = 18 cm, L = 60 cm, D = 7 cm in the NW corner (No. I) and W = 20 cm, L = 80 cm, D = 10 cm in the SW corner (No. 2). The distance between their central axes is 120 cm. Two slots aligned east have dimensions of W = 22 cm, L = 50 cm, D = 10 cm in the NE corner; and W = 12 cm, L = 60 cm, D = 10 cm in the SE corner.

G = 120 and 112 cm.

E = 31 on the left and 38 on the right in the NW corner and 26 on the left and 51 on the right in the SE corner.

F = 262 cm in the north-western corner and 250 cm in the south-eastern corner.

The grave was a burial for an 18–22-year-old male, a 15–17-year-old female, and two children of 9–10 and 10–12 years of age. The artefact assemblage consisted of nine vessels, nine stone arrowheads, numerous bronze ornaments, drilled canine teeth, a cheekpiece, and two votive cheekpieces. The antler cheekpiece belongs to the shield type, with four integral studs and visible wear from extensive use.

As the evidence is ambiguous, we would rather interpret this as the symbolic representation of a vehicle.

11. Ulubai Cemetery, Northern Kazakhstan

The Petrovka period cemetery of Ulubai is located at 53°34'45" N and 67°12'8" E, on the bank of the Sergeevskoe reservoir (the right bank of the Ishim River). Two burial mounds yielded evidence for two-wheeled vehicles.

Ulubai, Kurgan 1, Grave 1 (UK1G1)

The looted rectangular grave measured 4 m x 2.5 m x 1.5 m deep, and was aligned ESE–WNW. The wood planking of the ceiling was 0.3–0.45 m above the floor of the grave. The adjoining ritual Pit 2 contained three horses facing west and a caprid cranium.

In the eastern part of the grave, adjoining a short wall, were found two oval-shaped slots – right slot: W = 55 cm, L = 110 cm, W = 20 cm; left slot: W = 40 cm, L = 105 cm, D = 20 cm. The estimated diameters are 171 cm and 158 cm, respectively. It is very likely that these numbers are strong overestimations.

G = 120 cm.

E = 12 cm on the left and 10 cm on the right.

F = 210 cm.

As the ceiling is only 30–45 cm above the floor, it is very likely that no vehicle was in the grave once it was sealed

Human remains are represented by a lower jaw, a skull, and other bones scattered on the floor of the grave. The artefact assemblage consists of four ceramic vessels, metal braces, and small beads.[97]

Ulubai, Kurgan 4, Grave 1 (UK4G1)

The looted rectangular grave measured 4 m x 2.3 m x 1.3 m deep, and was aligned NE–SW, and 60 cm above the floor were ledges 15–30 cm wide, demarcating the location of the ceiling.

In the south-eastern part of the grave, adjoining a short wall, were two oval slots; right slot: W = 40 cm, L = 80 cm, D = 20 cm; left slot: W = 40 cm, L = 100 cm, D = 20 cm. The estimated diameter on the right is 100 cm, and 145 cm on the left.

G = 140 cm.

E = 5–10 cm.

F = 200 cm.

As the ceiling is only 60 cm above the floor and the estimated wheel diameter is up to 100 cm, it is very likely that no vehicle was in the grave once it was sealed.

Human remains were found at various depths within the filling of the grave. A horse cranium and other animal bones were in the south-eastern corner at a depth of 50 cm, located just above the ceiling.[98]

12. Vetlyanka IV Cemetery, Kurgan 14, Grave 6 (VIVK14G6), Southern Ural, Russia

The only burial site in the Cis-Urals where evidence for a chariot was found, is the cemetery of Vetlyanka IV. The site is located at 51°4'24" N and 54°46'46" E on the left bank of the Ilek River, a left tributary of the Ural River.

The looted and destroyed grave measured 3.7 m x 3.9 m x 0.5 m deep, with its long walls aligned W–E. There were two parallel slots near the short southern wall of the grave, in the depression in the floor, each measuring W = 10 cm, L = 43, D = 20 cm (the corresponding estimated diameter is 43 cm). The slots were aligned parallel to each other in a W–E direction.

G = 200 cm.

E = [cannot be specified]

F = 380 cm.

As the ceiling is only 50 cm above the floor, it is very likely that no vehicle was actually present. The only finds are a horse scapula and fragments of horse limb bones.[99]

---

[97] Zdanovich 1978.
[98] Zdanovich 1978.
[99] Gorbunov et al. 1990: 31–32.

11

Early Cheekpieces in Eurasia

Vadim S. Bochkarev and Pavel F. Kuznetsov

This paper presents the results of our study and analysis of Bronze Age cheekpieces across northern Eurasia (Volga-Urals, Don and Dnieper), Carpathian-Danube region, Southern Greece, and Western Asia. These items are an integral part of burial complexes along with chariots and weapons. Some of them were found in pairs *in situ* by the horse's jaw. We classify cheekpieces according to various features and consider their typological development in terms of chronology, regional and cultural links to understand borrowing and exchange across the region as well as pointing out independent local contributions.

The Emergence of Horse Equipment[1]

The use of horses especially in warfare is a characteristic feature of the first half of the second millennium BCE in the southern part of Eastern Europe and Western Asia. Until that time, no artefacts confirm that the horse was used as a transport animal. At the turn of the third/second millennia BCE, however, the first identifiable finds of horse bridle accessories made their appearance, in the form of cheekpieces.

In the English-language archaeological literature, the term "cheekpiece" is used due to its position on the side of the horse's jaw. The term "psaliy" is used in the Russian-language literature, borrowed from ancient Greek Ψάλιον (*psalion*), which has been mistakenly translated variously as "curb bit", "chain", "bond", and "bridle". The Russian term "psaliy" was used by academician L. E. Stephanie in 1865 in relation to cheekpieces in the Hermitage Museum,[2] although its original meaning was a metal adjunct to the bit, fitted like a dropped noseband, sometimes described as a cavesson.[3] Both terms now refer to the element at each side of a horse's bit, generally made of antler, bone or metal, and which was in use throughout the second millennium BCE.[4]

Types of Cheekpieces

In the northern part of Eurasia in the second millennium BCE, cheekpieces or unfinished items are often found in settlements and in burials among the grave goods. Depending on the use and material available, cheekpieces could be made of horn or antler, bone, metal and even wood. Some Mycenaean cheekpieces were made of ivory or baked clay.

Bronze Age cheekpieces are usually divided into two main categories[5] – **rod type** cheekpieces, made of antler tines, and those described in the Russian academic literature as "shield"-shaped because of their resemblance to the ancient Greek and Roman *parma, cetra* or *scutum* shields (Figure 11.1, I.II). We will refer to them in this paper as **shield type**. They are mostly made of antler and bone, though they may also have been manufactured from other materials, such as wood, which have not survived.

These two categories differ not only in shape, but also in design and use. As reported by H.-G. Hüttel, this difference is mainly explained by their function. In his opinion, rod type and shield type cheekpieces belong to two different systems of directional control.[6] Originally, shield type cheekpieces were provided with studs on the inside face, leading to the notion that they were intended to reinforce signals given through the reins for turning. Steering is particularly important for draught animals, when the driver may be two metres behind them, especially at speed.[7] Indeed, several cheekpieces (sometimes found in matching pairs) have been excavated from burials which include the remains of vehicles and the skeletons of horses.[8] A bronze bit with studded cheekpieces was also found in a sacrificial burial at Tel Haror.[9] All the reliable evidence where cheekpieces were found together with horse skulls is presented in Figure 11.2.

In our opinion, shield type cheekpieces might have been developed from a studded insert attached to a cavesson noseband, allowing for a bridle with such cheekpieces to have lacked a mouthpiece. A different principle applies to the design of rod type cheekpieces. These were used

---

[1] This research was supported by RSF grant No. 22-18-00194.
[2] Stephanie 1866:188; Usachuk 2013: 6.
[3] Littauer 1969: 492; 493 fn. 1.
[4] Bochkarev et al. 2015: 673.
[5] Hüttel 1981; Zdanovich 1986; Bochkarev and Kuznetsov 2010.
[6] Hüttel 1977: 76; 1981: 24; 1982: 42–43.
[7] Littauer 1969: 489; Dietz 1992; Brownrigg 2004: 485; Brownrigg 2006: 165-171.
[8] Alikhova 1955: 95–96; Ilchishin 2016: fig. 3.
[9] Bar-Oz et. al. 2013: fig 2.

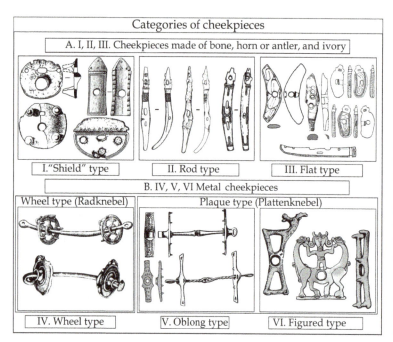

Figure 11.1. Categories of cheekpieces dated to the second millennium BCE classified according to their shape, materials used in manufacture, and equid control techniques. A: I, II, III – 'shield' type, rod type and flat type cheekpieces from Eastern, Central and South-Eastern Europe. B: IV, V, VI – wheel type and plaque type cheekpieces from Western Asia.

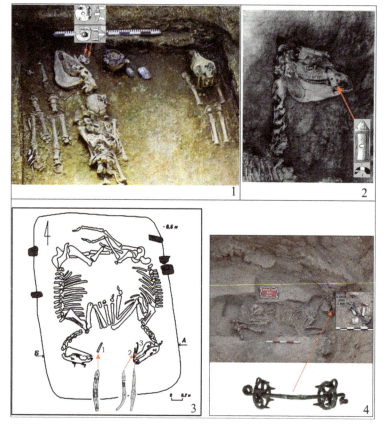

Figure 11.2. The location of the cheekpieces found *in situ* in burials with equids. 1 – Sintashta cemetery, grave 30, cheekpieces 1 and 2. Chelyabinsk region, the Southern Urals, Russia (after Gening et al. 1992: fig. 33); 2 – Kurgan cemetery at Komarovka, kurgan 5. Samara Volga region, Russia (after Alikhova 1955: 94); 3 – Kurgan at Gusyatin village. Ternopol region, Eastern Cis-Carpathian region, Ukraine (after Ilchishin 2016: fig. 3); 4 – Tel Haror settlement in western Negev, Israel (after Bar-Oz et al. 2013: fig. 3). 1–3 horse burials; 4 donkey burial.

to support the mouthpiece as well as to give directional control. Shield and rod types have never been found together in the same closed complexes.

A third category, the **flat type**, is until now represented by seven pieces only (Figure 11.1, III). All these cheekpieces are richly ornamented and have no studs, making us doubt their customary function and application. They have a relatively wide body and some rod-shaped elements and were manufactured from bone, horn or antler and are straight or curved in plan view (Figure 11.8, 110.111). We think that they combine the features of the rod and the shield type.[10] Their hybrid origin is reflected in their shape, design, and ornamentation.

Cheekpieces were used to control and guide horses harnessed to a vehicle: an ancient chariot was drawn by two horses, not one. Our work comparing the proportions of horses found in burials has shown that up to 90 % of them were between 128 and 144 cm high at the withers.[11] The majority are slender limbed or of medium build, that is, the first chariot horses were small and not robust. According to modern European classification, horses under the height of 147 cm at the withers are classed as ponies. Because these early chariot horses were of lighter build than ponies today, harnessing horses in pairs enabled them to draw a chariot with a crew consisting of two people. All animal traction was by means of paired draught under a yoke until the time of the Roman Empire in the west and Han China in the east, when shafts and suitable harness for single draught were invented.[12]

Historical and radiocarbon chronology suggest that chariots and cheekpieces appeared at about the same time at the end of the third millennium BCE to the beginning of the second millennium BCE in different regions and in entirely different cultural and social contexts.[13] Bridle bits with shield type cheekpieces developed among the pastoralist population of the Don-Volga-Ural region (the northern Eurasian steppe). Rod type cheekpieces appeared among farmers of the Carpathian-Danube region. Their invention was an important achievement in these two Bronze Age centres – or 'heartlands of culture genesis' as Bochkarev refers to them – in the northern part of Eurasia.[14]

---

[10] Bochkarev and Kuznetsov 2019: 52.
[11] Kosintsev 2010: 21–79.
[12] Brownrigg 2004; 2019; Brownrigg and Crouwel 2017.
[13] Hüttel 1977: 76; 1982: 42–44; Burmeister and Raulwing 2012.
[14] Bochkarev 2010: 45–51.

Over time, the two bridle systems became widespread and their areas of use partially overlapped. Apart from Eastern Europe and Kazakhstan, the Don-Volga-Ural cheekpieces spread to the Carpathian-Danube region and to the southern Balkan Peninsula.[15] On the other hand, rod type cheekpieces from the Carpathian-Danube region penetrated the territory of present-day Ukraine.[16] Hybrid forms with features of both shield type and rod type appeared in the Severskiy Donets area.[17] In the middle of the second millennium BCE, the shield type was replaced by the rod type before cheekpieces cast in metal appeared. Perhaps they proved to be more suitable for both steering horses harnessed to a chariot and riding them.

There is another region in Eurasia where bits with a mouthpiece and cheekpieces were used just as early – Western Asia. However, it remains unclear for what kind of equids this bridle was originally intended. These are always made of bronze (Figures 1,IV.V.VI). According to E. E. Kuzmina, this bridle was designed for onagers and donkeys or their hybrids, which were the original draught animals in the Ancient Near East.[18] Later this bridle was adapted for chariot horses. There are two types of metal mouthpieces known in Western Asia: straight bar and the more sophisticated jointed canons. As for the cheekpieces, all of them, with only one or two exceptions, are cast in bronze. These metal cheekpieces are usually divided into two groups – plaque type (Plattenknebel) and wheel type (Radknebel) cheekpieces.[19] But these data are based on unclear written sources and glyptic material. They do not provide any information about the construction and appearance of ancient bits. Comparatively recently, a ritual burial of a donkey was discovered in Israel (Tel Haror) in a Bronze Age shrine relating to layer III of the excavation (1700/1650–1550 BCE).[20] The bit had a rigid metal mouthpiece and a pair of wheel-shaped metal cheekpieces with studs.[21] So far, all the finds of equestrian equipment known in this area date to no earlier than the 17th century BCE, generally to the second half of the second millennium BCE.[22] In Western Asia and Egypt no cheekpieces made of bone or horn are known. The only exceptions are a few rod type and one (or two?) shield type cheekpieces from Central Anatolia. All of these date to no earlier than the middle of the second millennium BCE. Moreover, the fact that they were found in this region leaves an impression that they had been introduced from outside or represent a solitary instance.[23]

Originally all discoid cheekpieces seem to have had studs. As the cheekpieces evolved, the studs gradually disappeared. This change in cheekpieces is recognised throughout the northern part of Eurasia. From around the middle of the second millennium BCE, horses are regularly mentioned in ancient Near Eastern written sources in connection with chariots. According to E. E. Kuzmina, the more frequent use of horses and chariots was due to the appearance of Indo-Aryans in Western Asia.[24]

Apart from the countries of the ancient Near East, metal cheekpieces and mouthpieces of West Asian types penetrated Transcaucasia and the Aegean as well as the piedmont of Central Asia.[25] Still the links between the West Asian types of bit and those from the steppe zone of Northern Eurasia remain unproven. Both supporters of the West Asian origin of shield type cheekpieces[26] and supporters of the opposite hypothesis[27] failed to link them up. Obviously, it is time to accept the convergent origin of shield type cheekpieces in the two regions of Eurasia.

Another special region is southern Greece. The early cheekpieces found in the Mycenaean burial, grave IV, Grave Circle A, date to the Late Helladic I period (1670–1600 BCE according to radiocarbon dates). They are made of bone or horn and belong to the group of late Eastern European discoid cheekpieces. Later, bone cheekpieces, similar to the Carpathian-Danube examples, and metal cheekpieces, similar to the wheel type from West Asia, appeared here as did long, flat cheekpieces (oblong cheekpieces, type V in Figure 11.1).

Thus, the available data lead us to assume that at the beginning of the second millennium BCE there were three vast areas where a bridle bit for equid control appeared. They are the Carpathian-Danube area, the northern steppes of Eurasia, and West Asia. The bit in each of these areas has its own features. The former tends to rod type and the two latter ones opt for shield type cheekpieces. Metal mouthpieces equipped with cheekpieces of special types distinguish West Asia from the steppes.

In Northern Eurasia, shield type cheekpieces are the earliest. They are distributed over a vast area which stretches from the southern regions of Central Asia to the Carpathian-Danube region and the Southern Balkans (Figure 11.3). We have studied over three hundred shield type cheekpieces from this area. The most significant concentration of finds is in the Don-Volga-Ural region. The majority originate from burials, much smaller quantities were found in settlement excavations. Most often these cheekpieces are manufactured from elk and deer antler. Less frequently they are made from the bones of large ungulates. Some cheekpieces may have been carved from wood, but in most cases only rotted fragments have survived. Those made

---

[15] Hüttel 1981: 24, 38–51, 55, 56; Penner 1998: 31–70; Boroffka 1998: 101–117.
[16] Berezanskaya et al 1986: 100 fig. 29.1; Krushelnicka 1985: 16, fig. 4.1.
[17] Lyashko 1994: 161, 162, fig. 50.8; Gorbov and Usachuk 1999: 80, 81, fig. 1.6.
[18] Kuzmina 2008: 178.
[19] Potratz 1941: 39; Penner 1998: 81–100.
[20] Bar-Oz et al. 2013: 1–8.
[21] Bar-Oz et al. 2013: fig. 3, 4.
[22] Littauer and Crouwel 1979: 97, fn. 59.
[23] Hüttel 1982: 47.
[24] Kuzmina 2008: 179.
[25] Kuzmina 2008: 179–181.
[26] Littauer and Crouwel 1979; Hüttel 1977.
[27] Leskov 1964; Kuzmina 1980.

from horn and bone are far better preserved, though often found in fragmentary condition.

Regardless of which group the shield type cheekpieces relate to, they have several constructional and ornamental features in common. The body is the largest part of the cheekpiece. Its shape varies greatly. In the centre there is one or, less often, two holes. They can be round, oval or have a nearly square shape. The inner face of the cheekpiece has studs. The number of studs ranges from two to four. The studs can be integral (i.e. made in one piece) or inserted. They differ in shape (straight, ridged, waisted, wedge-shaped, etc.) and size (short or long, thin or thick). Most shield type cheekpieces have a tab – a projection to which we presume a noseband may have been attached. Most often this projection is recessed, made as a flatter step. The tab, as well as the body, can be of various shapes (trapezoidal, semi-oval, triangular, rod-shaped). Sometimes one, or more often, several perforations of different shapes and sizes are made in it. It has been suggested that a noseband attachment would go through these additional holes. Some holes for a noseband are made right in the cheekpiece body. Such holes are located either on the outer face, closer to the edges, or at the side. Sometimes they can be shaped as a protruding loop with one large aperture, or two small ones. A considerable number of shield type cheekpieces have carved decoration. The ornamentation is either applied on the outer face around the central hole, closer to the edges, or on the tips of the inserted studs.

In terms of design and typology, shield type cheekpieces are very diverse. In the Russian archaeological literature this group is usually subdivided into "discoid" and "fluted" categories. The former, cut from a cross-section of antler or horn, are more or less flat in profile but frequently provided with studs on the inside face. The group of discoid cheekpieces is the largest and the most diverse. It includes about 250 examples, while the second group is much smaller, including about 60 finds. Fluted cheekpieces are nearly rectangular or trapezoidal and are U-shaped in cross-section. They were made from long tubular bone. This material was more easily available compared to the antlers of wild animals. The ends were cut off and the bone was split longitudinally, then polished or serrated. Then a tab was cut out at one end. We have shown that fluted cheekpieces derive from the discoid form. They appeared two or three centuries later. Furthermore, both groups existed concurrently for quite a long time.[28]

These are the main characteristics of shield type cheekpieces. We will further use them to describe and classify these artefacts. Typological features are also based on these characteristics.

Discoid cheekpieces (group I) are found throughout the northern part of the Eurasian continent. The majority of them belong to the Sintashta, Potapovka and Pokrovskaya cultures. These are the first archaeological cultures of the Late Bronze Age. They are combined into a cluster of chariot cultures as they have similar burial customs and grave furnishings. Saying 'cluster' in this case we refer to a group of cultures associated with chariots, harnesses and the gear and equipment of charioteers. Most discoid type cheekpieces were discovered in sites related to these cultures. Significantly smaller number of cheekpieces were excavated at the archaeological sites known as Petrovka, Srubnaya and Alakul, considered to be the successors of the above-mentioned cluster of archaeological cultures. Discoid type cheekpieces disappeared in the fourth period of the Late Bronze Age (about the middle of the second millennium BCE).

Cheekpieces of discoid type are quite sophisticated in terms of design and decoration (Figure 11.4). They are distinguished by a number of principal features. The body can be round, oval, or nearly rectangular, it can be in the shape of a narrow or wide semi-disc or have a more complex configuration. Their thickness varies irrespective of the shape. In the centre there is a hole for the mouthpiece. Originally, it was always round, the diameter ranging from 10 to 20 mm ± 2 mm. While in use the edges became abraded, and the hole often became oval. Around the hole a raised rim reinforces the edges. This is usually made on the outer face of the cheekpiece, though sometimes it can also be found on the inner face. Later cheekpieces usually lack such reinforcement, even though they are thinner.

Apart from the hole for the mouthpiece there is sometimes another aperture, which is usually located at the edge, closer to the tab. We assume it was used to attach a cheek strap. This aperture can be round or presented as a transverse channel in the sidewall, or like a protruding loop. Such a lateral hole is typical of the cheekpieces from the Don-Volga region. It can also be recognized in the Ural-Kazakhstan items, but nearly all or most of the Ural-Kazakhstan cheekpieces with lateral holes are of later period.

The majority of discoid cheekpieces have studs. The studs can be either solid, made in one piece integral with the cheekpiece body, or inserted. As a rule, the cheekpieces with studs are thicker. Sometimes both integral and inserted studs are found on the same cheekpiece. Studs vary in shape and size. They can be shaped (e.g. of hourglass shape or ridged), or cylindrical, or wedge-shaped, or made like low bumps with rounded tips. The shaped ones are usually more substantial, while the cylindrical and wedge-shaped studs look more slender. They are all circular in cross-section. Their length can vary. Early cheekpieces tend to have long, sturdy studs. As mentioned above, studs can be integral or inserted: these features are of local and chronological significance. Integral studs are characteristic of the cheekpieces from the Ural-Kazakhstan region, while inserted studs are typical of the Don-Volga region. It is relevant whether a cheekpiece has studs or carries no studs. Notably, the studs tend to disappear over time.

The cheekpieces are often furnished with a tab perhaps used to attach a noseband. It is recessed and its edges are notched to form "hooks". The shape of the tab varies a good deal: it can be rectangular, trapezoidal, triangular,

---

[28] Bochkarev and Kuznetsov 2010: 320–322.

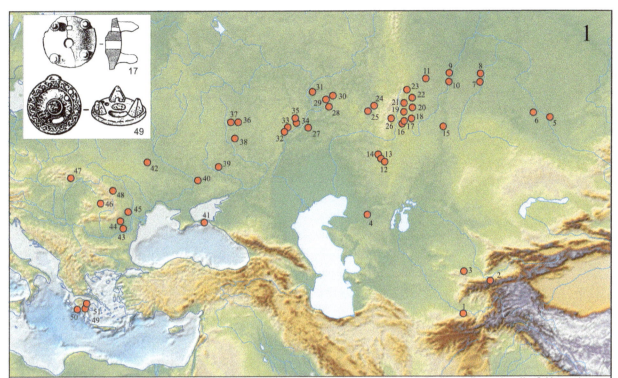

1-Jarkutan. 2-Zardcha-Khalifa. 3-Sazagan. 4-Toksanbay. 5-Ashchisu. 6-Ikpen. 7-Berlik. 8-Petrovka II. 9-Kamyshnoye. 10-Glyadyanskoye. 11-Shibayevo. 12-Zhaman Kargala. 13-Vostochniye Kurayli. 14-Tanabergen-2. 15-Bestamak. 16-Mirny IV. 17-Sintashta. 18-Krivoye Ozero. 19-Solntse II. 20-Kulevchi III. 21-Bolshekaraganskiy. 22-Kamenny Ambar-5. 23-Stepnoy VII. 24-Balanbash. 25-Babich. 26-Tavlykayevo IV. 27-Staritskoye. 28-Utevka VI. 29-Potapovka. 30-Surush. 31-Ouren II. 32-Kleshchevka. 33-Suvorovskiy. 34-Zolotaya Gora. 35-Storozhevka. 36-Filatovka. 37-Sofyino. 38-Otrozhka. 39-Ilichevka. 40-Boguslav. 41-Kamenka. 42-Trakhtemirovo. 43-Ulmeni. 44-Sărata Monteoru. 45-Cîrlomăneşti. 46-Berettyó. 47-Spišsky Štvrtok. 48-Brad. 49-Mycenae. 50-Kakovatos. 51-Dendra.

1-Toksanbay. 2-Zhaman Kargala. 3-Ilekshar I. 4-Bestamak. 5-Sintashta. 6- Kamenny Ambar-5. 7-Vesely. 8-Troitskiy. 9-Staritskoye. 10-Borodaevka II. 11-Krasnoselki. 12-Utevka VI. 13-Potapovka. 14-Ouren II. 15-Uvarovskiy II. 16-Dubovy Gai. 17-Novo-Yablonovka. 18-Storozhevka. 19-Berezovka. 20-Idolga. 21-Plyaskovatka. 22-Barannikovo. 23-Staroyurievo. 24-Selezni-1. 2. 25-Pichaevo. 26-Bolshaya Plavitsa. 27-Filatovka. 28-Vlasovka. 29-Bogoyavlenskoye. 30-Sofyino. 31-Kondrashevka. 32-Kondrashkinskiy. 33-Krasny I. 34-Ilichevka. 35-Varenovka. 36-Cândeşti. 37-Oarța de Sus. 38-Fűzesabony. 39-Mycenae.

Figure 11.3. The spread of early discoid cheekpieces in Eurasia. 1 – cheekpieces with integral studs; 2 – cheekpieces with inserted studs.

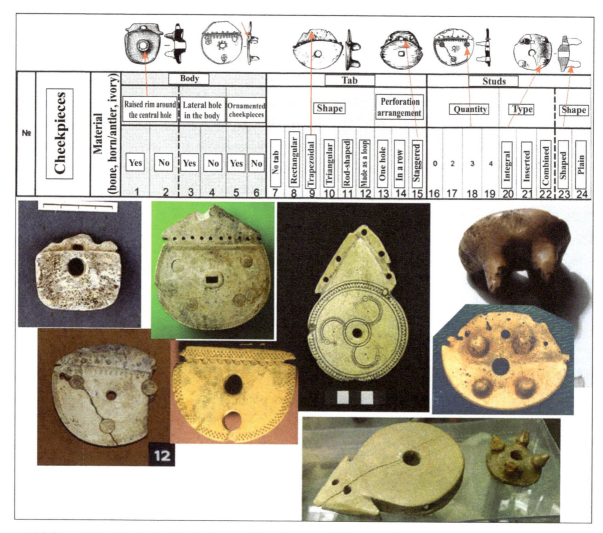

Figure 11.4. Description of each discoid cheekpiece with reference to 24 features of typological importance. In total 164 examples are described.

rod-shaped or in the form of a loop. The order and location of the perforations in the tab are of typological importance. They are usually round and small in size and can be staggered, or arranged in a row, though there are cheekpieces with only one hole in the tab. Sometimes the holes contain bone or horn pegs (rivets) used to fasten the noseband.

We can confidently state that the central hole in the cheekpiece body was used for the mouthpiece. The wear on the holes confirms this. However, we do not think that a mouthpiece was used with early horn/antler and bone cheekpieces. Our hypothesis is based on the location and placement of the cheekpieces by the jaws of sacrificed horses (Figure 11.2). We consider that the earliest cheekpieces were attached to a rigid and tight band around the horse's nose. The use of additional holes for attaching a noseband or a cheek strap is tentative. We presume that the lateral perforation on the cheekpiece body (Figure 11.9: 36, 37; Figure 11.10: 57, 68, 70, 74) would have been used to attach a cheek strap.

Cheekpieces are often decorated with engraved ornamentation. There may be a variety of geometrical figures applied along the edges, around the central hole, or on the inserted studs. The ornamentation is regarded as an important local characteristic. Decorated cheekpieces are typical of cultures in the Don and the Volga regions, and rare in the Urals and Kazakhstan. Ornamented cheekpieces from the Urals and Kazakhstan are of later periods.

These are the main features of discoid type cheekpieces of the Bronze Age from northern Eurasia. There are more than thirty features and they seem to almost completely distinguish this category. The presence or lack of some distinct characteristics is relevant. The overwhelming majority of them are of local or chronological significance, but there are characteristics combining both local and chronological categories. Below, we list the features used to classify discoid cheekpieces. They are presented in the order in which they are described above. The numbers in parentheses refer to the features used in our statistical analysis.

List of features:

1. Discoid body (Figure 11.8:109, 113, 115, 116, 127).

2. Elliptical body (Figure 11.9: 39–43).

3. Nearly rectangular body (Figure 11.6: 4, 17, 18, 21).

4. Narrow semi-discoid body (Figure 11.7: 80, 92–94, 104, 105).

5. Wide semi-discoid body (Figure. 6: 8, 20; Figure 11.9: 36, 37).

6. Shaped body (Figure 11.10: 49, 70).

7. Thickened body (Figure 11.6: 4, 11,20, 30; Figure 11.8: 113; Figure 11.11: 117).

8. Thin body (Figure 11.7: 80, 92–94, 104, 105; Figure 11.9: 39; Figure 11.10: 69; Figure 11.11: 137).

9. (1). Raised rim around the central hole (Figure 11.4: 1).

10. (2). No raised rim around the central hole (Figure 11.4: 2).

11. (3). Lateral aperture in the body (Figure 11.4: 3).

12. (4). No lateral aperture in the body (Figure 11.4: 4).

13. (16). No studs (Figure 11.4: 16).

14. (17). Two studs (Figure 11.4: 17).

15. (18). Three studs (Figure 11.4: 18).

16. (19). Four studs (Figure 11.4: 19).

17. (20). Integral studs (Figure 11.4: 20).

18. (21). Inserted studs (Figure 11.4: 21).

19. (22). Combined integral and inserted studs (Figure 11.4: 22; Figure 11.6: 8; Figure 11.9: 45).

20. (23). Shaped studs (Figure 11.4: 23; Figure 11.6: 11, 13, 21).

21. (24). Plain studs (Figure 11.4: 24; Figure 11.7: 92–96).

22. (7). No tab (Figure 11.4: 7; Figure 11.9: 34, 35, 38; Figure 11.11: 118, 121, 129, 135,136. 139; Figure 11.12:147, 148, 153, 156, 157).

23. (8). Rectangular tab (Figure 11.4: 8; Figure 11.8: 111; Figure 11.12: 151, 161).

24. (9). Trapezoidal tab (Figure 11.4: 9).

25. (10). Triangular tab (Figure 11.4: 10; Figure 11.7: 92, 93, 104, 105; Figure 11.8: 126, 128; Figure 11.9: 39; Figure 11.10: 70; Figure 11.12: 141).

26. (11). Rod-shaped tab (Figure 11.4: 11; Figure 11.8: 106, 107, 114, 116).

27. (12). Tab in the form of loop (Figure. 4: 12; Figure 11.12: 152).

28. (13). Tab with one hole (Figure 11.4: 13; Figure 11.6: 20, 30; Figure 11.7: 93, 95, 96; Figure 11.8: 115).

29. (14). Tab with perforations arranged in a row (Figure 11.4: 14; Figure 11.6: ,8, 11, 13, 16; Figure 11.8: 128; Figure 11.9: 36, 37, 44; Figure 11.10: 56–58, 68, 70, 74, 76, 77; Figure 11.11: 119, 125, 127, 134, 137, 138; Figure 11.1:,143, 149).

30. (15). Tab with staggered perforations (Figure 11.4: 15; Figure 11.6: 4, 17, 18, 25; Figure 11.7: 92, 93, 97; Figure 11.9,: 34, 40, 41, 42, 47, 48).

31. (5). Ornamented cheekpieces (Figure 11.4: 5).

32. (6). Cheekpieces with no ornamentation (Figure 11.4: 6).

We used multivariate data analysis (MDA) to identify significant combinations of these characteristics.[29] Our initial database includes 164 cheekpieces. These are the best-preserved artefacts providing the most complete information. We used 24 features (their numbers are given in parentheses in the list above), which we consider typologically significant. 164 cheekpieces were processed by Unscrambler software considering 24 features based on the Pearson correlation coefficient. We managed to obtain positive and negative correlation of all the samples. The multivariate data analysis considers a set of objects (cheekpieces) in the context of variables (features), determining the correlation degree of each sample with respect to all the others. It is impossible to render such an n-dimensional context on paper. Unscrambler software applies a visual approach to data analysis, as well as providing each sample and feature with a numerical value of its graphical location. One of the mathematical methods used by Unscrambler software is Principal Component Analysis (PCA), which is based on dimensionality reduction of the data with minimum possible information loss. PCA is widely used for structural analysis of multivariate data.[30] In the process of computing, PCA performs data mapping in such a way that multi-dimensional data is transformed into a reduced number of variables (principal components).

Based on the eigenvalues two principal components (further as PC) were extracted. Correlation of the samples related to PC1 and PC2 were visualised in two-dimensional diagrams – the score plot (samples) and loadings plot (features). The further away the sample (feature) is from the origin the more influence it has on the principal components.

The score plot obtained through the principal component analysis of the cheekpiece samples is shown in Figure 11.5. We can see the four quadrants of the coordinate plane where the cheekpieces are placed according to their positive or negative values relative to the two principal components.

The advantage of the PCA is that it shows the degree of influence (greater or lesser) of the features of each cheekpiece depending on how frequently they are clustered or outlying. PCA helps to identify interrelated features in particular quadrants of the coordinate plane. This is the way the features are clustered.

The following features have positive values (upper right quadrant):

---

[29] Esbensen 2006: 12–20.
[30] Esbensen 2006: 26–53.

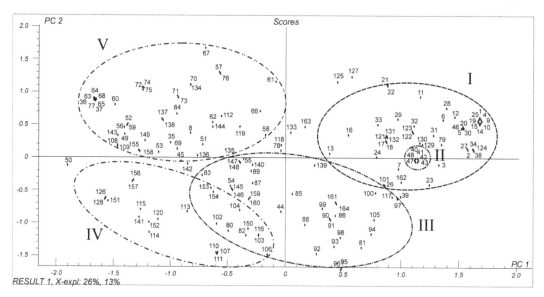

Figure 11.5. PCA score plot with 164 cheekpieces placed on the graph. I – location of the Sintashta cheekpieces (1–33); II – classic Potapovka cheekpieces (40–43, 47, 48); III – Petrovka cheekpieces (80–105); IV – Alakul cheekpieces (106–116); V – Pokrovskaya cheekpieces (49–79); Eurasian group of cheekpieces (117–154); Carpathian-Danube cheekpieces within the Eurasian group (140–154); Mycenaean group (155–164). See Appendix 1.

1) raised rim around the central hole (1);

2) trapezoidal tab (9);

3) four studs (19);

4) integral studs (20);

5) shaped studs (23).

Positive values of PC 1 and negative values of PC 2 (lower right quadrant) combine the following features:

1) no lateral hole in the body (4);

2) no ornamentation (6);

3) tab with one hole (13);

4) staggered perforations in the tab (15).

The following features have negative values of both PCs (lower left quadrant):

1) no raised rim around the central hole (2);

2) triangular tab (10);

3) no studs (16);

4) wedge-shaped studs (24).

The upper left quadrant (negative values of PC 1 and positive values of PC 2) contains the following features:

1) lateral hole in the body (3);

2) ornamented body (5);

3) additional holes in the tab arranged in a row (14);

4) three studs (18);

5) inserted studs (21).

Some features are located close to the origin of the coordinate plane, meaning they are neutral to the rest of the features, they have weak influence on the principal components. They are:

1) no tab (7);

2) rectangular tab (8);

3) rod-shaped tab (11);

4) tab made as a loop (12);

5) combined integral and inserted studs (22).

Too few cheekpieces have these features and this is probably the reason why these items are relatively neutral in the plot. The fact that these characteristics do not form systemic links can also explain their location closer to the origin. The former assumption is more likely to be correct.

Thus, several clusters of cheekpieces are quite clearly distinguished in the coordinate plane. These clusters cannot be considered as random group formations. They correspond to particular archaeological cultures. The Sintashta cheekpieces are located in the upper right quadrant of the scatterplot. The lower right quadrant of the coordinate plane is occupied by the cheekpieces of the Petrovka culture. Seventeen of the 26 Petrovka examples are here. The remaining eight cheekpieces are placed in the lower left quadrant of the coordinate plane. One item is found in the upper left quadrant of the scatterplot. In other words, the Petrovka cheekpieces combine features of both eastern and western regions.

In the lower left quadrant of the score plot are 13 of the 16 cheekpieces of the Alakul culture.

The upper left quadrant of the coordinate plane contains the majority of the Pokrovskaya cheekpieces. The statistics include 31 of the 67 recorded examples. All the cheekpieces related to the Srubnaya[31] culture are located in the lower left quadrant of the plot, i.e. together with the Alakul cheekpieces.

Special attention should be paid to the 15 cheekpieces found in Potapovka burials. Nine of them are located on the borderline between the Petrovka and Sintashta clusters, and one sample is in the Petrovka quadrant (No. 39), three cheekpieces coincide with the Pokrovskaya cluster (Nos. 35, 37, 38) and two samples lie in the Alakul quadrant close the Petrovka (No. 44) and Pokrovskaya (No. 45) quadrants (Figure 11.5). The neighbouring location of these finds is because one sample is ornamented, has a tab of undefined shape and three studs; and the other has a triangular tab with holes arranged in a row. Six samples form the core of this group (Figure 11.5). They are very similar to Sintashta cheekpieces in many characteristics, with one exception: they have no raised rim around the central hole. All these cheekpieces were found in kurgan cemetery Utevka VI. Two Potapovka cheekpieces contain all the classic features of the Pokrovskaya type (Figure 11.9, 36,37). Thus, the features of the Potapovka group show significant diversity. All this may indicate its intermediate position between the Early Pokrovskaya and Sintashta cultural traditions. In terms of territorial location, Potapovka is also in an intermediate position.

Individual cheekpieces have different cultural affinity and are scattered across all four quadrants of the scatterplot. We have temporarily brought them together into a so-called Eurasian group (Figure 11.11). This group includes 38 items. The finds were discovered over a vast area stretching from Central Asia, through Kazakhstan and Eastern Europe to the Balkan-Carpathian region. Obviously, they have different cultural affinity, but they do not form any closely-packed cluster or a distinct group. In typological terms they are just as diverse. However, these cheekpieces are of great interest because they show the extent to which the cheekpiece manufacturing tradition from the Don-Volga-Ural area affected the cultures in Northern Eurasia.

Thus, using the MDA method, we were able to identify several statistically stable groups or clusters of discoid type cheekpieces. Each of them is described by a certain combination of features. Some of them have a distinct cluster core. A number of features used to identify the core of each cultural group is referred to as a 'classic' set of features. It means a series of characteristics typical of a certain cultural and regional group. We therefore conclude that attributing a cheekpiece to an archaeological culture is an important classification technique. Hence, it seems reasonable to name these clusters after the cultures they relate to. Thus, the first cluster can be referred to as Sintashta (see Figure 11.5: I). It occupies the upper right quadrant on the coordinate plane, referred to below as the Sintashta quadrant. The second cluster relates to Petrovka. Its core is placed in the lower right quadrant, referred to below as the Petrovka quadrant (see Figure 11.5: III). Alakul (see Figure 11.5: IV) and Pokrovskaya (see Figure 11.5: V) clusters are located in the lower and upper left quadrants respectively (referred to below as the Alakul quadrant and the Pokrovskaya quadrant). The core of the Potapovka cluster (see Figure 11.5: II) is located directly on the PC1 axis between the Petrovka and Sintashta quadrants. It is important to note that cheekpieces of the 'Eurasian' group relating to different cultures are scattered over all four quadrants of the coordinate plane and do not form any cluster.

The fact that these clusters are easily related to certain archaeological cultures helps to clarify their classification and trace their typological development. In this regard, the great majority of discoid type cheekpieces can be related to a few cultures only. They are shared within two chronological sequences – the Ural-Kazakhstan and Don-Volga sequences. The former includes Sintashta, Petrovka and Alakul, while the latter includes Early and Late Pokrovskaya and Srubnaya cultures. The Potapovka culture discovered in the Samara Volga region can also be considered a part of the second group. It is contemporary with early Pokrovskaya and Sintashta cultures.

The Sintashta Cluster of Cheekpieces

We have analysed 33 items (Figure 11.6). All but five of them are placed in the upper right quadrant. However, four samples are placed in the lower right quadrant, i.e. among the Petrovka cheekpieces. Another is located in the Pokrovskaya quadrant. In the Sintashta cluster the core of eight cheekpieces is clearly distinguished (1, 4, 9, 10, 14, 15, 19, 25). All their correlation features coincide: 1) integral studs; 2) four studs; 3) shaped studs; 4) lack of ornamentation; 5) raised rim around the central hole; 6) trapezoidal tab; 7) tab with staggered perforation; 8) no lateral hole for the cheek strap.

The combination of these features determines the basic content of this group. However, the core can be increased to 13 pieces due to new finds recently discovered. Their features are the same eight characteristics of the Sintashta core from the PCA scatterplot. These 13 cheekpieces can be considered the basic classic variant of the Sintashta group. The other cheekpieces from this group deviate more or less from the classic set described above. They form separate variants.

Variant A2 includes six cheekpieces (11, 16, 21, 22, 32, 33). They do not form a compact group. There is a tab with holes arranged in a row, unlike the classic staggered perforations, which distinguishes them from the items of the classic variant (A1). This feature was obviously influenced by the Don-Volga (Pokrovskaya) cheekpieces. A row of perforations is the norm for the latter. It should also be noted that on the two cheekpieces (32 and 33), from the Glyadyanskoye settlement, related to variant A2, such holes are made in two rows (Figure 11.5).

Variant A3 includes three cheekpieces (5, 20, 30). They form a compact group placed close to classic variant A1. They have all eight common features and one characteristic

---

[31] In some publications Srubnaya is referred to as 'timber-grave' culture.

which distinguishes them from the samples of the previous two variants: there is only one hole in the tab. This feature is recognised as a local manufacturing technique of the Ural-Kazakhstan region. Almost all cheekpieces from the other regions lack this characteristic.

Only two items (17 and 18) relate to variant A4. They are just as uniform as the cheekpieces from the previous sets. Their common features, different from the other variants, include one hole in the tab, and the use of inserted instead of integral studs. The latter sets them far apart from the other Sintashta cheekpieces. It is highly likely that this feature was borrowed from the Pokrovskaya type.

Variant A5 is represented by four items (7, 8, 13, 26). They do not share all the features relating to a specific group. As a result, two examples (7, 26) are placed in the Petrovka quadrant, one (8) is in the Pokrovskaya cluster and one more cheekpiece (13) is located in the Sintashta quadrant very close to the borderline with Petrovka. The lack of a raised rim around the central hole is the main common characteristic. This feature can be considered in two ways. On the one hand, it could have been the result of local development. On the other hand, it could have been borrowed from the Pokrovskaya cheekpieces. It is worth noting that two examples of variant A5 carry three integral studs and two have four integral studs.

The cheekpiece (8) from grave 8, kurgan 2, kurgan cemetery Kamenny Ambar-5 is of special note. Five features set it apart from the classic Sintashta group. There are three studs, one of which is inserted. There is no raised rim around the central hole. Its unique feature is the tab with perforations arranged in a row. All these features place it closer to the western Pokrovskaya type. It is therefore no coincidence that it is located in the Pokrovskaya quadrant of the coordinate graph. Some features of this cheekpiece can obviously be explained by the influence of the Pokrovskaya tradition, while at the same time, it has certain Sintashta features – integral shaped studs, no lateral aperture, and a thickened body. Moreover, it was found together with a typical Sintashta cheekpiece.

Cheekpiece (7) from Solonchanka 1a, kurgan 2, grave 29 is also worth mentioning. It has three studs, like some cheekpieces from variant A5 (48 and 49). This relates them to the Petrovka type. One of the studs is located on the inner face of the tab. This feature is also typical of the Petrovka cheekpieces.

The other seven Sintashta cheekpieces (3, 6, 12, 23, 24, 28, 31) are diverse. They cannot be combined into one variant. One of them (24) is distinguished by two studs, while another (6) has two integral and two inserted studs. Both features are completely alien to Sintashta cheekpieces. A third cheekpiece (12) does not have any additional perforations. It is probably unfinished. The remaining four items are partially damaged and cannot provide the information required for classification.

To complete the typological characteristics of the Sintashta cheekpieces, we would also like to highlight another common feature. All of them are of relatively small size. Their height and width range within 9.5–3.5 cm. There is also a group of smaller cheekpieces

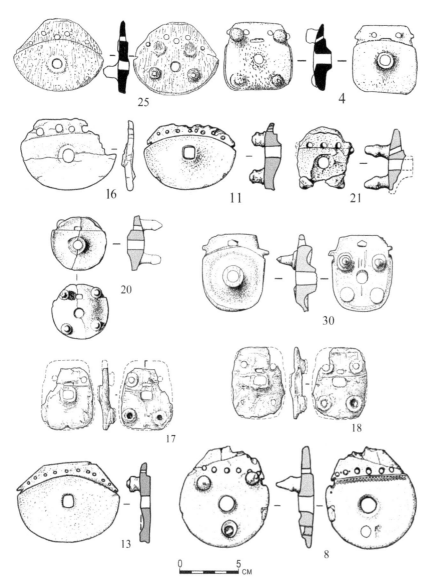

Figure 11.6. Cheekpieces in the Sintashta cluster. Classic cheekpieces, variant A1 (25, 4); variant A2 (11, 16, 21); variant A3 (20, 30); variant A4 (17, 18); variant A5 (13); special ornamented cheekpiece (8). The numbering corresponds to the reference numbers on the coordinate graph Figure 5 (4, 8, 11, 13, 16, 17, 18, 30: author's drawing after Usachuk 2013: figs. 3,2; 4,3; 5,6; 5,1; 9,5; 13,1; 13,2; 14,3; 20, 21, 25: author's drawing after Genlng et al.1992: figs. 75,3; 79,10; 114,6).

with sizes ranging from 4.5 cm to 3.5 cm.

To sum up the review of the Sintashta cluster, we conclude that this group of cheekpieces is a separate type consisting of five variants. Its features are most fully represented in variant A1, which we refer to as the classic one. Based on the characteristics of this variant, we can formulate a definition for the Sintashta type. It includes discoid type cheekpieces with four integral studs, a raised rim around the central hole, a trapezoidal tab with staggered perforations. There is neither a lateral hole for the cheek strap nor ornamentation. The cheek strap could have been attached to the tab of such a cheekpiece. The protrusions at both sides could have been used for that purpose. Each cheekpiece has these protrusions. This type, as mentioned above, consists of five variants, the first (A1) is the classic (basic) one and the other variants are derivative. They emerged as a kind of mutation of the basic variant because of both internal development and external influence. The most remarkable and dramatic is the influence of the Pokrovskaya tradition of cheekpiece manufacture from the Don-Volga region.

The Petrovka Cluster of Cheekpieces

Out of the 26 Petrovka cheekpieces in the PCA scatterplot, 17 are placed in the lower right quadrant (81, 86, 88, 90–101, 105). Eight are located in the Alakul quadrant (80–83, 87, 89, 102, 103, 104), one item is in the Pokrovskaya quadrant (84). Compared to the Sintashta type, the Petrovka cluster is not that numerous and its features are more scattered (Figure 11.7). Still, the core is quite well distinguished in the scatterplot. It includes six cheekpieces (86, 92, 93, 98, 104, 105). They have seven common features out of eight: 1) integral studs; 2) no lateral hole in the body; 3) no ornamentation; 4) two or three studs; 5) no raised rim around the central hole; 6) trapezoidal tab; 7) plain (not shaped) studs.

Only features 10, 11 and 12 are different, relating to the pattern of the holes in the tab. Cheekpieces 81, 86, 92, 93, and 98 within this core represent the classic variant of the Petrovka cluster. It is marked as B1. Compared to the Sintashta cheekpieces, these items have two new features – a triangular tab and plain (not shaped) studs. The other

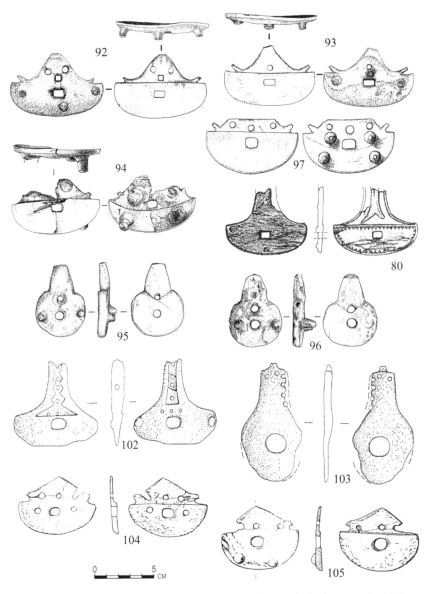

Figure 11.7. Cheekpieces in the Petrovka cluster. Classic cheekpieces, variant B1 (92, 93); variant B2 (94, 97, 102, 103, 104, 105); variant B3 (80, 95, 96). The numbering corresponds to the reference numbers on the coordinate graph Figure 5 (92, 93, 94, 95, 96, 97, 80: author's drawing after Usachuk 2013: figs. 7,1; 7,2; 7,3; 8,2; 8,3; 8,4; 113,2; 102, 103: author's drawing after Kupriyanova and Zdanovich 2015: figs: 17,1,2; 104, 105: author's drawing after Loshakova 2014: figs: 5,1,2).

cheekpieces in this group differ from the classic variant to some extent. They are grouped in two variants. Variant B2 includes four cheekpieces (94, 97, 104, 105), with such features as no raised rim around the central hole, no lateral hole, and wedge-shaped studs. Unlike the classic variant, these features do not occur regularly. They are sporadically replaced by features often found in the Sintashta type: staggered perforations or a single hole.

Variant B3 includes six cheekpieces (80, 95, 96, 100, 102, 103). They are very close to the previous variant, but they have a completely new feature – a rod-shaped tab. This is often found in later cheekpieces related to the Alakul and Srubnaya cultures. In this regard, special attention should be paid to the ornamentation of the two Petrovka cheekpieces. Ornamentation is also a widely recognized feature of the Srubnaya and Alakul cheekpieces.

Our analysis brings us to the conclusion that the Petrovka cheekpieces are an independent type, different from Sintashta, comprising three variants. Based on its classic set of features this group can be defined as follows: it includes cheekpieces with two or three integral studs of a plain shape, a triangular tab, without ornamentation and no lateral hole in the body. The central hole (for the mouthpiece) is not reinforced with a raised rim.

The Alakul Cluster of Cheekpieces

This is the smallest group (Figure 11.8). Eleven items are placed on the PCA plot. They retain features of cultural and technological importance. All (106, 107, 110, 111, 113, 114, 115, 116), except three (108, 109, 112), are concentrated in the lower left quadrant of the coordinate graph. The last three cheekpieces are placed in the Pokrovskaya quadrant of the scatterplot. It is typical that they share many but not all features. It is therefore reasonable to specify that the features of the Alakul cheekpieces are even more scattered than those of the Petrovka cluster. These are as follows: 1) no studs; 2) a loop-shaped protrusion used for headstall straps (Figure 11.8: 108, 109); 3) ornamentation; 4) a lateral hole in most of the cheekpieces; 5) no trapezoidal tab.

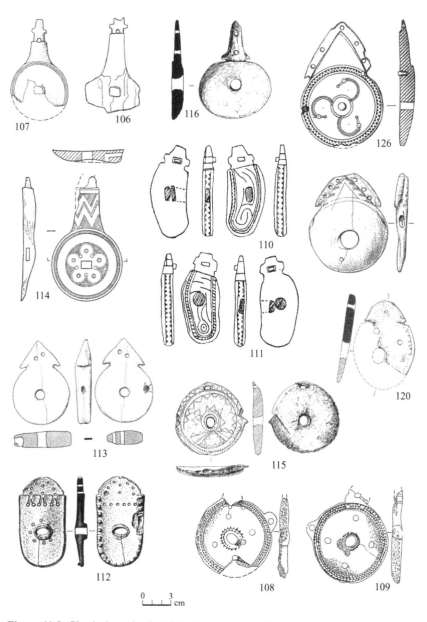

Figure 11.8. Cheekpieces in the Alakul cluster, type C. Alakul cheekpieces from the Ural-Kazakhstan region (106–116); the cheekpieces, placed in the Alakul quadrant, found in multilayer settlements of the Volga-Don region, perhaps related to Srubnaya (120, 126, 128). The numbering corresponds to the reference numbers on the coordinate graph Figure 5 (107, 108, 109, 112, 113, 128: author's drawing after Usachuk 2013: figs. 19,1; 93,3,4; 96,3; 19,4; 63,1; 110, 111: author's drawing from Bochkarev and Kuznetsov 2019: figs. 2,7,8.; 106, 116, 120: author's drawing after Bochkarev and Kuznetsov 2013: figs. 8, 2, 3, 10; 114: author's drawing after Zdanovich 1986: fig. 4,1; 115: drawn by P. Kuznetsov).

All these features are not regular, and we cannot group them into clearly defined variants of the Alakul type. We group all of them into Alakul type C. Tellingly, the shapes of these cheekpieces are far more varied than those of Sintashta and Petrovka. They are round or nearly oval, while the three cheekpieces (106, 110, 111) are nearly rectangular. The four cheekpieces look like an elongated rod. The origin of this shape can be recognised in the Petrovka items, though here we can see protruding nubs. The tabs were probably used for a noseband. It is possible that the loop-shaped tab was borrowed from the Carpathian-Danube cheekpieces. Lateral holes in the body follow the method of attaching cheekpieces to the bridle bit, which continued from western Pokrovskaya culture. The ornamentation of the Alakul cheekpieces is also very specific. It significantly differs in style from all the previous types and has no analogies. Such ornamentation, along with other characteristics, can be considered an innovation of this type of cheekpieces.

The Alakul cluster includes three cheekpieces which are related to other types. It is worth drawing attention to the Alakul cheekpieces from kurgan cemetery Ilekshar. Judging by their parameters, they are related to the Pokrovskaya type. However, they correspond to its later version. This is determined by such features as the small diameter of the studs and a round body. The cheekpiece from the Mirny settlement (112) is unique. It combines the features of several types from the Volga-Ural region. The body is rectangular. In size it is similar to the fluted cheekpieces, though it is flat in profile. It has integral studs and around the central oval opening there is a large, raised rim – typical characteristics of the Sintashta group. The studs are small. They are placed around the edge and are very close to one another like the teeth of a comb. Furthermore, there is a lateral perforation (a Pokrovskaya feature), which was broken. The shape of the tab and the perforation pattern are similar to the tabs of fluted cheekpieces.[32] The type of ornamentation on this item is most closely related to the Alakul cheekpieces. Thus, this cheekpiece combines the features of different regional groups and chronologically different cultures. It is therefore set apart.

The types of cheekpieces described make up the Ural-Kazakhstan series. At the same time, the cheekpieces of the Volga-Don sequence gained ground to the west of the Urals. This series includes clusters of Potapovka and Pokrovskaya types. It has not been confirmed so far whether there are any discoid type cheekpieces related to Srubnaya – the culture contemporary with Alakul. There are three examples presumably found in the Srubnaya horizon in the settlements of Boguslav, Varenovka and Nizhnyaya Krasavka. These are eastern European settlements with several cultural layers. In our study these three cheekpieces are considered within the Eurasian group.

The Potapovka Cluster of Cheekpieces

This is a relatively small and geographically compact group (Figure 11.9). In total 15 cheekpieces are considered. Three of them (34, 38, 46) are placed in the Sintashta quadrant, six are located right on PC1 axis (40–43, 47, 48), on the borderline between the Petrovka and Sintashta quadrants. One cheekpiece is placed in the Petrovka quadrant of the coordinate plane (39). Three items are found in the Pokrovskaya cluster (35–37) and two are placed in the Alakul quadrant (44 and 45) very close to the axes PC1 and PC2.

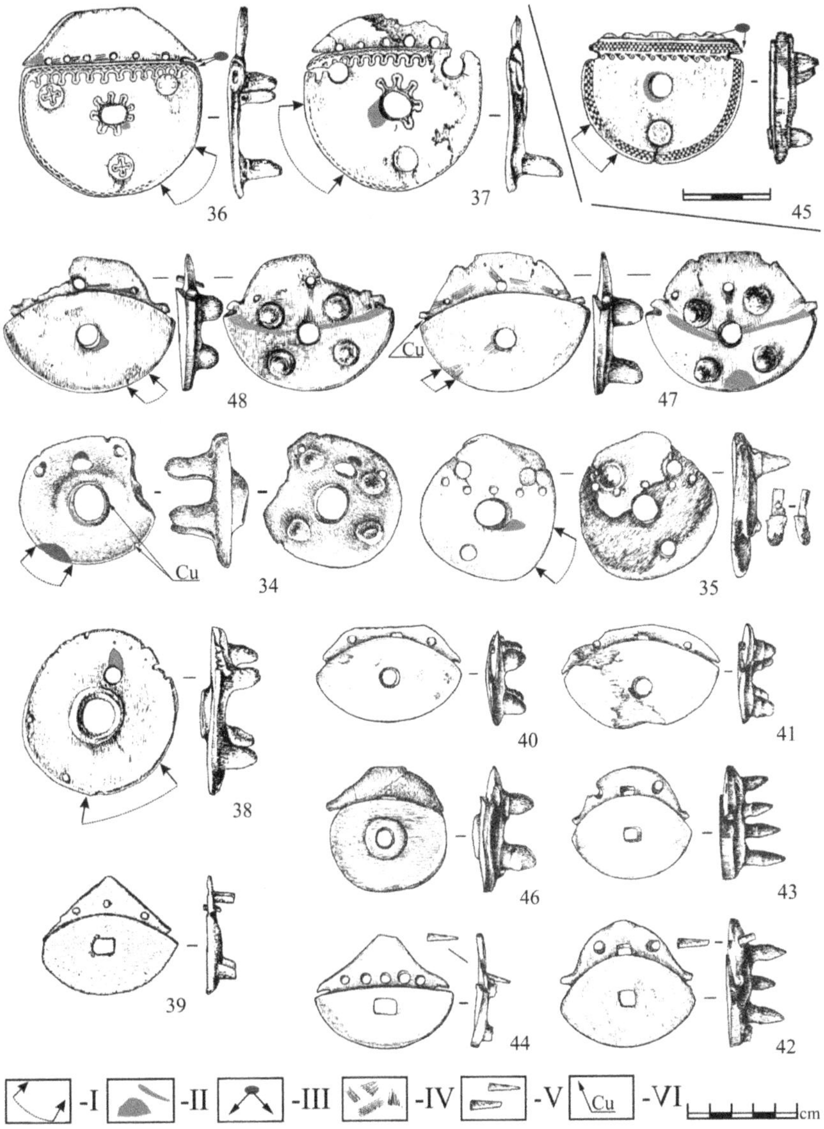

The core of this group is formed by six cheekpieces (40–43, 47, 48). They are identical to the classic Sintashta core, with one exception – they do not have a raised rim around the central hole. Therefore, they are placed on the borderline between the Sintashta and Petrovka quadrants. In fact, they can be considered as one of the Sintashta variants. Other Potapovka cheekpieces differ far more from the Sintashta items. Therefore, one group forms a separate variant of Potapovka, while the other belongs to the

[32] Bochkarev and Kuznetsov 2010: 138.

Figure 11.9. Cheekpieces in the Potapovka cluster. Classic cheekpieces (40–43, 47, 48); cheekpieces placed in the Sintashta quadrant (34, 38, 46); cheekpiece placed in the Petrovka quadrant (39); cheekpieces placed in the Pokrovskaya quadrant (35–37); cheekpieces placed in the Alakul quadrant (44, 45). The numbering corresponds to the reference numbers on the coordinate graph Figure 5. I Polished area at the edges abraded by the bridle straps; II polished area of the cheekpiece; III polished area at the protrusion of the tab (1, 3); IV regular scratch marks (nicks); V pegs in the lateral holes; VI traces of copper (drawn by P. Kuznetsov).

Early Pokrovskaya cheekpieces. Since these cheekpieces have only one difference from the classic Sintashta type, they are considered to be a variation. All these cheekpieces were excavated at kurgan cemetery Utevka VI.

One Potapovka cheekpiece (39), located in the Petrovka quadrant, found in grave 2, kurgan 2, kurgan cemetery Utevka VI, has an additional distinguishing feature – a triangular tab. However, it differs from the Petrovka cheekpieces since it has four studs instead of three. Apart from that, the item has an elliptical body, not trapezoidal, as in the case of the classic Petrovka cheekpieces.

One example corresponds to variant A1 of the Sintashta type. There is only one additional hole in the tab and it has a reinforcement around the central hole – a raised rim (46).

Three Potapovka cheekpieces have no tab and this feature distinguishes them. They were all found in the Potapovka kurgan cemetery. Two of them are located in the Sintashta quadrant (34 and 38). They are close to Variant A1 of the Sintashta type, though they have such classic features as a raised rim around the central hole and staggered perforations. The third cheekpiece includes the principal Pokrovskaya features, though it has no tab and no ornamentation (35). This cheekpiece is therefore placed in the Pokrovskaya quadrant.

The two cheekpieces from Potapovka kurgan cemetery can be clearly identified as the western Pokrovskaya type (36 and 37). Moreover, they have all the classic features. Both items were found together with Sintashta cheekpiece No. 38. The faces of the cheekpieces are ornamented with a zigzagging and oval meander. The studs are ornamented with tiny crosses incised into the meander.

Thus, the Potapovka cheekpieces are allocated in two quadrants of the coordinate plane: most items are placed in the Sintashta quadrant and the rest in the Pokrovskaya quadrant.

Two other cheekpieces are located in the Alakul quadrant (44 and 45). They are very different and cannot be attributed to the same type. Judging by the shape of the body and the two integral studs, cheekpiece 45 is similar to the eastern Sintashta-Petrovka group. Though the body is ornamented, the holes are arranged in a row and there is no raised rim around the central hole. Furthermore, it has one inserted stud. The body is embellished with carved squares in a staggered pattern placed in three rows separated by solid lines. In the upper part of the body there is a row of carved hooks with spiral tails. The tails are twisted clockwise. These features make this item similar to the Pokrovskaya cheekpieces. In general, it can be considered as a cheekpiece of a special hybrid group. While in use, the tab of the cheekpiece was broken. Probably, so was the lower stud. Then, the item was reworked: a slot for the inserted stud and new grooves were made, so that a part of the ornament was damaged. The cheekpiece had a practical value as it was large and substantial. That is the reason it would have been repaired. Cheekpiece 44 also has a number of hybrid features: three integral studs, a semi-disc body and a triangular tab. Additional holes in the tab, for the noseband, are placed in a row. They have pegs for fastening the straps of the noseband. Cheekpieces 44 and 45 were found together as a pair in grave 5, kurgan 6, kurgan cemetery Utevka VI. Thus, we can distinguish a special type of the Volga-Ural cheekpieces.

The Potapovka cluster demonstrates a great diversity of features, though it is based on the Sintashta core. All this makes the Potapovka cluster intermediate between the Early Pokrovskaya and Sintashta cultural spheres.

The Pokrovskaya Cluster of Cheekpieces

This group is geographically concentrated in the Don-Volga region. It is the most numerous group (Figure 11.10).

We know of at least 65 examples. At the same time, more than a half of those cheekpieces are in fragmentary condition. The Pokrovskaya items are far more fragile than the other cheekpieces as they are large but thin. Moreover, some cheekpieces are made of wood and have inserted bone studs and bone bushings in the central holes. Taking into consideration such characteristics as ornamentation along with all the aforementioned features, we can assume that they were designed for ceremonial (parade) rather than practical use.

We used 31 samples in the PCA. These items are the least damaged. 27 of them (49, 51–53, 56–78) are placed in the upper left quadrant of the plot. Three (50, 54, 55) are located in the lower left quadrant and one (79) in the Sintashta quadrant. The items sampled for the coordinate graph were found both in Early Pokrovskaya and Late Pokrovskaya sites. The core of this group consists of cheekpieces combining such features as: 1) inserted studs; 2) shaped studs; 3) three studs; 4) an ornamented outer surface and ornamented studs; 5) a trapezoidal tab; 6) a lateral hole in the cheekpiece body; 7) no raised rim around the central hole. Inserted studs, ornamentation and lateral holes are the most typical features of the Pokrovskaya cheekpieces. These are the features which distinguish them from Sintashta and Petrovka. Five samples combine all seven features listed above and represent the classic set of the Pokrovskaya group (63, 64, 65, 68, 77).

Geographically, the cheekpieces from the classic set are distributed along rather a narrow belt in the central forest-steppe zone of Eastern Europe, from the right bank of the Volga River in the Samara region (kurgan cemetery Uvarovskiy II, kurgan 11, grave 2) to the right bank of the Don in the Voronezh region (Kondrashkinskiy kurgan, grave 1). Perhaps the two cheekpieces (61 and 62) found in the kurgan near Kondrashevka on the right bank of the Don, excavated in 1912, can also be associated with the classic type. However, there is no information as to whether they were ornamented or not. These cheekpieces have not been preserved. Only the reconstruction of their inner face is available, which looks convincing enough.[33]

Apart from the classic type, there are four items from Pokrovskaya sites placed outside the Pokrovskaya quadrant. The most distinctive is cheekpiece 2 from grave 1, kurgan 6, kurgan cemetery Ouren II (79). It has Sintashta characteristics. It was found as one of a pair (78). The latter, however, has no raised rim around its central hole. It is placed in the Pokrovskaya quadrant, mid way between the two clusters. Both cheekpieces are likely to have been produced locally after the fashion of the Sintashta cheekpieces. These two items are among the little evidence testifying to the links between the cultural and technological traditions of Sintashta and Pokrovskaya. Cheekpieces 50, 54 and 66 are in the Alakul quadrant. Their location is explained by the incomplete data available for them. The cheekpiece excavated at Pichaevo single kurgan (66) is not

---

[33] Usachuk and Pustovoyt 2004.

Early Cheekpieces in Eurasia

Variant 2: The second cheekpiece (58) from kurgan cemetery Zolotaya Gora has no studs. This is a feature of later periods gaining widespread use in Srubnaya and Alakul. The site where this cheekpiece was found dates to the late Pokrovskaya period.

Variant 3: This cheekpiece (Figure 11.10: 69) without a tab is from grave 3, kurgan 1, kurgan cemetery Selezni-1. The central hole is reinforced with a raised rim on the inner face, not on the outer surface which is a distinctive feature of the Pokrovskaya cheekpieces. There are two more perforations in the body, one central and one lateral, made at right angles to each other. Probably one was used to fasten the noseband, while the other was used for the cheek strap. The body and studs are richly embellished. A 'Segner wheel'[34] is carved around the central hole consisting of six full-sized spirals and another small and rather unaesthetic one. It is likely that the number of spirals was important: there are seven spirals here. The spirals are twisted counterclockwise. The 'Segner wheel' imitates left rotation, although it usually imitates right rotation. The cheekpiece rims are decorated with two parallel lines and scalene triangles between them with the apexes tilted towards each other. Such ornamentation is quite frequently found on bone artefacts of the Late Bronze Age. It often seems to imitate a twisted cord. The studs are ornamented uniformly: with a circle with a large dot in the centre.

Apart from the variants described above, there are two types of Pokrovskaya cheekpieces which differ from the classic set in one or two features.

Type 1: 11 cheekpieces have four studs, not three (52, 54, 55, 56, 59, 67, 71, 72, 73, 74, 75). Two of them have a triangular tab (52, 59). Two others lack any ornamentation and may have had triangular tabs (54, 55). One cheekpiece is so badly damaged that it is impossible to tell how many studs there may have been (60).

The Pokrovskaya cheekpieces with four studs are much more widespread than the classic type with three studs: they are found from the Urals (Vesely Khuto – 54 and 55) to the Upper Don region (Staroyurievo kurgan 2, grave 1 – 74 and 75).

Type 2: The second type includes three cheekpieces with an unusual shape of the body (49, 50, 70). One of them is 'guitar'-shaped (70). This find from grave 4, kurgan 1, kurgan cemetery Selezni-2 was excavated together with a matching cheekpiece, which is not used in our statistical analysis because only a few fragments are available. They had three inserted studs and, probably, a triangular tab. The cheekpieces from Barannikovo are carved in the form of

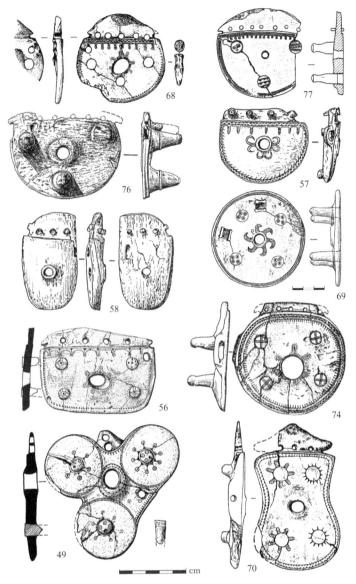

Figure 11.10. Cheekpieces in the Pokrovskaya cluster. Classic cheekpieces (68, 77). Variants of the classic type: Variant 1 (57, 76); variant 2 (58); variant 3 (69). Special types of the Pokrovskaya cheekpieces: type 1 (56, 74); type 2 (49, 70). The numbering corresponds to the reference numbers on the coordinate graph Figure 5 (49, 57, 58, 68, 69, 70, 74, 76, 77: author's drawing after Usachuk 2013: figs. 40,1; 39,1; 40,2; 46,2; 48,12; 49,1; 53,1; 42,1; 31,1. 56: author's drawing after Usachuk 2010: fig. 92).

ornamented. It is severely damaged. It is therefore unclear whether it once had a lateral hole.

The remaining finds on the periphery of the Pokrovskaya core can be divided into three variants and two special Pokrovskaya types of cheekpieces.

Variant 1: This includes cheekpieces from the ruined Suvorovskiy kurgan (76) and from kurgan cemetery Zolotaya Gora (57). Both sites are located on the right bank of the Volga, in the Saratov region. It is the integral studs that distinguish them from the others. They also have a raised rim around the central hole. The combination of these two features proves the eastern influence brought from Sintashta and Petrovka.

---

[34] A symbol of a rotating wheel used to decorate artefacts such as ceramics, cheekpieces, metal buckles, etc.

a rosette with three petals (49, 50). There is a central hole, and a stud is inserted in the middle of each petal. All these cheekpieces have intrinsic ornamentation, studied by A. N. Usachuk and his colleagues in detail.[35] The fragments of two other cheekpieces related to this type from the Saratov Volga region were published by N. M. Malov2.[36]

Conclusions

All the clusters within the discoid type considered above have several common features that are intended to ensure the most effective directional control of horses harnessed to a chariot. The origin of these effective cheekpieces is associated with the Don-Volga-Ural region. The Don-Volga-Ural sequence is subdivided into two contemporary categories: the Volga-Ural cheekpieces with integral studs and the Don-Volga cheekpieces with inserted studs. Meantime the influence of the Sintashta and Potapovka items with integral studs on the western manufacturing traditions was much stronger than the influence of the Pokrovskaya products with inserted studs on the eastern cheekpieces. Cheekpieces with integral studs spread up to the Balkans and southern Greece. At the same time, the main features of the early cheekpieces have common characteristics: body, studs, tabs, and additional perforation. The contours of the earliest Sintashta and Potapovka cheekpieces resemble the shape of cattle epiphyses. These round ends of long bones may have served as the first cheekpieces. As an example of such a cheekpiece we can consider sample 118 within the Eurasian group, found in the settlement of Balanbash.

The Eurasian Group of Cheekpieces

This group includes cheekpieces that are scattered across a vast area of the southern part of Eastern Europe and are also known in Central Asia. In most cases, we cannot associate these cheekpieces with any known culture. That is why they are brought together in one group based on geographic origin. This group includes accidental finds, items excavated at settlements with several cultural layers or sites which have not been related to any culture so far. These cheekpieces certainly pertain to different cultures and are not uniform in terms of typology (Figure 11.11). It is not surprising, therefore, that they are in all four quadrants of the scatterplot. In total 23 items were sampled for statistical processing.

Eurasian Cheekpieces in the Sintashta Cluster

We shall start by describing the Eurasian group of cheekpieces from those located in the Sintashta quadrant. Cheekpiece 124 from the Kamenka settlement in Eastern Crimea is related to the sites of the Kamenka-Liventsovka group and dates to the end of the Middle Bronze Age. The cheekpiece has four shaped integral studs, a raised rim around the central hole, and staggered perforations. These features make it similar to variant A1 of Sintashta cheekpieces with

---

[35] Myskov et al. 2004.
[36] Malov 2012.

no tab. At the same time, in the coordinate graph, it forms a dense group of items together with cheekpieces 34 and 38 from the Potapovka kurgan cemetery in the Samara Volga region. Cheekpiece 34 is absolutely identical with the Kamenka find.

Cheekpiece 125 is from the kurgan near Kleshchevka village (on the right bank of the Volga, not far from Saratov). The burial was damaged. The cheekpiece has four shaped integral studs and a raised rim around the central hole. There is no lateral perforation, though the holes in the tab are arranged in a row. A distinctive feature is the plain ornamentation applied on the edges, which shows a row of upside-down scalene triangles with dots. So this cheekpiece combines Sintashta and Pokrovskaya characteristics. It is undoubtedly of local Pokrovskaya origin, though it was influenced by Sintashta.

Cheekpiece 127 from the cultural layer of the Otrozhka settlement on the Middle Don is a hybrid combining both Sintashta and Pokrovskaya features. The Sintashta characteristics are four integral studs and rather a thick body. The Pokrovskaya features include the arrangement of additional holes in a row and a lateral aperture. This find can be classified as a special syncretic type, which combines both local Pokrovskaya and eastern Sintashta features equally. It is therefore quite natural that the cheekpiece is placed in the Sintashta quadrant, and very close to Pokrovskaya. Cheekpiece 125 from Kleshchevka is also placed here.

Cheekpieces 131 and 132 from Trakhtemirov are identical. They are remarkably thick and have no tab. These finds are located in the middle of the quadrant of the eastern Sintashta culture although they were found far to the west in the Trakhtemirov settlement in the Middle Dnieper region. The cheekpieces have distinct Sintashta traits: four integral studs and a raised rim around the central hole. At the same time, they have one large extra hole that could have been used to fasten a noseband and one additional small perforation. Moreover, there are small additional perforations made at the edge of the body. Some of the holes seem to have been damaged while in use. Such holes at the edges are a characteristic feature of the western cheekpieces without tabs. Similar perforations are seen in the cheekpieces from the Kamenka settlement (124) and in the cheekpieces from kurgan cemetery Potapovka (34, 38). An additional small hole can be associated with Pokrovskaya characteristics. In fact, we can also recognize a combination of the Sintashta and Pokrovskaya traditions in these cheekpieces (131, 132). At the same time, this combination looks unusual, and differs from the cheekpieces found in Kleshchevka (125) and Otrozhka (127). It is therefore possible to associate these two items with a special Trakhtemirov type. It is distinguished by the combination of the dominant Sintashta features (integral studs, a single hole for the noseband, reinforcement around the central hole) and one Pokrovskaya feature (a lateral hole). The unique nature of these cheekpieces leads us to assume that they were local products, probably within the context of the Babino culture.

Cheekpieces 121, 122, 123, 129, 130 from the Sintashta quadrant were discovered in the furthest south-eastern part of their distribution area, in Central Asia. Four locations of these cheekpieces are known in Uzbekistan and Tajikistan. Two items (129 and 130) were found in grave 2, Sazagan cemetery, in the old riverbed in eastern Uzbekistan. The cheekpieces have four shaped integral studs and a substantial raised rim around the central hole.

A similar cheekpiece was found in the Jarkutan site in a ritual complex (121). This site is also located in the old Sazagan riverbed.

Three or four cheekpieces were found in quite a rich grave at Zardcha-Khalifa near Panjakent in Tajikistan. Two of them, which are better preserved, are included in the statistics. These cheekpieces, with no ornamentation, four integral studs and a thickening around the mouthpiece hole, fit quite well into the Sintashta group. All of them have a groove carved along the sidewall. Such grooves are also made on the original Sintashta cheekpieces found in kurgan cemeteries Bolshekaraganskiy (1, 2) and Kamenny Ambar (3, 4, 6, 12, 13). Moreover, a similar groove is made on a cheekpiece from the Kondrashkinskiy kurgan in the Middle Don region (60).

In general, the cheekpieces from Central Asia can be associated with Sintashta variant A1 without a tab. They have such features as a substantial raised rim around the central hole and distinct grooves made on the sidewalls. It is therefore possible to assume that they are a local imitation of the Sintashta cheekpieces from the South Urals. In this regard, it is worth mentioning that there are other artefacts of north-western origin in this local cultural environment: metal knives, flint and metal arrowheads, jewellery.[37]

To complete our review of the finds placed in the Sintashta quadrant, we should mention the cheekpiece from Troitskoye village in Bashkiria (133). It has such Sintashta features as a raised rim around the central hole, no ornamentation and no additional perforation for a cheek strap. On the other hand, it has three inserted studs and additional holes arranged in a row, which are typical Pokrovskaya characteristics. The unique feature of this item is the studs, which are inserted into special bushings of a nearly square shape. To sum up, we can relate the Troitskoye cheekpiece to a separate subtype of the Sintashta cheekpieces.

Eurasian Cheekpieces in the Petrovka Cluster

The only cheekpiece in the Petrovka quadrant is the item found in the Balanbash settlement in the forest-steppe Ural zone in Bashkiria (117). It should be noted that in the scatterplot this cheekpiece is placed on the border with Sintashta. The Potapovka cheekpieces have a similar location in the plot. The cheekpiece from Balanbash does not have a marked tab. It has such Sintashta features as four integral studs, a thickened body, and no ornamentation. The

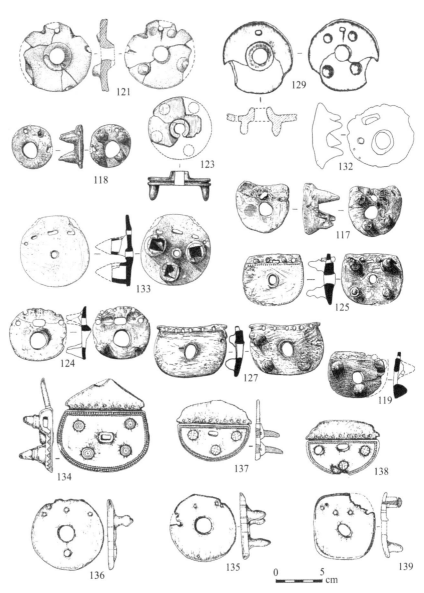

Figure 11.11. Cheekpieces in the Eurasian group. Cheekpieces from Central Asia (121, 123, 129); cheekpieces from the Southern Urals (117, 118, 133); the Volga region (125); the Don region (127, 134–139); the Dnieper region (119, 132); Eastern Crimea (124). The numbering corresponds to the reference numbers on the coordinate graph Figure 5 (117, 118, 121, 123, 124, 125, 127, 129, 133–139: author's drawing after Bochkarev and Kuznetsov 2013: figs. 6,5; 6,3; 6,1; 6,7; 6,6; 6,8; 6,2; 6,4; 6,9; 6,13; 6,12; 6,10; 6,11; 6,14; 119: author's drawing after Usachuk 2010: fig. 62,1; 123: author's drawing after Bobomulloev 1999: fig. 2,5; 132: author's drawing after Leskov 1964: fig.1).

---

[37] Avanesova 2010: 355, fig. 2,2.4.5; fig. 3,4; fig. 4,3.5–9.

distinctive feature is the lack of a reinforcement around the central hole. This feature is typical of the Potapovka cheekpieces. Considering all its features this cheekpiece can be considered as a variant of the Sintashta type. The cheekpiece from Balanbash is unique because it is made of the upper part of the left metatarsal of a large mammal, probably a cow or bull, according to N. V. Roslyakova.[38] Usachuk also mentions that a natural channel in the epiphysis of the bone was used as the additional perforation in the body.[39]

Cheekpiece 139 is located quite close to the Sintashta cluster. This is a cheekpiece with no tab. It has two integral and two inserted studs. The inserted studs are fixed in the bushings with the help of transverse holes in the studs. The inserted studs of the cheekpieces from the Potapovka cemetery and from Troitskoye are fixed in a similar way (35, 133). The cheekpiece is thin without any lateral hole; additional perforations are arranged in a row.

Eurasian Cheekpieces in the Alakul Cluster

The Alakul cluster includes three samples. Cheekpiece 126 was found in the Nizhnyaya Krasavka II settlement on the right bank of the Volga and on the left bank of the Medveditsa river, south of the Saratov region. The excavation director reports that the cheekpiece was found in the Pokrovskaya horizon.[40] There is also a Srubnaya horizon in the site, overlapping the Pokrovskaya layer.[41] It is a round cheekpiece with no studs and a distinct triangular tab. There had probably been a hole for a cheek strap. After it was broken, the groove was enlarged and a new hole with an additional peg was made. All these features assign the cheekpiece to the Alakul type. According to P. A. Kosintsev, the cheekpiece is made of elk antler.[42]

This type also includes cheekpieces found in the settlement of Polyany I, a multilayer site (128), located in the basin of the Donets River (Kharkov region, Ukraine). At present it is the furthest south-western find of the Alakul type. Its shape is like the previous cheekpiece, but it has a lateral hole made in the tab. Such a method of fastening the cheek strap is also common for the Alakul cheekpieces (110, 111, 113, 114). The tab is ornamented with horizontal notches and a fringe of vertical hatching below. The notches are placed very close to the perforation in the tab. The ornamentation seems to imitate the way the straps are presumed to be attached to this cheekpiece. In the Polyany settlement some Babino and Srubnaya pottery was also found. The cheekpiece is probably related to the Srubnaya horizon of the Late Bronze Age.

In the Alakul cluster there is a cheekpiece from the Varenovka settlement (120). The site is located in the Lower Don, Rostov region. Unfortunately, only some fragments of the cheekpiece are extant. The cultural layer of the site contained pottery of Babino, late Pokrovskaya and Srubnaya cultures. The cheekpiece had an elliptical body, a nearly triangular tab with a single hole and inserted studs. The edges are ornamented with an irregular zigzag, made in quite a negligent way. The hole for the mouthpiece is also likely to have been ornamented. The inserted studs combined with a narrow tab and ornamentation make it possible to classify the cheekpiece as a late Pokrovskaya item.

Cheekpieces of the Eurasian Group in the Pokrovskaya Cluster

There are only seven cheekpieces in this cluster. Three of them are found in graves 1 and 3 in the Filatovka kurgan (134, 137, 138). There are two cheekpieces without tabs placed close to the border with the Alakul cluster (135 and 136). Samples 135 and 136 were found together as a matching pair. They do not have a tab or a raised rim around the central hole. There is a small lateral hole and a row of perforations for the noseband. The cheekpieces have three shaped integral studs. Probably one of the studs of cheekpiece 136 was broken and then an additional slot was made for an inserted stud. All these features display a combination of eastern Sintashta-Petrovka and local Pokrovskaya traditions of horse bridle manufacture. In this regard, we can identify them as a special, hybrid type. Both cheekpieces are placed between the Alakul and Pokrovskaya quadrants.

Items 137 and 138 are twin cheekpieces with identical features: there are three inserted studs and an ornamented semi-discoid body; the trapezoidal tab with a small nub protruding on each side has a row of perforations. However, the cheekpieces have no lateral hole for the cheek strap. The combination of a trapezoidal tab and the lack of a lateral hole is typical of the eastern cheekpieces. It makes it possible to relate these items to the special Pokrovskaya type. Cheekpiece 134 also has a paired cheekpiece, which is not included in the statistics due to its fragmentary condition. It has all the Pokrovskaya characteristics: four shaped inserted studs, a body richly ornamented on both the inside and outside, and a triangular tab with several holes arranged in a row for the noseband. The attachment of the cheek strap is made on the inner side of the cheekpiece in the form of a pierced protrusion inclined towards the body. There is a similar hole with a peg in cheekpiece 126 found in the Nizhnyaya Krasavka II settlement. A remarkable feature of cheekpiece 134 from Filatovka is a distinctly raised rim around the central hole, a characteristic of the Sintashta cheekpieces. This feature allows us to classify this item as the early Pokrovskaya type.

Placed separately within the Pokrovskaya cluster is cheekpiece 119 from the Boguslav settlement (Ukraine, Dnepropetrovsk region, Pavlograd district) on the Samara River (a left tributary of the Dnieper). It has such Pokrovskaya features as a relatively thin body, lateral holes and additional perforations arranged in a row. However, it is not ornamented and has three integral studs. This cheekpiece can thus be related to the special hybrid Pokrovskaya-Sintashta group.

---

[38] Verbal communication 3 April 2013.
[39] Usachuk 2002: 90–96.
[40] Lopatin 2010: 138.
[41] Lopatin 2010: 129.
[42] Verbal communication 16 April 2013.

The last cheekpiece from the Eurasian group placed in the Pokrovskaya cluster of the scatterplot, is an accidental find from Bashkiria (118). This cheekpiece has neither tab and nor raised rim around the central hole, but has a lateral hole and two small additional perforations. Due to these features this sample is placed in the Pokrovskaya cluster. At the same time, it has four thick integral studs and a substantial body, which brings it closer to the Sintashta cheekpieces. It is therefore placed close enough to the Sintashta cluster. In shape this item resembles the cheekpiece found at Balanbash, a settlement in the same area of Bashkiria (117). The main characteristics of another example from Bashkiria (118) allow us to relate it to the special hybrid Sintashta-Pokrovskaya group.

Our review of Eurasian cheekpieces helps us to reach a number of important conclusions. 15 of 23 samples were found outside closed complexes. Most of them appeared in settlements. This suggests that the cheekpieces were of practical value. Most of them are placed in the Sintashta cluster (11 out of 23). But these cheekpieces are extremely scattered, from Central Asia to the Dnieper and Crimea. All of them were local products, though influenced by the Ural-Volga traditions. At the same time, not a single cheekpiece from this group is known in the territory of Sintashta. In this region there are cheekpieces found outside an archaeological context, but their cultural affinity is not in question. The absence of cheekpieces associated with Petrovka manufacturing traditions is probably due to their small quantity. The three cheekpieces (120, 126, 128) in the Alakul cluster do not raise any doubts about relating them to late Pokrovskaya or to the Srubnaya-Alakul culture. But the three Filatovka cheekpieces without tabs (135, 136, 139), placed in the same cluster, are older than all the Srubnaya-Alakul cheekpieces. Examples 136 and 139 have a unique combination of features, not recognised in any other cheekpiece. Sample 135 combines characteristics which can be recognised in the Petrovka cheekpiece from Bestamak cemetery (84), as well as in the late Pokrovskaya item found in the Zolotaya Gora cemetery (57).

All the Eurasian cheekpieces in the Pokrovskaya cluster have features typical of the eastern traditions of manufacturing. Two samples were found in settlements. At the same time, the Pokrovskaya cheekpieces appear only in funerary complexes. Accidental finds of such cheekpieces are unknown. Neither are they found in the cultural layers of settlements. Thus, the statistical and geographical distribution of the finds suggests the Pokrovskaya cheekpieces as being a relatively local phenomenon and having a ritual rather than a practical use. The geographical and statistical distribution of their features, which indicate the place of manufacture, allow us to assume that all of them had been produced locally. However, the influence of the Ural-Volga manufacturing traditions was significantly stronger than that of the western Don-Volga region.

Cheekpieces of the Danube Region

The cheekpieces of discoid type in the Danube region are represented by a small but very diverse group in terms of typology (Figure 11.12: 140, 141, 143-153). We have analysed 15 samples. All of them are placed in the Alakul and Pokrovskaya clusters.

The Alakul cluster contains a remarkable cheekpiece, No. 140, found in the settlement of Brad, Eastern Romania. This was found in the Monteoru cultural layer, related to phases C2-Ia (20th–17th century BCE). It is nearly round with two holes of almost equal size in the centre. There is a raised rim around the central hole. At the edge there is a protrusion with two perforations, which resembles a tab. The holes in it could have been used for the noseband. The two small holes in the body seem to have been used for the cheek strap. It has no studs. We classify it as a special Brad type due to its shape and design. The two holes in the centre are a distinguishing feature of this type.

One more sample, No. 150, can probably be attributed to this type. It comes from Tiszafüred in the Hungarian Plain. The site belongs to the Füzesabony culture. The disc-shaped cheekpiece is placed in the Alakul cluster. In the centre there are two holes, and two more holes, used to attach a cheek strap, are located at the periphery of the body. The purpose of a round aperture below the loop-shaped protrusion remains unclear.

The two Otomani examples found in the settlement of Oarta de Sus (145 and 146) are associated with a completely different type. They are placed in the Alakul cluster. This pair of cheekpieces was found *in situ* by the jaw of a horse laid on its side in a specially-made pit.[43] The cheekpieces have a nearly trapezoidal shape, one hole for the mouthpiece and four thin inserted studs. Two holes on one of the narrow sides of the cheekpiece may have been used to attach the noseband. These cheekpieces definitely form a separate group. They have neither lateral holes nor ornamentation. The cheekpieces belong to a later variant in that they have thin wedge-shaped studs. There is every reason to believe that they had been produced locally.

The cheekpiece discovered in the Hungarian settlement of Füzesabony in the Danube region (154) is distinguished by its unique design. It is placed in the middle of the Alakul cluster. There are three holes of small diameter for inserted studs. Two holes in the body are made to attach a noseband and there are two more holes in the centre. This feature makes it similar to the local Central Danube cheekpieces, but the discoid shape and especially the inserted studs point to links with the Pokrovskaya cheekpieces. In general, it is a hybrid example that can be classified as a special Füzesabony type. This item has neither a lateral hole nor ornamentation. Judging by the small diameter of

---
[43] Boroffka 1998: 92, Abb. 9. This pit was specially made for the horse to be buried. All the pits in a settlement are usually made as utility facilities for household use; this one is unusual in that it was made for a ritual purpose.

the inserted studs, it can be associated with the late Pokrovskaya group.

Another disc type cheekpiece with two elongated apertures was found in layer C of the Tószeg settlement in the Hungarian Danube region (151). It is located in the Alakul cluster. It has no studs. The tab is of nearly rectangular shape with no holes for attachment. Thus, the tab is only a decorative element. There is a large hole at the edge of the cheekpiece body used to attach the nose band. Thus, the cheekpiece may have been attached to the bridle in such a way that the decorative tab was turned downwards. Probably because of noseband tension, the edge of the cheekpiece body was damaged. Then it was reworked and two small perforations for a cheek strap were made. Judging by the location of the lateral holes in the cheekpiece body, it was attached to the left side of the horse's face. The front is decorated with a pattern of circles with dots. This cheekpiece presents a combination of the eastern Alakul-Srubnaya features and local Central Danube characteristics. Such a combination forms an independent Tószeg type.

The second cheekpiece from the Tószeg settlement (152) is also located in the Alakul cluster of the coordinate plane. This item, as well as cheekpiece 1, originates from layer C (20th–17th century BCE). The unique characteristic of this find is the combination of the features of discoid and rod type cheekpieces. An elongated prong, which is a feature of rod type cheekpieces, points in the opposite direction from one of two loop-shaped projections, the second appearing to have been broken off. There is also a central hole with a raised rim, which shows signs of wear. The rod-shaped prong has two protrusions, and is decorated with a band engraved with a pattern of circles with dots.

The Alakul cluster contains one of the cheekpieces from the settlement of Vatin, in Serbia, on the left bank of the Danube (141). It is a round cheekpiece with no studs, with two decorated holes of different diameters in the centre. It has a triangular projection resembling a tab without holes, which carries a relief ornament. A slanting perforation made through the side wall was used to attach the cheek strap. The central hole is decorated with a pattern of circles and dots. The disc rims are also ornamented. This item combines both local and eastern Srubnaya-Alakul features.

Another cheekpiece with no studs from the settlement of Vatin (142) is located in the Alakul cluster. It has a single hole in the centre and a raised rim around it, unlike the cheekpiece described above. The discoid body of the cheekpiece is decorated with an ornament in the form of circles with dots. At the side of the wall there is one lateral transverse perforation. Since only a fragment of the cheekpiece has survived, we do not have any information on the noseband attachment. This cheekpiece can be associated with the eastern Alakul group.

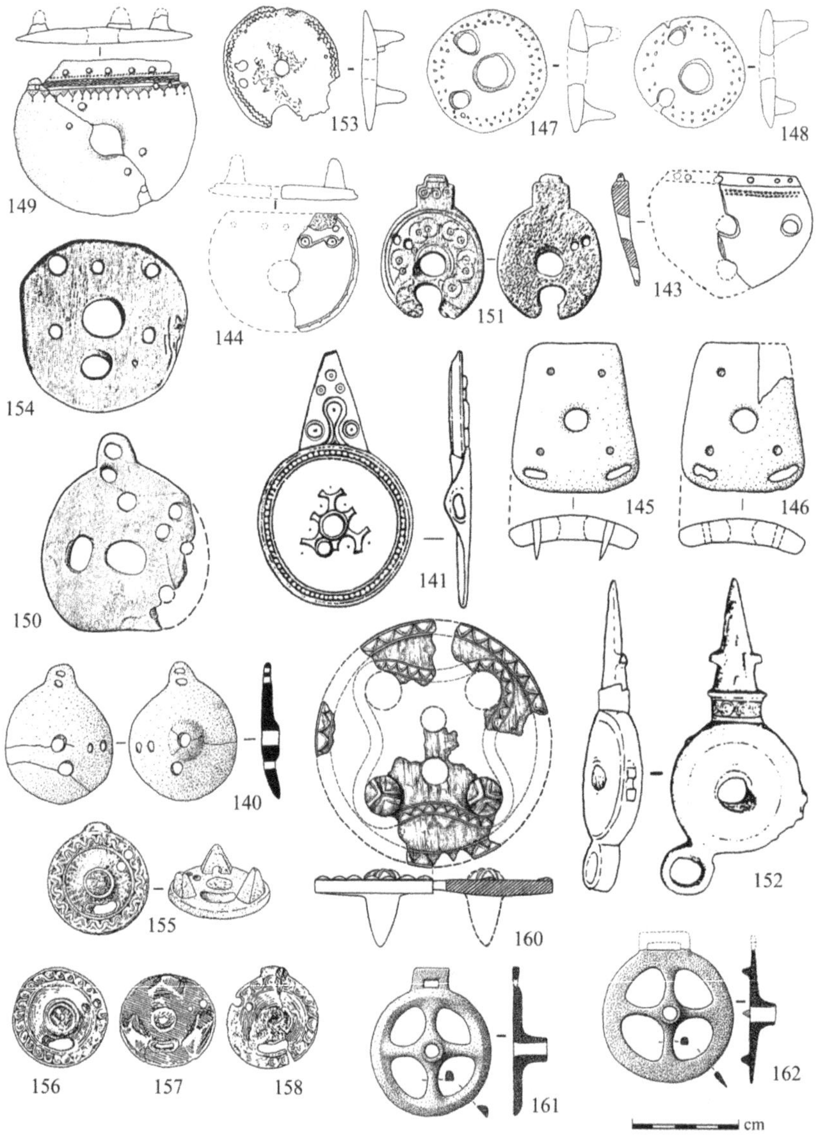

Figure 11.12. Cheekpieces of the Danube region and Mycenae. The Danube region: Eastern Romania (140); Serbia, the left bank of the Danube (141); Romania, the Carpathian region (143, 144, 153); Romania, the Danube region (145, 146, 147, 148); Romania, the Lower Danube region (149); Hungary, the Danube plain (150, 151, 152, 154). The region of Mycenaean Greece: Mycenae, Grave Circle A, grave IV (155–158); Kakovatos, tholos A (159); Mycenae, "House of Shields" (160); Mycenae, acropolis (161162); Mycenae, grave 81 (163); Thebes (164). The numbering corresponds to the reference numbers on the coordinate graph Figure 5; cheekpiece 159 is not to scale (140, 144–148, 153: author's drawing after Boroffka 1998: figs. 9,3; 8,5; 9,1; 9,2; 8,1; 8,2; 8,3. 141, 149–152: author's drawing after Hüttel 1981: figs. 4,34; 3,21; 3,24 A; 3,26; 4,27. 155–158: author's drawing after Karo 1930: fig. LXX, 532–535; 143: drawn by V. Bochkarev; 160: drawn by P. Kuznetsov; 161, 162: author's drawing after H. Matthäus 1977: figs. 2,1a; 2,2).

The next cheekpiece (153) of discoid type was found in the settlement of Ulmeni, located on the left bank of the Lower Danube, in Romanian Transcarpathia. It is placed in the Alakul cluster, though fairly close to Pokrovskaya in the scatterplot. The body is discoid. The shape of the tab is unclear, as this part of the cheekpiece is damaged. It has four integral studs. In the centre there is a round hole of small diameter. Two small perforations are made at the periphery of the body. The edge of the body is damaged, so the way in which the noseband was attached is unclear. The rims on the outer face are ornamented with an incised double zig-zag. The cheekpiece has distinct eastern features, but judging by the small central hole, it was produced locally. The next group of cheekpieces is placed in the Pokrovskaya cluster. We have studied three samples. On the territory of Romanian Transcarpathia is the settlement of Cândești, where cheekpiece 143 was discovered. The illustration of this cheekpiece is previously unpublished. It was found in layer 2A–2B of the Monteoru culture dating to 17th–15th century BCE. The cheekpiece has an oval body and carries three inserted studs. The tab is wide and has a row of perforations. Just below the tab, the outer face of the cheekpiece is ornamented with a horizontal line of zig-zags. The cheekpiece has survived only partially, so the way the noseband could have been attached is unknown. It is therefore tentatively classified as of Pokrovskaya type.

Of the four cheekpieces from the widely known settlement of Sărata Monteoru in Romania, three are included in our study. All have a discoid body.

Under circumstances that are not clear, two of them were found in the Sărata Monteoru settlement, so similar to each other that they could have made up a matching pair (147 and 148). They are located between the Alakul and Pokrovskaya clusters. They have a discoid body, four integral studs, two round holes, and rims ornamented with triangular notches. In general, these cheekpieces can doubtless be associated with a special type of early Eurasian cheekpieces without a tab.

One (149) was found in the Monteoru layer of the M1C3 phase dating to the 11th–10th century BCE. It is placed in the Pokrovskaya cluster. It has three integral studs and a distinctive wide trapezoidal tab with small perforations arranged in a row. The cheekpiece was broken. There are small holes in the body, made on either side of a diagonal crack. The lateral hole was damaged. The cheekpiece was repaired and two new perforations were made directly on the ornamentation below the tab. In terms of morphology, this cheekpiece has distinct Pokrovskaya features, due to the lateral holes in the body and the row of perforations in the tab. At the same time, it has integral studs, which are typical of the Sintashta and Petrovka examples. On the other hand, the ornamentation of the cheekpiece conforms to the local Carpathian-Danube tradition. It has to be assumed that this item was a local product but made in the eastern style.

In the settlement of Cîrlomănești in Romanian Transcarpathia, a fragment of cheekpiece No. 144 was found, which is placed in the central part of the Pokrovskaya cluster. The item has a semi-discoid body and a distinctive tab with two holes in it. The edge is ornamented with an ordinary spiral pattern. Below the tab there is a strip decorated with circles, of local Carpathian Danube origin. The cheekpiece combines Pokrovskaya and Petrovka features.

Apart from the samples included in our statistical study, we know of five more items from the Carpathian-Dniester basin, which have not been taken into account for a number of reasons. The fourth cheekpiece from the Sărata Monteoru settlement is disc-shaped, though it also has distinct characteristics of rod type cheekpieces. An unfinished item, or a cheekpiece prototype, from the Berettyó settlement in the Hungarian Danube region has no central hole, and this fact precludes its use as a cheekpiece. Two items from the Tószeg settlement, as well as the samples from the Spišský Štvrtok settlement in Slovakia, have both central and lateral holes in the body but have neither tab and nor studs. Therefore, identifying them as cheekpieces is currently in question.

Cheekpieces of Mycenaean Greece

Discoid cheekpieces in the southern Balkans are concentrated in the Peloponnese peninsula (Figure 11.12: 155-164). An exception is the cheekpiece from Thebes in central Greece.

Ten samples are included in the statistical processing. They are made of a variety of materials: bone, ivory and metal. However, their features are typical of discoid cheekpieces.

Four cheekpieces made of bone were found in grave IV of Grave Circle A at Mycenae. This is the richest and largest burial of this circle, investigated by H. Schliemann.[44] Three gold death masks were found there, probably depicting the face of the deceased. A gold ring with the image of a chariot drawn by a pair of horses was also found. The chariot has a single axle with four-spoked wheels. In the vehicle are two people: one is drawing a short bow and the second is probably a charioteer. The burial belongs to the early Late Helladic (Mycenaean) period of mainland Greece, 17th–16th century BCE.

In the scatterplot Mycenaean cheekpieces 1 and 4 (155 and 158) are combined and placed in the Pokrovskaya quadrant, close to the Alakul cluster. Both samples have three integral studs and a nearly trapezoidal tab. All perforations are made directly in the body. The tab is therefore a decorative element, without any practical application, and seems to have been pointing towards the ground when attached to the horse's bridle. Considering how similar the items are, it can be assumed that they are twin cheekpieces. The purpose of the hole at the base of one of the studs remains unclear (155). The edges of both cheekpieces are embellished with Mycenaean ornamental motifs.

---

[44] Schliemann 1878: 118–288, 506, figs. 373, 374.

Mycenaean cheekpieces 2 and 3 (156, 157) as well as the aforementioned pair, are also placed together in the scatterplot. They are located in the Alakul cluster. Each of the samples has three integral studs, and no tab. The straps which were attached to the holes were directed in opposite directions. If the elongated hole was used for the noseband, and not for the cheek strap, cheekpiece 2 (156) can be considered as the right one and cheekpiece 3 (157) as the left one. The artefacts are ornamented in Mycenaean style.

Thus, the four very similar Mycenaean cheekpieces from grave IV, Grave Circle A, may have formed a set to harness a pair of horses to a chariot. Cheekpiece 4 had been used, judging by the traces of wear.

It should be noted, that these items are the earliest among all the Mycenaean cheekpieces. The burials of Grave Circle A at Mycenae date to Late Helladic I (PE I A), i.e. 17th–16th century BCE according to 14C-dates.

Two cheekpieces made of ivory are also placed in the Alakul quadrant (159 and 160). One comes from tholos tomb A at Kakovatos (159), and the other from Mycenae (160), from the archaeological context of the "House of Shields" located outside the Mycenaean citadel, south of Grave Circle B. They date to Late Helladic II/III periods, 15th–13th century BCE. They have no tab and have two central holes without a raised rim. The studs are integral, although they are ornamented in the same way as inserted studs. The ornamentation is in the Mycenaean style. There are no obvious traces of wear.

Two cheekpieces made of bronze (161 and 162) come from the Mycenaean acropolis. They are located in the Petrovka quadrant. The discs of the cheekpieces resemble four-spoked wheels and are thickened around a mouthpiece hole in the form of a protruding bushing. The tabs are rectangular, with only one hole. There are no lateral holes. Cheekpiece 161 has no studs, while cheekpiece 162 has four integral studs. They belong to the Late Helladic III B–C period dating to 14th–13th century BCE.

The archaeological context of a bronze cheekpiece (164) found in Thebes is unknown. It is housed in the National Archaeological Museum of Athens. It is placed in the Petrovka quadrant and has common features with cheekpiece 1 from the Mycenaean acropolis. It has a rectangular tab with one hole. The shape of the cheekpiece resembles a four-spoked wheel with a raised rim around the central hole.

Bronze cheekpiece from grave 81 at Mycenae (163) is the only one that turned out to be placed in the Sintashta quadrant. It looks similar to sample 160 (Mycenae, "House of Shields"), made of ivory, as it has two central holes and four studs. But the studs in sample 163 are inserted.

This cheekpiece is placed in the Sintashta quadrant due to such features as a raised rim around the central hole, four studs, no tab and no ornamentation.

Thus, the materials used for Mycenaean cheekpieces tend to change: bone cheekpieces of Late Helladic I A (17th–16th century BCE) are replaced by metal cheekpieces of Late Helladic III B–C (14th–13th century BCE).

In the scatterplot the earliest Mycenaean cheekpieces occupy the boundary area between the Pokrovskaya and Alakul quadrants. The cheekpieces from the Carpathian-Danube region are also located here. Thus, our study confirms that this type of cheekpieces came to the southern Balkan Peninsula from the Carpathian-Balkan region. The later types of Mycenaean cheekpieces are uniform to a much greater extent. Tellingly, they are all made of bronze. It is significant that a metal bit with studded, wheel-shaped cheekpieces showing signs of wear and a long straight bar mouthpiece, dating from the 17th century BCE, was found in the the mouth of a donkey excavated at Tel Haror in the Levant (Figure 11.2: 4).[45] A similar bit had previously been excavated in Gaza in a context which included equids presumed to be horses.[46] The latter, however, is now considered to date from no earlier than the 15th century BCE.[47]

Thus, the manufacturing tradition of cheekpieces in Mycenaean Greece is first brought from the territory of the northern Balkans (the Danube region). The technology then developed with the influence of Western Asia, and probably Egypt. Judging by the images on the seals and murals from Mycenaean palaces, horses were harnessed to chariots throughout the Late Helladic period.

Transformation of Cheekpieces Through the Centuries in Terms of Cultural-Typological Classification

Our Late Bronze Age cultural and chronological chart has been developed for the southern part of Eastern Europe from the Urals to Carpathians (Figure 11.13).[48] Linked to P. Reinecke's Middle European chronology,[49] the chart consists of seven main stages. It covers a period of one thousand years beginning at the turn of the third/second millennia BCE and ending with 1000 BCE. Discoid cheekpieces existed in the Late Bronze Age only within the first three periods.

Period 1 includes the cheekpieces of the Sintashta, Potapovka and early Pokrovskaya cultures.

Period 2 includes the cheekpieces of the Petrovka and late Pokrovskaya cultures. During this period, shield type cheekpieces appear in the Danube region and in Central Asia.

Period 3 includes shield type cheekpieces of the Srubnaya and Alakul cultures. The features typical of the Carpathi-

---

[45] Bar-Oz et al. 2013; Littauer and Crouwel 2001: fig. 2.
[46] Hančar 1955: fig. 12; Petrie 1931: 88; Littauer 1969: 289–300, fig. 1a; Littauer and Crouwel 1979: 87 with fn. 59, fig. 48; Hüttel 1981, Taf. 43,C.
[47] Littauer and Crouwel 1979: 87, fn. 59; Clutton-Brock 1992: 83.
[48] Bochkarev 2017.
[49] Reinecke 1933.

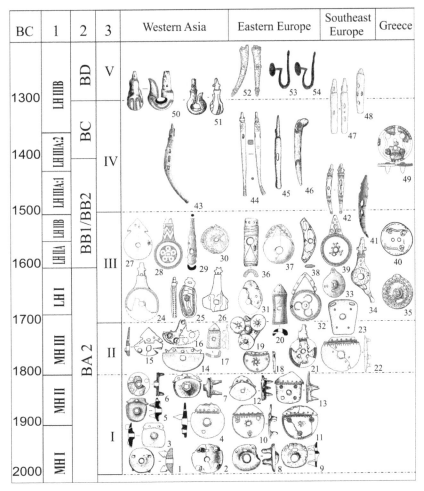

Figure 11.13. Cultural-typological chart of cheekpiece evolution according to chronological diagrams of the European Late Bronze Age. 1 – Helladic Bronze Age chronology after Furumark 1941; 2 – Central European chronology of the Bronze Age after Reinecke 1933; 3 – Eastern European chronology of the Late Bronze Age after Bochkarev 2017. The charts take into consideration actual radiocarbon dating.

an-Danube cheekpieces become apparent. During this period cheekpieces appear in Mycenaean Greece, the earliest of which correspond to the beginning of the Late Helladic I period–LH IA from the 17th to the first half of the 16th century BCE. It corresponds to the third stage of the Late Bronze Age in northern Eurasia.

In later periods, shield type cheekpieces completely fall out of use. Throughout the entire territory, they are replaced by rod type cheekpieces, which originated in the Danube region.

Conclusion

The domestication of horses and harnessing them to a chariot was a major factor in the invention of the bridle bit with cheekpieces which is evidenced in northern Eurasia.

We have shown that shield type cheekpieces existed during the first three periods of the Late Bronze Age. Shield type discoid cheekpieces appear at the turn of the third/second millennia BCE and exist until the 16th–15th century BCE. At the beginning of the second millennium BCE a bridle bit for equid control appeared in three large areas. These are the Carpathian-Danube region, the northern Eurasian steppe, and Western Asia. In the fourth period of the Late Bronze Age, 14th–13th century BCE, discoid and fluted cheekpieces were replaced by a rod-shaped type originating in the Carpathian-Danube region. During the same period, in the southern Balkan Peninsula, bone cheekpieces were superseded by a metal, wheel-shaped design which originated from Western Asia. In Western Asia, Egypt and Greece, plaque cheekpieces of various types became widespread.

For nearly a thousand years the war chariot drawn by horses controlled by bridle bits would remain the most advanced technological weapon so far known to civilisation.

Vadim S. Bochkarev
Senior researcher, Institute of Material Culture History, the Russian Academy of Sciences, St. Petersburg; Senior Lecturer, Department of Archaeology, St. Petersburg State University, RF

Pavel Kuznetsov
Head, Museum of Archeology of the Volga region, Samara State University of Social Sciences and Education, Samara, RF.

Bibliography

Alikhova, Anna E. 1955. Kurgany epokhi bronzy u s. Komarovka [Bronze Age Kurgans near the Village of Komarovka]. *Kratkie soobshcheniia Instituta istorii material'noy kul'tury* 59, 91–99.

Avanesova, Nona A. 2010. Proiavlenie stepnykh traditsii v Sapallinskoi kul'ture [The Genesis of Steppe Traditions in the Sapalli-Tepe Culture]. *Tsivilizatsii i kul'tury Tsentral'noi Azii v edinstve i mnogoobrazii. Materialy Mezhdunarodnoi konferentsii, Samarkand, 7–8 sentiabria 2009 g.*, 107–133, edited by Dilorom Alimova et al., 107–133. Samarkand, Tashkent: International Institute for Central Asian Studies/SMI–ASIA).

Bar-Oz, Guy, Pirhiya Nahshoni, Hadas Motro, and Eliezer D. Oren. 2013. Symbolic Metal bit and Saddlebag Fastenings in a Middle Bronze Age Donkey Burial. *PLoS ONE* 8, 3: e58648. DOI: 10.1371/journal.pone.0058648.

Berezanskaya, Sofia S., Vitaliy V. Otroshchenko, Nikolay N. Cherednichenko et al. 1986. *Kul'tury bronzovogo veka na territorii Ukrainy* [Archaeological Cultures of the Bronze Age in the Territory of Ukraine]. Kiev: Naukova dumka.

Bobomulloev, Saidmurod. 1999. Raskopki grobnitsy bronzovogo veka na verkhnem Zeravshane [The Excavations of the Bronze Age Burial in Upper Zeravshan). *Stratum plus* 1999 (2): 307–313.

Bochkarev, Vadim S. 2010. *Kul'turogenez i drevnee metalloproizvodstvo Vostochnoi Evropy* [Culture Genesis and Early Metal Production in Eastern Europe]. St. Petersburg: Info Ol.

Bochkarev, Vadim S. 2017. Etapy razvitiia metalloproizvodstva epokhi pozdnei bronzy na iuge Vostochnoi Evropy [Stages in the Development of Metal Production in the Late Bronze Age in the South-Eastern Europe]. *Stratum plus* 2017 (2): 159–204.

Bochkarev, Vadim S. and Pavel F. Kuznetsov. 2010. Fluted cheek pieces from the Eurasian steppes under the late Bronze Age. In: *Horses, Chariots and Chariot Drivers of the Eurasian Steppes*, edited by Pavel F. Kuznetsov et al., 292–343. Yekaterinburg, Samara, Donetsk: Rifey.

Bochkarev, Vadim S. and Pavel F. Kuznetsov. 2013. Kul'turno-tipologicheskie kharakteristiki drevneishikh diskovidnykh psaliev Severnoi Evrazii [Cultural-Typological Characteristics of the Earliest Discoid Cheekpieces from Northern Eurasia]. In: *Problemy periodizatsii i khronologii v arkheologii epokhi rannego metalla Vostochnoi Evropy: materialy tematicheskoi nauchnoi konferentsii*, edited by Evgeniy A. Cherlenok, Vadim S. Bochkarev, and Aleksandr I. Murashkin, 61–79. St. Petersburg: Scythia-print

Bochkarev, Vadim S., Sergey B. Valchak, and Pavel F. Kuznetsov. 2015. Psalii [Cheekpieces]. In: *Bol'shaia Rossiiskaia entsiklopedia, vol. 27*: 673. Moscow: "Bol'shaia Rossiiskaia entsiklopedia"

Bochkarev, Vadim S. and Pavel F. Kuznetsov. 2019. Ob odnoi raznovidnosti psaliev epokhi pozdnei bronzy Vostochnoi Evropy [About One Type of Cheekpieces of the Late Bronze Age of Eastern Europe]. *Arkheologiia Vostochnoevropeiskoi stepi* 15: 44–58.

Boroffka, Nikolaus. 1998. Bronze- und früheisenzeitliche Geweihtrensenknebel aus Rumänien und ihre Beziehungen. Alte Funde aus dem Museum für Geschichte Aiud, Teil II. *Eurasia Antiqua* 4: 81–135.

Brownrigg, Gail. 2004. Schirrung und Zäumung des Streitwagenpferdes. In: *Rad und Wagen. Der Ursprung einer Innovation. Wagen im Vorderen Orient und Europa*, edited by Mamoun Fansa and Stefan Burmeister, 481–490. Beiheft der Archäologischen Mitteilungen aus Nordwestdeutschland 40. Mainz: von Zabern.

Brownrigg, Gail. 2006. Horse Control and the Bit. In: *The Evolution of Equine-Human Relationships*, edited by Sandra L. Olsen, Susan Grant, Alice M. Choyke et al., 165–171. British Archaeological Reports, International Series 1560. Oxford: BAR Publishing.

Brownrigg, Gail. 2019. Harnessing the Chariot Horse. In: *Equids and wheeled vehicles in the ancient world: Essays in memory of Mary A. Littauer*, edited by Peter Raulwing, Katheryn M. Linduff and Joost H. Crouwel, 85–96. British Archaeological Reports, International Series 2923. Oxford: BAR Publishing.

Brownrigg, Gail and Joost H. Crouwel. 2017. Draught Systems in the Roman World. *Oxford Journal of Archaeology* 36 (2): 197–220.

Burmeister, Stefan and Peter Raulwing. 2012. Festgefahren. Die Kontroverse um den Ursprung des Streitwagens. Einige Anmerkungen zu Forschung, Quellen und Methodik. In: *Archaeological, cultural and linguistic heritage. Festschrift für Erzsébet Jerem in honour of her 70th birthday*, edited by Peter Anreiter, Eszter Bánffy, László Bartosiewicz et al., 93–113. Budapest: Archaeolingua.

Clutton-Brock, Juliet. 1992. *Horse Power. A History of the Horse and the Donkey in Human Societies*. Cambridge, MA: Harvard University Press and London: Natural History Museum Publications.

Dietz, Ute. 1992. Zur Frage vorbronzezeitlicher Trensenbelege in Europa. *Germania* 70: 17–36.

Esbensen, Kim. 2006. *Analiz mnogomernykh dannykh. Izbrannye gravy* [Analysis of Multivariate Data. Selected Chapters], edited by O. E. Rodionova. Samara: Samara State Technical University.

Furumark, Arne. 1941. *The Chronology of Mycenaean Pottery*. Stockholm: Kungliga Vitterhets Historie och Antikvitets Akademien.

Gening, Vadim F., Gennadiy B. Zdanovich and Vladimir V. Gening. 1992. *Sintashta. Arkheologicheskie pamiatniki ariiskikh plemen Uralo-Kazakhstanskikh stepei* [Sintashta. The Archaeological Sites of Aryan Tribes of the Ural-Kazakh Steppes]. Chelyabinsk: Iuzhno-Ural'skoe knizhnoe izd-vo.

Gorbov, Vladimir N. and Anatoliy N. Usachuk. 1999. O sisteme krepleniia psaliev s vydelennoi plankoi kolesnichnoi zapriazhki bronzovogo veka [On a Fastening System of Cheekpieces with a Protruding Plank to the Harness of a Bronze Age Chariot] In: *Problemy skifo-sarmatskoi arkheologii Severnogo Prichernomor'ia (k stoletiiu B. N. Grakova)*, edited by Petr P. Tolochko, 78–85. Zaporizh'e: Zaporozh'e State University. https://istina.msu.ru/collections/2819443/; accessed 29 April 2022.

Hančar, Franz. 1955. *Das Pferd in prähistorischer und früher historischer Zeit*. Wien: Herold.

Hüttel, Hans-Georg. 1977. Altbronzezeitliche Pferdetrensen. Ein Beitrag zur Geschichte des 16. Jahrhunderts v.Chr. *Jahresbericht des Instituts für Vorgeschichte der Universität Frankfurt am Main* 1977: 65–86.

Hüttel, Hans-Georg. 1981. *Bronzezeitliche Trensen in Mittel- und Osteuropa. Grundzüge ihrer Entwicklung*. Prähistorische Bronzefunde XVI.2. München: Beck.

Hüttel, Hans-Georg. 1982. Zur Abkunft des danubishen Pferd-Wagen-Komplexes der Altbronzezeit. In: *Prähistorische*

Archäologie in Südosteuropa zwischen 1600 und 1000 v.Chr., edited by Bernhard Hänsel, 39–63. Prähistorische Archäologie in Südosteuropa 1. Berlin: Moorland Editions.

Il'chyshyn, Vasyl' 2016. Pokhovannia konei epokhi bronzy v kurgani bilia Husiatina Ternopil'skoï oblasti [Burial Place of the Bronze Age horses in the Burial Mound Near the Husyatin, Ternopil' Region]. *Visnyk Riativnoï Arkheologiï* 2: 77–90.

Kosintsev, Pavel A. 2010. Chariot horses. In: *Horses, Chariots and Chariot Drivers of Eurasian Steppes*, edited by P. F. Kuznetsov et al., 21–79. Yekaterinburg, Samara, Donetsk: Rifey.

Krushel'nyts'ka, Larisa I. 1985. *Vzaemozv'iazky naselennia Prykarpattia i Volyni z plemenamy Skhidnoï i Tsentral'noï Evropy (rubizh epokh bronzy i zaliza)* [The Links of the Ciscarpathian and Volynia Population with Tribes from Eastern and Central Europe]. Kyïv: Naukova dumka.

Kupriyanova, Elena and Gennadiy D. Zdanovich. 2015. *Drevnosti lesostepnogo Zaural'ia: mogil'nik Stepnoe VII.* [Antiquities of the Forest-Steppe Transurals: The Kurgan Cemetery Stepnoe VII]. Chelyabinsk: Encyclopedia.

Kuz'mina, Elena E. 1980. Eshche raz o diskovidnykh psaliiakh Evraziiskikh stepei. [Once More About Discoid Cheekpieces of the Eurasian Steppes]. *Kratkie soobshcheniia instituta arkheologii* 161: 8–21.

Kuz'mina, Elena E. 2008. *Arii – put' na iug* [Aryans – the way to the south]. Moscow, St. Petersburg: Letnii Sad.

Leskov, Aleksandr M. 1964. Drevneishie rogovye psalii iz Trakhtemirova [Early Antler Cheekpieces from Trakhtemirov]. *Sovetskaia Arkheologiia* 1: 299–303.

Littauer, Mary A. 1969. Bits and Pieces. *Antiquity* 43: 289–300.

Littauer, Mary A. and Joost H. Crouwel. 1979. *Wheeled Vehicles and Ridden Animals in the Ancient Near East*. Handbuch der Orientalistik. Leiden and Cologne: Brill.

Littauer Mary A. and Joost H. Crouwel. 2001. The Earliest Evidence for Metal Bridle Bits. *Journal of Archaeology* 20 (4): 329–338.

Lopatin, Vladimir A. 2010. Pokrovskii kul'turnyi kompleks poseleniia Nizhniaa Krasavka II (po materialam issledovanii 2007–2009 godov) [The Pokrovskaya Cultural Complex at the Settlement of Nizhniaya Krasavka II [Research Materials of 2007–2009]. *Arkheologiia Vostochno-Evropeiskoi stepi* 8: 126–156.

Loshakova, Tatiana N. 2014. Psalii poseleniia Toksanbai [Cheekpieces from the Toksanbai Settlement]. *The Culture Genesis Process at the Beginning of Late Bronze Age in the Volga-Ural Region. Questions of Chronology, Periodization, Historiography. Proceedings of the International Scientific Conference, Samara, May 12–14, 2014*, edited by Pavel F. Kuznetsov, 81–88. Samara: SGSPU.

Lyashko, Svetlana N. 1994. *Kostoreznoe proizvodstvo v epokhu bronzy. Remeslo epokhi eneolita-bronzy na Ukraine* [Bone Carving in the Bronze Age. Crafts in Ukraine in the Eneolithic – Bronze Age Periods]. Kiev: Naukova dumka.

Malov, Nikolay M. 2012. Pogrebenie pokrovskoi kul'tury s fragmentami shchitkovykh psaliev iz Tarumovskogo individual'nogo kurgana 2 [A Burial of the Pokrovskaya Culture with Fragments of Shield-Type Cheekpieces from the Tarumovka Individual Kurgan]. *Arkheologiia Vostochno-Evropeiskoi stepi* 9: 74–91.

Matthäus, Hartmut. 1977. Mykenische Trensen mit Radknebeln. *Archäologisches Korrespondenzblatt* 7: 37–40.

Myskov, Yevgeniy P., Aleksey V. Kiyashko, Roman A. Litvinenko, and Anatoliy N. Usachuk. 2004. Pogrebeniia kolesnichego iz basseina Dona [A Charioteer's Burial in the Don River Basin]. *Psalii.Elementy upriazhi i konskogo snariazheniia v drevnosti*, edited by A. N. Usachuk, 128–138. Arkheologicheskii almanakh 15. Donetsk: Donetskii oblastnoi kraevedsheskii musei.

Penner, Silvia. 1998. *Schliemanns Schachtgräberrund und der Europäische Nordosten: Studien zur Herkunft der frühmykenischen Streitwagenausstattung*. Saarbrücker Beiträge zur Altertumskunde 60. Bonn: Habelt.

Petrie, W. M. Flinders. 1931. *Ancient Gaza I. Tell el Ajjul*. Egyptian Research Account 53. London: British School of Archaeology in Egypt.

Potratz, Johannes A. H. 1941. Die Pferdegebisse des zwischenstromländischen Raumes. *Archiv für Orientforschung* 14: 1–39.

Potratz, Johannes A. H. 1966. *Die Pferdetrensen des Alten Orient*. Analecta Orientalia 41. Rome: Pontificum Institutum Biblicum.

Reinecke, Paul 1933. Zur Chronologie des Frühen Bronzealters Mitteleuropas. *Germania* 17: 11–13.

Schliemann, Heinrich. 1878. *Mycenae. A Narrative of Researches and Discoveries of Mycenae and Tiryns*. London: Murray.

Stefani, Ludolf E. 1866. *Obiasnenie neskol'kikh drevnostei, naidennykh v 1864 g. v Iuzhnoi Rossii. Otchet Imperatorskoi arkheologicheskoi komissii za 1865 god* [The Explanation of Some Antiquities, Found in 1864 in Southern Russia. Report of the Imperial Archaeological Commission for 1865]. 3–223. St. Petersburg: Tipografiia Imperatorskoi Akademii Nauk.

Usachuk, Anatoliy N. 2002. Psalii s poseleniia Balanbash [The Cheekpiece from the Balanbash Settlement]. In: *Arkheologicheskie pamiatniki Vostochnoi Evropy*, edited by Arsen T. Siniuk, 90–96. Voronezh:VGPU.

Usachuk, Anatoliy N. 2010 Reconstruction of Ancient Cheek Pieces Attachment in the System of Horse Head Bands: Contradictions and Prospects. In: *Horses, Chariots and Chariot Drivers of Eurasian Steppes*, edited by by P. F. Kuznetsov et al., 257–291. Yekaterinburg, Samara, Donetsk: Rifey.

Usachuk, Anatoliy N. 2013. *Drevneishie psalii (izgotovlenie i ispol'zovanie)* [The Earliest Cheekpieces (Production and Use)]. Kiev, Donetsk: Institut arkheologii NAN Ukrainy.

Usachuk, Anatoliy N. and Oleg V. Pustovoyt. 2004. Psalii Pervogo Kondrashevskogo kurgana [Cheekpieces from the First Kondrashevsky Kurgan]. In: *Psalii.Elementy upriazhi i konskogo snariazheniia v drevnosti, Arkheologicheskii almanakh 15*, edited by Anatoliy N. Usachuk, 46–61. Donetsk: Donetskii oblastnoi kraevedsheskii musei.

Zdanovich, Gennadiy B. 1986. Shchitkovye psalii iz Srednego Priishim'ia [Shield-Shaped Cheekpieces from the Middle Ishim Region]. *Kratkie soobshcheniia instituta arkheologii* 185: 60–65.

Appendix 1
List of Cheekpieces Grouped According to Archaeological Cultures and Sites (Figure 11.5)

Sintashta Culture

1. Bolshekaraganskiy, kurgan 24, grave 1
2. Bolshekaraganskiy, kurgan 24, grave 2
3. Kamenny Ambar-5, kurgan 2, grave 5, cheekpiece 1
4. Kamenny Ambar-5, kurgan 2, grave 5, cheekpiece 2
5. Kamenny Ambar-5, kurgan 2, grave 5, cheekpiece 3
6. Kamenny Ambar-5, kurgan 2, grave 5, cheekpiece 4
7. Kamenny Ambar-5, kurgan 2, grave 6
8. Kamenny Ambar-5, kurgan 2, grave 8, cheekpiece 1
9. Kamenny Ambar-5, kurgan 2, grave 8, cheekpiece 2
10. Kamenny Ambar-5, kurgan 2, grave 8, cheekpiece 3
11. Kamenny Ambar-5, kurgan 4, grave 8, cheekpiece 1
12. Kamenny Ambar-5, kurgan 4, grave 8, cheekpiece 2
13. Kamenny Ambar-5, kurgan 4, mound layer
14. Krivoye Ozero, kurgan 9 grave 1, cheekpiece 1
15. Krivoye Ozero, kurgan 9, grave 1, cheekpiece 2
16. Krivoye Ozero, kurgan 9, grave 2
17. Sintashta I, grave 14, cheekpiece 1
18. Sintashta I, grave 14, cheekpiece 2
19. Sintashta, cemetery, grave 11, cheekpiece 1
20. Sintashta, cemetery, grave 11, cheekpiece 3
21. Sintashta, cemetery, grave 12, cheekpiece 1
22. Sintashta, cemetery, grave 12, cheekpiece 2
23. Sintashta, cemetery, grave 5, cheekpiece 1
24. Sintashta, cemetery, grave 30, cheekpiece 1
25. Sintashta, cemetery, grave 30, cheekpiece 2
26. Sintashta, cemetery, grave 39, cheekpiece 1
27. Sintashta, cemetery
28. Tanabergen-2, kurgan 7, grave 22, cheekpiece 1
29. Solonchanka IA, kurgan 2
30. Solntse II, kurgan 4, grave 1
31. Arkaim, accidental find
32. Glyadyanskoye, cheekpiece 1
33. Glyadyanskoye, cheekpiece 2

Potapovka Culture

34. Potapovka, kurgan 3, grave 4, cheekpiece 1
35. Potapovka, kurgan 3, grave 4, cheekpiece 2
36. Potapovka, kurgan 5, grave 8, cheekpiece 1
37. Potapovka, kurgan 5, grave 8, cheekpiece 2
38. Potapovka, kurgan 5, grave 8, cheekpiece 3
39. Utevka VI, kurgan 2, grave 1
40. Utevka VI, kurgan 6, grave 4, cheekpiece 1
41. Utevka VI, kurgan 6, grave 4, cheekpiece 2
42. Utevka VI, kurgan 6, grave 4, cheekpiece 3
43. Utevka VI, kurgan 6, grave 4, cheekpiece 4
44. Utevka VI, kurgan 6, grave 5, cheekpiece 1
45. Utevka VI, kurgan 6, grave 5, cheekpiece 2
46. Utevka VI, kurgan 6, grave 6, cheekpiece 1
47. Utevka VI, kurgan 6, grave 6, cheekpiece 2
48. Utevka VI, kurgan 6, grave 6, cheekpiece 3

Pokrovskaya Culture

49. Barannikovo, kurgan 1, grave 2, cheekpiece 1
50. Barannikovo, kurgan 1, grave 2, cheekpiece 2
51. Berezovka, kurgan 3, grave 2, cheekpiece 1
52. Bogoyavlenskoye, kurgan 1, grave 3, cheekpiece 1
53. Borodaevka II, kurgan 1, grave 2, cheekpiece 1
54. Vesely Khutor kurgan, cheekpiece 1
55. Vesely Khutor kurgan, cheekpiece 2
56. Dubovy Gai, kurgan 1, grave 4, cheekpiece 1
57. Zolotaya Gora, kurgan 4, grave 1, cheekpiece 1
58. Zolotaya Gora, kurgan 4, grave 1, cheekpiece 2
59. Idolga, kurgan 3, grave 1
60. Kondrashkinskiy kurgan, grave 1
61. Kondrashevka, kurgan 1, grave 1, cheekpiece 1
62. Kondrashevka, kurgan 1, grave 1, cheekpiece 2
63. Krasny I, kurgan 1, grave 2, cheekpiece 1
64. Krasny I, kurgan 1, grave 2, cheekpiece 2
65. Pichaevo kurgan, grave 1, cheekpiece 1
66. Pichaevo kurgan, grave 1, cheekpiece 2
67. Selezni-1, kurgan 1, grave 1, cheekpiece 1
68. Selezni-1, kurgan 1, grave 1, cheekpiece 2
69. Selezni-1, kurgan 1, grave 3, cheekpiece 1
70. Selezni-1, kurgan 1, grave 4, cheekpiece 1
71. Selezni-2, kurgan1, grave 4, cheekpiece 3
72. Selezni-2, kurgan 1, grave 4, cheekpiece 4
73. Staritskoye, destroyed burial, grave, cheekpiece 1
74. Staroyurievo, kurgan 2, grave 2, cheekpiece 1
75. Staroyurievo, kurgan 2, grave 2, cheekpiece 2
76. Suvorovskiy, kurgan 3, grave 2
77. Uvarovskiy II, kurgan 11, grave 2
78. Ouren II, kurgan 6, grave 1, cheekpiece 1
79. Ouren II, kurgan 6, grave 1, cheekpiece 2

Petrovka Culture

80. Ashchisu, kurgan 1, grave 1
81. Berlik, kurgan 10, grave 1, cheekpiece 1
82. Bestamak, cemetery, grave 7, cheekpiece 1
83. Bestamak, cemetery, grave 7, cheekpiece 2
84. Bestamak, cemetery, grave 7, cheekpiece 3
85. Vostochniye Kurayli-I, kurgan 11, grave 4, cheekpiece 1
86. Vostochniye Kurayli, kurgan 11, grave 4, cheekpiece 2
87. Vostochniye Kurayli, kurgan 11, grave 4, cheekpiece 3
88. Zhaman Kargala, kurgan 14, grave 2, cheekpiece 1
89. Zhaman Kargala, kurgan 14, grave 2, cheekpiece 2
90. Zhaman Kargala, kurgan 14, grave 2, cheekpiece 3
91. Zhaman Kargala, kurgan 14, grave 2, cheekpiece 4
92. Krivoye Ozero, kurgan 1, grave 1, cheekpiece 1
93. Krivoye Ozero, kurgan 1, grave 1, cheekpiece 2
94. Krivoye Ozero, kurgan 1, grave 2
95. Krivoye Ozero, kurgan 1, grave 3, cheekpiece 1
96. Krivoye Ozero, kurgan 1, grave 3, cheekpiece 2
97. Krivoye Ozero, kurgan 1, grave 2, cheekpiece 1
98. Kulevchi III, settlement
99. Novonikolskoye, settlement
100. Petrovka II, settlement, cheekpiece 1
101. Petrovka II, settlement, cheekpiece 2
102. Stepnoy VII, kurgan 5, grave 2, cheekpiece 1
103. Stepnoy VII, kurgan 5, grave 2, cheekpiece 2

104 Toksanbay, settlement, cheekpiece 1
105 Toksanbay, settlement, cheekpiece 2

Alakul Culture

106 Adybel, accidental find
107 Alakul, kurgan 13, grave 2
108 Ilekshar I, kurgan 6, grave 3, cheekpiece 1
109 Ilekshar I, kurgan 6, grave 3, cheekpiece 2
110 Kazangulovo, settlement, cheekpiece 1
111 Kazangulovo, settlement, cheekpiece 2
112 Mirny IV, settlement, cheekpiece 1
113 Mirny IV, settlement, cheekpiece 2
114 Novonikolskoye, kurgan 5, grave 2
115 Tanalyk, settlement
116 Tasty-Butak, settlement

Eurasian Group

117 Balanbash, settlement
118 Bashkiria, accidental find
119 Boguslav, settlement
120 Varenovka, settlement
121 Jarkutan, settlement
122 Zardcha-Khalifa, grave, cheekpiece 1
123 Zardcha-Khalifa, grave, cheekpiece 2
124 Kamenka, settlement
125 Kleshchevka, distroyed kurgan
126 Nizhnyaya Krasavka II, settlement
127 Otrozhka, settlement
128 Polyany I, settlement
129 Sazagan, grave 2, cheekpiece 1
130 Sazagan, grave 2, cheekpiece 2
131 Trakhtemirovo, cheekpiece 1
132 Trakhtemirovo, cheekpiece 2
133 Troitskiy, accidental find
134 Filatovka, kurgan, grave 1, cheekpiece 1
135 Filatovka, kurgan, grave 1, cheekpiece 3
136 Filatovka, kurgan, grave 1, cheekpiece 4
137 Filatovka, kurgan, grave 3, cheekpiece 1
138 Filatovka, kurgan, grave 3, cheekpiece 2
139 Filatovka, kurgan, grave 3, cheekpiece 3

Carpathian-Danube Region

140 Brad, settlement
141 Vatin, settlement, cheekpiece 1
142 Vatin, settlement, cheekpiece 2
143 Kyndeshti, settlement
144 Kyrlomaneshti, settlement
145 Oarta de Sus, grave of horses, cheekpiece 1
146 Oarta de Sus, grave of horses, cheekpiece 2
147 Sărata Monteoru, settlement, cheekpiece 1
148 Sărata Monteoru, settlement, cheekpiece 2
149 Sărata Monteoru, settlement, cheekpiece 3
150 Tiszafüred, settlement
151 Tószeg, settlement, cheekpiece 1
152 Tószeg, settlement, cheekpiece 2
153 Ulmeni, settlement
154 Fűzesabony, settlement

Mycenaean Greece

155 Mycenae, Grave Circle A, grave IV, cheekpiece 1
156 Mycenae, Grave Circle A, grave IV, cheekpiece 2
157 Mycenae, Grave Circle A, grave IV, cheekpiece 3
158 Mycenae, Grave Circle A, grave IV, cheekpiece 4
159 Kakovatos, tholos A
160 Mycenae, "House of Shields"
161 Mycenae, acropolis, cheekpiece 1
162 Mycenae, acropolis, cheekpiece 2
163 Mycenae, grave 81
164 Thebes, cheekpiece 1

Appendix 2
Numbering of the cheekpieces in Figure 11.13

1 Sintashta, cemetery, grave 39, cheekpiece 1 (26)
2 Sintashta, cemetery, grave 11, cheekpiece 3 (20)
3 Kamenny Ambar-5, kurgan 2, grave 5, cheekpiece 2 (4)
4 Kamenny Ambar-5, kurgan 2, grave 8, cheekpiece 1 (8)
5 Solntse II, kurgan 4, grave 1 (30)
6 Zardcha-Khalifa, grave, cheekpiece 2 (123)
7 Bolshekaraganskiy, kurgan 24, grave 1, cheekpiece 1 (1)
8 Potapovka, kurgan 3, grave 4 cheekpiece 1 (34)
9 Kamenka, settlement (124)
10 Potapovka kurgan 5, grave 8, cheekpiece 1 (36)
11 Uvarovskiy II, kurgan 11, grave 2 (77)
12 Utevka VI, kurgan 6, grave 4, cheekpiece 3 (42)
13 Bogoyavlenskoye, kurgan 1, grave 3, cheekpiece 1 (52)
14 Krivoe Ozero, kurgan 2, grave 1 (97)
15 Berlik, kurgan 10, grave 1, cheekpiece 1 (81)
16 Novonikolskoye I, settlement
17 Satan, cemetery
18 Krasny I, kurgan 1, grave 2, cheekpiece 1 (63)
19 Barannikovo, kurgan 1, grave 2, cheekpiece 1 (49)
20 Komarovka, kurgan 5, grave 1
21 Borodaevka II, kurgan 1, grave 2, cheekpiece 1 (53)
22 Sărata Monteoru, settlement, layer M1C3, cheekpiece 3 (149)
23 Oarţa de Sus, settlement, burial with horses, cheekpiece 1 (145)
24 Alakul, cemetery, kurgan 13, grave 2 (107)
25 Kazangulovo, settlement, cheekpiece 1 (110)
26 Adybel, accidental find, (106)
27 Mirny IV, settlement, cheekpiece 1 (112)
28 Novonikolskoye, cemetery, kurgan 5, grave 2 (114)
29 Chelkar, settlement
30 Ilekshar I, kurgan 6, grave 3, cheekpiece 2 (109)
31 Varenovka settlement (120)
32 Nizhnyaya Krasavka II, settlement (126) 33 Brad, settlement (140)
34 Tószeg, settlement, cheekpiece 3
35 Mycenae, Grave Circle A, grave IV, cheekpiece 1 (155)
36 Kapitonovo I, settlement
37 Polyany I, settlement (128)

38 Nizhne-Semenovsky Island, accidental find
39 Vatin, settlement, cheekpiece 1 (141)
40 Kakovatos, tholos A (159)
41 Tiszafüred, settlement
42 Sălacea settlement
43 Kent, settlement
44 Suskanskoye I, settlement
45 Skelki [Ukraine], settlement
46 Kirovo, settlement
47 Bucharest [Romania], settlement
48 Coroteni, settlement
49 Mycenae, "House of Shields" (160)
50 Kent, settlement
51 Myrzhyk [Kazakhstan], settlement
52 Postnikov Ovrag, settlement
53 Ingul, treasure of bronze artefacts
54 Ingul, treasure of bronze artefacts

12

Chariots on the Central Asian Rocks: The Dating Problem

Viktor Novozhenov

Recently, in Central Asian Rock Art, new multi–figure compositions including chariots, different in design and in their probable purpose, have been published. The technique of their execution is very informative: shallow dotted carvings with polishing of the patina made it possible to depict many significant details and features on the rocks. Such close attention of the artists to details and design features made it possible to highlight important typological and iconographic features that determine their more accurate dating and ethno–cultural affiliation, and also clarify many of the design features of the vehicles depicted. Early chariot petroglyphs are associated with the initial stage of the Andronovo Pictorial Tradition (APT) already identified in Central Asian rock art, in contrast to the series of chariots from the Koksu valley (Yeshkiolmes) dated to the Karasuk (Begazy–Dandybai) period. Analysis of the chariot images of the entire area enables us to distinguish two artistic layers in the petroglyphs of the Middle and Late Bronze Age of Central Asia: early and late, correlated with the first part of second millennium BCE and a second one at the end of the second/first half of the first millennium BCE, which can be associated respectively with the Andronovo and Karasuk (Begazy–Dandybai) pictorial traditions in Central Asian rock art.

Introduction

According to most researchers, at the turn of the third and second millennia BCE and the first centuries of the second millennium, Andronovo sites appeared in the Trans–Urals, Kazakh Steppe, Western Turkestan, South Siberia possibly in Xinjiang, Persia and the Hindustan Peninsula.[1]

A new wave of immigrants was reflected in recent data on population genetics for the Sintashta genotype, confirming the genetic relationship of the Sintashta population with tribes from the western regions of the Eurasian steppe, which can be proven by both their migration from the western regions and the genetic relationship with their earlier Yamnaya (Pit–Grave) relatives of the *first wave of migration*, who settled in the area several generations before the Sintashta period and successfully developed in new territories. Population genetics do not confirm the relationship of the Sintashta people with any population groups in Anatolia or other regions of Asia, indicating a west–Eurasian, steppe origin[2] but agreed with the hypothesis of their possible migration from Anatolia.[3]

Sites of the Sintashta–Petrovka type (in our understanding, the early Andronovo sites, corresponding to the initial stage of the formation of the Andronovo archaeological cultures) contain a convincing set of evidence for the acquaintance of the population with the chariot.[4] The total interval of Sintashta AMS dating obtained to date is 2010–1770 BCE (68.2 % accuracy) or 2200–1650 BCE (95.4 %) and it can be synchronised with the Ancient Babylonian Kingdom no later than the reign of Hammurabi (1848–1806 BCE according to the *long* chronology). The appearance of the Mitanni chariot complex can be dated to the 17th century BCE and associated with the migration of Indo–European population groups to Mesopotamia from the north.[5] The beginning of the Second Transition Period in the radiocarbon chronology system of Egypt dates from 1746–1645 BCE (68.2 % accuracy) or 1871–1616 BCE (95.4 %). The end can be dated to 1596–1582 BCE (68 %) or 1601–1573 BCE.[6]

In the south of Central Asia, in Margiana and Bactria, complex ethnocultural processes associated with the population of the steppes, Harappa and the Middle East were also taking place.[7] The outpost of these communications was Sarazm,[8] and especially Gonur–depe.[9] For the material at the latter site, there is a solid series of 59 calibrated radiocarbon dating determining the period of existence of the Margianan capital within the 25th–15th centuries BCE. The most intensive occupation period of the site was at the turn of 2000 BCE, and the site ceased by 1500 BCE.[10]

By the beginning of the second millennium BCE in the steppe communities of Eurasia, all the necessary prerequisites were present for the use of light, fast and manoeuverable two–horse vehicles – chariots. They were developed

---

[1] Anthony 2007; Chernykh 2009; Epimakhov 2014; Deopik 1979; Kozintsev 2019; Kristiansen et al. 2018; Kuzmina 2007; 2008; 2010; Nikolaeva 2019a; 2019b; Novozhenov and Sidikov 2019; Vinogradov 2003; Xiashan Qi and Wang Bo 2008.
[2] Damgaard et al. 2018; Jeong et al. 2020; Mallory et al. 2019; Sikora et al. 2019; Wang et al. 2020; Yang et al. 2020
[3] Grigoriev 2015; 2021; 2023.
[4] Chechushkov and Epimakhov 2018.

[5] See Wilhelm 1989 16–20 and the contribution of Burmeister and Raulwing in this volume.
[6] Chechushkov 2014.
[7] Frankfort 2011; Masson 2006.
[8] Kasparov and Avanesova 2017
[9] Sarianidi 2010; Novozhenov 2016.
[10] Zaitseva et al. 2008.

with an undoubted military and ritual function, as a means of herding domestic animals (first, very mobile and hard–to–graze herds of horses) and for hunting as an important source of replenishing the resources of these communities. The function of reconnoitring – the search for new fertile pastures and the survey of new steppe territories – was also relevant. In addition, a pair of harnessed horses was already the most effective step and a means of taming the horse (Figure 12.1)[11]

The development of vehicles during the previous period in the steppes indicates serious attempts to modernise the heavy four–wheeled wagon – reduction of weight and increased manoeuverability to adapt to the physiological characteristics of a new harness animal in comparison with cattle and camels[12] – the horse.[13]

Finds in burials with chariots of the Shang dynasty (also known as the Yin dynasty, 16th to 11th centuries BCE) and the early and late Zhou (1046–256 BCE), Spring and Autumn (770–481 BCE) and Warring States (481–256 BCE) periods enable us to recognise the structure of steppe chariots. A Taiwanese researcher, Hsiao–yun Wu,[14] published the most complete and detailed summary and analysis of burials with chariots from China. She analyses more than 230 examples of actual chariots from burials of the Shang period to the vehicles of Emperor Qin Shihuang (259–210 BCE), as well as features of the funeral rites and the topography of the burial grounds in which they were found. The author also identifies a significant series of burials in which an imitation of chariot installation is found.[15] She examines in detail the typology of chariots, based on the development of some technical features for their manufacture and practical application.[16]

In all the variety of chariot burials in the steppe zone, two traditions can be clearly traced: the placing of real chariots in grave and the imitation installation. If the Shang period is characterised by single burials with one chariot (or its imitation), a pair of horses and one or two buried charioteers (as in the Sintashta and Petrovka tombs), then in the early Zhou and later periods the number of options and their combinations increases significantly.

In recent years, a series of calibrated radiocarbon dates for steppe chariot graves have been published,[17] corresponding with the 20th–17th centuries BCE.

Figure 12.1. Undocumented horse figurine from the Buzykai river valley in Bashkiria, Russia. Museum of South Ural University. Author's photo (see: Botalov and Vasina 2014: 860-866).

This period gives fairly accurate dating for chariot petroglyphs on the rocks and compositions in which they are present. At the same time, some technological details in actual chariot design are singled out; these date more precisely certain images during the period defined above. It seems that in the framework of the pictorial traditions detailed below, and in combination with other images which can be dated, vehicles and especially chariots become a chronological reference point and can adjust and determine the dating of both the compositions in which they are present and offer a framework for the series of images and styles which constitute these particular visual traditions.

There is no doubt that later, up to the turn of the millennia, chariots were used in real life, art, mythology and in army units, but were then supplanted by cavalry, though for a long time they still retained their military, representational and ritual significance.[18] Of course, the tradition of building chariots in the steppe continued in subsequent historical periods along with improvement in the design of light vehicles, horse harness and equipment. There are finds of actual vehicles in the Pazyryk barrows (4th–3rd centuries BCE) and other contemporary and even earlier pictorial evidence, such as a carved miniature on a unique comb with a chariot in a battle scene from Taksai 1 burial complex of the early Sarmatian period in the western part of the Kazakh steppe (Figure 12.2),[19] and paintings on the walls of a wooden tomb chamber in Tatarli (Anatolia) dated to the 6th century BCE,[20] as well as later finds in Bulgaria – in Kazanluk and Sveshtari, for example.

Chariot petroglyphs in Central Asia

The objects of this study here will be images of horse–drawn chariots. Their totality, in our opinion, changes the established ideas about the construction of Bronze Age

---

[11] Fages et al. 2020; Gaiduchenko 2014; Gaunitz et al. 2018; Kosintsev 2010; Librado et al 2017; 2021; Novozhenov 2020; Outram 2014; Usmanova et al. 2018.
[12] Sarianidi 2010 ; Teufer 2012; Izbitser 2010; Gey 2000.
[13] Chechushkov and Epimakhov 2010; Chechushkov et al. 2018; 2020; Cheremisin et al. 2019; Esin 2012; Fansa and Burmeister (eds.) 2004; Jacobson–Tepfer 2012; Kozhin 2015; Kukushkin 2011a; 2011b; Kukushkin and Dmitriev 2019; Kupriyanova et al 2017; Kuznetsov 2006; Littauer and Crouwel 1979; 1996; Lindner 2020; 2021; Miller 2012; Piggott 1983; 1992.
[14] Wu 2009; 2011; 2013.
[15] Wu 2009: 49–59.
[16] Wu 2009: 22–42.
[17] Hanks, Epimakhov and Renfrew 2007; Cherlionok 2021; Lindner 2020; Wang 2019.

[18] Sun Tzu 2014: 46–47; 49–50; 65–67; 76; 106–110; 124–128; Sima Qian 1993.
[19] Sdikov and Lukpanova 2013; Altinbekov 2013; 2014.
[20] Novozhenov 2015: 57–88; Summerer 2007.

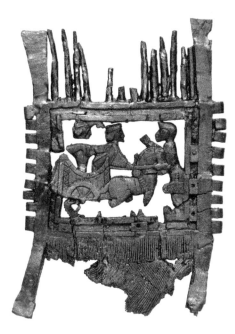 

Figure 12.2. Left: Western Kazakhstan. Taksai 1. Early Sarmatian wooden comb with double-sided chariot composition. Sixth century BCE. Author's photo (see: Sdikov and Lukpanova 2013; Altinbekov 2013; 2014). Right: reconstruction of the comb.

vehicles and details the picture of technological solutions that are not accessible through direct study from other sources.[21]

Currently, more than seven hundred petroglyphs of chariots are known with images of chariots on the rocks, while more than fifty sites with the remains of actual chariots, weapons of charioteers and their equipment have been excavated in the Ural–Kazakhstan steppe[22] plus further chariot remains (230 examples) in China.[23] Many types of complex weapons for use in chariots from Andronovo graves are depicted in compositions on the rocks: chariots, spears, club–bearers in battle or with clubs on their shoulders, with shields (?) and various types of bows.[24]

Analysis of the rock engravings of chariots, carts, and wagons from different regions of Eurasia reveals several clear patterns and features of the development of the design of chariots, which, as a rule, was reflected in their images on the rocks, regardless of the artistic style or their technique of manufacture. The noticeable similarity of chariot images in the petroglyphs and their remains in actual graves, the consistency of the sets of characters involved in these scenes, the commonality of the funeral rite, harness sets and weapons, including specialised ways of managing and protecting the crew, raise the question of how to place these artefacts within the Asian chariot complex.[25]

Methods

In general, the clear chronological position of chariot petroglyphs on rocks coincides with the period of the existence of actual chariots among local communities, or reflects the prevalence of myths associated with them, which would not be possible without knowledge of such vehicles and their use in the everyday life of these groups. The development of vehicle design and the weapons used in chariot petroglyphs in combination with a set of characteristic types of weapons used, and draught horses make it possible to clarify the dating of specific images and holistic compositions in which they are present.

We consider the pictorial, figurative, ornamental and megalithic traditions as a means of visual communication in accordance with the postulates of communication theory. These pictorial traditions have become an important form of internal and external activity of local groups, recorded by archaeological methods in the form of identified archaeological cultures and cultural–historical communities. They have become a reliable indicator of self–identification within these communities, and their study and analysis make it possible to clarify many controversial issues of ethno–cultural history.

For analysis and copying of images, the method of processing digital photographs, recognition and computer 3D modelling of images was used, based on the automatic separation of dots (pixels) of a carving or drawing from similar traces of natural origin. In combination with modern powerful graphic editors, photogrammetry and computer simulation, this method eliminates the subjective factor in the process of creating a copy of an image and can be considered an objective source obtained on the basis

---

[21] Novozhenov 2012a; 2012b; 2020; 2021; Novozhenov and Altinbekov 2014; Rozwadowski 2020; Rogozhinski and Novozhenov 2018; Rogozhinski 2004; Clottes 2011; Jacobson–Tepfer and Novozhenov 2020.
[22] Chechushkov 2014; Anthony 2007; Anthony and Vinogradov 1995; Kukushkin et al. 2018; Littauer and Crouwel 1996; Kuznetsov 2006; Checkushkov and Epimakhov 2018.
[23] Wu 2009; 2013; Wagner 2004.
[24] Novozhenov 2012a: 137–140.
[25] Novozhenov 2012a; 2012b; 2020; 2021.

Figure 12.3. Eastern Kazakhstan. Tarbagatai mountains, Moldazhar (Shimailly) area. General view and indexed panorama of the monument. The location of boulders with chariot petroglyphs is marked in red (after Samashev 2018: 60–61).

Figure 12.4. Moldazhar. Boulder 1. Left and right faces of the stone and a horizontal surface with petroglyphs. Photo and rendering (after Samashev 2018: 63–87, figs. 18–47).

of hardware data.[26] This method is used along with other traditional methods of archaeological research for dating, classification and typology of artefacts, searching for systemic analogies, and determining the cultural affiliation of objects under consideration.[27]

This study also uses the results of computer and mock–up modelling based on comprehensive analysis of materials and ancient technologies developed in the restoration laboratory 'Ostrov Kirim' and protected by Author's certificates of the Republic of Kazakhstan,[28] as well as the results of previously proposed graphic reconstructions[29] and field experiments.[30]

Results: The Earliest Rock Art Chariots

The most ancient chariots were designed for one standing charioteer, with an open platform and drawn by a pair of horses by means of a central draught–pole. This type of chariot was used and was most likely dominant in the Early Srubnaya (also known as Timber–grave culture 1900–1200 BCE) and Early Andronovo cultures (flourished c. 2000–1150 BCE), including Sintashta, Petrovka and Early Alakul). The earliest chariots found in China date from about 1200 BCE, during the late Shang dynasty.[31]

In the petroglyphs of Tarbagatai (Eastern Kazakhstan), battle and transport vehicles of the Bronze Age are of particular interest. Petroglyphs of the Moldazhar area, in the centre of the watershed of the Tarbagatai Mountains, in the east of Kazakhstan, were discovered by Alekei Rogozhinskiy (2011a, b) and partially published and described in detail by Zenolla Samashev (2018) under the name Shimaily I. The most informative and multi–temporal petroglyphs and tamgas are located on the top and slopes of the Sardongal hill, on rounded boulders which are probably of moraine origin (Figure 12.3).

In the diversity of the multi–temporal repertoire of this unique monument, the pictorial layer of the Bronze Age stands out sharply with a rich set of armed anthropomorphic figures (archers, opposing club–bearers, charioteers) and zoomorphic images (bovids, decorated horses, steppe antelopes) shown in battle and hunting compositions, as well as in scenes well known in Central Asian petroglyphs as *Master of horses*.[32] In all the variety of images on this stone (Figure 12.4), realistic figures of horses stand out, reminiscent of the appearance of a Przewalski horse, and horses whose bodies are

---

[26] Novozhenov and Ilyin 2021; Monna et al. 2022: 91–101; Rolland et al. 2022.
[27] Sher 1980, Shvets 2012.
[28] Altinbekov and Novozhenov 2020.
[29] Esin et al. 2021: 600–620.
[30] Spruytte 1983; Chechushkov and Semyan 2022.
[31] See Chechushkov and Epimakhov and Wu in this volume.
[32] Sher 1980; Savinov 2021: 243–249.

decorated with hatched triangles and ornamental elements characteristic of Sintashta and Petrovka ceramics found in the chariot burials.³³

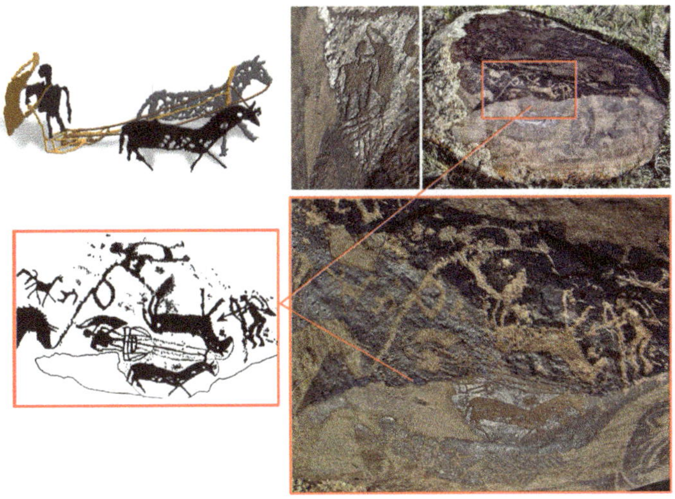

Three vehicles are depicted on the boulder, two are standard for their time – two–horse chariots, shown with spoked wheels, and in one case a charioteer is armed most likely with a spear. The chariots have a central draught pole equipped with special braces that fix the yoke in a rigid position, since when manoeuvring such a vehicle, centrifugal forces and the main stress are transferred to the junction between yoke and pole.³⁴ A line is shown in front of the muzzles of the horses, indicating one element of the harnessing system, the link which connects the inner cheekpieces of the draught horses for convenience and greater efficiency in controlling them. At the same time, the reins can be confidently interpreted as extending from the heads of the horses on the outside, from the outer cheekpieces back to the chariot. This method of control allows not four, but only two reins to be used. A similar, but more complex control system was recorded for later chariots depicted in the valley of the Koksu River in southern Kazakhstan.³⁵

Figure 12.5. Moldazhar. Boulder 1. The third vehicle is a war sled with a charioteer and an opposing archer. Photos show the location on the stone, fragments; graphic drawing by the author and 3-D projection.

The third vehicle (Figure 12.5) is depicted on the shoulder of a boulder in the standard Central Asian rock chariot tradition: a pair of draught horses is depicted with their backs to each other, in *'top plan view'*, a central draught pole, reins, and a charioteer standing on a platform with a quiver behind his back containing a bow. With his left hand, he holds a rope tied to the base of a rectangular platform with a D–shaped front (vertical handrail?), and with his right hand he controls the moving vehicle by means of the reins. An archer on foot is shown in front of the two–horse team, with a quiver on his back. The arrow of his bow is directed at the vehicle opposing him. The only deviation from the 'canon' is the presence of skids instead of traditional wheels, which leads to the interpretation of this image as a sled used as a combat vehicle. The battle character of the scene is beyond doubt and is typical of classical chariot scenes of the Ancient World.³⁶

Figure 12.6. Moldazhar. Boulder 34. Photo detail and drawing of a composition with chariots (after Samashev 2018: figs.133-142).

The images are characterised by the detailed drawing of the yoke. All three vehicles are equipped with the neck–yoke system.³⁷ This method of harnessing was widespread in Northern Eurasia and did not cause discomfort to the horses. Realism is also emphasised by the constant number of spokes depicted in the wheels (six or seven), generally consistent with archaeological observations.³⁸

On boulder 34 (Figure 12.6), part of another multi–figured composition with the participation of hunters, mountain sheep, horses and a bovid with curved horns, two chariots

---

³³ Novozhenov 2022.
³⁴ Gail Brownrigg (pers. comm.) suggests that these braces run from the bottom of the inner side of the yoke fork to the pole, as on the bronze models found in the mausoleum of Emperor Shihuang (Wu 2013: fig. 1.2(2)), rather than from the yoke itself as was usual in ancient harnessing in the Near East (Spruytte 1983: 53). Such braces are probably also intended on the plan views of *bigae* on plaques from China (fig. 14) and *quadrigae* on the rock carvings at Somon Bogd, (Novozhenov 2012a: fig. 44, no. 6.3.HS2) and at Jamani Us, both in Mongolia (Novozhenov 2012a: fig. 59 no. 6.3.YU3(P)).
³⁵ Novozhenov and Rogozhinski 2019; see below.
³⁶ Novozhenov 2012a; 2021.
³⁷ Spruytte 1983.
³⁸ Chechushkov and Epimakhov 2018: 458.

are depicted. One is shown with a charioteer shooting a bow and carefully depicted details of the construction of the vehicle, while the other without a driver, is more abstract and lacks detailed implementation on the surface of the stone.[39] Among the design features of the first chariot, we note the presence of rows of straps or ropes parallel to the central draught–pole, connecting the front edge of the sub–square platform with the yoke, fixing it in a position strictly perpendicular to the central draught–pole, like stretched cords, and increasing the strength of this main structural unit for such a chariot when manoeuvring at speed. Of at least nine such stretched cords, two may be the reins, and these are depicted tied to the front of the platform, thereby freeing the hands of the charioteer. It is also possible that the front rail of the body of the chariot is shown here, which is less likely. The charioteer stands in a fixed position on the platform (the legs are shown spread apart) and he is depicted at the moment of shooting a long bow at a herd of mountain sheep, as evidenced by the tip of his arrow directed at these animals. This can thus be interpreted exclusively as a hunting scene. A curious detail in the scene is a little horse tied behind the chariot (a spare horse?).

There are other documented and undocumented chariot compositions at this site (Figure 12.7).[40]

The Late Rock Art Chariots

The figurative monuments of the Koksu river valley and the Yeshkiolmes ridge are located in the intermountain depression, about 50 km south of the city of Taldykurgan, in the spurs of the Dzungarian Ala–Tau in southern Kazakhstan.[41] The majority of the petroglyphs at these sites were dated to the 13th–12th centuries BCE by Begazy–Dandybai and Sargary–Alekseyevo ceramics and to the tenth–eighth centuries BCE by material of the Dongal type found here under the rocks with petroglyphs (Figure 12.8).[42] Medieval images, Kazakh drawings and inscriptions (including Arabic ones) were also revealed, though the number is insignificant in comparison with petroglyphs of the Bronze Age and Early Nomadic periods.

Figure 12.7. Moldazhar. Undocumented images of vehicles. Photo (left) and drawings (right) after Samashev (2018: 334, 348-354, 362, fig. 430).

All chariots are depicted in motion (Figures 12.9–12.13), possibly in battle; in front of them are flying arrows. The procession is led by an archer on foot, whose size is intentionally enlarged. Behind the chariots is shown a smaller human figure with raised right hand. An indefinitely shaped object, perhaps some kind of weapon, is depicted in his fist. Two upper chariots are similar in design, the differences are only in some details: the upper is larger than the lower; the diameter of the four–spoked wheels is greater, and they are drawn by larger horses.

The draught animals of all chariots are pairs of horses of elongated proportions, quite stylised, showing the ears in detail, triangular protrusions of unclear purpose on the

Figure 12.8. Southern Kazakhstan. Yeshkiolmes. General view showing the concentration of chariot scenes. Author's photo.

---

[39] Samashev 2018: figs. 133–142.
[40] Samashev 2018: 334; 348–354; 362, fig. 430.
[41] Maryashev and Rogozhinski 1991; Maryashev and Goryachev 2002.
[42] Novozhenov and Rogozhinski 2019.

croup of the upper pair of stallions, and the end of the tail of the lower stallion decorated with carved lines. All chariot horses are depicted in a standard way, *positioned one above the other,* with long tails but without manes, and with visible thickenings on the ends of the legs indicating the hooves, in a single fine style and reflecting the appearance of horses of the same breed.

The design of all chariots is standardised: wheels with four spokes rotate on the axle, with a massive central draught–pole and with a special thickening in the centre of the wheel. The chariot platform is D–shaped or sub–rectangular, lightweight, and located in front of the axle for proper balance. The platform of the lower chariot is without any visible barrier, but the platform of the upper chariot most likely has such a guard rail, as evidenced by a thin line of a sub–rectangular shape adjacent to its massive axle and supporting the spear shaft. The tractive force from the draught animals is transmitted by a transverse yoke fixed at the end of the central pole without visible yoke saddles (yoke forks) or other attachments at their withers.

Figure 12.9. Yeshkiolmes. Unit of chariots. Photo detail (left) and drawings (right) by the author.

The design of the chariot is shown very realistically, as it is drawn with thin carved lines, in contrast to the outline figures of draught horses and charioteer. Wheels of large diameter with ten spokes are depicted with small round hubs. The platform body is rectangular in shape, located in front of the axle, and rests in the middle on the central draught–pole. The platform is depicted by carved intersecting lines, indicating the peculiarity of its design, namely a platform made of interwoven willow twigs or rawhide strips for shock absorption during movement – a very practical, lightweight and reliable technical solution for a comfortable ride on rough terrain. There are vague carved lines adjacent to the platform at the rear. Perhaps this is how the handrail was situated for convenience in the daily operation of the vehicle.

Figure 12.10. Yeshkiolmes. Battle with chariots and archers. Photo (left) and drawings (right) by the author.

Control of the draught animals

The tractive force of the animals is transmitted by the central pole and the yoke fastened at its front end, depicted in the form of two carved lines between the horses' withers. The draught animals are controlled using a pair of reins attached to the ends of each horse's bit and held in the hands of the charioteer: two reins from the right–hand horse held in the right hand and, correspondingly, two reins from the other horse in the left. Additionally, the horses' heads are connected by separate lines (straps) connecting the inner ends of both horses' bits for tighter control: in this case, pulling a pair of reins on one side with one hand (for one horse) at the same time gives a command to turn the other horse, which enabled one horse to turn the team to the right or left.

On three chariots the harness straps are clearly shown as components of the original control system for draught animals, which consists of long reins leading from the horses' heads and which the charioteer holds in his left hand (Figure 12.10). Two separate crossed straps connect the horses' heads, the ends probably attached to the bits, or are fixed crosswise, linking the inside ends of the bits on to the yoke.

The top image clearly shows the system of priority control over the principal horse, whose head is controlled by two reins fixed in the standard way – on either side of the bit. In this case, to control the second horse, it was enough to have one rein attached to the outside of the bit, while on the inside its bit was probably constantly connected by another strap to the inside of the bit of the principal horse or fixed on the yoke of the chariot.

It is also possible that the second reins are depicted behind the horse's croup and the charioteer manages the reins from two horses, holding them in pairs in his left hand. At the same time, two crossed straps are shown in front of the animals' muzzles, which probably connected the sides of the bits of both horses, effectively duplicating the commands to each horse and controlling the turns by tightening only one rein. In any case, such a system greatly facilitated driving and ensured the necessary manoeuvrability of the chariot and efficiency during hunting or combat operations. And most importantly, it allowed the charioteer to control a pair of horses with only his left hand, freeing his right hand for using weapons – a spear or a mace (club), a whip or a goad.

The control system depicted for a pair of horses probably required the use of additional distribution rings for reins and special devices that prevent harness straps from twisting and provide the necessary manoeuvrability for these chariots.

It should be noted that the control system described was not suitable for archery from a moving chariot – both hands had to be free, which implies the presence of other devices such as handrails or a special buckle on the charioteer's belt, where the reins were temporarily attached when shooting. Or, as the Egyptian pharaohs are shown, the reins tied around his waist.[43] But the easiest thing for the charioteer was to simply stop the chariot in a strategically advantageous place, shoot the bow, and then continue driving.

Charioteers and chariot attributes

Seen from above two vehicles the charioteers are shown quite realistically and in detail. They are depicted in a dynamic position, clearly balancing on the platform of a moving chariot, standing on the rear edge of the platform (almost on the axle). In their left hand they hold the reins tightly, providing themselves with the necessary stability and balance, shifting their centre of gravity by leaning as far back as possible, and in their right hand they hold certain objects: the upper charioteer holds a whip or goad, and the lower one holds either a mace (club) or a goad (or whip). Perhaps his palm is open – the fingers are shown, and the object is held on to his wrist with a strap as he waves his hand.

Behind the charioteers are large quivers like a modern backpack, attached to their body at two or three points (obviously with special straps) and shifted backwards, as they balance on a moving platform. At the same time, the quiver of the upper chariot is shown open and the arrowheads in it are visible, while the quiver of the lower chariot is depicted with the cover open (?) and obscure thin objects nearby, hanging from its upper edge, possibly held by cords or some kind of straps.

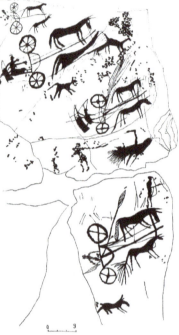

Figure 12.11. Yeshkiolmes. Chariot scene, charioteers with bows and spear. Photo (left) and drawings (right) by the author.

Figure 12.12. Yeshkiolmes. Chariot with platform clearly delineated. Author's photo.

---

[43] In reality, the Pharaoh was accompanied by a charioteer, but in order to show his power, he is depicted alone in his chariot, the reins tied around his waist being an artistic convention.

Figure 12.13. Yeshkiolmes. Chariot with platform construction clearly shown. Photo 13a) and processed photo (13a) by the author.

In the scenes under consideration, the charioteers are dressed in long, fitted tunics or caftans probably reaching to their knees, they obviously have belts, a quiver on their backs and a fairly standard set of weapons: bows with quivers full of arrows, bows, clubs (?), whips, spears or javelins.

An indispensable attribute of these chariots is a spear, or a javelin vertically mounted on the body of the chariot with a clearly depicted tip. This position of the spear perhaps confirms a light rail or siding around the platform, especially in the upper vehicle, since it would provide a reliable point of attachment for the spear during movement. At the same time, there are some technical solutions for reliably fastening the shaft of such a spear directly to the supporting struts of the axle or the platform body of the chariot without additionally fixing it in this position on the handrail. It is an important point that a similar position of the spear on the chariot was already noted by researchers in the petroglyphs of the Kazakh Altai (see above), in the sites of Moldazhar, Moinak, Kurchum, where horses of a different appearance – with a *forelock* and round–shaped bodies, clearly depicted in the Seima–Turbino style – were harnessed to a carriage platform without visible handrails and with a spear vertically mounted on.

Dating discussion

In general, along with realistic and well–detailed images of chariots in the Moldazhar (Shymayly) area, more conventional, schematic images were found showing harnessed and unharnessed vehicles of various types, with and without charioteers, including carts with disc wheels which appear to be articulated two–wheeled structures attached one behind the other, widely known in contemporary petroglyphs from other regions of Eurasia.[44] Four–wheeled wagons or baggage vehicles were not recorded. Draught animals are exclusively a pair of horses, though in one case a two– humped camel (Bactrian) is depicted pulling a rectangular platform without wheels (a transportation platform, like a sledge) with traces (ropes?) which might be interpreted instead as reins. The dating of the Moldazhar images is clearly evidenced by rather archaic designs of exclusively single–occupant (personal) chariots, the presence of horses in the Seima–Turbino style, and most importantly, the presence of ornaments in the decoration on the horses: hatched triangles and vertical zigzags. While the first elements are characteristic of all Adronovo ceramics (Alakul, Fedorovo), the vertical zigzags are more indicative of ceramic and cheekpiece decoration of Sintashta–Petrovka appearance in the chariot burials.[45] Ceramics from burials with chariot associations recorded in the Sintashta cemetery (burials 11, 12, 30) and in Kamennyi Ambar 5 (burials 5 and 8) in the Southern Urals, have a repeating and limited set of ornamental motifs – triangles and vertical zigzags and pronounced decoration.[46] Similar ornamentation is observed in Central and Northern Kazakhstan (Satan, Senkibay 2, Taldy 1, Atshisu, Bestamak, etc), and in the Potapovsky burial mound (Volga region) in central burial 4 (combined with burials 1, 2, 5 and 10) of kurgan 3 and in burial 8 in the fifth kurgan.[47] This comparison makes it possible to date realistic images of chariots to around the turn of third and second millennium BCE, with a later dating – towards the middle of the second millennium BCE – of sketchy images of vehicles on this remarkable monument.

From the middle of the second millennium BCE, innovations took place in the design of chariots: they became larger, specialisation with a crew of two people appeared – an archer and a charioteer – and there were *trigae* and *quadrigae* harnessed with a central draught pole, yoke–saddles, traces for the outriggers and other special harness straps. The shape of the body changed from an open platform to a structure with sides and special handrails for the crew. These constructions, along with other types of vehicles, became widespread in Andronovo, Karasuk and Zhou communities and were used by the Sakas and Sarmatians, Huns, Persians, Greeks, and Chinese until the turn of the millenium.[48]

It is in this classic form that a war chariot on spoked wheels became recognisable and widespread throughout the Eurasian continent in art, architectural and statuary monuments, including petroglyphs. It is these chariots,

---

[44] Novozhenov 2012:101–102.
[45] Novozhenov 2022.
[46] Vinogradov 2003; Lindner 2020: 374; 377–378; figs. 5; 6; 9.
[47] Cherlionok 2021: 87–100; Kuznetsov 2006; Kukushin et al. 2018a; 2018b; Kuzmina 2007; 2008.
[48] Novozhenov 2014a; 2018b; 2019.

combined with special armaments, that became a formidable military force, as evidenced by the battles at Kadesh or Megiddo between the Egyptians and the Hittites or the famous Greco–Persian wars, and the power of the first Assyrian empire was ensured by exceptionally competent communications, including the first in the world by courier service, excellent roads built on its territory and, of course, military chariots.

The appearance of the harness animals at Yeshkiolmes differs from the iconography of the horses of the Seima–Turbino style depicted on more northerly sites in similar scenes, and probably indicates different types of horses. The Sintashta and Petrovka peoples had already used horses of a different appearance from the Botai (Przewalski) horses, and draught horses as depicted in the chariot scenes under consideration could have appeared even later than the events described above, most likely at the turn of the second to first millennium BCE – though larger horses shown with a sub–rectangular body were identified from the earliest layers in the petroglyphs of the Koksu Valley dated to the 13th–10th centuries BCE,[49] and the chronological range of the areas discussed covers the period from the 13th to the 8th centuries BCE.

Clarification of the dating allows the analysis of the designs of chariots and the control system for draught animals, as mentioned above. It was established that chariots initially developed from individual single occupancy towards their technical improvement and design complexity.[50] To judge by Chinese chariots, the appearance of additional devices in the form of handrails on the body occurs only during the Western Zhou Dynasty (c. 1045–771 BCE).[51]

The features of the chariots on the Yeshkiolmes petroglyphs indicate their highly developed technical level. The practical use of such structures in battle or hunting required considerable driving skills and outstanding acrobatic abilities from charioteers. At the same time, the designs presented on the rocks of Yeshkiolmes provided a fairly comfortable ride and the necessary springing.

The presence of original control systems for draught animals also indicates a high level of horse training, when it became possible to control only the principal horse of a pair, and an innovative system for positioning and securing the reins was developed, greatly simplifying the task of manoeuvring. The triangular protrusions visible on the croups of the harness horses are associated with the general complex system of straps of this harnessing and require additional explanation and special research.

It is clear that such a complex reining system is based on the use of additional devices for their proper distribution and attachment, such as the bronze zoomorphic finials with rings and plaques found in the Arzhan I burial mound,[52] a complex of horse and chariot equipment carved from horn at the Kent site,[53] similar objects found in Karasuk, Tasmola, Tagar and early Sarmatian sites, and the complexes of Taksay I or Kyryk–oba.[54] The radiocarbon dating of the contemporary Western Zhou chariots is quite well developed, basically corresponding with the dynastic chariot, and it also fits into the chronological range indicated above. The rod–shaped cheekpiece made of horn in the Baifu burial, whose calibrated radiocarbon dates of the wooden chamber are 1120 ± 90 BCE[55] or 1085 ± 130 BCE, can help clarify the dating of Zhou finds (Zhong Suk–Bae 2000: 121). This Western Zhou burial has clear steppe features, similar to materials from Lulihe. It corresponds to the ancient principality of Yan (11th century BCE–222 BCE), controlled by the Western Zhou dynasty in Northern China, which, judging by archaeological and written data, had active contacts with both the Late Yin population of the Central Plain of China and with tribes from the steppe and foothill regions of Central Asia.

It is noteworthy that Karasuk knives with a loop were used as money in the Yan state. However, such currency was also used in some other neighbouring states in the north in the Warring States period before the unification of China by Emperor Qin Shihuang in 222 BCE and even much earlier. Separate images of such Karasuk knives are carved on the rocks among the petroglyphs at Maimak in South Kazakhstan, which also testifies to their special symbolic and communicative function.

The radiocarbon dating of the Baifu burial given above does not correspond with the data of traditional early Chinese chronicles, which recorded the migration of the Yan population from Henan to Hebei province only in the reign of King Cheng in 1024–1005 BCE.[56] This fact indicates the constant earlier and later migrations of the steppe nomadic population to the territory of the Yan state and the existence of a permanent channel of communication with the northern steppe tribes.

The Shangzunling necropolis is associated with the ancient principality of Guo, defeated by another state – Jin – in 655 BCE, during the Warring States period. According to inscriptions on the vessels from those burials, they belonged to high officials of this state who lived during the times of King Huang (ruled 827–782 BCE). This site is traditionally dated according to the dynasty chronology from the second half of the ninth to the first half of the seventh centuries BCE, which also contradicts the radiocarbon dating. Zhangjiaopo also dates from the reigns of King Cheng and King Kang (1004–967 BCE) and the late 11th – first half of the 10th century BCE.[57]

---

[49] Rogozhinski 2004: 80–85.
[50] Novozhenov 2012a: 300–308; 2019.
[51] Wu 2009; 2011; 2013.
[52] Smirnov 2012.
[53] Varfolomeev et al. 2017.
[54] Novozhenov and Altinbekov 2014; Novozhenov 2018b.
[55] Komisarov 1988: 55
[56] This is where the modern city of Beijing is located, in the vicinity of which the Baifu cemetery was excavated, and where, according to written sources, the capital of the Yan state was located and other large cemeteries of two bright, but later Scythian cultures, of the Nanshan'gen and Yuhuangmiao types were excavated.
[57] Zhong Suk–Bae 2000: 123.

Spears in chariots are placed in an upright position, which indicates the presence of a special device for holding them or the presence of a rail that supports them. The obvious probability is a combination in the design. An Etruscan bronze chariot from Monteleone, decorated with images of birds of prey and scenes from the life of the Greek hero Achilles, exhibited at the Metropolitan Museum of Art, is dated to the second quarter of the sixth century BCE.[58] On the draught pole there is a special device in the form of a tube into which the shaft of a spear, a javelin or a whip (or goad) was inserted vertically.

In the chariots of Yeshkiolmes, spears on long shafts or javelins with tips similar to finds from Begazy–Dandybai sites are placed as standard weapons. All these types of weapons and horse equipment were recorded on the earliest town in the Kazakh steppe, the Kent settlement, which existed in the Begazy–Dandybai period (14th–10th centuries BCE).[59] The armoury complex found over many years of excavation: spear heads, javelins and arrows made of bronze, horn, bone and stone, as well as various types of cheekpieces, a unique collection of products made of horn and bone decorated with carved lines, including decorative ornamental horn plaques intended to lie on the chariot horses' shoulders, similar to those found in the Arzhan I burial mound, most closely matches the attributes of the harness pictured on the rocks of the Koksu Valley. This horse harness corresponds to the complex type of control system for draught animals depicted in the scenes discussed, where a significant number of devices were required for the correct distribution of straps including special hooks made of horn.[60] It is the largest of the excavated sites of the final Bronze Age in the Kazakh steppe, well dated to the 14th–10th centuries BCE.

At the same time, although the arrows in the scenes examined are shown with detailed tips, nevertheless they are only partly similar to the two–bladed bronze arrowheads from excavations I, V, VI at Kent.[61] It is difficult to identify their exact cultural affiliation. Perhaps, part of the arrowheads, judging by the presence of special lines on them, are made of stone or bone, which certainly affected their shape, not to mention the possible artistic license of the maker of the petroglyphs and the intentional fantastic, imaginative perception of these images. Such tips are very similar to the bone and stone blanks found in the Kent dwellings in significant numbers, and finished arrowheads of various shapes made of horn, bone and stone.

In the contemporary layer of images there are certain types of arrowheads of a triangular shape (Yazdepe, Lugavskoye); or leaf–shape, characteristic of contemporary sites in the Kazakh Steppe and Kazakh Altai, also known amongst the antiquities of the Tagar culture in the Minusinsk Basin. These scenes correspond to the IV and V types of petroglyphs of the entire Yeshkiolmes complex dated to the 13th/12th–8th/early 7th centuries BCE.[62]

At the same time, the forms of arrows and javelins – types of weapons found in the contemporary petroglyphs of Yeshkiolmes – have analogies in material from the sites and burial grounds of the final Bronze Age excavated here under the rocks with petroglyphs. Among them, two chronological groups of sites stand out for the period of interest: the sites of Talapty I (dwelling 3), Kuygan II and the burials of Talapty I–III dated to the 13th–11th centuries BCE and the site of Talapty (dwellings I, II) and sites and the burial grounds of Kuygan I and II dated to 11th–10th centuries BCE.[63]

The relative dating of the chariot groups under consideration can also be evidenced by ornaments consisting of shaded isosceles triangles typical for the decoration of Andronovo dishes, found near this cluster of chariot petroglyphs in the same gorge.

In general, taking into account the foregoing, the chariot scenes as well as the accompanying petroglyphs find exact analogies in sites of the Mongolian and Russian Altai (Kalbak Tash and Tsagan–Salaa), Dzhungarian Alatau (Zhaltyrak Tash), geographically reflecting possible migrations of the authors of these compositions, and are directly related to the Begazy–Dandybai period and the Karasuk artistic tradition.[64] The specific dating of the chariot scenes is the 14th–10th centuries BCE with a clear stratification between earlier realistic battle scenes within this chronological range and later rather sketchy chariot groups with scenes depicting the hunting of wild animals, which possibly existed up to the eighth century BCE.

During the period under consideration there were complex historical processes and significant migrations of the population which directly affected the Koksu Valley. The initiators of such movements were, apparently, for the most part not whole communities of people or even tribes, but relatively small groupings – elite and self–sufficient clans of blood relatives – quickly dissolving among the autochthonous population and subordinating them due to their possession of the most advanced and progressive innovations such as advanced chariot designs and weapons.

Identification, migrations and figurative traditions

Based on Chinese written sources, it turns out that these nomadic waves of migration, proven by archaeological finds, coincide exactly with the periods of activity and widespread settlement of steppe tribes known in Chinese records as the Rong (Xirong, Shanrong) and Di.[65]

---

[58] www.metmuseum.org/art/collection/search/247020.
[59] Varfolomeev et al. 2017: 20–21; 40; 45–46; 56–57; 255–272; 314–324.
[60] See the illustration in Varfolomeev et al. 2017: 13.
[61] Varfolomeev et al. 2017: 20–21; 44–46.

[62] Rogozhinski 2004: 81–82.
[63] Rogozhinski 2004: 78–79.
[64] Novozhenov 2014b; 2020.
[65] Kruykov 1970; Maliavkin 1981; Piankov 2013; 2015: 233–243; Kovalev 1998; 2008; 2014: 124–136; 2015; Tairov 2007; Novozhenov 2017; 2018; 2019; 2020.

Peoples from the northern states in Eastern Turkestan lived in conflict with the Chinese on the border, as is confirmed by the ancient Chinese inscriptions on oracle bones (ox shoulder-blades and tortoise plastrons) of which several thousand were found in the late Shang and pre-dynastic Zhou centres of the late second millennium BCE. They are evidence of the real threat from the north for the dynastic Chinese, but also document different kinds of contacts (intermarriages and intermingling) with the steppe populations to their north and north–west showing that there was not constant warfare.

These nomadic steppe groups could have been related to the groups known as the Gui–Fang, Tu–Fang, and Hun–Fang who were thought to populate what is now Xinjiang Autonomous Region of the PRC and lived in the state of Yan (one of the states of Western Zhou, in the area of modern Beijing) and with whom the Shang and Zhou rulers frequently entered into conflict.[66] It is noteworthy that the earliest sources refer to all the northern neighbours of the ancient Chinese as *rong,* which has been translated as meaning: warrior, battle chariot and a large military campaign.[67]

In North China, two main sites were excavated – the cemeteries at Nanshan'gen and Yuhuangmiao – where many objects of steppe type dating from the ninth–sixth centuries BCE were discovered (Figure 12.14). The earlier is a site of Upper Xiajiadian type at Nanshan'gen, which existed in the territory northeast of Beijing in the ninth–seventh/sixth centuries BCE. To a large extent, the Yuhuangmiao finds (second half of the seventh–sixth centuries BCE) are related to this material. The burials are located in a mountainous area of about 400 x 200 km, like an arc covering the north of the plain with the city of Beijing, on the site of which in the seventh–sixth centuries BCE the capital of the Kingdom of Yan was located. The southern border of the cultural range was only 40–50 km from this capital. A large quantity of steppic material has been located there, clearly indicating the presence of non–dynastic Chinese peoples, forming part of a historical and cultural community which existed in the ninth–sixth centuries BCE in the territory from Transbaikalia to the Ordos. Though there does not appear to have been direct contact with the cultures of Xinjiang, Southern Siberia and Kazakhstan, there were many similarities with them.

In a series of earlier studies, the main figurative traditions in the petroglyphs of the Central Asian Bronze Age have already been identified and substantiated.[68] Here, only the main features of the pictorial traditions identified for petroglyphs of the Middle and Final Bronze Age which are still the subject of discussion are repeated.

Andronovo pictorial tradition (APT)

The *Andronovo pictorial tradition (APT)* developed on the basis of the original Pit–grave/Afanasievo tradition, of which the bearers and their descendants during the third millennium BCE settled throughout the Great Belt of the steppes of Northern Eurasia. The southern impulse for the spread of this pictorial tradition, which retained a significant Sumerian (Near Eastern) component, spread to the central and northern regions of Asia through the tribes that left the monuments of the Bactria–Margiana archaeological complex (BMAC). The influence and striking similarity of designs from the excavations of Gonur and Central Asian petroglyphs have already been noted by researchers[69] and found vivid expression in the ancient petroglyphs of Saimaly–Tash in the form of an original *bi–triangular* style of goats as on Near Eastern painted ceramics. The combination of these two impulses in Turan, in the Ural–Kazakhstan steppes and the foothills of the Altai at the turn of the third to second millennium BCE led to the emergence of this pictorial tradition.[70]

Pictorial series of the APT

The *sun–headed, masked* zoomorphic hero is the key character of this tradition. The Solar deity in the Andronovo petroglyphs corresponds to the main functions of the cosmogony of the Indo–Europeans and the pronounced cult of the horse. This deity controls the chariots and is present on the altar compositions of the pictorial monuments of the Bronze Age.

The APT code fragments are reconstructed as follows: → sun–headed character in canonised poses (or a man with emphasised genitals and a *tail*, sometimes with a ball at its end) a chariot (with spoked wheels, drawn by horses in a standard position with their backs to one another, and the chariot itself shown exclusively in the *top view* position) → different types of Andronovo weapons → cult of the horse: a horse with a detailed mane/tail => great bovids with large horns curved forward → Bactrian camels → solar symbolism (cross signs) → (...)

Karasuk (Begazy–Dandybai) pictorial tradition (KPT)

Another, the *Karasuk (Begazy–Dandybai) pictorial tradition (KPT)*, developed in the rock art of Southern Siberia, Altai, Ordos and in the steppes and foothills of Kazakhstan starting from the Middle Bronze Age and coexisting with *APT* in the second half of the second millennium BCE, and later became the artistic basis of the emerging Scythian–Saka animal style during the early nomadic period.[71]

We fully share the chariot hypothesis, which interprets some horse burials of the Arzhan I kurgan as an imitation of burials with chariots, including a four–horse team – a *quadriga.*[72] An image of a chariot depicted in a peculiar

---

[66] Maliavkin 1981; Komisarov 1988; Khodzhaev 2010 38–40; see also Kovalev 2008; 2014.
[67] Khodzhaev 2010: 33; 38–46.
[68] Rogozhinski and Novozhenov 2018; Novozhenov 2014b; 2020.

[69] Mariashev 2011.
[70] Novozhenov 2020: 399–430.
[71] Savinov 2021; Novozhenov 2020.
[72] Smirnov 2012.

 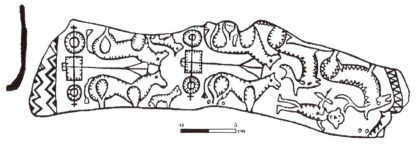

Figure 12.14. Nothern China. Western Zhou. Central Asian chariots in the style of the petroglyphs. Left – Bronze plaque in the form of a two-horse chariot. Metropolitan Museum of Art, New York. No. 2002.201.12, gallery 207. Eighth–seventh centuries BCE; author's photo. Right – Nanshangen necropolis, grave 102, bone plaque with an engraved image of a chariot and triangles decoration (after Novozhenov 2012a: 67, fig. 27:3)

manner was found on one of the slabs of the Arzhan II burial mound and on deer stones. The significant role of charioteers in Karasuk society is clearly evidenced by the finds of images of chariots on the inner walls of stone cists – Karasuk graves (Khara Khaya burial grounds in Tyva, the Northern bank of the Varcha River, etc.).

The pictorial series of the KPT is very similar to Andronovo but has a number of fundamental differences. First of all, this concerns the interpretation of the image of a person – there are no *sun–headed* characters, which are replaced by a conventional image of a person without sexual characteristics and are probably transformed into the form of anthropomorphic megalithic structures – deer stones, symbolising charioteer ancestors.

A feature of the Karasuk chariot petroglyphs is the depiction of draught horses in profile projection (placed *one above the other*), despite the fact that the chariot itself can be shown only in the traditional perspective – *seen from above in a plan view*. Karasuk chariots are often shown unharnessed, including on the slabs of dated Karasuk graves; very often combined with images of deer (Mongolia, Minusinsk Basin) and the design *Horses by the World Tree*. Trigae and quadrigae appear. The horses are also shown without additional detailing of the exterior features. There are images of large bovids and – very rarely – camels.

Fragments of the visual code of the KPT are reconstructed as follows: → symbolic image of a person without gender differences → weapons (on deer stones) → a chariot with a special manner of depicting draught horses (or unhanessed) → symbolic image of a horse → a deer with branched horns → a massive bovid → various signs → (…)

Conclusions

The new collection of Central Asian chariot petroglyphs significantly supplements our information about the design of early vehicles of the population of the Eurasian steppes in the Middle and Final Bronze Ages. Special construction details, harnessing, horse control systems and ornamental decoration similar to those found in dated archaeological material from chariot complexes of the Volga region, the Urals, the Kazakh steppe and China are shown in detail.

The selection of new structural details of the chariot images has become possible on the basis of modern methods of digital image processing and computer modelling.

The classic pair–horse chariots of the rock carvings under consideration are shown in scenes of hunting with dogs for steppe antelopes and wild cattle, accompanied by archers on foot. In addition, they are depicted in battle scenes, surrounded by people fighting with clubs and bows.

The dating of the Moldazhar chariot petroglyphs is based on the dates published by AMS for specific burials of the chariot complex from Sintashta and Petrovka including actual chariots. A certain semantic connection and a striking similarity between two–component ornaments on ceramics in such burials were found. This makes it possible to confidently date the realistic images of the sledge and chariots of Moldazhar to around the turn of the third–second millennium BCE and associate them with the bearers of the Sintashta, Petrovka and Early Alakul archaeological cultures, while the schematic images of vehicles are dated to a later period – to the middle of the second millennium BCE within the framework of the Andronovo pictorial tradition (APT), identified in the petroglyphs of Central Asia for the Middle Bronze Age.

The semantic connection revealed between certain motifs of the ornament, the vessel itself, the chariot theme and the charioteer may indicate the presence of special graphic visual markers or identity marks indicating that they belong to a certain strata, group or caste, similar to generic clan signs – *tamgas*, the use of which was actively developed in the Eurasian steppes at a much later time. Zoning in on the decoration of horses may indicate the stage of domestication of each type of horse and the degree of readiness to be harnessed to a vehicle, and most importantly, the position of this horse in the mythological world view and the possible hierarchy of specific horses as potential sacrificial animals.

Early chariot petroglyphs are associated with the initial stage of the Andronovo pictorial tradition (APT) already identified in the rock art of Central Asia, in contrast to the series of chariots from the valley of the river Koksu (Yeshkiolmes, Zhetysu), dated to the Karasuk (Begazy–

Dandybai) period. An analysis of the chariot groups of the entire area enables us to distinguish two artistic layers in the petroglyphs of the Middle and Late Bronze Age of Central Asia: early and late, correlated with the first part of second millennium BCE and a second one with the end of second/first half of first millennium BCE, which can be associated respectively with the Andronovo and Karasuk (Begazy–Dandybai) pictorial traditions in the rock art of Central Asia.

Acknowledgements

I am very grateful to my colleagues Andrei Epimakhov, Katheryn Linduff and Gail Brownrigg who are more experienced in this topic and who discussed with me various aspects of this text and definition of English terms. Without this discussion, this text would probably contain many inaccuracies. And my special thanks to Gail and Katheryn for correction of some provisions in this work and correction of my English mistakes.

Viktor Novozhenov
Lead Researcher, International Dialogue Department, UNESCO Center for the Rapprochement of Cultures, Almaty, Kazakhstan.

Bibliography

Altinbekov, Kirim. 2013. *Vozrozhdionnaya iz pepla. Rekonstruktsiya zhritsy po materialam pogrebeniya v mogil'nike Taksay I* (Reborn from the Ashes. Reconstruction of the Priestess Based on the materials of the burial in the burial ground Taksay I cemetery). Almaty: Ostrov Kirim Press.

Altinbekov, Kirim. 2014. *Vozrozhdionnye sokrovishcha Kazakhstana: opyt nauchnoy restavratsii* (Revived Treasures of Kazakhstan: The Experience of Scientific Restoration). Almaty: Ostrov Kirim Press.

Altinbekov, Kirim and Viktor A. Novozhenov. 2020. Image of a Chariot of the Andronovo Period. Copyright Certificate of the Republic of Kazakhstan # 8494 of March 02, 2020. https://copyright.kazpatent.kz.

Anthony, David W. 2007. *The Horse, the Wheel and Language. How Bronze–Age Riders from the Steppes Shaped the Modern World*. Princeton and Oxford: Princeton University Press.

Botalov, Sergei G. and Yuliya V. Vasina. 2014. Kamennaya skulpturka loshadi: sluchainaya Nakhodka iz Buzykaya (Stone Sculpture of Horse: Random Find from Buzykai). In: *Nauka na Yuzhnom Urale*. Science in South Ural University: Proceedings of 66th Conference. Section of Humanitarian Science, edited by Sergei G. Botalov, 860–866. Chelyabinsk: South Ural University.

Anthony, David W. and Nikolai B. Vinogradov. 1995. Birth of the Chariot. *Archaeology* 48 (2): 36–41.

Chechushkov, Igor. V. 2014. Rasprostranenie koliosnogo transporta v svete radiouglerodnoi khronologii (The Distribution of Wheeled Transport in the Light of Radiocarbon Chronology). In: *Tainstvo etnicheskoi istorii rannikh kochevnikov stepnoi Evrazii* (Sacrament of the Ethnic History of the Ancient Nomads of Steppe Eurasia) edited by Andrei V. Epimakhov: 274–285. Almaty: Ostrov Kirim.

Chechushkov, Igor V. and Andrei V. Epimakhov. 2010. Kolesnitsy i upriyazh kak kul'turnyi indicator evolutsii konskogo snartazheniya (Chariots and Harness as a Cultural Indicator of the Evolution of Horse Breeding. The Chariot Complex of the Ural–Kazakhstan Steppes). In: *Horses, Chariots and Chariot's Drivers of Eurasian Steppes*, edited by Pavel F. Kuznetsov, Anatolii N. Usachuk, Pavel A. Kosintsev et al.: 182–229. Yekaterinburg, Samara, Donetsk: Rifey.

Chechushkov Igor V. and Andrei V. Epimakhov. 2018. Eurasian Steppe Chariots and Social Complexity During the Bronze Age. *Journal of World Prehistory* 31: 435–483. DOI: 10.1007/s10963–018–9124–0.

Chechushkov Igor, Andrei Epimakhov and Andrei Bersenev. 2018. Early Horse Bridle with Cheekpieces as a Marker of Social Change: An Experimental and Statistical Study. *Journal of Archaeological Science* 97: 125–136. DOI: 10.1016/j.jas.2018.07.012.

Chechushkov, Igor. V. and Ivan A. Semyan. 2022. Eksperimental'noe issledovanie stepnoi kolesnitchy po materialam Sintashtinsko–Petrovskikh pamyatnikov Pozdnei Bronzy (Experimental Study of the Steppe Chariot Based on the Materials of the Sintashta–Petrovka Monuments of the late Bronze Age). *Russian Archaeology* 4: 21–34.

Chechushkov, Igor V., Emma R. Usmanova and Pavel A. Kosintsev. 2020. Early Evidence for Horse Utilization in the Eurasian Steppes and the Case of the Novoil'inovskiy 2 Cemetery in Kazakhstan. *Journal of Archaeological Science: Reports* 32. DOI: 10.1016/j.jasrep.2020.102420.

Cheremisin, Dmitriy V., Sergei A. Komissarov and Alexandr I. Solovyov. 2019. Izobrazheniya kolesnits Tsentral'noi Azii kak marker mobil'nosti i migratsii (Images of Chariots of Central Asia as a Marker of Mobility and Migration). In: *Mobil'nost' i migratsiya: kontseptsii, metody, rezultaty* (Mobility and Migration: Concepts, Methods, Results) edited by Viacheslav I. Molodin: 215–228. Novosibirsk: Institute of History, Archaeology and Ethnography of Siberian Brunch of Russian Academy of Sciences.

Cherlionok, Eugeni A. 2021. Kolesnichnaya upryazh nachala epokhi pozdnei bronzy Povolzhia: otnositel'nay khronologiya pogrebal'nogo obryada i ornamentatsiya psaliev (Chariot Harness of the Beginning of the Late Bronze Age in the Volga–Don Region: Relative Chronology of the Funeral Rite and Ornamentation of Cheekpieces). In: *Tvorets kul'tury. Material'naiya kul'tura i dukhovnoie prostranstvo cheloveka v svete arkheologii, istorii i etnografii* (Creator of Culture. Material Culture and Spiritual Space of Man in the Light of Archaeology, History and Ethnography: Sat. Scientific Art., Dedicated to the 80th Birthday of Professor Dmitri Glebovich Savinov) edited by Nikolai Yu. Smirnov: 87–100. St. Petersburg: Institute for the History of Material Culture of Russian Academy of Sciences.

Chernykh, Eugeni N. 2009. *Stepnoi poyas Evrazii: phenomen kochevykh kul'tur* (Steppe Belt of Eurasia: The Phenomenon of Nomadic Cultures). Moscow: Drevniye rukopisi Rossii.

Clottes, Jean (ed.). 2011. *Rock Art in Central Asia*. A Thematic Study. Paris: ICOMOS. https://archive.org/details/rock-art-central-asia.

Damgaard, Peter de B., Nina Marchi, Simon Rasmussen et al. 2018. Ancient Human Genomes from Across the Eurasian Steppe. *Nature* 557: 369–375.

Deopik, Dmitriy V. 1979. Kul'tura vsadnikov v verkhov'yakh Yantsy i vostochnaya versiya "zverinogo stilya" (Horseman Culture in the Upper Yangtze and the Eastern Version of the "Animal Style". In: *Kul'tura i iskusstvo narodov Srednei Azii v drevnosti i srednevekov'e* (Culture and art of the peoples of Central Asia in Antiquity and the Middle Ages), edited by Mikhail Kriukov: 67–79. Moscow: Nauka.

Epimakhov, Andrei V. 2014. Dinamika kommunikatsii epokhi bronzy na Urale (The Dynamics of Communications of the Bronze Age of the Urals). In: *Tainstvo etnicheskoi istorii rannikh kochevnikov stepnoi Evrazii* (Sacrament of the Ethnic History of the Most Ancient Nomads of Steppe Eurasia). Collective Monograph in Memory of Elena E. Kuzmina, edited by Andrei V. Epimakhov: 125–205. Almaty: Ostrov Kirim.

Esin, Yuri N. 2012. Drevneishie izobrazheniya povozok Minusinskoi kotloviny (The Earliest Images of the Carts of the Minusinsk Depression). *Scientific Review of Sayano Altai* 1 (3): 14–47.

Fages, Antoine, Andaine Seguin–Orlando, Mietje Germonpré and Ludovic Orlando. 2020. Horse Males Became Over–Represented in Archaeological Assemblages During the Bronze Age. *Journal of Archaeological Science: Reports* 31. DOI: 10.1016/j.jasrep.2020.102364.

Fansa, Mamoun and Stefan Burmeister (eds.). 2004. *Rad und Wagen. Der Ursprung einer Innovation. Wagen im Vorderen Orient und Europa*. Mainz: von Zabern.

Filippova, Elena E. 1997. Pogrebal'nye petrogliphy srednego Eniseya i ikh mesto v ideologicheskikh predstavleniyakh Karasukskikh plemion (Funeral Petroglyphs of the Middle Yenisei and Their Place in the Ideological Representations of the Karasuk Tribes). *Arkheologicheskaya kollektsiya. Pogrebal'nyy obryad. Trudy Gosudarstvennogo Istoricheskogo muzeya Moskva* (Archeological Collection. Funeral Rite. Proceedings of the State Historical Museum Moscow) 93: 62–69. Moscow: State Museum of History.

Frankfort, Henri–Paul. 2011. Some Aspects of Horse Representation in the Petroglyphs of Inner Asia from Earliest Periods to the 1st Millennium BCE. In: *Arkheologija Juzhnoj Sibiri. Sbornik nauchnykh trudov, posvjashchennuj 80–letiju so dnja rozhdenija Jakova Abramovicha Shera* (Archeology of Southern Siberia. Collection of Scientific Papers Dedicated to the 80th Anniversary of the Birth of Yakov Abramovich Sher) 25, edited by Lubov N. Ermolenko and Vladimir V. Bobrov: 54–64. Kemerovo: Kemerovo State University.

Gaiduchenko, Leonid L. 2014. Sem' tysyacheletii istorii kazakhskoi loshadi (Seven Millennia of the History of the Kazakh Horse). In: *Vsadniki Velikoy Stepi: traditsii i novatsii* (Riders of the Great Steppe: Traditions and Innovations). Proceedings of the Branch of the Institute of Archeology Named after Alikey Kh. Margulan, IV, edited by Akhan Ongar: 300–310. Astana: Alikey Kh. Margulan Institute of Archaeology.

Gaunitz, Charleen, Antoine Fages, Kristian Hanghøj et al. 2018. Ancient Genomes Revisit the Ancestry of Domestic and Przewalski's Horses. *Science* 360, (6384): 111–114. https://doi.org/10.1126/science.aao3297.

Gey, Alexandr N. 2000. *Novotitorovskaya kul'tura* (Novotitorovskaya culture). Moscow: Old Garden.

Grigoriev, Stanislav A. 2015. *Ancient Indo–Europeans*. Chelyabinsk: Cicero.

Grigoriev, Stanislav A. 2021. Archaeology, Genes and Language, The Indo–European Perspective. *Journal of Indo–European Studies* 49 (1–2): 187–230.

Grigoriev, Stanislav A. 2023. Horse and Chariot. Critical Reflections on one Theory. *Archaeologica Austriaca* 107: 1–32.

Jacobson–Tepfer, Esther. 2012. The Image of the Wheeled Vehicle in the Mongolian Altai: Instability and Ambiguity. *The Silk Road* 10: 1–28.

Jacobson–Tepfer, Esther and Viktor Novozhenov (eds.). 2020. *Naskal'nyye Letopisi Zolotoy Stepi ot Karatau do Altaya* (Rock Art Chronicles of the Golden Steppe: From Karatau to Altai). Vol. II. Almaty: UNESCO Center for the Rapprochement of Cultures.

Jeong, Choongwon, Ke Wang, Shevan Wilkin et al. 2020. A dynamic 6,000–Year Genetic History of Eurasia's Eastern Steppe. bioRxiv preprint. https://www.biorxiv.org/content/10.1101/2020.03.25.008078v1.

Hanks, Bryan K., Andrei V. Epimakhov and Colin Renfrew. 2007. Towards a Refined Chronology for the Bronze Age of the Southern Urals, Russia. *Antiquity* 81: 353–367. DOI: 10.1017/S0003598X00095235

Izbitser, Elena V. 2010. Kolesnitsa s tormozom ili reconstructsia bez tormozov (The Chariot with a brake or a reconstruction without brakes). *Stratum plus*. 2: 187–194.

Kasparov, Aleksei R. and Nina A. Avanesova. 2017. Ot Volgi do Zerafshana: mezhkul'turnye vzaimodeistviya v epokhu paleometalla (From the Volga to Zeravshan: Intercultural Interactions in the Era of the Paleometal). In: *Naslediye i sovremennost' v dialoge kul'tur ot Volgi do Zeravshana: Samara–Samarkand* (Heritage and Modernity in the Dialogue of Cultures from the Volga to the Zeravshan): Samara–Samarkand. Materials from the International Scientific Conf. (Samara, 2016) 2nd Edition Supplemented, edited by Vladimir I. Ionesov: 204–228. Samara: Institute of Culture.

Khodzhaev, Alijon. 2010. *Iz Istorii Rannikh Tyurkov* (From the History of the Ancient Turks). Tashkent: Publishing House of the Academy of Sciences of Uzbekistan.

Komisarov, Sergei A. 1988. *Kompleks Vooruzheniya Drevnego Kitaya. Pozdnyaya Bronza* (Battle Complex of Ancient China. Late Bronze Age). Novosibirsk: Nauka.

Kosintsev, Pavel A. 2010. Kolesnichnye loshadi (The Chariot Horses). In: *Horses, Chariots and Chariot's drivers of Eurasian Steppes*, edited by Pavel F. Kuznetsov, Anatolii N. Usachuk, Pavel A. Kosintsev, et al.: 21–79. Yekaterinburg, Samara, Donetsk: Rifey. https://www.academia.edu/31041303/Horses_chariots_and_chariots_drivevers_of_Eurasian_steppes_2010.

Kovalev, Alexei A. 1998. Drevneishie datirovannye pamyatniki skifo–sibirskogo zverinogo stilya (Nanshangan) (The Earliest Dated Monuments of the Scythian–Siberian Animal Style (Nanshangen type)). In: *Drevniye Kul'tury Sredney Azii i Sankt–Peterburga* (Ancient Cultures of Central Asia and St. Petersburg). Materials of the All–Russian Scientific Conference Dedicated to the 70th Anniversary of the Birth of A. D. Grach, edited by Sambu Ivan U. and Alexandr M. Reshetov: 122–131. St. Petersburg: Cult–Inform–Press.

Kovalev, Alexei A. 2008. Lokalizatsiya narodov 6–3 vekov do n.e. na severnykh granitsakh kitaiskikh gosudarstv po arkheologicheskim i pis'mennym dannym (Localization of the Peoples of the 6th–3rd Centuries BCE on the Northern Borders of Chinese States (According to Archaeological and Written Sources)). *Zapiski Instituta istorii material'noy kul'tury Rossiyskaya Akademiya Nauk*. Notes of the Institute of the History of Material Culture of the Russian Academy of Sciences 3: 181–202.

Kovalev, Alexei A. 2014. Proiskhozdenie skifov iz Dzungarii: proiskhozhdenie gipotezy i sovremennoe sostoyanie (The Origin of the Scythians from Dzungaria: The Basis of the Hypothesis and its Current State). In: *Arii Stepey Yevrazii: Bronzovyy i Ranniy Zheleznyy Veka vYyevraziyskikh Stepyakh i na Sopredel'nykh Territoriyakh* (Aryans of the Steppes of Eurasia: Bronze and Early Iron Ages in the Eurasian Steppes and in Adjacent Territories): Collection of Papers in Memory of Elena E. Kuzmina, edited by Konstantin E. Razlogov, Elena V. Antonova, Andrei V. Epimakhov et al.: 124–137. Barnaul: Publishing House of the Altai State University.

Kozhin, Pavel M. 2015. Drevnii koliosnyi transport: problemy i rabochie gipotezy (Ancient Wheeled Transport: State of Problems and Working Hypotheses). *Nauchnoye obozreniye Sayano–Altaya* (Scientific Review of Sayano–Altai) 1 (9). Series: Archaeology Vol. 2: 2–18.

Kozintsev, Alexandr. 2019. Proto–Indo–Europeans: The Prologue. *The Journal of Indo–European Studies* 47(3/4): 293–380.

Kristiansen, Kristian, Thomas Lindkvist and Janken Myrdal (eds.). 2018. *Trade and Civilisation: Economic Networks and Cultural Ties, from Prehistory to the Early Modern Era*. Cambridge: Cambridge University Press.

Kryukov, Mikhail V. 1970. *Etnicheskaya kartina mira v drevnekitaiskikh pis'mennykh istochnikakh II–I tysyacheletii do n. e.* (On the Ethnic Picture of the World in Ancient Chinese Written Monuments of the II–I Millennium BCE). *Ethnonyms*. Moscow: Nauka.

Kukushkin Igor A. 2011a Metallicheskie izdeliya ranneandronovskogo mogil'nika Atshisu (Metal Products of the Early Andronovo Burial Ground at Ashchisu). *Russian Archaeology* 2: 110–116.

Kukushkin, Igor A. 2011b. Arkheologicheskie kompleksy Kazakhstana s kolesnichnoi atributikoi (Archaeological Complexes of Kazakhstan with Chariot Attributes. A New Aspect in the Archaeology of Bronze of Kazakhstan). In *Svideteli Tysyacheletiya: Arkheologicheskaya Nauka Kazakhstana za 20 let (1991–2011)*. (Witnesses of the Millennium: 20 Years of Archaeological Science in Kazakhstan (1991–2011)) edited by Baurzhan Baitanayev and Arman Beisenov: 97–113. Almaty: Alikey Kh. Margulan Institute of Archaeology.

Kukushkin, Igor A. and Evgenii A. Dmitriev. 2019. Chariot Complex of the Tabylda Burial Ground (Central Kazakhstan). *Archaeology, ethnography and anthropology of Eurasia* 47(4): 43–52. https://rep.ksu.kz/handle/data/11885.

Kukushkin, Igor A., Eugeny A. Dmitriev and Alexei I. Kukushkin. 2018a. Pogrebenie petrovskoi kul'tury u sela Taldy v Karkaralinskom raione Karagandinskoi oblasti (Burial of Petrovka Culture Near the Village of Taldy (Karkaraly District of the Karaganda Region)). *Samarskiy nauchnyy vestnik* (Samara Scientific Herald), 2(23): 150–155.

Kukushkin, Igor A., Eugeny A. Dmitriev and Alexei I. Kukushkin. 2018b. Markery sotsial'noi stratifikatsii v epokhu bronzy (Markers of Social Stratification in the Bronze Age. In: *Margulan Readings. Spiritual Modernization and Archaeological Heritage* edited by Baurzhan Baitanayev and Arman Beisenov: 98–100. Almaty–Aktobe: Alikey Kh. Margulan Institute of Archaeology.

Kupriyanova, Elena, Andrei Epimakhov, Natalia Berseneva, and Andrei Bersenev. 2017. Bronze Age Charioteers of the Eurasian Steppe: a Part–Time Occupation for Select Men? *Prähistorische Zeitschrift* 92: 40–65.

Kuzmina, Elena E. 2007. *The Origin of the Indo–Iranians*, edited by James P. Mallory. Leiden Indo–European Etymological Dictionary Series 3. Leiden and Boston: Brill.

Kuzmina Elena E. 2008. *Arii – put' nay ug* (Aryans – The Path to the South). Moscow and St. Petersburg: KomKniga.

Kuzmina Elena E. 2010. *Predistoria Velikogo Shiolkovogo puti* (The Background of the Great Silk Road: Dialogue of Cultures Europe – Asia). Moscow: KomKniga,

Kuznetsov, Pavel F. 2006. The Emergence of Bronze Age Chariots in Eastern Europe. *Antiquity* 80(309): 638–645.

Kuznetsov, Pavel F., Anatolii N. Usachuk, Pavel A. Kosintsev, et al. (eds.). 2010. *Horses, Chariots and Chariot's Drivers of Eurasian Steppes*. Yekaterinburg, Samara, Donetsk: Rifey.

Librado, Pablo, Cristina Gamba, Charleen Gaunitz et al. 2017. Ancient Genomic Changes Associated with Domestication of the Horse. *Science* 356 (6336): 442–445. DOI: 10.1126/science.aam5298. PMID: 28450643.

Librado, Pablo, Naveed Khan, Antoine Fages et al. 2021. The Origins and Spread of Domestic Horses from the Western Eurasian Steppes. *Nature* 598: 634–640. DOI: 10.1038/s41586-021-04018-9.

Lindner, Stephan. 2020. Chariots in the Eurasian Steppe: a Bayesian Approach to the Emergence of Horse–Drawn Transport in the Early Second Millennium BCE. *Antiquity* 94 (374): 361–380. DOI: 10.15184/aqy.2020.37

Lindner, Stephan. 2021. *Die technische und symbolische Bedeutung eurasischer Streitwagen für Europa und die Nachbarräume im 2. Jahrtausend v. Chr.* Berliner archäologische Forschungen 20. Rahden/Westf.: Leidorf.

Littauer, Mary A. and Joost H. Crouwel. 1979. *Wheeled Vehicles and Ridden Animals in the Ancient Near East.* Leiden and Cologne: Brill.

Littauer, Mary A. and Joost H. Crouwel. 1996. The Origin of the True Chariot. *Antiquity* 70 (270): 934–939. (Reprinted in Littauer and Crouwel 2002, *Selected Writings on Chariots and Other Early Vehicles, Riding and Harness*, edited by Peter Raulwing. Culture and History of the Ancient Near East 6, 45–52. Leiden: Brill).

Mallory, James P., Anastasia Dybo and Oleg Balanovsky. 2019. The Impact of Genetics Research on Archaeology and Linguistics in Eurasia. *Russian Journal of Genetics*: 55 (12): 1472–1487. https://doi.org/10.1134/S1022795419120081.

Maliavkin, Igor G. 1981. *Istoricheskaya Geographia Sredney Azii* (Historical Geography of Central Asia). Novosibirsk: Nauka.

Mariashev, Aleksei N. 2011. Naskal'noie iskusstvo v Kazakhstane: rezul'taty 20 let izuchenia i problemy (Rock Art of Kazakhstan: Results of a 20-Year Study and Problems). In: *Arkheologiya Kazakhstana v Epokhu Nezavisimosti: Itogi i Perspektivy* (Archaeology of Kazakhstan in the Era of Independence: Results and Prospects). Materials of the International Scientific Conference Dedicated to the 20th Anniversary of Independence of the Republic of Kazakhstan and the 20th Anniversary of the Institute of Archaeology Named after A. Kh. Margulan. Vol. 1, edited by Baurzhan A Baitanaev and Arman Z. Beisenov: 36–40. Almaty: Alikey Kh. Margulan Institute of Archaeology.

Mariashev, Aleksei N. and Aleksei E. Rogozhinsky. 1991. *Petroglyphy v Gorakh Eshkiolmes* (Petroglyphs in the Mountains of Yeshkiolmes). Alma Ata: Alikey Kh. Margulan Institute of Archaeology.

Mariashev, Aleksei N. and Alexandr Goryachev. 2002. *Naskal'noe Iskusstvo Semirech'ya* (Rock Art of Semirechie). Almaty: Alikey Kh. Margulan Institute of Archaeology.

Masson, Vadim M. 2006. *Kul'turogenez Drevnei Srednei Azii* (Cultural Genesis of Ancient Central Asia). St. Petersburg: Institute for the History of Material Culture of Russian Academy of Sciences.

Miller, Bryan. 2012. Vehicles of the Steppe Elite: Chariots and Carts in Xiongnu Tombs. *The Silk Road* 10: 29–38.

Monna, Fabrice, Tanguy Roland, Jerome Magail et al. 2022. ERA: A New, Fast, Machine Learning–Based Software to Document Rock Painting. *Journal of Cultural Heritage* 58: 91–101. https://doi.org/10.1016/j.culher.2022.09.018.

Nikolaeva, Nadezhda A. 2019a. The Most Ancient History of the Ciscaucasia in the Light of the Concept of Indo–European Migrations (Part 1). *Oriental Studies* 43 (3): 355–366. https://doi.org/10.22162/2619-0990-2019-43-3-355-366.

Nikolaeva, Nadezhda A. 2019b. The Most Ancient History of the Ciscaucasia in the Light of the Concept of Indo–European Migrations (Part 2). *Oriental Studies* 44 (4): 570–579. https://doi.org/10.22162/2619-0990-2019-44-4-570-579

Novozhenov, Viktor A. 2012a. *Chudo Kommunikatsii i Drevneyshiy Kolesnyy Transport Yevrazii* (Communications and Earliest Wheeled Transport of Eurasia). Moscow: Taus Publishing. https://www.academia.edu/5159110/Communications_and_the_Earliest_Wheeled_Transport_of_Eurasia

Novozhenov, Viktor A. 2012b. Ranneandronovskie kolesnichnye innovatsii i nekotorye aspekty genezisa kitaiskoi tsivilizatsii (Early Andronovo Chariot Innovations and Some Aspects of the Genesis of Chinese Civilization). In: *Kul'tury Evraziiskoi Stepi i Ikh Vzaimodeistvie s Drevneishimi Tsivilizatsiyami* (Cultures of the Eurasian Steppe and Their Interaction with Ancient Civilizations). Materials of the International Scientific Conference Dedicated to the 110th Birthday of the Outstanding Russian Archaeologist Mikhail P. Gryaznov). Vol. 2, edited by Vadim A. Aliokshin, Maya E. Kashuba et al.: 183–187. St. Petersburg: Institute for the History of Material Culture of Russian Academy of Sciences.

Novozhenov Viktor A. 2014a. Velikaya step': chelovek v sisteme drevnikh kommunikatsii. (The Great Steppe: A Human in the System of Ancient Communication). In: *Tainstvo Etnicheskoi Istorii Rannikh Kochevnikov Stepnoi Evrazii* (Sacrament of the Ethnic History of the Ancient Nomads of Steppe Eurasia) edited by Andrei V. Epimakhov: 18–267. Almaty: Ostrov Krim.

Novozhenov, Viktor A. 2014b. Andronovskaya izobrazitel'naya traditsiya v petroglifakh epokhi bronzy Tsentral'noi Azii (Andronovo Fine Tradition in the Petroglyphs of the Bronze Age of Central Asia). In: *Arii Stepey Yevrazii: Bronzovyy i Ranniy Zheleznyy Veka vYyevraziyskikh Stepyakh i na Sopredel'nykh Territoriyakh* (Aryans of the Steppes of Eurasia: Bronze and Early Iron Ages in the Eurasian Steppes and in Adjacent Territories): Collection of Papers in Memory of Elena E. Kuzmina, edited by Konstantin E. Razlogov, Elena V. Antonova, Andrei V. Epimakhov et al.: 455–468. Barnaul: Publishing house of Altai State University.

Novozhenov, Viktor A. 2015. Wheeled Transport and Eurasian Communications of the Early Nomads. *Stratum plus* 3: 57–88.

Novozhenov, Viktor A. 2016. Kommunikatsii i transport strany Margush v prostranstve i vo vremeni (Communication and Transport of the Country of Margush in Space and in Time). In: *Raboty Margianskoy Arkheologicheskoy Ekspeditsii* (Works of the Margiana Archaeological Expedition) vol. 6. In Memory of Victor Ivanovich Sarianidi, edited by Nadezhda A. Dubova: 361–377. Moscow: Starii Sad.

Novozhenov, Viktor A. 2017. Indoiranskaya mifologicheskaya traditsiya v petroglifakh Kazakhstana i Trentral'noi Azii: mif sozdaniya cheloveka i chudesnye povozki (Indo–Iranian Mythological Tradition in Petroglyphs of Kazakhstan and Central Asia: The Myth of the Creation of Man and the "Wonderful" cart). In: *Religions of Kazakhstan and Central Asia on the Great Silk Road.* Materials of the International Scientific and Practical Conference, June 12–13, 2017, edited by Karl M. Baipakov and Viktor A. Novozhenov: 334–358. Almaty: UNESCO Centre for the Rapprochement of Cultures.

Novozhenov, Viktor A. 2018. Kommunikatsii i koliosnyi transport na Velikom Shiolkovom puti (Communications and Wheeled Transport on the Great Silk Road). In: *Central Asia on the Great Silk Road: A Dialogue of Cultures and Faiths from Antiquity to the Present,* edited by Karl M. Baipakov and Viktor A. Novozhenov: 241–263. Almaty: UNESCO Center for the Rapprochement of Cultures.

Novozhenov, Viktor A. 2019. Model' kommunikatsii rannikh kochevnikov Tsentral'noi Azii (The Communication Model of the Early Nomads of Central Asia). In: *Skifiya i Sarmatiya* (Scythia and Sarmatia) (Materials of the International Scientific Conference "New in the Studies of the Early Iron Age of Eurasia: Problems, Discoveries, Methods"), edited by Nikolai Markov: 159–181. Moscow: Institute of Archaeology of Russian Academy of Sciences.

Novozhenov, Viktor A. 2020. *The Rock Art Chronicles of Golden Steppe: Model of Communication in Antiquity and Middle Ages.* Vol. 1. Almaty: UNESCO Centre for the Rapprochement of Cultures.

Novozhenov, Viktor A. 2021. Naskal'nye izobrazheniya kolesnits kak istochnik rekonstruktsii (Rock Carvings of Chariots as a Source of Reconstruction). In: *Ancient Art in the Context of the Cultural and Historical Processes of Eurasia: on the 300th Anniversary of the Scientific Discovery of the Tomsk Pisanitsa,* edited by Anna Mukhareva, Elena Miklashevich et al.: 214–237. Kemerovo: Kemerovo University Press.

Novozhenov, Viktor A. 2022. Boevye sani i kolesnitsy Moldazhara (Battle Sledge and Chariots of Moldazhar). In: *Eurasia from the Aeneolithic (Chalcolithic) Era to the Early Middle Ages (Innovaton, Contacts, Transmission of Ideas and Technology).* Proceedings of the International Conference Dedicated to the 120th Anniversary of the Outstanding Researcher of Southern Siberian and Central Asian Antiquities Mikhail Petrovich Gryaznov (1902–1984), edited by Maya T. Kashuba, Nikolai Yu. Smirnov, Evgeniy O. Stoyanov et al.: 387–391. St. Petersburg: Institute for the History of Material Culture of Russian Academy of Sciences.

Novozhenov, Viktor A. and Kirim Altinbekov. 2014. Ob ispol'zovanii kolesnits v epokhu rannikh kochevnikov (On the Use of Chariots in the Era of the Early Nomads). In: *Voskhozhdeniye k Vershinam Arkheologii* (Ascent to the Heights of Archaeology): A Collection of Materials of the International Scientific Conference "Ancient and Medieval States in Kazakhstan" Dedicated to the 90th Anniversary of the Birth of Kimal A. Akishev, edited by Karl M. Baipakov: 231–247. Almaty: Alikei Kh. Margulan Institute of Archaeology.

Novozhenov, Viktor A. and Aibek Zh. Sidikov. 2019. Bronze Age Transeurasian Communications. *Otan Tarikhy.* 3 (87): 183–204.

Novozhenov, Viktor A. and Aleksei E. Rogozhinsky. 2019. Novye syuzhety s kolesnitsami v petrogliphakh doliny reki Koksu (Eshkiol'mes) (New Chariot Plots in the Petroglyphs of the Koksu River Valley (Yeshkiolmes)). In: *Istoriya i Arkheologiya Semirech'ya* (History and Archaeology of Semirechye): Collection of Articles and Publications. Vol. 6: 170–196. Almaty: Alikey Kh. Margulan Institute of Archaeology.

Novozhenov, Viktor A. and Roman V Ilin. 2021. Tsifrovaya tekhnologiya kopirovaniya izobrazitel'nykh pamiatnikov (Digital Technology of Copying Pictorial Monuments). In: *Proverka Garmonii Algebroy* (Verifying Harmony by Algebra). Collection of Articles in Memory of Yakov Abramovich Sher, edited by Leonid B. Vishniatsky and Konstantin V. Chugunov: 192–206. St. Petersburg: Institute for the History of Material Culture of Russian Academy of Sciences.

Outram, Alan K. 2014. Animal Domestications. In: *The Oxford Handbook of the Archaeology and Anthropology of Hunter – Gatherers,* edited by Vicki Cummings, Peter Jordan and Marek Zvelebil: 749–764. Oxford: Oxford University Press.

Piankov, Igor V. 2013. *Srednyaya Aziya i Evraziiskaya Step' v Drevnosti.* (Central Asia and Eurasian Steppe in Antiquity). St. Petersburg: Petersburg Linguistic Society.

Piankov, Igor. V. 2015. Etnokul'turnye protsessy v evraziiskoi stepi (Ethnocultural Processes in the Eurasian Steppes (Late 2nd – First Half of 1st Millennium BCE) In: *Saka Culture of Saryarka in the Context of the Study of Ethno–Socio–Cultural Processes in the Steppe Eurasia.* Collection of Scientific Articles Dedicated to the Memory of Archaeologist Kimal Akishevich Akishev edited by Arman Z. Beisenov: 233–243. Almaty: Alikei Kh. Margulan Institute of Archaeology.

Piggott, Stuart. 1983. *The Earliest Wheeled Transport from the Atlantic Coast to the Caspian Sea.* London: Thames and Hudson.

Piggott, Stuart. 1992. *Wagon, Chariot, and Carriage. Symbol and Status in the History of Transport.* London: Thames and Hudson.

Rogozhinski, Aleksei E. (ed). 2004. Rock Art Monuments of Central Asia. Public Participation, Management, Conservation, Documentation. Almaty: Iskander.

Rogozhinski, Aleksei E. and Viktor A. Novozhenov. 2018. Cultural Landscapes with Petroglyphs of Central Asia: Questions and Answers. Samarkand: International Institute for the Central Asian Study.

Rolland, Tanguy, Fabrice Monna, Jean F. Buoncristiani et al. 2022. Volumetric Obscurance as a New Tool to Better Visualize Relief from Digital Elevation Models. *Remote Sensing* 44 (4): 941. DOI: 10.3390/rs14040941.

Rozwadowski, Andrjei. 2020. Rock Art as a Source of History in Central Asia. In: *Encyclopédie des Historiographies: Afriques, Amériques, Asies*: Volume 1: Sources et genres historiques (Tome 1 et Tome 2) edited by Nathalie Kouamé, Éric P. Meyer and Anne Viguier: 1520–1535. Paris: Presses de l'Inalco. DOI: 10.4000/books.pressesinalco.29472.

Samashev, Zeinolla. 2018. *Petroglyphs of Tarbagatai. Shimaily.* Astana: Kazakh Research Institute of Culture.

Sarianidi Victor I. 2010. *Zadolgo do Zaratushtry. Arkheologicheskiye svidetel'stva protozoroostrizma v Baktrii i Margiane* (Long Before Zarathustra. Archaeological Evidence of Protozoroostrism in Bactria and Margiana). Moscow: Starii Sad

Savinov, Dmitri G. 2021. Na puti izucheniya coderzhaniya pamyatnikov naskal'nogo iskusstva (On the Way to Discover the Content of Rock Art Monuments). In: *Ancient Art in the Context of the Cultural and Historical Processes of Eurasia: on the 300th Anniversary of the Scientific Discovery of the Tomsk Pisanitsa,* edited by Anna Mukhareva, Elena Miklashevich et al. 238–249. Kemerovo: Kemerovo University Press.

Sdikov, Murat N. and Yana A. Lukpanova. 2013. Rannie kochevniki Zapadnogo Kazakhstana (Early Nomads of Western Kazakhstan (the Example of the Taksai I Complex)). Uralsk: Polygraphservice.

Sikora, Martin, Vladimir V. Pitulko, Victor C. Sousa et al. 2019. The Population History of Northeastern Siberia since the Pleistocene. *Nature* 570: 182–188. DOI: 10.1038/s41586-019-1279-z

Sima Qian. 1993. *Records of the Grand Historian. Han Dynasty,* II Translation by B. Watson. Hong Kong and New York: Columbia University Press.

Sher, Yakov A. 1980. *Perogliphy Sredney Azii.* (Petroglyphs of Central Asia). Moscow: Nauka.

Shvets, Irina N. 2012. *Studien zur Felsbildkunst Kasachstans*. Materialien zur Archäologie Kasachstans. Bd.1. Darmstadt and Mainz: von Zabern.

Smirnov, Nikolai Yu. 2012. What did the Arzhan "King" Ride on? In: *Kul'tury Evraziiskoi Stepi i Ikh Vzaimodeistvie s Drevneishimi Tsivilizatsiyami* (Cultures of the Eurasian Steppe and Their Interaction with Ancient Civilizations). Materials of the International Scientific Conference Dedicated to the 110th Birthday of the Outstanding Russian Archaeologist Mikhail P. Gryaznov). Vol. 2, edited by Elena V. Bobrovskaya et al.: 424–431. St. Petersburg: Institute for the History of Material Culture of Russian Academy of Sciences.

Spruytte, Jean. 1983. *Early Harness Systems. Experimental Studies*. London: Allen. (Translation by Mary A. Littauer of *Etudes Expérimentales sur l'Attelage,* Paris: Crepin Lebond 1977*).*

Summerer, Latife. 2007. Picturing Persian Victory: The Painted Battle Scene on the Munich Wood. Achaemenid Culture and Local Traditions in Anatolia, Southern Caucasus and Iran. New Discoveries. In: *Ancient Civilizations from Scythia to Siberia* 13 (1–2) edited by Ascold Ivantchik: 3–30. Leiden: Brill. DOI: 10.1163/157005707X212643.

Sun Tzu. 2014 (edition). *The Art of War*. Translation and Commentary by Nikolai I. Conrad. St. Petersburg: ABC–Atticus.

Tairov, Alexandr. D. 2007. *Rannie Kochevniki Zhayik–Irtyshskogo Mezhdurechiya v 8–6 Vekakh do n. e.* (Early Nomads of the Zhayyk–Irtysh Interfluve in the 8th–6th Centuries BCE). Astana: Alikei Kh. Margulan Institute of Archaeology.

Teufer, Mike. 2012. Der Streitwagen: eine «indo-iranische» Erfindung? Zum Problem der Verbindung von Sprachwissenschaft und Archäologie. *Archäologische Mitteilungen aus Iran und Turan* 44: 271–312.

Usmanova, Emma R., Igor V. Chechushkov, Pavel A. Kosintsev et al. 2018. Loshad' v dukhovnoi kul'ture i v sotsial'noi structure naseleniya uralo–kazakhstanskikh stepei (The Horse in the Spiritual Culture and Social Structure of the Population of the Ural–Kazakhstan Steppes in the Bronze Age (Based on Materials from Novoilinovski II Burial Ground)). In: *Yevraziyskaya Step' v Eepokhu Bronzy: Kul'tury, Idei, Tekhnologii* (The Eurasian Steppe in the Bronze Age: Cultures, Ideas, Technologies). Collection of Scientific Articles on the Occasion of the 80th Anniversary of Gennady Borisovich Zdanovich, edited by Dmitri G. Zdanovich: 198–215. Chelyabinsk: State University Press.

Varfolomeev, Victor V., Valery G. Loman and Valery V. Evdokimov. 2017. *Kent – gorod epokhi bronzy v tsentre Kazakhskoi stepi.* (Kent – The Bronze Age City in the Center of the Kazakh Steppes*).* Materials and Research on Cultural Heritage XI. Astana: Kazakh Research Institute of Culture.

Vinogradov, Nikolai B. 2003. *Mogil'nik Epokhi Bronzy Krivoie Ozero v Yuzhnom Zaural'e* (Bronze Age Burial Ground Krivoie Ozero in the South Trans–Urals). Chelyabinsk: South Ural Publishing House.

Wagner, Mayke. 2004. Wagenbestattungen im bronzezeitlichen China. In: *Rad und Wagen. Der Ursprung einer Innovation Wagen im Vorderen Orient und Europa*, edited by: Mamoun Fansa and Stefan Burmeister*:* 107–122*.* Mainz: von Zabern.

Wang Pan. 2019. Proiskhozhdenie kolesnits Yangsu 1. (On the Origin of Yinxu 1 Chariots). *Bulletin of the Novosibirsk State University.* Series *History, Philology.* 19 (4): 9–18.

Wang, Chuan–Chao, Hui–Yuan Yeh, Alexander N. Popov et al. 2020. The Genomic Formation of Human Populations in East Asia, bioRxiv preprint. DOI: 10.1101/2020.03.25.004606

Wilhelm, Gernot. 1989. *The Hurrians*. Warminster: Aris & Phillips.

Wu, Hsiao–yun. 2009. Zhongguo zaoqi zhanche muzang yanjiu 中国早期战车墓葬研究 (*Study on Chariot Burials in Early China, 1200–210 BCE.*) Aurora Center for the Study of Ancient Civilization. Peking University Publication Series 20. Beijing: Kexue chubanshe.

Wu, Hsiao–yun. 2011. Mache zai zaoqi dongxi jiaoliu Zhong di diwei yu jiaoliu moshi Xiyuan qian 2000-1200 馬車在早期東西交流中的地位與交流模式：西元前2000-1200年 (The Role of the Transmission of Chariots in Early East–West Interaction: 2000–1200 BCE. *The National Palace Museum Research Quarterly* 28 (4): 119–132.

Wu, Hsiao–yun. 2013. *Chariots in Early China: Origins, Cultural Interaction and Identity* BAR International Series (S2457). Oxford: BAR Publishing.

Xiaoshan Qi and Wang Bo. 2008. *The Ancient Culture in Xinjiang along the Silk Road*. Xinjiang: Xinjiang People's Publishing House; Xinjiang–Uygur Autonomous Region International Cultural Exchange Association.

Yang, Jianhua, Huiqi Shao and Ling Pan. 2020. *The Metal Road of the Eastern Eurasian Steppe. The Formation of the Xiongnu Confederation and the Silk Road.* Singapore: Springer. DOI: 10.1007/978-981-32-9155-3_1.

Zaitseva, Galina I., Nadezhda A. Dubova, Alexandr A Sementsov et al. 2008. Radiouglerodnaya khronologiya pamyatnika Gonur tepe (Radiocarbon Chronology of the Gonur–depe Monument). In: *Raboty Margianskoy arkheologicheskoy ekspeditsii* (Works of the Margiana Archaeological Expedition) 2: 166–178. Moscow: Nauka.

Zhong, Suk–Bae. 2000. O datirovke kompleksov s kinzhalami epokhi pozdnei bronzy iz severnogo Kitaya (On the Chronology of Complexes with Daggers of the Late Bronze Age from North China). In: *Archaeology, Paleoecology and Paleodemography of Eurasia* edited by Vadim Olshansky: 110–137. Moscow: Geos; Institute of Archaeology of Russian Academy of Sciences.

13

When Chariots Were First Known in China: Early Cheekpiece Development in the Late Shang Dynasty Around 1250 BCE

Hsiao-yun Wu

Horse drawn chariots suddenly appeared in the Shang dynasty, around 1200 BCE. The Shang elite buried horses and chariots with splendid bronze ornaments and weapons in royal ritual places and cemeteries at the Shang capital at present day Anyang, Henan. The great number of Shang style items and weapons indicates that chariots became accoutrements of war and marks of prestige for royalty soon after their introduction. Previous studies have paid attention to the role of chariots as war and prestige items in Shang society and their association with the steppes. How to deal with the new technology in practical terms is much less discussed. When the Shang elite decided to build and use their own chariots, how to control chariot horses efficiently was one of the problems to deal with. To further explore the Shang elite's adoption of steppe chariot driving, this article will explore the harness technology by examining the earliest Shang cheekpieces found at Anyang, dating to the 13th century BCE. This article aims to analyse the variation in shape of those cheekpieces to present the Shang elite's earliest consideration of the adoption of horses and chariots and the decisions they made. What happened when the Shang elite faced driving and riding people? Did they ever have the opportunity to choose which skills to adopt? This article will also discuss contemporary steppe groups in the eastern part of the Eurasian steppes to provide a further understanding of the possible multiple sources of chariot knowledge.

Introduction

In contrast to the long and gradual development in the Eurasian Steppes, the sudden appearance of horse drawn chariots in early China is a totally different story. In the archaeological record, well-developed chariots with their horse teams appeared in royal ritual places and cemeteries at the Shang capital at present day Anyang, Henan. They were soon used as accoutrements of war and markers of prestige, as indicated by the countless bronze accessories and weapons buried with them.[1]

The earliest examples known today are dated to the latter half of the 13th century BCE, the time of the best known and longest reigning late Shang ruler, Wu Ding. His reign was a highly active period of cultural interactions and trade. As seen in the tomb of Fu Hao, one of his consorts, exotic burial goods, including mirrors from the northwest, weapons associated with the Shang frontier, and jades from the north, east and south, demonstrate strong links to the world beyond Shang territory.[2] In addition to the possession of exotic artefacts, her tomb also yielded a pair of small jade horses, a pair of cheekpieces and a set of bronze bridle ornaments (Figure 13.1).[3] Their presence implies the extraordinary possession of the newly introduced horses and driving skills, which were previously unknown.

The jade horses from the tomb of Fu Hao are rendered in a realistic style. They have short necks, legs and manes. Scholars have shown that although horses had appeared in several parts of modern China as early as in the late Pleistocene, Neolithic, and early Bronze periods, they were rare, and there is no evidence that they were used for transportation.[4] As shown by the archaeological finds at Anyang, when horses suddenly appeared in great numbers in burial contexts along with chariots in the heartland of the Central Plain, they were already domesticated and well-trained for draught.

Since the horse drawn chariot is a new feature in the burial context in Wu Ding's time, the horse and the chariot are thought to have been introduced into China as a package. However, woodworking skills for chariot building and the veterinary specialist knowledge needed for horse raising and training belong to quite different types of knowledge systems. The finds from the tomb of Fu Hao seem to suggest a more complex situation. They do not include chariot fittings, but there was a set of horse bridle fittings in the lower part of the shaft of the tomb. The presence of one pair of cheekpieces (Figure 13.1) and one headstall seems to indicate that they belong to only one horse. While a chariot needs paired horses for draught, the presence of only one bridle set in the tomb suggests that horses could be used singly. The most likely use of a single bridled horse would be for riding. Accompanying the bridle was a typical weapon-and-tool set, including *ge* blades,

---

[1] Wu 2013: 29–56.
[2] Many articles discuss the exotic items of the tomb of Fu Hao. For a most recent one, see He 2020.
[3] Institute of Archaeology, CASS 1980.
[4] Linduff 2003: 141–148; Flad et al. 2007: 167–203; Kikuchi 2019: 139–141.

arrows, and a steppe style bow-shaped object. The two terminals of the bow-shaped object are in the shape of horse heads in realistic style similar to the jade horses (Figure 13.1). The finds indicate an emphasis on the unusual status of horses in Shang society. Furthermore, several scholars have suggested that Fu Hao probably came from the steppe.[5]

While most previous researchers treat the horse and chariot related finds of the late Shang period as a whole, this article will particularly focus on a rather short period, the Wu Ding reign, ca. 1258–1200 BCE.[6] It was the time when the chariot and horse had just been introduced to the Central Plain. When the Shang elite decided to build and use their own chariots, one of the problems they faced must have been how to manage steppe horses effectively. This article will examine the harness items to explore the Shang elite's adoption of steppe equestrian skills. In the late Shang burial context, most headstalls, mouthpieces, and bridle straps were made of organic materials, which have vanished after being buried for thousands of years. However, a number of bronze cheekpieces and bridle-related items have survived. They provide useful information on the possible structure of horse bridles, and their variation can represent the Shang elite's adaptation to the newly introduced horse and chariot skills. This article aims to analyse the variation of the cheekpieces and related items to present the Shang elite's earliest consideration of the adoption of horses and chariots and the decisions they made. What happened when the Shang encountered driving and riding people? Did they have the opportunity to choose which skills to adopt? This article will also discuss contemporary steppe groups in the eastern part of the Eurasian steppes to provide a further understanding of the possible multiple sources of knowledge of horse behavior and chariot technology.

Early Horse and Chariot Burial Context at Anyang

Chronology

The chronology of the late Shang dynasty at the capital of Yin 殷 at present day Anyang has been established from transmitted texts, oracle bone inscriptions and archaeology. It is believed that King Pan Geng 盘庚 moved to this thirteenth capital of the Shang, which was the last and most long-lasting of the dynasty. Wu Ding was the fourth ruler at the capital. The lineage of the Shang kings settled at Yin is documented in the oracle bone inscriptions discovered at Xiaotun, Anyang on the southern bank of the Huan 洹 River, where the royal palaces were located. In addition, large cemeteries of the royal family were found to the north of the Huan River at Xibeigang, Anyang. Koji Mizoguchi and Junko Uchida's recent study demonstrates a sequence for the tombs of the Shang kings buried there, and suggests tomb HPKM1400 is the tomb of Wu Ding,[7] though this issue is still debated.[8]

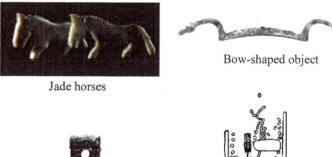

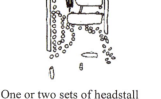

Figure 13.1. Horse and chariot related items from the tomb of Fu Hao. After Institute of Archaeology, CASS 1980: fig. 4, plates 30, 74, 75.

After Anyang was identified as the capital Yin by archaeologists in the early twentieth century, the site is usually referred to Yinxu, the ruins of Yin, and the period of the Shang dynasty there is called the Yinxu period or the late Shang period. Traditionally, the Yinxu period is divided into four phases. The major part of the Wu Ding reign belongs to Yinxu phase II. With the discoveries at Huanbei Shangcheng on the northern bank of the Huan river from 1997, the divisions of the late Shang period became more complex. More and more scholars now believe that it was Wu Ding who moved the palace from Huanbei to Xiaotun, where some of the earliest horse-and-chariot burials were found.[9]

If it is accepted that horses and chariots were exotic items from the borderlands to their north and west, it is also necessary to address the question about who were the contemporary inhabitants there during the reign of Wu Ding. As many studies have shown, the northern artefacts from the tomb of Fu Hao were associated with areas which include the steppes in present day Xinjiang, Mongolia, the Hexi Corridor in Gansu and Qinghai, and the Loess Highland in Shanxi and Shaanxi.[10] Horse herders and chariot builders and drivers probably lived in those areas and many have been associated with horse and chariot using peoples in the further northern and western steppes. In the northwest, particularly in Xinjiang, archaeological finds show strong

---

[5] So and Bunker 1995: 27; Linduff 2006: 365.
[6] The date of the reign of Wu Ding follows Hwang 2018.
[7] Mizoguchi and Uchida 2018: 709–723.
[8] Wang 2018: 23–37.
[9] Wang 2006, 2018; Mizoguchi and Uchida 2018: 720.
[10] Lin 1998b: 262–288; Bagley 1999: 197–198; Linduff 2006: 364–367; Wu 2017: 14–15.

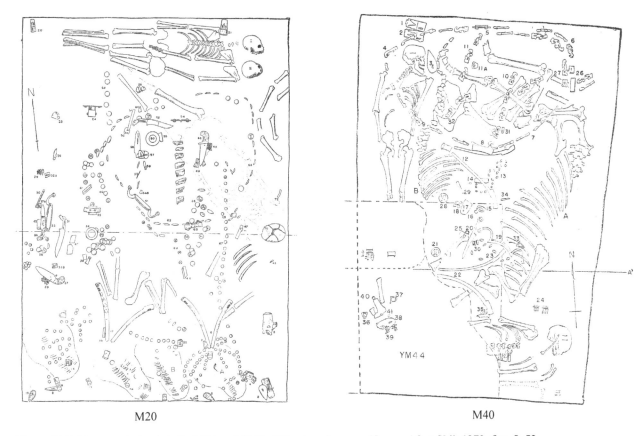

Figure 13.2. Horse-and-chariot pits M20 and M40 at Xiaotun, Anyang, Henan. After Shih 1970: figs. 8, 52.

features of the Andronovo culture (ca. 1800–1200 BCE).[11] As many scholars have pointed out, it was through this culture that the concept of chariot use was possibly transmitted from the eastern Eurasian steppes and eventually to the Central Plain.[12] The bow-shaped objects and a knife with an animal-head pommel from the tomb of Fu Hao can be linked to the Karasuk culture (ca. 1400–1000 BCE) in the Minusinsk basin in Southern Siberia.[13]

Tombs

Remains of chariots are rarely found in tombs, although remains of chariot boxes are reported from a royal tomb, HPKM 1001, at Xibeigang, Anyang.[14] Unusual examples are known from two tombs with ramps, M1 and M18, at a cemetery of a Shang outpost at Qiaobei, Shanxi. One complete chariot with two horses is well displayed on the upper part of the ramp. In M1, a human figure is placed in front of the chariot.[15]

Unlike the tomb of Fu Hao, horse and chariot related items are seldom found in tombs. Only one C-shaped mouthpiece is known from a small contemporary tomb M33 in a Shang cemetery at Hougang, Anyang (Figure 13.3).[16]

Horse-and-Chariot Pits

Horses and chariots are mainly buried together in pits specific to them, and positioned as if in use. In a small number of cases, horses and chariots are placed in separate pits.

Elements of horse bridles similar to those from the tomb of Fu Hao are found in horse-and-chariot pits at the palace area at Xiaotun where there are five known horse-and-chariot pits. All the pits contain human sacrifices,[17] where pits YM20 and YM40 are well preserved (Figure 13.2). YM40 contains a chariot drawn by two horses. The horse heads no longer exist, but the pit yielded cheekpieces identical to those from the tomb of Fu Hao. YM20 contains two pair-horse chariots. On the four horse heads are bronze headstall ornaments and cheekpieces next to the horses' mouths. The chariots in the two pits are dismantled, but since their arrangement is basically according to the chariot structure, it is easy to identify their sizes and shapes. The round chariot boxes are particularly distinctive.[18]

In addition to Xiaotun, horse and chariot burials are also found in the royal cemetery at Xibeigang. The largest tomb in the cemetery is HPKM1400, including the one

---

[11] Kuzmina 1998: 63–93; Peng 1998:573–580; Mei and Shell 1999: 570–578; Mei 2000: 66–67; Kohl 2007: 237–241; Shui 2001: 6–46; Shao 2009: 81–97.
[12] Barbieri-Low 2000; 2010; Kuzmina 2008: 57–58; Anthony 2007: 456–457; Wu 2013: 29–56.
[13] Lin 1986: 265–267; Wu and Wagner 1999; Legrand 2006: 855–858.
[14] Liang 1962: 66–67.
[15] Qiaobei Archaeology Team 2006: 347–394.
[16] Institute of Archaeology, CASS 1993: 891, 896; Chang 2019: 60.
[17] Apart from one pit which is seriously damaged, the other four pits contain human remains. Shih 1970: 15–233.
[18] Shih 1970: 15–233.

that probably belonged to Wu Ding, as mentioned above.[19] Around HPKM1400 are close to one thousand sacrificial pits, including the largest chariot pit and horse pit of the Shang dynasty known today. Different from the arrangement at Xiaotun, chariots and horses there were buried in separate pits on a large scale. The chariot pit HPKM1136-1137, dating to ca. 1200 BCE, contains more than forty chariots. As Ming-chorng Hwang suggests, three adjacent large horse pits, HPKM 1162, 1220, and 1221 together with the chariot pit form a burial set. The chariots had been dismantled before being buried and the chariot bodies and other parts were placed in a disorderly fashion in the pit, while the dismounted axles were located together on the southern side.[20] Apart from numerous splendid chariot ornaments, the chariot pit yielded several kinds of cheekpieces. No detailed information on the three horse pits has been published, but we at least know that HPKM 1162 yielded cheekpieces.

Horse Pits

Horse pits were also found at Anyang, including a group of horse pits belonging to tomb HPKM1001 at Xibeigang. The tomb used to be assigned to Wu Ding, but now scholars tend to think it belonged to Wu Ding's predecessor, the Shang king Xiao Yi, who was buried on the orders of Wu Ding.[21] The horse pits are sacrificial pits also dated to the Wu Ding period. Each contains two, three, or four horses. No chariot related items were excavated, but delicate headstalls were found on the horses' heads. Among them, the bridle from horse pit HPKM1911 has cheekpieces similar to those from the tomb of Fu Hao.[22]

A much debated example of the Wu Ding period, as I will show below, is the horse pit M164 in the palace area at Xiaotun. The pit contains one horse and one human figure. On the horse's head is a frontlet ornament composed of a shell and jades. In front of its mouth is a C-shaped mouthpiece (Figure 13.1). The man is next to the horse and is accompanied by a weapon-and-tool set similar to those found in YM20, YM40, and the tomb of Fu Hao.[23]

Early Types of Cheekpieces and Related Items

The cheekpieces are particularly numerous in the above burial context, and they have many variations in shapes. Hwang divides late Shang cheekpieces into four categories: plaque-shaped, plaque-shaped with animal design, L-shaped, and rod-shaped.[24] Only the second category, a later variation of the first type, does not date to the Wu Ding period. I will examine the cheekpieces and related items of the Wu Ding period in further detail below.

Plaque Cheekpieces

The plaque cheekpiece is the favoured type of cheekpiece of the time. It is a square plaque with a round hole in the centre and two parallel tubes attached to two sides. According to its attachments, this type can be further divided into three sub-types: square plaque, square plaque with a loop, square plaque with a loop and two protruding tubes.

The square plaque cheekpiece is the simplest in shape (Figure 13.1). It was found in the tomb of Fu Hao, in horse-and-chariot pits YM40, YM202 and in horse pit HPKM1162. This is the simplest design and represents the most basic requirement for a cheekpiece: the central hole held a mouthpiece; the two tubes functioned as guides for straps to pass through so that the cheekpiece could be attached to a headstall.

The square plaque cheekpiece with a loop is similar to the previous type (Figure 13.3.2). It has been found in horse-and-chariot pit YM20 and horse pit HPKM1162. While no attachments have been found in burial contexts, there is evidence to show the function of the loop. However, from later Shang horse-and-chariot pits, M41 at Qianzhangda, Shandong for example, we know that the loop is on the side when fastened on a headstall[25] (Figure 13.4.1).

The third type is similar to the second, but the tubes protrude from one side. The terminals of the tubes are flattened (Figure 13.3.3). This type has only been found in the large chariot pit HPKM1136-1137. The very long and flat tubes indicate a need to separate the two cheek straps of the headstall. The flat terminals show the possible width and shape of the straps, and made the straps steadier than the short round tubes.

In later periods, the second type became the most commonly used type of cheekpiece and they are frequently found in Shang burial contexts of the Yinxu phase III and IV. They are also frequently unearthed in early Western Zhou dynasty contexts which succeeded the Shang.[26]

L-shaped Cheekpieces

This type has only been found in the large chariot pit HPKM1136-1137. It looks like a simplified plaque cheekpiece. The body is thin, and bent into an L-shape. There is a large round hole for a mouthpiece in the centre of one side, and two small round perforations in place of the tubes, on the other side (Figure 13.3.4–5). Some of them have a bar equivalent to the loop of the plaque cheekpiece, connecting the edges of the two sides (Figure 13.3.5).

In later Shang sites, this type is only known from a horse-and-chariot pit, M40, at Qianzhangda, Tengzhou, Shandong. Compared to the earlier example from HPKM1136-1137, the side with two small round perforations is much shorter than the side with a central hole. The bar has disappeared. Instead, there is a narrow slot along the edge of

---

[19] Mizoguchi and Uchida 2018: 709–723.
[20] For the information on HPKM1136-1137, 1162, 1220, and 1221, see Hwang 2018.
[21] Mizoguchi and Uchida 2018: 718–719.
[22] Shih 1964: 332–335.
[23] Shih 1972: 5–35.
[24] Hwang 2015: 154–155.

[25] Institute of Archaeology, CASS 2005: 131–133.
[26] Wu 2002: 222–225, 241.

Figure 13.3. Earliest types of Shang cheekpieces. 1-5. Cheekpieces from chariot pit HPKM1136-1137; 6. Cheekpieces from horse pit HPKM1162. Courtesy of the Institute of History and Philology, Academia Sinica.

the larger side. In M40, the cheekpieces were excavated together with pronged U-shaped items. Bronze headstall ornaments were found on the two horse heads as if intact. The excavators' reconstruction provides a clear structure of the headstall.[27] (Figure 13.4.2) The two small holes were used to attach straps, but there is no information to show the function of the narrow slot.

Hwang's third type of Shang cheekpieces, a plaque with animal design, seems to be a derivation from the L-shaped cheekpiece. Examples come from horse-and-chariot pit M45, at Qianzhangda, Tengzhou, Shandong. They are flat plaques in the shape of stylised animal heads with a central hole and a narrow slot. Two half loops on the back are for attaching straps (Figure 13.5).[28]

Rod-shaped Cheekpieces

This type has only been found in horse pit HPKM 1162. The body is long and thick with a central hole for a mouthpiece and a loop on the lower side. On the sides are parallel thin perforations for attaching cheek straps (Figure 13.3.6). The loop corresponds to that of the plaque cheekpieces and the bar of the L-shaped cheekpieces. This type is very limited and is not seen in later sites.

Hwang pointed out that its structure and design are comparable to the above types of cheekpieces;[29] however, the rod shape and thick body are very different from the square and L-shaped examples. They can be linked to the rod-shaped cheekpieces of the Eurasian Steppes. Elena Kuzmina has shown that the earliest type of Eurasian cheekpieces were shield-shaped examples of the Sintashta-Petrovka culture, followed by the plaque and the rod-shaped types.[30] They were used by different cultural groups at different times. In this context, the coexistence of plaque and rod-shaped examples in horse pit HPKM 1162 is worth noting. The appearance of rod-shaped cheekpieces at Anyang, though small in number, might indicate a source of horses and related knowledge other than that represented by the thin, plaque cheekpieces.

Mouthpieces

Plaque cheekpieces are frequently found as parts of a horse's bridle but no mouthpiece of the Wu Ding period has yet been found. This suggests that bits of that time were most possibly made of organic materials, probably soft cords or rigid bars of wood or antler as were also used in steppe examples. Gail Brownrigg and Igor Chechushkov et al. have argued that bits of soft rope or rigid bars were used in the Bronze Age of the Eurasian steppes, based on reconstructions of studded shield cheekpieces of the Potapovka culture. The ends of the cord bits pass through the central holes, and have a knot on the outer side of the cheekpiece.[31] Metal straight bar bits can be traced to the seventeenth century BCE in the Near East,[32] and single bar bits made of antler, dating to the late second millennium BCE, are known from a site at Yanghai, Xinjiang.[33]

It is worth noting that bronze bits, together with cheekpieces, were found in burials of the Yinxu Phase IV, dating

---

[27] Institute of Archaeology, CASS 2005: 125–127, 360–361 (vol. 1). For the reconstruction, see CASS 2005: 640–641 (vol. 2).
[28] Institute of Archaeology, CASS 2005: 360–361 (vol. 1).
[29] Hwang 2015: 155.
[30] Kuzmina 1994; Chechushkov et al. 2018: 126–128; see also Kusnetsov and Bochkarev, this volume.
[31] Brownrigg 2006: figs. 3, 4; Chechushkov et al. 2018: fig. 1.
[32] Littauer and Crouwel 2001; Bar Oz et al. 2013.
[33] Niyazi and Tanaka 2011: 200, fig. 7; Turfan City Bureau of Cultural Relics et al. 2019: fig. 1001 (vol. 2).

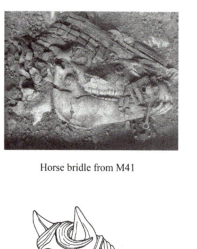
Horse bridle from M41

Horse bridle from M40

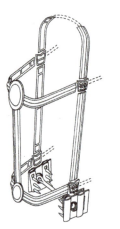
Reconstruction

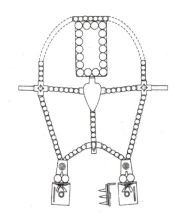
Reconstruction

Figure 13.4. Horse bridles from Qianzhangda, Tengzhou, Shandong. After Institute of Archaeology, CASS 2005: 641, 643, plates 29, 32

to ca. 1100 BCE, at Qianzhangda, Tengzhou, Shandong. The horse-and-chariot pit M41 yielded two bronze bar bits, 133 mm long, in the form of a plain bar mouthpiece with loop terminals. They were found *in situ* in the two horses' mouths (Figure 13.4.1). Similar bits, 143 mm long, but with twisted-rope decoration are known from tomb M18 (Figure 13.5).[34] The imitation of rope probably indicates the previous existence of soft bits.

C-shaped Object with Prongs

The C-shaped objects interpreted by most authors as mouthpieces are shaped in a C-curve with three sharp prongs on each inner side (Figure 13.6.1).[35] They have two button-like attachments set at a right angle to the prongs. The one from M164 at Xiaotun is made of jade (Figure 13.6.1) and measures 115.5 mm x 61mm x 6 mm thick, and weighs 31.5 g. Two attachments in the form of a human face have become separated from the main body. The small holes on the upper parts of the body and on the back of the attachments indicate that they could be joined together. Other examples, made of bronze, were cast in one piece. A slightly later bronze example from M33, dating to ca. 1150 BCE, at Hougang, Anyang is more like a flattened, wider U-shape, measuring 156 mm long and 73 mm high, with a loop next to the attachment on the left (Figure 13.6.3).[36] A very similar example is known from a late Shang tomb at Qianzhangda, Tengzhou, Shandong (Figure 13.6.4).[37]

Many scholars suggest how the C-shaped objects were used as mouthpieces. Jing Zhongwei compares them with studded cheekpieces from the Eurasian steppes and the Near East, and suggests that the C-shaped 'mouthpiece' was created by the Shang elite for better control of horses.[38] Chang Huaiying argues that the C-shaped object is a combination of bit and cheekpiece.[39]

Shih Chang-ru made a plastic replica of the find from M164 and argues that it fits and works well when put in a horse's mouth. He suggests that the object should be placed in the mouth with the open ends backwards. When the reins were pulled, the sharp prongs would prick the horse's tongue. In a personal communication with William Schulz, a horse rider from Arizona, Schulz proposed that the open end should be downwards, making a comparison with bits with a high port used by horsemen in the Spanish tradition to control their mounts by causing pain. In the excavated context, the open ends of the jade object are indeed forward, but it is not in the horse's mouth. It is possible that the bridle was not intact when it was buried, and the C-shaped item was displaced from the horse's mouth, while the two small stone human face ornaments were gathered to one side.[40] Shih's illustration shows the mouthpiece lying almost horizontally, with the prongs inside the mouth

---

[34] Institute of Archaeology, CASS 2005: 359, fig. 264.6 (vol. 1).
[35] Shih 1972: 5–35; Yang 2002: 136; Wang 2002: 28; Jing 2010: 77–78; Hwang 2015: 143.
[36] Institute of Archaeology, CASS 1993: 896.
[37] Institute of Archaeology, CASS 2005: 360, fig. 265.4 (vol. 1).
[38] Jing 2010: 77–78.
[39] Chang 2019: 59–61.
[40] Shih 1972: 25, fn. 2.

Early Cheekpiece Development in the Late Shang Dynasty Around 1250 BCE

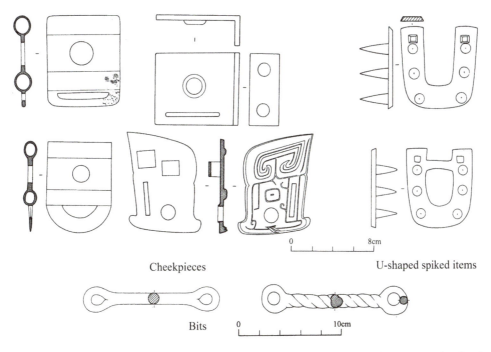

Figure 13.5. Cheekpieces, U-shaped spiked items and bits from Qianzhangda, Tengzhou, Shandong. After Institute of Archaeology, CASS 2005: 359, 361.

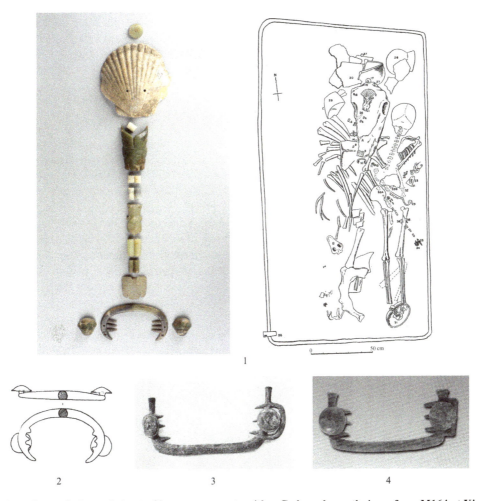

Figure 13.6. C-shaped mouthpieces. 1. A set of horse ornaments with a C-shaped mouthpieces from M164 at Xiaotun, Anyang, Henan. Courtesy of the Institute of History and Philology, Academia Sinica; tomb plan from Shih 1972: 8. 2. C-shaped mouthpiece from Shanchengcun, Wuxiang, Shanxi. After Wang and Yang 1992: 91; 3. C-shaped mouthpiece from M33 at Hougang, Anyang, Henan. After Institute of Archaeology, CASS 1993: plate 4.2. 4. C-shaped mouthpiece from BM9 at Qianzhangda, Tengzhou, Shandong. After Institute of Archaeology, CASS 2005: plate 150.4.

and the button-like attachments visible outside, with the headstall and reins apparently attached to them.

Hwang, on the other hand, like Schulz, suggests that the open side should be placed downwards. He suggests that the reins are attached by the buttonlike attachments. He also envisages that when the reins are pulled, the prongs will prick the horse's tongue or gums.[41]

However, if the piece were placed inside the horse's mouth, the button-like attachments, which largely overlap the prongs, would not only be invisible, but they would prevent the prongs from functioning. Nonetheless it would be possible to put the mouthpiece into the mouth of a small horse like a bit, as suggested by Chang Huaiying, supported by a headstall, with the prongs outside pressing on the lips or the jaw. Alternatively, such an item might have been used over the nose or even under the chin, perhaps for leading or training. Taking into account the precious material from which it was made, the jade example from Xiaotun could be considered as a symbolic offering made especially for the burial rather than for actual use.

Pronged U-shaped Items

Pronged U-shaped items, approximately 70 mm x 60 mm, are known from sites of the latest phase of the Shang dynasty and the early phase of the Zhou dynasty, dated to about the 11th century BCE (Figure 13.5). They typically have six studs on the inner face. On the two terminals are small holes for attachment to a cheekpiece or headstall.[42] Like examples from the horse-and-chariot pits at Meiyuanzhuang and Dasikong at Anyang, Henan[43] and M41 at Qianzhangda, Tengzhou in Shandong,[44] they are placed on the inner side of cheekpieces (Figure 13.4). An unusual example from M6 at Guozhuang, Anyang even combines the looped plaque cheekpiece and pronged U-shaped item into one piece.[45]

When the item was in use, the studs were next to the corner of the horse's mouth. Its combination with cheekpieces, particularly the example from Guozhuang, is very similar to the studded cheekpieces widely found in the Europe, the Near East, and the Eurasian steppe, as many scholars have pointed out.[46] Mary Littauer and Joost Crouwel have shown that the studs of the European and Near Eastern counterparts dating to the second half of the second millennium BCE were used to reinforce directional control.[47] Gail Brownrigg's experiment on the use of studded cheekpieces from the Potapovka culture in the Eurasian steppes, dated between 2000 and 1800 BCE, shows that the internal studs can reinforce the driver's signal to turn.[48] Studs on the cheekpieces are useful to reinforce steering, but the finds of the C-shaped object and the pronged U-shaped item of the Shang are only found in very small numbers, particularly if compared with the number of cheekpieces. This might indicate that, for the Shang elite, such items were not considered essential for driving.

While the C-shaped objects have been found in association with an awl-shaped whip ornament in small tombs, Hwang suggests that these two items were probably indicators of mounted soldiers of the Shang dynasty.[49] Following Hwang, Jing further focuses on whip ornaments, and pronged U-shaped items, and suggests that riding appeared in the Central Plain of China in the late Shang period.[50] However, the very limited finds of the C-shaped objects (two dated to the Wu Ding reign and the other two dated to later Shang phase), do not seem to support the existence of a specific kind of mounted soldier in Shang society. Furthermore, a chariot axle-cap and two linchpins were found in associated pit H115 in the upper part of M164. The excavator suggests that the burial might also indicate chariot use.[51] If the studded items were useful for guiding horses, their appearance might be associated with other purposes. In modern horse training, there is a kind of harsh mouthpiece which can depress the horse's tongue to cause discomfort. This is particularly useful for training stubborn horses. Similarly, the C-shaped object and the pronged U-shaped items might have been used in horse training rather than for riding.

Discussion

The above horse bridle items of the Wu Ding period show great variety. Hwang says that although the cheekpieces of the late Shang period can be categorised into different types, they all have similar structures.[52] However, their variations still demonstrate the need for different types and uses. The plaque cheekpiece with no loop found in some of the earliest burials with horse and chariot related artefacts, including HPKM1911, YM40, YM202, and the tomb of Fu Hao, was the earliest form. A loop was added and then became a basic component of later cheekpieces. The L-shaped cheekpiece without tubes presents a rather different means of attachment from that of the plaque type. The rod-shaped cheekpiece seems to be another simplified type of the plaque cheekpiece, as Hwang suggests.[53] It looks as if the two sides had been cut away, keeping the central part to maintain a minimum form. However, its long, thick body recalls many counterparts widely seen in the Eurasian steppes. It is also possible that the Shang elite learned of this type from steppe neighbours other than those using plaque cheekpieces. All these variations suggest that the Shang elite of the Wu Ding period were experimenting with the development of horse bridles, and that they learned horse skills from more than one source.

---

[41] Hwang 2015: 146.
[42] Wu 2002: 225–226; Jing 2010: 79–81; 2013:309–313.
[43] Institute of Archaeology, CASS 2014: 465–471; Anyang Archaeological Team, IA, CASS 1998: 56–62.
[44] Institute of Archaeology, CASS 2005: 127–129.
[45] Anyang Archaeological Team, IA, CASS 1991: 906–907.
[46] Jing 2013: 313–317; Wang 2019: 83–84; Takahama 2020: 47–48.
[47] Littauer and Crouwel 1979: 87–89; 2001.
[48] Brownrigg 2006: 170.
[49] Hwang 2015: 142.
[50] Jing 2013: 306–307.
[51] Shih 1972: 30–32.
[52] Hwang 2015: 154–155.
[53] Hwang 2015: 155.

In a later development, as shown by the numerous finds of the later Shang and early Zhou periods, the plaque cheekpiece with a loop was selected as the major type, while the L-shaped cheekpieces were still used, though rarely. And the rod-shaped type, which was most popular in contemporary eastern part of the Eurasian Steppe,[54] was discarded by the Shang elite.

While most horse and chariot pits yielded paired horses, the single set of horse bridle elements found in the tomb of Fu Hao is worth noting. Does it indicate the existence of horse riding? Shih, Hwang and Jing suggest that there were mounted soldiers in the late Shang dynasty based on the presence of the C-shaped mouthpieces and awl-shaped whip ornaments, as mentioned above.[55] But if we consider what the horse feels when such an item is put in its mouth, the C-shaped mouthpiece is not ideal for a rider to deliver subtle messages to his mount. A horse's tongue and the corners of the mouth are very sensitive. They are places to receive signals when a horse is wearing a bridle. If it is accepted that the relationship between driver/rider and horses should be harmonious rather than tense, bits and bridles should provide subtle messages to the well trained animal. Putting the hard and pronged C-shaped mouthpiece in the horse's mouth would make the tongue feel much more pressure, compared to that felt from a soft or bar bit. The pronged U-shaped item, when placed on the inner side of the cheekpieces, would also cause discomfort to the corner of the horse's mouth. This is particularly clear if we consider that most of the mouthpieces do not have prongs, and most Shang cheekpieces are not lined with pronged U-shaped accessories. These studded items seem to have had limited use, for example, only if the horse was difficult to manage. It is also possible that the very limited number of human figures buried in the pits with the C-shaped mouthpiece might have been horse trainers of the time.

If we are to discuss the possibility of horse riding and the appearance of mounted soldiers in the Shang period, we should consider the horse related people around the Shang. Who were the driving and riding peoples with whom the Shang elite had contact? What happened when the Shang elite met them? These are questions to be asked before suggesting that the Shang had skillful mounted soldiers.

Equestrian Neighbours of the Shang

Bridle cheekpieces are key to revealing the relationship between the equestrian skills of the Shang elite and the peoples from the Eurasian steppes. Cheekpieces were found with the horses of the earliest chariots in the Sintashta culture (ca. 2000–1800 BCE) on the borders of Eastern Europe and Central Asia. Made of bone or antler in round or oval shield-like shapes, they have a central hole probably for a mouthpiece, and several studs on the inner side.[56] A thinner protruding tab at the top has several small holes or studs for attaching to a headstall or noseband.[57] Kuzmina suggests that they were developed based on the cheekpieces of Eastern Europe.[58] Their body gradually changed shape into plaque form in the Petrovka (c. 1800–1740 BCE) and the Alakul (ca. 1900–1450 BCE) and later in the Timber-Grave cultures (ca. 1800–1200 BCE).[59] The latest phase of the Timber-Grave culture was contemporary with Wu Ding.

Several scholars have compared the Shang square cheekpieces with their steppe counterparts to explore their origins. Jing and Shū Takahama particularly focus on the similarity between the studded cheekpieces of the Eurasian steppe and the Near East and the pronged U-shaped items, suggesting that they have a close relationship.[60] Wang Peng thinks that the plaque cheekpiece was introduced along with the chariot. He traces the development of cheekpieces in the steppe and makes a comparison with the plaque cheekpieces and pronged U-shaped items of the Shang. He points out that the structural similarity between them indicates borrowing from the steppe. Furthermore, according to the accepted chronology, Wang suggests that it is most possible that the Shang plaque cheekpiece originated in the Alakul and the Timber-Grave cultures distributed in the western Eurasian steppe, and perhaps from the Fatyanovo culture (ca. 2800–1700 BCE) in the central Eurasian steppe, though no cheekpieces have been reported from there.[61]

As they observed, the Shang plaque cheekpiece shares many features with those from the Eurasian steppe and the Near East. However, the Shang system of passing the straps through tubes and the steppe method of utilising holes, still indicate significant variation. In addition, the earliest Shang cheekpieces did not incorporate prongs, suggesting that studs were not considered crucial. Because the pronged U-shaped items appeared about a hundred years later in the Yinxu phase IV, the Shang must have accepted the ideas of cheekpieces and studded linings separately.

If it is accepted that the Shang elite adopted cheekpieces from their steppe neighbours, the appearance of plaque and rod-shaped cheekpieces and other horse related items most possibly suggests that there were variations in cheekpiece design in the contemporary eastern Eurasian steppe. Rather than focus on the issue of studs, I will trace the driving and riding peoples who had direct or indirect contact with the Shang to explore further the possible external network during the Wu Ding period.

Southern Siberia

When the Shang adopted horse-drawn-chariots in ca. 1250 BCE, they were greatly influenced by their contemporaries in the steppes, particularly peoples of the Karasuk culture

---

[54] Podobed et al. 2014.
[55] Shih 1964: 338–339; Hwang 2015: 142; Jing 2013: 306–307.
[56] See Bochkarev and Kuznetsov, this volume.
[57] For examples and reconstruction, see Brownrigg 2006.
[58] Kuzmina 2008: 52–53.
[59] Wang 2019: 83; Chechushkov et al. 2018: 126–130.
[60] Jing 2013: 313–319; Takahama 2020: 47–48.
[61] Wang 2019: 83–85.

(ca. 1400–1000 BCE) in Southern Siberia. Many scholars have pointed out the close relationship between the Shang and the Karasuk culture based on the appearance of bronze items with Karasuk features, including celts, knives with an animal-headed, ringed, or capped pommel, bow-shaped objects, and chariots at Anyang.[62]

Although no chariot remains have been excavated, rod-shaped cheekpieces are found in many Karasuk sites. They are made of bone or antler, curved in the centre, and usually with pointed terminals. There are three holes, the central one for a bit, and the upper and lower two for bridle straps. The three holes are usually in the same plane, while in a small number of examples the upper and lower holes are vertical to the central perforation.[63] They suggest a different harnessing system from that presented by the steppe plaque cheekpieces.

With abundant finds of horse bones and cheekpieces, Sophie Legrand suggested that the people of the Karasuk culture used horses for traction and riding.[64] The experiment conducted by Igor Chechushkov et al. suggests that, though both shield- and plaque-shaped cheekpieces can be used for both riding and driving, the rod-shaped cheekpieces are most suitable for rigid control of a ridden horse.[65] As no plaque cheekpieces are known from Karasuk sites, the rod-shaped cheekpieces could have been used for both driving and riding.

Mongolian Steppes and the Loess Highland

Artefacts and representations with Karasuk features have been widely found in the Mongolian steppe and the Loess Highland in northwest China.

In Mongolia, representations of horse-drawn-chariots and bow-shaped objects are seen in rock carvings and on deer stones.[66] Knives with a ring or an animal-headed pommel are also found there.[67] As William Taylor et al. show, horses played important roles in the 'Deer Stone-Khirigsuur Complex' in the late Bronze Age, from 1300 to 700 BCE. Horses there were used as sacrifices and transportation, probably for chariot driving, horse riding or harnessing to carts, as early as 1300 BCE.[68]

Numerous knives with Karasuk features have been found in the Loess Highland. The appearance of those Karasuk features led scholars to suggest that there was a route through Mongolia and the Loess Highland linking the Karasuk people and the Shang.[69] Horses have been found in sites contemporary with the late Shang period, including one from Gaohong, Liulin and seven from Xicha in Shanxi.[70] Though small in number, they still indicate the role played by horses in local societies. Like chariots in the Minusinsk basin and Mongolia, they were probably not frequently buried.

It seems that no cheekpieces have been reported from these areas. However, a bronze C-shaped object very similar to that of M164 at Anyang, together with several ritual bronzes and weapons in typical early Anyang style, were unearthed from a small contemporary tomb at Shanchengcun, Wuxiang, Shanxi (Figure 13.6.2).[71] The Shanchengcun site is located on a possible route by which the Shang elite may have introduced horses from regions to their north.[72] Since the C-shaped object was probably used to train horses as discussed above, the man in the M164 burial was possibly a horse trainer associated with the Loess Highland.

Further Northwest

Much overlooked riding neighbours are those living in present-day Xinjiang. Many scholars have demonstrated the close relationship between Xinjiang and the Andronovo culture which was the major late Bronze Age culture in the eastern Eurasian steppes extending from the Urals to the Altai and Xinjiang.[73] As scholars, including Elena Kuzmina have shown, it was through the expansion of the Andronovo culture that chariots were introduced to the eastern part of the Eurasian steppe.[74] They were then further transmitted to the Central Plain of China in the Wu Ding period.[75] No reliable evidence has yet been found to prove the existence of chariots contemporary with the Andronovo culture or the late Shang period in Xinjiang. As in the Karasuk culture, chariots were probably not used as burial goods, but horses are quite frequently found in tombs there.[76]

Bridles contemporary with the late Shang period have been discovered in Xinjiang. Rod-shaped cheekpieces with three holes, dating to before 1000 BCE, were found in tombs at Wubao, Hami.[77] The most important finds are those from cemeteries at Yanghai, Shanshan in the Turfan depression. The site was used from the 13th century BCE to the second century CE and the earliest group of burials is dated from the 13th to the 10th century BCE, roughly contemporary with the late Shang period. Many tombs contain horses and several yielded leather bridles, preserved in the dry environment. In addition, antler and wooden mouthpieces are reported from the site. The antler example is slightly curved with a perforation at each end.[78]

---

[62] Watson 1978; Lin 1998a: 258–261; So and Bunker 1995; Wu 2013: 37–42.
[63] Podobed et al. 2014.
[64] Legrand 2006: 855–857.
[65] Chechushkov et al. 2018: 135.
[66] Novogrodova 1989: 188; Saruulbuyan et al. 2009: 26, 29; Taylor et al. 2015: 855–856.
[67] Saruulbuyan et al. 2009: 26, 29.
[68] Talyor et al. 2015.
[69] Legrand 2004; Wu 2013: 37–45.
[70] Yang 1981; Cao and Hu 2001; Cao 2014: 201–202.
[71] Wang and Yang 1992.
[72] Cao 2014: 201–205.
[73] Kuzmina 2008: 98–107; Peng 1998; Mei and Shell 1999; Mei 2000: 66–67; Shui 2001: 30–31; Han 2007: 40–51; Kohl 2007: 237–241; Shao 2009; Guo 2012: 270–275.
[74] Kuzmina 2008: 49–59.
[75] Wu 2013: 32–45.
[76] Guo 2012: 419.
[77] Xinjiang Institute of Cultural Relics and Archaeology 1992.
[78] Turfan City Bureau of Cultural Relics et al. 2019: fig. 1001 (vol. 2). For the antler bit, see Niyazi and Tanaka 2011: 195, fig. 5.4. For the

A fully published tomb, M21, dated from the 12th to 8th century BCE, provides further information on the early horse bridles of the Yanghai site.[79] The tomb contains the mummified body of a man holding a whip in his hand, and a bridle hangs next to him.[80] The bridle from M21 is one of the earliest from the site. It is made of leather and has small bronze ornaments on the straps (Figure 13.7). The arrangement of bronze ornaments also recalls the bronze round ornaments decorating the bridles from the horse-and-chariot pits YM20 and YM40 at Xiaotun, Anyang as discussed above. The bridle also includes a pair of rod shaped wooden cheekpieces, but no mouthpiece has survived (Figure 13.7).[81] These are grooved to hold the bifurcated bridle straps through which they are slotted at each end, while a third groove in the centre indicates that there may once have been an organic mouthpiece. Similar cheekpieces are known from tomb M208, also dated from the late second millennium BCE.[82] The short whip has a leather thong. On the surface of the whip is a shallow spiral carving decorated with thin bronze strips (Figure 13.7). This recalls the gold flakes decorating the rotted wooden whip in horse-and-chariot pit YM20 at Xiaotun, Anyang.[83]

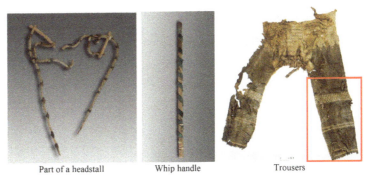

Figure 13.7. Some artefacts from M21 at Yanghai, Shanshan, Xinjiang. After Turfan City Bureau of Cultural Relics et al. 2019: plates 167.4, 223.1, 238.1.

A pair of woollen trousers worn by the deceased provides further clues to the possible connection between peoples living in Xinjiang and the Shang elite. The trousers have been recognised as the earliest trousers known to date and are seen as the marker of horse riding and local mobile pastoralism (Figure 13.7).[84] As the reconstruction team points out, the trousers with 'straight-fitting legs and a wide crotch-piece seem to be a predecessor of modern riding trousers.' Together with the horse bridles and weapons, including a bronze axe, a bow, and arrows, found in M21, 'the invention of bifurcated lower body garments is related to the new epoch of horseback riding, mounted warfare and greater mobility.'[85]

The research has demonstrated the importance of this pair of trousers, but what caught my attention is the most significant pattern band in the central part of the legs (Figure 13.7). The interlaced T-shaped pattern is very similar to a typical interlaced pattern on Chinese ritual bronzes. This pattern is not only frequently seen on Shang ritual bronzes (Figure 13.8), but also seen on later Zhou bronzes, such as

Figure 13.8. Ritual bronze with interlaced T-shaped pattern, ca. 11th century BCE. Collection of the National Palace Museum.

the 8th century BCE bronzes excavated from Shandong and Hebei.[86]

Victor Mair also points out that the ornamental band of interlocking fretwork round the knees can be seen on a late Shang bronze in the Royal Ontario Museum[87] as well as on textile fragments from the southeastern and northeastern rim of the Tarim Basin. He shows that this type of ornament was first used on textiles, and then on other materials. An interesting example comes from the royal cemetery of the Shang. This pattern appears on the decorative band of the robe of a stone elite figure from royal tomb HPKM1004 at Anyang, attributed to the Shang ruler who followed Wu Ding (Figure 13.9).[88] Next to the T-shaped pattern decorative bands are geometric decorative bands with an arrow pattern, which recall the simple zigzag decorative bands around the lower legs of the Yanghai trousers. The

---

wooden bit, see Guo 2012: 423; Niyazi 2019: 166.

[79] Academia Turfanica, Xinjiang and Xinjiang Institute of Cultural Relics and Archaeology 2011: 14; Turfan City Bureau of Cultural Relics et al. 2019: 39–43 (vol. 2).

[80] Wagner and Tarasov 2018: 18, 21, 146; Turfan City Bureau of Cultural Relics et al. 2019: 39–41 (vol. 2).

[81] Academia Turfanica, Xinjiang and Xinjiang Institute of Cultural Relics and Archaeology 2011: 103–106; Turfan City Bureau of Cultural Relics et al. 2019: 42 (vol. 2).

[82] Niyazi and Tanaka 2011: 195, fig. 5.8; Turfan City Bureau of Cultural Relics et al. 2019: fig. 1001 (vol. 2).

[83] Shih 1970: 128–130.

[84] Wagner and Tarasov 2018: 145. The ¹⁴C dates of the trousers they provided is 2900–3100 BP.

[85] Beck et al. 2014: 224.

[86] For the Shandong one, see Qiguo gucheng yizhi bowuguan 2015: 43; for the Hebei one, see Editorial Committee of Complete Collection of Chinese Bronzes 1997: 114.

[87] Mair 2021. The date of the bronze with interlocking fretwork mentioned in the article should be late Shang period, ca. 12th century BCE.

[88] The figure is composed of fragments found in looted parts of HPKM1004 and HPKM1217. Reference no. R001580. Collection of the IHP, Academia Sinica, Taiwan. For the date of HPKM1004, see Mizoguchi and Uchida 2018: 718–721.

Figure 13.9. Marble robed and kneeling human figure. Courtesy of the Institute of History and Philology, Academia Sinica.

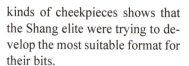
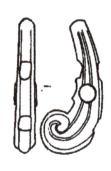

Figure 13.10. Horn-shaped cheekpieces of the Early Western Zhou period from M28, Zhangjiapo, Changan, Shaanxi. After Feng Hao Archaeological Team, IA, CASS 1987: 30.

presence of these patterns on the trousers, Shang bronzes and a Shang elite robe suggests a possible link between the two areas.

Driving or Riding? The Choice after Encountering Horses and Chariots

The robes of the Shang elite and the trousers of the steppe people present a vivid contrast in their cultures and lifestyles. We have no evidence of the existence of trousers in Shang society. Transmitted texts say that it was not until 307 BCE in the Warring States period, when a ruler of the Zhao state decided to introduce mounted fighting and ordered his soldiers to wear trousers, that they became prevalent in Central China. But Mair suggests that the distribution of the interlocking fretwork could represent the expansion of pastoral peoples and the predecessors of the Scythians.[89] It would be interesting to ask, if the Shang elite had contact, and even knew riding and associated equipment, i.e. trousers, why mounted warriors were adopted so late as a significant force in warfare?

The efforts of the Shang elite in dealing with horses and their use can be demonstrated by the variation of cheekpieces and related items of the Wu Ding period, as this article has shown. If compared with counterparts elsewhere, the shapes of the Shang cheekpieces are unique. The variation suggests that the Shang probably learned about the concept of cheekpieces and their usefulness in training and use through their contacts with several driving and riding groups, particularly those in the Loess Highland and Xinjiang. In this rather short period, the presence of the various kinds of cheekpieces shows that the Shang elite were trying to develop the most suitable format for their bits.

While the square cheekpiece became the principal type in use over the next two hundred years, the scarce rod-shaped cheekpiece was abandoned after the Wu Ding period. It was not until the early Western Zhou period, in the early 10th century BCE, that rod-shaped cheekpieces appeared again in the Zhou states, and became the major type in the later Zhou period.[90] There are two early examples similar to the one from HPKM 1162. One is from the Zhou capital at present day Zhangjiapo, Changan, Shaanxi (Figure 13.10).[91] Like the Shang rod type cheekpiece, it has a thick body, a central hole for a mouthpiece and two vertical perforations for bridle straps. The other is from the Yu state at Baoji, Shaanxi.[92] Its structure is similar to the Zhangjiapo example, and it has a ring terminal recalling the same part of the Shang cheekpiece. Both have a curved end to imitate the shape of horn or antler. It is clear that the curved terminal of the Yu example does not have an actual function. Their presence probably suggests that the Zhou people adopted specific horse bridles from steppe peoples who used horn shaped cheekpieces. Even though the horn shape recalls the cheekpieces widely seen in Eurasia,[93] the presence of a loop on the cheekpiece of the Yu and many other Zhou states seems to indicate that the Zhou elite also adapted the design of Shang bits and their harness system.

It was not until the late Western Zhou period around the 8th century BCE, that cheekpieces with a central hole and a loop began to disappear. Horn-shaped cheekpieces with two small holes for bridle straps became the major type. Now the cheekpieces pass through the two outer ring terminals of the mouthpiece. As Takahama Shu has pointed out, this new way of connecting bits and cheekpieces indicates an innovation in the horse harnessing method in the Central Plain which is different from previous examples.[94]

Though we do not have solid evidence to show where the prototypes of the Shang cheekpieces came from, the development of cheekpieces of the Wu Ding period can provide a further understanding of the process of horse adoption in Shang society. If the Shang elite learned the uses of horses and chariots directly or indirectly from peoples in the Loess Highland and Xinjiang and the peoples

---

[89] Mair 2021.
[90] Wu 2002: 223.
[91] Feng Hao Archaeological Team, IA, CASS 1987: 30–31.
[92] Lu and Hu 1988: 123
[93] Takahama 2014: 30–32. For more discussion on the cultural contacts presented on horse equipment, including those from the Yu state, see Rawson et al. 2021.
[94] Takahama 2020: 53.

of the Andronovo and of the Karasuk cultures, it is highly possible that they were aware of riding as well as driving. Many scholars, including Edward Shaughnessy and Emma Bunker, suggest that chariots were first deployed as prestige display items rather than war machines.[95] Or, as Magdalene von Dewall and Edward Shaughnessy point out, the very limited number of chariots among archaeological finds and excavated texts, including oracle-bones and bronze inscriptions, indicates that chariots were only used as command platform in battle.[96] While the Shang chariots and related items were made locally, the limited use of horses and chariots suggests the difficulty in obtaining or maintaining horses locally, which pushed the Shang elite to consider how many horses were affordable, what they needed from them, and how to use them. In such a situation, the Shang elite made their decision to manufacture their own horse-and-chariot accessories, and to adopt driving rather than riding for military use and ceremonial occasions, thus transforming customs from elsewhere into their own cultural traditions.

Hsiao-yun Wu
Vice-head of the department of antiquities and senior researcher at the National Palace Museum, adjunct associate professor at Graduate Institute of Art History, National Taiwan Normal University

Bibliography

Academia Turfanica, Xinjiang (Xinjiang Tulufanxue yanjiuyuan 新疆吐鲁番学研究院) and Xinjiang Institute of Cultural Relics and Archaeology (Xinjiang wenwu kaogu yanjiusuo 新疆文物考古研究所). 2011. Xinjiang Shanshan Yanghai mudi fajue baogao 新疆鄯善洋海墓地发掘报告 (Excavation in the Yanghai Cemetery in Shanshan (Piqan) County, Xinjiang). *Kaogu xuebao* 考古学报 1: 99–150.

Anthony, David W. 2007. The Horse, the Wheel, and Language: How Bronze-age Riders from the Eurasian Steppes Shaped the Modern World. Princeton and Oxford: Princeton University Press.

Anyang Archaeological Team, IA, CASS (Zhongguo shehui kexueyuan kaogu yanjiusuo Anyang gongzuodui 中国社会科学院考古研究所安阳工作队). 1991. Henan Anyang Guozhuang cunbei faxian yizuo Yin mu 河南安阳郭庄村北发现一座殷墓 (A Yin Tomb Discovered North of Guozhuang Village, Anyang). *Kaogu* 10: 902–909.

Anyang Archaeological Team, IA, CASS (Zhongguo shehui kexueyuan kaogu yanjiusuo Anyang gongzuodui 中国社会科学院考古研究所安阳工作队). 1993. 1991 nian Anyang Hougang yinmu de fajue 1991 年安阳后冈殷墓的发掘 (Excavation of Yin Tombs in 1991 at Hougang, Anyang, Henan). *Kaogu* 10: 880–903.

Anyang Archaeological Team, IA, CASS (Zhongguo shehui kexueyuan kaogu yanjiusuo Anyang gongzuodui 中国社会科学院考古研究所安阳工作队). 1998. Henan Anyang shi Meiyuanzhuang dongnan de Yindai chemakeng 河南安阳市梅园庄东南的殷代车马坑 (Horse-and-Chariot Burial Pits of the Yin Period Southeast of Meiyuanzhuang, Anyang City, Henan). *Kaogu* 10: 48–65.

Bagley, Robert W. 1999. Shang Archaeology. In: *The Cambridge History of Ancient China*, edited by Michael Loewe and Edward L. Shaughnessy, 124–231. Cambridge: Cambridge University Press.

Bar-Oz, Guy, Pirhiya Nahshoni, Hadas Motro, and Eliezer D. Oren. 2013. Symbolic Metal Bit and Saddlebag Fastenings in a Middle Bronze Age Donkey Burial. *PLOSOne* 8 (3): e58648. Doi.org/10.1371/journal.pone.0058648.

Barbieri-Low, Anthony. 2000. *Wheeled Vehicles in the Chinese Bronze Age (c. 2000–741 B.C.)*. Sino-Platonic Papers 99. Philadelphia/PA: University of Pennsylvania. http://www.sino-platonic.org/complete/spp099_wheeled_vehicles_china.pdf.

Barbieri-Low, Anthony. 2010. The Chariot Comes to China. *Dig* 12 (5): 22–25.

Beck, Ulrike, Mayke Wagner, Xiao Li, Desmond Durkin-Meisterernst, and Pavel E. Tarasov. 2014. The Invention of Trousers and its likely Affiliation with Horseback Riding and Mobility: A Case Study of Late 2nd Millennium BC Finds from Turfan in Eastern Central Asia. *Quaternary International* 30: 224–235.

Brownrigg, Gail. 2006. Horse Control and the Bit. In: *Horses and Humans: the Evolution of Human-Equine Relationships*, edited by Sandra L. Olsen, Susan Grant, Alice M. Choyke and László Bartosiewicz. BAR International Series 1560. 165–171. Oxford: BAR Publishing.

Cao Dazhi. 2014. *The Loess Highland in a Trading Network (1300–1050 BC)*. Ph.D., Princeton University.

Cao Jian'en 曹建恩 and Hu Xiaonong 胡晓农. 2001. Qingshuihe xian Xicha Yizhi Fajue Jianbao 清水河县西岔遗址发掘简报 (Preliminary Report on the Site at Xicha, Qingshuihe County). In: *Wanjiazhai Shuili Shuniu Gongcheng Kaogu Baogao Ji* 万家寨水利枢纽工程考古报告集 (Collection

---

[95] Shaughnessy 1988: 199; Bunker 1995: 26.
[96] von Dewall 1964: 175; Shaughnessy 1988: 198. See also Robin Yates, this volume.

of Archaeological Reports of Wanjiazhai Yellow River Diversion Project), 6–78. Huhehaote: Yuanfang chubanshe.

Chang Huaiying 常怀颖. 2019. Yinxu chemaqi buyi 殷墟车马器补议 (A Supplementary Discussion of Yinxu Chariots). *Jianghan kaogu* 江汉考古 5: 59–70.

Chechushkov, Igor V. and Andrei V. Epimakhov. 2018. Eurasian Steppe Chariots and Social Complexity during the Bronze Age. *Journal of World Prehistory* 31 (4): 435–483.

Chechushkov, Igor V., Andrei V. Epimakhov, and Andrei G. Bersenev. 2018. Early Horse Bridle with Cheekpieces as a Marker of Social Change: An Experimental and Statistical Study. *Journal of Archaeological Science* 97: 125–136.

Dewall, Magdalene von. 1964. *Pferd und Wagen im frühen China*. Bonn: Habelt.

Editorial Committee of Complete Collection of Chinese Bronzes (Zhongguo qingtongqi quanji bianji weiyuanhui 中国青铜器全集编辑委员会). 1997. Zhongguo qingtongqi quanji 中国青铜器全集 (Complete Collection of Chinese Bronzes), vol. 9. Beijing: Cultural Relics Press.

Hao Archaeological Team, IA, CASS (Zhongguo shehui kexueyuan kaogu yanjiusuo Feng Hao gongzuodui 中国社会科学院考古研究所沣镐工作队). 1987. 1984–85 nian Fengxi Xizhou yizhi muzang fajue baogao 1984–85 年沣西西周遗址墓葬发掘报告 (Excavation of the Western Zhou sites and Tombs at Fengxi in 1984–85). *Kaogu* 1: 15–32.

Flad, Rowan K., Jing Yuan and Shuicheng Li. 2007. Zooarcheological Evidence for Animal Domestication in Northwest China. In: *Late Quaternary Climate Change and Human Adaption in Arid China*, edited by David B. Madsen, Fahu H. Chen, and Xing Gao, 167–203. Amsterdam: Elsevier.

Guo Wu 郭物. 2012. Xinjiang shiqian wanqi shehui de kaoguxue yajiu 新疆史前晚期社会的考古学研究 (Archaeological Research on the Societies of the Late Prehistoric Xinjiang). Shanghai Chinese Classics Publishing House, Shanghai.

Han Jianye 韩建业. 2007. Xinjiang de qingtong shidai he zaoqi tieqi shidai wenhua 新疆的青铜时代和早期铁器时代文化 (Cultures in Xinjiang from the Bronze Age to the Early Iron Age). Beijing: Science Press.

He Yuling 何毓灵. 2020. Yinxu 'wailai wenhua yinsu' yanjiu 殷墟'外来文化因素'研究 (On the Exogenous Features at Yinxu). Zhongyuan wenwu (中原文物) 2: 33–49, 128.

Hwang Ming-chorng (黃銘崇). 2015. Cong Shangdai de 'C xing maxian' yu 'jianzhui ceshi' kan Shangdai de qibing wenti 從商代的'C形馬銜''尖錐策飾'看商代的騎兵問題 (C-Shaped Horse Mouthpieces and Pointed Whip Ornaments and Related Problems of Shang Mounted Warriors). In: *Jinian Yinxu fajue 80 zhounian xueshu yantaohui lunwenji* 紀念殷墟發掘八十週年學術研討會論文集 (Proceedings of the Conference Commemorating the 80th Anniversary of the Anyang Excavations), edited by Yung-ti Li, 141–187. Taipei: The Institute of History and Philology, Academia Sinica.

Hwang Ming-chorng (黃銘崇). 2018. Shangwang de lanbaojianzi 商王武丁的「藍寶堅尼」(The Shang King Wu Ding's 'Lamborghini'). https://kam-a-tiam.typepad.com/blog/2018/12/商王武丁的藍寶堅尼.html; accessed 1 November 2019.

Institute of Archaeology, CASS (Zhongguo shehui kexueyuan kaogu yanjiusuo 中国社会科学院考古研究所). 1980. *Yinxu Fu Hao mu* 殷墟妇好墓 (The Tomb of Lady Hao at Yinxu in Anyang). Beijing: Cultural Relics Press.

Institute of Archaeology, CASS (Zhongguo shehui kexueyuan kaogu yanjiusuo 中国社会科学院考古研究所). 2005. *Tengzhou Qianzhangda mudi* 滕州前掌大墓地 (*The Qianzhangda Cemetery in Tengzhou*). Beijing: Cultural Relics Press.

Institute of Archaeology, CASS (Zhongguo shehui kexueyuan kaogu yanjiusuo 中国社会科学院考古研究所). 2014. *Anyang Dasikong: 2004 nian fajue baogao* 安阳大司空 2004年发掘报告 (*Dasikong, Anyang: Report of the 2004 Excavation*). Beijing: Wenwu chubanshe.

Jing Zhongwei 井中伟. 2010. Xiajiadian shangceng wenhua de qingtong dingchi maju—beifang caoyuan yu zhongyuan qingtong wenhua jiaowang de xinzheng zhiyi 夏家店上层文化的青铜钉齿马具—北方草原与中原青铜文化交往的新证之 (Bronze Horse Harness with Tine-shaped Cheekpieces of the Upper Xiajiadian Culture—New Evidence in Cultural Association with the Central Plain Region, the Northern Culture Zone of China and the Eurasian Steppe). *Bianjiang kaogu yanjiu* 边疆考古研究 9: 75–84.

Institute of Archaeology, CASS (Zhongguo shehui kexueyuan kaogu yanjiusuo 中国社会科学院考古研究所). 2013 Zhuice, dingchiqi yu dixian: gongyuanqian erqianji zhi qian sanshiji zhongxifang yumaqi bijiao yanjiu 鍱策、钉齿器与镝衔—公元前二千纪至前三世纪中西方御马器比较研究 ('Zhuice', 'dingchibiao' and 'dixian': a Comparative Study of Horse-Controlling Devices in China and the West from the 2nd Millennium to the 3rd Century BCE). *Kaogu xuebao* 考古学报 3: 297–324.

Kikuchi Hiroki 菊地大树. 2019. Zhongguo gudai jiama zaikao 中国古代家马再考 (Rethinking Domestic Horses in Ancient China). *Nanfang wenwu* (南方文物) 1: 136–150.

Kohl, Philip L. 2007. *The Making of Bronze Age Eurasia*. Cambridge: Cambridge University Press.

Kuzmina, Elena E. 1994. *Otkuda prishli indoarii? Material'naya kul'tura plemen andronovskoy obshchnosti i proiskhozhdeniye indoirantsev* (Whence came the Indo-Aryans? The material culture of the tribes of the Andronovo community and the origin of the Indo-Iranians). Moscow: Kalina.

Kuzmina, Elena E. 1998. Cultural Connections of the Tarim Basin People and Pastoralists of the Asian Steppes in the Bronze Age. In: *The Bronze Age and Early Iron Age Peoples of Eastern Central Asia*, edited by Victor H. Mair, 63–93. Journal of Indo-European Studies, Monograph 26 (2 vols.). Washington, D.C: Institute for the Study of Man.

Kuzmina, Elena E. 2008. *The Prehistory of the Silk Road*. Philadelphia: University of Pennsylvania Press.

Legrand, Sophie. 2004. Karasuk Metallurgy: Technological Development and Regional Influence. In: *Metallurgy in Ancient Eurasia from the Urals to the Yellow River*, edited by Katheryn M. Linduff, 139–156. Lewiston: Edwin Mellen Press.

Legrand, Sophie. 2006. The Emergence of the Karasuk Culture. *Antiquity* 80 (310): 843–789.

Lian Siyong 梁思永. 1962. *Houjiazhuang. dierben. 1001 hao damu* 侯家莊.第二本.1001號大墓 (*Hou Chia Chuang Volume II: HPKM-1001*). Taipei: The Institute of History and Philology, Academia Sinica.

Lin Yun. 1986. A Reexamination of the Relationship between Bronzes of the Shang Culture and of the Northern Zone. In: *Studies of Shang Archaeology*, edited by Kwang-chih Chang, 237–274. New Haven and London: Yale University Press.

Lin Yun 林沄. 1998a. Guanyu qingtong gongxiangqi de ruogan wenti 关于青铜弓形器的若干问题 (Some Issues on Bronze Bow-shaped Artefacts). In: (*Lin Yun xueshu wenji* 林沄学术文集 (*Scholastic Collections of Lin Yun*), 251–261. Beijing: Encyclopedia Publishing House of China.

Lin Yun 林沄. 1998b. Shang wenhua qingtongqi yu beifang diqu qingtongqi guanxi zhi zaiyanjiu 商文化青铜器与北方地区青铜器关系之再研究 (A reconsideration of the relationship Between Shang Dynasty Bronzes and Northern-style Bronzes). In: *Lin Yun xueshu wenji* (*Scholastic Collections of Lin Yun*), 262–288. Beijing: Encyclopedia Publishing House of China.

Linduff, Katheryn M. 2003. A Walk on the Wild Side: Late Shang Appropriation of the Horse in China. In: *Prehistoric Steppe Adaption and the Horse*, edited by Marsha Levine, Colin Renfrew and Katy Boyle, 139–162. Cambridge: McDonald Institute.

Linduff, Katheryn M. 2006. Why have Siberian Artifacts been Excavated within Ancient Chinese Dynastic Borders? In: *Beyond the Steppe and the Sown*. Proceedings of the 2002 University of Chicago Conference on Eurasian Archaeology, edited by David L. Peterson, Laura M. Popova and Andrew T. Smith, 358–370. Colloquia Pontica 13. Leiden and Boston: Brill.

Littauer, Mary A. and Joost H. Crouwel. 1979. *Wheeled Vehicles and Ridden Animals in the Ancient Near East*. Leiden and Köln: Brill.

Littauer, Mary A. and Joost H. Crouwel. 2001. The Earliest Evidence for Metal Bridle Bits. *Oxford Journal of Archaeology* 20 (4): 329–338.

Lu Liancheng 卢连成 and Hu Zhisheng 胡智生. 1988. *Baoji Yu guo mudi* 宝鸡 国墓地. (*Yu State Cemeteries in Baoji*). Beijing: Cultural Relics Press.

Mair, Victor. 2021. What a Prehistoric Pair of Pretty Pants Can Tell us about the Spread of Early Languages. https://languagelog.ldc.upenn.edu/nll/?p=50713; accessed 6 April 2021.

Mei Jianjun. 2000. *Copper and Bronze Metallurgy in Late Prehistoric Xinjiang: Its Cultural Context and Relationship with Neighbouring Region*. Oxford: BAR Publishing.

Mei Jianjun and Colin Shell. 1999. The Existence of Andronovo Cultural Influence in Xinjiang during the 2nd Millennium B.C. *Antiquity* 73 (281): 570–578.

Mizoguchi, Koji and Junko Uchida. 2018. The Anyang Xibeigang Shang Royal Tombs Revisited: A Social Archaeological Approach. *Antiquity* 92 (363): 709–723.

Niyazi Aikebaier 艾克拜尔·尼牙孜. 2019. Xinjiang Tulufan pendi Yanghai mudi chutu maju jiqi zuheyanjiu 新疆吐鲁番盆地洋海墓地出土马具及其组合研究 (Study on the Horse Harnesses and Their Compositions Unearthed from the Yanghai Cemeteries of the Turpan Basin in Xinjiang). In: *Jucai lancui zhuxinpian— Meng Fanren xiansheng bazhi huadan songshou wenji* 聚才揽粹着新篇—孟凡人先生八秩华诞颂寿文集 (*Proceedings of Celebrating the 80th Birthday of Professor Meng Fanren*), 165–171. Beijing: Science Press.

Niyazi Aikebaier 艾克拜尔·尼牙孜 and Yuko Tanaka 田中裕子. 2011. Torufan bonchi Yanhai bochi ni okeru haka to syutu bagu no bunseki トルファン盆地洋海（ヤンハイ）墓地における墓と出土馬具の分析 (Analysis of Graves and Harness in the Yanghai Cemeteries of the Turpan Basin). *Chugoku koko gaku* 中国考古学 11: 189–202.

Novgorodova, Elena A. 1989. *Srednyaya Mongoliya* [*Ancient Mongolia*]. Moscow: Nauka.

Peng Ke. 1998. The Andronovo Bronze Artifacts Discovered in Gongliu County in Yili, Xinjiang. In: *The Bronze Age and Early Iron Age Peoples of Eastern Central Asia*, edited by Victor H. Mair, 573–580. Journal of Indo-European Studies, Monograph 26 (2 vols.). Washington, D.C.: Institute for the Study of Man.

Piggott, Stuart. 1978. Chinese Chariotry: An Outsider's View. In: *The Arts of the Eurasian Steppelands*, edited by Philip Denwood, 32–51. Colloquies on Art and Archaeology in Asia 7. London: Percival David Foundation of Chinese Art.

Podobed, Vyacheslav A., Anatoliy N. Usachuk and Vitaliy V. Tsimidanov. 2014. Vznuzdavshiye loshad' (sterzhnevidnyye psalii Yevrazii kontsa II — nachala I tys. do n.e.: tipologicheskiye i khronologicheskiye sopostavleniya Vznuzdavshiye loshad' (sterzhnevidnyye psalii Yevrazii kontsa II — nachala I tys. do n.e.: tipologicheskiye i khronologicheskiye sopostavleniya) [Those Who Bridled a Horse — Rod-like Cheek-pieces of Eurasia of the Late 2nd–Early 1st Millennium BC: Typological and Chronological Comparisons]. In: *Drevnosti Sibiri i Tsentral'noy Azii. Sbornik nauchnykh trudov, posvyashchennyy yubileyu* (*Antiquities of Siberia and Central Asia. Collection of Scientific Papers dedicated to the Aniversary*), edited by Vasili I. Soenov: 85–118.

Qiaobei kaogudui 桥北考古队 (Qiaobei Archaeology Team). 2006. Shanxi Fushan Qiaobei Shang Zhou mu 山西浮山桥北商周墓 (The Shang and Western Zhou Tombs at Qiaobei in Fushan, Shanxi). *Gudai wenming* 古代文明 5: 347–394.

Qi Heritage Museum (Qiguo gucheng yizhi bowuguan 齐国故城遗址博物馆). 2015. *Qiguo gucheng yizhi bowuguan guancang qingtongqi jingpin* 齐国故城遗址博物馆馆藏青铜器精品 (*Selection of Bronzes from the Collection of the Qi Heritage Museum*). Beijing: Cultural Relics Press.

Rawson, Jessica, Limin Huan, and William Timothy Treal Taylor. 2021. Seeking Horses: Allies, Clients and Exchanges in the Zhou Period (1045–221 BC). *Journal of World Prehistory* 34: 489–530. Doi.org/10.1007/s10963-021-09161-9.

Saruulbuyan, J., G. Eregzen and J. Bayarsaikhan. 2009. *The National Museum of Mongolia*. Ulaanbaatar: The National Museum of Mongolia.

Shao Huiqiu 邵会秋. 2009. Xinjiang diqu Andeluowonuo wenhua xiangguan yicuntanxi 新疆地区安德罗诺沃文化相关遗存探析 (An Analysis of the Related Remains of the Andronovo Culture in Xinjiang). *Bianjiang kaogu yanjiu* 边疆考古研究 2: 81–97.

Shaughnessy, Edward L. 1988. Historical Perspectives on the Introduction of the Chariot into China. *Harvard Journal of Asiatic Studies* 48: 189–237.

Shih Chang-ru 石璋如. 1964. Yindai de gong yu ma 殷代的弓與馬 (Bow and Horses of the Yin-Shang People). *Bulletin of IHP* 35: 321–342.

Shih Chang-ru 石璋如. 1970. Xiaotun diyiben, Yizhi de faxian yu fajue, bing bian: beizu muzang 小屯第一本遺址的發現與發掘丙編殷墟墓葬之一北組墓葬 (*Hsiao-T'un Volume 1: The Site Its Discovery and Excavations Fascicle 3: Burials of the Northern Section*). Taipei: The Institute of History and Philology, Academia Sinica.

Shih Chang-ru 石璋如. 1972. Xiaotun, diyiben, yizhi de faxian yu fajue, bingbian, Yinxu muzang zhier, zhongzu muzang 小屯第一本遺址的發現與發掘丙編殷墟墓葬之二中組墓葬 (*Hsiao-T'un Volume 1: The Site Its Discovery and Excavations Fascicle 3: Burials of the Middle Section*). Taipei: The Institute of History and Philology, Academia Sinica.

Shui Tao 水涛. 2001. Xinjiang qingtong shidai zhu wenhua de bijiao yanjiu—fulun zaoqi zhongxi wenhua jiaoliu de lishi jincheng 新疆青铜时代诸文化的比较研究—附论早期中西文化交流的历史进程 (A Comparative Study of Bronze Cultures in Xinjiang— with a Discussion of the Process of Early Cultural Exchange between the East and West). In: *Zhongguo xibei diqu qingtong shidai kaogu lunji* 中国西北地区青铜时代考古论集 (*Papers on the Bronze Age Archaeology of Northwest China*), 6–46. Beijing: Science Press.

So, Jenny F. and Emma C. Bunker. 1995. *Traders and Raiders on China's Northern Frontier*. Seattle and London: Arthur M. Sackler Gallery, Smithsonian Institution, in association with University of Washington Press.

Takahama Shū 高濱秀. 2011. Seisyūzidai no kokkakusei no hyō no issyu nituite 西周時代の骨角製の鑣の一種について (About a Kind of Western Zhou Cheekpiece Made of Bone or Horn). *Kanazawadaigaku kōkogaku kiyō* 金沢大学考古学紀要 32: 1–12.

Takahama Shū 高濱秀. 2014. Chuugokushoki no kutsuwa wo megutte: seisyuujidai no iwayurukakugatahyou wo chuushinni 中国初期のくつわをめぐって:西周時代のいわゆる角形鑣を中心に (Cheekpieces of Early China: A Discussion Focusing on Horned-shaped Cheekpieces of the Western Zhou Period). *Kanazawadaigaku kōkogaku kiyō* 金沢大学考古学紀要 35: 25–44.

Takahama Shū 高濱秀. 2020. Two Technical Traditions of Casting Horse Bits in China and their Relationships with the Steppe Area. *Asian Archaeology* 3:47–57.

Taylor, William Timothy Treal, Jamsranjav Bayarsaikhan, and Tumurbaatar Tuvshinjargal. 2015. Equine Cranial Morphology and the Identification of Riding and Chariotry in Late Bronze Age Mongolia. *Antiquity* 88 (346): 854–871.

Turfan shi wenwuju 吐鲁番市文物局 (Turfan City Bureau of Cultural Relics). Xinjiang Institute of Cultural Relics and Archaeology, Academy of Turfanology (吐鲁番学研究院), and Turfan Museum (吐鲁番博物馆). 2019. (*Xinjiang Yanghai mudi* 新疆洋海墓地 (*Report of Archaeological Excavations at Yanghai Cemetery*). Beijing: Cultural Relics Press.

Wang Haicheng 王海城. 2002. Zhongguo mache de qiyuan 中国马车的起源 (The Origins of Chinese Chariots). *Ouya xuekan* 欧亚学刊 3: 1–75.

Wang Jinxian 王进先 and Yang Xiaohong 杨晓宏. 1992. Shanxi Wuxiangxian Shangchengcun chutu yipi wanshang tongqi 山西武乡县上城村出土一批晚商铜器 (A Group of Bronzes of the Late Shang Period found in Shangcheng, Wuxiang, Shanxi). *Wenwu* 4: 91–93.

Wagner, Mayke and Pavel E. Tarasov. 2018. *Die Erfindung der Hose: Buch und Film*. Mitmach- und Entdeckerbücher zur Ostasiatischen Archäologie 1. Oppenheim: Nünnerich-Asmus.

Wang Peng 王鹏. 2019. Zhouyuan yizhi qingtong lunya mache yu dongxi wenhua jiaoliu 周原遗址青铜轮牙马车与东西文化交流 (Horse Wagon With Bronze Wheel Felloe From Zhouyuan – Implication to the Exchanges Between the East and West). *Kaogu* 2: 74–88. Translated into English by Xinru Liu, published in: *The world of the ancient Silk Road*, edited by Xinru Liu, 2023, 103-115. The Routledge worlds. Abingdon; New York: Routledge.

Wang Qi 王祁. 2018. Yinxu wenhua fenqi ji xiangguan zhu wenti zaiyanjiu 殷墟文化分期及相关诸问题再研究 (A Renewed Study of the Phases of Yinxu Culture and Related Issues). *Zhongguo guojia bowuguan guankan* 中国国家博物馆馆刊 10: 23–37

Wang Zhenzhong 王震中. 2006. 'Zhong Shang wenhua' gainian de yiyi jiqi xiangguan wenti '中商文化'概念的意义及其相关问题 (Meaning and Related Issues of the Concept of the 'Middle Shang culture'). *Kaogu yu wenwu* 考古与文物 1: 44–49.

Watson, William. 1978. The Chinese Chariot: An Insider's View. In: *The Arts of the Eurasian Steppelands*, edited by Philip Denwood, 1–31. Colloquies on Art and Archaeology in Asia 7. London: Percival David Foundation of Chinese Art.

Wu En and Mayke Wagner. 1999. Bronzezeitliche Zugleinenhalter in China und Südsibirien. *Eurasia Antiqua* 5: 111–133.

Wu Hsiao-yun 吴晓筠. 2002. Shang zhi Chunqiu shiqi Zhongyuan diqu qingtong chemaqixingshi yanjiu 商至春秋时期中原地区青铜车马器形式研究 (A Typological Study of the Bronze Chariot Fittings in the Central Plains from the Shang Dynasty to the Spring and Autumn Period). *Gudai wenming* 1: 180–277.

Wu Hsiao-yun. 2013. *Chariots in Early China: Origins, Cultural Interaction, and Identity*. BAR International Series S2457. Oxford: BAR Publishing.

Wu Hsiao-yun 吳曉筠. 2017. Shang Zhou shiqi tongjing de chuxianyu shiyong 商周時期銅鏡的出現與使用 (The Emergence and Use of Mirrors During the Shang and Zhou Dynasties). *The National Palace Museum Research Quarterly* 35 (2): 1–66.

Xinjiang Institute of Cultural Relics and Archaeology. 1992. Xinjiang Hami Wubao mudi 151, 152 hao muzang 新疆哈密五堡墓地 151, 152 号墓葬 (Tomb Nos. 151 and 152 in the cemetery in Wubao, Hami, Xinjiang). *Xinjiang wenwu* 新疆文物 3.

Yang Baocheng 杨宝成. 2002. Yinxu wenhua yanjiu 殷墟文化研究 (*Study on Late Shang Culture*). Wuhan: Wuhan daxue chubanshe.

Yang Shaoshun 杨绍舜. 1981. Shanxi Liulin xian Gaohong faxian Shangdai tongqi 山西柳林县高红发现商代铜器 (Bronzes of the Shang Dynasty Found in Gaohong, Liulin Country, Shanxi). *Kaogu* 3: 211–212.

14

Early Chinese Chariots, Carriages, and Carts in War and Peace: Evidence from New Textual and Archaeological Sources

Robin D. S. Yates

Chariots, carriages and carts played central roles in the lives of those living in Warring States, Qin and Han China, roughly fifth century BCE to the second century CE, both in war and in peace. They marked status, rank and official position; they were a main means of communication on land; they accompanied the elite into the afterlife in burials, sometimes in enormous numbers, and were later represented in murals in tombs; chariots were important machines employed on the battlefield: they feature prominently in the pits of terracotta warriors to the east of the First Emperor of China's mausoleum. Carts, pulled either by horses, oxen, or even by men, carried essential supplies, both in military campaigns and in peacetime. Horses were both worshipped as deities and butchered in sacrifices in ceremonies. Horses and wheeled vehicles had both symbolic, religious, and practical functions and cost their owners immense financial and other resources to build, maintain, and destroy. This essay will explore some of the wide range of new textual sources, especially legal and administrative documents, pertaining to chariots, carriages and carts that have been discovered in the last fifty years within the confines of the current People's Republic of China.

Introduction

It is well-known that China's Zhou dynasty (ca. 1045 BCE–265 BCE) was the heyday of the chariot's dominance on the field of battle. It evolved in many ways from a fairly rudimentary, unstable vehicle introduced from steppe cultures to a highly sophisticated machine, and there were many regional variations, including in the equipment wielded by the warriors riding aboard, as can been seen from the numerous excavated examples.[1] By the later stages of that 800-year time span, the states contending with each other in the so-called Warring States period of the Eastern Zhou were fielding hundreds if not thousands of these impressive machines in the increasingly ferocious military campaigns. At the same time, however, the age of the war chariot was coming to an end and it was gradually replaced by large infantry armies of conscript soldiers and eventually by cavalry forces. The demise of the chariot was, however, not swift. Chariots continued to be employed in war for many centuries after the introduction of cavalry, again from steppe cultures. Further, chariots evolved into carriages for use in civil affairs and they became ubiquitous machines in the daily lives of those living under the imperial administrations of the unified Qin and Han dynasties (221 BCE–220 CE).

This essay in honour of one of the great experts in the history of the chariot, Joost Crouwel, will explore the developments in the four hundred-plus years of the Qin and Han and will lay special emphasis on data, both textual and material, that has been brought to light in the last fifty or so years through archaeological discoveries. I will particularly emphasise the new textual evidence as seen in legal and administrative documents, as these materials provide fascinating insights into the roles that chariots, carriages, and carts played in daily life, both military and civilian, and how these machines were treated by both officials and members of the lower orders.[2]

The information that these newly recovered documents contain is not to be found in the transmitted historical sources. Indeed, these new sources bring into question the reliability and sometimes veracity of the transmitted sources, such as the well-known *Historical Records* (*Shi ji* 史記) of Sima Qian 司馬遷 (ca. 145–ca. 86 BCE). These documents cannot be ignored if we are to gain a better understanding of the realities of those times: they completely transform our understanding of many aspects of society in the late pre-imperial and early imperial periods, including manufacturing organisation and protocols. Hence in this chapter I will not be discussing the transmitted text that has often been cited in studies of chariots and chariot-making, the *Kaogong ji* 考工記 (The Artificer's Record), an originally independent work that was added to the *Zhou li* 周禮 or *Zhou guan* 周官 (the Rites of Zhou or Offices of Zhou) to replace the lost last section. This latter work, which purports to record the bureaucratic organisation of the early Western Zhou state, was incorporated into the Confucian canon, but its dating is much in dispute. One scholar now suggests that it contains late Warring States

---

[1] Wu, Hsiao-yun 2013; Barbieri-Low 2000. For an early study, see Shaughnessy 1988; and, more recently, Wang Haicheng 2002. For an overview of studies in Chinese of pre-Qin chariots and horses, see Luo 2014; cf. von Dewall 1964.

[2] Many aspects of the culture of chariots and other wheeled vehicles in early China are reviewed by Yu (2015) in his well-researched and valuable *Zhongguo gudai che wenhua*, but he does not emphasise the new textual evidence.

and Qin material and was assembled in the early Han dynasty.³ The *Artificer's Record* is itself in a poor state of preservation with numerous problematic technical words and passages and it may have been written not as a technical manual to guide artisans in their tasks, but rather for officials who supervised them.⁴ Its origins are as murky as the *Rites of Zhou* itself.⁵

I will not consider the reconstructions of the two miniature bronze chariots excavated from the First Emperor of Qin's mausoleum that have been the subject of intense analysis which throw so much light on many aspects of two types of Qin vehicles.⁶ Nor will I discuss the four types of military chariots, the command, the light, the 'supplementary' heavy used in conjunction with both infantry and cavalry, and the 'riding' chariot that accompanied the cavalry, within the formations of pottery figurines that have been excavated and identified by archaeologists in the pits to the east of his tomb mound.⁷ These chariots reveal that the technology of chariot warfare was still evolving in the late third century BCE, less than a hundred years before chariot warfare was abandoned in the mid-second century BCE by the subsequent Han dynasty.⁸

Preliminary Considerations

First, it is important to recognise that the term *che/ju* 車 was used for all vehicles, machines, and other apparatuses that used wheels in some form. It was not a word that was exclusively reserved for chariots, carriages, and carts.⁹ The word for a pulley wheel used especially above wells to draw water also incorporated the graph *che*¹⁰ and wheels obviously played a key role in silk and other textile technology, as they were used to spin thread.¹¹ In this essay, I will review new data that pertains to *che/ju* in a relatively broad sense. I will barely touch on other essential aspects of the chariot, for example on the terminology of the various components of wheeled vehicles or on the means of traction, primarily horses and oxen, but also humans. These have been studied intensively by other scholars and I will not introduce their results here.¹² I will, however, consider some evidence as it relates to armouries (*ku*). Given that the Chinese graph for these installations is an image of a chariot or carriage under a roof 庫, it is tempting to translate the term as a 'carriage house.' However, although clearly chariots were stored in these buildings from at least Eastern Zhou times (eight to third centuries BCE), when they first appeared as identifiably independent structures, they also functioned as sites for the manufacture of weapons that were stored with the chariots. I shall review some evidence concerning the armoury of the Qin county of Qianling as well as the great armoury of the Western Han dynasty later in this essay (Figure 14.1).

Second, the functions of *che/ju* were varied: they were not just used as fighting machines in warfare or as a means of transportation or communication. Of course, in the pre-unification period prior to 221 BCE, the primary function of the chariot was for use in warfare with a secondary use in hunting—hunting was a means of training for war and so the two were closely connected.¹³ At the same time, as a number of scholars have demonstrated, chariots, chariot accoutrements, flags and banners that adorned the chariots, as well as various types of specially made weapons, served also as means of reward for military and other types of success and as marks of grace and favour of subordinate individuals by higher authorities, most notably in the Western Zhou by the Zhou kings themselves.¹⁴ These status symbols were flaunted by the recipients.

Another extremely important function of chariots was their employment in funeral ritual. It is hard to decide whether one should call these vehicles chariots or carriages, especially as the practice of riding in a vehicle in a funeral cortege continued from Zhou times into the Han.¹⁵ In the Zhou and earlier in late Shang times,¹⁶ chariots and sometimes their drivers, as well as wheels, horses, and chariot fittings were buried to accompany the dead, the greater number, type and quality of the object depending on the status of the deceased.¹⁷ In addition, there were regional variations and historical traditions.¹⁸ In the tomb of Yi, Marquis of the state of Zeng in the Chu cultural region of late fifth century BCE date, a unique record of the carriages with their dignitaries who attended the funeral of the Marquis was recovered by archaeologists. This record, written in Chu-style script on slips of bamboo, has been the subject of a number of epigraphic and other analytic studies.¹⁹ What they reveal

---

3   Wu Tinghai 2019.
4   For a problematic rendition of this work into English, see Wen 2013.
5   This is not to say that the text was not important later in Chinese history; see Elman and Kern 2009.
6   Qin Shihuang bingmayong bowuguan and Shaanxi sheng kaogu yanjiusuo 1998; Sun 2001; Dang 2011; Shi 2017; Li, Cheng 2010.
7   Wang, Xueli 1994: 123–142.
8   An 2005.
9   For the Han views of the subject of various terms associated with *che* 車, see the words categorised under *che* in the etymological dictionary *Shi ming* 釋名 'Explaining Terms' compiled by Liu Xi 劉熙 ca. 200 CE: https://ctext.org/shi-ming/shi-che/zh. For example, Liu explains the term *rongche* 容車, literally 'face carriage' as a type of carriage in which a married woman rides as it carries screens which hide the face of the occupant.
10 See below under 'wheelbarrows'; cf. Zhao 1989.
11 Sun 2008: 64–69.
12 See, for example, Wang Shaohua 2005; Wang Zhenduo 1997; Yu 2013; Chen, Ning 2015.

13 Exactly how chariots were deployed on the field of battle is not entirely clear, despite many descriptions of battles in the *Zuo zhuan*, the primary source for the Spring and Autumn period. See Durrant et al. 2016; Byrne 1974; Kierman 1974. Presumably both the horses and the occupants of the chariots had to be extremely highly trained.
14 Cook 1997; Lu Liancheng 1993: esp. 381, where the author cites an inscription from the Mao gong *ding* (Lord Mao cauldron) translated by Shaughnessy 1991: 81. For an overall view of the changing patterns of social organisation in the Zhou dynasty, see von Falkenhausen 2006.
15 The symbolism and meaning of these funeral corteges in the early imperial period will be reviewed later in this article.
16 One should probably also include the imperial Qin, too.
17 In Han times, these were replaced by models. See, for example, *Shandong sheng wenwu kaogu yanjiusuo* and *Zibo shi Linzi qu wenwu guanli ju* 2016, possibly the grave of Liu Hong 劉閎, King of Qi 齊王, a son of Emperor Wu of the Han Dynasty who died while still young.
18 For the Qin, see Liu and Liang 2015.
19 Jiang 2011; Luo 2015; 2017.

is that the Chu had their own names and types of carriages that were evidently different from those in the northern states, but to date these have not been studied by any Western scholars. Research has not yet developed sufficiently to reveal whether the war chariots of the state of Chu and their method of deployment on the battlefield in the final stages of the wars of unification in the late third century BCE were inferior to those of the state of Qin and whether the disparities in chariot technology between the two contenders played any role in the defeat of the Chu by the Qin.

A third extremely important function of chariots (carriages) that developed as their use in warfare diminished was that of transporting civil officials in the burgeoning bureaucracy of the late Warring States and imperial Qin and in the Han dynasty. A clear distinction of rank in the bureaucratic hierarchy was made between those higher-level officials who had the right, and even obligation, to ride in a carriage and those lesser functionaries who were forbidden to do so. Indeed, it was specifically legislated that women were not allowed to ride in official carriages, which indicates that carriages were embedded in the developing gender regime of the early imperial period. Needless to say, in the Han the empresses and other high-ranking female imperial consorts did have the right to ride in carriages and these were distinguished from "male" carriages by the hanging silk curtains or drapes that protected the occupants from prying eyes (Figure 14.2).[20]

Rapid communication became essential for the newly founded imperial regimes and wheeled vehicles could ob-

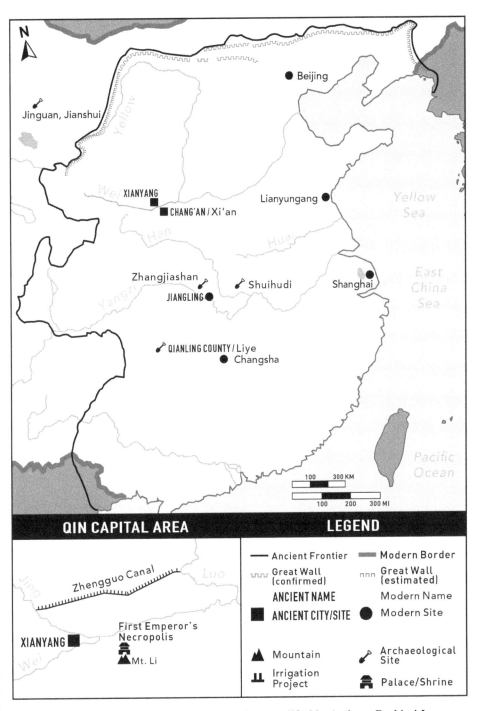

Figure 14.1. Map of Qin China. Drawn by QZ Lau, modified by Anthony Barbieri-Low.

viously not travel fast and far without an expanding road network.[21] This network has been extensively studied, but it is ancillary to the present endeavor, and so I will leave its consideration aside.[22]

Carts as a means of transportation of goods, equipment, and other materials obviously fulfilled a fourth function of wheeled vehicles which were equally important in both

---

[20] *Hou Han shu* 1965: 3647 (the treatises were composed by Sima Biao 司馬彪, died ca. 306 CE). Each rank of consort determined the type of silk curtains or at least the design of the weave. These types of carriages were called *pengche* 軿車, and probably derived from earlier war chariots that had leather curtains draped in front and rear to protect the occupants from arrows and other projectiles.

[21] Transportation by water was also essential, especially in the Yangzi River basin in the south, and various types of boats were constructed, but the river network and riverine transportation are beyond the scope of this essay.

[22] Wang Zijin 2015a; 2015b. For the importance of communication in the Qin, see Sanft 2014.

Figure 14.2. Rubbing of a carriage with curtains or drapes, possibly for female occupants (from Sun Ji 2020: 123, Figure 25-1; originally published by Shanghai guji chubanshe 2008: 117, Figure 25-1; with permission of Zhonghua shuju).

Figure 14.3. Photograph of a brick tomb tile depicting a market scene with a single-wheeled wheelbarrow in the collection of the Sichuan Provincial Museum, Chengdu, Eastern Han period (photograph by Dr. Hajni Elias with her permission).

civil and military daily life. In the Han dynasty, the single wheeled wheelbarrow was invented (Figure 14.3), as was, supposedly, the 'south-pointing chariot' (*zhinan che* 指南車) that used a complex system of gearing allowing for the image of a man standing on top of the chariot always to point south.[23] Perhaps the sedan chair (*jiaoche* 轎車), used for travel in difficult mountainous terrain,[24] was also invented but it seems to have become popular only from the Song dynasty (960–1279 CE) on, although it was obviously known from at least the period of division after the Han. In this essay, I shall say a few words on the wheelbarrow and leave the latter two contraptions aside.

Last, chariots were supposedly employed in one of early China's most fearsome punishments, the ripping apart of criminal tied to four chariots with a subsequent exposure of the corpse (*chelie yi xun* 車裂以徇) for treason and rebellion.

The term 'chariot' also was coined for the titles of many officials in the Han dynasty, especially for those responsible for security and for various units of the armed forces, but these will not be considered here.[25] There was a horse deity that was worshipped in early and later imperial times, but the rituals associated with it will not concern us, either.[26] Further, in the laws, precise distinctions regarding the types of horses that could be used to pull different types of chariots and carriages or that could be ridden were also laid down, as were rules regarding the renting of horses from the common people for government or state use.[27] But these will only be referred to in passing, as they are not germane to the substance of present essay. Let us now turn to that substance.

Chariots

Chariot Production and Repair in Legal and Administrative Documents

Who built the chariots and carriages and who maintained and repaired them? Was there a profession of 'coachbuilder' or anything comparable to the English guild of the Worshipful Company of Coachmakers and Coach Harness Makers that was incorporated in London in 1670? Was there a separate profession of harness-maker or of wheelwright? There is no real evidence of guilds in China until the late Ming dynasty,[28] but the tradition of craft specialisation goes back at least until the Warring States period and the Qin and Han dynasties. Carpenters of late imperial times worshipped as a patron deity Lu Ban a master carpenter who is said to have competed with the philosopher Mozi in an engineering battle (he lost).[29] The earliest visual evidence for wheelwrights at work comes from the Eastern Han, and images on decorative stone tomb-tiles of wheelwrights at work have been discovered (Figure 14.4).[30] But there is no indication of whether they were working in a private studio or in a government workshop. The story that the Daoist philosopher Zhuangzi tells of the conversation between Wheelwright Pian and Duke Huan of Qi, although entirely ahistorical and completely apocryphal, suggests that in the Warring States there were carpenters who specialized in the making of chariot- and

---

[23] Needham with Wang Ling 1965: section 27e(5) pp. 286–303.
[24] There is one possible reference to the sedan chair in a transmitted source from the Han in the biography of Yan Zhu 嚴助, an official favoured by the young Han Wudi. See *Han shu* (Yan Zhu zhuan 嚴助傳), 64A.2779–2780.
[25] See Bielenstein 1980: passim.
[26] Sterckx 1996; Weng Mingpeng 2019. As no horses were ridden in pre-imperial times and all horses were harnessed to chariots, presumably this horse deity was associated in some way with chariots, but it is not clear how. It does not appear that the so-called 'Heavenly Horses of Ferghana' sought by Emperor Han Wudi were assimilated to this deity. For these horses, see Linduff 2019.
[27] For horses in early China, see Wan, Xiang 2013; Yates 2003; Chen Ning 2015. For important and still valuable earlier studies, see Hayashi '1959a; 1959b; 1960.
[28] Rowe 1992.
[29] Ruitenbeek 1996; Barbieri-Low 2007: 106.
[30] Chavannes 1893, pl. XLIII, stone discovered in Liu Village, Jiaxiang County, Shandong Province, ca. 1st century CE. Cf. Barbieri-Low 2007: 93, Fig. 3.15.

Figure 14.4. Rubbing of a wheelwright's workshop from Chavannes 1893, plate XLIII, stone discovered in Liu Village, Jiaxiang County, Shandong Province, ca. 1st century CE (from Chavannes 1893: pl. XLIII).

cart-wheels, but it is not clear whether Pian was a government worker or whether he was an independent artisan.[31]

In the Qin, it appears as though chariots for use in war were built in state workshops by artisans who were a combination of permanent state workers, convicts, and even slaves.[32] Indeed, it appears that both state-owned chariots and official carriages were built in armouries (*ku* 庫), but no Qin statutes or ordinances relating to armouries have so far been discovered.[33] In addition, it seems as though the imperial Qin had an office called the Bureau of Chariots (*Che cao* 車曹), most likely at either the commandery (i.e., regional) and/or capital level(s), possibly at the county level, too,[34] but it does not seem as though this bureau was in charge of manufacture or of storage – chariots and carriages were stored in the armouries. Without more evidence, it is difficult to determine the functions of the Bureau of Chariots, although it may have been concerned with the deployment and management of state chariots and carriages. In the Han, the official with the overall responsibility for all matters to do with horses and chariots/carriages for the army and the imperial court as well as with the imperial stables was the Grand Coachman (*Taipu* 太僕).[35] Whether he had a Bureau of Chariots underneath him is not known; perhaps the Han dispensed with the bureau.

In the Qin, the evidence regarding the management of horses is far more limited. However, in contrast with the Han, who seem to have had 30,000 government slaves originating from steppe tribes taking care of the horses, the Qin seem to have had convicts herd the horses, for one short statute in the Yuelu hoard reads as follows:[36]

When wall-builders of the Grand Stables are herding[37] horses without supervision, abscond and are caught, cut off their left legs, and again make them wall-builders. When later they again abscond, do not cut off (the right leg), as is so in the case of other wall-builders.

From this statute, we know, of course, that the Qin had an office called the 'Grand Stables' that managed at least some of the state's horses, probably those based at the Qin capital of Xianyang in the northwest, modern Shaanxi Province; others were managed at the county level, as we know from the archive of the Qin County of Qianling that was thrown down as well – Qianling is the modern Liye Township in extreme Western Hunan Province.[38] The punishment inflicted on the convicts who fled their posts but who were subsequently caught is rather horrifying, but not uncommon for the Qin.

The official supervising the armoury at the county level in the Qin was a full-time bureaucrat often referred to as the Bailiff of the Armoury (*ku sefu* 庫嗇夫) who was responsible for the management of the armoury, its products, and the workforce.[39] It is quite possible that some of the workers in the armouries were also artisans who had their own independent workshops and were seconded to the armouries to fulfil their tax obligations to the state by working a certain number of days a year for the government. In the recently discovered Qin legal and administrative documents, there is no indication that there was a special rubric of the law that concerned chariot-making, in other words there were no statutes (*lü* 律), ordinances (*ling* 令), or other legal regulations concerned with their manufacture, but there are a considerable number of rules directly relevant for chariots and carriages categorised under different headings. There are, however, general rules that could apply to chariots and chariot-making (or carriages) as well as many other products of state workshops. Some are directly related to chariots or carriages. An example of the latter, although not entirely without its problems of interpretation, is an excerpt from the Statutes of the Director of Convict Labour:

For one lubrication when repairing one cart use one ounce of glue and two *chui* (ca. 10 grams) of grease.

---

[31] Watson 1968: 152–153. Duke Huan was reading a book containing the words and deeds of past sages and Pian, who was at work on a wheel in the courtyard below, pointed out to him that writings of the past were merely the dregs of dead men; in other words, the way was not to be found in books or in the past.

[32] The question of slavery in the Qin and early Han is very complex and contentious as is the terminology of various types of slaves either bought on the open market or enslaved by the state because members of their families had committed crimes. There were both government or state slaves and private slaves, and it is not always easy to distinguish between them. For the most recent discussion, see Yates 2021.

[33] A text titled 'Laws on Armouries' *Ku fa* 庫法 was discovered in Tomb no. 1, Yinqueshan, Linyi, Shandong Province, in 1972, dating from the early years of Han Emperor Wu's reign (probably in the 130s BCE). Some scholars have suggested that these were laws of the state of Qi in Warring States times, but that is not yet proven. See Wu Jiulong 1984.

[34] Two fragmentary documents recovered from level 8 of Well no. 1, Liye, discarded from the archives of the Qin county of Qianling 遷陵, mention a 'Bureau of Chariots': see Chen Wei 2012: document nos. 8-405, p. 144; 8–562 and 8–1820, pp. 179–180.

[35] For this functionary and his staff and the various stables and other units for which he was responsible as revealed by transmitted historical sources, see Bielenstein 1980: 34–38.

[36] Chen, Songchang 2016: slip no. 49 (archaeological number 1997).

[37] The editors understand *cong* 從 'follow' as *zong* 縱 'give free rein to,' interpreting the word as *mu (ma)* 牧馬 'herd horses.'

[38] It was excavated by archaeologists in 2002. See Yates 2012–2013.

[39] Chen, Wei 2012; Lu, Shan 2019.

When repairing (pieces that have) fallen apart, the glue is to be divided according to their number. In this way, the cart will not (move with) difficulty; it is to be greased according to the circumstances.[40]

Another from the same rubric states:

Wall-builders and grain-pounders[41] are to be dressed in red clothes and to wear red head-cloths; they are to be manacled and fettered. Elderly wall-builders are not to lead or supervise (others); those who have been nominated to lead and supervise are to lead and supervise them. Grain-pounders and wall-builders who are going out for statute labour must not venture to go to a market as well as to remain outside the outer gate of the building. When they would be obliged to pass through a market, they are to make a detour; they must not pass through. When wall-builders or grain-pounders break pottery vessels or iron tools, or wooden tools, or when making carts they break wheel rims, they are to be bastinadoed immediately ten strokes for the value of one cash; if the value is twenty cash or more, they are to be thoroughly beaten. The tool (or vessel) is to be written off. If they are not immediately beaten, the official in charge is to be charged with half (the value).

(Statutes of the) Director of Convict Labour[42]

The first article reveals the close attention that the Qin state paid to the minutiae of production and repair, whereas the second clearly reveals that convicts were engaged in production and repair of chariots and their related equipment. That this was indeed the case can be seen from several documents preserved in the Liye (Qianling County) hoard, where, in addition, it is recorded that one convict was sent to 'study chariots/carriages' (*xueche* 學車) at another county downriver.[43] It is most likely that this individual was sent either to learn how to drive a chariot or carriage or how to build one.

A third article in the Shuihudi collection excerpted from an unnamed statute reads:

Venturing to make other objects when these do not belong to the annual production (quota), as well when there has been no royal command, the Master of the Artisans as well as his Assistant are each fined two suits of armour.[44] When a county workshop for the first time presents (work) and it is poor, the County Bailiff, his Assistant, his (subordinate) functionaries and the Head of the bureau are each fined one shield. When wall-builders working as artisans are rated as inferior, (each) man is given a hundred strokes. When carts are inferior, the Director of Convict Labour and the Overseer (are fined) one shield; the workers are given fifty strokes.[45]

This article reveals one of the principal features of the Qin system of production that was extended to the entire population, namely the system of mutual responsibility. Should the unit produce something not specifically ordered by higher authorities or if the quality of a product manufactured by a unit was judged inferior, every level of the unit was held responsible, not only the workers and their immediate superiors, but those in management positions, too, and the punishments increased in severity the further up the administrative chain – except, of course, for the convicts at the bottom who were given heavy corporal punishment, presumably because they were not thought to be capable of paying a heavy monetary fine – the fines calculated in suits of armour and in shields were actually levied in cash. How did the Qin determine the quality of products from their workshops? They must have had quality-control specialists who assessed the goods. The Qin had a type of statute called the 'Statutes on Checking' (Xiao lü 效律) and these seem to have been the rules primarily under which the quality of products was determined and the procedures to be followed for checking the performance of administrators and functionaries.[46] Two groups of excerpts from these statutes have been preserved in the Shuihudi Tomb no. 11 collection. The early Han officials seem to have adopted this category of statute with modifications, as can be seen from a smaller selection found in Tomb no. 247, Zhangjiashan, dating from roughly 186 BCE.[47]

Chariots as Seen in the Han Chang'an Armoury Inventory

That chariots were not completely abandoned after the mid-second century BCE can be seen in the remarkable inventory of the holdings of what was probably the largest armoury in the Han dynasty, located in the Han capital of Chang'an, modern Xi'an, Shaanxi Province. Built in roughly 200 BCE, this armoury was located by archaeologists and thoroughly excavated from 1975–1980.[48] The inventory, however, was retrieved from the tomb of a relatively low-ranking functionary in what is now Lianyungang, Jiangxi Province.[49] In addition to listing the holdings of military equipment for the exclusive use of the emperor, the inventory catalogues a huge number of weapons, chariots, and other objects, such as flags and pennons, that were employed by regular forces.[50]

---

[40] Hulsewé 1985: 75–76, A76, slightly amended; Xia 2019: 148–149.
[41] These were male and female convicts condemned to the longest sentences and to perform the most strenuous types of hard labour.
[42] Hulsewé 1985: 72–73, A70, slightly amended; Xia 2019: 154–155.
[43] Document no. 9–2289; Chen, Wei 2018: 456.
[44] The issue of fines in the Qin and Han is highly complicated. See Barbieri-Low and Yates 2015: 202–207 and the explanation below.
[45] Hulsewé 1985: 110–111, C12, slightly amended; Xia 2019: 201–202.
[46] Two groups of similar selections from these statutes were deposited in Tomb no. 11, Shuihudi: see Hulsewé 1985: 93–101; Caldwell 2018: esp. 131–179.
[47] Barbieri-Low and Yates 2015: 823–832.
[48] Zhongguo shehui kexueyuan kaogu yanjiusuo 2005.
[49] For a transcription with commentary on this inventory and all the other texts excavated in the tomb, see Zhang and Zhou 2011.
[50] It has been estimated that 23,268,487 items in 240 categories are to be found in the inventory. The ink of a number of items has been lost, so these figures cannot be completely verified.

Among the various types of chariots are light war chariots, those to be ridden in by officers and generals, drum chariots (Figure 14.5), bell chariots, chariots carrying multiple-bolt arcuballistae,[51] chariots with mounted crossbows, chariots with mounted battering-rams, chariots that had long poles erected on them which could be climbed up and from the top of which a keen-eyed look-out could scan the surrounding landscape, and what are called 'Entertainment chariots or carriages'. It is clear from this inventory that generals still rode in chariots while commanding their troops, even though the bulk of the Han military forces were cavalry, for they are seen riding in 'ax chariots' (*fuche* 斧車; Figure 14.6).[52] The 'entertainment chariots' might have been used in training exercises. Some of these types of chariots are depicted in Eastern Han tomb tiles (Figure 14.7), although the image of the 'entertainment chariot' does not seem to represent a version that would have been useful in the army. What is not recorded are trebuchets mounted on wheels, tanks, ladders and other similar offensive and defensive machines that are recorded in the Mohist military chapters of perhaps pre-Qin date. The reason for this is, perhaps, because such machines were built on the spot during military engagements and would not have been useful to keep in storage in the armoury.

Figure 14.5. Rubbing of a Drum chariot (from Sun Ji 2020: 127, Figure 26-3; originally published by Shanghai guji chubanshe 2008: 121, Figure 26-3; with permission of Zhonghua shuju).

Chariots for Hunting Tigers

Tigers appear to have been a danger that the Qin authorities had to face and apparently tigers were capable of penetrating the palace grounds in the capital of Xianyang, modern Shaanxi province. They also roamed the forests of central and south China.[53] It seems as though there were specially designed chariots for hunting (or shooting) tigers (射虎車) or at least there were units trained to catch tigers which involved men both mounted in chariots and on foot. This can be seen from an item in the Shuihudi Tomb no. 11 statutes which reads as follows:

Figure 14.6. Ax chariot (from Sun Ji 2020: 127, Figure 26-1; originally published by Shanghai guji chubanshe 2008: 121, Figure 26-1; with permission of Zhonghua shuju).

> For hunting tigers, two chariots form a squad. When the tiger has not yet crossed the fencing(?) and they pursue it and the tiger returns, they are fined one suit of armour. When the tiger escapes and they do not catch it, (the occupants of) the chariots are fined one suit of armour. When the tiger is about to attack, the foot-soldiers are to come out and shoot it; if they are not successful at it, they are fined one suit of armour.
>
> When a leopard escapes and it is not caught, the fine is one shield.
>
> Statutes on Hunting of the Major of the Gate Traffic Control Office[54]

A fragmentary document preserved in the Qin Qianling County archive indicates that another law specified that six men were to be released from statutory labour duty for catching one tiger.[55] Another document broken into multiple pieces reveals that the Qin state sold meat from a tiger caught by members of the commoner population to a garrison soldier performing his turn of duty in the county,

---

[51] This was a type of heavy siege crossbow that could fire at the same time ten long iron-tipped arrows with ropes attached, perhaps hundreds of metres. After firing, it would appear that the arrows could be retrieved by winding the ropes back by means of a large windlass. For these devices and for the Mohist machines mentioned below, see Needham and Yates 1994; for a detailed description and the later history of this machine, see pp. 187–203.
[52] The axe was the symbol of a general's authority to conduct executions in the field.
[53] These were probably South China tigers that were virtually eliminated from the wild after 1949. There is an ongoing effort to reintroduce them.

[54] Revised translation based on Hulsewé 1985: 112–113; Xia 2019: 204–206, notes that the meaning of the term that I have tentatively translated as "fencing" has been the subject of considerable scholarly debate.
[55] Yates 2018: 425; Zhuang 2018.

Figure 14.7. Rubbing of an 'Entertainment' chariot (from Sun Ji 2020: 121, Figure 26-2; originally published by Shanghai guji chubanshe 2008: 121, Figure 26-2; with permission of Zhonghua shuju).

presumably for consumption, at a rate of twenty cash per *dou* 斗 of meat (roughly 2 litres or 2.11 quarts).[56] Whether this was a common or standard practice is not known.

Chariots Used in Executions

In the transmitted texts there are several mentions of the use in the pre-Qin period of chariots to carry out unusually savage executions for treason. The four limbs of the condemned man were tied with ropes that were attached to chariots and then, at a given command, the horses of all four chariots galloped forward, dismembering the individual's body.[57] Examples include Lord Shang in the state of Qin in 338 BCE, Lao Ai who attempted a coup-d'état against King Zheng, later the First Emperor of Qin, in 238 BCE, and Li Si, the Chancellor of the Qin, on the orders of the Second Emperor (died 208 BCE). Recently, another version of the collapse of the Qin has been retrieved from a looted tomb and is preserved at Peking University. In this work, called the *Zhao Zheng shu* 趙正書 (Book of Zheng of Zhao), Li Si is not stated to have been torn apart by chariots.[58] So it is possible that this punishment was not actually implemented in Qin or in other pre-Qin states as the Han records claim. It may have been a fantasy dreamed up by Han writers to criticise the Qin for cruelty and enhance the Han's reputation for moral governance. Nevertheless,

historical records indicate that this punishment was employed in later times, imitating the ancient practice.

Carriages

At the same time as the Qin was developing its technology for chariot warfare, it also expanded its use of carriages for civilian purposes. As it conquered its rivals, it expanded its control over larger and larger swathes of territory. Consequently, its needs for communication also increased. So, the Qin road system rapidly expanded (of course, the system of water transport also expanded at the same time) and the government began to specify which officials could use what means of transportation and which types of communication could be transmitted using what forms of transportation. It also composed manuals specifying the distance between one node in the transportation network to another. It seems that it distributed these manuals to all the counties it established for administration and control of the local areas. These nodes were built according to official specifications and acted as checkpoints where the travellers were required to show their passports and other documents that gave them permission to travel and to what services they were qualified to access—for example grain rations, cooking equipment, and personnel such as cooks. All travel and all movement were carefully regulated.

The state calculated the distance different types of transportation should travel per day depending on the activity, the time of year (for water transportation, whether it was going upstream or downstream) and on the load, and then issued regulations specifying how long it should take for a given communication or mode of transportation to move between one point and another. For example, a Qin Statute on Government Service reads:

> During transportation and deliveries, a heavy cart or [a person with] a shouldered burden, should travel sixty *lǐ* (approx. 24.95 km) per day; an empty cart should travel eighty *lǐ* (approx. 33.3 km) per day, and [walking] personnel should travel a hundred *lǐ* (approx. 41.6 km) per day.[59]

Another Qin ordinance states:

> An Ordinance states: Functionaries return home for rest forty days per year. On dangerous roads, they are to travel 80 *lǐ* per day; on easy roads, 100 *lǐ* (per day). All functionaries who do not have the privilege of riding in carriages are to travel 80 *lǐ* per day; when going to their office, they are to travel 50 *lǐ* (per day). Functionaries on leave who match

---

[56] Chen, Wei 2018: 57 – document nos. 9-56, 9-1209, 9-1245, 9-1973.
[57] Li, Guyin 2005: 27–33.
[58] Beijing daxue chutu wenxian yanjiusuo 2015.

[59] Slip no. 248 (1394) in volume 4 of the Yuelu hoard. The parallel early Han dynasty Zhangjiashan statute states: 'During transportation and deliveries, a heavy cart, [or a person with] a shouldered burden, should travel fifty *lǐ* (approx. 20.8 km) per day; an empty cart should travel seventy *lǐ* (approx. 29 km) per day, and [walking] personnel [who have delivered their shouldered burdens] should travel eighty *lǐ* (approx. 33.3 km) per day.' Thus clearly, in comparison with the Qin, the Han reduced the distance that those on government service were expected to travel per day.

travelling as well as (those who) are released to return to dwell at home in all cases are not to use this ordinance. Supplementary(?) Ordinance C no. 51[60]

Another reads:

> The Ordinance states: All those who ride official conveyances,[61] ride official carriage horses, ride horses (that are normally) hitched to the carriages of envoys, as well as (those who) are travelling to county governments to re-investigate cases, when they delay more than ten days in all cases do not feed (them) from the government (stores), but supply rice (grain) according to the passport, lend cauldrons and steamers (so that) they (can) cook it. [Should they have] their own runners, servants, and drivers accompanying (them), order that they cook for themselves. Those who lack runners, servants, and drivers, the county governments are to lend staff to cook (for them) but in all cases they are not to give firewood or vegetables. The rest is as according to the statutes.

Ordinance of the Bureau of Granaries in the Capital Region C no. 46[62]

Yet another reads:

> The Ordinance states: 'When Acting Scribes of (the Commandant of) the Court, Scribes of (the Commandant of) the Court, and Accessory Scribes are re-investigating law cases and they are riding horses (that are normally) hitched to the carriages of envoys,[63] as well as official carriage horses, and (the horses) die unexpectedly, what if (they were to) add (a horse) from a team of three or four horses?' The deliberation: 'Order that they may ride on (horses used by) document scribes, servants, and runners; they may not get (a horse) from a team of three or four horses. Other cases are to be comparable to the office of the Controller of Standards being able to ride on horses (that are normally) hitched to the carriages of envoys to travel to county courts to re-investigate cases as well as (to deal with) other county court business.'

Ordinances on 'Side' Gold and Cloth of the Governor of the Capital Area B no. 9[64]

Official scribes were required to seal a document in the proper fashion, to write down on the document exactly when a despatch arrived and who delivered it, whether by day or by night: each office was issued with a water-clock by which the functionaries could determine to the hour when a communication arrived. Punishments were issued depending on the length of delay during transportation not explained by, for example, bad weather or floods. Officials were required to keep logs of their movements. All these types of regulations were continued by the Han after the Qin collapse. Needless to say, these regulations must have had a major impact on the daily lives of ordinary individuals.

Both the Qin and the early Han used different types of carriages for official communications and for travel of functionaries and they issued sumptuary regulations for this form of travel, depending on the circumstances (e.g., whether there was a military emergency or not), the rank or function of the official and what type of business that he was engaged in, etc. So, for example, only officials above a certain salary rank could ride in carriages, low-ranking functionaries did not have the right to ride in carriages, they had to walk. In the Han, the cut-off point in salary rank was 160 *shi* (bushels) of grain per year. Only those whose annual salary ranked above that grade could ride in a carriage. Women were specifically forbidden to ride in official carriages, as the Qin law stated:

> Carrying women in one's official carriage – how is this to be sentenced? Fine two suits of armour. As for harnessing official horses to one's private carriage and riding in it, do not sentence (the person).[65]

'Two suits of armour' was a heavy cash fine (2688 cash). This regulation was carried over into the early Han and provides the background to one of the legal cases recorded in the Zhangjiashan Tomb no. 247 collection in which an official tried to escape from the Han capital region and return east while driving his newly-wed wife in the carriage. He dressed his wife up as a man to try to fool the officials, but was caught.[66]

Of course, some individuals were wealthy enough to afford the purchase of their own private wheeled vehicles, but the state regulated what type of transportation could travel on what type of road. The carriage technology therefore evolved to meet these complex demands. As the Han developed, these regulations seem to have fallen into relative abeyance, although they seem to have been kept on the books, and there was much movement on the road system for both official purposes, whether military or civilian, for economic reasons (i.e., for trade), and for pleasure. As a consequence, travel by carriage became common-place and, as in the modern world, pests could be carried from one region to another and from one state to another. Before the unification in 221 BCE, the Qin required the following procedure:

---

[60] Slip nos. 134 (1903) and 135 (1905) in volume 5 of the Yuelu hoard. See below.
[61] For the ambiguity of this term, see Barbieri-Low and Yates 2015: 686, note 1.
[62] Slip nos. 257 (166 3) and 258 (1779) in volume 5 of the Yuelu hoard.
[63] For the term *shima* 使馬, which appears in the Zhangjiashan corpus, see Barbieri-Low and Yates, 2015: 934, note 35.
[64] Slip nos. 261 (1924) and 262 (1920) in volume 5 of the Yuelu hoard. The Commandant of the Court was the chief legal official in the Qin (and also later in the Han dynasty), Accessory Scribes were officials at the central as well as commandery (regional) levels and the Controller of Standards was an official at the commandery, and possibly central levels, particularly responsible for legal affairs. The position of Controller was abolished by the Han and he only appears in newly excavated and retrieved documents, such as this one.

[65] Hulsewé 1985: 170, D155 (slightly revised).
[66] Barbieri-Low and Yates 2015: 1195–1206.

When guests from the regional lords (i.e., envoys from the courts of Qin's rivals) come, the transverse bar and the yokes (of their carriages) must be singed with fire. Why are they singed? If the regional lords do not treat the gadflies, the gadflies all attach themselves to the transverse bar and the yokes, to the neck-straps, the girths, the shafts (and) the straps; therefore they are singed.[67]

We do not know whether this procedure continued in the post-unification period and whether the same precautions were taken in the Han to reduce the risk of transmission of problematic species (nowadays we might call them invasive species) from one region to another.

Travel by carriage even influenced the development of tomb art. The various types of carriages were displayed on the walls of the tombs especially from the turn of the millennium and this ritual and artistic practice expanded dramatically in the Eastern Han (23–220 CE). These have been the subject of extensive research by art historians. For example, Wu Hung begins one of his essays on tomb art in the following way: 'Images of chariots are abundant in Han period (206 BCE–CE 220) tombs and serve different purposes. Some indicate the official rank of the tomb occupant or pertain to events in his life, while others depict funerary processions as well as imaginary tours taken by the soul. … Because of their dual function of representing actual ritual events and a fictional time/space after death, these images link life and afterlife into a continuous metaphorical journey, in which death is conceived as a liminal experience.'[68] From them, we have a much better idea of what different types of Han carriages looked like in reality, even though one has to recognise that the artisans who carved the images may have exercised a certain amount of artistic license in their representations.

Carts

After the defeat of all his rivals in 221 BCE, at the time when King Zheng of Qin adopted his new title of "First Emperor," it appears that he ordered a massive change in the nomenclature of many other titles and terms that were to be changed in official documents. Among these changes was the change in official terminology of 'big carts' (*dache* 大車) to 'ox carts' (*niuche* 牛車).[69] It is the latter term that is seen in administrative documents after that date, while *dache* is seen before then. Whether the change in the term signalled any technological change in the form of the cart (for example, whether it became more common after that

Figure 14.8. Rubbing of an Ox cart (from Sun Ji 2020: 123, Figure 25-3; originally published by Shanghai guji chubanshe 2008: 117, Figure 25-3; with permission of Zhonghua shuju).

date for carts to be increased in size, to have four wheels, and to be pulled by oxen rather than horses) is not known (Figure 14.8).

In the following Qin statute preserved in the Yuelu collection as reconstructed by the editors[70], the state is forbidding stallions and mares of a certain height and of a young age to pull a wheeled vehicle called a *ju*. According to a comment on the Han dictionary *Shuowen jiezi* this was a cart with a straight draught-pole, otherwise known as a 'large cart,'[71] which was, of course in official Qin terminology after the unification an 'ox-cart.' In other words, it was a cart to which normally an ox was yoked and was used in farming. The state also is banning the use of such horses to 'open up fields' which must refer to them pulling ploughs,[72] and it also objects to them being rented out for private transportation purposes. Note, too, that merchants were similarly banned from using horses above a certain height to pull their vehicles. So presumably it was not uncommon for merchants to load their stock onto horse-drawn vehicles to take to the markets.[73] The Qin state apparently wanted all horses to be put at the disposal of the state, to be used for all these purposes if they were tall enough. If they were, they were branded to indicate that they had passed inspection and could be employed. Most likely, taller, stronger animals were incorporated into its cavalry forces. Finally, it is worth noting that the horses are relatively small in comparison to modern day animals: Emperor Wu of the Han dynasty is famous for having introduced a new breed of horses from Central Asia, although some examples of the new breeding stock may have entered the Han before his time.[74] Of course, that the Qin state explicitly wished to ban the above-mentioned practices implies that they were, in fact, being carried on by the population at large, but we have no means of determining how prevalent these practices were.

---

[67] Hulsewé 1985: 171–172, D158, slightly amended; Xia 2019: 278–282.
[68] Wu, Hung 1998; cf. Wu, Hung 1994; Shao 2018.
[69] A document is preserved in the Liye archive listing many of these changes in nomenclature. Unfortunately, much of the writing has not survived. But the change in the terms to be used for carts survived. See Chen, Wei 2018: 155–160, document no. 8-461. Because of its historical significance, the document has been studied extensively by scholars.

[70] See note 36 above.
[71] *Shuowen jiezi* 說文解字, *pian* 14A.49b, p. 726.
[72] The Qin were particularly anxious to expand agricultural production by opening up what they considered to be uncultivated wastelands. Of course, by doing so, they were disrupting the ecology of the natural landscape and destroying the habitat for the local flora and fauna.
[73] The Qin also issued a number of market regulations, but these are not germane to the topic of chariots, carriages, and carts.
[74] See Linduff 2019; Yates 2003, and the scholarship cited therein.

A Statute on Finance states:

> It is strictly forbidden: do not dare to have stallions or mares more than five *chi* five *cun* (i.e., 1.2925 metres or 4.24 feet) tall and less than a full four years old pull *ju* carts,[75] open up fields, or be rented out for transportation by others; and it is strictly forbidden: traders are not to be able to use stallions or mares more than five *chi* five *cun* (i.e., 1.2925 metres or 4.24 feet) tall to transport (goods) for sale in the market as well as to be rented out for transportation by others. For violating the ordinance, in every case fine each person two sets of armour, and confiscate and submit the horses to the state. As for those who are able to arrest or denounce (such activity), give them the horses. When the Bailiffs of the District or Police Stations do not catch them, fine each one set of armour, and fine the Assistant, the Magistrate, and the Scribe Directors each one shield. As for horses more than a full four years old who match pulling *ju* carts, opening up fields, or being rented out for transportation, order the Bailiff of the Stables to measure and age the horse in the presence of the Assistant and the Magistrate, and brand it on the right shoulder; the brand mark should say: 'Matches being ridden/harnessed.' Should it not match being ridden/harnessed and to stealthily brand (it) as well as to fraudulently and counterfeitedly allow someone else to brand (it), in every case exile them and confiscate and submit the horse to the state.[76]

In the Qin, the state allowed individuals to pay off their debts to the government, as well as redemption fees and fines that had been levied on them for criminal acts, by means of loaning out the horses or oxen that they owned.[77] In addition, such a person could hire a replacement and slave-owners could depute their male and female slaves to work off their crimes for them, too. The rate of exchange for an individual's labour is given in the Shuihudi laws (it was 8 cash per day if the individual paid for his own food, 6 cash per day if the state provided the food)[78] but it is not known at what rate horses or oxen could pay off a debt or a fine.

When carts and oxen owned by the state were calculated by the functionaries to be insufficient for a particular project initiated under the rules of a government service (or corvée labour), one of the forms of tax imposed by the Qin state, carts owned by the population at large were requisitioned for corvée labour projects. This can be seen in various statutes and in the documents preserved in the Liye archive. For example, one item in the Yuelu hoard reads:

A Statute on Government Service states:

> When levying a government service as well as carts and oxen and they do not match (being levied) as well as without authorisation making the dependents and disciples of others,[79] the sons of those who are tax exempt, non-adult stalwart youths,[80] and crossbowmen,[81] as for the Bailiff of the District and the officials in charge, fine each two sets of armour. When the Commandant, the Commandant's Scribes, the Sergeant Majors, the Assistant, and the Scribe Directors see (the situation) as well as when they perhaps report, yet do not lodge an official accusation about it, they share the same crime. Should they not see it and not report it, fine each one set of armour. When providing service in a township, and delivering and transporting, first provide it with all the government's carts and oxen as well as labourers. When it is an emergency that cannot be delayed, then levy a government service according to the statutes. For not first (using) all the government's carts, oxen, and labourers and to levy the black-headed ones[82] as well as initiate a government service, when the (amount of labour) force is sufficient to be equal (to the task) and not to make it equal,[83] sentence them.

Another statute in same category states (see above):

> A Statute on Government Service states: During transportation and deliveries, a heavy cart or [a person with] a shouldered burden, should travel sixty *li* (approx. 24.95 km) per day; an empty cart should travel eighty *li* (approx. 33.3 km) per day, and [walking] personnel should travel a hundred *li* (approx. 41.6 km) per day.[84] Those who have ... enrol (them) in the accounts, and order the labourers to

---

[75] According to the *Shuowen jiezi, pian* 14A.49a, p. 726, this type of cart had a straight draught-pole.
[76] Chen, Songchang 2016: slip nos. 127 (1229), 128 (1279), 128 (1279), 130 (1298), 131 (1365).
[77] Hulsewé 1985: 69, A68.
[78] Hulsewé 1985: 68, A68. This rate is confirmed by a Statute of the Director Convict Labour in the Yuelu hoard, slip nos. 257 (0350) and 258 (0993); see Chen, Songchang 2016.

[79] This might be a single term, "dependent disciples."
[80] The term *aotong* appears in the Shuihudi legal texts. See Hulsewé 1985: 115, C20, and note 2. 'Stalwart' refers to those who were categorised as not 'disabled'. Non-adult stalwart youths were below the age when they were required to perform labour duty for the state.
[81] The editors suggest that these are either crossbowmen who had their skills tested twice yearly in spring and autumn, or an alternative way of writing *nu* 奴 'male slave.' The former is more likely: the state probably wished for the crossbowmen to be on active duty and not to waste their energies engaging in labour projects.
[82] The 'black-headed ones' was the official Qin term for members of the tax-paying population registered on the official population registers. It was introduced at the beginning of the Qin Empire in 221 BCE, as mentioned above.
[83] Officials were required to estimate ahead of time exactly the amount of labour and materiel needed to accomplish a given task. This was called 'equalising' *jun* 均.
[84] The parallel early Han dynasty statute from Tomb no. 247, Zhangjiashan, states: "During transportation and deliveries, a heavy cart, [or a person with] a shouldered burden, should travel fifty *li* (ca. 20.8 km) per day; an empty cart should travel seventy *li* (ca. 29 km) per day, and [walking] personnel [who have delivered their shouldered burdens] should travel eighty *li* (ca. 33.3 km) per day." Thus clearly, in comparison with the Qin, the Han reduced the distance that those on government service were expected to travel. See above for another Qin ordinance on a similar subject.

grease the axles of the carts well.⁸⁵ Feed the oxen. When the oxen are thin, the leaders of the oxen are not to get a contract for the government service.

Completely levy the bond servants and bondwomen, the robber guards, those resident for paying off a fine, redemption [fee], or debt. The government … them … transport and deliver them. When it is an emergency, and it cannot be delayed, then levy a government service for it.

Those who have fines, redemption [fees], or debts are to choose the days and then be personally resident. As for those who are in residence for the government/state, if the county where they are resident has/holds a government service or garrison (duty), and these types (of individual) match getting to be sent out, order (them) (to perform) the government service or garrison (duty). When the government service or garrison (duty) is finished, they are immediately to be resident again. As for matching government service or garrison (duty), when (a person) is sick and cannot go out as well as when he works for more than a full year, exempt the government service for the year that he was sick, and do not follow up … sentence (them) for detention; exempt the days of detention when (they are performing) government service or garrison (duty), and employ them according to the days that they went out.

The assembly for the project was reckoned to have started when the carts arrived and late arrival or abscondence (in other words, missing the levy entirely or running away before arriving at the location where the project was to be undertaken) was punished by the state by beating.⁸⁶

The Qin state was well-known for promoting agriculture, and especially noted for encouraging the population to use oxen for ploughing and other agricultural purposes.⁸⁷ It comes, therefore, as no surprise that the Qin state loaned out carts and oxen for use of the ordinary population. It took great care of its property, as can be seen from the following statute:

When government storehouses loan government carts and oxen … to the location of the borrower. When the borrower perhaps privately uses a government cart and oxen, as well as when the borrower does not feed the oxen well, and the oxen grow thin; if he does not repair the cart, if the cart is neglected, if the cart's shafts are crooked, as well as when the cart has not been covered, or if the carriage's hood or canopy have been violently broken or torn, the person in charge of the cart and oxen as well as the functionary (and) the head of the office will have committed a crime.⁸⁸

Of course, carts pulled by oxen continued to be used in the Han dynasty and they even came to be favourite modes of transportation for scholars in the later part of the period.

The Prices of Carts and Carriages

What was price or value of a cart or carriage in the Han dynasty? There is very limited evidence, and what is recorded in the transmitted texts suggests that prices were extremely high. Was that really the case? Ding Bangyou and Wei Xiaoming have recently published a book that gathers the prices of many Han articles. They have found two citations to the price of a cart in excavated documents. The first, from the so-called Jinguan Han slips from Jianshui in the desert on the northwest frontier, gives the price of one carriage or cart (*che*) as 3,000 cash and another from Juyan in the same region specifies an ox cart priced at 2,000 cash.⁸⁹ Both of these prices are likely to derive from documents of the late Western Han dynasty, although the exact date cannot be determined with any precision.

In contrast to the paucity of information on the price of carriages and carts, the evidence they have gathered on the price of horses is much more substantial and Ding and Wei have been able to retrieve evidence from both excavated documents and transmitted texts, and the calculations of previous scholars. The price seems to have fluctuated quite widely, varying according to the supply and demand, and on the geographical location as well as on the age of the animal, its gender and its general health condition, and the type of work that it was capable of doing. Suffice it to say that in general the price of a horse was more than an ox cart, sometimes substantially higher, double, triple, or even more. When an animal died, all parts of its body were gathered and carefully priced and, of course, the price was well below that of a cart, frequently not even reaching 1,000 cash.⁹⁰

Of course, it would be most helpful if the dates of the records that Ding and Wei have gathered were available and it would also be useful to have a comparative value: in other words, the value of other objects at the same time. One document retrieved from Juyan does provide the comparative values as it is a listing of the property of a man, but the date of its composition has not survived. The document, no. 37.35 reads as follows:⁹¹

---

⁸⁵ The Yuelu editors interpret as *gongjian* 攻閒 as *gangjian* 釭鐧. The term appears in the Shuihudi "Statutes of the Director of Convict Labour," which Hulsewé, following the Shuihudi editors, interprets as "repair." See Hulsewé 1985: 75–76, A76.
⁸⁶ Hulsewé 1985: D143 and D144, p. 167.
⁸⁷ This is said to have originated with the ideas of Lord Shang (Gongsun Yang), the 'legalist' advisor and chief minister under Duke Xiao of Qin in the fourth century BCE. See Pines 2019. The form of ploughing with an ox or oxen saw extensive developments in the Han which were related to the developments in the production of different types of cast iron ploughshares, especially those manufactured in state foundries and distributed by it. For images of the various types of ploughing with oxen in the Han and relevant analysis, see Zhang Xuanyi 2020.
⁸⁸ Hulsewé, *Remnants of Ch'in Law*, A74, pp. 74–75, slightly amended.
⁸⁹ Ding and Wei 2016: 130–131.
⁹⁰ Ding and Wei 2016: 138, 148.
⁹¹ Xie Guihua et al. 1987: 61.

Li Zhong, 30 years old; of Royal Conveyance rank,[92] Guangchang Ward, Lude Platoon Leader:

    2 non-adult male slaves value 30,000   5 usable horses value 20,000   one house 10,000

    1 adult female slave 20,000   2 ox carts 4000   5 *qing*[93] of cultivated fields 50,000

    2 light carriages value 10,000   a weight-bearing ox 26,000   Total property value 150,000[94]

While there are a number of points that could be made on this document,[95] what is interesting for our purposes is that the light carriage (*yaoche*) was valued at 5000 cash while ox cart was valued at 2000 cash. The ox was the most valuable possession, followed by the slaves. Li Zhong was certainly a wealthy man.

Wheelbarrow

As far as can be determined, the single-wheeled wheelbarrow, known as a "deer cart" (*luche* 鹿車) first appeared in the Eastern Han period.[96] It was pushed, rather than pulled as the *wanche* 輓車 was, and usually by a single individual. Images of wheelbarrows appear in Eastern Han tomb tiles, especially in Sichuan Province, where the device may have been invented (Figure 14.3). They are shown being used to transport alcohol,[97] but textual sources also indicate that they were also a means of carrying a human. They were later deployed for transporting military equipment especially along narrow mountainous roads and pathways. The term itself may have derived from the term for a pulley, as the terms *luche* and *jing luche* (井鹿車) appear in recently published documents found in a well in downtown Changsha, the capital of Hunan Province.[98] In the latter documents, the terms clearly refer to the pulleys placed above a well from which water was to be drawn.

Brief Concluding Remarks

This essay has been a summary exploration of some of the new legal and administrative documents and texts dating primarily from the Qin and early Han empires discovered in the last fifty years that concern chariots, carriages, and carts. There is obviously much more that could be said on each of the types of wheeled vehicles discussed. The subject is almost inexhaustible, especially given the numerous archaeological excavations of objects, as well as the ongoing discovery of new textual sources, some of which have been published, but many more of which are awaiting publication. Each new discovery enriches our understanding. Wheeled vehicles played a central role in warfare and in civilian daily life, especially for officials and functionaries, but for the common people, too, in economic and social terms and in ways that we barely comprehend at present. While not being allowed to ride in a carriage obviously constrained an individual's freedom of movement and limited her/his experience, those individuals entitled to ride in them were enabled to travel to distant locations, even if only potentially, and as a consequence of this possibility they undoubtedly expanded their geographical knowledge and their sense of place in the world and in the cosmos as a whole. Indeed, early imperial Chinese saw chariots in the sky among the constellations: something that I have had no space to discuss. Clearly, by Eastern Han times, many individuals hoped or expected to travel in carriages in the world after death, even if they were legally barred from riding in them in this world.

Robin D. S. Yates
James McGill Professor Emeritus, East Asian Studies and History and Classical Studies, McGill University, Montreal, Canada

---

[92] This was rank 8 in the 20-rank Han system, the highest that a commoner could reach.
[93] A *qing* was roughly 4.61 hectares or 11.39 acres.
[94] The total of 150,000 does not match the figures given in the list: so either the scribe made an error in calculation, or the document is a draft that may have been corrected in the fair copy. Alternatively, one or more of the figures listed is incorrect. I am not comfortable in deciding between these alternatives.
[95] For example, the total is incorrect.
[96] For reconstructions and discussion, see Wang Zhenduo 1997: 23–32.
[97] Women seem to have been particularly involved in the manufacture and sale of alcohol: see Elias 2020.
[98] Wu Meijiao 2020. Wu cites four documents in her study. The corpus has yet to be published in its entirety.

Bibliography

An Zhongyi 安忠義. 2005. Han Wudi shiqi qibing de xingqi yu junzhi gaige 漢武帝時期騎兵的興起與軍制改革 (The Rise of Cavalry in Han Wudi's Time and the Reforms in the Military) *Yantai shifan xueyuan xuebao (zhexue shehui kexue ban)* 煙臺師範學院學報(哲學社會科學版) 22 (4): 44–49.

Barbieri-Low, Anthony J. 2000 (1997). *Wheeled Vehicles in the Chinese Bronze Age (c.2000–771 BC)*. Sino-Platonic Papers 99. Cambridge, MA: M.A. thesis, Harvard University.

Barbieri-Low, Anthony J., and Robin D. S. Yates. 2015. *Law, State, and Society in Early Imperial China: A Study with Critical Edition and Translation of the Legal Texts from Zhangjiashan Tomb no. 247*. Leiden: Brill.

Beijing daxue chutu wenxian yanjiusuo 北京大學出土文獻研究所, ed. 2015. *Beijing daxue cang Xi-Han zhushu (san)* 北京大學藏西漢竹書 (參) (The Bamboo Books Held by Peking University [3]). Shanghai: Shanghai guji chubanshe.

Bielenstein, Hans. 1980. *The Bureaucracy of Han Times*. Cambridge: Cambridge University Press.

Byrne, Rebecca Zer. 1974. *Harmony and Violence in Classical China: A Study of the Battles of the "Tso Chuan."* Unpublished Ph.D. Dissertation. Chicago: University of Chicago.

Caldwell, Ernest. 2018. *Writing Chinese Laws: The Form and Function of Legal Statutes Found in the Qin Shuihudi Corpus*. London and New York: Routledge.

Chen Ning 陳寧. 2015. *Qin Han mazheng yanjiu* 秦漢馬政研究 (Studies on the Management of Horses in the Qin and Han). Beijing: Zhongguo shehui kexue chubanshe.

Chen Songchang 陳松長, ed. 2016. *Yuelu shuyuan cang Qin jian (si)*. 嶽麓書院藏秦簡(肆) (The Qin Bamboo Slips Held by the Yuelu Academy [4]). Shanghai: Shanghai cishu chubanshe.

Chen Wei 陳偉. 2016. Guanyu Qin Qianling xian 'ku' de chubu kaocha 關於秦遷陵縣"庫"的初步考察 (Preliminary Investigation concerning the Qin Qianling County 'Armory'). *Jianbo* 簡帛 12: 161–177.

Chen Wei 陳偉, chief ed. 2012. *Liye Qin jiandu jiaoshi (di yi juan)* 里耶秦簡牘校釋(第一卷) (Collations and Explanations of the Qin Slips and Boards from Liye 1). Wuhan: Wuhan daxue chubanshe.

Chen Wei 陳偉, chief ed. 2018. *Liye Qin jiandu jiaoshi (di er juan)* 里耶秦簡牘校釋(第二卷) (Collations and Explanations of the Qin Slips and Boards from Liye 2). Wuhan: Wuhan daxue chubanshe.

Cook, Constance A. 1997. Wealth and the Western Zhou. *Bulletin of the School of Oriental and African Studies* 60 (2): 253–294.

Dang Shixue 黨士學. 2011. Qin ling tong liche cheyu jiegou ji yibi jiexi 秦陵銅立車車輿結構及衣蔽解析 (Analysis of the Structure and Trappings of the Bronze Standing Chariot from the Qin Mausoleum). *Qin Shihuangling bowuyuan* 秦始皇陵博物院: 191–212.

Dewall, Magdalene von. 1964. *Pferd und Wagen im frühen China*. Bonn: Habelt.

Ding Bangyou 丁邦友 and Wei Xiaoming 魏曉明. 2016. *Qin Han wujia shiliao huishi* 秦漢物價史料匯釋 (Compilation and Explanations of the Historical Materials on Prices in the Qin and Han). Beijing: Zhongguo shehui kexue chubanshe.

Durrant, Stephen, Wai-yee Li, and David Schaberg, trans. 2016. *Zuo Tradition: Commentary on the "Spring and Autumn Annals"*, 3 vols. Seattle: University of Washington Press.

Elias, Hajni. 2020. Women's Role in the Production and Sale of Alcohol in Han China as Reflected in Tomb Art from Sichuan. *Early China* 43: 247–284.

Elman, Benjamin and Martin Kern, ed. 2009. *Statecraft and Classical Learning: The Rituals of Zhou in East Asian History*. Leiden: Brill.

Falkenhausen, Lothar von. 2006. *Chinese Society in the Age of Confucius (1000–250 BC): The Archaeological Evidence*. Los Angeles: Cotsen Institute of Archaeology, University of California.

Hayashi Minao 林巳奈夫. 1959a. Chūgoku senshin jidai no basha 中国先秦時代の馬車 (Horse-drawn Chariots of the Pre-Qin Period in China). *Tōhō gakuhō* 東方學報 29: 155–284.

Hayashi Minao 林巳奈夫. 1959b. Chūgoku senshin jidai no uma (I) 中国先秦時代の馬 (I) (Horses in the Pre-Qin Period in China (1)). *Minzokugaku kenkyū* 民族學研究, 23 (4): 387–409.

Hayashi Minao 林巳奈夫. 1960. Chūgoku senshin jidai no uma (II) 中国先秦時代の馬 (II) (Horses in the Pre-Qin Period in China 2). *Minzokugaku kenkyū* 民族學研究, 24 (1–2): 33–57.

Hou Han shu 後漢書 (Book of the Later Han); compiled by Fan Ye 范曄 (398–445 or 446); treatises by Sima Biao 司馬彪, died ca. 306 CE. 1965. Beijing: Zhonghua shuju.

Hulsewé, A.F.P. 1985. *Remnants of Ch'in Law: an Annotated Translation of the Ch'in Legal and Administrative Rules of the 3rd Century B.C., Discovered in Yün-meng Prefecture, Hu-pei Province, in 1975*. Leiden: Brill.

Jiang Yan 蔣艷. 2011. *Zeng You Yi mu tongwen zhushi* 曾侯乙墓筒文注釋 (Explanatory Commentary on the Scripts in the Tomb of Yi, Marquis of Zeng). MA thesis, Xi'nan daxue.

Kierman, Frank A., Jr. 1974. Phases and Modes of Combat in Early China. In: *Chinese Ways in Warfare*, edited by Frank A. Kierman, Jr. and John K. Fairbank, 27–66. Cambridge MA: Harvard University Press.

Li Cheng 李成. 2010. "Cong qingtong cheqi guishi xian-Qin mache de fazhan" 從青銅車器窺視先秦馬車的發展 (A Peek into the Development of the Pre-Qin Bronze Chariot from the Perspective of Bronze Chariot Equipment). *Wenbo* 文博 6: 15–22.

Li Guyin 李古寅. 2005. *Zhongguo gudai xingju de gushi* 中國古代刑具故事 (The Story of Ancient Chinese Instruments of Torture). Beijing: Zhongguo wenshi chubanshe.

Linduff, Katheryn M. 2019. The Heavenly Horses Visualized in Han China (220 BCE–220 CE). In: *Equids and Wheeled Vehicles in the Ancient World: Essays in Memory of Mary A. Littauer*, edited by Peter Raulwing, Katheryn M. Linduff, and Joost H. Crouwel, 171–180. Oxford: British Archaeological Reports.

Liu Ting 劉婷 and Liang Yun 梁雲. 2015. Qin ren chema xun fangshi ji qi yuanyuan 秦人車馬殉葬方式及其淵源 (The Form and Origin of the Chariot and Horse Burial Sacrifice of the Qin People). *Qin Shihuangling bowuyuan* 秦始皇陵博物院: 164–175.

Liu Yonghua 劉永華. 2002. *Zhongguo gudai cheyu maju* 中國古代車輿馬具 (Ancient Chinese Chariots and Horse Trappings). Shanghai: Shanghai cishu chubanshe.

Lu Liancheng. 1993. Chariot and Horse Burials in Ancient China. *Antiquity* 67 (257): 824–838.

Lu Shan 盧珊. 2019. Qin Qianling xian junbei wuzi guanli yanjiu 秦遷陵縣軍備物資管理研究 (Studies on the Management of Armaments in the Qin County of Qianling). MA thesis, Dongbei shifan daxue.

Luo Xiaohua 羅小華. 2014. Xian-Qin chema yanjiu zongshu 先秦車馬研究綜述 (Summary of Studies on Chariots and Horses in the Pre-Qin Period). *Zhongguo shi yanjiu dongtai* 中國史研究動態 2: 5–11.

Luo Xiaohua 羅小華. 2015. Zeng hou Yi mu zhujian suojian mache zhuangbei wupin zonghe fenxi 曾侯乙墓竹簡所見馬車裝備物品綜合分析 (A Comprehensive Analysis of the Items of Horse-drawn Chariot Equipment Found on the Bamboo Slips of the Tomb of Yi, Marquis of Zeng). *Chutu wenxian* 出土文獻 7: 42–49.

Luo Xiaohua 羅小華. 2017. Zeng hou Yi mu zhujian zhong de chezhen 曾侯乙墓竹簡中的車陣 (The Parade of Chariots in the Bamboo Slips in the Tomb of Yi, Marquis of Zeng). *Chutu wenxian* 出土文獻 11: 165–171.

Needham, Joseph, with Wang Ling. 1965. *Science and Civilisation in China vol. 4 Physics and Physical Technology, Part II Mechanical Engineering*. Cambridge: Cambridge University Press.

Needham, Joseph and Robin D. S. Yates. 1994. *Science and Civilisation in China vol. 5, part 6 Military Technology: Missiles and Sieges*. Cambridge: Cambridge University Press.

Pines, Yuri, trans. 2019. *The Book of Lord Shang: Apologetics of State Power in Early China*. New York: Columbia University Press.

Qin Shihuang bingmayong bowuguan 秦始皇兵馬俑博物館 and Shaanxi sheng Kaogu yanjiusuo 陝西省考古研究所, ed. 1998. *Qin Shihuang ling tong chema fajue baogao* 秦始皇兵陵銅車馬發覺報告 (Report of the Excavation of the Bronze Chariots and Horses in the Mausoleum of the First Emperor of Qin). Beijing: Wenwu chubanshe.

Raulwing, Peter, Katheryn M. Linduff, and Joost H. Crouwel, eds. 2019. *Equids and Wheeled Vehicles in the Ancient World: Essays in Memory of Mary A. Littauer*. BAR International Series 2923. Oxford: BAR Publishing.

Rowe, William T. 1992. Ming-Qing Guilds. *Ming-Qing yanjiu* 1: 43–55.

Ruitenbeek, Klaas. 1996. *Carpentry and Building in Late Imperial China: A Study of the Fifteenth-century Carpenter's Manual, Lu Ban jing*. Leiden, New York: Brill.

Sanft, Charles. 2014. *Communication and Cooperation in Early Imperial China: Publicizing the Qin Dynasty*. Albany: State University of New York Press.

Shandong sheng wenwu kaogu yanjiusuo 山東省文物考古研究所 and Zibo shi Linzi qu wenwu guanli ju 淄博市臨淄區文物管理局. 2016. Shandong Linzi Shanwang cun Han dai bingma yongkeng fajue jianbao 山東臨淄山王村漢代兵馬俑坑發掘簡報 (Brief Report of the Excavation of the Han Dynasty Pottery Figurines of Warriors and Horses at Shanwang Village, Linzi, Shandong). *Wenwu* 文物 6: 4–29.

Shao Jingjing 邵菁菁. 2018. Cong Han dai mushi bihua kan mache lizhi yu chema chuxing tu yiyi 從從漢代墓室壁畫看馬車禮制與車馬出行圖意義 (The Ritual System of Horse-drawn Carriages and the Meaning of the Images of the Emergence of Carriages and Horses Seen in Han Dynasty Tomb Murals). *Meishu shi lun yanjiu* 美術史論研究 6: 75–80.

Shaughnessy, Edward L. 1988. Historical Perspectives on the Introduction of the Chariot into China. *Harvard Journal of Asiatic Studies* 48 (1): 189–237.

Shaughnessy, Edward L. 1991. *Sources of Western Zhou History*. Berkeley CA: University of California Press.

Shi Dangshe 史黨社. 2017. Qin mache de wenhua shi yiyi—cong Qin ling chutu tong chema tanqi 秦馬車的文化史意義—從秦陵出土銅車馬談起 (The Cultural and Historical Significance of Qin Horse-drawn Chariots – Talking from the Bronze Horse-drawn Chariot Excavated from the Qin Mausoleum). *Qin Shihuangling bowuyuan* 秦始皇陵博物院: 338–356.

Shi ming 釋名 (Explaining Terms); compiled by Liu Xi 劉熙 ca. 200 CE: https://ctext.org/shi-ming/shi-che/zh.

Shuowen jiezi 說文解字 (Discussing Writing and Explaining Graphs), comm. Duan Yucai 段玉裁 (1735–1815); rpt. of the copy held by the Jingjun lou (Duan Yucai's own collection). 1986 (1981). Shanghai: Shanghai guji chubanshe.

Sterckx, Roel. 1996. An Ancient Chinese Horse Ritual. *Early China* 21: 47–79.

Sun Ji 孫機. 2001. *Zhongguo gu yufu luncong (zengding ben)* 中國古輿服論叢(增訂本) (Collected Discussions on Ancient Chinese Chariot Accessories [Revised Edition]). Beijing: Wenwu chubanshe.

Sun Ji 孫機. 2020. *Han dai wuzhi wenhua ziliao tushuo (zengding ben)* 漢代物質文化資料圖說(增訂本) (Illustrated Explanations of Data on Han Material Culture, revised edition). Beijing: Zhonghua shuju; originally published by Shanghai: Shanghai guji chubanshe 2008.

Wan Xiang. 2013. The Horse in Pre-imperial China. Unpublished PhD dissertation, University of Pennsylvania.

Wang Haicheng 王海城. 2002. Zhongguo mache de qiyuan 中國馬車的起源 (The Origins of Chinese Horse-drawn Chariots). *Ouya xuekan* (*Eurasian Studies*) 歐亞學刊 3: 1–75.

Wang Shaohua 汪少華. 2005. *Zhongguo gudai cheyu mingwu kaobian* 中國古車輿名物考辨 (Textual Research on Well-known Objects Related to Ancient Chinese Chariots). Beijing: Shangwu yinshuguan.

Wang Xueli 王學理. 1994. *Qin yong zhuanti yanjiu* 秦俑專題研究 (Special Studies on Qin Terracotta Figures). Xi'an: Sanqin chubanshe.

Wang Zhenduo 王振鐸; ed. and suppl. Li Qiang 李強. 1997. *Dong-Han chezhi fuyuan yanjiu* 東漢車制復原研究 (Studies on the Restoration of the System of Carriages in the Eastern Han). Beijing: Kexue chubanshe.

Wang Zijin 王子今. 2015a. *Qin Han jiaotong shi xinshi* 秦漢交通史新識 (New Understandings of the History of Communications in the Qin and Han). Beijing: Zhongguo shehui kexue chubanshe.

Wang Zijin 王子今. 2015b. *Zhanguo Qin Han jiaotong geju yu quyu xingzheng* 戰國秦漢交通格局與區域行政 (Patterns and Regional Administration of Communications in the Warring States Period, and Qin and Han Dynasties). Beijing: Zhongguo shehui kexue chubanshe.

Watson, Burton, trans. 1968. *The Complete Works of Chuang Tzu*. New York: Columbia University Press.

Wen Renjun. 2013. *Ancient Chinese Encyclopedia of Technology: Translation and Annotation of the Kaogong ji (The Artificers' Record)*. New York: Routledge.

Weng Mingpeng 翁明鵬. 2019. Shuo Shuihudi Qin jian 'Ma mei' deng pian yu Beida cang Qin jian 'Cizhu zhi dao' de chaoxie tedian he niandai wenti 說睡虎地《馬禖》等篇與北大藏秦簡《祠祝之道》的抄寫特點和年代問題 (Discussion of the 'Ma Mei' and Other (Related) Sections in the Qin Slips from Shuihudi and the Question of the Date (of Composition) and of the Copying of the 'Way of Sacrificing and Offering Prayers' in the Qin Slips Held by Peking University). *Jianbo yanjiu 2019 (qiu-dong juan)* 簡帛研究 2019 (秋冬卷): 157–175.

Wu Hsiao-yun. 2013. *Chariots in Early China: Origins, Cultural Interaction, and Identity*. BAR International Series 2457. Oxford: British Archaeological Reports.

Wu Hung. 1994. Beyond the 'Great Boundary': Funerary Narrative in the Cangshan Tomb. In: *Boundaries in China*, edited by John Hay, 81–104. London: Reaktion Books.

Wu Hung. 1998. Where Are They Going? Where Did They Come from? – Hearse and 'Soul-carriage' in Han Dynasty Tomb Art. *Orientations* 29(6): 22–31. Partially trans. Zheng, Yan 鄭岩. 2004. Cong nali lai? Dao nali qu? – Han dai yishu zhong de chema tuxiang 從哪裡來？到哪裡去？– 漢代藝術中的車馬圖像 (Where Are They Going? Where Did They Come from? The Images of Carriages and Horses in Han Dynasty Art). *Zhonguo shuhua* 中國書畫 4: 50–53.

Wu Jiulong 吳九龍. 1984. Yinqueshan Han jian Qi guo falü kaoxi 銀雀山漢簡齊國法律考析 (Analysis of the Laws of the State of Qi in the Han Slips from Yinqueshan). *Shixue jikan* 史學集刊 4: 14–20.

Wu Meijiao 吳美嬌. 2020. 'Luche' chengming kaoxi – Cong Zoumalou Xi-Han jian suojian jingluche shuoqi '鹿車'稱名考析 – 從走馬樓西漢簡所見井車說起 (Analysis of the Term 'luche' [Deer Cart/Pulley] – Starting from the Well-Pulley Seen in the Zoumalou Western Han Slips). *Chutu wenxian* 出土文獻 3: 106–114.

Wu Tinghai 武廷海. 2019. *Kaogong ji* chengshu niandai yanjiu – jianlun Kaogong ji jiangren zhishi tixi 《考工記》成書年代研究 – 兼論考工記匠人知識體系 (Studies on Date of Composition of the Record of Artisans – Simultaneously Discussing the Knowledge System of Carpenters in the Record of Artisans). *Zhuangshi* 裝飾 10: 68–72.

Xia Liya 夏利亞. 2019. *Shuihudi Qin jian wenzi jishi* 睡虎地秦簡文字集釋 (Collected Explanations of the Graphs in the Qin Slips from Shuihudi). Shanghai: Shanghai jiaotong daxue chubanshe.

Xie Guihua 謝桂華, Li Junming 李均明, and Zhu Guozhao 朱國炤. 1987. *Juyan Han jian shiwen hejiao* 居延漢簡釋文合校 (Transcriptions and Combined Interpretations of the Han Slips from Juyan). Beijing: Wenwu chubanshe.

Yates, Robin D. S. 2003. The Horse in Early Chinese Military History. In: *Junshi zuzhi yu zhanzheng* (Military Organization and War: Papers from the Third International Conference on Sinology, History Section), edited by Huang Kewu, 1–78. Taipei: Institute of Modern History Academia Sinica.

Yates, Robin D. S. 2012–2013. The Qin Slips and Boards from Well No. 1, Liye, Hunan: A Brief Introduction to the Qin Qianling County Archives. *Early China* 35–36: 291–329.

Yates, Robin D. S. 2018. Evidence for Qin Law in the Qianling County Archive: A Preliminary Survey. *Bamboo and Silk* 1 (2): 403–445.

Yates, Robin D. S. 2021. L'«esclavage» dans l'ordre social aux temps des premiers empires chinois. In: *Les mondes de l'esclavage. Une histoire comparée*, edited by Paulin Ismard, 39–45. Paris: Éditions du Seuil.

Yu Liangming 余良明. 2015. *Zhongguo gudai che wenhua* 中國古代車文化 (Culture of Ancient Chinese Chariots). Fuzhou: Fujian jiaoyu chubanshe.

Zhang Xiancheng 張顯成 and Zhou Qunli 周羣麗. 2011. *Yinwan Han mu jiandu jiaoli* 尹灣漢墓簡牘校理 (Collation of the Slips and Boards in the Han Tomb at Yinwan). Tianjin: Tianjin guji chubanshe.

Zhang Xuanyi 張宣逸. 2020. Han dai huaxiang zhong de 'niugeng tu' 漢代畫像中的 ('Images of Ploughing with Oxen' in Han Dynasty Paintings). *Nongye kaogu* 農業考古 4: 258–263.

Zhao Huacheng 趙化成. 1989. Han hua suojian Han dai cheming kaobian 漢畫所見漢代車名考辨 (Textual Research on the Names of Chariots/Carriages Seen in Han Dynasty Paintings). *Wenwu* 4: 76–82.

Zhongguo shehui kexueyuan kaogu yanjiusuo 中國社會科學院考古研究所. 2005. *Han Chang'an cheng wuku* 漢長安城武庫 (The Han Armoury in Chang'an City). Beijing: Wenwu chubanshe.

Zhuang Xiaoxia 莊小霞. 2018. Liye Qin jian suojian Qin 'dehu fuchu' zhidu kaoshi – jianshuo zhonggu shiqi Hunan diqu de huhuan 里耶秦簡所見 '得虎復除' 制度考釋 – 兼說中古時期湖南地區的虎 (Explanation of the Qin System of 'Tax Relief for Catching Tigers' Seen in the Qin Slips from Liye – Simultaneously Discussing Tigers in the Region of Hunan in Ancient China). *Chutu wenxian yanjiu* 出土文獻研究 17: 115–128.

15

Majiayuan Chariots and the Lustre of Eurasia

Xiaolong Wu and Katheryn M. Linduff

Dozens of lavishly decorated chariots have recently been excavated from the Majiayuan cemetery in present day northwestern China located in a contact zone between Chinese agricultural and Eurasian pastoral groups. Ongoing excavations at Majiayuan have already revealed thousands of artefacts made from a variety of materials, including gold, silver, bronze, iron, tin, clay, bone, glass, faience, agate, and turquoise. The tombs are thought to date to the third century BCE and belong to a local Rong group dominated by the Qin State during the late Zhou Dynasty. The nature of the hybrid and innovative features of the Majiayuan chariots and their ornaments as well as the question of how and why these tombs were achievable in a distant frontier of the Zhou realm far from the regional capital of the Qin State are examined. We propose that the remote and topographically circumscribed location aided in bringing wealth and a strategic role to both the Qin and the Majiayuan peoples. The chariot was the signifier not only of the importance of its owner, but also of the role of this outpost in relation to the ambitions of the rising Qin state and the larger world of Eurasia to their west and dynastic Zhou to their east.

Introduction[1]

Since August 2006, a rescue excavation has been carried out on looted tombs in Majiayuan 马家塬 (Figure 15.1) and other sites in Zhangjiachuan 张家川, Autonomous County of the Hui Nationality, Tianshui 天水 Area, Gansu 甘肃 Province,[2] and to date 69 tombs have been identified, 37 tombs have now been excavated, and 26 tombs have been published, although many more await public notice. Most of the tombs were of catacomb type, many with chariot pits (Figures 15.1, 15.2). In addition to elaborately decorated chariots, tens of thousands of funerary objects have been unearthed, including items made from clay, bronze, gold, silver, bone, iron, agate, turquoise, and coloured glass. Judging from the tomb type, the styles and type of objects buried in these tombs, the excavators have suggested that the interred belonged to the Rong 戎 leadership. The Rong were mentioned in literary texts as a powerful regional population who had become part of the Qin state apparatus during the Warring States period of the late Zhou Dynasty, or in the fifth to third centuries BCE.

The extravagance of these tombs raises an obvious question. How did the owners of these tombs, located in the distant frontier of the Zhou realm and far from the regional capital of the Qin State, accumulate such wealth? What we shall propose here is that it was their remote and topographically circumscribed location that aided in bringing them wealth and giving them a strategic role in Qin history. This group of sites near Majiayuan was located at the gateway to the outside world and was a hub through which trade and tribute were controlled and provided commodities valuable to the emerging ambitions of the Qin and their quest to create an empire. Although chariots were associated with rank and often military accomplishment in Zhou China, their diverse types and the extravagant embellishment in gold, silver and paint on their exteriors at Majiayuan mark them as very special luxury items. They displayed both technological and iconographic debt to traditions found further to their west into eastern Eurasia where the Qin kings sought horses and cattle.[3] Control of technological knowledge, exotic materials and access to the 'foreign' accredited to and amassed by the local Majiayuan elite allowed them to flaunt their economic abundance as well as affording them political advantage within the fading Zhou confederation. The chariots were the signifiers not only of the importance of their owner, but also of the role of this outpost in relation to the ambitions of the rising Qin state and the larger world of Eurasia to their west and dynastic Zhou to their east.

The Site and its Contents

The Majiayuan site is located in Zhangjiachuan Hui Autonomous County, Gansu Province, west of the Longshan Mountain which divides the Guanzhong 关中 Plain in the Wei River Valley and the pastoral tribes further west. Most tombs at Majiayuan have a ramp with steps leading down

---

[1] The authors would like to acknowledge the contribution of Joost Crouwel to their thinking on this topic. Without his guidance as evidenced in his many publications and more recently in his encouragement and interest in the Chinese and Eurasian chariot types, this research would not have been forthcoming. It is the sign of a true scholar who inspires and welcomes thinking beyond his own knowledge and experience. For this, we thank Joost!

[2] Gansu and Zhangjiachuan 2008; Zaoqi and Zhangjiachuan 2009; 2010; 2012; 2018.

[3] Wan 2013; Wong 2017; 2020.

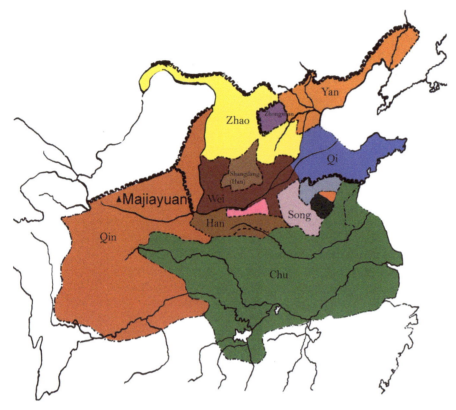

Figure 15.1. Location of the Majiayuan cemetery on a map of China at around 350 BCE.

to the bottom of an earthen pit, on one side of which was a side chamber or catacomb (Figure 15.2). The deceased was buried in the catacomb in a coffin. Chariots were usually placed in the earthen pit, but some large tombs also contain a chariot in the catacomb along with the coffin. Representative grave goods at Majiayuan include chariots and chariot fittings, chariot decorations comprised mainly of plaques made of gold, silver, bronze, iron, and tin, body ornaments such as earrings, belt plaques, buckles, and hooks, iron and bronze weapons and tools, and bronze or pottery vessels. Beads of various materials were used to decorate chariots and the clothes of the deceased. The mortuary culture including the style of the artefacts is hybrid, borrowed from both Zhou/Qin and Eurasian models.

The layout of the cemetery is a semi-circle centred on M6, the largest tomb (around 33 m long, 10 m wide at the opening, and 14 m deep) at the burial ground. M6 (Figure 15.3) is a shaft tomb and the only one with a ramp; the ramp is flanked by nine tiers of steps. Most of the excavated tombs are of a catacomb type with an L-shaped plan (Figure 15.2). All the catacomb tombs have steps in their west wall. Based on the number of steps, these tombs can be divided into five ranked categories: with nine, seven, five, three, and one step respectively. Although the ramp and steps of M6 could have been used for accessing the bottom of the tomb during interment, steps in other tombs are irregular in shape and are too narrow and steep for practical use; instead, the number of steps probably primarily symbolises social rank.[4] Each catacomb, usually at the east end of the north wall of rectangular earthen pits, contains a single skeleton in a supine extended position.

In addition to its large size and unique structure, M6 also stands out because of its contents. Although more severely looted than other tombs, M6 still yielded some precious gold and silver ornaments unseen in other tombs (Figure 15.4) and it is the only Majiayuan tomb so far excavated that contains complete intact sacrificial horses (four). Other tombs were only provided with heads and hooves of horses, cattle and goats. Since the late Shang period, it had been a common practice for the aristocrats in central China to sacrifice whole horses and chariots in tomb ramps or in separate pits near tomb chambers; the horses and chariots were either in the same pit or in separate pits, and the chariots were disassembled in some cases.[5] This practice continued during the early Western Zhou period (ca. 1050 – eighth century BCE), but was altered beginning in the Middle Western Zhou period (roughly ninth century BCE) when chariots were usually disassembled and placed directly in the tomb chamber, although horses were still buried in separate pits.[6] During the Eastern Zhou period (770–256 BCE), horse and chariot pits were still a typical feature of the high-ranking elite tombs in the Central Plain area (middle and lower Yellow River Valley), such as in the states of Jin 晋,[7] Qi 齐[8] and Zhongshan 中山,[9] and this practice continued in the tomb of the first emperor of the Qin Dynasty.[10] During the first millennium BCE, chariot and horse burials constituted an important part of the mortuary rituals and reflected the high social status of the deceased in Eurasia as well, as seen in the large kurgans at Pazyryk and Berel in the Altai Mountains.[11] In contrast, among the pastoralists on China's Inner Asian Frontier, the typical burial practice involved placing heads and hooves of domesticated animals in the tomb fill, as seen in a majority of the tombs of the Taohongbala 桃红巴拉, Maoqinggou 毛庆沟, Yuhuangmiao 玉皇庙 and Yanglang 杨郎 cultures.[12] M6 at Majiayuan is unique be-

---

[4] Wu Xiaolong 2013: 123.
[5] Zheng 1987; Lu 1993: 824.
[6] Lu 1993: 835; Zhongguo Shehui Kexueyuan 2004: 75; Zhang Liyan 2010; Wan 2013.
[7] Shanxisheng 1996.
[8] Shandongsheng 1984.
[9] Hebeisheng 1995.
[10] Shaanxisheng Kaogu Yanjiusuo and Qin Shihuang Bingmayong 2000: 18.
[11] Rudenko 1970: 39–44; Rubinson 2012; Samashev 2012.
[12] Tian 1976; Tian and Guo 1986; Beijingshi 1989; Ningxia 1993; Linduff 1997; Wu Xiaolong 2004.

cause it contains entire horses and chariots within the tomb chamber, instead of dismembered animals as in the Inner Asian Frontier or whole horses in separate pits as in the Central Plains area. Those hybrid burial practices and artefacts adopted from different cultures help to confirm the paramount social status of the deceased in M6, probably the leader of this community.

The Chariots

Lavishly decorated wooden chariots are the most dramatic grave goods so far excavated at Majiayuan (Figure 15.5). Most tombs contain chariots in the main chamber; some large tombs also contain a chariot in the catacomb. Based on structure and decoration, these chariots can be categorised into five types.[13] The most lavishly decorated belong to Type I. These chariots are completely painted with black lacquer, and have animal-shaped plaques and abstract openwork designs made of gold, silver, tin, and bronze attached to the passenger boxes and wheels. The doors at the back of the boxes are reinforced with iron and bronze fittings at the corners. The sides and wheels of some chariots were covered with tightly strung colourful glass and agate beads, including some made with Han purple and Han blue (barium copper silicate) pigments. Type II chariots are often painted red and decorated with bronze openwork plaques but lack the gold and silver ornaments and the beads of Type I.

The boxes of type I and II chariots have a grid structure formed with horizontal wooden bars pierced by vertical wooden posts, and with taller sides added to the woven structure of the box. The vertical posts of the back of the box are decorated and reinforced with either bronze elements or iron pieces inlaid with gold or silver: reverted L-shaped tubes on the top to tie beams and posts together, thin vertical straps in the middle, and figure 8 shaped plaques toward the bottom (Figure 15.6). The joining methods for the wooden elements of Majiayuan chariots

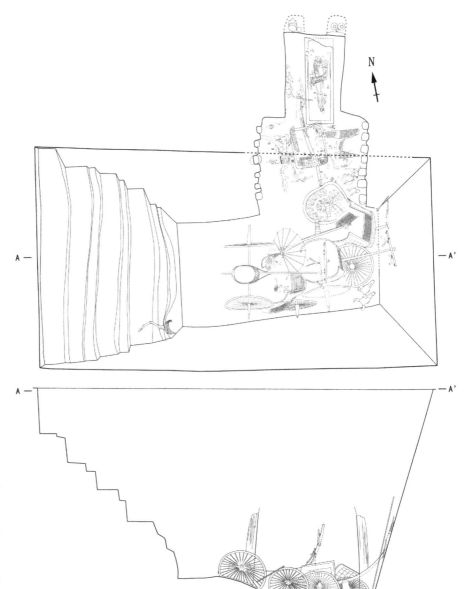

Figure 15.2. A catacomb tomb (M16) at Majiayuan (drawing courtesy of Wang Hui).

include the use of mortise and tenon structures (mostly on wheels and umbrellas) and cords (mostly to connect boxes with draught poles and axles, and draught poles and yokes). Nails and rivets were also used to secure metal ornaments to wooden members. The inverted Y-shaped yoke saddles, decorated with iron, gold, silver, and bone, are tied onto the yoke bars, which have projecting metal rein loops or holes on the bar itself for the reins to thread through. The poles for chariot umbrellas are usually tied to the side of the passenger box and curve toward the centre; some are also directly secured close to the centre of the bottom of the box.[14]

Type III chariots have passenger boxes formed with a grid of wooden slats and both sides have flat armrests. The boxes are lacquered black and the wheel spokes and hubs are

---

[13] Zhao 2010b.

[14] Zhao 2018: 44–52.

Wu and Linduff

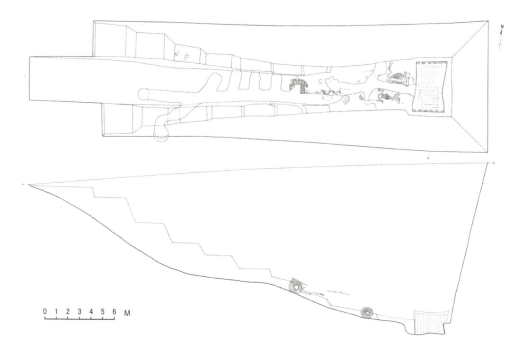

Figure 15.3. Plan and section of Tomb M6 at Majiayuan (drawing courtesy of Wang Hui).

Figure 15.4. Some surviving artefacts from M6 (photographs courtesy of Wang Hui): (a) human-face-shaped gold ornaments, height 1.6 cm; (b) horse ornaments made of gold and silver rings and buttons, diameter 6cm; (c) gold ornament with tubes and granulation, height 1.1 cm; (d) gold ornament with sard and turquoise inlay, length 2.4 cm, width 1.4 cm.

painted with a red and black ground with blue and green patterns. Type IV chariots also have passenger boxes that are made of wooden slats and are lacquered black, but they are much smaller and do not have any other decoration. The boxes could be square, round or oval. Type V chariots are the simplest in structure and decoration; the passenger box is made of wooden boards and the whole structure is unpainted and undecorated. Larger tombs at Majiayuan usually contain a greater variety of chariots, and those chariot types suggest different functions, such as ceremony, war and hunting.[15]

Despite these broad categories, each chariot is unique in size, structure and measurement, which suggests that each is individually designed and manufactured.[16] In addition, their design and decoration emphasise extravagant display at the cost of practicality[17] and some details indicate that they were made especially for funeral ceremonies, not for practical use.[18]

Within the dynastic Zhou tradition, the number and type of bronze ritual vessels buried in tombs reflect a graduated symbolic system correlating to a social hierarchy among the elite,[19] and the number and decoration of chariots, along with horses and banners, also seem to constitute a

---

[15] Wu Xiaolong 2013: 126.
[16] Zhao 2010b: 96.
[17] Zhao 2010a: 75.
[18] Zhao 2010b: 96.
[19] Yu and Gao 1979; Zhang Wenjie 2012.

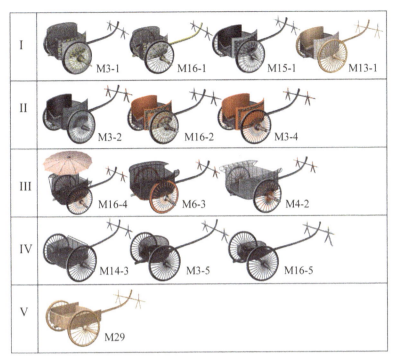

Figure 15.5. Five Types of chariots excavated at Majiayuan (drawing courtesy of Wang Hui & Zhao Wucheng).

Figure 15.6. Bronze decorative elements on the back door of the chariot in M25 (photograph by Xiaolong Wu).

bers; however, they also have a few unique features. One of the main differences is that Majiayuan chariots have larger wheels and more spokes. The size of the wheels varies from tomb to tomb and from chariot to chariot, but most chariots from relatively larger tombs (such as M1 and M16) in the cemetery have wheels with a diameter between 140 and 160 centimetres, and 30 to 40 spokes. In contrast, the wheels on chariots excavated at M1 (tomb of King Cuo) in Pingshan 平山, Hebei province (State of Zhongshan, late fourth century BCE) are only 80 centimetres in diameter, with 26 spokes.[23] Although the height of wheels and number of spokes increased gradually on examples from the Chinese/Zhou states, they are still outmatched by the Majiayuan chariots; for instance, the two examples from Ma'anzhong 马鞍冢, Huaiyang 淮阳, Henan 河南 Province (State of Chu, third century BCE) have wheels that are 136 centimetres in diameter with 28–32 spokes.[24] The vast majority of the chariots found in China from the Shang Dynasty to the end of the Zhou Dynasty (thirteenth to third centuries BCE) have wheels that are between 100–140 centimetres in diameter.[25] It has been pointed out that taller wheels and more numerous spokes are typical features of chariots from the Eurasian Steppes.[26] For instance, the carriage (not a chariot) from Pazyryk Barrow no. 5 in the Altai Mountains have wheels that are 150 centimetres in height and have 34 spokes.[27] Another exclusive feature of the type III chariots at Majiayuan is the use of wide armrests on the left and right sides of the boxes, which emphasised extravagance and enhanced the stability and comfort of the passengers. These were distinctly not battle machines but were constructed for parade and spectacle. Moreover, their innovative features show that the designers and builders of the Majiayuan chariots could design, build and embellish their chariots with some amount of freedom and flexibility.

hierarchical system in mortuary practice and they served as important signifiers of the owner's social rank.[20] At Majiayuan, the size of tombs, the number of steps in the wall of the tomb chamber and the quantity and types of chariots buried in them are all graduated and correlate with each other. The local rulers were obviously familiar with the dynastic Zhou ranking system and adopted it to signify their wealth and social status.[21]

The construction of Majiayuan chariots is similar to those found in the Zhou states to the east such as two wheels and a single draught pole,[22] the design of chariot boxes and umbrellas, and the practice of lacquering the wooden mem-

Also unique are three ox-drawn carts (M57-2, M19-1, M18-3) found along with horse-drawn chariots in three tombs at Majiayuan. They were identified as such because ox skulls (as opposed to the usual horse skulls) were found under their yokes, and their draught poles also differ in structure from those of the horse chariots. While horse-drawn Chinese chariots have only one draught pole which starts from the centre under the box and curves upward toward the end, the ox-drawn carts have two additional draught poles that are attached on the two sides of the bot-

[20] Lu 1993: 835–837.
[21] Wu Xiaolong 2013: 127.
[22] Wan 2013: 60–63.
[23] Hebeisheng 1995: 305–310, 514–523.
[24] Henansheng 1984.
[25] Wu Xiaoyun 2009: 211–231.
[26] Wang Hui 2009: 72.
[27] Rudenko 1970: 189–193.

tom of boxes and converge in the front to form a triangle, and the two side poles are connected with the central pole and a crossbar in the middle. The yokes of the ox-carts are twice as long (2.5 m) as the chariot yokes (0.92–1.42 m), and they rest on the two side poles which are lower than the central curved pole. The yoke saddles are simplified into two vertical bars. Other than the draught poles, yokes, and yoke saddles, the ox-carts are similar to type III chariots in structure. And all ox-carts have an umbrella rising from the centre of the box.[28] This type of ox-cart is unknown from other sites and could have been an adaptation of chariots by the Majiayuan community for burial purposes. When information on the sex of the deceased is available, it will be interesting to see whether the use of ox-carts was gender specific.

The Decorative Designs on the Chariots[29]

The metal plaques that decorate the Majiayuan chariots (Figure 15.7) were mainly inspired by the iconography and style of steppe art. The so-called golden warrior from the Issyk Kurgan, dated to the third or second century BCE, was probably a warrior chief or member of royalty,[30] and the 4000+ gold plaques and ornaments which covered the body are full of animal imagery and mark royal status. The decorative plaques shaped like ibexes and lions from Majiayuan (Figure 15.7, lower panel) are reminiscent of the gold headdress ornaments from the Issyk mound in Kazakhstan, and are similar in both motif and style of representation.[31] Similar artefacts were also found in northern Xinjiang along the Tianshan 天山 Mountains, and these finds suggest a route of cultural exchange between Zhangjiachuan and Eurasia through northern Xinjiang.[32] Motifs such as stylised S-shaped bird-heads and goldsmith techniques such as granulation and sheet metal techniques link the Majiayuan site with finds from further west and north on the Eurasian Steppe, such as those from Kurgan I at Filippovka along the Volga River,[33] dated to the fourth century BCE. Granulation is a Near Eastern and ultimately a Mediterranean technique that was transmitted to China through the Eurasian steppes.[34]

Among the iconographic themes represented in the décor, the most identifiable animals are ibex and tiger, both represented on flat metal plates. These plaque-like attachments for the chariot in M3, for instance, are decorated with a big-horned ibex motif and are made from either cast bronze or silver foil (Figures 15.7, 15.8, 15.9). These plaques are distinguishable from those typically cast in high relief that came from foundries found in Guyuan 固原 and the Ordos region because the ibex images are flat casts, have recurved horns and stand on four separately articulated legs and feet. Contrary to these flat cast images, the tiger shaped decorations were made by hammering gold or silver over a model probably made of wood. The gold foil tigers that adorned the side panels of the carriages in M3 stand with manes and tails curled upward and across the back of the animal to form opposing arcs (Figures 15.7, 15.8, 15.9).

In addition to these animal shaped decorations, openwork ornamental plaques also adorned the vehicles, for example those on the wheels of chariots in M3. The complex openwork decorations are bilaterally symmetrical designs with curvilinear stripes reaching toward each other forming converging curves (Figure 15.8). Alternatively, the ornamental openwork decorations attached to the spokes of the chariot wheels in M3 are made of rows of openwork silver foil decorations (Figure 15.8). These decorative motifs plus the hammering and low relief casting technology used to produce the artefacts are atypical in Qin territory but have direct analogies far to the west of Majiayuan in eastern Kazakhstan, and according to Raphael Wong (2007, 2020) the overall patterning of those designs is akin to textile designs found in materials excavated at Pazyryk in the Russian Altai.

These Majiayuan chariot features denote local innovation in design, such as the bronze plaques arranged in a circular pattern on wheel rims (Figure 15.7, upper panel). For instance, most Majiayuan bronze plaques have outer frames shaped as triangles or wave patterns, and their inner open-

Figure 15.7. Metal decorative plaques on chariot wheels and passenger boxes from M3 (photograph courtesy of Wang Hui).

---

[28] Zhao 2018: 52–54. See chapter 14 by Robin D. S. Yates, this volume.
[29] The following section is informed by the research presented in the following article: Yang and Linduff 2013: 74–79; see also Wong 2017, 2020 who attributes overall patterning of designs on the chariots at Majiayuan to textile designs known especially from Pazyryk, kurgan 5.
[30] Akishev 2006: 61; Chang and Guroff 2006: 112.
[31] Yang 2010: 52–54.
[32] Yang 2010: 54–55.
[33] Aruz et al. 2000: pl. 17.
[34] Huang Wei et al. 2009: 83.

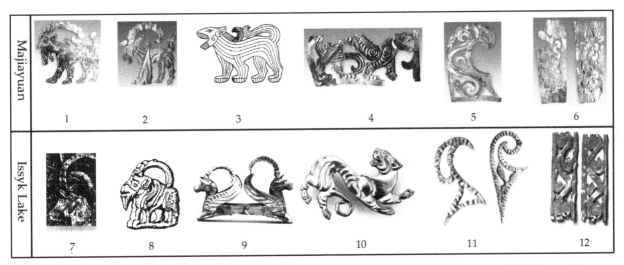

Figure 15.8. The comparison of plaques from Issyk and Majiayuan (adapted from Yang and Linduff 2014: Fig. 1; with permission of Yang Jianhua).

Figure 15.9. The comparison of the patterns of ibex and tiger from Issyk and Majiayuan (adapted from Yang and Linduff 2014: Fig. 2; with permission of Yang Jianhua).

work designs are formed with different arrangements of the reversed letter S, which is actually a highly simplified and stylised griffin-head design.[35] Although the S-shaped design was popular on the Eurasian Steppe during the first millennium BCE,[36] similar bronze plaques for chariots had not been seen before. And many of those design and artefact sources can ultimately be found in Eurasia and further west,[37] the Majiayuan chariot decorative items are hybrid forms that draw upon various sources to create original designs.

Moreover, many iconographic and aesthetic features recorded on items found at the Majiayuan cemetery can be distinguished from materials made based on 'Zhou dynastic' iconographic and technical standards in four distinct ways. First, the animal decorations mainly depict tigers and ibex, especially ones that emphasise the recurved horns of the ibex. An upwards-curling horn style is also reflected in the disposition of the manes and tails of tigers and on openwork ornamental plaques. Second, the objects were primarily made from hammered gold or silver sheeting, although some flat, cast bronze figures were also found. These gold and silver adornments created the image of wealth and displayed assets of the donor and the deceased. Third, the gold and silver designs were hammered into the strips both longitudinally and horizontally. Finally, funerary chariots decorated with these images bore subjects popular to the west of Gansu and far beyond the Qin state or the dynastic lands of the Zhou but displayed the animals in a distinctive relationship to each other. For instance, in most examples from sites further west, the tiger and ibex appear as predator and prey respectively, while those depicted on the plaques from Majiayuan do not tussle with each other, thus confirming another local adaptation (Figures 15.8, 15.9).

The Geographical Context and the Choice of Decorative Imagery

The Tianshan mountain area borders on both southeast Kazakhstan and Xinjiang. In the Iron Age (seventh to second centuries BCE), the Saka were thought to have lived in this area. The important discovery made near Issyk-Kul in southeastern Kazakhstan mentioned above yielded the body of a 16 to 18 year-old interred with warrior's equip-

---

[35] Wu Xiaolong 2013: 128.
[36] Aruz et al. 2000: pls. 1–4, 24–55, 69–72, 185; Linduff 1997: figs. A29, A35; Stark et al. 2012: 40, 42, 173.
[37] Wong 2017; 2020 traces the sources of motifs and overall patterns to west Asia where most predate those at Majiayuan. The issue of how they got to Xinjiang is addressed in Linduff and Rubinson 2022: 113–126, where exchanges, for instance of lacquerware, between the Altai in Russia and China are outlined from as early as the fifth century BCE.

ment and rich funerary goods including 4000+ gold ornaments. The kurgan is dated from the third to the second centuries BCE,[38] or comparable to the elaborate Majiayuan tombs, and brings to light a shared decorative imagery.

In several ways, both in technique and ornamental detail the Issyk golden pieces anticipate the animal décor at Majiayuan. The decorations representing big-horned sheep found in the Issyk kurgan are made from hammered gold and silver foil, and several more gold plaques representing ibex have been discovered in Kargaly valley near Issyk-Kul. These are similar to the ibex plaques in Majiayuan where the big horn curls backwards and four feet are rendered separately. The plaques from Kargaly are dated from the Wusun 乌孙 period during the second to first century BCE, or somewhat later than the Issyk kurgan.

The golden horse image on the hat of the occupant of the 'tomb of the golden warrior' has wings and horns. The curved horns and wings form adjoining spirals and are disposed similarly to the manes and tails of the golden tigers found in the debris of the chariot in M3 at Majiayuan. The Issyk representation of a snow leopard jumps upward and looks back. Its body is engraved with longitudinal and horizontal indentations using a technique similar to that used on the silver tigers from Majiayuan. Likewise, the openwork gold foil plaques from Issyk are similar to the curvilinear openwork plaques found in Majiayuan (Figure 15.8).

The similarities between the decorative remains found at Majiayuan to those yielded from the excavations in the area of Issyk-Kul are many and close: animal style decorations are made in two-dimensional relief (Figure 15.8), unlike the popular three-dimensional animal style objects found in the Ordos Plateau; gold and silver foil is more frequently used than bronze; the dating of both remains are contemporary with the late Warring States period of the dynastic Zhou. The gold and silver ornamental plaques attached to the chariots in Majiayuan (M1 and M3) and the occupant in the Issyk kurgan, illustrate a similar aesthetic predilection for luxurious effect. This aesthetic choice is very different from the less elaborate and practical uses of the three-dimensional bronze animal decorations found in other tombs in the region. Very few three-dimensional animal decorations are found in earlier tombs on northern bank of the northernmost Ili River,[39] which had affinities to the northern steppe area. The emergence of these two treatments of animal décor in northern dynastic Zhou China documents different time periods: the three-dimensional animal style belongs to an earlier stage in the north between the late fourth and third centuries BCE, or from the middle and late Warring States period in the Zhou; and, the two-dimensional style belongs to a later stage, or from the third centuries BCE during the late Warring States period.[40] This observation confirms that there was communication between northern dynastic China and the frontier areas from the west and north over a long period.

Two main animal representational types that decorate the gold and silver ornamental plaques: one is the ibex standing firmly on four separate feet; the other represents felines with longitudinal and horizontal, engraved lines on their bodies. The details of these types also bear some similarity to each other; the recurved horns connect with the upward turning tails or wings. The two main types denote predator and prey, but the animals do not fight each other in the Majiayuan examples. The floral ornamental plaques also have similarities: the petals curls upwards to form hooked shapes and strips that are filled with floral patterns. These similarities in decorative approach to décor and aesthetic effect, as well as in tomb type do not appear to be coincidental but must rather be a reflection of some sort of reciprocal knowledge exchange among peoples in the region. Since these cultural features have a long history and appear frequently in southeast Kazakhstan, a network of contact and exchange in the third to second centuries BCE can be assumed.

Technological Transfer

In addition to iconographic and stylistic affinities between the region and the materials recently unearthed at Majiayuan, a shared technology can be pointed out as another feature of exchange. The hammering of pliable metals is documented throughout the eastern Kazakh region and belongs to a larger region of sharing. For instance, the excavated frozen tombs found nearby in the Altai,[41] (Figure 15.8) in the Ukok plateau at Ak-Alakha[42] and at Berel[43] in eastern Kazakhstan assume a contemporary regional mortuary practice and artefact style. Beginning in 1997 an international team began to excavate Tomb 11 at Berel, and several features of the tomb suggested to the excavators that it had belonged to an important member of the local leadership.[44] The owner's high status was seemingly indicated in this case by the size of the kurgan (63 m in diameter) and the tomb chamber (2x4 m), the fine construction of the tomb chamber (pine and larch board framework with a ceiling of birch bark sheets, felt, and a layer of twigs), as well as the presence of large gilded wooden ibex horns (70 cm) attached to two of thirteen sacrificed horses (Figure 15.10). Berel Tomb 11 contained two remarkably well-preserved bodies of a young man and an older woman, as well as many funerary goods and well-preserved architecture. Perhaps of the greatest interest here, are the frozen corpses of sacrificed horses wearing preserved leather masks with attached horns analogous to the recurved ibex horns displayed on Issyk and Majiayan artefacts. Like the artefacts found at Majiayuan, these objects include the same iconography, and used a technology that hammered

---

[38] Chang and Guroff 2006: 112, fig. 39.
[39] Yang and Zhang 2012.
[40] Yang 2004.

[41] Rudenko 1970.
[42] Polys'mak 1992; 2001.
[43] Francfort 1999; Samashev 2006.
[44] Francfort 1999.

Figure 15.10: Decoration of a horse from Berel with wooden recurved horns like ibex (adapted from Yang and Linduff 2014: Fig. 3; with permission of Yang Jianhua).

gold and silver over wooden models as at Berel.[45] Even the cast items from Majiayuan appear to be modelled on a prototype of wooden carved examples, a technique not previously documented within the Qin dynastic territory.

A deliberate repetition of decoration with local flavour as described above parallels the choice to use chariots as a sign of both control of wealth and power by force. These shining gold and silver decorated chariots must have been central to local pageantry confirming both their local wealth and valued display of contact with the outside. Control of both depended on the revival and adoption of Eurasian models that met the needs of the local elite as well as the Qin.

Historical Context

The connections between eastern Kazakhstan and western Gansu at Majiayuan show inspiration that came from continued contact, but was newly inspired once in the hands of local designers and artisans encouraged by new, presumably prosperous, patrons. What can explain the newly amassed wealth at the moment of the burials at Majiayuan? This cemetery is located in an area to the north and west of the Qin where many pastoralist groups, collectively known as the Xi Rong 西戎 (Western Rong), were active during the first millennium BCE (Figure 15.1). After the conquest of the Yiqu Rong 义渠戎 (local sub-group of Rong) in this area, King Zhao of Qin established the Longxi 陇西 Prefecture in south-eastern Gansu around 279 BCE, and the Zhangjiachuan area belonged to this new administrative unit.[46] In 271 BCE, King Zhao built a series of defensive walls at the north and west borders of the Qin territory, which ran from Lixian 礼县 County in southeastern Gansu, through southern Ningxia and north-ern Shaanxi, to Junger Banner in Inner Mongolia.[47] The Majiayuan region was enclosed within this newly built border wall. The Majiayuan cemetery, however, is fundamentally different from other Qin cemeteries in terms of burial practice and grave goods, and probably represents the remains of the rulers of a Rong pastoralist group newly affiliated with the state of Qin. Their ability to distinguish themselves with such ostentatious presentation must represent their strength and perceived independent position within the Qin orbit.

The fourth and third centuries BCE were a time of intense cultural borrowing between the Chinese states and their northern neighbours. This trend is partly demonstrated by a record in the *Shiji* 史记 (Historical Records) that recounts the adoption of nomadic dress and mounted archery of the Hu tribes by King Wuling of Zhao 赵武灵王 to reform his military around 307 BCE.[48] Meanwhile, gold artefacts popular among the northern pastoral groups started to appear in tombs of the social elite in the Chinese states during the third century BCE. We are not sure to what extent the Chinese aristocracy in the Zhou states adopted cultural practices of their northern neighbours but it is clear that they had adopted heterogeneous visual symbols and related status markers to display their power and status as a foil to the changing Zhou ritual system.[49]

On the other side of the interaction, the luxury chariot and body ornaments of gold, silver and other materials found in this contact zone suggest the emergence of a new class of aristocracy in the local nomadic or pastoral society, whose social position depended on their success in managing diplomatic and commercial relations with the Chinese and other neighbours.[50] The finds at Majiayuan represent the burial practices of such a new elite class. As one of the Rong groups under the control of the state of Qin, the society represented by the Majiayuan cemetery must have played an important role in the exchange between the Qin and trading partners to the west. During the third century BCE when the state of Qin was engaged in combat with other states to its east, its rulers had to maintain peaceful commercial relations with the Rong groups under its control and traded with them for horses, an important resource for the state.[51] According to the *Shiji*, the first emperor of the Qin Dynasty honoured a merchant of the Wuzhi Rong 乌氏戎 group for his contribution to the trade between the Qin and the Rong groups, and 'gave orders to honour Lo as though he were an enfeoffed lord, and to allow him to join the ministers in seasonal audiences at court'.[52] The luxury objects found at Majiayuan suggest that the rulers buried there probably acquired great wealth through trade with Qin and through acting as intermediaries between Qin and nomadic peoples further to the west, as the northern groups often did through a down-the-line trade network

---

[45] Mylnikov and Samashev 2004.
[46] Zhangjiachuan 1999: 56.
[47] Wang Xueli 1994: 199.
[48] *Shiji* 43.1806–9.
[49] Wu Xiaolong 2013: 133.
[50] Linduff 2009: 95; Linduff and Rubinson 2022: 113–126.
[51] Wang Hui 2009: 75.
[52] *Shiji* 129. 3260; Swann 1950: 430.

connecting China with the Eurasian Steppes.[53] The cultural hybridity at Majiayuan, therefore, demonstrates commercial and cultural connections which the local elite had with various peoples to their west, and visualises the political, diplomatic, and economic powers controlled by the Majiayuan elite through these connections.[54]

Conclusion

Foreign objects, materials and imagery helped concentrate and channel the energy and power associated with domains lying outside local societies, and individuals who were able to acquire or possess those extraordinary objects were often endowed with the same powers associated with those potent outside worlds.[55] In addition, the original meanings for these objects were probably adapted to invent a new cultural practice in the service of the socio-political needs of its users.[56] The highly mixed culture at Majiayuan was not the static result of cultural encounters, simply reflecting cultural exchanges, but was consciously created by social agents and artisans to negotiate power and status. The luxury artefacts of diverse cultural origins such as the chariots and their decorations found at Majiayuan are the result of symbolically and politically charged activities such as long-distance acquisition and skilled craftworking. The Majiayuan elite adopted luxury goods and status markers from elites in other power centres to create a hybrid culture that legitimised their social status in the local community[57] but also in relation to the Qin. Chariots and their varied designs tell a story about the Qin control not only of foreign interaction, but also of invaluable technology and the ability to restrict access to knowledge and exchange with the outside world.

Xiaolong Wu
Professor of Art History, Hanover College,
Hanover, IN.

Katheryn M. Linduff
Professor Emerita, East Asian and Eurasia Art History and Archaeology, University of Pittsburgh,
Pittsburgh, PA.

---

[53] So and Bunker 1995: 60.
[54] Wu Xiaolong 2013: 134–135.
[55] Helms 1993: 9, 170.
[56] Van Dommelen 2006: 119.
[57] Wu Xiaolong 2013: 131.

Bibliography

Akishev, Kemal A. 1978. *Kurgan Issyk:Iskusstvo sakov Kazahstana* (*Issyk Mound: The Art of Saka in Kazakhstan*). Moscow: Iskusstvo Publishers.

Akishev, Kemal A. 2006. Golden Warrior: Sun God, Shaman, or Mythological Hero. In: *Of Gold and Grass: Nomads of Kazakhstan*, edited by Claudia Chang and Katharine S. Guroff, 57–62. Bethesda, MD: Foundation for International Art and Education.

Aruz, Joan, with Ann Farkas, Andrei Alekseev, and Elena Korolkova, eds. 2000. *The Golden Deer of Eurasia*. New York: The Metropolitan Museum of Art.

Beijing shi Wenwu Yanjiusuo Shanrong wenhua kaogudui 北京市文物研究所山戎文化考古队. 1989. Beijing Yanqing Jundushan dongzhou shanrong buluo mudi fajue jilue 北京延庆军都山东周山戎部落墓地发掘记略 (Summary of the Excavations of the Cemetery of Shanrong Tribes at Jundushan, Yanqing County, Beijing). *Wenwu* 8: 17–35.

Chang, Claudia and Katharine S. Guroff, eds. 2006. *Of Gold and Grass: Nomads of Kazakhstan*. Bethesda, MD: Foundation for International Art and Education.

Francfort, Henri-Paul. 1999. The Frozen Mausoleum of the Scythian Prince. *Ligabue Magazine* 35: 42—63.

Gansu sheng wenwu kaogu yanjiusuo 甘肃省文物考古研究所, and Zhangjiachuan huizu zizhixian bowuguan 张家川回族自治县博物馆. 2008. 2006 niandu Gansu Zhangjiachuan huizu zizhixian Majiayuan Zhanguo mudi fajue jianbao 年度甘肃张家川回族自治县马家塬战国墓地发掘简报 (Report of the 2006 Excavation at the Majiayuan Cemetery of the Warring States Period in Zhangjiachuan Autonomous County of Hui Nationality in Gansu). *Wenwu* 文物 9: 4–28.

Hebeisheng Wenwu Yanjiusuo 河北省文物研究所. 1995. *Tomb of Cuo, the King of the Zhongshan State in the Warring States Period*. Beijing: Wenwu Chubanshe.

Helms, Mary W. 1993. *Craft and the Kingly Ideal: Art, Trade, and Power*. Austin: University of Texas Press.

Henansheng Wenwu Yanjiusuo 河南省文物研究所. 1984. *Henan Huaiyang Ma'anzhong Chu mu fajue jianbao* 河南淮阳马鞍冢楚墓发掘简报 (Brief Report on the Excavation of the Chu Tombs at Ma'anzhong, Huaiyang, Henan Province). *Wenwu* 10: 1–17.

Huang Wei, Wu Xiaohong, Chen Jianli and Wang Hui. 2009. Zhangjiachuan Majiayuan mudi chutu jin guanshi de yanjiu 张家川马家塬墓地出土金管饰的研究 (Studies on the Gold Tubular Ornaments Excavated from the Majiayuan Cemetery in Zhangjiachuan). *Wenwu* 10: 78–87.

Linduff, Katheryn M. 1997. An Archaeological Overview. In: *Ancient Bronzes of the Eastern Eurasian Steppe from the Arthur M. Sackler Collections*, edited by Emma C. Bunker, Trudi S. Kawami, Katheryn M. Linduff, and Wu En, 18–98. New York: Arthur M. Sackler Foundation.

Linduff, Katheryn M. 2009. Production of Signature Artifacts for the Nomad Market in the State of Qin During the Late Warring State Period in China (4th–3rd century BCE). In: *Metallurgy and Civilization: Eurasia and Beyond. The 6th International Conference on the Beginnings of the Use of Metals and Alloys (BUMA VI)*, edited by Jianjun Mei and Thilo Rehren, 90–96. London: Archetype.

Linduff, Katheryn M. and Karen S. Rubinson. 2022. *Pazyryk Culture Up in the Altai*. London and New York: Routledge.

Lu Liancheng. 1993. Chariot and Horse Burials in Ancient China. *Antiquity* 67: 824–838.

Ningxia Wenwu Kaogu Yanjiusuo 宁夏文物考古研究所. 1993. Ningxia Guyuan Yanglang qingtong wenhua mudi 宁夏固原杨郎青铜文化墓地 (Cemetery of a Bronze-using Culture at Yanglang, Guyuan City, Ningxia). *Kaogu Xuebao* 1: 13–56.

Mylnikov, Vladimir and Zainola S. Samashev. 2004. *Woodworking of the Ancient Cattle-Breeders of the Kazakh Altai: Materials of Complex Analysis of Wooden Objects from Barrow 11 at the Berel Burial Ground*. Almaty: Exxon Mobil.

Qianwei et al. 潜伟等. 2001. Xinjiang Hami Tianshan- beilu mudi chutu tongqi de chubu yanjiu 新疆哈密天山北路墓地出土铜器的初步研究 (A Preliminary Study of the Unearthed Bronze Objects in the North of Tianshan Mountains in Hami, Xinjiang). *Wenwu* 文物 6: 79–89.

Polos'mak, Natalia V. 1992. *Cteregushchiye zoloto grify* (*Griffins Watching over Gold*). Novosibirsk: Nauka.

Polos'mak, Natalia V. 2001. *Vsadniki Ukoka* (*The Riders in Ukok*). Novosibirsk: INFOLIO Press.

Rubinson, Karen S. 2012. Burial Practice and Social Roles of Iron Age Mobile Pastoralists. In: *Nomads and Networks*, edited by Soeren Stark, Karen S. Rubinson, Zainola S. Samashev, and Jennifer Y. Chi, 77–90. Princeton, NJ and Oxford: Princeton University Press.

Rudenko, Sergei I. 1970. *Frozen Tombs of Siberia: The Pazyryk Burials of Iron Age Horsemen*. Berkeley and Los Angeles: University of California Press.

Samashev, Zainolla S. 2006. Culture of the Nomadic Elite of Kazakhstan's Altai Region (Based on Materials from the Berel Necropolis). In: *Of Gold and Grass: Nomads of Kazakhstan*, edited by Claudia Chang and Katherine S. Guroff, 35–44. Bethesda, MD: Foundation for International Art and Education.

Samashev, Zainolla S. 2012. The Berel Kurgans: Some Results of Investigation. In: *Nomads and Networks*, edited by Soeren Stark, Karen S. Rubinson, Zainola S. Samashev, and Jennifer Y. Chi, 31–49. Princeton, NJ and Oxford: Princeton University Press.

Shaanxisheng Kaogu Yanjiusuo and Qin Shihuangdi Bingmayong Bowuguan 陕西省考古研究所, 秦始皇帝兵马俑博物馆. 2000. *Qin Shihuangdi lingyuan kaogu baogao* 秦始皇帝陵园考古报告 (*Archaeological Report of the Funerary Park of the First Emperor of the Qin Dynasty*). Beijing: Kexue Chubanshe.

Shanxisheng Kaogu Yanjiusuo 山西省考古研究所. 1996. *Taiyuan Jinguo Zhaoqing mu* 太原晋国赵卿墓 (*Tomb of a Zhao Minister of Jin State near Taiyuan*). Beijing: Wenwu Chubanshe.

Shandongsheng Wenwu Kaogu Yanjiusuo 山东省文物考古研究所. 1984. Qi gucheng wuhao dongzhou mu ji daxing xunmakeng de fajue 齐故城五号东周墓及大型殉马坑的发掘 (The Excavation of the Eastern Zhou tomb No. 5 and the Large Pit of Sacrificial Horses at the Old Capital of the Qi State). *Wenwu* 文物 9: 14–19.

Shiji. 1997. *Shiji (Records of the Grand Historian)*, by Sima Qian (ca. 145 – ca. 85 BCE). Beijing: Zhonghua Shuju.

So, Jenny and Emma C. Bunker. 1995. *Traders and Raiders on China's Northern Frontier*. Seattle, London: University of Washington Press and Arthur M. Sackler Gallery, Smithsonian Institution.

Stark, Soeren, Karen S. Rubinson, Zainola S. Samashev, and Jenny Y. Chi, eds. 2012. *Nomads and Networks*. Princeton, NJ and Oxford: Princeton University Press.

Swann, N. L. 1950. *Food and Money in Ancient China: The Earliest Economic History of China to AD 25*. Princeton, NJ: Princeton University Press. [Ban Gu (Author), Nancy Lee Swann (Translator)].

Tian Guangjin 田广金. 1976. Taohongbala de Xiongnu mu 桃红巴拉的匈奴墓 (Xiongnu Tombs at Taohongbala). *Kaogu Xuebao* 考古学报 1: 131–144.

Tian Guangjin and Guo Suxin 田广金, 郭素新. 1986. *E'erduosi shi qingtongqi* 鄂尔多斯式青铜器 (*Ordos Style Bronzes*). Beijing: Wenwu Chubanshe.

Van Dommelen, Peter 2006. Colonial Matters: Material Culture and Postcolonial Theory in Colonial Situations. In: *Handbook of Material Culture*, edited by Christopher Tilley, Webb Keane, Susan Kuchler, Michael Rowlands, and Patricia Spyer, 104–124. London: Sage.

Wan Xiang. 2013. *The Horse in Pre-Imperial China*. Unpublished dissertation, University of Pennsylvania. https://repository.upenn.edu/cgi/viewcontent.cgi?article=1878&context=edissertations

Wang Hui 王辉. 2009. Zhangjiachuan Majiayuan mudi xiangguan wenti chutan 张家川马家塬墓地相关问题初探 (Preliminary Discussions on Questions Related to the Cemetery at Majiayuan, Zhangjiachuan County). *Wenwu* 文物 10: 70–77.

Wang Xueli 王学理, ed. 1994. *Qin wuzhi wenhua shi* 秦物质文化史 (*History of Qin Material Culture*). Xi'an: San Qin Publishing House.

Wong, Raphael. 2017. Carpets, Chariots and the State of Qin. *Tenzing Asian Art* 48 (2): 60–70.

Wong, Raphael. 2020. Steppe Style in Southeast Gansu Province (China) in the 4th and 3rd Centuries BC. In: *Masters of the Steppe: The Impact of the Scythians and Later Nomadic Societies of Eurasia, Proceedings of a Conference held at the British Museum 27–29 October 2017*, edited by Svetlana V. Pankova and St John Simpson, 650–659. Oxford: Archaeopress Archaeology.

Wu Xiaolong. 2004. Female and Male Status Displayed at the Maoqinggou Cemetery. In: *Gender and Chinese Archaeology*, edited by Katheryn M. Linduff and Yan Sun, 20–35. Walnut Creek, CA: AltaMira.

Wu Xiaolong. 2013. Cultural Hybridity and Social Status: Elite Tombs on China's Northern Frontier during the Third Century BCE. *Antiquity* 87: 121–136.

Wu Xiaoyun 吴晓筠. 2009. *Shang Zhou shiqi chema maizang yanjiu* 商周时期车马埋葬研究 (*Study on Chariot Burials in Early China, 1200–221 BCE*). Beijing: Kexue Chubanshe.

Yang Jianhua 杨建华. 2004. *Chunqiu Zhanguo shiqi Zhongguo beifang wenhuadai de xingcheng* 春秋战国时期中国北方文化带的形成 (*The Formation of a Culture Belt in North China during the Spring and Autumn Period and Warring States Period*). Beijing: Wenwu.

Yang Jianhua 杨建华. 2010. Zhangjiachuan muzang caoyuan yinsu xunzong 张家川墓葬草原因素寻踪 (Origins of the Steppe Elements in the Zhangjiachuan Tombs). *Xiyu yanjiu* 西域研究 4: 51–56.

Yang Jianhua and Katheryn M. Linduff. 2013. A Contextual Explanation for 'Foreign' or 'Steppic' Factors Exhibited in Burials at the Majiayuan Cemetery and the Opening of the Tianshan Mountain Corridor; with Yang Jianhua. *Journal of East Asian Archaeology* 1: 73–84.

Yang Jianhua 杨建华 and Zhang Meng 张盟. 2012. Zhongya Tianshan, Feiergana yu Pamier diqu de zaoqi tieqi shidai yanjiu: yu Xinjiang diqu de wenhua jiaowang 中亚天山、费尔干纳与帕米尔地区的早期铁器时代研究—与新疆地区的文化交往 (A Study of the Early Iron Age in the Tianshan Mountain Region, Ferghana and Pamir Areas: Cultural Communication with Xinjiang Area). *Bianjiang kaogu yanjiu* 边疆考古研究 9: 85–104.

Yu Weichao 俞伟超 and Gao Ming 高明. 1979. Zhoudai yongding zhidu yanjiu (xia) 周代用鼎制度研究（下）(Studies on the Zhou Dynasty System of the Use of Ding Vessels). *Beijing daxue xuebao (zhexue shehui kexue ban)* 北京大学学报（哲学社会科学版）Beijing University Journal (Philosophy and Social Sciences Edition) 1: 83–96.

Zabneprovskiy, Yu. A. 1992. Ranniye Kochevniki Yuzhnogo Kazakhstana i Tashkentskogo Oazisa [The Early Nomadic People in the Kazakhstan and Tashkent Oasis]. In: *Stepnaya polosa Aziatskoĭ chasti SSSR v skifosarmatskoye vremya (The Steppe Zone of the Asian Part of SSSR during the Scythysian-Sarmatian Period)*, edited by M. G. Moshkova, 224–235. Arkheologiya SSSR. Moscow: Nauka.

Zaoqi Qin wenhua lianhe kaogudui 早期秦文化联合考古队 and Zhangjiachuan huizu zizhixian bowuguan 张家川回族自治县博物馆. 2009. Zhangjiachuan Majiayuan Zhanguo mudi 2007—2008 nian fajue jianbao 张家川马家塬战国墓地 2007~2008 年发掘简报 (Report of the 2007—2008 Excavation at the Majiayuan Cemetery of the Warring States Period in Zhangjiachuan, Gansu). *Wenwu* 文物 10: 25–51.

Zaoqi Qin wenhua lianhe kaogudui 早期秦文化联合考古队 and Zhangjiachuan huizu zizhixian bowuguan 张家川回族自治县博物馆. 2010. Zhangjiachuan Majiayuan Zhanguo mudi 2008—2009 nian fajue jianbao 张家川马家塬战国墓地 2008~2009 年发掘简报 (Report of the 2008—2009 Excavation at the Majiayuan Cemetery of the Warring States Period in Zhangjiachuan, Gansu). *Wenwu* 文物 10: 4–26.

Zaoqi Qin wenhua lianhe kaogudui 早期秦文化联合考古队 and Zhangjiachuan huizu zizhixian bowuguan 张家川回族自治县博物馆. 2012. Zhangjiachuan Majiayuan Zhanguo mudi 2010—2011 nian fajue jianbao 张家川马家塬战国墓地 2010~2011 年发掘简报 (Report of the 2010—2011 Excavation at the Majiayuan Cemetery of the Warring States Period in Zhangjiachuan, Gansu). *Wenwu* 文物 8: 4–26.

Zaoqi Qin wenhua lianhe kaogudui 早期秦文化联合考古队 and Zhangjiachuan huizu zizhixian bowuguan 张家川回族自治县博物馆. 2018. Zhangjiachuan Majiayuan Zhanguo mudi 2012–2014 nian fajue jianbao 张家川马家塬战国墓地 2012~2014 年发掘简报 (Report of the 2012—2014 Excavation at the Majiayuan Cemetery of the Warring States Period in Zhangjiachuan, Gansu). *Wenwu* 文物 3: 4–25.

Zhang Liyan 张礼艳. 2010. Luelun Feng Hao diqu xizhou shiqi chema maizang de tedian 略论丰镐地区西周时期车马埋葬的特点 (A Brief Discussion of the Chariot and Horse Burials in the Feng-Hao Area during the Western Zhou Period). *Zhongguo lishi wenwu* 中国历史文物 5: 47–56.

Zhang Wenjie 张闻捷. 2012. Zhou dai ying ding zhidu shuzheng 周代用鼎制度疏证 (Commentaries on the Zhou Dynasty System of the Use of Ding Vessels). *Kaogu Xuebao* 考古学报 2: 131–162.

Zhangjiachuan Huizu Zizhixian Difangzhi Bianzuan Weiyuanhui 张家川回族自治县地方志编纂委员会. 1999. *Zhangjiachuang Huizu zizhixian zhi* 张家川回族自治县志 (*Annals of Zhangjiachuan Hui Autonomous County*). Lanzhou: Gansu Renmin Chubanshe.

Zhao Wucheng 赵吴成. 2010a. Gansu Majiayuan zhanguo mu mache de fuyuan 甘肃马家塬战国墓马车的复原 (Restoration of Chariots from the Warring States Period Tombs at Majiayuan, Gansu Province). *Wenwu* 6: 75–83.

Zhao Wucheng 赵吴成. 2010b. Gansu Majiayuan zhanguo mu mache de fuyuan (xu yi) 甘肃马家塬战国墓马车的复原（续一）(Restoration of Chariots from the Warring States Period Tombs at Majiayuan, Gansu Province [Supplement I]). *Wenwu* 文物 11: 84–96.

Zhao Wucheng 赵吴成. 2018. Gansu Majiayuan zhanguo mu mache de fuyuan (xu er) 甘肃马家塬战国墓马车的复原（续二）(Restoration of Chariots from the Warring States Period Tombs at Majiayuan, Gansu Province [Supplement II]). *Wenwu* 文物 6: 44–57.

Zheng Ruokui 郑若葵. 1987. Shilun Shangdai de che ma zang 试论商代的车马葬 (A Preliminary Discussion of the Shang Dynasty Chariot and Horse Burials). *Kaogu* 考古 5: 462–469.

Zhongguo Shehui Kexueyuan Kaogu Yanjiusuo 中国社会科学院考古研究所. 2004. *Zhongguo kaoguxue (liangzhou juan)* 中国考古学（两周卷）(*Chinese Archaeology [Zhou Dynasty Volume]*). Beijing: Zhongguo Shehui Kexue Chubanshe.

Part III

Chariot Findings, Chariots in Action, Their Construction, and Experimental Archaeology

16

The Ancient V-spoked Chariot Wheel: Why was It Made that Way? Some Thoughts Based on Some Observations and the Experience of Making Chariot Reconstructions

Robert Hurford

The ancient Egyptians did not make chariots – perhaps that is too strong a statement. They imported them, in parts, sometimes perhaps as complete vehicles, and embellished and refined them. For over a thousand years the wheels of these beautifully light chariots were made using a curious design. I describe how craft manufacturers in areas of the Near East making and often exporting chariots may have worked in economic alliance with vine-growers to produce chariots for the elite to use in display and warfare.

Introduction

In this paper I hope to draw together some rather scattered observations relating to the place of chariots in the economy of the ancient Near East. For over a thousand years the chariot played a role of considerable importance in society. Here I try to show some ways in which ancient economies and trade networks may have been organised towards supplying them.

It has been my good fortune to make a number of chariot reconstructions in the last couple of decades. The majority of them have been for TV documentaries, and these projects brought opportunities for research.

Figure 16.1. Mike Loades at Saqqara driving one of the chariots we made. The boy jumped on as the chariot turned; Mike did not notice (author's photo).

In 2012 we made a film with TV6 about Egyptian chariots, constructing two chariots in Cairo (Figure 16.1).[1] During the filming we visited, in a party which included the Egyptologist Dr. Stephen Harvey, a tomb which is normally closed to the public: TT86 (Menkheperraseneb), in the Valley of the Nobles on the west bank of the Nile near Luxor. It contains some chariot-making scenes, of which there are about ten in Egypt as a whole.[2] TT86 also contains a wall painting depicting a procession of tribute bearers, in which one man carries the frame of a chariot, a wheel and a yoke, which appears to be unique among Egyptian tomb paintings (Figure 16.2). This is plainly an unfinished chariot. The handrail and skirt (together making what many authors call the 'siding') were not present, nor is the woven floor in place. When examined closely, as we were able to do, it was clear that the axle was square-ended (Figure 16.3). The figure carrying this frame is dressed as a Levantine. My thanks are due to Stephen Harvey for this and other interpretative details.

The only conclusion possible is that this is an example of a part-made import, a kit, to be assembled and finished in Egyptian workshops.

Three Egyptian Wheel Designs

The earliest vehicle builders had been restricted to making vehicles with wheels of various types developed from solid discs.[3] Later, designs using spokes were developed, enabling the wheel to become lighter, and eventually to be made larger in diameter. The spokes have tenons which are inserted into mortices in a stock (otherwise known as a hub or nave), the rim is fitted to the ends of the spokes, and

---

[1] *Building Pharaoh's Chariot* (2013) Nova, Season 40, Episode 5. TV6 Limited. Broadcast: PBS America, 6 February 2013. Available online: https://www.youtube.com/watch?v=0Loti-WBK_k&t=1851s; last accessed 18 February 2021.
[2] Herold 2006: 51–78.
[3] Piggott 1983: 23–27; Littauer and Crouwel 1979a: 18–19; passim.

Figure 16.2. The image of the tribute bearer in TT 86 (author's photo).

Figure 16.3. Detail from the previous image from tomb TT86 enlarged (author's photo).

several methods of preventing the assembly from falling apart under the stresses of use were developed.[4] The earliest known spoked wheels, both dating from the early second millennium BCE, are on a model wagon from Acemhöyük in Anatolia, apparently made with V-spokes,[5] and from Sintashta on the Eurasian steppes.[6] The latter represent a different construction method with spokes tenoned into the hub, which continued to be used and developed, including for the large multi-spoked wheels still in use in China. There has been an assumption that the V-spoked wheels were more difficult to make than the familiar, 'modern', mortised cylinder and tenoned spoke type.[7] This would be true for a modern wheelwright, whose working habits, the infrastructure of his timber supplies and available tools are all geared to making the latter kind of wheel. The Bronze Age wheel maker had fewer effective chisels, but he may well have had a ready supply of timber in the form of grown bends, which in most modern situations are difficult to come by. In that case a significant part of the job is done for him. Making a wheel that way becomes more obvious, the tree is 'talking' to the workman and the strength of the construction runs through the grain.[8] The final form in Europe was the iron encircling and compressing tyre first seen in the Hallstatt culture.[9] This construc-

tion became the norm, and the most recent wooden wheels are of this type.[10]

The V-spoked wheels of the ancient Near East and actual specimens from the Egyptian New Kingdom survive. The Florence chariot[11] probably predates those of Amenophis III and Tutankhamun, though only the latter can be firmly dated to the fourteenth century BCE.

The surviving Egyptian chariots have been described in masterly fashion by Howard Carter,[12] and by Mary Littauer and Joost Crouwel.[13] The wheels of Tutankhamun's chariots (and the Lidar Höyük wheel[14]) follow one constructional type which is described in their publications.[15] This type of wheel comprises a hub made of three sections, fitted together with exquisitely made taper joints. The six composite spokes are V-shaped, fitting into the middle section of the hub, each glued back-to-back to its neighbours. These tenon[16] into the rim, which is made of two sections scarfed[17] together (Figure 16.4). The hub is waterproofed with birch bark or sometimes covered with metal foil (gold or electrum). The whole assembly is secured together with a rawhide tyre.

A second, related, type can be seen in the hub of the wheel from the tomb of Amenophis III in the Ashmolean

---

[4] The options available over the span of history are: rawhide to encircle the rim, glue holding the spokes into the wheel hub (which I believe was essential in making the large Chinese multi-spoked wheels); the ultimate development was the encircling and compressing iron tyre. When the iron tyre ceased to be used from the "dark ages" until its revival in early modern times, a ring or rings of strakes, in iron (or in the one exceptional case of the 1602 coach sent by Elizabeth I to Boris Godunov in Russia, brass) was used as a substitute.

[5] Littauer and Crouwel 1986: 291.

[6] Chechuschkov and Epimachov 2018; see also Chechuschkov and Epimachov this volume.

[7] 'A different, simpler, and far more familiar wheelwright's technique' (Littauer and Crouwel 1986: 292).

[8] Jean Spruytte made an experimental construction of this type of wheels using only simple tools of local Saharan stone (Spruytte 1983: 80); see also Brownrigg this volume.

[9] Pare 1992: 45–51.

[10] The tyre is otherwise called a 'bond'. The accepted etymology of the word 'tyre', said to derive from 'attire', always seems questionable to me as it ties or compresses the wheel joints together, it is a tie-er.

[11] Spruytte 1989.

[12] Carter 1972.

[13] Littauer and Crouwel 1985; 1991.

[14] Littauer and Crouwel 1991.

[15] See also Spruytte 1995.

[16] A projecting piece of wood is inserted into a mortise in another piece.

[17] Tapered ends overlap and are glued together.

Figure 16.4. Model of a six-spoked Egyptian wheel of the type found in Tutankhamun's tomb (author's photo).

Figure 16.6. Model of four-spoked Egyptian wheel of the "Florence" type (author's photo).

Figure 16.5. Amenophis III wheel hub, Ashmolean Museum, Oxford (author's photo).

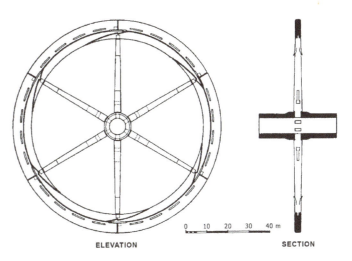

Figure 16.7. The wheel in the Brooklyn Museum, New York (after Littauer and Crouwel 1979b: fig. 1).

Museum, Oxford (Figure 16.5).[18] Being largely disassembled, this is in a very convenient condition for inspecting and understanding its construction.

The difference lies in the Vs of which the spokes are formed, which fit together to make the centre of the hub. The outer cylindrical sections of the hub have tenons fitting between the spokes where they meet. The wheel of the 'Florence chariot'[19] can also be assumed to be of the Amenophis type, though made with four rather than six spokes (Figure 16.6). Perhaps a future investigation inside the hub will confirm this assumption. My 'exploded' models of the Tutankhamun and Florence types aim to explain the difference. The Amenophis III wheel has six spokes, and the Florence ones have four, but the construction of these two specimens is assumed to be the same, apart from the angles involved and the numbers of components.

There is a third type of spoked wheel known from Egypt. This is represented by the unique specimen now in the Brooklyn Museum, New York (Figure 16.7),[20] which has been carbon dated to the fifth century BCE.[21] The hub is of one piece, the six spokes are simply fitted to it with rather short tenons, and the rim is similar to the designs previously described. Some shapes are worked on to the outer ends of the spokes and they have T-shaped slots near their junction with the hub. By assuming that there were rawhide bindings from the spokes to the hub, I made a not unsuccessful interpretation of the function of these slots when making some reconstructions of Assyrian chariots in Sanliurfa, Turkey (Figures 16.8-16.9).[22] This, incidentally, was the first occasion when I met Joost Crouwel (Figure 16.9). I have since learned of Jean Spruytte's interpretation of the construction, incorporating

---

[18] Western 1973; Littauer and Crouwel 1985: 67–68; Spruytte 1995: 239.
[19] Littauer and Crouwel 1985: 68–69, 105–108; Spruytte 1983: 25–26; 1989; 1999; Cavillier et al. 2002.
[20] Littauer and Crouwel 1979b; Spruytte 1995; 1996: 41–58 with figs. 32–54.
[21] Spruytte 1996: 74.
[22] The film entitled *Machines Time Forgot, Chariot* S01E04, made by Windfall Films and directed by Michael Barnes, was broadcast in the UK on Channel 4, and in the USA by Discovery in 2003. It can still be found on YouTube: https://www.youtube.com/watch?v=QRipPsvL-Z0.

Figure 16.8. My interpretation, partly made, of the Brooklyn wheel. The thongs are arranged to brace the spokes (author's photo).

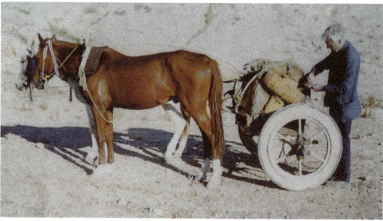

Figure 16.9. Joost Crouwel examining a reconstruction of an Assyrian chariot in Turkey (author's photo).

a wooden ring passing through the slots. Though mentioned in the original inventory of the find, the ring is no longer present. Spruytte identified rock drawings of Saharan chariots, whose wheels show a ring which might represent this missing part.[23] If I approached the task again, I would combine my ideas with his. This construction method does not, however, enter my story here.

Timber Bending for the V-spoked Egyptian Wheels

At this point first-hand experience in making chariot wheels becomes relevant. The wheels we made in Cairo used the Tutankhamun design (Figure 16.4). The hubs of these wheels are very small in diameter (80–90 cm) and to make them the V-shaped, spokes must be bent at a very sharp angle. This proves to be only just possible using modern techniques, involving steel tension straps and a species of timber which is very amenable to heat bending. Even with these provisos it is difficult. In making the film *Building Pharaoh's Chariot* we were using mulberry timber, which was available and proved suitable. I shall call the peak of this V-shape the 'knuckle'. As can be seen from my models, in the Tutankhamun type the knuckle is thin (Figure 16.4), but in the Amenophis and Florence type it is much thicker (Figure 16.6). There is no possibility of bending this thicker knuckle into the sharp angle required from a straight piece of timber using heat.[24] This certainly meant that for the purpose of making this documentary film, the Tutankhamun design was the only viable one of those two alternative methods of construction.

The process of bending timber requires the application of considerable force, and equipment to direct that force, together with quite a bit of effort to apply heat to the timber. In modern practice the usual technique also involves a thin steel tension strap (Figure 16.10). If timber is prepared by using cutting tools some of the fibres will be cut. These cut fibres will tend to break out as the timber bends because the timber will be compressed on the inside and stretched at the outside of the bend, and the stretching will tear the fibres apart. The strap helps prevent the grain breaking out and compresses it on the inside of the bend more strongly than can happen without a strap. I once tried a rawhide strap and found not only that it was nowhere near strong enough for the job but that the heat made the rawhide actually fall apart – and even a steel tension strap will sometimes distort with the pressure when in use. I do not think bronze would be as suitable as steel. I can only imagine that the way to use bronze as a compression strap would be to make a flat chain, and I am unaware of any archaeological finds which might represent such a strap. Consequently, I think I can say that the ancient chariot builders did not use tension straps. In Turkey we used coppiced timber, which was more suitable for bending than sawn wood. In coppicing, the tree is used as it grew, the grain of the young poles is not cut. This avoids introducing points where breakout may start, and so the bend will have less need of tension straps, but there are still severe limits to the possible radius of the bend which can be obtained.

It is interesting to note that in all the Egyptian tomb paintings the equipment depicted in timber bending activities

Figure 16.10. Modern bending jig and steel tension strap (author's photo).

---
[23] Spruytte 1996: 46–58, figs. 32–54.
[24] Heat bending is a more general term than "steam bending". Timber is heated using steam, or boiling water; this softens the lignin, and renders the timber pliable and capable of being bent into a different shape. When the moisture level is reduced after steaming, the shape will be retained.

Figure 16.11. Author's model (now in the International Museum of the Horse, Lexington, Kentucky) of the wall painting in the tomb of Intef, TT155, based on Herold 2006: 59 (author's photo).

is rather scanty, and the workmen do not seem to be applying much force.[25] In every case only one workman is pulling at the workpiece (Figure 16.11). Of course, artistic licence may be at play here, but I would suggest that in most of these scenes the workmen may well be merely correcting an already bent piece of timber. In consequence of all these considerations, I am sure that most of the timber being bent was grown to a shape approximating to its desired bend.

The last step in the bending process is to dry the workpiece. Drying serves to fix the shape, locking the timber fibres in position. If this is not done, the shape will revert to its original form, particularly if the piece is exposed to any substantial degree of humidity. While working in Cairo we found it sufficient to place the work on the workshop roof for a couple of days to bake in the sun, but drying cabinets are needed in less desiccating climates.

Rock Cut Channel Moulds

The Urartian rock cut 'moulds' demand attention.[26] These are channels cut in the rock of hillsides near the sites of Urartian cities (Figures 16.12a-16.12b).[27] They are certainly made in the exact form of a variety of chariot components of the kind found in Tutankhamun's tomb, notably the 60° V-shape in the size necessary to make chariot wheels. The section of the cut is between 4 and 10 cm deep and 10–15 cm wide. We might guess at a number of possible functions for these channels. The obvious suggestion is that they are the formers within which the timber is bent, but they do not seem to me immediately suitable for that purpose. I could not use them exactly as they are to form the shapes required: some additions, such as slots for wedges, for example, might begin to make them work. Alternatively, perhaps they may be considered as a possible way of exposing the bent parts to drying heat if the rocks are hot on sunny days. Or maybe they were a method

Figure 16.12a. Rock cut channels at an Urartian fortress, Upper Anzaf (after Konyar 2006: figure 1; by kind permission of Dr. E. Konyar).

of standardising shapes and sizes, perhaps of timber growing naturally in approximately the required form. Whatever their precise purpose, these channels cut into the rock would appear to be associated with the production of parts for chariots, and thus indicate that this was an industry of the region.

At least one site in Jerusalem contains rocks with similar channels, all cut in the V-shape, which are open to the some of the same interpretations. These, however, were in rock-cut chambers and therefore unlikely to be warmed by the sun (Figure 16.13).[28]

Geographical Distribution of these Wheel Designs

I have referred to the Tutankhamun type of wheel as an Egyptian form, but it has also been found in south eastern Anatolia. The six-spoked wheel, excavated in 1982 at Lidar Höyük, and dated to the early twelfth century BCE, which is now in the museum in Sanliurfa in Turkey, is of the same construction.[29] The timber used has been analysed as elm, which is also noted in the Egyptian wheels in Cairo and Oxford which have been subjected to analysis.[30] There is a strong case to be made that the six-spoked wheels shown in such perfect detail in the Assyrian reliefs from Nimrud and Nineveh are of the same construction, and this comment could also be applied to the well-depicted wheels in the Mycenaean frescoes of the thirteenth century BCE from Tiryns.[31]

Urartian rock cut moulds from Lake Van (and possibly Jerusalem), plainly show that components of similar wheels were being worked on in those areas.

We can therefore demonstrate from this evidence that wheels of this sophisticated technological construction were being used in Egypt, and in Lidar Höyük, perhaps in the whole Assyrian empire, and possibly in Mycenaean

---

[25] For workshop scenes see Herold 2006: 51–78 with illustrations: Timber bending: TT155, Tomb of Intef (reign of Hatshepsut/Thutmoses III) – bending of pole (58–59); TT95, Tomb of Meri (reign of Amenhotep II) – bending of wood (62–63); Egyptian Museum Cairo RT 17/6/24/12 = Tomb of Ipuja, Saqqara (possibly late 18th Dynasty) – bending of pole (?) (68–69); TT36, Tomb of Ibi (26th Dynasty) – bending of wood (76–77).
[26] These are in the eastern Anatolian region around Lake Van, probably dating from the ninth or eighth centuries BCE.
[27] Belli 2001; Konyar 2006; 2013; Danişmaz 2018.
[28] Amit et al. 2011; and see my several web links from www.chariotmaker.com.
[29] Littauer and Crouwel 1991.
[30] Dittman 1934; Western 1973; Littauer and Crouwel 1985: 92.
[31] Crouwel 1981: 81–85, pl. 95.

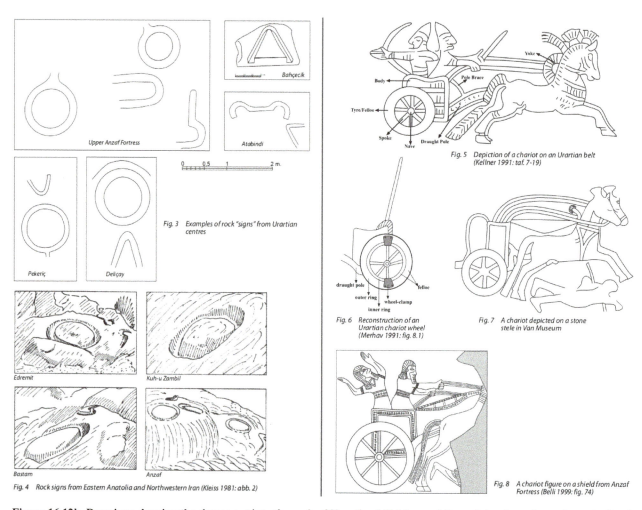

Figure 16.12b. Drawings showing the shapes cut into the rock of Urartian hillsides, and the points where those elements fitted on chariots of the time (after Konyar 2006: figure 3–8; by kind permission of Dr. E. Konyar).

Figure 16.13. Professor Ronny Reich in Chamber 5, excavated in fortifications near the Gihon spring in Jerusalem (photograph by kind permission of R. Reich and E. Shukron).

Greece. Such wheels, or at the very least parts for them, were evidently being produced in Urartu, and perhaps in Jerusalem. Other production sites which have not been discovered must have existed as well.

Going with the Grain

It might seem that there would be an easier way to create the V shape by using naturally forking branches. At first sight the crotch of beechwood illustrated (Figure 16.14) looks as though it would be the right material for a 60°, or 45° V-shape, suitable for six or eight spokes. However, on closer inspection, it can be seen that the grain in the crotch is not continuous and would thus be liable to split. This same weakness is clearly visible in the branch of *Liriodendron* (Figure 16.15) which has broken away from the trunk (the species is prone to doing this). The break has started, as the picture shows, in the confused grain in the crotch. The rest of this branch rambles, and it demonstrates that the grain can run in curves, turning through 90° in places. The beech crotch also shows this irregular grain, illustrating that the grain does not flow continuously across the shape. Because of the weakness in this confusion or discontinuity of the woodgrain, these branched growth patterns are not suitable for use as spokes. The strength of a naturally grown bend lies in the continuity of the grain.

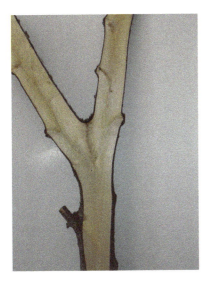

Figure 16.14. Fork (or crotch) of beech (author's photo).

Figure 16.15. Branch torn from a tree (*Liriodendron*) (author's photo).

The shipbuilders of early modern times knew this, and the well-known quest for 'knees' for wooden ships in the eighteenth century[32] was only part of an established market between foresters, merchants and shipbuilders with, at least in English history, a certain amount of governmental involvement to encourage growing the right timbers, in order to equip the Royal Navy. There was indeed, recorded in Europe, a considerable amount of deliberate distortion of tree growth to supply the demand.[33]

Why Do it that Way?

My interest was piqued many years ago when I heard that Homer states that chariot spokes are made from vinestocks. Unfortunately, I have never been able to track down a source, so it may be a bit of false information. I collected a small truckload of cut vinestocks from my local vineyard, but they proved to be an interesting failure for the intended purpose and were quite quickly consumed by some surprisingly large beetle larvae. Nevertheless, this set ideas in motion and the concepts involved are central to this investigation.

These highly sophisticated wheels constructed with V-spokes were evidently being produced over a wide area. But why were they made in the way they were? To a modern eye it is not the obvious way to do the job. Indeed, it seems an oblique and downright difficult solution to the challenge of creating a robust but lightweight wheel, though it certainly produces a beautiful and elegant result.

The answer to this question must lie partly in the limitations of available tools, particularly the quality of the saws at the time. This would lead to thin bent elements from small trees being easier to use than parts sawn from large logs. The solution must also depend on the availability of bentwood elements for making this design. In order to make enough chariots to equip an army, these parts must have been readily available, and in quantity, over a large geographical range. As we have seen, elm was used for these V-shaped elements.

The Elm and the Vine

It is apparent that elm was an important element in the production of chariot parts. The genus *Ulmus* in Britain is a complex combination of clones, cultivars and crossbreeding. It is said that elms may have been introduced to Britain by Lucius Columella,[34] who was a Roman of Iberian origin. He, Virgil and a number of other Roman authors write of the 'marriage' of vine and elm, where an elm is planted alongside a vine, to give it support.[35] Genetic studies of the common hedgerow elm tend to suggest that much of the population is a sterile clone, which may have its origin in Iberia. Whatever the truth of that, it led to an interest in this cultivation method, which was widespread around the Mediterranean, and remained in use up to the 1950s (Figure 16.16). It was certainly practised before the time of the Roman authors: vines growing on trees can be seen in Assyrian palace reliefs (Figure 16.17). But *Ulmus* does not seem to have been a common tree genus in Egypt. Maps of the modern distribution of *Ulmus minor* suggest that it does not extend to most of Turkey or any parts of Egypt, but the Lebanon and Armenia, mainland Greece, Crete and many other areas do have populations.

Elm was cultivated in ancient times to support growing vines. Columella explains in great detail how the tree should be pruned, trained to form horizontal branches at vertical stages three feet apart with clear intervals between (an ideal arrangement and measurement to yield pieces for V-spokes). In modern viniculture vines are frequently

---

[32] A curved piece of wood forming a brace, used to strengthen a junction of major components, especially frames and deck beams in boat building.
[33] Barker 2007; 2019; Jarvis Bay Maritime Museum 2015.
[34] Richens 1983: *passim*.
[35] The Roman author Lucius Columella (first century CE) dedicates Chapter 6 of Book V in his *De Re Rustica* to the plantation of elms in vineyards; see Fuentes Utrilla 2004: 10; Motta 2020.

Figure 16.16. Harvesting grapes. Byzantine ivory panel from a box, 10th–11th c. CE; Museum für Byzantinische Kunst (inv. no. 573; from the Radowitz collection), Bode-Museum, Berlin (image in the public domain: Wikimedia Commons).

Figure 16.17 Assyrian vine growing up a tree. Detail of a wall panel relief 7th century BCE (after George Rawlinson, Five Great Monarchies of the Ancient World. Vol 1 London: Murray 1862).

Figure 16.18. Modern vines in France, trained in espalier form, along wires (author's photo).

Figure 16.19. Trees trained to carry vines in the Po valley, northern Italy (after Motta 2020; photograph by kind permission of Dr. Angelo Sarti).

trimmed as espaliers (Figure 16.18):[36] this, though in the vine itself and not an accompanying elm, gives examples of the exact shape best suited to produce parts for the V-spoked wheel. Trained elms, grown over many thousands of acres of vineyards, would have had the potential to provide quantities of elements growing naturally at a right angle (Figure 16.19). These would be a useful by-crop for a grower if there were a market for them, and a market would surely be a natural result of the demand which certainly must have existed for the manufacture of chariots.[37] Indeed, the angles of the espaliers could be adjusted in growing the elms to provide the 60° V-shaped elements required for six-spoked wheels, and eight-spoked wheels could be catered for in the same way. If the market was thriving in such things, as it must have been at the period which we are considering, these could be supplied in quantity by vine growers.

Ancient 'Self Assembly' Chariots

The unfinished chariot included in the Levantine tribute, the presence of rock-cut moulds suitable for producing the basic shapes of the parts required for the manufacture of wheels and yokes, and the workshop scenes on wall paintings showing the finishing and final construction of chariots, lead to the conclusion that chariots were assembled from parts that could well have been made elsewhere and

---

[36] With the branches encouraged to grow flat, often against a wall or support.

[37] The effect of a market in bentwood parts on the shipbuilding industry in early modern times has been documented (Barker 2007). This reinforces the notion that making an elm by-crop suitable for the chariot-makers would have been economically attractive.

Figure 16.20. These delicate looking wheels are strong structures; testing the lateral stability of a Tutankhamun type of wheel (author's photo)

imported in the large quantities needed for the Egyptian army. Elm did not grow in Egypt, and it can be concluded that for the origin of the woods we should be looking at countries lying to the northeast.

Indeed, beside one of the chariots depicted on the wall of the tomb of Kenamun in Thebes, a well preserved inscription says: "The woods for it (the chariot) were brought from ... the mountain lands of Naharain." This is the Egyptian term for the land of Mitanni, which extended either side of the Euphrates and included the hill country to the north of the Mesopotamian desert, and probably south Armenia. During the New Kingdom, Egypt carried out regular trade with these lands, the greater part of which were under Egyptian control. Quantities of raw materials were imported both as trade goods and tribute. There is thus no reason to doubt that the woods from the region of Naharain-Mitanni were brought to Egypt as raw material.[38]

It would make better economic sense to import the various parts ready shaped than to transport large quantities of raw timber over long distances. Like the flat-pack assembly kits of modern Ikea furniture imported from Scandinavia, the component parts brought from foreign lands would then have been adjusted, assembled and finished to Egyptian tastes and standards in the local workshops.

Conclusion

An observant genius must once have devised a method of making the lightweight type of wheel I have been describing, using glue and bentwood parts. Its use became widespread, greatly helped by the habit of cultivating elms with vines. The cultures of the Near East and Europe which have left much of the most graphic evidence of chariot use embraced it over a long period of time.

Why? There must have been influences which made the V-spoked wheel so successful, and I propose that the reason this design became viable is that it made use of a readily available by-product of viniculture, in the shape of elms grown to support the vines.

I come close to asserting that when wheels of this kind were in strong demand, the growers of vines must have held counsel with the chariot-makers to supply the best shapes for their needs. I think that these ready-formed elements became traded to the mutual benefit of the two parties (Figure 16.20).

Acknowledgements

I have used ideas and imagery from many sources, gaining a number of delightful friends and heavy books. Specifically in the writing of this paper I must thank, of course, Joost Crouwel himself. Those fine drawings and dimensions of the Tutankhamun chariots and many other papers were a primary resource. Thanks are due to the television directors, Michael Barnes and Richard Reisz, who took me to the Near East, Dr. Stephen Harvey for an insight I would have missed, Professor Erkan Konyer for his publication of Urartian rock channels, and to Kristina Howell for skilful help with the manuscript.

I would never have been running on this road if Mike Loades had not wound me up and set me off, and in writing this paper Gail Brownrigg has been tirelessly and generously helpful.

Robert Hurford
Master Wheelwright, Independent Scholar, UK

---

[38] Dittmann 1934: 250–251.

Bibliography

Amit, David, Guy D. Stiebel, and Orit Peleg-Baskar, eds. 2011. *Ḥidushim ba-arkhe'ologyah shel Yerushalayim u-sevivoteha* (*New studies in the Archaeology of Jerusalem and its region*) 5. Jerusalem: Israel Antiquities Authority/ The Hebrew University of Jerusalem, Institute of Archaeology.

Barker, Richard. 2007. Two Architectures – A View of Sources and Issues. In: *Creating Shapes in Civil and Naval Architecture: A Cross-Disciplinary Comparison*, Vol. I, edited by Horst Nowacki and Wolfgang Lefèvre, 41–133. Berlin: Max Planck Institute for the History of Science.

Barker, Richard. 2019. Seeking the Truth of Yarranton's 17th Century Hamburg *Krummholz*: The Supply of Timber in and from Germany. In: *Opus Opificem Probat. The Commemorative Book Dedicated to Jerzy Litwin*, edited by Robert Domżal, Marii Durka, and Anna Ciemonska, 205–220. Gdansk: National Maritime Museum of Gdansk.

Belli, Oktay. 2001. Surveys of Monumental Urartian Rock Signs in East Anatolia. In: *Istanbul University's Contributions to Archaeology in Turkey (1932–2000)*, edited by Oktay Belli, 365–369. Istanbul: İstanbul University Rectorate Research Fund.

Carter, Howard. 1972. *The Tomb of Tutankhamun* (abridged edition). London: Sphere Books.

Cavillier, Giacomo, P. Roberto Del Francia, and Alberto Rovetta. 2002. *Il Carro e le Armi del Museo Egizio di Firenze*. Florence: Giunti.

Chechushkov, Igor V. and Andrei V. Epimakhov. 2018. Eurasian Steppe Chariots and Social Complexity during the Bronze Age. *Journal of World Prehistory* 31: 435–483. DOI: 10.1007/s10963-018-9124-0.

Crouwel, Joost H. 1981. *Chariots and other Means of Land Transport in Bronze Age Greece*. Allard Pierson Series 3. Amsterdam: Allard Pierson Museum.

Danişmaz, Harun. 2018. Palu Kalesi'ndeki Urartu Kaya Işaretleri. In: *Urartian Rock Signs in the Palu Fortress/Uluslararasi Palu Sempozyumu Bildirtler* 1, edited by Enver Çakar, Kürşat Çelik, and Yavuz Kisa, 193–199. Harput Uygulama ve Araştirma Merkezi 4. Elâziğ: Firat Üniversitesi.

Dittmann, Karl H. 1934. Die Herkunft des altägyptischen Streitwagens in Florenz. *Germania* 18: 249–252.

Fuentes-Utrilla, Pablo, Ruby A. López-Rodríguez, and Luisa Gil. 2004. The Historical Relationship of Elms and Vines. *Forest Systems* 13 (1): 7–15. DOI: 10.5424/808.

Herold, Anja. 2006. *Streitwagentechnologie in der Ramses-Stadt. Knäufe, Knöpfe und Scheiben aus Stein*. Die Grabungen des Pelizaeus-Museums Hildesheim in Qantir-Piramesse; Forschungen in der Ramses-Stadt 3. Mainz: von Zabern.

Jarvis Bay Maritime Museum. 2015. Crooks and Knees in Shipbuilding. *Jarvis Bay Maritime Museum blog*, 4 April 2015. http://jervisbaymaritimemuseum.blogspot.com/2015/04/crooks-and-knees-in-shipbuilding.html; accessed 6 August 2020.

Konyar, Erkan. 2006. An Ethno-Archaeological Approach to the "Monumental Rock Signs" in Eastern Anatolia. *Colloquium Anatolicum* 5: 113–126.

Konyar, Erkan. 2013. Turkey: Secrets of the Chariot Makers. *Current World Archaeology* 57. https://www.world-archaeology.com/features/turkey-secrets-of-the-chariot-makers/; accessed 9 July 2020.

Littauer, Mary A. and Joost H. Crouwel. 1979a. *Wheeled Vehicles and Ridden Animals in the Ancient Near East*. Leiden and Cologne: Brill.

Littauer, Mary A. and Joost H. Crouwel. 1979b. An Egyptian Wheel from Brooklyn. *Journal of Egyptian Archaeology* 65: 107–120 [reprinted in Littauer and Crouwel 2002: 296–313].

Littauer, Mary A. and Joost H. Crouwel. 1985. *Chariots and Related Equipment from the Tomb of Tut'ankhamūn*. Tut'ankhamūn's Tomb Series 7. Oxford: Griffith Institute.

Littauer, Mary A. and Joost H. Crouwel. 1986. The Earliest Three-Dimensional Evidence for Spoked Wheels. *American Journal of Archaeology* 90 (4): 395–398 [reprinted in Littauer and Crouwel 2002: 289–295].

Littauer, Mary A., Joost H. Crouwel, and Harald Hauptmann. 1991. Ein spätbronzezeitliches Speichenrad vom Lidar Höyük in der Südost-Türkei. *Archäologischer Anzeiger* 1991: 349–358 [reprinted as "A Late Bronze Age Spoked Wheel from Lidar Höyük in Southeast Turkey" in Littauer and Crouwel 2002: 314–326].

Littauer, Mary A. and Joost H. Crouwel. 2002. *Selected Writings on Chariots and Other Early Vehicles, Riding and Harness*, edited by Peter Raulwing. Culture and History of the Ancient Near East 6. Leiden and Cologne: Brill.

Motta, Annalisa. 2020. *The Vineyards of Ancient Rome, Between the Owner's "Otium" and the Work of the Winemaker*; 25 June 2020. http://www.guadoalmelo.it/en/the-vineyards-of-ancient-rome-between-the-owners-otium-and-the-work-of-the-winemaker; accessed July 18 2020.

Pare, Christopher F. E. 1992. *Wagons and Wagon-Graves of the Early Iron Age in Central Europe*. Oxford University Committee for Archaeology, Monograph 35. Oxford: University Committee for Archaeology.

Piggott, Stuart. 1983. *The Earliest Wheeled Transport, from the Atlantic Coast to the Caspian Sea*. London: Thames and Hudson.

Richens, Richard H. 1983. *Elm*. Cambridge: Cambridge University Press.

Spruytte, Jean. 1977. *Études expérimentales sur l'attelage. Contribution à l'histoire du cheval*. Paris: Crépin-Leblond.

Spruytte, Jean. 1983. *Early Harness Systems*. Translated by Mary Littauer from Spruytte 1977. London: Allen.

Spruytte, Jean. 1989. Le char antique du musée archéologique de Florence. *Traveaux du Laboratoire d'Anthropologie de Préhistoire et d'Ethnologie des Pays de la Méditerranée Occidentale (LAPMO)* 1989: 185–190.

Spruytte, Jean. 1995. Technologie d'une roue du XVe siècle av. J-C (Char A4 de Toutankhamon, No, 332 de l'inventaire de H. Carter. In: *L'Homme méditerranéen. Mélanges offerts à Gabriel Camps*, edited by Robert Chenorkian, 239–247. Aix-en Provence: Presses de L'Université de Provence.

Spruytte, Jean. 1996. *Attelages Antiques Libyens. Archéologie saharienne expérimentale*. Paris: Maison des Sciences de l'Homme.

Spruytte, Jean. 1999. L'attelage égyptien sous la VIIIᵉ Dynastie: étude technique et technologique. *Kyphi* 2: 77–87.

Western, A. C. 1973. A Wheel-Hub from the Tomb of Amenophis III. *Journal of Egyptian Archaeology* 49: 91–94.

17

Jean Spruytte – Horseman, Scholar, Chariot Builder

Gail Brownrigg

Jean Spruytte was a French riding teacher and carriage driver who constructed first scale models and then full-sized chariots based on the study of visual evidence for vehicles and harnessing in antiquity. His practical experiments demonstrated clearly that the long-held theory that ancient harness had choked the draught horses was untrue, and was based on confusion between two harness systems. Bringing to bear the eye and knowledge of a horseman, he analysed the relationship between the type of harness used and the design and balance of chariots in the ancient world. He published numerous articles and two books. Although the importance of his work was not always recognised by academics at the time, his studies informed the work of some distinguished scholars such as Joost Crouwel and Mary Littauer. Jean Spruytte's research and working reconstructions have made a substantial contribution to the history of chariots and harnessing.

Introduction

Jean Spruytte (Figure 17.1) meticulously researched and reconstructed ancient harness and chariots. Combining his knowledge of horses with great practical ability, an enquiring mind and a scholarly attention to detail, he published a large number of papers in French, including his studies of Egyptian, Greek and Saharan wheels, chariots and harness as well as wider equine themes. His small book, intended for the general reader with an interest in equine history, *Études expérimentales sur l'attelage. Contribution à l'histoire du cheval* (1977), translated into English by Mary Littauer in 1983 as *Early Harness Systems. Contribution to the History of the Horse,* summarised the conclusions he had reached about the function of ancient harness and its links with the design and balance of chariots in Egypt, Assyria, Etruria, Greece, the Sahara and ancient China. A further book examined in depth the subject which had first sparked his interest in ancient technology – the early Saharan rock paintings depicting chariots: *Attelages Antiques Libyens* (1996).

Figure 17.1. Jean Spruytte (1919–2007).

His experiments were all carried out for his own interest and at his own cost in his spare time. He contributed frequently to the equestrian magazine *Plaisirs Équestres*, but also to academic publications, with a focus on the technology of ancient vehicles. Spruytte held that only practical experiments could indicate how a particular harness system would function in a way that purely theoretical reasoning could never achieve. Emphasising the importance of extensive trials to demonstrate the feasibility of his reconstructions, he said that, while a successful experiment did not prove that the harness was actually used in antiquity, if it did not function well, it showed that it could not have existed.

Jean Spruytte was a very private man. Despite corresponding for over thirty years with Mary Littauer, the acknowledged expert on ancient vehicles, he continued to address her as 'Madame,' and she would respond: 'Cher Monsieur Spruytte.'[1] His long-standing friend and collaborator Franck David, with whom he had many discussions about ancient vehicles and harness and to whom he referred as his 'heir' in this field, always speaks of him with respect as 'Monsieur Spruytte'.

His knowledge of ancient vehicles was gained through practical experience combined with years of in-depth study of both published material and representations. Like Mary Littauer, he found that few horse riders shared his interest in history or in the function of the harness, vehicles and equipment, while many academics failed to understand the technological basis and practical significance of his conclusions.

His interest in vehicle technology led him to make model wheels from different periods, to examine how they had

---

[1] Much of this correspondence is held in the Littauer archives at the Museum of the Horse in Kentucky.

been constructed.² One interesting finding was the result of accidentally leaving a solid plank wheel out in the rain: it became distorted from the wet, whereas a wheel with interstices such as are depicted on early vehicles maintained its shape – hence the need for the gaps to allow for expansion and contraction in hot or damp conditions. Following his initial research, he constructed beautifully made chariot models, down to sculpting each horse to scale. The larger ones represented hours of meticulous craftsmanship: the 1/5 scale model of a Greek chariot and four horses took 268 hours to make. He then built full sized reconstructions and spent many hours testing them with the help of his wife and his son Alain, who can be seen driving the chariots in the illustrations for his book on early harness systems.³

He emphasised the importance of rigorous experimental trials to try out his ideas. Using ponies of a suitable size – around 13–13.2 hh (130–137 cm) – he drove each chariot for many hours and tested its manoeuvrability and stability at walk, trot and gallop, including tight circles and sharp turns, carefully observing the function of the vehicle and the harness. He kept records and photographs of the manufacture of the chariot parts and his trials of the finished reconstruction. The conclusions he reached were based on thorough examination of the evidence available, including articles and publications, images and archaeological finds, combined with hands-on practical reconstruction with real vehicles and flesh-and-blood ponies which would soon begin to show rubs and sores, breathing difficulties or behavioural problems if the harness was not effective. This series of reconstructions and trials were made before experimental archaeology was recognised as a discipline which could make an important contribution to understanding the technology of the past.

Military Service in North Africa

Jean Spruytte's interest in ancient vehicles and harness was first sparked by the opportunity to visit and study the rock paintings of chariots in the Tassili n'Ajjer, in the central Sahara on the borders of Algeria and Libya, where he was posted while serving with the Méhariste camel regiments.⁴ This arid, mountainous region conceals large numbers of rock paintings and engravings which he examined and photographed, observing them with the eye of a horseman and making careful notes.

He had joined the army in search of adventure in distant lands. Since reading tales of heroism and adventure as a boy – especially those describing the exploits of camel corps officers in the Saharan desert – it had been his dream to travel to North Africa. When he was nearly sixteen, he went to the gendarmerie office to enrol in the African army. He was told that he was too young and that he needed to wait two years. Showing his determination, he applied again on the day of his eighteenth birthday. On 16th November 1937, Spruytte signed on for three years with the Third Regiment of the Algerian Spahis,⁵ garrisoned at Batna in the south of the country. He received all the equestrian and military training of a cavalry regiment, acquiring the specialist knowledge of a true horseman. It was principally on horseback that he was to discover a large part of the Maghreb and its desert expanses. Extensive cavalry manoeuvres across Tunisia, intended to demonstrate the presence of the French army, gave him the opportunity to visit much of that region.

In 1940 the young officer transferred to the Camel Corps (Compagnie Méhariste) of Hoggar, where he was to see active service. Now he was a member of that elite regiment of which he had read so much. The camel regiments, whose principal mission was to assure the presence of French authority in the Saharan regions, were widely dispersed, with their means of communication a radio and their means of transport dromedaries – the only way of travelling in this difficult and immense desert terrain. Thus, for twelve years Spruytte lived with the local people, learning their language, their customs and their values. There he discovered the realities of nomad life and laws of survival in the depths of the vast Saharan desert before the invasion of mechanised vehicles – a way of life that was soon to disappear for ever. The poverty and the harsh living conditions in the huge expanse of the Sahara imbued him with a certain difference of outlook and independence which the true 'people of the Sahara' seem to share.

With this unit he took part in the action against the town of Ghat (Libya) on 20th January 1943, which led to the surrender of the Italian forces and thus freed the passage for General Leclerc's column arriving from the south two days later. In November 1943 he transferred to the Tassili Camel Corps, based at Fort Polignac, remaining with the regiment until his retirement from the army on 16th November 1952, with the rank of adjutant (Figure 17.2). He remained in North Africa supervising the construction of wells, especially in Mauretania. In 1945 and in 1948, he again spent time at Tamadjert in the Tassili n'Ajjer, where he had the opportunity to explore the isolated region and study from a horseman's perspective the many rock paintings depicting chariots and horses which inspired his future research.

Spruytte had come to know the desert and its people well, developing a great interest in the Sahara and its history. He never forgot the years he spent travelling throughout the

---

² Spruytte 1977; 1983: pls. 31–34.
³ Spruytte 1977; 1983.
⁴ With their local tribal links, plus their mobility and flexible tactics, the locally recruited *Compagnies Méharistes* provided an effective means of policing the desert. Operating in wide-ranging platoons of 50 to 60 men under French officers, they administered local laws, provided medical assistance, inspected wells and reported on the state of pastures in the oasis areas. During World War II the Méhariste companies saw service against Axis forces in the Fezzan and southern Tunisia. After the war they resumed their role as desert police until they were disbanded at the end of French rule in 1962, see https://en.wikipedia.org/wiki/Méhariste; accessed 7 September 2020.

⁵ The Algerian cavalry in French service.

Figure 17.2. Adjutant Spruytte, commander of the 2nd platoon of the Tassili Camel Corps in Algeria, in May 1948.

Figure 17.3. Jean Spruytte driving his carriage in 1977 (photo by courtesy of Franck David).

Figure 17.4. Early experiment with a reconstructed Saharan chariot, made using very simple tools, based on the images in the Tassili rock paintings (after Spruytte 1977/1983: pl. 22.7; by permission of Alain Spruytte).

region as a Spahi, a Méhariste and as a civilian. He became truly a 'man of the desert' – it was perhaps the happiest time of his life. The experience helped to shape his personality, and he found it hard to adapt to the restrictions of modern society and European conventions. More than once he said that he should never have left Africa.

Horseman and Teacher

Nonetheless, he returned to France. In 1962, now married with young children, he settled at Vinon sur Verdon, north of Marseille in Provence. His innate love of horses, combined with his depth of equestrian experience – legacy of his cavalry training – enabled him to set up a successful equestrian centre which he named 'l'Éperon d'Argent' (the 'Silver Spur'). His ability to transmit his knowledge to others, together with the patience to relate to younger generations, made it a very friendly place, but he found he also needed to arrange a private space suitable for his studies – as those who knew him at that time could well appreciate. He was instrumental in organising the first long-distance ride, 178 km run over two days (2nd–3rd October 1965) from Vinon to Le Muy, in the Haut-Var region, opening the way for the sport of endurance riding which is now so popular. He trained many successful competitors in this field. He taught both riding and carriage driving, something that was quite unusual for the time (Figure 17.3). He became highly respected as a top-class instructor; his experience and ability were recognised by the carriage driving qualification awarded him by the French Equestrian Federation in 1964. He contributed to the development of this discipline as a competition judge. One of his young pupils, Jean-Luc Berrard, became French carriage driving champion not once, but three times, in 1980, 1981 and 1982, going on to set up a successful driving centre of his own.[6]

Research and Experimentation

Though a busy man, with four children, Spruytte found time to continue his research into the history of the Sahara and its ancient horsemen, widening his interest to the whole of the Mediterranean and the Near East. His interest in chariots first sparked by seeing the rock paintings in North Africa, he began to study the history of early vehicles and to examine the publications and especially the depictions available. He contacted museums and obtained photos, books and articles to build up the background information he needed to study early vehicles and harness. He did not follow the accepted view that there was a lack of innovation in antiquity which led to stagnation in technological development and hence to ineffective harness for horses involving a yoke placed on the withers[7] – which would have rubbed and caused sores. Clever with his hands, he reconstructed ancient vehicles, first as wooden models, even carving the horses carefully to scale. He then built full sized chariots, which could be harnessed and driven and thus fully tested.

---

[6] http://attelage.org/f_article_read.php?aid=33377.

[7] Lefebvre des Noëttes 1924; 1931; Needham 1965: 304–306, 312–315; White 1962.

One of his early projects was to build a light chariot similar to those he had seen on the Saharan rock paintings, without using metal tools (Figure 17.4).[8] This was intended partly to show that such vehicles could have existed in the central Sahara before the introduction of metal to that remote region, and, more importantly, to enable him to experiment with a harnessing system that would resemble the Tassili depictions. Other reconstructions included Egyptian, Assyrian, Greek and Etruscan chariots and harness. His conclusions about the balance of a vehicle and the function of the relevant harnessing system would have been impossible to reach without practical experimentation.

Ancient Harnessing

Until the time of the Roman Empire in the west and the Chinese Han Dynasty (202 BCE–220 CE) in the east, all animal traction, whether for wheeled vehicles or agricultural implements, was in pairs by means of a yoke attached at the front of a central draught pole. While cattle had been exploited in this way since at least the fourth millennium BCE, the earliest incontrovertible evidence for domesticated horses and their use for draught comes from the Bronze Age site of Sintashta in the southern Russian Urals dating to around 2,000 BCE (see Chechushkov and Epimakhov, this volume).

The French army officer, Commandant Richard Lefebvre des Noëttes, had studied numerous depictions from antiquity and reached the mistaken conclusion that the harness comprised a 'throat strap' to which the yoke was attached, joined to a girth to keep it in place (Figure 17.5e). He examined statues, carvings and early paintings of horses in his extensive research covering early harnessing, as well as the use of saddles, stirrups and horseshoes. He also reconstructed what he considered to be the ancient 'throat and girth' harness and experimented with a pair of cab horses pulling a wagon.[9] He found that they could only manage with ease a load of about 500 kg, which corresponded with the maximum weight allowed for the *cursus velox* ('speedy post') vehicles under the regulations laid down in the Theodosian Code published in Byzantium in 438 CE,[10] thus reinforcing his argument that the harness was inefficient. He published his findings in two books, *La Force Motrice Animale à Travers les Âges* (1924) and *L'attelage et le cheval de selle à travers les âges* (1931) which became widely quoted. Highly respected authorities such as the medievalist Lynn White junior[11] and the sinologist Joseph Needham[12] relied on his research, with-

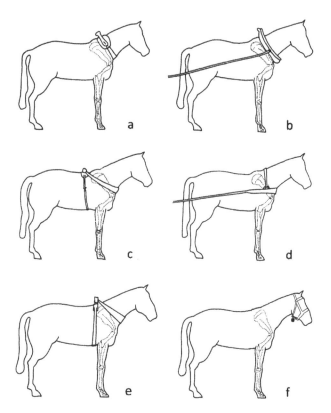

Figure 17.5. Harness systems. Shoulder traction: a – neck yoke with yoke fork; b – modern collar. Breast traction: c – dorsal yoke with neckstrap; d – modern breastcollar. Incorrect combination: e – 'throat and girth' harness proposed by Lefebvre des Noëttes. Frontal traction: f – position of traction bar used with Saharan chariots (adapted from Spruytte 1977/1983).

out questioning the flawed premise on which it was based. Though the core theme of his thesis – that lack of effective animal transport led to human slavery[13] – has been forgotten, his theory that the design of harness in antiquity was not only ineffective but detrimental until the 'invention' of the horse-collar in the Middle Ages, entered the history books and is still repeated today.[14] For the best part of a century, it has been accepted and repeated that early horse harness virtually strangled the poor beasts drawing chariots or wagons by putting pressure on their windpipes, making it hard for them to breathe and thus to use their strength to its full potential. Not only does this oft-repeated myth fail to recognise that chariot horses were prized for their agility in pulling a lightweight vehicle at speed, rather than slow and cumbersome wagons – oxen were used for heavy draught and ploughing – but it would seem highly unlikely that generations of horsemen would continue to use defective equipment for more than two thousand years. Nonetheless, authors writing about equine history continue to quote from one another without thinking to query the description given by Lefebvre des Noëttes.

---

[8] Spruytte 1964; 1967; see also Spruytte 1977: 82–83; 1983: 80.
[9] Lefebvre des Noëttes 1924: 85–86, figs. 1–2; 1931: 162–164 with drawings; see also http://www.humanist.de/rome/rts/introduction.html#WHOWAS.
[10] Lefebvre des Noëttes 1924: 67–70; 1931: 157–160. Under Diocletian (emperor from 284 to 305 CE) the *cursus publicus*, the state-run courier and transportation relay system, had been subdivided into the mule-drawn *cursus velox* which concentrated on rapid transport, and the *cursus clavularius* which was responsible for carrying heavy items on ox-drawn wagons.
[11] White 1962: passim.
[12] Needham 1965: 304–306, 312–315.

[13] Lefebvre des Noëttes 1931: 174–183 (slavery as a consequence of inefficient harnessing), 184–188 (conclusion); Weller n.d.: http://www.humanist.de/rome/rts/introduction.html#WHOWAS.
[14] Kelekna 2009: 161, following Needham 1965; Wikipedia, s.v. Horse collar. https://en.wikipedia.org/wiki/Horse_collar; accessed 4 April 2019.

Spruytte demonstrated that the Commandant had confused two types of harnessing (Figure 17.5), neither of which would put pressure on the windpipe, and by amalgamating them had reconstructed his false 'throat and girth' harness, leading to the concept of its inefficiency and choking effect. The myth of strangled horses and technological stagnation should have been laid to rest at last, yet it still continues to circulate both in academic circles and in popular literature. 'Received wisdom' is seldom questioned!

Egypt and the Near East – Yoke with Yoke Forks

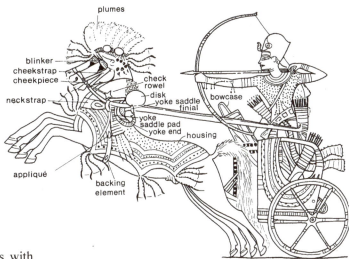

Spruytte, on the other hand, looked at the images with a fresh eye, and researched the archaeological material available. Carefully examining the evidence, he concluded that rather than pressing on the sensitive bony projection which forms the withers, the equine yoke must have been placed further forward, resting on the firm crest of the neck, where there is often a small dip. He realised that in order to prevent it from slipping back, the Y-shaped objects which had been discovered in Tutankhamun's tomb would come into play, lashed tightly to the yoke and lying against the upper part of the horses' scapulae (Figure 17.5a). This would represent a form of shoulder traction, comparable to the use of the modern collar (Figure 17.5b), as distinct from breast traction consisting of a broad strap across the neck and shoulders as in the breastcollar which is in widespread use today (Figure 17.5d).

Having made scale models, Spruytte then built a full-sized chariot, experimenting with the wheel construction and the harnessing method. He conducted extensive trials, which showed that this harnessing system functioned effectively, and that it was associated with the rear position of the axle, as is clearly visible in Egyptian reliefs and tomb paintings. The weight of the charioteer standing ahead of the axle was transferred in part to the front of the pole, helping to prevent the yoke from lifting and keeping it down on the draught animals' necks. A strap under the neck did not tighten when the animals pulled, but simply held the yoke in place and prevented their stepping out from under it. Another long strap led from the outside 'leg' of each yoke fork, under the belly behind the elbows and up to the front of the pole to act as a brake when slowing down or stopping (Figure 17.6).[15] Traction is by means of yoke forks lying on the horses' shoulders; when slowing or stopping, the braking element attached to the end of the pole prevents these from sliding up the horses' necks.

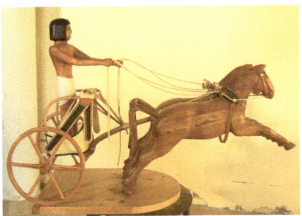

Figure 17.6. a (top) – Egyptian chariot, harness and accessories (after Littauer and Crouwel 1985: fig. 2; by permission of Joost Crouwel). b (middle) – Trial with Spruytte's reconstructed chariot and harness (after Spruyttte 1977, 1983: pl. 7.2; photograph Jean Spruytte, by permission of Alain Spruytte). c (bottom) – Spruytte's hand-carved model 1:5-scale (photograph Jean Spruytte, by permission of Alain Spruytte).

By coincidence, Mary Littauer reached the same conclusion as to the function of the yoke forks,[16] by examining closely the material from the tomb of Tutankhamun and various images including Assyrian reliefs of the 9th century BCE which show unharnessed chariots being transported in a boat.[17] Spruytte was impressed by the fact that she had arrived by deduction at the same interpretation of the harness as he had by practical experimentation. Their mutual respect and long correspondence led to her trans-

---

[15] Spruytte 1977: 41, pls. 7–8; 1983: 40–41, pls. 7–8.
[16] Also known as a yoke saddle.

[17] Littauer 1968.

Figure 17.7. Spruytte's scale model of an Assyrian chariot with outrigger. If the outside horse is killed or injured, it can be released (photographs Gail Brownrigg, Jean Spruytte).

lation of his first book,[18] and to a friendship lasting more than three decades.

Assyria

Similar harness can be identified throughout the Near East and the Aegean in the second millennium BCE.[19] In the early first millennium, an extra horse is sometimes harnessed alongside the team under the yoke. Again using a carefully made scale model, Spruytte demonstrated his theory that the outside horse of an Assyrian triga was not, in fact, attached to the yoke, but was used as a kind of equine shield in battle. He suggested that if it was killed or injured, it could simply be set loose by letting go of its reins, allowing the whole chariot with its crew to continue instead of being disabled and rendered useless (Figure 17.7).[20]

Later Assyrian reliefs show four horses harnessed together under a long yoke which had curved bays instead of the yoke forks, but which still transferred the draught on to top of the animals' scapulae – another form of shoulder traction.[21]

Etruria

In most forms of shoulder traction – right up to the late invention of the harness saddle which carries the shafts and helps maintain the longitudinal balance of a two-wheeled vehicle – the axle is attached at the rear part of the body to produce an imbalance towards the front, thus maintaining the yoke in contact with the neck in all circumstances. However, extant remains of Etruscan vehicles indicate that many were relatively narrow,[22] so there would not have been room for two people to stand side by side. Spruytte

Figure 17.8. Joost Crouwel chose to use Spruytte's hand-carved model of an Etruscan chariot for the front cover of his book *Chariots and other Wheeled Vehicles in Italy before the Roman Empire* (2012; photograph Jean Spruytte).

suggested that in the Etruscan world there were draught systems using shoulder traction (neck yoke), in which the body of the vehicle, longer than it was wide, was balanced over the axle (Figure 17.8). A vehicle of this kind, carrying two people standing one behind the other, could have been designed to reduce the amount of weight which would have pressed on the horses' necks with two people standing in front of the axle.[23]

Mainland Greece

Images on Greek vase paintings from the 8th century BCE onwards, however, showed a different type of harnessing. The chariot axle was placed centrally and though sometimes obscured by the outside horse of the team of four, when visible – for example in harnessing scenes – the yoke was not shown resting on the horses' necks, but rather on their backs. A long, broad neckstrap extended from the yoke itself across their shoulders and chests (Figure

---

[18] Spruytte 1983.
[19] Littauer and Crouwel 1979a: 84–86; Brownrigg 2019: 87–89.
[20] Spruytte 1993: 4, fig. 5.
[21] Littauer and Crouwel 1979a: 114, 116–117, figs. 61–62; Brownrigg 2019: fig. 27.
[22] Emiliozzi 1999; Crouwel 2012a.

[23] Spruytte 1999: 72.

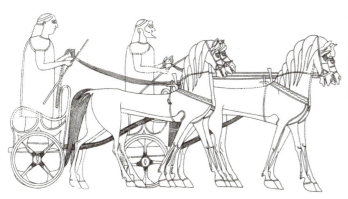

Figure 17.9. Greek racing chariot with dorsal yoke. The driver stands over the central axle.
a (top left) – Detail of an Attic black-figure neck amphora 600–590 BCE; National Museum, Athens, 353 (after Crouwel 1992: pl. 9, by permission of Joost Crouwel). b (top right) – Spruytte's hand-carved model of a Greek racing chariot 1/5 scale took 268 hours to make (photograph Jean Spruytte, by permission of Alain Spruytte). c (bottom left) – Spruytte's full-size Greek racing chariot (photograph by permission of Franck David). d (bottom right) – Experimenting with the chariot (after Crouwel 1992, pl. 37c, by permission of Joost Crouwel).

17.9a).[24] Making first scale models (Figure 17.9b) and then an actual reconstruction of a Greek vehicle (Figures 17.9c-d), Spruytte demonstrated that a dorsal yoke was associated with breast traction, corresponding with the modern type of harnessing known as a breastcollar which is today used with traces and a swingletree[25] (Figures 17.5c–d). The outer horses of a quadriga wore a wide neckstrap to which was attached a single trace leading back to the vehicle. Spruytte later showed that these traces passed through the side of the vehicle and were attached to the floor on the opposite side, counteracting the centrifugal force and the tendency of the vehicle to tip over on fast turns.[26] Again the reconstruction was subjected to extensive trials at walk, trot and gallop (Figure 17.9c). No matter what the gait or the movement performed, the neckstraps did not ride up, while the yoke, held firmly in place by the girth, functioned efficiently as a braking and backing element. This type of harnessing is evidenced for mainland Greek racing chariots. When the driver stands slightly behind the axle the horses bear absolutely no weight.[27] Any tendency for the front end of the pole to lift up is prevented by the girth which holds the yoke on to the backs of the horses, while the fact that the yoke was held firmly in place would allow more accuracy on the tight turns which were the most dangerous point of a race. Though the talented painters who decorated the red and black figure vases often chose to depict heroes and warriors of the Homeric epics mounting or riding in their war chariots, they took as their models the lightweight racing vehicles which they could see in their own day.

An advantage of the dorsal yoke is that its function in supporting and balancing the vehicle is separate from the traction element (the neckstrap). These are combined in any kind of neck yoke. With the axle placed centrally, the weight on the draught animals is almost negligible.[28] The load that they can pull is thus limited only by the strength and soundness of the harness, the yoke and the vehicle (especially the axle and the wheels) and the robustness and even more importantly the weight of the animals.[29] Spruytte demonstrated that, unlike the experiment carried

---

[24] Spruytte 1977: pl. 12.1; Brownrigg 2019: 89–90; Crouwel 1992: 42.
[25] Also known as a whippletree, it transfers the bilateral pull to a single point on the vehicle or implement. The earliest evidence of its use, for single draught with long traces, is a ploughing scene on carvings on the North Mausoleum at Ghirza in Libya from the time of the Roman Empire. http://www.livius.org/ga-gh/ghirza/ghirza_north-d-g.html and http://www.livius.org/ga-gh/ghirza/ghirza_south-c.html. Whippletrees are also used to balance out the pull of two horses harnessed side by side.
[26] Spruytte 1978.
[27] Spruytte 1977: 64; 1983: 57.
[28] Spruytte 1977: 63; 1983: 57.
[29] Spruytte 1977: 107 ff; 1983: 99 ff.

Figure 17.10. Chinese harnessing, Eastern Han dynasty. Single draught with traction by means of a breastcollar. a – Carriage depicted on a moulded brick, 2nd century CE (after Sun Ji 2001: fig. 21, 10.1, by permission of Mr. Sun Ji). b – Harnessing experiment. The cart is a modern training vehicle fitted with shafts of Chinese design (after Spruytte 1977/1983: fig. 15.3, by permission of Alain Spruytte).

out by Lefebvre des Noëttes in 1910 with his 'throat and girth' harness, in which a pair of large cab horses could manage only 500 kg,[30] two horses harnessed with a properly fitting dorsal yoke and suitable neckstraps could easily draw a laden wagon weighing, with its driver, some 975 kg on a difficult surface in a sand arena.[31] A team would thus be capable of moving even greater loads efficiently on a hard road.

Nonetheless, Georges Raepsaet, whose studies focused on ancient technology and the efficiency of animal traction systems in the classical world, rejected Spruytte's concept of a dorsal yoke.[32] He considered the iconography to be ambiguous, pointing out that the yoke often appeared to be erroneously shown on the horses' withers instead of clearly in front or behind. He did not see any reason to assume an innovation in the harnessing of Greek racing chariots which could perhaps have improved speed and mobility, since chariots had already been driven at the gallop in Egypt and the Near East. He cited evidence for the use of a neck yoke in mainland Greece on donkeys, mules and cattle for utilitarian transport, including agricultural settings, as well as in East Greek depictions of horse-drawn chariots. He admitted that Spruytte's reconstructed breast traction system was functional, but despite illustrating harnessing scenes from a black-figure hydra in Berlin and a vase in Athens, both clearly showing the long, flexible neckstrap lying below the line of each horse's scapula and passing in front of its breast just above the point of the shoulder,[33] he insisted that there was insufficient iconographical evidence showing what he referred to as the 'so-called' dorsal yoke. It seems that Raepsaet failed to recognise the important association between 'this imaginative draught harness based on the curious dorsal yoke' ('ce harnais de traction original fondé sur ce curieux joug

dorsal') and the central position of the axle placed directly under the body of the vehicle. He also overlooked the fact that the two types of harness were being used for different purposes: oxen and mules under the traditional neck yoke are depicted transporting heavy loads at walking pace, whereas the small, agile horses pulling lightweight chariots designed for speed wear broad neckstraps attached to a dorsal yoke.

Single Draught in China

The technology of a two-wheeled vehicle with a central axle in combination with a harnessing system in which the traction element is independent of the support element is also evidenced in Han China (202 BCE–220 CE). While early Chinese harness was based on the yoke-and-pole system with long yoke forks lying in front of the shoulders, under the Western Han dynasty (202 BCE–9 CE) single draught between shafts was introduced. A broad breastcollar was attached to the shafts, while support was assured by a crossbar resting on a single arched yoke fork placed high on the neck (Figure 17.10). The reins were carried very high in order to have a lifting effect and to prevent the horse from lowering his head to the ground, which would cause the vehicle to tilt forward. Although Lefebvre des Noëttes had described its function correctly,[34] Spruytte experimented with this harnessing system[35] in order to compare it with Gallo-Roman vehicles. He found that at a walk, contrary to what one might expect, any swaying of the shafts from the action of the neck was negligible, while when trotting it was entirely absent since the horse holds his head and neck still at this gait. In fact, both ridden and harnessed horses depicted in Han imagery are shown travelling at a smooth amble or 'tölt'[36] (Figure 17.10a), a

---

[30] Lefebvre des Noëttes 1924: 85–86, figs. 1–2; 1931: 162–164 with drawings.
[31] Spruytte 1977: 101–107, pls. 27–29; 1983: 98–99, pls. 27–29; see also http://www.humanist.de/rome/rts/load.html; accessed 27 October 2020.
[32] Raepsaet 2002: 161–167.
[33] Raepsaet 2002: figs. 87, 88.

[34] Lefebvre de Noëttes 1931: 108–109.
[35] Spruytte 1977: 70–71, pl. 15; 1983: 61, 73, pl. 15.
[36] The footfall corresponds with the 'running walk' of the American saddlebred and the Tennessee walking horse, the 'paso llano' of the Peruvian Paso and similar gaits performed by many other horse breeds, though little known in modern Europe. '[The] paces [of the Han horse] are the amble, a conventional and high-stepping walk, the gallop, and very rarely

Figure 17.11. Gallo-Roman harness. a – Funerary monument in Igel (Austria) depicting a mule between the shafts with another alongside (after Spruytte 1977/1983: pl. 35.2; Raepsaet 2002: fig. 135; Brownrigg and Crouwel 2017: fig. 2); b – Spruytte's experiment with an attempted reconstruction of the harness. The vehicle is modern, fitted with suitable upward-curving shafts (photograph Jean Spruytte, by permission of Alain Spruytte).

four-beat gait still much prized in the Icelandic horse: the head is carried high and the animal seems to skim along with hardly any movement in its neck and back.

Gallo-Roman Harness

In addition to the two principal harnessing systems of antiquity – shoulder traction and breast traction – Spruytte recognised that the equid harness depicted on Gallo-Roman reliefs was clearly different from that previously known.[37] Figured documents from widely separate areas illustrate a new type of harness and vehicles, including two-wheelers pulled by a single draught animal between shafts, or sometimes with a companion alongside. These are shown at walk (Figure 17.11a), as are the pairs and teams harnessed to four-wheeled wagons.[38] He attempted a reproduction (Figure 17.11b) of the harness depicted in the iconography of the western provinces and attested by material from Bulgarian Thrace described by Venedikov in 1960.[39] However, he did not publish his experiment and trials fully because he was not satisfied with the results.[40] Spruytte hoped that more actual archaeological finds from the relevant period would come to light, and that his friend and colleague Franck David would thus be able to continue with this research.

An experienced horseman and dressage trainer who collaborated on many of the experiments, David now holds all Spruytte's archives, the carefully compiled documentation and many of the scale models, which he is willing to put at the disposal of researchers who wish to draw on the information or obtain explanations. He says: 'I owe this in respect for his memory and all that he has taught me during fifteen exciting years with him. I am continuing the work which I began with him and hope thus to bring my own contribution to the overall body of research. We must continue to bring a technical approach to help researchers to understand the reality of harness and equitation.'

David has concentrated on the Gallo-Roman harness system which was touched on only briefly in *Etudes Expérimentales* as 'a new traction system, clearly different from those previously known in antiquity,' and has benefitted from access to archaeological finds, which Spruytte had always hoped would help to clarify the images on tombs and monuments. He has published his studies in two articles,[41] demonstrating the details and function of this new harness, which was used on horses or mules yoked in pairs, as well as for single draught between shafts. Spruytte would have been most interested to see the curved wooden sidepieces found at Le Rondet in Switzerland,[42] still joined by a metal U-shaped element which enabled them to fit on either side of the animal's neck, holding in place the single or double yoke. A similar find of a carved wooden plaque from Reims[43] confirmed the shape of the sidepieces depicted on the monuments, while another excavated during work on the new underground railway system in London and securely dated to the first century CE[44] has shown that this new harness system was already in use at that time. He would have been pleased to see that his work is being carried on, following his example in reconstruction and experimental trials.

The Enigmatic Saharan Rock Paintings

Spruytte considered that the two principal harnessing methods in antiquity were shoulder traction, exemplified by the Egyptian and Assyrian chariots (Figures 17.5a,

---

the trot. The amble predominates, perhaps because this smooth gait restricts to a minimum the up-and-down movements of the neck and as a result it had the advantage of reducing considerably any swaying of the carriage caused by the strange position of the yoke.' Lefebvre des Noëttes 1931: 106 (author's translation).
[37] Spruytte 1977: 132–133, pls. 35–37; 1983: 126–127, pls. 35–37.
[38] Spruytte 1977: 132–138; 1983, 126–133; Raepsaet 1982; see also Brownrigg and Crouwel 2017; Brownrigg, Crouwel and Linduff 2023: 166–171.
[39] Venedikov 1960.
[40] Personal communication 2003.
[41] David 2011; 2015; see also Brownrigg and Crouwel 2017; Brownrigg, Crouwel and Linduff 2023: 169–171.
[42] Schwab 1973; 2003.
[43] David 2015: 15, figs. 13–14.
[44] Personal correspondence with Michael Marshall, Museum of London Archaeology, April 2019.

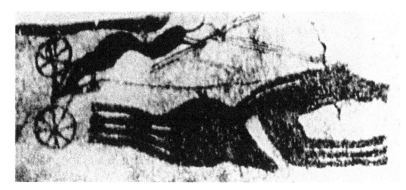

Figure 17.12. Tamadjert rock painting, Tassili n'Ajjer (after Spruytte 1977/1983: pl. 18.1; photograph Jean Spruytte, 1948, by permission of Alain Spruytte).

17.6–17.8), and breast traction, used for the Greek racing chariots (Figures 17.5c; 17.9).

However, he also tried to analyse the enigmatic type of harness system which had attracted his attention in the North African desert during his service in the Camel Corps. As commander of Fort Gardel, 50 km from Djanet, in 1941–1942[45] and posted to Tamadjert in 1945 and 1948, he had the opportunity to explore the area. He found numerous paintings of chariots and horses in rock shelters beneath the cliffs, which he examined and recorded with sketches and photographs (Figure 17.12).

At that time, the rock art of Africa, though briefly mentioned by early travellers,[46] was hardly known in Europe. Rock paintings and engravings are found throughout the Sahara, of different styles, and dating to different periods. The earliest engravings on the cliffs and in the caves beneath show huge wild animals such as elephants, giraffes and rhinoceros, which are found today in the African savannah. There are also strange anthropomorphic figures which have been the subject of much debate, scenes of a cattle raising society, of hunting and chariots, and during the most recent period – reflecting the desertification of the region – images of camels used to transport both people and goods.

Like Lieutenant Gabriel Gardel who had served in the Tassili region before the First World War, but whose notes have not been published,[47] other French legionaries such as Lieutenant Brenans recorded and sketched the images in 1933–1934. He submitted some of his drawings to the director of the Bardo Museum in Algiers, who sent them to the famous French prehistorian, Abbé Henri Breuil, the acknowledged expert on prehistoric rock art.[48] Abbé Breuil had copies made of these drawings, which were not published until 1954.[49] Hearing of these discoveries, Henri Lhote, the explorer and anthropologist and pupil of Abbé Breuil, made his way to the Tassili in 1935, where he met Brenans and saw the paintings for himself. Determined to return one day to make life-sized copies in colour, he was not able to realise his dream until 1956. The reproductions he made with his team on that expedition were exhibited in Paris in 1957 and 1958,[50] bringing Saharan art to the attention of the public as well as historians. Lhote's book describing the adventures and obstacles involved in the project, *A la découverte des Fresques du Tassili,* was published in 1958.[51] In the meantime, Yolantha (Yolande) Tschudi, a young Swiss anthropologist, also visited the Tassili and made several copies of the figures, which she published in 1955 with one of the first tentative attempts at the chronological classification of the material.[52]

In Saharan rock art, images of horses harnessed to chariots have been among the subjects that have attracted most attention in recent years. Whilst the great majority of them are engraved, painted chariots are concentrated essentially in the central Sahara, in the rock shelters beneath the cliffs in the Tassili n'Ajjer[53] and Tadrart.

Spruytte decided to concentrate on the paintings from Tamadjert which he had been able to examine himself, looking at them with the eye of a horseman. Characterised by 'stick-headed' figures wearing short kilts or belted tunics, they include light chariots and hunting scenes on foot with bow and arrow and short lances, while other figures dressed in long skirts go about typical domestic tasks. Some vehicles are shown unharnessed, often with horses standing beside them. Most are depicted travelling at speed, usually drawn by two horses at a stylised 'flying gallop'. The chariots are very simple, consisting of an open platform, with no front or side panels, resting on a long rear axle joining the two spoked wheels, and a single draught pole. The paintings seem to show no harness except four reins held by the single standing charioteer (Figures 17.12; 17.13a).

Again using carefully executed scale models (Figure 17.13b), Spruytte replicated the appearance of the scenes in the paintings. The yoke is seldom easily visible, as the horses are shown from the side, but it is clear that the draught pole extends to just behind their heads. Thus this is not a system of shoulder traction with a neck yoke and yoke forks. It would not be possible to place a yoke just behind the ears on the first cervical vertebrae, partly because this is a sensitive area and it would need plentiful padding in this position. More importantly it could not be held in place without a strap around the throat which would hinder the horses' breathing and tend to strangle them – as Lefebvre des Noëttes had pointed out in his faulty

---

[45] http://saharayro.free.fr/bordjs/fortsc01.htm.
[46] Barth 1857; Duveyrier 1864.
[47] http://lesamisdalgerianie.unblog.fr/2018/03/07/lieutenant-gabriel-gardel-un-heros-saharien/
[48] Keenan 2002.
[49] Breuil 1954.
[50] Lhote 1957.
[51] Translated into English as *The Search for the Tassili Frescoes. The Story of the Prehistoric Rock Paintings of the Sahara.*
[52] Tschudi 1955; 1956.
[53] Coulson and Campbell 2010.

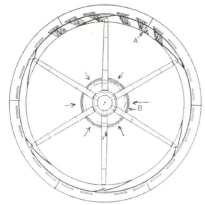

Figure 17.13. a (top row, left) – Tamadjert rock painting, Tassili n'Ajjer (photograph J. Kunz, after Spruytte 1977/1983: pl.18.3 and Spruytte 1996: fig. 8, by permission of Alain Spruytte). b (top row, right) – Spruytte's model of the chariot and harness depicted at Tamadjert with its stabilising hoop and wheels similar to an Egyptian wheel in the Brooklyn Museum. Traction is by a bar under the horses' heads (photograph copyright Musée Saharien, Le Crès, Montpellier, France, by permission). c (middle row, left) – Spruytte's reconstruction of the wheel in the Brooklyn Museum, New York, with 'tensioning collar' (after Spruytte 1996: fig. 34, by permission of Alain Spruytte). d (middle row, right) – Full-sized reconstruction of a Saharan chariot with stabilising hoops and traction bar, as depicted on the Tamadjert rock paintings (photograph copyright Musée Saharien, Le Crès, Montpellier, France, by permission). e (bottom right) – A later reconstruction of the Tassili chariot, based on the wheel in the Brooklyn Museum, which confirmed the functionality of the traction bar and the manoeuvrability of the vehicle (after Spruytte 1996: fig. 82, by permission of Alain Spruytte).

reconstruction of ancient harnessing. Spruytte deduced that instead of a yoke placed high on their necks, the element which could be seen projecting to one side and was also visible on the unharnessed vehicles, must be some kind of bar placed beneath their jaws. The problem was to work out how this could be attached in such a way that it could not hurt the horses or cause injury. In order to experiment with the unusual harnessing system in the Tassili chariot scenes, Spruytte had built a light vehicle resembling those on the rock paintings, using simple stone tools that would have been available to prehistoric inhabitants of the region (Figure 17.4).[54] This first experimental chariot – which he considered unsuccessful because the wheels, instead of rotating independently, were fixed on the axle, putting great strain on it and thus inhibited tight turns – was intended to show that such a chariot could have been made before the introduction of metal to the region, More importantly, Spruytte wanted to try out a possible novel means of traction and its feasibility. A second version, incorporating the independently rotating wheels from the Egyptian chariot he had made, had a curved rail based on that of the chariot in Florence,[55] but this proved unnecessary as the driver did not need to hold on to remain in balance.[56] He quite naturally adopted a position like that shown on the paintings, with his knees bent.

---

[54] Spruytte 1977: 82–83; 1983: 75, 80.

[55] In 1828/29 a chariot had been found in a shaft grave in western Thebes, Upper Egypt during excavations by Rosellini and Champollion. It was, however completely broken into pieces. It was packed into cases and shipped to Florence, where it was incorrectly reconstructed on the basis of ancient Egyptian representations. See Littauer and Crouwel 1985: 108.

[56] Spruytte 1977; 1983: pls. 23–26.

Frontal Traction

After extensive trials, Spruytte concluded that, strange as it may seem, a light bar lashed to the forward end of the pole and suspended from a form of headstall similar to a modern leather halter, functioned most effectively (Figures 17.5f; 17.13). This was confirmed by several paintings visible in later photographs taken by Jürgen Kunz[57] showing very clearly the 'traction bar' in position beneath the jaws of the horses. The few technical details revealed by the paintings were not improvised by the artist, but actually corresponded to reality and enabled reconstruction of a draught system which replicated them and which functioned effectively. With this simple harnessing method, the ponies could indeed pull the lightweight chariot and were easily controlled at all gaits, from walk to gallop.[58] If the driver stood almost over the axle, hardly any weight was carried on the bar, but to prevent it from lifting when the driver mounted the vehicle, it was essential that the wheels were at the rear of the floor rather than positioned centrally. An additional benefit of such a bar would be to link the animals together so that they would turn and work as a team – a method still used today in training harness horses.

Saharan Chariots and Horses

Another observation made by Spruytte was that almost all the horses in the chariot paintings appeared to have docked tails. This must have been due to the risk that the reins, running from the horses' heads directly to the hands of the charioteer with no terret rings to hold them in place, could catch underneath long tails – which, as any horseman knows, could have resulted in panic, kicking, and total loss of control leading to a serious accident. Rare depictions of long tails, from Tamadjert[59] and Oued Allarama,[60] show horses about to be harnessed up. Though many of the paintings show mere stumps, could this be artistic convention, like the flying gallop? Actual docking of horses' tails (illegal in Britain since 1949 for welfare reasons) is not easy and carries a risk of infection. Perhaps the tails were either shaved or bound up short, rather than docked (Figures 17.12; 17.13a),[61] as is done on plough horses today, for the same reason.

When Spruytte began his experimental trials in the 1960s,[62] very little had been published about Saharan rock art and the chariot paintings that interested him. His friendship with the photographer Jürgen Kunz, who was also researching the Tassili chariots, enabled him to examine more recent photographs and add to the material he had collected whilst there himself and confirm the accuracy of his own sketches. With his usual rigour and attention to detail, he was determined to use only the evidence from good quality photographs rather than drawings which could easily result in misinterpretation – or at worst even falsification – of the original. Having seen the rock art *in situ*, he was also well aware that even though images were juxtaposed in a single scene, that did not mean that they belonged together or were even contemporary. For example, a galloping chariot depicted near a group of armed figures fighting one another was not proof that the vehicle was actually taking part in the battle. It was difficult to decipher not only the technical details of the vehicles and their draught system, but also the purpose for which they were used. It would be easy to jump to the conclusion as others did, and as Lhote was determined to prove,[63] that they were 'war chariots'. Spruytte felt this was unlikely, since they usually carried only a single person, whereas in other cultures the charioteer accompanied a warrior who used both hands for his weapons. The mystery of the Tassili chariots – even their dating – led to much discussion amongst historians and ethnographers.

'With regard to harnessing and vehicles, either something is materially possible, or it is not.... The experimental results obtained must be relevant to the safety and ease of control, the handling and feasibility of the turnout, and lastly, the robustness and balance of the vehicle at all gaits, including the gallop'.[64] The reconstructed chariots, based on the photographic evidence of the Tamadjert paintings, proved successful and functioned well in experimental trials. Nonetheless, Henri Lhote, who liked to be considered not only the 'discoverer' of the Tassili rock art, but also the expert on its history and interpretation, dismissed them as the work of a 'clever handyman'[65] which could have had no basis in reality.

He claimed that in contrast to the Egyptian chariot in Florence which weighed about 80 kg, and Tutankhamun's chariots which he erroneously stated comprised metal elements,[66] the simple, lightweight Saharan vehicle was impractical and could not travel far. In fact, Spruytte's first experimental chariot, despite having wheels fixed on the axle instead of rotating independently, was nonetheless driven some 20 km in the course of various trials.[67]

Lhote argued that leather tyres would not have lasted long on rough and stony ground, proposing that the Saharan chariots might have had metal protection on the rim or even complete wheels made of bronze.[68] This ignores the fact that Egyptian chariots operated in desert conditions and on terrain similar to those of Algeria and Libya. Reconstructed chariots with rawhide tyres, used in the shooting of the film *Troy*, covered substantial distances, which

---

[57] Spruytte 1996; Kunz 1982.
[58] Spruytte 1977: 71–99; 1983: 73–97.
[59] Kunz 1982: fig. 9.
[60] Spruytte 1996: fig. 38, pl. v.
[61] Kunz 1982: 88.
[62] Spruytte 1964; 1966; 1967.
[63] Lhote 1963: 233–234; 1982b: 95–111.
[64] Spruytte 1996: 21–22.
[65] Lhote 1982b: 72.
[66] 'The chariots are almost entirely constructed of two materials – wood and leather, the latter dressed or in the form of rawhide' (Littauer and Crouwel 1985: 92). Bronze was used for some linchpin shafts and outer nave hoops and for the small pins used in attaching decorative roundels, bosses or terminals; Littauer and Crouwel 1985: 94.
[67] Spruytte 1977: 83; 1983: 80.
[68] Lhote 1982b: 74.

must have run into tens of miles.[69] Metal reinforcements nailed to the felloes were known in the Near East during the Bronze Age[70] but have not been found in either Egypt or North Africa. Iron tyres encircling and compressing the rim appear in Europe in the Hallstatt culture, dating to the eighth–sixth centuries BCE. However, Tutankhamun's chariots A4 and A5[71] and a wheel now in Brooklyn [see below][72], had a wooden tyre or outer rim, which must have been fitted in order to take the wear, and could be easily replaced.

Lhote thought that the Saharan chariots must have resembled those of the Egyptians,[73] well known from actual finds[74] as well as depictions on temple reliefs, tomb paintings and stelae, and that the reason no superstructure was shown must have been due to the difficulty of painting in such inaccessible places as the rock shelters.[75] Though in the caption to a very clear photo from Tamadjert,[76] he described the curved yoke as emerging from beneath the throats of the animals, he considered it 'indisputable' that it would have been placed high up on the horses' necks, albeit without the yoke forks used in Egypt, and held in place instead by the straps or cords seen hanging from it on some unharnessed chariots.[77] As had been pointed out by Spruytte, this would have resulted in a choking effect when in draught. Lhote would have seen Spruytte's demonstrations of both the Egyptian and the Saharan chariots at the 1981 Sénanque conference *Les Chars Préhistoriques du Sahara*,[78] which he attended, but it seems that he failed to understand or chose to ignore the principles behind the technology of early harness systems.[79]

Multiple Shafts

Spruytte continued to study and experiment with the unusual Saharan chariots and harness, working with Jürgen Kunz to examine more images, which continued to be discovered. In addition to the Tassili paintings showing the horses harnessed either side of a central draught pole, rock engravings from many sites across the Sahara depict chariots as if seen from above, with multiple parallel shafts or poles. Spruytte surmised that these would allow several animals to be placed side by side, linked by a long 'traction and support bar' in the same way as the pairs from Tamadjert. He experimented with four ponies abreast.[80] To his surprise, he found that not only was this bar very effective in keeping the ponies together, but it also restrained them from bucking, rearing or other bad behaviour, allowing their breaking and training to proceed more quickly than with traditional methods and harness. When put between the multiple shafts they learned very quickly to stay straight and to work together as a team.

The Sahara vehicles date from different periods. Some were considered by researchers to have been contemporary with the use of fast horse-drawn chariots in the Aegean, Egypt and the Near East, dating from the middle of the second millennium to the end of the first millennium BCE.[81]

Spruytte's focus, however, was principally on their function and the harnessing system. Unlike other authors who presumed that they were war chariots,[82] he pointed out that, though they could have been used for hunting, the vehicles do not have protective front or side panels, nor is there any evidence that they were associated with weaponry or scenes of battle in the Tassili paintings. The charioteer is usually alone with no accompanying warrior. Spruytte proposed that these were training vehicles for locally raised animals which would then be sold on to places where the countryside was less suitable for raising horses and the people less skilled in their training. Whilst in North Africa, Spruytte had come to know and admire the agility and endurance of the tough little Barb horses native to the region. Perhaps their ancestors had pulled the chariots depicted in the rock paintings.

The Brooklyn Wheel[83]

One particular photograph, taken by Jürgen Kunz at the Oued Allarama (near Tamadjert), showed a man standing with two horses facing an unharnessed chariot. The traction bar at the end of the pole and the stabilising hoop on the floor of the vehicle were clearly visible.[84] A striking

---

[69] Pers. comm. with their maker, Robert Hurford, 2 September 2020.
[70] Crouwel 2012b.
[71] Littauer and Crouwel 1985: 77.
[72] Littauer and Crouwel 1985: 77 fn. 1; Spruytte 1996: figs. 48–53.
[73] Lhote 1982b: 67, 71.
[74] Howard Carter excavated the tomb of Tutankhamun in 1922, and one of the chariots was exhibited in Paris in 1976. A chariot found in western Thebes (Upper Egypt) by Rosellini and Champollion in 1828/29, (incorrectly reconstructed on the basis of ancient Egyptian representations) was exhibited in Florence. Shortly after the turn of the 20th century another was found in the Valley of the Kings, in the tomb of the parents in law of Amenophis II (1388–1350 BCE).
[75] Lhote 1982b: 76.
[76] Lhote 1982b: fig. 17 – the chariot is that illustrated in our Figure 17.13a.
[77] Lhote 1982b: 71–72.
[78] Spruytte 1982.
[79] Henri Lhote has come in for sharp criticism in his turn. According to the British anthropologist, Jeremy Keenan 'Lhote's work is now recognized for its denigration of almost all and sundry' (Keenan 2000: 284). He failed to mention previous studies of the Tassili frescoes, such as the first tentative attempts at the chronological classification of the material by Yolande Tschudi, published in 1955 – the year before he undertook the expedition in which he claimed to have 'discovered' them. Moreover, it is now suggested that he undertook what might be regarded today as the systematic vandalism of the sites, not only by liberally washing the paintings to restore their colour, but by removing quantities of artefacts from the area. It is even suggested that some of his drawings were manipulated or even fabricated to make them more attractive to the general public or to support his theories of contact between pharaonic Egypt and the central Sahara.

[80] Spruytte 1986; 1996: 27–38, figs. 23–30.
[81] Lhote 1963: 233–234; Camps and Gast 1982, 3; Muzzolini 1982; Le Quellec 2019; Lhote 1958; 1959: passim; Striedler 2004: 160–161, 164–165.
[82] Lhote 1982a: 25; 1982b: 95–111; 1958; 1959: passim; Striedler 2004:161.
[83] See also Hurford this volume.
[84] Spruytte 1996: 38–39, fig. 18.

detail was the delineation of the wheels, which closely resembled the one in the Brooklyn Museum (New York), reportedly brought from Dashur in Egypt by Doctor Abbott in 1843 and obtained by the museum in 1948 (Figure 17.13c).[85] In 1986 this was carbon dated to the fifth century BCE).[86]

With his interest in solving technical problems, Spuytte had already studied this wheel and made a model at 1/5 scale in 1980.[87] Unlike the wheels of Tutankhamun's chariots and the one in Florence, comprising V-shaped elements fitted back to back to form the hub and the spokes[88] (see Figure 17.6c and Robert Hurford this volume), the spokes of the Brooklyn wheel were mortised individually into the hub and part way into the rim, enabling them to be removed easily should the wheel need to be dismantled. A unique feature was the wooden ring (currently missing from the wheel but mentioned in the 1948 inventory) passing through slots in the spokes and encircling the hub. In his full-sized reconstruction (Figures 17.13c–e) Spruytte used bands of rawhide, which shrank and tightened as they dried, to hold this ring – which he described as the 'tensioning collar' ('*collier de serrage*') – firmly in place, as well as to lash the wooden tyre on to the rim.[89]

He built another chariot, incorporating the stabilising hoop, the traction bar and wheels of this design, and continued to experiment with the stability and manoeuvrability of the turnout. Together with the preliminary scale model, this is now in the Musée Saharien du Crès in Montpellier (Figures 17.13d–e).[90] As with the previous experimental trials, the vehicle with its unique harnessing system was put to the test with a pair of agile ponies moving at all gaits. The apparently fragile wheels proved remarkably resilient, even at speeds of up to 25 km per hour on turns so sharp that they resulted in skidding. The rawhide bindings holding the various elements together created a rigid structure. The hoop in the centre of the platform helped the driver to keep his balance and, as before, the traction bar, while providing longitudinal equilibrium to the chariot, enabled him to control the ponies easily as it kept them together and they pulled one another round on the turns. In appearance this later vehicle closely resembled the chariots depicted in the paintings preserved in the shelters beneath the Tassili rocks (Figures 17.12, 17.13a). Close examination of these images reveals details which can be recognised with knowledge of Spruytte's reconstruction, including evidence for the 'Brooklyn' type of wheel with its remarkable tensioning collar and clear representation of a tyre around the rim.

A Lifetime of Research

Jean Spruytte's extensive studies of the chariots and harness depicted in the Saharan rock paintings resulted in a well illustrated book, including photographic documentation by Jürgen Kunz, which makes an important contribution to the study of early vehicles. Combining his interest in the history of the horse, his love of Africa, his technological knowledge and his practical expertise, *Attelages Antiques Libyens* published in 1996 – nearly twenty years after *Études Expérimentales* – essentially sums up a lifetime of research. This extensive study of chariots in the Tassili rock paintings presents technical analysis of both harnessing and vehicles, together with a detailed description of their reconstruction and the experimental trials undertaken at all paces from walk to gallop. The chapter on the technology of the unique wheel in the Brooklyn Museum, carbon dated to the fifth century BCE,[91] which he analysed and painstakingly reconstructed for his experiments, suggests a plausible context for the Tamadjert paintings, helping to place them in their geographical and historical setting. Spruytte knew the region well and could envisage the training sessions in the narrow valleys at a time when the vegetation could support cattle and horses, before the onset of arid conditions meant that camels came to dominate the lifestyle and the art of the inhabitants. He concluded that 'the experiments provide evidence of the existence ... in ancient Libya[92] of a system of training harness horses perfectly adapted for this purpose and appropriate for the geographical conditions of this region, as well as the presence of a sedentary population specialised in this activity.'[93]

The introduction evokes the desert landscape among strange rock formations on the Tassili plateau which Spruytte knew so well from his military posting as a Méhariste – a formative period in his life and an experience which he never forgot. Though he settled with his family in Provence, at heart he always remained 'a man of Africa'. He wrote numerous articles relating to the Sahara, covering historical as well as equestrian themes. One of his first publications, 'Cavaliers et cochers sahariens de l'antiquité' ('Horsemen and charioteers of the Sahara in antiquity'), appeared in *Plaisirs Équestres* in 1964. For the next two decades he would continue to be a regular contributor to this magazine. He widened his research to include the whole of the Mediterranean world and beyond, developing a truly international network of correspondents who shared his interests and exchanged ideas. Chief among these was Mary Littauer, who supplied him with much of the archaeological material which formed the basis for his research, and one of the few people who really understood the importance of his work from a hippological perspective.

---

[85] https://www.brooklynmuseum.org/opencollection/objects/118224; Littauer and Crouwel 1979b; Spruytte 1996: 41, xi and fig. 38.
[86] Spruytte 1996: 74.
[87] Spruytte 1996: 41.
[88] Spruytte 1977: 25–27; 1983: 25–27.
[89] Spruytte 1996: figs. 34–37; see also Robert Hurford, this volume.
[90] http://museesaharien.fr/qui-sommes-nous/evenements/20170311-conference-chars-garamantiques.

[91] Spruytte 1996: 74.
[92] The 'Libya' of Herodotus comprised a large swathe of North Africa, including present-day Algeria and modern Libya.
[93] Spruytte 1996: 74 (author's translation).

Spruytte's Legacy

Jean Spruytte – horseman, scholar and pioneer in experimental archaeology – passed away in 2007 aged 88. His ashes were scattered on the Tassili plateau in southeast Algeria, where he had so happily roamed the desert and first saw the enigmatic rock paintings which inspired the studies which became part of his life.

The work of some distinguished scholars such as Joost Crouwel and Mary Littauer was informed by his meticulous reconstructions and experiments, yet his studies have not yet received all the recognition they deserve amongst researchers, historians and archaeologists. This paradox is perhaps partly due to Spruytte himself. He was a very private man, who never sought publicity. He was an excellent teacher for those who came to learn about the history of the horse and of driving, willing to share his knowledge with people he thought would understand and appreciate his research. He worked only for his own pleasure and for that of the colleagues he respected. His articles, though numerous, are written in French and are dispersed among publications of all kinds, such as *Plaisirs Équestres* and journals specialising in Saharan history. Free of preconceived ideas, Spruytte was not afraid to question long-held theories amongst the scientific community, even if standing up against historical misconceptions meant ruffling a few feathers. Some well respected 'authorities' did not like to be contradicted by a 'mere' riding teacher, a self-taught researcher with no academic qualifications. Such critics failed to recognise the importance of his practical experience of horses and vehicles, combined with a depth of knowledge acquired through years of research.

As Joost Crouwel said in his review of *Attelages Antiques Libyens*:[94] 'Over the years Spruytte has made substantial contributions to our understanding of two-wheeled, horse-drawn chariots of the ancient world – their construction, harness systems and performance.' Combining his equestrian expertise with an ability to analyse the available iconographical and archaeological evidence, he demonstrated that there were several different methods of harnessing horses in the ancient world. His studies put an end to the long-standing myth of a single, inefficient 'throat and girth' harness unchanged for centuries, which was thought to throttle the draught animals, and showed instead that each system was not only effective for the purpose for which it was used but was also closely related to the design and function of the vehicle. His legacy lies in the major contribution he has made to the history of the horse, to better understanding of early harnessing, and to chariot research.

Gail Brownrigg
Independent Scholar, UK

---

[94] Crouwel 1997.

Bibliography

Barth, Heinrich. 1857. *Reisen und Entdeckungen in Nord- und Central-Afrika in den Jahren 1849 bis 1855. Tagebuch Seiner im Auftrag der Brittischen Regierung Unternommenen Reise*. Gotha: Perthes (5 vols.). Vol. I: *Travels and Discoveries in North and Central Africa: Being a Journal of an Expedition Undertaken Under the Auspices of H.B.M.'s Government, in the Years 1849–1855*. London: Longman, Brown, Green, Longmans and Roberts. Available online: http://www.columbia.edu/cu/lweb/digital/collections/cul/texts/ldpd_7721375_001/index.htm; accessed 6 December 2020.

Breuil, Heinrich. 1954. Les roches peintes du Tassili-n-Ajjer d'après les relevés du Colonel Brenans avec la collaboration de Henri Lhote. In: *Extrait des Actes du Congrès Panafricain de Préhistoire, IIe Session, Alger 1952*, 65–219. Paris: Arts et Métiers Graphiques.

Brownrigg, Gail. 2004. Schirrung und Zäumung des Streitwagenpferdes. Funktion und Rekonstruktion. In: *Rad und Wagen. Der Ursprung einer Innovation. Wagen im Vorderen Orient und Europa*, edited by Mamoun Fansa and Stefan Burmeister, 481–90. Beiheft der Archäologischen Mitteilungen aus Nordwestdeutschland 40. Mainz: von Zabern.

Brownrigg, Gail. 2019. Harnessing the Chariot Horse. In: *Equids and Wheeled Vehicles in the Ancient World: Essays in Memory of Mary A. Littauer*, edited by Peter Raulwing, Katheryn M. Linduff and Joost H. Crouwel 85–96. BAR International Series 2923. Oxford: BAR Publishing.

Brownrigg, Gail and Joost Crouwel. 2017. Draught Systems in the Roman World. *Oxford Journal of Archaeology* 36 (2): 197–220.

Brownrigg, Gail, Joost Crouwel and Katheryn Linduff. 2023. Developments in equid harnessing and draught in the Roman Empire and Han China: independent or interconnected? *Oxford Journal of Archaeology* 42 (1): 166–182.

Camps, Gabriel and Marceau Gast, eds. 1982. *Les chars préhistoriques du Sahara. Archéologie et techniques d'attelage. Actes du colloque de Sénanque, 21–22 mars 1981*. Laboratoire d'Anthropologie et de la Préhistoire de la Méditerranée Occidentale. Aix-en-Provence: Université de Provence.

Coulson, David and Alec Campbell. 2010. Rock Art of the Tassili n'Ajjer, Algeria. *Adoranten* 2010: 1–15. https://s3.amazonaws.com/media.africanrockart.org/wp-content/uploads/2018/12/26145312/Coulson-article-A10-proof.pdf.; accessed 20 September 2020.

Crouwel, Joost H. 1992. *Chariots and Other Wheeled Vehicles in Iron Age Greece*. Allard Pierson Series vol. 9. Amsterdam: Allard Pierson Museum.

Crouwel, Joost H. 1997. Review of 'Attelages antiques libyens: Archéologie saharienne expérimentale' by Jean Spruytte. *American Journal of Archaeology* 101 (4): 814.

Crouwel, Joost H. 2012a. *Chariots and Other Wheeled Vehicles in Italy Before the Roman Empire*. Oxford: Oxbow.

Crouwel, Joost H. 2012b. Metal Wheel Tyres from the Ancient Near East and Central Asia. *Iraq* 74: 89–95.

David, Franck. 2011. Les jouguets des attelages gallo-romains: études expérimentales. *Histoire et Sociétés Rurales* 35(1): 7–58. DOI: 10.3917/hsr.035.0007.

David, Franck. 2015. Les harnais des attelages gallo-romains. Nouvelles études expérimentales. *Histoire et Sociétés Rurales* 43 (1): 7–44. DOI: 10.3917/hsr.043.0007.

Dupuy, Christian. 2017. Henri Duveyrier et la charrerie antique du Sahara. *Le Saharien* 222: 50–70. https://www.academia.edu/35664452/2017_Henri_Duveyrier_et_la_charrerie_antique_du_Sahara_Henri_Duveyrier_and_Saharan_antique_carts.pdf; accessed 12 September 2020.

Duveyrier, Henri. 1864. *Les Touareg du Nord*. Paris: Libraire-éditeur Challamel Ainé.

Éligune (obituary). http://eligunepigouy.com/Spruytte.html; accessed 2 August 2016.

Gauthier, Yves and Christine Gauthier. 2011. Des chars et des Tifinagh : étude aréale et corrélations. *Les cahiers de l'AARS* 15: 112–113.

Gauthier, Yves and Christine Gauthier. 2018. Petit manuel d'attelage: gravures et peintures de chars sahariens. *Les Cahiers de l'AARS* 20: 37–38 (with further bibliography).

Gauthier, Yves and Christine Gauthier. 2020. Compléments à l'inventaire des chars: La route des chars, Aouineght, el-Gallaouiya et autres sites sahariens. *Les Cahiers de l'AARS* 21: 67–106.

Keenan, Jeremy. 2000. The Theft of Saharan Rock Art. *Antiquity* 74: 287–288.

Keenan, Jeremy. 2002. The Lesser Gods of the Sahara. *Public Archaeology* 2: 131–150.

Kelekna, Pita. 2009. *The Horse in Human History*. Cambridge: Cambridge University Press.

Kunz, Jürgen. 1982. Contribution à l'étude des chars rupestres du Tassili-n-Ajjer occidental, In: *Les chars préhistoriques du Sahara. Archéologie et techniques d'attelage. Actes du colloque de Sénanque, 21–22 mars 1981*, edited by Gabriel Camps and Marceau Gast, 81–97. Aix-en-Provence: Laboratoire d'Anthropologie et de la Préhistoire de la Méditerranée Occidentale, Université de Provence.

Le Quellec, Jean-Loïc. 2019. Central Saharan Rock Art. Review: *Inference* 5 (1). https://inference-review.com/article/central-saharan-rock-art; accessed 28 September 2020.

Le Quellet, Jean-Loïc and Annie Mouchet. 2020. A propos d'un panneau ornée de Yalanyela qui fit couler beaucoup d'encre. *Les Cahiers de l'AARS* 21: 177–200.

Lefebvre des Noëttes, Richard. 1924. *La force motrice animale à travers les âges*. Nancy, Paris, Strasbourg: Berger-Levrault. Available online: https://gallica.bnf.fr/ark:/12148/bpt6k3413457x/f11.image.r=Lefebvre des Noëttes.

Lefebvre des Noëttes, Richard. 1931. *L'attelage et le cheval de selle à travers les âges. Contribution à l'Histoire de l'Esclavage*, 2 vols. Paris: Picard.

Lhote, Henri. 1953. Le cheval et le chameau dans les peintures et gravures rupestres du Sahara. *Bulletin de l'Institut français d'Afrique noire* 15 (3): 1138–1228. DOI:10.2307/3887334.

Lhote, Henri. 1957. *Peintures préhistoriques du Sahara: Mission H. Lhote au Tassili. Exposition, Pavillon de Marsan, Palais du Louvre Paris novembre 1957–janvier 1958*. Paris: Musée des Arts Décoratifs.

Lhote, Henri. 1958. *A la découverte des fresques du Tassili*. Paris: Arthaud.

Lhote Henri. 1959a. *The Search for the Tassili Frescoes. Rockpaintings of the Sahara*. (Translation from the French by Alan Houghton Brodrick from *À la découverte des Fresques du Tassili*). London: Hutchinson.

Lhote, Henri. 1959b. *The Search for the Tassili Frescoes; the Story of the Prehistoric Rockpaintings of the Sahara*. New York: Dutton.

Lhote, Henri. 1963. Chars rupestres du Sahara. *Comptes Rendus de l'Académie des Inscriptions et Belles Lettres* 107 (2): 225–238.

Lhote, Heni 1966. La route des chars de guerre lybiens Tripoli-Gao. *Archaeologia* 9: 28–36.

Lhote, Henri. 1976. *Vers d'autres Tassilis: nouvelles découvertes au Sahara*. Paris: Arthaud.

Lhote, Henri. 1982a. Les chars rupestres du Sahara et leurs rapports avec le peuplement dans les temps protohistoriques. In: *Les chars prehistoriques du Sahara: Archéologie et techniques d'attelage. Actes du colloque de Senanque 21–22 Mars 1981*, edited by Gabriel Camps and Marceau Gast, 23–34. Aix-en-Provence: Laboratoire d'Anthropologie et de la Préhistoire de la Méditerranée Occidentale, Université de Provence.

Lhote, Henri. 1982b. *Les chars rupestres sahariens des Syrtes au Niger par le pays des Garamantes et les Atlantes*. Toulouse: Éditions des Hespérides.

Littauer, Mary A. 1969. The Function of the Yoke Saddle in Ancient Harnessing. *Antiquity* 42: 27–31. [Reprinted in Littauer and Crouwel 2002: 479–486].

Littauer, Mary A. and Joost H. Crouwel. 1979a. *Wheeled Vehicles and Ridden Animals in the Ancient Near East*. Handbuch der Orientalistik Abt. 7: Kunst und Archäologie, Bd. 1: Der Alte Vordere Orient, Abschnitt 2: Die Denkmäler, B: Vorderasien Lfg. 1. Leiden and Cologne: Brill.

Littauer, Mary A. and Joost H. Crouwel. 1979b. An Egyptian Wheel in Brooklyn. *The Journal of Egyptian Archaeology* 65: 107–120. [Reprinted in Littauer and Crouwel 2002: 296–313 with figs. 139–148].

Littauer, Mary A. and Joost H. Crouwel. 1985. *Chariots and Other Related Equipment from the Tomb of Tut'ankhamūn*. Tutankhamūn's Tomb Series 7. Oxford: Griffith Institute.

Littauer, Mary A. and Joost H. Crouwel 2002. *Selected Writings on Chariots and Other Early Vehicles, Riding and Harness*, edited by Peter Raulwing. Culture and History of the Ancient Near East 6. Leiden and Cologne: Brill.

Muzzolini, Alfred. 1982. La 'période des chars' au Sahara. L'hypothèse de l'origine égyptienne du cheval et du char. In: *Les chars prehistoriques du Sahara: Archéologie et techniques d'attelage. Actes du colloque de Senanque 21–22 Mars 1981*, edited by Gabriel Camps and Marceau Gast, 45–56. Aix-en-Provence: Laboratoire d'Anthropologie et de la Préhistoire de la Méditerranée Occidentale, Université de Provence.

Needham, Joseph. 1965. *Science and Civilisation in China* 4, 2. Mechanical Engineering. Cambridge: Cambridge University Press.

Raepsaet, Georges. 1982. Attelages antiques dans le nord de la Gaule. Les systèmes de traction par equidés. *Trierer Zeitschrift* 45: 215–273.

Raepsaet, Georges. 2002. *Attelages et Techniques de Transport dans le Monde Gréco-Romain*. Bruxelles: Le Livre Timpermann.

Schwab, Hanni. 1973. Le Rondet – Eine römische Militärbrücke im Grossen Moor. *Archäologisches Korrespondenzblatt* 3: 335–343.

Schwab, Hanni. 2003. *Archéologie de la deuxième correction des Eaux du Jura, 4. Ponts et ports romains sur la Broye inférieure de la Thielle moyenne*. Archéologie fribourgeose 17. Fribourg: Edition universitaires Fribourg.

Spruytte, Jean. 1964. Cavaliers et cochers sahariens de l'antiquité. *Plaisirs Equestres* 14: 116–118.

Spruytte, Jean. 1966. Les chars et les chevaux de Tamadjert. Contribution à l'étude des peintures rupestres du Tassili-n-Ajjer. *Bulletin de la Société Royale Belge d'Anthropologie et Préhistoire* 76: 73–78.

Spruytte, Jean. 1967. Un essai d'attelage protohistorique. *Plaisirs Équestres* 34: 279.

Spruytte, Jean. 1977. *Études expérimentales sur l'attelage. Contribution à l'histoire du cheval.* Paris: Crépin-Leblond.

Spruytte, Jean. 1978. Le quadrige de course grec. *Plaisirs Èquestres* 102: 418–424.

Spruytte, Jean. 1982. Démonstrations expérimentales de biges d'après quelques oeuvres rupestres Sahariennes. In: *Les chars préhistoriques du Sahara. Archéologie et techniques d'attelage. Actes du colloque de Sénanque, 21–22 mars 1981*, edited by Gabriel Camps and Marceau Gast, 163–172. Aix-en-Provence: Laboratoire d'Anthropologie et de la Préhistoire de la Méditerranée Occidentale, Université de Provence.

Spruytte, Jean. 1983. *Early Harness Systems. Contribution to the History of the Horse* (translation by Mary A. Littauer of Spruytte 1977). London: Allen.

Spruytte, Jean. 1985. La roue pleine et ses dérivés. Par où passe la technologie II. *Techniques et Cultures* 6: 99–110.

Spruytte, Jean. 1986. Figurations rupestres sahariennes de chars à chevaux. Recherches expérimentales sur les véhicules à timons multiples. *Antiquités africaines* 22: 29–55.

Spruytte, Jean. 1989. Le char antique du musée archéologique de Florence. *Travaux du Laboratoire d'Anthropologie et de la Préhistoire de la Méditerranée Occidentale* 18: 185–190.

Spruytte, Jean. 1993. Le trige de guerre assyrien au IXe siècle avant J.-C. *Préhistoire Anthropologie Méditerranéennes* 2: 1–8.

Spruytte, Jean. 1996. *Attelages antiques libyens. Archéologie saharienne expérimentale.* Paris: Maison des Sciences de l'Homme.

Spruytte, Jean. 1999. L'attelage égyptien sous la VIIIe dynastie. Étude technique et technologique. *Kyphi* 2: 77–87.

Spruytte, Jean. 1999. L'aggogiamento degli equini nel mondo antico. Aspetti tecnici generale. In: *Carri da Guerra e Principi Etruschi: Catalogo della Mostra, Museo del Risorgimento 27 Maggio–4 Luglio 1999*, edited by Adriana Emiliozzi, 69–72. Rome: L'Erma di Bretschneider.

Striedler, Karl Heinz. 2004. Bronzezeitliche Wagen in der Sahara? In: *Rad und Wagen. Der Ursprung einer Innovation. Wagen im Vorderen Orient und Europa*, edited by Mamoun Fansa and Stefan Burmeister, 157–166. Mainz: von Zabern.

Sun Ji. 2001. *Zhongguo Gu Yu Fu Luncong* (Essays on Ancient Chinese Chariots and Garments). Beijing: Wenwu Chubanshe.

Tschudi, Yolande. 1955. *Nordafrikanische Felsmalereien (Tassili n Ajjer).* Florence: Sansoni.

Tschudi, Yolande. 1956. *Les peintures rupestres du Tassili-n-Ajjer* (translated from German by Georges Piroué). Neuchâtel: La Baconnière.

Venedikov, Ivan. 1960. *Trakiyskata Kolesnitsa.* Sofia: Bulgarian Academy of Sciences (in Bulgarian, with French summary).

Weller, Judith, n.d. *Roman Traction Systems.* http://www.humanist.de/rome/rts/, with links to 'The harness systems' – http://www.humanist.de/rome/rts/harness.html and 'Who was Lefebvre des Noëttes?' – http://www.humanist.de/rome/rts/introduction.html#WHOWAS; accessed 21 March 2021.

White, Lynn Townsend Jr. 1962. *Medieval Technology and Social Change.* Oxford: Clarenden Press.

18

Some Observations on Chariotry and Chariot Warfare in the Near Eastern Late Bronze Age and the Battle of Kadesh

Steven Weingartner

This paper analyses the technological development and combat employment of Hittite and Egyptian chariotry in the Late Bronze Age from a military history point of view. The discussion is premised on the assumption that chariots were Ground Combat Vehicles (GCV) designed and built to incorporate a trio of essential attributes (or capabilities) collectively known in contemporary military engineering parlance as the 'Iron Triangle,' and consisting of (1) protection, (2) firepower and (3) mobility. As with modern GCV (e.g., main battle tanks and lesser tracked and wheel fighting vehicles) it was not technically possible to simultaneously maximise the performance levels of all attributes at the same time due to the natural conflict that exists between them; one attribute perforce always takes precedence over the other two. The decision as to which attribute will be dominant arises from the complex interplay between technology and tactics and is determinative in formulating a warfighting methodology that will maximise the combat strengths of a particular chariot design while minimizing its weaker aspects. The Battle of Kadesh will be analysed as a paradigmatic example of a clash of chariotry forces involving two technologically different types of chariots with different tactical objectives, predicated by their respective technical characteristics, governing their combat employment.

Chariots in the Light of Military History[1]

Introduction

In the mid–second millennium BCE chariotry dominated the battlefields of the Near East and clashes between armies deploying groupings of massed chariotry decided the fate of nations. Foremost among the practitioners of chariot warfare were the empires of Egypt and Hatti, rivals in a long ongoing struggle for control of northern Syria. In 1274 BCE Egypt and Hatti went to war to decide the issue once and for all, staking their geopolitical fortunes in the region on a single decisive battle. Marching into the disputed region with veteran armies of roughly the same size and composition, the Egyptian and Hittite forces collided just outside the city of Kadesh, a Hittite client state located on the Orontes River some 29 kilometres southwest of modern Homs in the Arab Syrian Republic.[2] The combatant forces fielded a combined total of 6,000 chariots, and although infantry was present in substantial numbers, the mighty clash of arms that ensued is primarily and properly regarded as a clash of chariotry, with infantry operating in a subsidiary role.[3] In what is known to history as the 'Battle of Kadesh' it was chariotry not infantry that shaped the character, course, and outcome of what proved to be the climactic encounter between the two greatest military powers of the Late Bronze Age.[4]

Not incidentally, the Battle of Kadesh was also a defining event in the evolution and development of chariot warfare. The adversaries were both masters of chariot combat, but their chariots were quite different in design, with different capabilities that were reflected in the tactics developed for their use. This had long been the case, but whereas Egyptian chariot design and employment had remained largely unchanged for several centuries preceding the battle, the Hittites had been experimenting in both areas. The fruit of their efforts was unveiled at Kadesh: the Hittites introduced a new type of chariot and a new system of chariot combat, capable of destroying the Egyptian army.

In the following we take a closer look at chariotry and chariot warfare in the Near Eastern Late Bronze Age from the military history point of view. In chapter I the focus is on chariot tactics,[5] strategy, advantages, and limitations of chariot forces. Chapter II deals with the Battle of Kadesh and its three distinct phases (Figure 18.1).

---

[1] Elements of this paper were previously published in other articles and essays written by the author on the subject of chariots, chariotry, and chariot warfare. See also S. Weingartner, When Chariots Collide: Understanding the Battle of Kadesh as a Clash of Competing Chariot Technologies and Tactical Systems *(forthcoming)*. – All URLs have been accessed September 9, 2023.
[2] On the Egyptian military see Schulman 1963; 1964; 1995; Spalinger 1981; Gnirs and Hoffmeier 2001. On the Hittite military see Beal 1992; 1995; Lorenz and Schrakamp 2011.
[3] For the size, composition, and organization of the Egyptian and Hittite armies in the period under discussion in this paper, see Beal 1992; Gabriel and Metz 1991; Gabriel 2002; 2004; 2006; 2009; and Schulman 1962; 1963; 1964 and 1981.
[4] See fn. 58.
[5] See also de Backer 2009 on the 'Evolution of War Chariot Tactics in the Ancient Near East' and Schrakamp 2013 on warfare in the ancient Near East.

Early Ground Combat Vehicles

In the Late Bronze Age Near East the origin of purpose–built ground combat vehicles (GCV) is traceable to the mid–third millennium BCE and the employment by warring Sumerian city–states of a four–wheeled wagon, pulled by equid hybrids, as a mobile weapons platform.[6] This so–called battle wagon cannot be categorised as a 'true' chariot,[7] which it resembled only superficially, and in much the same way that a Model T resembles (or, more precisely, fails to resemble) a late–model Porsche. The capacity for nimble movement, which was the hallmark trait of the chariot, was absent from the battle wagon's performance capabilities portfolio. This deficiency was attributable to the vehicle's technical characteristics, which suffer considerably by comparison with the chariot. In particular, the two–axle configuration was detrimental to vehicle agility, the more so because the battle wagon lacked a swiveling front axle. Instead, the front axle was fixed rigidly to the frame, which resulted in poor handling and instability in turns, especially in turns made at speed. Relatedly, it rolled into battle on heavy, solid wood disks with none of the 'give,' or flexibility, afforded by lightweight spoked wheels, the invention of which lay well into the future. The result was a bone–jarring, teeth–rattling ride on even moderately irregular ground and, overall, an inability to engage in the sort of swirling melees that would in later centuries come to typify chariotry combat.

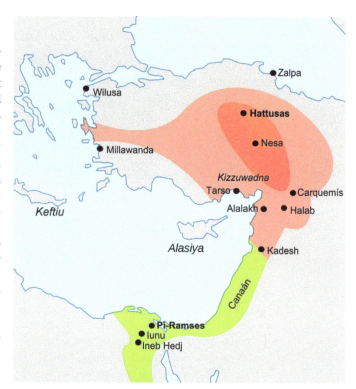

Figure 18.1. Hittite and Egyptian empires in the Late Bronze Age (Wikipedia Commons; https://en.wikipedia.org/wiki/File:Hititas_1300_adC.svg).

The 'True Chariot'

It was not until the appearance of the spoked–wheel horse-drawn chariot in the Near East in the early second millennium BCE[8] that the weaponization of wheeled conveyances achieved the status of what is now known as a 'Major Military Innovation' (MMI). This is defined, in part, as

> the creation of a weapons system whose capabilities are shown to be significant in scope and impact (consequential) as a result of technological change and systems development used in an operationally innovative manner, and which causes organizational adaptation significant enough to change the way one of the primary combat arms of a service conducts its operations or results in the creation of a new combat arm.[9]

The adoption of the chariot and its inclusion in the force structure of Late Bronze Age armies – the set of military units in an armed force or in all of the armed forces as the potential military capability of the armed forces – did indeed result in the creation of a new combat arm: namely, chariotry. It hardly needs to be said that this did not happen overnight. The learning curve was steep, and the ascent was made over time at different rates, along different paths, and in different locations. For example, whereas the Hittites were known to have employed chariotry as early as the reign of King Anitta (ca. 1740–1725 BCE)[10] the Egyptians did not develop chariotry and incorporate it into their order of battle until they undertook to expel the Hyksos from Lower Egypt in the first half of the sixteenth century.[11]

It is important to grasp in this regard that the adoption of chariots and employment of chariotry owed as much if not

---

[6] See Littauer and Crouwel 1979a: 15–47; Moorey 1986 and Crouwel 2019. With a wider approach Pinheiro 2010.

[7] On this term Littauer and Crouwel 1996; see also Burmeister and Raulwing 2012: 98–106.

[8] The origin of the spoked–wheel horse drawn–chariot remains at issue. For example, Mary A. Littauer and Joost Crouwel (1996), advocates of a multiple–origins theory, theorise that the Near Eastern variant was developed locally, independent of the development of chariots elsewhere. Stuart Piggott (1992: 48), on the other hand, contends that the chariot was an innovation of northern tribal peoples of the Eurasian Steppe; see also the contributions on the Steppe vehicles in this Festschrift. It was in this region, asserts Piggott, that 'the first experiments were made in light spoke–wheeled vehicles, a technological reservoir on which Mesopotamia could draw, and then create the chariot, and its later development of organised chariotry and chariot warfare, which a sophisticated political setting alone could make possible'. For a wider context see Piggott 1983 and Raulwing 2000. This topic is, however, beyond the scope of this article.

[9] Wiener 2010: 4; see also Krepinevich 2009: 30–42.

[10] A passage in the text informs readers that King Anitta, preparatory to going on campaign, assembled in the city of Neša 1,400 troops and '40 teams of horses,' i.e., 40 chariots. Neu 1974: § 18 and Beckman 2006: 216–219.

[11] See especially in this regard Shaw 2001; Gabriel 2009: 51–53; Raulwing and Clutton-Brock 2009: 66–82. On Egyptian chariots see Littauer and Crouwel 1985; the editions of Veldmeijer and Ikram 2013 (e.g., Spalinger 2013 'Egyptian Chariots: Departing for War') and 2018a; 2018b. Technical studies have been published by Rovetta et al. 2000; Sandor 2004a; 2004b, and Wiegand 2018.

more to developments in the socio–economic–political spheres as to technological innovations and the domestication of equines.[12] Roger Moorey, discussing the use of chariots by Hattusili I (mid–sixteenth century BCE), correctly observes that 'the emergence of an elite corps of charioteers, with a complex social and military organization, is evident only in the Late Bronze Age at a time of conflict between major rulers with the extensive resources and motivation needed to maintain and equip substantial bodies of men and horses with all the paraphernalia chariotry requires.'[13] Similarly Stuart Piggott observes that the 'adoption of the whole techno–social package–deal in its complex maturity in early Mesopotamia and its neighbor states led to an international rivalry and the arms race of the early second millennium BC.'[14] In the same vein P.A.L. Greenhalgh emphasises 'the vast and complex bureaucratic palace–administrations which maintained large chariot forces of both the Greek and the Near and Middle Eastern chariot–using powers of the Late Bronze Age'; citing Elena Cassin, he points to 'how the mass–production and maintenance of chariotry reveals a complex technology requiring the collaboration of various bodies of professionals and a centralised, bureaucratic administration to collect and control the raw materials, organise the work of the many specialist craftsmen, and distribute the new or repaired chariots.'[15] Mary A. Littauer's and Joost H. Crouwel's *Selected Writings on Chariots and other Early Vehicles, Riding and Harness* (2002) offers readers interested in the subjects of chariots, chariotry, and chariot warfare a comprehensive and indispensable compendium on the subject.[16]

Of course, knowledge of how to use chariots in battles had to come subsequent to the acquisition process: one takes as axiomatic that technologies cannot be used until they are in hand; and that it is only once they are in hand that one can learn to use them properly and successfully. This would, perforce, have entailed considerable experimentation with tactical doctrine, i.e., the employment of chariots and chariotry groupings in combat. Again, the learning curve was steep, but quickly ascended. Early practitioners of chariot warfare would have recognised right from the start that mobility was the primary attribute of the chariot and, by extension, chariotry; and that chariotry's effectiveness as a combat arm was a function and expression of mobility realised chiefly through movement in and about the space between armies, or 'battlespace.'

For the purposes of this discussion, 'battlespace' refers to the space between armies drawn up for battle, typically about 100 yards apart.[17] The formation of the battlespace was the necessary prelude to fighting the 'setpiece battle' – alternately: 'parallel battle or 'linear battle', so–called because the opposing forces array and fight on parallel lines. The advance into the battlespace ('movement to contact') by opposing forces consisting of massed infantry was ideally conducted with methodical precision in order to preserve the cohesion which is foundational to the retention and application of force combat power. In the setpiece/parallel/linear battle scheme, therefore, extensive tactical maneuver is largely obviated, movement is predictable, and as a result there are few if any surprises in the battle's unfolding.

> [T]he stage is elaborately set, parts are written for all the performers, and carefully rehearsed by many of them. The whole performance is controlled by a time–table, and, so long as all goes according to plan, there is no likelihood of unexpected happenings, or of interesting developments.[18]

Phalanx combat is the epitome of this type of warfare; chariotry combat, its antithesis.

Mobility, the Iron Triangle, and Tactics

Mobility is part of the design trinity of essential capabilities found in all GCVs, including chariots. Traditionally referred to as the Iron Triangle, the trinity comprises mobility, protection, and firepower (Figure 18.2).[19]

The Iron Trinity's three capabilities are functions of the vehicle's technical characteristics, or physical components, which collectively comprise the vehicle's architectural hardware.[20] In the case of the chariot, the components include the yoke and centre pole, axle, wheels, chariot box – even the horses. In a well–designed vehicle the technical characteristics are configured to interact synergistically, with all three 'contributing positively toward vehicle efficacy.'[21] In such circumstances the capabilities associated with the technical characteristics are said to be in proper balance, achieving performance levels commensurate with their positions in the vehicle's design objective hierarchy.[22] The design objective is based on the operating concept developed for the use of the GCVs both individually and *en*

---

[12] See, e.g., Pinheiro 2010; Turchin 2013.
[13] Moorey 1986: 204.
[14] Piggott 1992: 49.
[15] Greenhalgh 1973: 11.
[16] Littauer and Crouwel 2002. See especially Littauer's and Crouwel's important summary on 'Military Use of the Chariot in the Aegean in the Late Bronze Age' (1979b); see also Crouwel 1981, Chapter VII 'Chariots, their use (pp. 119–144) and Chapter VIII 'Summary of Use of Chariots' (pp. 145–146).
[17] Gabriel and Metz 1991: 70.
[18] Monash 1920: 206.
[19] One may refer to 'key attributes' or 'requirements' instead of 'essential capabilities,' and 'survivability' and 'lethality' instead of 'protection' and 'firepower.' In the event, the concepts are the same and the terms are interchangeable; see, e.g., Keena 2011: 62.
[20] Burgess and Gaidow 2015: 1; see also Loffler et al. 2001: 176.
[21] Keena 2011: 270.
[22] Wong 2016: 118–119. See also Blackmore 2011: 72: 'Somewhere in the triangle is a balance point between the three. To make a tank fast means surrendering weight in armour and firepower; a well–protected, heavily armoured tank makes for sluggish movement, one that can be wiped out by more agile weapons. A tank that carries a heavy gun must also carry heavy rounds for the gun. Without speed, an immobile juggernaut will eventually be destroyed. Without armour, a speedy machine will be destroyed. Without sufficient firepower, even a tank that can fire and move quickly will be destroyed by a tank with a long–range gun. Properly drawing the triangle of speed, armour, and firepower will result in what the U.S. Army calls 'survivability' – both the weapon and its operators will survive encounters with the enemy'.

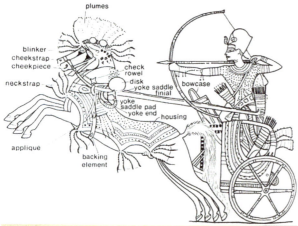

Figure 18.2 Top: Schematic drawing of a harnessed Egyptian chariot and its harnessing parts (after Littauer and Crouwel 1985: 4 Fig. 2). Bottom: Typical Late New Kingdom war chariot. Note the rear axle placement, fenestrated side, slack backing element, shoulder traction harness, neck yoke seated above the withers, and blinkers. Protection for the horses consists of a body trapper, head covering topped by a plumed headdress, and the shoulder strap, possibly bronze–plated. The depiction of the pharaoh working his bow while steering the chariot with the reins tied around his hip is an artistic convention. In actual combat, a driver would be handling the reins, and a runner (i.e., a dismounted man–at–arm) would be jogging alongside the vehicle (NYPL digital collections; public domain).

Figure 18.3. Detail of coloured plate from the Ramesseum in Thebes. The fenestrated sides of the Egyptian chariot provided no protection for the occupants. This configuration was consistent with the Egyptian chariotry operating concept, which privileged the mobility 'side' of the Iron Triangle over protection and firepower (NYPL digital collections, public domain).

masse, at the three levels of war: strategic, operational, and tactical.[23]

The ideal GCV would realise simultaneous capabilities maximization at all levels, delivering 100 percent performance against all desired design criteria.[24] Such perfection is, however, impossible due to the interdependencies between and limitations of the technical characteristics, which result in 'competing demands and inherent conflicts between design considerations.'[25] A large, heavily armored main battle tank, for example, gains protection and (usually) firepower at the expense of mobility, which is negatively affected by the weight of the armor and armament. Conversely, an agile GCV sacrifices protection and firepower in exchange for enhanced mobility (Figure 18.3).

Given that this is the case, it follows that designers of Egyptian chariots must prioritise the GCV's capabilities; which is to say, they must establish a hierarchy of capabilities/attributes whereby the vehicle's internal structure is configured so as to best support the operating concept.[26] This involves compromises and trade–offs, which entail the manipulation of the technical characteristics in particular and the hardware architecture overall in order to privilege the capability best suited for fulfilling the vehicle's operating concept. It is here that the zero–sum nature of the process is revealed.[27] In the circumstances 'no one objective function can be improved without a simultaneous detriment to at least one of the other objectives.'[28] Thus, proper balance is the condition in which the vehicle achieves a superior performance level with one essential, *dominant* capability and less efficacious (but still satisfactory) performance levels with the remaining two capabilities.

The operating concept for all two–man chariots (including, notably, for the Egyptian chariot) emphasised mobility – specifically, *tactical* mobility – over protection and firepower. This emphasis produced a vehicle design that privileged the technical characteristics associated with this capability (Figure 18.4).

One might expect that mobility is privileged at the expense of vehicle survivability (in combat); but this is not necessarily the case. For the vehicle's mobility, if properly exploited, can serve as protection in lieu of 'passive protection,' e.g., armour. The latter may actually be detrimental to vehicle survivability insofar as it adds weight which adversely impacts mobility – and increases a vehicle's vulnerability on the battlefield, thus diminishing its survivability. By contrast, explains Wei Jun Goh, a lightweight, high–mobility platform is, or should be, capable of leveraging its movement 'to avoid threats and enhance

---

[23] Schmitt 2002: 7–9: 'In simplest terms, operating concepts describe how military forces operate. (...) they describe what is to be done militarily in a type of situation and how it is to be done; that is, how military power is to be brought to bear'.
[24] Kelly et al. 2011: xviii and 106.
[25] Keena 2011: 23.
[26] Department of the Army 2015: 20–21.
[27] Wong 2016: 118; Kelly et al. 2011: 69.
[28] Keena 2011: 30.

Figure 18.4. Drawing of an Egyptian chariot horse with armored trapper and head covering. The vehicle's two-horse teams provided Egyptian chariot crews with excellent protection across the frontal arc of the vehicle (after Stillman and Tallis 1984: 142).

its survivability through susceptibility reduction.'[29] Thus, mobility not only provides vehicle protection; mobility *is* protection. This mobility–as–protection concept, premised on the assumption that a moving target is hard to hit, is valid if, and only if, movement in and through the battlespace is more or less continuous.

What this entailed for chariotry–infantry encounters was the use of fire–and–movement tactics by chariots operating in the battlespace, just beyond reach of the infantry grouping (e.g., a phalanx) it is attacking, to deliver stand–off missile fire in the form of archery.

This was a simple concept, no doubt readily grasped by early chariotry users. But, as the Prussian general and military theoretician Carl von Clausewitz (1780–1831) observed, '[E]verything in war is very simple, but the simplest thing is difficult,' and 'the difficulties accumulate and end by producing a kind of friction that is inconceivable unless one has experienced war.'[30] Foremost among the accumulating difficulties users of chariotry encountered was the enemy, and the actions taken by the enemy to stymie chariotry's movement and thus neutralise its mobility. There were many means for achieving this goal. The learning curve for defending against chariotry was also quickly ascended. In all wars the enemy gets a vote and is usually not slow to exercise it. Such is the way of war:

> Whenever an adversary is discovered to have or to be working on a significant new military capability or, in the absence of such evidence, is thought capable of developing a particular capability, attention is necessarily directed toward a counter to that capability[31]

As we shall see, this was the dynamic at work in the development of the Hittite three–man chariot.

One of the more creative gambits for neutralizing chariotry was attempted in Egypt's war with Kadesh, in the forty–second regnal year of Pharaoh Thutmose III in 1462 BCE. The Egyptian army, commanded in person by the pharaoh, was arrayed for battle just outside the gates of Kadesh, with the chariotry lined up in front of its infantry opposite the chariotry of the Durusha, prince of Kadesh. The fighting was due to begin soon in customary fashion, with the clash of opposing chariotry, when Durusha caused a mare to be released in the open space between the armies.[32]

Presumably the prince thought the mare would fire the passions of the stallions that drew Thutmose's chariots, supplanting their martial ardor with lustful desire and making them uncontrollable at the precise instant he unleashed his own chariotry against the Egyptians. And who knows but that his gambit would have worked, were it not for the quick thinking and quicker actions of an Egyptian officer named Amenemhab. In his tomb biography, inscribed on the walls of his funeral chamber near the New Kingdom Egyptian capital of Thebes, he proudly recalls how 'I pursued after her on foot, with my sword, and I ripped open her belly; I cut off her tail, I set it before the king while there was thanksgiving to god for it!'[33] The crisis passed: the horses' lust was cooled, and they could turn their attentions to the job at hand. Shortly thereafter the Egyptians defeated Durusha's army and stormed the city, with Amenemhab leading the assault.[34]

Durusha's tactic for dealing with the elite Egyptian chariotry might seem an act of desperation, and rather comical, and not least because most chariot horses were geldings,[35] but at least it shows a sensitivity to and understanding of the nature of horses – which were, for obvious reasons, key to chariotry operations and thus an important factor in the tactical development of chariotry and chariot warfare.

That being the case, chariotry would generally have eschewed frontal assaults on massed close–order infantry. The prospects for the success of what one historian described as the 'penetration of a horizontal line by a vertical wedge' of chariotry[36] could not have been great. The plain fact is, horses won't run into solid objects; and horses tend to perceive a formation of massed, close–order infantry as just such an obstacle, seemingly solid as a stone wall. As if that weren't discouragement enough for the horses, the formation is also bristling with spears and composed of men who are shouting and gesticulating in a manner most terrifying to the animals. Horses can be made to charge into such formations but in doing so they are going against

---

[29] Goh 2014: 16.
[30] Von Clausewitz 1989: 119.
[31] Greenwood 1990: 419. See also, in the same vein, Creveld 2007: '[W]ar is an imitative activity par excellence. To win, it is necessary to understand the enemy; to understand the enemy means learning from him and, to some extent, becoming like him. If only because any weapon used in war will inevitably fall into the hands of the enemy and be copied, technological superiority, even if achieved, rarely lasted for very long' (no pagination).
[32] Breasted 1906: 233.
[33] Gabriel 2009: 179.
[34] Radner et al. 2022: 154.
[35] Gabriel 2009: 58.
[36] Liverani 2001: 116.

their own better instincts. And they are liable at any time to obey those instincts rather than the commands of their charioteer, balking in front of the formation or shying away it. Their behaviour is no mystery; it is actually quite intelligent, self–protecting, and sane. They do not want to bull their way into formation because, it hardly needs be said, horses are not bulls.

Late Bronze Age army commanders were equally reluctant to employ their chariotry in direct frontal assaults, and not only because their horses were disinclined to execute this tactic. It is important in this regard to grasp that, while chariotry was the elite combat arm in Near Eastern armies of the Late Bronze Age, infantry was the primary combat arm, outnumbering chariotry by a significant margin. In the Egyptian New Kingdom field army, for example the ratio of chariots to infantry was usually about 1:10, that is, one chariot (with a crew of three comprising driver, warrior, and the so–called third man, i.e., a runner/man–at–arms) for every ten infantrymen.[37]

The main–body infantry of civilised armies was no mere armed rabble, but rather a sophisticated combat arm comprising a mix of foot soldiers and archers, organised in unit–groupings of various sizes usually based on multiples of five or ten. The battle alignment was the formation of densely packed spearmen generically known as a phalanx. In addition to spears, the foot soldiers were armed with secondary weapons such as swords and daggers; and they were highly disciplined and trained to fight in cohesive formations. Archers were arrayed by unit on the phalanx's flanks or just behind it, and though they wore lighter protective gear to facilitate the use of the bow and enhance their ability to swiftly displace and redeploy as circumstances dictated, they too carried secondary edged weapons for close–quarters fighting.[38]

Given the competency and numerical superiority of infantry in civilised armies, chariotry was not practicable for use in frontal assaults, as a weapon of 'shock'; that is, as a weapon that could be hurled against an infantry phalanx in order to rupture the formation with the shock of collision. In this context 'shock' refers to the weight and inertial momentum or impetus of an object moving at speed to shatter a stationary entity. Simply put, the Late Bronze Age chariot was not a kinetic–energy weapon.

Nor was a chariotry formation a solid body. It was, rather, a grouping of individual vehicles. Even when moving at speed, chariots in formation lacked the numbers and the close configuration, hence the weight and mass, required to generate phalanx–shattering force. The average phalanx was sturdier and stronger than most chariotry formations and could not be ruptured by a frontal assault of chariotry so long as the foot soldiers kept their nerve and held their positions.

If the foot soldiers did hold their positions, and if a commander of chariotry was foolish enough to launch his squadrons into them, the encounter would likely end in disaster for the chariotry. The first chariots to strike the phalanx would certainly inflict some casualties among the foot soldiers and a few vehicles might penetrate into the secondary ranks. Even so, infantrymen who remained steadfast and unyielding would break the charge, with most of the vehicles that composed the chariotry formation coming to grief on the phalanx's hedge of spears. The horses, pierced by one or more spears, would be rearing and twisting in pain, and many of the chariots would be overturned, spilling the crewmen onto the ground. In the next instant the following chariots would crash into the leading vehicles; a pileup would ensue, resulting in fearful carnage as the foot soldiers swarmed amidst the wreckage to slaughter the dismounted chariot crewmen.

The annals of warfare are filled with accounts of failed chariotry and cavalry charges against massed, close–order infantry. Diodorus Siculus, writing in the first century BCE, describes what happened at the Battle of Gaugamela (331 BCE) when the Persian king, Darius, launched his chariotry brigade – two hundred vehicles, with scythes attached to the wheel hubs – in a frontal assault against Alexander the Great's Macedonian infantry.

> First the scythed chariots swung into action at full gallop and created great alarm and terror among the Macedonians'; however, 'as the [Macedonian] phalanx joined shields (…) all beat upon their shields with their spears as the king had commanded and a great din arose. As the horses shied off, most of the chariots were turned about and bore hard with irresistible impact against their own ranks. Others continued on against the Macedonian lines, but as the soldiers opened wide gaps in their ranks the chariots were channeled through these.[39]

The Macedonian infantry was not unscathed, however. 'In some instances,' wrote Diodorus, 'the horses were killed by javelin casts and in others they rode through and escaped, but some of them, using the full force of their momentum and applying their steel blades actively, wrought death among the Macedonians in many and various forms.'[40]

Although the Battle of Gaugamela took place well after the heyday of Near Eastern chariotry (c. 17th–13th century BCE), the critical tactical error Darius committed in hurling his chariotry against an infantry phalanx is nonetheless relevant to any discussion of chariot warfare in the Late Bronze Age, and in most of the Iron Age as well — a period spanning eleven–hundred years, from about 1700 to 600 BCE. Equally relevant is the Persian king's second mistake, closely related to the first, of charging his chariots at the gallop. No doubt he did so because he believed that vehicle momentum (the product of mass plus velocity), along with the use of scythed wheels, would enable the

---

[37] Gabriel 2006: 173: 'The basic ratio of chariots to infantry seems to have been one chariot for every ten infantrymen, a ratio that provided each division with at least 500 machines as an organic force.'

[38] See also Littauer and Crouwel 1979b; recently on thrusting spears also Wernick 2013 following Littauer and Crouwel.

[39] Welles 1963: 283–284.

[40] Welles 1963: 283–284.

use of his chariots as weapons of directly applied physical shock. He was wrong. His chariotry was soon destroyed; ultimately, his army suffered the same fate.

Alexander the Great achieved similar results five years later in the Battle of the Hydaspes in 326 BCE, against the chariotry of the Indian king Porus. The Indian chariots were huge vehicles, drawn by four horses and carrying a crew of six — two archers, two shield–bearers, and two drivers. According to Curtius, the drivers also performed as men–at–arms: 'When the fighting was at close–quarters they dropped the reins and hurled dart after dart against the enemy.'[41] Porus dispatched one hundred of these machines along with four thousand mounted horsemen to contest the advance of Macedonian army, which had recently completed a surprise crossing of the River Hydaspes (modern Jhelum) in the immediate aftermath of a torrential downpour. But the chariots had trouble getting into position; they 'kept sticking in the muddy sloughs formed by the rain and proved almost immoveable because of their great weight.' The fighting was well underway by the time they finally managed to deploy, at which point 'the drivers rode at full speed into the midst of the battle, thinking they could thus most effectively succor their friends.' The author's choice of words implies that the battle had devolved into a melee between infantry and cavalry by the time the chariots arrived on the scene: the Macedonian *phalangites* must have been dispersed, allowing the chariots to charge into their 'midst.' In the event, the Indian chariots slammed into the Macedonians with tremendous force, and the ensuing carnage was such that 'it would be hard to say which side suffered most from this charge, for the Macedonian foot–soldiers, who were exposed to the first shock of the onset, were trampled down.' However, the chariotry, as always when attacking infantry head–on, got the worst of the encounter:

> [T]he charioteers were hurled from their seats, when the chariots in rushing into action jolted over broken and slippery ground. Some again of the horses took fright and precipitated the carriages not only into the sloughs and pools of water, but even into the river itself.[42]

After what could not have been more than a few minutes of fighting, the Indian chariotry was shattered: the wreckage of overturned chariots and the bodies of their slain crewmen lay strewn on the sodden battlefield; other vehicles were 'wandering about without their drivers,' the forlorn horses making their own way back to the main body of the Indian army.

Over two thousand years after the battle on the Hydaspes, the mounted cuirassiers under Napoleon's Marchal of the Empire Michel Ney (1769–1815) experienced similar futility when they charged British infantry squares in the Battle of Waterloo in 1815. Each square was firmly positioned with a hedge of bayonets presented, while the men

Figure 18.5. Egyptian crown prince Amenhotep II demonstrating his skill as a chariot archer shooting at a target. Working his bow while steering the chariot with the reins tied around his hips, as depicted here, might have been impressive as performance art but was impractical for actual combat. In battle, a driver would have handled the chariot (public domain; https://exploreluxor.org/amenhotep-ii/).

behind the bayonets, encouraged by their officers to shout and 'make faces,' did so enthusiastically; whereupon, as a British veteran of the battle recalled,

> the horses of the first rank of cuirassiers, in spite of all the efforts of their riders, came to a stand–still, shaking and covered with foam, at about twenty yards' distance from our squares, and generally resisted all attempts to force them to charge the line of serried steel.[43]

How Chariotry Fought

If chariotry was not used against infantry in direct frontal assaults, how, then, did these formations actually fight? An inscription on the Great Sphinx Stele of Amenhotep II in Giza recounts a demonstration of chariot archery certainly indicative of chariotry attack methodology in engagements with enemy infantry groupings. The demonstration was conducted by the crown prince himself,[44] who is said to have driven his chariot parallel to a line of four copper targets, each 'one palm in thickness,' mounted on poles set in the ground at 34–foot intervals.[45] Working his bow 'like the god Montu in his panoply' he loosed his arrows in quick succession, with 'each arrow coming out at the back of its target while he attacked the next post.' It was, exalted the author of the text, 'a deed never yet done, never yet heard reported: shooting an arrow at a target of copper, so that it came out of it and dropped to the ground' (Figure 18.5).

We may forgive the author for his hyperbole, which was certainly required of him. In point of fact, however, Amenhotep really did nothing out of the ordinary – shooting arrows from a moving chariot was part of the basic skill-set of every chariot warrior. As well, the crown prince's performance benefited from the controlled conditions in

---

[41] McCrindle 1896: 113 and the following quotations in this paragraph.
[42] McCrindle 1896: 208.
[43] Gronow 1892: 191.
[44] He was the son and eventual successor of Thutmose III (1479–1425 BCE), and just 18 years old at the time.
[45] Lichtheim 2006: 41–42 and all following quotes in this paragraph.

which it was enacted: the ground was no doubt level, and there were no enemy chariots or foot soldiers to contest his passage. That said, the exercise does indeed provide insight into one aspect of chariot warfare.

Here I would also note that Amenhotep's job was made all the easier by the moderate speed at which he drove his chariot. It is my contention that this was a standard feature of chariot warfare.[46] Late Bronze Age chariotry typically did not gallop into battle. Although chariots could achieve a top speed of about 40 km on level ground for a certain amount of time, the advance into the battlespace, also known as 'movement to contact,' probably took place at the speed of a running man, between 13 and 19 km. Attacking at speed was conducive neither to the effective use of the bow, the chariot warrior's primary weapon, nor the javelin. A chariot driven at speed on even the most favorable terrain provides a very rough ride for its passengers, who must brace themselves against the sides of the chariot box, clutching whatever they can — rim, rails or reins, a 'balance thong' attached to the rim, or to each other — to avoid being pitched out the rear or otherwise tossed from the jolting vehicle. In the circumstances the chariot warrior would find it most difficult if not downright impossible to fit an arrow to his bowstring, much less to shoot with any accuracy. Needless to say, the chariot warrior would experience the same problems in attempting to aim and throw a javelin.

There were other reasons for not driving at speed, apart from the negative effects of vehicle instability on weapons use. Galloping exhausted the horses, and it wore them out quite quickly, and to little or no tactical or strategic gain. Why charge a phalanx at speed if one weren't going to charge into it? But, as contended, Late Near Eastern Bronze Age chariotry did not normally employ the tactic of the frontal assault–to–collision against infantry. So, the galloping charge served no military purpose, even as it put the chariots in jeopardy faster by bringing them too quickly within range of the phalanx's archers and auxiliary missile troops such as slingers and javelin–throwers.

Also at issue was the number of arrows the chariot warrior could shoot, if indeed he could shoot any at all, before he found that his fast approach had brought him right up against the phalanx's front rank. The faster the approach, the fewer the arrows that could be shot at the phalanx before the chariot was forced to either turn aside, wheel about, or charge headlong into the formation. As well, at this critical juncture those chariots that had driven too close to the phalanx might be further imperiled by small parties of men–at–arms specially detailed to rush out of the formation to attack the vehicles.

Chariot warriors could fire more arrows at a phalanx by advancing toward it at a slower pace, e.g., a fast trot. As well, they could do more damage to the phalanx, and at less danger to themselves and to their drivers and runners, if they advanced no further than to within maximum effective bowshot of the infantry formation.

Here one would note that archery employed against massed, close–order infantry equipped with shields is only effective when used for plunging fire, that is, for arrows shot in a high arcing trajectory so that they fall, or plunge, into the middle and rear ranks of the infantry mass. Arrows shot at the front ranks of an infantry phalanx are necessarily shot in flatter trajectories. The targets are fewer because the archer is shooting at the first line only; and, because the infantry would be carrying shields, most of the arrows, not counting the rare lucky shot, would inflict few casualties on the foot soldiers.

Velocity–and–penetrating force performance tests such as those conducted by Richard Gabriel and Karen Metz reveal that arrows, even those shot from powerful composite bows, could not penetrate the shields that well–equipped infantry carried:

> A wooden, hide–covered shield measuring 2 by 4 feet adds 1,152 square inches of protection, enough to protect the entire target area of the individual soldier, 1,059 square inches. If the soldier was armored, the combination of armor and shield reduced the probability of an arrow strike to a vulnerable area to almost zero and rendered arrows fired in salvo at range almost totally ineffective in generating casualties within an infantry formation. Unless a lucky shot struck a particularly inattentive or poorly trained soldier, *the infantry formations of ancient armies had little to fear from archery fire.*[47]

Additional protection may have been provided to chariot warriors and, possibly, chariot runners and heavy infantry in the form of bronze helmets or leather skullcaps, textile body armour, and corselets made of bronze or leather scales or lamellae.[48]

Therefore, in an engagement between chariotry and infantry, the chariotry would attack the phalanx from a distance (i.e., maximum effective bowshot), shooting arrows in high arching trajectories to bring plunging fire on the formation's middle and rear ranks.[49] The tactics used by the Normans at the Battle of Hastings in AD 1066 provide an analog for how Late Bronze Age chariotry might have been employed against infantry. In that battle Norman cavalry attacked the Saxon shield wall with alternating arrow volleys and cavalry charges. The horsemen would intermittently charge, forcing the Saxons to lower their shields to defend against the slashing swords and thrusting spears of the mounted attackers. After a few seconds of inconclusive combat, the horsemen withdrew, at which point archers loosed clouds of arrows in high trajectories at the Saxons. On each occasion most Saxons managed to raise their shields, thus protecting themselves from the plunging arrows; but also, on each occasion a few Saxons

---

[46] Deborah Cantrell offers an opposing (and possibly the majority) view, arguing strongly and persuasively for galloping chariots in battle in *The Horsemen of Israel* (Cantrell 2011).

[47] Gabriel and Metz 1991: 72; emphasis added.
[48] Gabriel and Metz 1991: 70–72.
[49] See Leprévost and Bernage 2002.

failed to get their shields up in time. Struck in the head or upper body by arrows, they were either slain outright or severely wounded. Dead or incapacitated, it made no difference: they removed themselves, or were removed, from the shield wall, causing the wall to contract by the width of several men. By alternating arrow volleys and cavalry charges throughout that long day of battle (the fighting lasted some ten hours, from early morning until after nightfall), the Normans took a steady toll on the Saxon soldiery, reducing their ranks a few men at a time, and forcing the shield wall to contract with each reduction. Eventually the shield wall's contractions left its flanks exposed (hitherto the shield wall had at either end been anchored on and protected by steep drop–offs). Whereupon the Norman cavalry charged around the flanks into the Saxon rear, and the Saxons, realizing that their position was no longer tenable, broke and ran – and were slaughtered.

Late Bronze Age chariotry probably employed similar tactics. Thus, we may envisage a battle between chariotry and infantry unfolding as follows.

First, let us assume, for the sake of conjecture, the battle order of an Egyptian chariotry grouping – typically, 500 vehicles, divided into ten squadrons of 50 vehicles.[50] Each chariot had a crew of three: the driver/shield–bearer (charioteer); the warrior (archer); and the 'third man' (a dismounted man–at–arms, alternately referred to as a 'runner,' who ran or jogged, as circumstances warranted, into battle next to his assigned vehicle). Thus, a chariotry grouping comprising 500 vehicles would number 1,500 combat personnel.

The chariotry would assault by squadrons, with possibly four of the units committed to action while the fifth was held in reserve. Each squadron, comprising five troops of ten vehicles, might advance in a single line abreast, in one or more columns, or in some combination of columns and lines–abreast, with a man–at–arms running alongside each vehicle. When the vehicles had advanced to within maximum effective bowshot of the phalanx, the chariot warriors would salvo their arrows. The chariots might then halt to allow the firing of several stationary volleys, or they might keep moving, pivoting in unison to execute a half–turn, or caracole, to the left or right; or divide at the centre with the two wings driving in opposite directions; or wheel about in a 180–degree turn. If the chariots turned right or left, they would drive parallel to the phalanx's battle line, while the warriors fired their arrows continuously into the infantry mass (see, e.g., Figure 18.8).

The chariot warriors would not fire at the front rank, which would present as a shield wall and thus be more or less impervious to missile attack. Instead, they would direct high trajectory fire into the middle and rear ranks, thereby endeavouring to attrit the infantry mass through plunging fire.

When the chariots reached the end of the battle line they would break contact, drive back to their start point, and reform and briefly rest up for another attack (Figure 18.6).

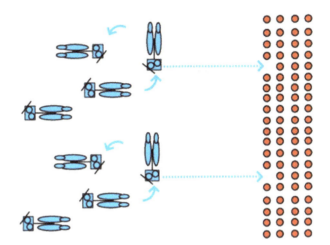

Figure 18.6. Chariotry attacking massed infantry with missile fire, using a caracole–like maneuver to avoid direct physical contact with the enemy. This was the only viable means for engaging massed infantry with chariotry. The goal was attrition not destruction: to progressively thin the enemy formation's ranks and disrupt its cohesion, thereby setting it up for a knock–out blow by the massed infantry of the attacking army (courtesy of Nicola Zotti).

In the meantime, the third men attached to the chariots probably stayed on the battlefield to establish a skirmish line at the point of the vehicles' halting/turning. The skirmish line would serve to 'hold the ground,' repelling sorties by infantrymen and archers from the phalanx and providing an initial impact/line–of–resistance for opposing chariotry that was sent to contest the ownership of the open space.

Alan Schulman compares the third man to modern armoured infantry.[51] The comparison is apt. As mentioned, the spoke–wheeled war chariot was one of warfare's earliest crew–served ground combat vehicles. And, like its modern variants (tanks in particular, but also the infantry/cavalry armoured family of vehicles such as the Bradley series),[52] chariots were most effective when they were supported by infantry. Chariots, like tanks, could and did fight without infantry support, but this was always a dangerous proposition. For that reason, the third man was a key component to every chariot crew, providing infantry support and protection against enemy foot soldiers and, eventually, against the crews of enemy chariots as well (Figure 18.7).

---

[50] Gabriel and Metz 1991: 14. See also the still indispensable studies of Schulman 1963 and 1964 as well as Gnirs 1996; 1999; 2000 and Gnirs and Hoffmeier 2001 for a survey of the military establishment of New Kingdom Egypt.

[51] Schulman 1963: 90: 'Egyptian foot soldiers are frequently illustrated marching, as individuals, alongside the chariot-horses, and once, in a Sakkara tomb-relief, a squad of four of them are pictured running there. These could have been Egyptian chariotry runners. Their function in battle was probably to protect the horses from the enemy foot and runners. If I may use a modern analogy here, I might compare this with the use of modern armored infantry. Tanks usually go into action with an accompanying complement of infantry who, acting as support troops, protect the armor from the hostile infantry, and hold the ground taken until the regular infantry comes up.'

[52] For information on the Bradley fighting vehicle systems see Ling 1993 and Blair 1999.

Figure 18.7. New Kingdom Egyptian chariot advancing into battle with a runner (a.k.a 'third man') trotting alongside. The runner's presence was critical to the success of Egyptian chariotry operations, providing an element of protection lacking in the vehicle's construction while adding to the vehicle's overall combat power. However, the fact that he was dismounted imposed limitations on the chariot's battle speed, thus diminishing the chariot's mobility (Artwork by Angus McBride from *New Kingdom Egypt* © 2013 Osprey Publishing).

As mentioned, the third man in most Near Eastern chariotry ran or jogged into battle alongside his vehicle. In the ideal set–piece battle, he did not have far to go: the opposing armies initially formed up at a distance of about 100 yards, and the third men and their chariots advanced about half that distance, or 50 yards, to bring them within effective bowshot of the enemy phalanx. At this distance the chariot warriors would fire their arrows and turn their vehicles to drive parallel to the phalanx, shooting arrows at the infantry mass.[53]

The movement of the chariots through the battlespace, as imagined and described here, resembled the caracole manoeuvrings of European cavalry of the Early Modern Period (specifically the sixteenth and seventeenth centuries), with chariot archers shooting arrows instead of mounted horsemen discharging pistols (see Figure 18.6). As with the cavalry units executing caracole manoeuvres, so too the squadrons in a chariotry host: while the chariots of one squadron were clearing the battlespace the chariots of another squadron were entering it. The squadrons performed these movements repeatedly, cycling through the battlespace until the horses were blown, the crews were exhausted, the arrows expended (Figure 18.8).

In such a battle men and horses alike who would find themselves much taxed in energy and spirit by the physical and psychological strains of battle. The chariot warrior would suffer the most in this regard, more than his driver, more than his horses. The main cause of exhaustion was his use of the composite bow. This was a difficult weapon to master, requiring a well–trained man at the peak of physical conditioning to employ effectively in combat. Richard Gabriel and Karen Metz assert that an ancient archer was expected to shoot accurately five to six arrows per minute and could get off ten to twelve arrows at maximum pull before his performance was seriously degraded by fatigue. In other words, a chariot warrior could use his bow for about two minutes at most before he had to retire from the battlespace to rest his arm.[54]

The foot soldiers would also be dealing with fatigue, however, and there would no rest for them if the chariot squadrons maintained their cycle of attacks. Plunging arrow fire from the chariots would steadily attrit the phalanx's ranks, causing the formation to contract and thereby disrupting its cohesion. Eventually the phalanx's cohesion would be fatally compromised, and the formation would begin to fragment, at which point the chariotry would retire from the fray, whereupon its own phalanx would advance into the now–vacant battlespace to deliver the death blow to the enemy infantry formation.

The only effective counter to this tactic of attrition was to oppose chariotry with chariotry. Thus, major Late Bronze Age battles tended to be set–piece affairs, in which the clash of chariotry comprised the first phase. It was in this phase that the third man came into his own as a combatant. He would then undertake to attack enemy chariot crews and slay their horses, actions that occurred when the opposing chariot squadrons became intermingled and the resulting traffic jams slowed the movement of the chariots or stopped them altogether. In the ensuing melee the third man would also find himself battling his counterpart, the third man attached to enemy chariots.

This initial clash of chariotry often decided the outcome of the battle. The foot soldiers who remained on the battlefield while their chariotry was either destroyed or driven off might well conclude that the battle would inevitably end in their own defeat. Daunted by this prospect, their morale would plummet along with any willingness to stand their ground. The foot soldiers might then break formation and run away, whereupon the opposing army commander would release his reserve chariotry squadron. Racing at speed along the flanks of the fleeing troop mass (and note that this was an instance where chariot horses would indeed have galloped), the reserve chariots would overtake the hapless foot soldiers and cut off their escape route, thus setting the stage for a battle of annihilation, to be executed by follow–on infantry. Meanwhile other chariots would pursue and harry the retreating soldiers to keep

---

[53] Gabriel and Metz 1991: 70.

[54] Gabriel and Metz 1991: 68. Of course, rates of fire varied, depending on a host of circumstances. For an in-depth discussion on rates of fire see Davis 2013: 87–93 and fn. 291.

Figure 18.8. Egyptian chariotry in the Battle of Megiddo (ca. mid–15th century BCE) engages massed infantry in the prescribed manner, by driving parallel to the enemy's infantry battle line and deluging it with plunging arrow fire; see also Figure 6 (courtesy of Giuseppe Rava).

them dispersed, maximise their confusion, and prevent them from reforming.

The basic tactics of chariot warfare remained unchanged for most of the second millennium: with chariotry attacking infantry using fire–and–movement and stand–off missile fire to achieve results; chariotry–versus–chariotry encounters taking the form of chaotic, swirling, and fiercely fought melees. In either instance, most of the fighting took place within the battlespace, the pursuit outside the battlespace of routed infantry or chariotry forces was the exception that proved the rule. However, sometime around the beginning of the 13th century BCE the Hittites adopted the three–man chariot and in doing so changed the character of chariot warfare.

The Battle of Kadesh

The practice of war, indeed its 'art,' is to achieve an asymmetry over the opponent; one way to achieve advantageous tactical asymmetry is through the use of superior technology – or through the superior use of technology.[55]

The goal [in combined arms warfare] is to confuse, demoralize, and destroy the enemy with the coordinated impact of combat power. The enemy cannot comprehend what is happening; the enemy commander cannot communicate his intent nor can he coordinate his actions. The sudden and devastating impact of combined arms paralyzes the enemy's response, leaving him ripe for defeat.[56]

The Battle of Kadesh has generated a vast historiographical *corpus*. First and foremost, among the historical accounts are those authored by the Egyptians themselves relatively soon after the battle was fought. These include two texts known respectively as 'The Poem of Pentaur' (hereafter, 'the Poem') and 'The Bulletin,' as well as numerous captioned wall reliefs depicting key events in the battle. The Poem provides the most detailed account of the battle's unfolding and is important for what it reveals, both implicitly and explicitly, about chariotry and chariot combat in the late Late Bronze Age.[57] Any list of modern treatments should start with James Henry Breasted's 'The Battle of Kadesh. A Study in the Earliest Known Military Strategy.' Breasted's work is foundational to Battle of Kadesh historiography. From its publication in 1903 to the present, Breasted's work has provided generations of military historians and scholars with the sturdiest of historiographical underpinnings for constructing their own analyses and interpretations of the battle (Figure 18.9).[58]

Background

The Battle of Kadesh may be understood as three distinct battles fought serially, or as a single battle fought in three distinct phases. I prefer the latter interpretation. The battle's three phases were: shock; siege; melee. The Hittites won the first phase, shock; the second phase, siege, was a stalemate; and the Egyptians won the third phase, melee. It was mostly, and most famously, a clash of chariotry:

---

[55] Milevski 2014: 83.
[56] Department of the Army 1993: 2–3.
[57] See Gardiner 1960; Fecht 1984a; 1984b; Kitchen 1994: 2–23; Lichtheim 2006: 57–71; von der Way 1984.
[58] See Burne 1921 'Being a Military Commentary on Professor J. H. Breasted's Book' and Searles 1924. Breasted also published a brief account of the battle with three maps and one figure for a wider readership in 1909: 424–435. See furthermore on the Battle of Kadesh (in selection): Cavillier 2006; Goedicke 1985; Guidotti and Peccioli Daddi 2002; Healy 1993; Heinz 2001: 281–293 (on the Egyptian illustrations of the battle); Hofer 2006; Kenning 2014; Kuschke 1979; 1984; Mayer 1982; Mayer and Mayer–Opificius 1994; Murnane 1990; Santosuosso 1996; Schulman 1962; Spalinger 1985; 2002 (here 347–365 'XI. Military Compositions as Literature'); 2003: 163–199; 2005: 209–234; 2018a: 127–200; 2018b; see also Spalinger 2018a: 137–199 on Ramesses II: Pharaoh as Warrior'; Sturm 1996; Trimm 2017 [see Index p. 719 s.v. Qadesh (Kadesh)], and most recently Brand 2023: 115–180. See also Bell 2007. The Hittite sources are scarce: See Edel 1949; Mauer 1985.

Figure 18.9. Depiction of a pivotal episode in the Battle of Kadesh: Phase II, 'Siege,' (see below). Having annihilated the Egyptian Re battlegroup, the Hittite chariotry strike force attacks the Amun camp, initiating a highly kinetic siege of Egyptian forces trapped within. In response the pharaoh sallies forth from the camp with the remnant of the Amun chariotry grouping that had not fled the Hittite onslaught. In the course of the battle, he would lead six counterattacks against his foes (courtesy of Giuseppe Rava).

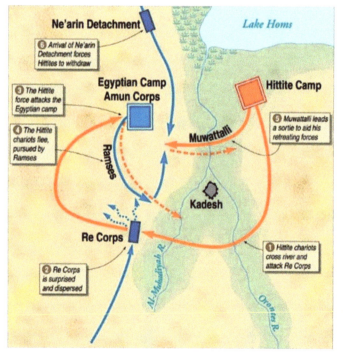

Figure 18.10. Synopsis of the main phases of the Battle of Kadesh http://dusttears.blogspot.com/2022/10/cotswold-wargaming-day-2022-kadesh-lite.html.

the Hittite infantry groupings (there were two, both quite large) did not take part in the actual fighting, playing no role in the battle until the end, when it played a critically important role indeed, as a force in being, i.e. a presence that would deter the Egyptians from taking further action that might have turned a transitory tactical setback by the Hittites into a decisive victory for the Egyptians. The Egyptian infantry – specifically, the infantry component of the Nearin battlegroup (see below) – took part in the third

phase only, helping to drive the Hittite chariotry from the battlefield and thus saving the pharaoh and his battlegroup from destruction, but proving unable to follow up on its success due to the presence of the aforementioned Hittite infantry groupings assembled just north of the city of Kadesh.

It hardly needs be said that the battle did not unfold as intended by either side. As is so often the case in the realm of military endeavour, happenstance and luck (bad and good in nearly equal measure) trumped intent. Both sides made mistakes, manifested most glaringly in their failure to perform basic reconnaissance and in the breakdown of command–and–control functions during critical moments in the fighting. As a result both sides lost the ability to impose their will on the battle through deliberate action: instead, the battle took on a life of its own to impose its will on them. And yet the battle's unfolding did have a certain logic to it, a consequence of the shifting applications of the two tactical paradigms and the tactical systems developed for their implementation. With a respectful nod to German military theorist and historian Hans C. Delbrück (1848–1929), I would contend that the clash started as a battle of annihilation and morphed into a battle of exhaustion: from a decisive battle to an attrition battle.[59] In battle the key to success often lies in creating an asymmetric confrontation with the enemy. At Kadesh, this happened twice (Figure 18.10).

At issue in this climactic military encounter between the two Late Bronze Age superpowers was control of the Kingdom of Amurru and the Bekaa Valley region, which included the kingdom and city of Kadesh. Long a bone of contention between Egypt and Hatti,[60] Kadesh was located at the confluence of the Orontes River and the Mukadiyah tributary steam some five kilometres south of what is now Lake Homs in modern Syria. Neither the Egyptians nor the Hittites were interested in a larger program of conquest; neither was desirous of fighting a long, drawn–out war, aiming rather to settle the matter with a single decisive battle. Assembled to that end in their respective homelands were two powerful armies, both highly mobile and strong in chariotry, both composed of veteran troops with considerable experience in combined arms warfare, and both commanded and led by their respective sovereigns, Ramesses II of Egypt (c. 1303–1213 BCE) and Muwatalli II of Hatti (1295–1272 BCE).

By the time of the Battle of Kadesh the Hittites had formulated a different concept of chariotry combat and

---

[59] Jarymowycz 2001: 10–11: 'Hans Delbrück (…) identified two types of strategies, *Niederwerfungsstrategie*, or battle of annihilation, the complete destruction of the enemy mass, and *Ermattungsstrategie*, the battle of exhaustion. (…) The choice was between strategic maneuver leading to one decisive battle and attrition warfare.' See also Freedman 2013, Chapter 9: 'Annihilation or Exhaustion,' 108–122, in *Strategy: A History*.
[60] It was a Hittite tributary kingdom at the time of the battle. See Bryce 2005: 234. See also Murnane's study of Kadesh in the context of Late Bronze Age geopolitics, *The Road to Kadesh* (Murnane 1990).

developed a very different chariot to realise it – a three–man chariot. The new vehicle evidently entered service early in the reign of Muwatalli II, who was in overall command of the Hittite field army at the Battle of Kadesh in 1274 (his younger brother and eventual successor, Hattusili III, apparently exercised tactical command over the chariotry arm in the battle). Walter Mayer is correct in asserting that it was developed and adopted around this time by the Hittites and their allies specifically as a counter to the Egyptian chariot and chariotry tactical system and, even more specifically, for a war they expected fight with Egypt for control of Syria.[61] 'This was a completely singular measure,' wrote Mayer, 'and only intended for the special conditions of this attack,' i.e. the powerful blow by massed chariotry the Hittites conducted at Kadesh. 'The 'fire power' of the cars was thereby doubled – the ultimately only *minor impairment of the mobility* was well accepted for it.'[62]

It thus seems evident that Muwatalli formulated his plan of campaign with considerable care, in order to employ his new machines to their best advantage (Figure 18.11).

The Hittite king's army disposed of around 50,000 combat troops of all types. Its offensive punch resided in a chariotry component totalling 3,500 machines and 10,000 men, divided into two groupings: a strike echelon comprising 2,500 three–man chariots organised into four sub–groupings each comprising 625 vehicles, and a tactical reserve grouping of 1,000 machines (probably two–man chariots accompanied by runners). The infantry was likewise divided into two brigades of approximately 18,000 and 19,000 men respectively.[63]

The army's 'big battalions' configuration is indicative of the way the army was meant to fight. The chariotry strike echelon was the centrepiece of a tactical system developed to maximise the capabilities of its three–man chariots. The unique ability of these machines to carry three armed men over distance to the point of contact with the enemy would enable the strike echelon to conduct what was literally a freewheeling battle of tactical manoeuvre, ranging across a wide and open battlefield to deliver a concentrated blow against an enemy force. While the chariotry maneuvered into attack position the infantry was to engage and fix the enemy firmly in place, thus serving as the anvil for the chariotry's hammer. The reserve chariotry would be held back until it was needed, to be committed to the battle if and when the circumstances warranted its employment (Figure 18.12).

In this scheme of battle the chariotry was the arm of decision and, potentially, the instrument of total victory. In the set–piece battle, by contrast, the chariotry fixed the enemy force for the infantry, which finished the job the chariotry had started; the infantry was the arm of decision. The aim of the set–piece battle was the defeat of the enemy via attrition; the aim of the manoeuvre battle was the destruction of the enemy via annihilation. In the so–called battle

Figure 18.11. Hittite three–man chariot carrying a javelin–armed warrior, driver, and 'third man' armed with a spear. The latter has not deployed his weapon: as Littauer and Crouwel have observed (see fn. 38), effective use of the spear requires that he dismount from the vehicle and fight on foot. Note the chariot's relatively spacious dimensions, wood construction, centre–mounted axle, and horse armour (Courtesy of Warlord Games).

Figure 18.12. Hittite chariot warriors with their three–man chariots and prisoners taken in a recent chariotry engagement. The three–man vehicle with its capacity for carrying two warriors in the cab had double the firepower of the two–man (single–warrior) variant employed by the Egyptians, and its sturdy hard–sided, slat–wood construction, possibly reinforced by the armouring of the side panels with bronze or copper discs (as pictured here), provided protection for its crew that was entirely lacking in fenestrated Egyptian models. Withal Hittite chariot design privileged battlefield lethality and survivability over agility and speed, which were hallmark attributes of the Egyptian chariot. In making this trade–off the Hittites must have determined that any vehicle deficiencies consequent to its larger size and heavier weight were more than offset by its positive attributes (courtesy of Angel Gracia Pinto).

---

[61] Mayer 1982: 344: 'Die ägyptischen Quellen berichten ausdrücklich, daß die hethitischen Wagen mit einem zweiten Kämpfer bemannt gewesen seien. Dies war eine völlig singuläre Maßnahme und nur für die speziellen Bedingungen dieses Überfalls gedacht. Die 'Feuerkraft' der Wagen war dadurch verdoppelt worden – die letztlich nur geringfügige Beeinträchtigung der Beweglichkeit konnte dafür gut in Kauf genommen werden'.

[62] Mayer 1982: 344, my translation; emphasis added.

[63] Beal 1992: 291–296, see especially notes 1101–1106. Beal's figures for a Hittite army are approximately twice the size estimated by many scholars, and are based, quite correctly in my view, on Alan Gardiner's 'reading of the numbers' in the relevant Egyptian texts. 'Breasted and others,' Gardiner wrote in this regard, ' (…) failed to recognize the sign for 10,000,' a mistake which led to the lower estimations; Gardiner 1960: 42; see also fn. 60.

of attrition (alternately, as told, 'exhaustion') the enemy was worn down to a point beyond his capacity to continue fighting; in a battle of annihilation the enemy force was utterly shattered, if not erased altogether from existence. The adoption of the three–man chariot provided Muwatalli with the primary technological means for achieving annihilation; and it was to that end as well that he selected the Kadesh vicinity, which featured terrain suitable for operations employing his three–man chariots across a broad area, as his venue for battle.

The Egyptian army was the Hittite army's numerical and qualitative equal, a veteran professional fighting force with up to 50,000[64] experienced troops of every type populating its ranks at every level of every Late Bronze Age military occupation specialty. But its force structure was quite different from that of the Hittites to the extent that it was an expression of a different warfighting philosophy, one shaped by the concept of the set–piece battle.

The army's basic tactical formation was a combined arms battlegroup roughly analogous to the Roman legion and the modern mechanised infantry division.[65] Each battlegroup had a nominal strength of 10,000 fighting men.[66] These were organised into three infantry brigades and two archery brigades of equal size (c. 1,500 men) plus a chariotry grouping of 500 vehicles operated by 1,500 men organised into three–man crews consisting of a warrior, driver, and dismounted runner.[67] The ratio of chariots to foot soldiers was, typically, 1:10, i.e., one chariot for every ten infantrymen and archers. Small contingents of lightly equipped auxiliary troops (e.g., skirmishers, slingers, javelin throwers) were also attached to each battlegroup.

Ideally, the chariotry functioned as the battlegroup's tactical–level mobile *force de frappe*, initiating offensive battle and using its unique capacities for rapid manoeuvre to gain advantageous position in the battlespace for the purpose of meleeing with enemy chariotry and attriting enemy infantry formations with stand–off (albeit moving) missile fire. In this scheme of battle, it was the infantry that functioned as the arm of decision, fighting in close formation (i.e., as a phalanx) to finish the battle the chariotry had started. Archers, slingers, and skirmishers operated in support of the infantry and chariotry, providing security for both (especially on the flanks) while augmenting the combat effectiveness of both through the exercise of combat capabilities particular to their respective armaments.

In essence, each battlegroup was a small army unto itself, capable of conducting complex military operations, including sustained combat, independently of any parent formation. It was the sort of formation employed by imperial powers down through the ages for policing their domains and responding forcefully to internal threats from refractory populations and external threats from tribal groups appearing suddenly on their borders. It could also be readily united with other battlegroups to form a larger army of substantial size and power, one capable of power projection over distance and of fighting and defeating the armies of rival powers in battles meant to conclusively decide the issue or issues that had brought the antagonists into conflict with each other. It was just such a battle Ramesses now sought with the Hittites.

Each battlegroup had its own baggage train for transporting the vast camp and field equipage required for a formation of its size and complexity. This enabled logistical self–sufficiency, which was key to the ability of each battlegroup to operate autonomously.[68] Attached to each baggage train was an indeterminate number of noncombatant support personnel. These 'civilians' performed the battlegroup's myriad services and supply functions, which included managing and caring for the pack animals (mules and donkeys, heavily laden), and oxen (pulling two–wheeled carts loaded with cargo).

On route marches horses were relieved of their chariot–pulling duties, traveling in remudas (herds) following close on to their respective battlegroups. Chariots were accordingly disassembled for the journey, with their constituent parts (wheels, chariot boxes, yoke saddles, and harness) packed on ox–drawn carts and, possibly, donkeys and mules. This was done to save wear and tear on both the chariots and the horses – especially the horses.

---

[64] The size of the Egyptian army in the Battle of Kadesh, like that of the Hittite army, is disputed. Figures of 20,000–25,000 appear consistently in the traditional scholarship, perhaps most notably in Breasted's writings (Breasted 1903), but also in the works of many others too numerous to list here. Beal believes they are too low by half, as does Trevor Bryce (Beal 1992: 291–298; Bryce 2005: 235). Beal's argument for the higher totals is convincingly made in Beal 1992: 291–296, wherein the author states that 'a figure of between 40,000 and 50,000 men for the forces that the Great Kings could muster [for the Battle of Kadesh] is likely to be correct.' Similarly, Bryce avers: 'The total figure given by Ramesses for the enemy forces is 47,500, including some 3,500 chariotry and 37,000 infantry. While Ramesses *may* have exaggerated the figures, it is quite conceivable that the Hittites did in fact gather such a force from the sources available to them' (Bryce 2005: 235, emphasis in original). Beal's figures are used in this paper.

[65] 'Battlegroup' is a modification of the term 'battle force,' which identifies this formation type in Lichtheim's translation of the Poem [of the scribe Pentwere or Pentaur]. E.g., in reference to the Nearin, 'his majesty had made a first battle force from the best of his army, and it was on the shore of the land of Amor' (Lichtheim 2006: 64). 'Battlegroup' is my preferred term because of its greater specificity. Note in this regard that a battlegroup, in modern military parlance, is 'the minimum militarily effective, credible and coherent, rapidly deployable force package capable of stand–alone operations or for the initial phase of larger operations. It is based on a combined–arms, battalion–sized force, reinforced with combat–support and combat service–support elements' (Council of the European Union 2014: 9). Although the Egyptian battlegroup greatly exceeded in numerical size its modern counterpart, the terminological modification seems otherwise appropriate.

[66] Following Richard Beal's figures for the combined total (40,000) of the four battlegroups comprising the main body of the Egyptian army (Beal 1992: 293). This is a substantial increase over the traditional figure of c. 5,000 total combat troops for each battlegroup. See especially in the latter regard Breasted's and Schulman's discussion of Egyptian army and unit size: Breasted 1903: 8–11; Schulman 1964.

[67] Based on Richard Gabriel's unit breakdown of Egyptian army battlegroups (Gabriel 2006: 71–172; 2004: 73). Note that Gabriel adheres to scholarly tradition in citing a battlegroup size of 5,000–6,000 total combat troops. I have adjusted the figures upward in accordance with Beal's figures.

[68] See Wernick 2011 on *The Logistics of the New Kingdom Egyptian Military in the Levant*.

It is important to grasp in this regard that the Late Bronze Age war chariot was a tactical–level not an operational–level nor a strategic–level weapons system. The mobility the chariot brought to Late Bronze Age warfare was exclusively tactical in nature, confined to the battlefield and its near approaches. Chariotry did not facilitate operational manoeuvre involving road marches over distance nor did it enhance operational mobility. Armies conducting operational manoeuvres (either on roads or cross–country) did not move faster because of chariotry nor did chariotry perform fast *Blitzkrieg*–style thrusts into the depth of the enemy's rear. In fact, chariotry typically did not take part in long–range operational movements of any kind. There were no 'chariotry *Blitzkriege*.' The pursuit and exploitation of a routed enemy force was limited in space and time to the battlefield and its environs. This was primarily a consequence of terrain and equine physiology; which is to say, of the limitations (in terms of capability, durability, etc.) of the chariot–as–a–weapons system.

The herds could be quite large, given that they included, in addition to the horses already assigned to chariots, sizeable numbers of replacement horses, held in reserve to take the place of those that were killed or wounded in battle, or otherwise incapacitated over the course of the campaign. The five battlegroups of the Egyptian army that fought at the Battle of Kadesh each had a 500–vehicle chariotry grouping with 1,000 active horses and at least 250 in reserve, for a total of 6,250 equines.[69]

Their food requirements, like the fuel requirements of a main battle tank, were vast, as befitting any hard–working internal combustion engine (albeit an organic one). According to Richard Gabriel,

> a horse consumes twelve to fourteen pounds of hard fodder (grain) and fourteen to sixteen pounds of green (grass) or dry (hay) fodder a day. In addition, horses need between twenty and thirty–five quarts of water per day and more in hot climates. The logistical requirement for a single [Egyptian] chariot brigade therefore was 13,000 to 15,000 pounds of grain and fodder and 2,500 [ca. 9,500 liter] to 4,000 [ca. 15,000 liter] gallons of water a day to keep the animals in fighting trim.[70]

Of course, food and water consumption would have been higher, perhaps considerably so, when the horses were 'on the job,' i.e., pulling chariots.

All of this is to say nothing of the army's beasts of burden (the aforementioned oxen, mules, donkeys) plus cattle and sheep on the hoof. Numbering in the many thousands, their food requirements were commensurate with those of the horses: 'For every 10,000 animals of all kinds, the yield of 247 acres of cultivated land was needed *every day* to feed them'.[71]

For road movement an army comprising multiple battlegroups marched in a 'columnar format of gap–separated segments or 'serials.''[72] Each serial consisted of a battlegroup plus its baggage train. This configuration provided the only practicable means by which multiple self–sustaining battlegroups, each possessing what amounted to its own mobile supply depot, could travel as a united force. Even so, columnar movement was a tricky proposition. Each serial underwent continuous variations in length. The gaps between serials varied accordingly. The variations in the serials and gaps, occurring from minute to minute, were due to factors of METT–TC[73] coming into play. Thus,

> during movement, elements within a column of any length may encounter many different types of routes and obstacles simultaneously. Consequently, parts of the column may be moving at different speeds, which can produce an undesirable accordion–like effect.[74]

The animals could be especially troublesome in this regard. Men will submit to march discipline, but equids are not so obliging: horses are high–strung, mules stubborn, donkeys eccentric. Oxen are generally placid but almost preternaturally indifferent to notions of haste. All these traits tend to work to the detriment of efficient columnar movement. In order to minimise the problems associated therewith, the gaps between the battlegroups would be increased. This facilitated movement, but it also rendered each battlegroup more vulnerable to a surprise flank attack and defeat in detail by a larger enemy force concentrated against it. The bigger the gap, the more vulnerable the battlegroup, and the less able it was to provide timely assistance to another battlegroup under attack.

Of course, the best way to forestall a surprise attack was to prepare for it, which was chiefly accomplished by reconnoitring the region into which the army was advancing, and by using an army's intelligence operatives to ascertain the location, activities, and aims of the enemy. Ramesses failed utterly in this regard – not because he was incompetent per se, but, perhaps, because he was relatively young and impetuous and overconfident. And, surely, because Muwatalli had probably taken this into account and used his knowledge to deceive his opponent and catch him off balance. Muwatalli, however, would himself be caught off balance by the Egyptians toward the end of the battle.

---

[69] Gabriel 2009: 62–63. This is probably a conservative estimate. According to Gabriel, a Neo-Assyrian field army with a chariot force of 4,000 machines required 12,000 horses at the very minimum and *16,000 at the maximum*' (Gabriel 2002: 134; emphasis added). Based on the latter figure, the Egyptian army may have had as many as 10,000 horses: i.e., 1,000 combatant horses and 1,000 'spares' in each of its five battlegroups.
[70] Gabriel 2009: 62–63.

[71] Gabriel 2006: 99, emphasis in the original.
[72] Cockrell 1978: 55.
[73] 'Mission, Enemy, Terrain and weather, Troops and support available – Time available, Civilians' defined as 'mnemonic used by the United States Army to help commanders remember and prioritize what to analyze during the planning phase of any operation' (https://metttc.com/).
[74] Military Field Manuals FM 3-90, chapter 14–19.

To Kadesh

Ramesses departed Egypt with the main body of his army in late in the spring of 1274, probably toward the end of April, arriving at Kadesh some thirty days later at the end of May.[75] The army was composed of four battlegroups named after Egypt's primary gods. First in the line of march came the Amun battlegroup, followed by battlegroups Re, Ptah, and Seth in that order. Pharaoh marched in the van with Amun, exercising personal command over that formation, and accompanied by his bodyguard of elite Sherden swordsmen (Figure 18.13).

There was, in addition to the main–body battlegroups, a fifth battlegroup known rather enigmatically as the 'Nearin,' a Semitic loanword that translates as 'young men' or 'youths.'[76] The identity and composition of the Nearin is still under discussion, but wall reliefs showing them advancing into the battle as a combined–arms chariotry–and–infantry force indicate that they were organised along the same lines, and thus probably in the same numbers, as the main–body battlegroups. And, as Santosuosso observed, the troops look to be ethnic Egyptians, outfitted and equipped like Egyptian soldiers, which casts doubt on a commonly held theory that they were Canaanite mercenaries. If the Nearin was indeed an Egyptian battlegroup like the others, total army combat troop strength would, as Richard Beal posited, have reached 50,000 (including 2,500 chariots crewed by 7,500 men).[77] These are impressive numbers on the face of it, until one realises that there never was nor could ever be any intention by Ramesses and his captains of using them *en masse* – the set–piece battle tactical system obviated such employment by restricting the size of the chariotry formations – hence the number of chariots – that could operate in the limited confines of the battlespace.

The Egyptian army's four main–body battlegroups Amun, Re, Ptah, and Seth took an inland route into Syria,[78] marching at a necessarily slow pace set by the plodding oxen pulling the army's supply carts and, not least, by the complexities of managing the herds of spirited chariot horses trailing each battlegroup. The Nearin, meanwhile, had journeyed up the coast, possibly by ship, to the mouth of the Eleutheros River.[79] Upon reaching this destination it was to turn inland and march up the river valley to affect a junction with the main body at Kadesh. Its mission as

Figure 18.13. Ramesses and his chariot on the road to Kadesh, accompanied by two members of his elite Sherden bodyguard (courtesy of Giuseppe Rava).

initially conceived seems to have been to secure the expedition's Sea Lines of Communication (SLOC) with Egypt and to serve as a covering force for the main body's left flank. But as fate would have it, the Nearin would serve yet a third and vastly more important purpose, that of the savior of the pharaoh and his army in the coming battle.

Ramesses could not then imagine and certainly had no inkling of what a near–run thing the Battle of Kadesh would turn out to be. No doubt he was brimming with confidence about Egyptian prospects for victory not only because confidence seems to have been an essential part of his character but also because he commanded what was in all respects a fighting force of superior quality. His confidence was further bolstered by information provided by two Shosu (Bedouin) tribesmen who had gained an audience with the pharaoh to inform him that the Hittite army was then ensconced in Halab (Aleppo), some 200 kilometres north of Kadesh.

The pharaoh's meeting with the Shosu took place while the army was camped just below Shabtuna (modern Riblah) on the right bank of the Orontes, about 11 kilometres south of Kadesh. Upon being told that the Hittites were as yet far to the north, he threw caution to the proverbial wind and ordered an immediate advance on the city. And why not? If what the Shosu told him was true, Kadesh was his for the taking. Except what the Shosu told him was not true. Perhaps they were Muwatalli's agents, baiting a trap for the Egyptians with false information. Alternately, they may have honestly believed that the Hittite army was in Aleppo. The result was the same in either case.

---

[75] Santosuosso 1996: 429. The author reflects modern scholarly consensus in stating that the Battle of Kadesh was 'probably fought at the end of May.'

[76] Schulman 1981: 8; Santosuosso 1996: 431–433 (and for the following information).

[77] Beal 1992: 293–294 allows for the possibility of a much lower figure of '1,000 or so' for the Nearin. But his previously mentioned (and evidently preferred) figure of a 50,000–strong army size would require a Nearin battlegroup totaling 10,000 combat troops, like the other battlegroups. For an in–depth discussion on the identity of the Nearin see Schulman 1962: 47–52; 1981: 7–19; Gardiner 1947: 171; 188–189. See also Obsomer 2016.

[78] See Kuschke 1979 and 1984.

[79] Santosuosso 1996: 431–433. Present-day Kabir River (Nahr al-Kabir), 'Eleutheros' is the name given to it in Classical antiquity. The river's mouth is located in northern Lebanon on the border with Syria.

The Egyptians broke camp early the next morning after the previous day's meeting with the Shosu. The pharaoh, eager to get to Kadesh as soon as he could, must have set a brisk pace for his troops, marching them at the quick–step. The battlegroup's baggage train straggled along slowly behind it. The combination of relatively speedy movement by the battlegroup Amun's combat elements and slow movement by its baggage train would have stretched the column exceedingly, to an unusual length – and much to the detriment of movement by the other battlegroups. The other battlegroups, similarly, encumbered by their own baggage trains, and by the road–clogging presence of Amun's long baggage train ahead of them, would follow at their customary snail's pace. As a result, Amun reached its destination – an open field just northwest of Kadesh and west of the Orontes River – well before the rest of the army; even before the Ptah and Seth battlegroups had left the Shabtuna camp.

Thus, in his haste to reach Kadesh, Ramesses had also taken his battlegroup into a perilously isolated position in enemy territory where a hostile city, strong walled with soaring towers, loomed over them on a high mound a short distance to the east of their encampment. Amun would remain in this isolated state for several hours, given the agonizingly slow rate of march maintained by its companion battlegroups. Ramesses was unconcerned by this state of affairs. Convinced that the Hittites were as yet far away in Aleppo, he had not bothered even to shield his column's advance with a screening force or to reconnoitre the area into which it was marching. One of the few security measures his troops did undertake was a routine one, that of building a palisade of shields around the camp. Patrols were also sent out. One doubts that the pharaoh thought they would find anyone or anything noteworthy.

Battle Phase I, 'Shock': Re Destroyed

> What was new in this military clash was its unheard–of violence (due to the concentration of energy) as well as the degree of attrition of its elements; the latter occurred in direct proportion to the degree of energy concentration. Again, we encounter what we have called, in the context of technical accidents, the 'falling height' of a mechanical apparatus: the greater the degree of concentration/mechanization of the two colliding bodies of troops, the more violent the shock of their clash, the greater the attrition of the elements that constitute the whole.[80]

> Taking the offensive position with lethality and speed regardless of an enemy's best efforts to resist can cause shock. The enemy can be rendered physically and mentally paralyzed and thus incapable of any meaningful action. This can be caused by surprise, violent and sustained fires, mass casualties, isolation and/or the sudden appearance of armed, aggressive enemy soldiers on and around his posi-

Figure 18.14. Hittite chariotry strike force equipped with three-man chariots charging into battle (courtesy of Radu Oltrean).

> tion. This paralysis is, however, temporary. This is 'shock effect.' We should aim to create it.[81]

Let us pause here to take stock of the situation. Muwatalli had successfully undertaken to convince Ramesses that the Hittite army would be far away from Kadesh when the Egyptians approached the city. He had accomplished a deftly executed piece of operational footwork, masked by deception, in order to construct a trap baited with Kadesh itself. Like all traps this one now depended on the actions of the intended prey to complete its work. It could be said that Muwatalli was gambling on Ramesses to make strategic mistakes, but this would be to underestimate Muwatalli's acumen as a judge of the pharaoh's impetuous character (Figure 18.14).

The precise location of the Hittite host at this juncture is not known and the Egyptian accounts of the battle are imprecise in this regard. In the 'Poem' we are told that 'the vile foe from Khatti and the many foreign countries with him stood concealed and ready to the northeast of the town of Kadesh' and that the Hittites' strike force of three–man chariots 'had been made to stand concealed behind the town of Kadesh.'[82] Pentaur wrote that

> his majesty was alone by himself with his attendants, the army of Amun marching behind him, the army of Re crossing the ford in the neighborhood south of the town of Shabtuna at a distance of 1 iter from where his majesty was, the army of Ptah

---

[80] Schivelbusch 2014: 153.

[81] Hickey 2004: 28.
[82] Lichtheim 2006: 64.

being to the south of the town of Ironama, and the army of Seth marching on the road.[83]

We may deduce from this passage that the Re battlegroup was then strung out on the road to Kadesh, occupied in the laborious, time–consuming – and cohesion–disrupting – process of crossing the Shabtuna ford, while Ptah was well behind Re, south of Ironama, and Seth was still further back on the road to Shabtuna, and thus at least a day's march from the Amun camp.

From this many scholars have concluded that the Hittite chariotry strike force lay hidden on the *left* bank of the Orontes, i.e., on the northeast side of Kadesh in the very shadow of the city's walls, in the triangle of land formed by the confluence of the Orontes and the Mukadiyah stream.[84] This same interpretation usually carries with it the presumption that the main body of the army (the infantry groups plus the reserve grouping of two–man chariots) were positioned, if not in the confluence triangle, then somewhere close by.

This is highly unlikely. The triangle simply was not sufficiently spacious to accommodate the Hittite chariotry strike force of 2,500 chariots (much less the entire army of 50,000 infantry troops and its noncombatant personnel and supply trains). It is also unlikely that the Hittite chariotry had assembled on the right bank of the Orontes, immediately opposite the city, waiting for an opportune moment to attack. The most opportune moment imaginable to attack had, in fact, already come and gone. If the Hittite chariotry had been in a position to attack the Amun battlegroup while it was on the march it would surely have done so. Failing that, the Hittites would have attacked while the Egyptians were setting up their camp. In either instance they would almost certainly have destroyed the Amun battlegroup and killed Ramesses in the bargain. That they did not seize one of these two opportunities to win the war in a single stroke is indicative of the fact they were not positioned for an attack, hence not in the city's immediate vicinity.

It is my contention that the Hittite army was positioned some four to eight kilometres north of Kadesh, on the right bank of the Orontes near a marsh located at what is now the southern shore of Lake Homs. Here the Hittites were equally well situated to meet an enemy thrust from either the Eleutheros Valley through the Homs Gap or from Shabtuna. In this scenario Muwatalli would not yet have ascertained the location of the main body of the Egyptian army and was, perhaps, waiting for the situation to clarify before making his next move.

Alternately, it is equally possible that the Hittite army was still strung out on the road from Aleppo when the Amun battlegroup appeared on the plain northwest of the city. Had that been the case, we may conjecture that Muwatalli, informed by scouts of Amun's arrival, had ordered the chariotry strike force and tactical reserve to detach from the army's main body and hasten to the city. The strike force would engage the Egyptians and keep them occupied until the slow–marching infantry arrived to take part in the battle.

In either case – whether the army was encamped north of the city or still marching down from Aleppo – Muwatalli committed what appears to have been a grievous tactical error in directing all of his forces, infantry and chariotry, to proceed to the city post–haste. In doing so he apparently failed to station units astride the Eleutheros Valley road at its point of egress from the Homs Gap. He should have established a blocking position at that location to forestall the advance of an Egyptian battlegroup approaching from the coast. As well, he should have ordered scouting units to reconnoiter the valley. Evidently, he did neither. His failure to take these very elemental precautionary measures had tremendous – and, from Muwatalli's standpoint, immensely deleterious – consequences for the battle's course and outcome. Perhaps his decision to leave the Homs Gap unguarded stems from a belief that he needed every man and every unit available to him to deal with the large enemy force marching up from the south. Perhaps he believed that force constituted the full might of the Egyptian army and not four separately marching battlegroups in strung–out columns. Finally, events may have been unfolding faster than he had anticipated, with the Egyptians arriving on the scene sooner than he expected.

Indeed, Muwatalli may have been as surprised by the rapidity of the Egyptian march on Kadesh as Ramesses was soon to be surprised by the presence nearby of the Hittite army. This would explain why Muwatalli chose to go on the attack with his chariotry alone before the infantry arrived on the scene. He had no choice. He was seizing the moment which had been thrust on him. Even at that, he was too late to attack the Amun battlegroup when it appeared, with the pharaoh in command, just outside the city. Ramesses' impetuousness to get to Kadesh had, in this instance, benefited the Egyptian king, however inadvertently. As it was, the Hittite chariotry – both the strike force and the tactical reserve – was clearly not in position to attack Amun before it could complete the process of establishing and fortifying its encampment.

One can only speculate on the unfolding and outcome of the battle had the Hittite army in its entirety reached Kadesh before the Egyptians, with time to spare for setting up to ambush the Amun battlegroup while it was still marching in column of route or before pitching camp. Attacking from concealment behind the city with the strike echelon of three–man chariots and one or both of the infantry brigades, using a hammer–and–anvil tactical scheme for which the Hittite army was so splendidly equipped and configured (and, no doubt, trained), the Hittites must certainly have achieved the annihilating results they sought, and in very short order. In doing so they would surely have killed or captured Ramesses, ending the war then and there and sending the course of Bronze Age history down paths that can scarcely be imagined. In the event Muwatalli, having been informed that the Re battlegroup was marching

---

[83] Lichtheim 2006: 64.
[84] See, e.g., Santosuosso 1996: 436.

up from Shabtuna some distance behind the Amun battlegroup, and knowing that it was too late to attack Amun, must have ordered his chariotry strike force to drive down at once from the northern encampment (or its position on the road from Aleppo, as the case may be) so that it could fight the battle of tactical manoeuvre he had planned upon and for which his three–man chariots had been designed and built.

At about the same time this was happening an Egyptian patrol discovered two Hittite scouts lurking on the fringes of the Amun camp, possibly in a thicket on the bank of the Orontes, using the brush as cover for spying on their enemies. Flushed from what proved a dubious concealment, these unfortunates were seized and hauled before the pharaoh, where they were beaten into revealing the nearby presence of the Hittite army. Alarmed by this news, and surely dismayed by the realization that the wily old Hittite king had played him for a fool, Ramesses sprang into action, ordering his troops to stand to arms and dispatching his vizier and other messengers (including at least one mounted rider) to his laggard battlegroups with instructions to 'hasten the army . . . as it marched on the way to the south of the town of Shabtuna, so as to bring it to where his majesty was.'[85] According to this account 'the army' is still south of Shabtuna when the Hittites attack. For the sake of narrative consistency, however, we must assume that the Re battlegroup – or at least the bulk of it – had passed through Shabtuna, forded the Orontes, and was marching on the road to Kadesh.

In all likelihood Ramesses assumed, quite understandably, that the Hittites had targeted the Amun camp for their opening attack. He could not yet have known that his adversaries now had something quite different in mind. It would seem that Muwatalli, recognizing that he had missed his opportunity to attack Amun while it was marching in column of route and thus eminently vulnerable to an annihilating blow by the Hittite chariotry strike force, had determined to bypass the fortified Amun camp and fall upon the next Egyptian battlegroup (Re) in the Egyptians' line of march.

This course of action, which Muwatalli had conceived on the fly, instantaneously revising his original plan of battle in response to changed circumstances, had much to recommend it. If the attack on the Re battlegroup was successful – and there was every reason to believe that it would be, with the destruction of that battlegroup being the most likely outcome – Muwatalli would achieve in a single stroke the elimination of a major formation from the Egyptian order of battle while at the same accomplishing the isolation on the battlefield of another major formation (the Amun battlegroup). As well, while his strike force busied itself with exterminating Re his two huge infantry formations would arrive on the right bank of the Orontes just above Kadesh, where the tactical reserve chariotry grouping awaited them. Together they would then cross the river and assault the isolated Amun camp with an exceedingly powerful combined arms force comprising about 37,000 infantry troops and 1,000 chariots.

At the same time, the chariotry strike force, having dealt with Re, could deploy across the road from Shabtuna as a blocking force to prevent the Ptah and Seth battlegroups from intervening in the battle at the Amun camp. Upon completing the destruction of Amun, the bulk of the combined arms force would move south to link up with the strike force and proceed with the destruction of the two remaining battlegroups.

Thus, Muwatalli would achieve the desiderata of all mobile warfare practitioners, the defeat in detail of an enemy army. With its strike force of three–man chariots, his own army was uniquely equipped and ideally configured to fight such a battle. By the same token the Egyptian army with its battlegroup configuration was uniquely susceptible to a defeat–in–detail strategy.

The possible existence of a fifth Egyptian battlegroup marching in from the coast through the Eleutheros River valley, however, seems not to have occurred to Muwatalli. As mentioned, the Hittite king ordered no scouting parties into the valley, nor did he position units in the vicinity of the Homs Gap to guard against the appearance of an Egyptian force approaching from that direction. Perhaps this neglect was deliberate on his part. Perhaps he believed that he could finish off Amun and the remnants of the Egyptian army before a fifth battlegroup could arrive to make its weight felt. If so, he was sorely mistaken. The pace of events was accelerating, and the fog of war generated thereby was thickening by the minute, forcing him to make decisions based increasingly on best–guess assumptions and hope. The complicated mechanisms of what would prove to be an exceedingly complex battle were fully in motion, no one on either side knew what was really going on – and all this before the actual fighting had even begun.

That situation was soon to change. The movement of the Hittite chariotry strike force from its encampment northeast of the city on what is now the south shore of Lake Homs had gotten underway. It must have gone unseen but, in due course, not undetected by the Egyptians in the Amun camp. Stands of tall wheat[86] in the field east of the

---

[85] Lichtheim 2006: 61.

[86] It is interesting to note in this regard that the start of the campaign season in the Near East – famously referred to in 2 Samuel 11:1 as the time 'when the kings go forth [to battle]' – coincided with the winter grain harvest. The ancient Hebrew grain harvest festival, the Feast of the Weeks, took place from about May 14 through June 15, which is exactly the time of the Kadesh War in 1274. In New Kingdom reckoning, May is summer, which is known as 'Shomu,' the 'Season of the Harvest' or 'Low Water.' The march of the Egyptian army to Kadesh and the battle itself takes place circa Shomu 2 or 3, that is, May/June. (Note, according to the 'Poem,' Ramesses and his army departed Egypt in the 'second month of summer'; according to the 'Bulletin,' in the 'third month of summer', Lichtheim 2006: 60 and 64 respectively). The earlier start date seems likely, and if the army did indeed get underway in May, the battle would have taken place sometime in June. In the Bronze Age and before (going back as far as the 7th millennium BCE) emmer wheat (*Triticum turgidum dicoccoides*) was the primary cereal crop, a staple of civilizations, abundant in the region to the degree that it virtually 'carpeted the full length of the Fertile Crescent' (Sagona and Zimansky 2009: 67). This ancient

camp as well as trees and foliage growing on the banks of the two watercourses may have blocked the Egyptians' line–of–sight view of the Hittite chariotry, but billowing dust clouds raised by its passage would have revealed both its presence and its general direction. We may well imagine the ensuing frenzy and tumult in the Amun camp, with blaring horns sounding assembly, the booming of drums beating the troops to quarters, the frantic running to–and–fro, the proverbial confused sounds of alarm and fright as the Egyptians scrambled to meet the onslaught.

But that onslaught did not come – not yet, at any rate. Instead of turning to ford the Orontes just above the confluence to attack the Amun camp, the Hittite strike force of three–man chariots continued south, disappearing behind the city. Whatever relief Rameses might have felt at this development would have been tempered by his recognition that the Hittite strike force was manoeuvring to attack the Re battlegroup. The reprieve to the Amun battlegroup was only temporary. The full force of the Hittite chariotry forces was about to be unleashed on Re. Well might Ramesses at this point have wondered, with considerable anxiety, whether his messengers would reach Re in time to warn the battlegroup of the impending Hittite attack, or whether Re, having been so informed, would be able to deploy for battle before the attack commenced.

The pharaoh was right to worry about Re. The Hittite strike force rolled down along the right bank of the Orontes, passing south of both Kadesh (situated atop what is now known as Tell Nebi Mend) and the smaller tell (Laodiceia) below it. The tactical reserve grouping followed the strike force as far as the confluence of the Mukadiyah stream and the Orontes, taking up station just above the joining of the two watercourses (and due east of the Amun camp), where it stood in readiness for commitment as needed in the coming battle.

Muwatalli's decision to forgo an immediate attack with his strike force on the Amun camp merits some comment. Such an attack would have entailed the strike force crossing the Orontes above the confluence, where the tactical reserve halted. Upon doing so the strike force would shortly have found itself with Amun to its front (west) and the advancing Re column on its left (south): a most perilous position indeed that would have exposed the Hittite chariotry to attack from two directions. Meeting this simultaneous threat to front and flank would have required the Hittite king to commit that (arguably) most egregious of tactical errors, dividing one's force in the face of the enemy. Muwatalli evidently decided to hold back his reserve chariotry and begin the battle with a concentrated attack by his strike force on Re. This meant crossing two watercourses, a potentially difficult undertaking: the Orontes first, then the Mukadiyah stream. Muwatalli really had no choice in the matter, at least from the standpoint of sound tactics: this was the unavoidable situation he had to confront.

Fortunately for Muwatalli, the two watercourses presented no significant obstacle to the Hittite strike force. In a modern photograph of the Orontes (see Figure 18.15), taken in high summer at a location slightly south and east of Tell Nebi-Mend – approximately where the Hittite chariotry might have crossed it, and at the same time of year — the river is much reduced in width and depth. We cannot know whether these conditions precisely obtained in the summer of 1274 BCE but, as Kuschke observed, they must have been similar.[87] Thus, upon drawing up adjacent to the Laodiceia tell, the strike force pivoted to the right and crossed the river – an easy passage, accomplished in one continuous movement. There was no slowing of the chariots and no breaking of stride by the horses pulling them.

Once across the Orontes the strike force drove west in what must have been a narrow column though the gap separating Tell Laodiceia from a neighbouring village to its south, then fanned out by sub–groupings across the plain beyond. Having reached open ground they might have accelerated slightly, moving at a good clip (but not galloping, and for reasons aforestated) toward the next watercourse in their path, the Mukadiyeh stream. In doing so the drivers would have taken great care to maintain their spacing in the formation, straining at the reigns to steer their chariots and control their horses so as to avoid collisions and prevent the traffic tie–ups to which a large body of vehicles in motion are prone. They were transitioning to the movement–to–contact stage of the operation, and this warranted increasing the pace somewhat, but without the chaos and calamity that might otherwise ensue and, just as importantly, without exhausting their horses. In this instance as in many others Late Bronze Age chariotry groupings operated in a fashion identical to that of modern armoured formations. Controlling the flow of traffic proved of no less concern to the chariotry commanders of antiquity as to the armoured formation commanders of the present: controls must be imposed, or chaos will ensue. The best way to achieve control is by regulating speed. Thus, the lateral extension of the Hittite strike force after it emerged from the Tell Laodiceia gap was a precision movement neither hurried nor dilatory in its execution.

This movement was the opening expression of the innovative tactical scheme for which execution the three–man chariot had been developed. The goal of the Hittites was to broaden attack frontage sufficiently to commit the largest number of chariots possible to the initial clash without loosening the 'clenched fist' that force concentration entailed. Movement was conducted at a moderately lively pace – *allegro moderato*, to borrow from the lexicon of music composition. The headlong charge was absolutely

---

cultivar was much taller at its ripening than modern varieties, reaching heights of nearly five feet, with some varieties growing to eight feet and more (Vergauwen and Smet 2017: R859; Barkley and Barkley 2013: 62). Did uncut wheat affect the dispositions of the two armies and the course of the battle? I think it is very possible, even probable; and, if so, it would have hindered Egyptian mobility and manoeuvre, while facilitating the movement of Hittite chariotry by concealing its approach when it came pounding down and around Kadesh and crossed the Orontes River and the Mukadiyah stream to ambush the Re battlegroup. On the reconstruction of the march from Egypt to Kadesh see Kuschke 1979.

[87] Kuschke 1979.

Figure 18.15. The Orontes River presented no serious obstacle to the movement of the Hittite strike force, as this modern photo indicates. It was taken in the summer, at around the same time the Battle of Kadesh was fought, when the water level was very low. Quite possibly this spot is very close to where the Hittite chariotry forded the river. Tell Nebi Mend, i.e., the city of Kadesh, stands in the background, a short distance northwest of the crossing (after Jona Lendering and Marco Prins; https://www.livius.org/pictures/international/orontes/the-orontes-at-kadesh/).

Figure 18.16. Tank desant in practice: Red Army 'tank riders' (tankodesantniki) leap from their tanks during a battle with German forces on the Eastern Front in World War II (Sovfoto; https://www.billdownscbs.com/2015/04/1943-russias-tank-desant-tactic.html).

eschewed. Formation cohesion within and between the subgroupings was strictly maintained. There would have been no intent on the part of the Hittites to approach to within bowshot of the Egyptian column and then turn ninety degrees and drive parallel to the enemy's line, shooting arrows into the ranks of the marching foot soldiers. They had not come to Kadesh in their heavy three–man–chariots to fight an Egyptian–style attritional battle. Rather, their intent was to use the surprise and positional advantage they had gained through a sweeping cross–county manoeuvre to conduct a massive, combined arms assault on the Egyptian battlegroup. Momentum and the weight of the assault would combine to overwhelm the Egyptians: the third crewmen, brought to the point of contact by their chariots, would dismount to operate in their support, and this resultant mixed force of rolling chariots and swarming men–at–arms would shatter the enemy column with a single concentrated blow.

Here it bears mentioning that World War II Red Army tank formations conducting movements to contact typically proceeded at the same 'moderately lively' pace and for the same reasons as the Hittites. And they did so with infantrymen riding on the tanks. When contact with the enemy was imminent, they leapt from the tanks to continue their part of the advance on foot, trotting or walking alongside the tanks which drove slowly so as not to outpace the infantrymen. In Soviet military parlance this was known as 'tank desant' (*tankovyy desant*) and the tank riders were called *tankodesantniki* (Figure 18.16).[88]

In March 1943 CBS radio correspondent Bill Downs, reporting from Moscow on the war in Russia, introduced his American audience to the concept of *tankovyy desant* and to the *tankodesantniki* who implemented it.[89] Characterizing the latter as 'hitchhike troops,' Downs explained that these were highly trained specialists who played an important role, distinct from that of regular line infantry, in the success of the Red Army's 1942–1943 winter offensives. Although *tankovyy desant* was not unique to the fighting on the Eastern Front (Loyalist forces in the Spanish Civil War had experimented with its use under the tutelage of Soviet advisors),[90] the Red Army had since made it a cornerstone of their combined arms offensive methodology. 'What this tactic really boils down to,' Downs explained,

> is that a group of Tommy gunners[91] and riflemen are piled on to a tank, hanging onto anything they can grab and riding into the battle in style. (…) The men ride into battle until the going gets too hot for the safety of the operation. Then, at the command of the officer in charge, they roll off together. (…) The tank either slows down so that it can cover hitchhike troops, or else lines are attached to the back of the tank and the men run along behind being pulled at a gallop by their tank. (…) These tank–borne troops often direct the fire of the tank. And if it is a night operation, they act as scouts, going ahead of the tank to protect it against ambushes. (…) Finally, when an objective is taken, it is the job of the hitchhikers to hold the place until the main infantry forces can arrive.[92]

A better description of the purpose and function of the third man in the Hittite three–man chariot crew cannot be found. These third men must have been highly trained specialists like the *tankodesantniki*, probably chariot warriors themselves who could fill in for the warrior should the latter be killed or otherwise incapacitated. As military theorists Richard K. Simpkin and John Erickson observed, tank desant was used to achieve the fundamental goals

---

[88] See the memoir of World War II Red Army *tankodesantnik* Evgeni Bessonov (2017). For the American equivalent of tank desant, see *War Department Field Manual FM 17–40: Armored Infantry Company*, especially Appendix: Armored Infantry Transported on Tanks: 164–176 (United States War Department 1944).
[89] Downs 1943.
[90] Downs 1943.
[91] Zaloga 1999.
[92] Downs 1943.

of manoeuvre theory, namely 'surprise, leverage, simultaneity and interchangeability';[93] and this was precisely the aim of the Hittites in formulating the tactic of what may well be termed 'chariot desant' and in developing a chariot specifically for the implementation thereof. The attack on Re by the Hittite chariotry strike force was an instance of chariot desant carried out to perfection, with all four goals cited by Simpkin and Erickson achieved in what was literally one very fell swoop. More than 3,000 years before a group of talented Soviet military thinkers – Mikhail Tukhachevsky (1893–1937), Vladimir Triandafillov (1894–1931), and Georgii Isserson (1998–1976) foremost among them – developed the doctrines of tactical deep battle and deep operations in the 1920s–30s, the Hittites were executing tactical deep battle doctrine with great effectiveness and notable (if temporary) success on the battlefield of Kadesh.[94]

The Hittite chariotry juggernaut pounded on toward the Mukadiyah stream, steadily closing the distance to that watercourse and the Egyptian column beyond. The Egyptians meanwhile continued their slow incautious march to the Amun camp, slogging along the Shabtuna road with mindless disregard for the dangers attendant to columnar movement in a war zone, utterly clueless that their doom was fast drawing nigh. The potential for enemy action seems to have eluded them and, as noted previously, they made no effort to guard against it or even to determine whether an enemy force might be operating in the vicinity. No scouts were dispatched across the Mukidiyah stream to reconnoitre what even the most dimly witted foot soldier could have identified as the Hittites' likeliest avenue of attack. No horses were hitched to chariots and thus no chariots were sent out to patrol the column's vulnerable Kadesh–facing right flank where it might offer at least some resistance however slight to an assault from that quarter. Evidently the messenger sent by Ramesses to summon the column had not yet reached it. Events were unfolding faster than information about them could travel – a common occurrence in warfare up to and through the First World War and the advent of portable wireless radios.[95]

What the Egyptians did not know, however, their horses probably suspected. The latter with their keen equine sense of smell could scarcely have failed to notice that a great number of horses were headed their way, even as the strike force was yet on the far side of the Mukadiyah stream.[96] From this they must have intuited that a battle was in the offing and, like the horse in Job 39:19–25 who 'smelleth the battle afar off,' greeted the prospect with a kind of anxious excitement, becoming much agitated and vocal in their eagerness for combat.[97] But inasmuch they were herded together in the remuda at the trailing end of the column only the drovers charged with their handling would have seen this bellicose change in their temper and comportment. The drovers might have guessed the cause of their agitation and passed word of the warning explicit in the horses' behaviour to the front of the column, but if so, it went unheeded or came too late to the battlegroup commander for him to take any meaningful action.

The Mukadiyah stream, shallower and narrower than the Orontes, presented even less of an obstacle to the chariotry advance than the river. The Hittite chariots splashed across it and drove on without pause toward the Egyptian battlegroup. A number of scholarly analyses of the battle have suggested that an orchard or a line of trees abutted the stream's left bank.[98] If so, this too plainly did not hinder the strike force. Nor did the expanse of tall ripening wheat that might well have stood between the stream and the road inhibit its movement. Unlike the prohibitively lightweight Egyptian chariot – which, as Jean Spruytte observed, lacked the bulk to force its way through a field of fully grown wheat[99] – the Hittite three–man chariot would not have experienced any problems in this regard. Ease of passage in the circumstances was ensured by the combined weight of the robustly built vehicle and its three–man

---

[93] Simpkin and Erickson 1987: 55.
[94] Trout 1992: 'The concept of deep battle is to deny the enemy commander the ability to employ his forces not yet engaged at the time, place, or in the strength of his choice. It is to hit him as deep in his own territory as possible, thereby preventing those yet–to–be–committed forces from reaching the battlefield.'
[95] Kuschke 1979: 22; 30.
[96] Cantrell 2011: 22–23: 'The horse's sense of smell is far more acute than a human's. It acts as an early–warning system for danger. When alarmed, a horse flares its nostrils, sniffing toward the perceived threat. (...). With a light breeze, a horse can smell a single mare in season from over a half mile away. Likewise, a horse can sense the unfamiliar smell of an opposing army's horses, mules, asses, and camels from over a mile away, long before they can be seen. The horse's physical reaction to such unpleasant and unfamiliar smells, usually a snort, a stomp, or a toss of the head, can serve to alert its rider to an approaching threat.'
[97] In addition to smelling the Hittite horses, the horses might have heard the enemy chariotry force approaching even before it crossed the Mukadiyeh stream. Observing that horses have 'extremely sensitive hearing,' Deborah Cantrell writes (2011: 18–19) that horses 'can hear approaching danger much sooner than a human and before either can see the origin of the sound. When strange sounds startle a horse, it will prick its ears toward the sound and prepare for flight, or in the case of the seasoned and brave war–horse, prepare to run toward it. Running toward battle instead of fleeing is an anomaly and is something the horse must be trained to do'.
[98] Breasted 1903: 101 f.: 'Moreover, a reference in Extract No. 18 (p. 29 below) shows that there was a forest between Shabtuna and Kadesh, on the west side of the river, and the skilfully masked manoeuvres of the Hittite king would indicate that there must have been a good deal of forest in the plain around Kadesh'; p. 29 under no. 18: 'His majesty was camping alone, no army with him: – his and his troops had [not yet ?] arrived, and the division with which Pharaoh, L. P. H., was had not finished setting up the camp. Now the division of Re and the division of Ptah were (still) on the march; they had not (yet) arrived and their officers were in the forest of Baui (B'wy). These statements hardly need any comment. Ramses, with the division of Amon, has passed along the west side of Kadesh and gone into camp early in the afternoon on the northwest of Kadesh. Of his other three divisions the Egyptian scribe only knows that Re and Ptah are somewhere on the march, with their officers evidently separated from them in the forest south of Kadesh.'
[99] Spruytte 1983: 51: 'The lightness of the [Egyptian] vehicle and team launched at a gallop could never have made it a vehicle of impact, and although a single man could not have stopped it and would inevitably have been knocked down, a simple field of wheat would have sufficed to obstruct its progress and immobilize it.' Cantrell 2011: 11 fn. 2; 63 fn. 8: 'The Egyptian chariot's lightness might also be an issue when moving at speed on open, unobstructed terrain, where '[t]he main problem was loading the chariots with enough weight to keep them grounded' and 'the light weight of the chariots was a serious problem, they often bounded out of control and wrecked.'

crew, and further boosted by the strong horses pulling it, shouldering effortlessly through the wheat, trampling and flattening the stems beneath their pounding hooves.

By now, surely, the Egyptians knew that a massive Hittite chariotry host was bearing down on them. Shortly, with the ground quaking and the air filled with the din of hoofbeats and turning wheels, the first line of Hittite chariots could be discerned – but only partially so. If, as one can reasonably assume, a field of ripening emmer wheat or barley lay between the Mukadiyah stream and the Shabtuna road, the awns extending upward from the spikelets of those mature and very tall ancient cultivars would have topped out at about the same height (c. 132 centimetres, or 13 hands) as the withers of the average–size Late Bronze Age chariot horse. Thus, all that could be seen of the horses were their heads and necks protruding above the grain. The horses were crowned with plumed headdresses (typically made of ostrich feathers) and these would have bounced and swayed in rhythm with their movements. Similarly, all that could be seen of the three men in each chariot were their torsos and heads. Of these the most notable, and impressive, was the warrior wearing a helmet crested with a brightly coloured horsehair plume and a long scale–armour hauberk glittering in the sun: chariot warfare in the Late Bronze Age was in its accoutrements as sumptuous and splendid in appearance as it was deadly in practice. The vehicle frames would be mostly hidden from view. Thus, each vehicle would present as a pair of horses' heads followed by the heads and upper torsos of three–man crew, standing shoulder–to–shoulder skimming almost magically across the wheat on an invisible conveyance.

We cannot know whether the cultivated zone, if it indeed existed, extended from the stream bank (or, alternately, from the grove of trees that possibly abutted the stream) right up to the road, or whether it stopped well short of the road leaving an open space between the two. In any event, once the chariots came within bowshot one or both the two fighting men in each vehicle would have begun lofting arrows into the Egyptian column. The chariots would be moving at a brisk pace, from between ca. 19 to 30.5 km, using a gait (probably variations of the trot or canter) that would minimise to the extent possible the deleterious effects of terrain irregularities (such the furrows they would surely encounter in cultivated fields) on the use of the bow. Collection might be imposed on the horses for the same purpose.[100] The primary concern of the archers was volume of fire not accuracy.[101] The intent was to provide 'area fire,' which is to say, to deluge the targeted area with arrows rather than shooting at individual targets. Hittite chariot warriors were capable of shooting five to six arrows per minute (this was the standard rate of fire for all

Figure 18.17. Movement to contact! Having forded two watercourses (the Orontes River and the Mukadiyah stream), the Hittite chariotry fans out to attack the Egyptian Re battlegroup marching north toward the Amun camp. The Hittites achieved complete surprise and annihilated the Egyptian force in the ensuing battle (Artwork by Brian Delf from *Hittite Warrior* © 2007 Osprey Publishing).

Late Bronze Age archers) and thus, within the space of a mere sixty seconds, they could have loosed several thousand arrows at the Egyptians. The plunging arrows must have wreaked havoc among the Egyptians, killing some and wounding many others, and, most importantly, disrupting the battlegroup's overall cohesion (Figure 18.17).

In this instance area fire functioned primarily as a shock tactic, where 'shock,' as defined by Wolfgang Schivelbusch, is understood to be:

> a violent act compounded from the concentration of many individual elements. (…) the kind of sudden and powerful event of violence that disrupts the continuity of an artificially/mechanically created motion or situation, and also the subsequent state of derangement. The precondition for this is a highly developed general state of dominance over nature, both technically (military example: firearms) and psychically (military example: troop discipline).[102]

Thus shock causes disruption; which generates chaos; which hinders where it does not obviate outright attempts by the victimised force to organise for defence, culminating in force disintegration.

The process of disintegration in the Re battlegroup probably began before the Hittite strike force came into physical contact with the pharaoh's troops, possibly while the chariots were still pushing through the wheat, almost certainly during the arrow bombardment. It did not start everywhere at once. Mass panic typically begins as an individual phenomenon. But in war, in the midst of desperate battle, it can burst suddenly into flame and flash among the ranks like a wildfire racing through dry prairie grass. A few men quit the battle line, running away from the fighting; and then, suddenly, everyone is running.

It seems most likely that the breaking point for the Egyptians came when the forward echelons of the Hittite strike

---

[100] See also Cantrell 2011: 11, fn. 2: 'There are distinct changes in speed among the various types of canters: collected canter, 7.2 mph [ca. 11.5 km]; working canter, 8.7 mph [ca. 14 km]; medium canter, 10.9 mph [ca. 14.5 km]; and extended canter, 13.2 mph [ca. 21 km]. Horses are taught to use these gaits on command after months and years of training'; see also Clayton 2002.
[101] Cantrell 2011: 25 fn. 2.
[102] Schivelbusch 2014: 157.

force emerged from the cultivated zone bordering the Mukadiyah stream to be fully revealed to the hapless trudging foot soldiers. In World War II the term 'tank terror' was coined to describe the effect a mass tank attack could have on even battle–hardened infantrymen.[103] What the Egyptian soldiers experienced was closely akin to tank terror; one might call it 'chariot terror.' The chariot horses, resplendently accoutred in plumed headdresses and brightly coloured armour trappings, stepping high and shaking and tossing their heads, snorting and baring their teeth and roaring as they came on, were especially fearsome – and fear–inducing. The neck of each horse, Job 39 informs us, is 'clothed … with thunder' and 'the glory of his nostrils is terrible':

> [H]e paweth in the valley and rejoiceth in his strength; he goeth on to meet the armed men. He mocketh at fear, and is not affrighted; neither turneth he back from the sword. The quiver rattleth against him, the glittering spear and the shield. He swalloweth the ground with fierceness and rage' and 'he saith among the trumpets, Ha! Ha!'[104]

Seeing the Hittite horses in the fullness of their battle fury, and hearing, as the horses did, 'the thunder of the captains and shouting' from the men in the chariots, many of the Egyptians threw down their weapons and took to their heels.[105] Of course there must have been others more resolute who stood their ground, turning to face their attackers even as their terrified comrades tried to make good their escape. At a certain point – when the chariots were within 75–50 yards of the column – the vehicles would have decelerated in order to employ the chariot desant tactic. Thus, the third man in each chariot crew would dismount and, sprinting alongside his vehicle, charge the Egyptian column with his spear held before him.

According to the Poem, the Hittite chariotry 'came forth from the south side of Kadesh and attacked the army of Re *in its middle*, as they were marching unaware and not prepared to fight'[106] (emphasis added). A lesser element, however, would have raced at speed to the front of the column to block its movement toward the Amun camp while another would have driven to the column's rear to cut off retreat. This was, and still is, standard operating procedure for attacking a marching column. The goal was to envelop the column, thus sealing off any possibility of escape, and strike it a blow so mighty as to shatter it upon impact.

And that, in fact, is what happened. Smashing into and through the column, the Hittite chariots, working in tandem with their dismounted men-at-arms, swiftly routed the Egyptian soldiery with much bloodshed and slaughter. The few Egyptian troops who survived the encounter scattered in all directions, with most fleeing north to the putative refuge of the Amun camp. with the Hittite chariots in pell–mell pursuit, shooting and spearing and cutting down those overtaken in the rout.[107]

The shattering and scattering of Re marked the end of what I have termed the 'shock phase' of the Battle of Kadesh. The Hittites had fought what amounted to a battle of tactical manoeuvre, the effects of which were enhanced and intensified by the sheer impetus and weight of their attack, to achieve a sudden, annihilating victory over their adversaries. The Hittite chariotry was alone among Late Bronze Age military establishments in possessing the capability – and the technology – to fight a manoeuvre battle over distance. The ability to function as a combined arms force comprising chariots and what may be properly termed 'mechanised infantry,' with the latter riding on the chariots to the point of contact with the enemy, was unique to the Hittite military. An operation made possible by the three–man chariot and the tactical system that inspired its development, it provided a foretaste of modern mechanised warfare (Figure 18.18).

Figure 18.18. The Hittite chariotry strike force attacked en masse, probably in multiple unit columns on a narrow front (as pictured here), applying the principle of concentration of force (public domain; NYPL digital collection).

Battle Phase II, 'Siege': Amun Embattled

The battle now entered its second stage, the 'siege phase.' The Hittites' galloping pursuit of Re's remnants brought them swiftly to the Amun camp and the shield wall that surrounded it. Here the Hittite charioteers would have been well-advised to invest the camp without attacking it, holding themselves passively in check until the Hittite infantry arrived on the scene. But perhaps this was too much to ask of men who has just scored a stunning victory over

---

[103] Bagdonas 2014: 11: '[The Germans'] phrase for it, Panzerschreck, meant 'tank terror,' and they [the Germans] spent a great deal of time, effort, training and weaponry to overcome it.'

[104] Translation from the King James Bible (https://holy-bible.online/kjv.php). Deborah Cantrell (2011: 11–32) analyses this passage both for what does and does not reveal about horses in war as part of a broader discussion on the nature of warhorses and their behaviour in battle.

[105] Lichtheim 2006: 64: 'Then the infantry and chariotry of his majesty weakened before them on their way northward to where his majesty was.'

[106] Lichtheim 2006: 64.

[107] Heidenreich and Roth 2020: 136: 'Military panic is most commonly associated with soldiers running away from the battlefield. There are numerous descriptions of this; indeed, it is so common as to be a topos of ancient historical writing. Despite the fact that the rhetoric of flight is often repetitive, running uncontrollably is indeed the most common reaction of soldiers seized with panic.'

their foes, eliminating fully one-fifth of the pharaoh's army from the Egyptian order of battle. In the event the mass of Hittite chariotry came surging up to the camp and swirled around the shield wall like a river in full spate, '[surrounding] the followers of his majesty who were by his side.'[108]

The Hittites would not have driven their chariots into the palisade, and for reasons previously stated; rather, they would have driven parallel to it, with the warriors lofting arrows at the defenders inside the camp even as their spear-armed third men dismounted and formed ad hoc assault parties for attacking the barrier at multiple points. Muwatalli, who was surely watching the battle from a suitable vantage point – possibly one of Kadesh's ramparts or towers – must have understood that the battle was spinning out of his control: a common occurrence in high–tempo, fast–paced operations. As military analyst and theoretician Huba Wass de Czege has noted: 'When speed and rapid, decisive results are important, the potential for chaos and loss of mutual support will go up.'[109]

At certain point in the course of the fighting a group of Hittite chariots achieved a penetration, breaking through the barricade and charging into the camp. They had not gotten far before the chariot crews stopped and alighted from their vehicles to loot the place of everything of value, they could lay hands upon. Dazzled by the variety and abundance of riches they found in and among the tents, they lost sight of their true purpose and paid the ultimate price for their greed when they were set upon by swarming Egyptian infantry, who sealed the breach behind them and slew them to the man.

In this dire hour when his fate and the fate of his army hung in the balance Ramesses firmly grasped the nettle of battlefield command, acting with swift and certain resolve to stave off annihilation: 'When his majesty caught sight of [the Hittite chariots] he rose quickly, enraged at them like his father Mont.'[110] Taking up weapons and donning his armour he was 'like Seth in the moment of his power.' In doing so, he covered himself in glory – and, more importantly, bought critical time for his beleaguered battlegroup. He would have known that the Nearin battlegroup was somewhere *en route* from the coast, advancing through the Eleutheros Valley, and that the Ptah and Seth battlegroups were marching up from the south. He also would have known that several hours might elapse before the three battlegroups arrived. Amun would just have to hold out until they did. Its ability to do so, however, was cast in doubt by a number of his charioteers. Infected with the contagion of panic spread by the fleeing troops of the Re battlegroup, they leapt aboard their vehicles and bolted from the camp. No doubt many Egyptian foot soldiers also took flight (Figure 18.19).

While they made good their escape Ramesses battled the Hittites from his chariot. His later claims that he acted alone may be dismissed as boilerplate rhetoric of the sort

Figure 18.19. Hittite chariotry strike force attacking the Amun camp (courtesy of Giuseppe Rava).

that all kings in that age, and in the ages that followed, employed in praising their deeds and the splendour of their persons. His bodyguard of elite Sherden swordsmen and Egyptian men–at–arms accompanied him everywhere he went on the battlefield, loping alongside his chariot, breaking into a run when Ramesses charged the enemy, and fighting with untrammelled ferocity to protect him from swarming Hittite spearmen and chariots. Likewise, Menena, his chariot driver and shield bearer, never wavered in the performance of his highly exacting duties, keeping ever at his side throughout the battle and performing his highly exacting duties with unremitting courage, skill, and devotion to the pharaoh. As well, probably many Egyptian charioteers, those who had not succumbed to panic like those who had taken flight, joined Ramesses in these forays; and it was certainly the case (evidenced by the fact that the Hittites did not succeed in overrunning the camp) that the majority of his troops, infantry and archers and various auxiliaries, remained steadfastly at their posts behind the shield wall, resisting and repulsing each successive Hittite assault in its turn (Figure 18.20).

Yet all their efforts would have gone for naught absent the pharaoh's courageous leadership. The Egyptian army's centre of gravity resided in his royal person, and had Ramesses been killed in the fighting or had he been a lesser

Figure 18.20. With the battle's outcome hanging in the balance, Ramesses rallied his troops, leading them in six counterattacks from the Amun camp (after Brian Palmer; https://arrecaballo.es/edad-antigua/el-imperio-egipcio/batalla-de-kadesh-1-274-ac/).

---

[108] Lichtheim 2006: 61.
[109] Wass de Czege 2010: 26.
[110] Lichtheim 2006: 61.

man who lacked the backbone and ability to organise and conduct an active defence of the camp, Egyptian resistance would have soon collapsed and Amun in its entirety would have been wiped out. Fortunately for the Egyptians (and for Egypt) Ramesses more than rose to meet the challenge thrust upon him. Drawing on his seemingly depthless reservoirs of courage, he staged as many as six counterattacks, directing his chariot straight into the swirling Hittite host, working his bow without pause, shooting arrows left, right, and centre at the Hittites in their chariots; he 'charged their ranks fighting as a falcon pounces (…) like Sakhmet in the moment of her rage' (Figure 18.21).[111]

At the same time Menena, would have been throwing the vehicle around the crowded battlefield, careening and weaving precipitously among the hurtling Hittite chariots, darting and dashing this way and that, starting and stopping abruptly, careening through turns on one wheel – and occasionally grabbing the pharaoh by the latter's left arm to prevent him from being thrown from the vehicle during its most violent manoeuvrings, or by raising his small hand–held shield to protect His Majesty from Hittite arrows. Menena held the shield in his right hand, and he also held in this hand the two reins leading to the right–side horse, and he was required to handle both simultaneously: an arguably harder job than the pharaoh's. Ramesses knew that he owed much to Menena for his brave and skilful handling of their chariot, and he later saw to it that the driver was mentioned by name in Pentaur's account (Figure 18.22).

Also mentioned by name are Ramesses' two horses, Victory–in–Thebes and Mut–is–Content, which he called 'my *great* horses' declaring: 'It was they whom I found supporting me when I alone fought many lands, it was they whom I found in the midst of battle.'[112] They too were accorded a tremendous (and unprecedented) honour, one that might well have been the envy of his human retainers: 'They shall henceforth be fed in my presence, whenever I reside in my palace' (Figure 18.23).[113]

Also mentioned in the accounts are the Sherden. It is likely that these mercenary soldiers were chariot–killing specialists who served the pharaoh not only as his personal bodyguard but as chariot runners tasked with engaging enemy chariots and their runners in chariotry melees.[114] They were uniquely well–equipped for the job by virtue of their primary armament, a large sword with an approximately 38–inch blade, a raised spine, and a wide base tapering to a needle–like point. Thus configured, it was ideal for stabbing into the gaps and joins of the body armour worn by Late Bronze Age chariot warriors. 'The sword's length,' observes Richard Gabriel,

> gave the Sherden warrior superior 'reach' to get at his target while on foot and below the enemy charioteer. The sharp point could easily penetrate

Figure 18.21. Ramesses engaging a Hittite three–man chariot on the plain of Kadesh. Handling the reins is his trusted driver, Menena, and his two beloved horses, Victory–in–Thebes and Mut–is–Content, pull the vehicle (after Johnny Shumate; https://arrecaballo.es/edad-antigua/el-imperio-egipcio/batalla-de-kadesh-1-274-ac/).

Figure 18.22. Ramesses II charging the Hittite chariotry, 'fighting as a falcon pounces (…) like Sakhmet in the moment of her rage' (Artwork by Adam Hock from *Bronze Age War Chariots* © 2006 Osprey Publishing).

Figure 18.23. Sherden at Kadesh, equipped with round shields and armed with their distinctive long swords. Broad at the base and tapering to a narrow point, these were designed for stabbing into the joins and gaps of scale body armour: ideal tools of the Sherdens' trade as 'chariot–killers' (public domain; https://periplusca.files.wordpress.com/2013/03/0sea-peoples-2.png).

---

[111] Lichtheim 2006: 62.
[112] Lichtheim 2006: 70, emphasis added.
[113] Lichtheim 2006: 70.
[114] Gabriel 2006: 71–72, with fn. 27.

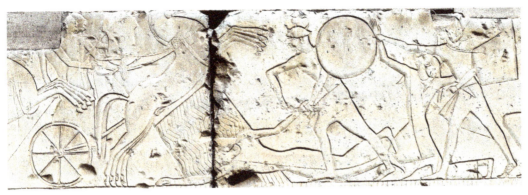

Figure 18.24. The fighting was ferocious, with no quarter asked or given by either side. Here a Sherden swordsman cuts off the hand of a Hittite chariot warrior (courtesy of Mohamed Raafat Abbas. http://www.enim-egyptologie.fr/revue/2017/2/Abbas_ENiM10_p7-23.pdf).

leather, lamellar, and, perhaps, even thin (two millimeters) bronze scale armor. Striking from below, the needle–like point could find a seam or slide under the overlapping scales of the charioteer's armor coat.[115]

It was a heavy weapon but well balanced for one–handed use due to having its balance point (centre of gravity) located just above the hilt in its wide base. This was where the sword held much of its weight and from which it accordingly derived significant strength. The long narrow rapiers then in widespread use among Aegean warriors were also excellent stabbing weapons but they had a tendency to break when stressed due to their uniform width from hilt to point. By contrast the Sherden sword's triangular configuration transferred stress at or near the point (produced, e.g., when a Sherden warrior thrust into the scale–armour hauberk of a Hittite chariot warrior) to the base where it was dissipated. One–handed use further benefitted the Sherden warrior for carrying a sturdy round shield, which provided much–needed protection in the close–quarters combat that was his stock in his trade.

Being swordsmen, the Sherden did not fight in phalanxes after the fashion of spear–armed infantry. The densely packed infantry mass where spearmen stand shoulder to shoulder with shields locked or overlapping is certainly necessary for forming the shield wall and presenting the hedge of spears from which it both derives and generates combat power. But such formations are a constraint on swordsmen who need a degree of open space, and the freedom of movement open space enables to wield their weapons effectively. It is therefore likely that the Sherden fought in small loosely organised groups using battle–swarm tactics against enemy chariotry forces.

Their origins are unknown and a subject of debate.[116] Western Anatolia, the Caucasus, Sardinia, and, more generally, the 'islands in the sea' have all been proposed as possible homelands. They had frequent but conflicting relations with the Egyptians going back at least to the fourteenth century. Alternately fighting both for and against the pharaoh and his armies, they plied their trade as soldiers of fortune with notable success in an age abundant with such men.

The Sherden who served Ramesses in the Kadesh War were brought to Egypt as captives taken in an abortive piratical raid on the Nile Delta in the second year of the pharaoh's reign.[117] Evidently impressed by their skills as fighting men, Ramesses caused them to be settled in Lower Egypt and incorporated them into his army's force structure. Ultimately, they were brought into his household as armed retainers charged with protecting the pharaoh's royal person. Loyalty to one's employer is a prerequisite for the job, and the Sherden evidently possessed this quality in spades.

In the Battle of Kadesh they remained steadfastly at the pharaoh's side when many native–born Egyptian troops, elite charioteers as well as foot soldiers, had taken to their heels in headlong flight. The Sherden kept fighting even when it seemed that they must all be killed in the Hittite onslaught. Ramesses had chosen well in selecting these fierce men to serve as his bodyguards.

Ramesses and his Sherden fought as a combined–arms unit: six times they burst forth together from behind the shield wall, the pharaoh in his chariot charging at speed into the 'midst of the foe' with his 'household butlers'[118] (i.e., the Sherden) sprinting alongside the vehicle, with swords at the ready and shields up. They would not have had to go far before engaging the Hittites. While Ramesses fought the Hittites with bow and arrows, the Sherden would have fanned out ahead and to either side of his vehicle to engage the now–dismounted Hittite spearmen and the chariots that had borne them to the battlefield. The countless 'small combats' pitting sword–armed Sherden warriors against Hittite third men armed with their long spears must have been savage in the extreme. Equally savage where the swarming attacks by two or more Sherden on Hittite chariots. This is no mere conjecture: one of the Egyptian wall reliefs of the battle depicts Sherden warriors cutting the hands off a Hittite warrior they pulled from his vehicle later as a means of counting how many enemies they killed (see Figures 18.23 and 18.24).

---

[115] Gabriel 2006: 71–72.
[116] On the Sherden, see Abbas 2017 and Cavillier 2010.
[117] Abbas 2017 and Cavillier 2010.
[118] Lichtheim 2006: 70.

In the battle for the Amun camp the combatants on both sides provided, cumulatively, a textbook example of mobile mechanised warfare as it should be fought on the tactical level, with chariots and infantry operating in support of each other. This is the essence of the combined arms approach, which is key to success on the mechanised battlefield – which the Kadesh battlefield most certainly exemplified, and in all three phases of the encounter. Swarming centripetal attacks of the sort conducted by chariotry's third men (Sherden runners on the one hand, dismounted Hittite spearmen on the other) may appear haphazard and anarchic to an eye untrained in swarming tactics, but there is actually purpose to the apparent madness: that being the overcoming of defences through violent, relentless, and unpredictable assaults from multiple directions. Here it bears repeating that the brilliance of the new Hittite tactical system lay in the ability of the Hittites' three–man chariots to transport their third men over distance to a point on the battlefield where they might be advantageously deployed to form ad hoc swarming parties, ideally in numbers superior to those of the enemy encountered at the point of contact and without exhausting themselves in transit.

Unfortunately for the Hittites at this juncture, the contest had devolved from a battle of tactical manoeuvre battle into a battle of position. What's more, the position at issue was protected against assault by a shield wall. This was not, in the circumstances, an insubstantial fortification. From the standpoint of the Hittites, the shield wall might just as well have been built of cyclopean stone blocks, and to a towering height. The wall robbed the Hittite chariotry of its force mobility and in so doing obviated mobility's advantages. The Hittite chariotry could not, on its own, break through the shield wall; and for so long as the Egyptian troops stood firm behind it, they could continue holding out (Figure 18.25).

However, they could not hold out indefinitely. Perhaps an hour, maybe more, had elapsed from the arrival of the Hittite chariotry and the completion of Ramesses' sixth surging counterattack. In that time hard fighting must have taken its toll on the Egyptians, eroding their stamina and with it their combat effectiveness. The same must be assumed for the chariot horses. The battle of position was morphing ineluctably, as all such battles do, into a battle of exhaustion. The Egyptians including their horses were suffering casualties. They were expending arrows that could not be retrieved (although they could retrieve the arrows the Hittites were shooting at them). And, most worrisome of all, they were in danger of running out of water.

We do not and cannot know how much water the Egyptians had laid up in the camp prior to the Hittite attack. Probably very little in the few hours since making camp. Until just a short while before the outbreak of fighting the nearby Orontes River and the Mukadiyah stream would have provided for all their water needs. Then the Hittite chariots came and cut them off from the two watercourses. Their water stocks would have begun to run low almost immediately. The situation would have soon turned dire. The effect on the horses would have been especially prob-

Figure 18.25. Swarming Egyptian foot soldiers assault Hittite chariots from the rear, where the vehicles were most vulnerable to attack (public domain; NYPL digital collections).

lematic. Much more than humans, horses require large quantities of water if they are to perform at peak levels over an extended period.[119] This was the greatest threat to the Egyptians: the possibility that they would run out of water for the horses in case the Hittites cut off the water sources, and that the animals would begin dropping dead in harness for want of it. Without horses there could be no chariotry; and without chariotry, Egyptian resistance would soon collapse.

Ramesses' predicament was then akin to that faced by the Duke of Wellington (1769–1852) in late afternoon during the Battle of Waterloo in 1815. With the battle going badly for the Seventh Coalition, Wellington, assessing his deteriorating position, was famously heard to comment: "Give me night or give me Blücher."[120] Ramesses must have had similar thoughts concerning his battlegroups marching up from the south, and the Nearin approaching from the coast. He must have wondered in this moment about their exact location. Would they get to him in time, before Amun ran out of water – before the Hittite infantry joined the fight?

As for the latter: around this time the lead elements of the two Hittite infantry brigades must have been arriving on the opposite bank of the Orontes, just above Kadesh, where it was deploying for battle alongside the tactical reserve chariotry grouping. We may assume that these formations were to merge with the reserve chariotry to form an immensely powerful combined arms force comprising about 37,000 foot soldiers (line infantry plus auxiliaries) and 1,000 chariots. But it would be some time yet before

---

[119] McKeever and Lehnhard 2014: 79: 'The volume of water that must be consumed by the horse to ward off, or alleviate, dehydration will obviously vary with the individual animal and conditions. (...) Some studies have documented that an active horse, under warm conditions, can consume 100 L (26 gallons) of water per day.' See also McKeever 1997: 79. In a prolonged battle such as the Battle of Kadesh, in the torrid heat of a Near Eastern summer's day, the water intake needs of chariot horses must have been greater still.
[120] Chandler 1988: 143. Alternatively, 'Night or the Prussians must come,' see Howarth 1968: 162.

the infantry was fully assembled and properly arrayed for battle. Only then would Muwatalli commit the combined arms force in its entirety to the battle. The force would cross the Orontes and attack the Amun camp, eliminating it in short order. Having delivered the knockout blow to Amun it could then pivot to face south and engage and defeat, in detail, the Egyptian battlegroups advancing from that direction. The battle would be over, the fighting ended, the war won: and the Hittite king could return home in triumph.

In the meantime, the battle at the Amun camp continued – albeit with what surely would have been a considerable lessening in the tempo and scale of the fighting. This was only to be expected; it is a natural, almost inevitable, occurrence in lengthy hard–fought battles. Soldiers (and their horses) cannot fight at peak levels of intensity for very long. They are drained by their exertions, diminished by what they are doing and by what has been done to them (including injuries). The toll exacted is both physical and psychological, an exhaustion of both mind and body. In some instances, shock sets in: soldiers break down mentally, run away, lapse into catatonia.[121] Mostly, however, there is merely a slackening of effort. Men remove themselves from the battle without quitting the battlefield: they pause for breath, as it were; they stop to rest, gather their wits, reorder their thoughts.

This is never an across–the–board phenomenon: it never happens to everyone, everywhere on the battlefield, at the same time. Thus, combat becomes fragmented, dispersed, intermittent; the battle is fought in multiple discrete 'pulses' occurring spontaneously, distributed randomly around the battlefield. There are flashpoints of extreme violence and broad stretches of inaction and calm. Groups of men engage in furious combat while others just a few yards distant stand idly by. The ground is strewn with the detritus of mayhem and slaughter: dead men and horses, body parts and pooled blood, overturned chariots, detached wheels, broken weapons, splintered shields, and cloven helmets. Amidst the battle wrack the wounded, men and horses alike, cry out and lone figures stagger aimlessly about, faces devoid of expression, gazing into an infinite distance with thousand–yard stares that see everything and comprehend nothing.

To be sure, many if not most of the Hittite charioteers were probably not so stricken; although tired, they were still fit for duty, still eminently capable of further operations. Or they would be presently, after taking a short break. The relative let–up in the fighting was a boon to these men, giving them the respite they needed. They would have used that time productively, by leading their horses to the Orontes or Mukadiyah steam for a quick splash–down and a cooling drink; by replenishing their chariot quivers with more arrows and javelins; by combining their casualty–depleted squadrons for the next combat pulse. As they did so they might have voiced their frustration at the course the battle had taken following their annihilation of the Re bat-

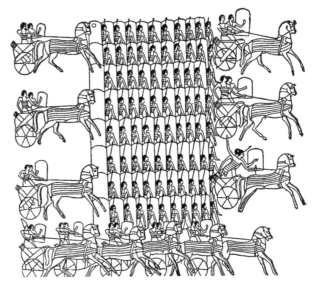

Figure 18.26. Ramesses and his battlegroup were on the brink of annihilation when the Nearin battlegroup arrived on the scene to save the day for the Egyptians. Marching down from the Eleutheros Valley to the north, the Nearin conducted a textbook combined arms attack, with phalanxed infantry flanked by Egyptian chariotry (public domain; https://en.wikipedia.org/wiki/Military#/media/.jpg).

tlegroup. The exhilaration they surely felt upon obliterating that force had surely passed due to their failure to mete out the same fate to Amun. Heretofore they had assaulted the Egyptian shield wall tenaciously and often, but to no decisive result. The defenders had held firm and beaten back every attack. The Hittite charioteers were thus reacquainted with a fundamental tenet of mechanised warfare, one they well knew but had either forgotten or ignored in their initial lunge at the Amun camp: all other things being more or less equal, stalwart troops defending a fortified position will generally prevail over combat vehicles attacking without infantry support.

Were they angry about this state of affairs? One assumes they were. A few might have vented their anger by driving along the shield wall, shooting arrows and hurling taunts at the defenders, a futile but satisfying gesture. Some battled Rameses and his Sherden during his periodic sallies from the camp. Most would have bided their time. They knew the situation was about to change. Reinforcements were on the way. The tide of battle was about to turn in their favour. Or so they thought.

It turned out that they were wrong. The Nearin battlegroup, with exquisite timing, marching down from the Eleutheros Valley, finally arrived on the scene. It came literally at the last possible moment, when yet another Hittite chariotry thrust had succeeded in penetrating the camp's shield wall: 'And the Narn [sic] broke into the host of the wretched Fallen one of Khatti as they [the Hittites] were entering into the camp of Pharaoh' (Figure 18.26).[122]

Muwatalli countered by committing his tactical reserve chariotry grouping to the battle.

---

[121] Lichtheim 2006: 62.

[122] Gardiner 1960: 37.

Figure 18.27. An Egyptian combined arms battlegroup in full battle array, with phalanxed infantry accompanied by chariotry. The illustration seems to have been based on an Egyptian wall relief depicting the attack of the Nearin in the Battle of Kadesh (public domain; https://avatars.mds.yandex.net/get-mpic/4341821/img_id639537024769813140.jpeg/orig).

Then [Muwatalli] caused many chiefs to come, each one of them with his chariots, and they were equipped with their weapons of warfare. (…) Their total of a thousand chariots came straight into the fire.[123]

This was something of a desperation move on Muwatalli's part. With the outcome of the battle hanging in the balance he could wait no longer for his infantry brigades, still forming up on the right bank, to complete their preparations. The moment had arrived to take action, which he did by sending his reserve chariotry across the river to engage the Nearin and prevent the Egyptian battlegroup from breaking the siege of the Amun camp. Certainly, he would have much preferred to commit his infantry brigades with the chariotry reserve grouping, but this option was not available to him, except by committing them piecemeal, which was really no option at all – which was, in fact, a course that would put them at great risk of piecemeal annihilation by the Egyptian battlegroups hastening up from Shabtuna (Figure 18.27).

Battle Phase III 'Melee': Battlegroup Amun Rescued

Thus began the 'melee phase' of the battle. The third and final act in this violent drama of Late Bronze Age warfare took place on the plain west of the city of Kadesh, between the Amun camp and the Orontes. The Nearin, deploying for battle off their line of march – an intricate manoeuvre flawlessly executed by the experienced, battle–wise 'boys' – made the move to contact in perfect combined arms battle array. The Abu Simbel relief depicts an infantry phalanx 10 ranks deep and 8 files broad, supported by chariotry squadrons in line abreast formations. One squadron leads the advance, another brings up the rear, and a third moves alongside the right flank. A fourth squadron likely guarded the left flank but is not depicted due to lack of space.

The Abu Simbel relief is obviously meant to represent a far larger force, one probably comprising approximately 10,000 foot soldiers (phalanxed infantry plus archers, slingers, and skirmishers) accompanied by 500 chariots. That said, it should also be noted that the positioning of the infantry and mechanised elements is nearly identical to that of a twenty–first century combined arms task force advancing to contact in open battle. The tactical logic is the same in either instance: the leading mechanised element would deliver the initial blow, using shock to damage and disrupt the cohesion of the opposing force preparatory to the main attack by the infantry, functioning as the arm of decision. Mechanised elements also provide flank and rear security and may, depending on how the battle unfolds, be employed as a tactical reserve to bolster a faltering effort or to conduct exploitation and pursuit in the event that the enemy is routed.

Similarities between the ancient and modern mechanised formations extends to their rate of advance. The chariot horses as represented in the relief are clearly moving at what appears to be a slow walk. They are, most definitely, *not* galloping. The restraint imposed on them by their drivers was, of course, necessitated by the slower foot speed of the infantry: a faster pace by the chariots would separate the chariotry from the infantry to the detriment of both. Combined arms operations are effective to the extent that the constituent elements remain combined, and that is why modern combined arms tank–infantry forces advance at walking speed, just like the chariots of their Late Bronze Age predecessors. Tanks typically do not go barrelling at speed across a battlefield without infantry support, and neither did chariots: and for the same reasons. Infantry and combat vehicles in a combined arms force move at the same speed so that each provides security for the other while increasing the combat power of the formation as a whole.

Just moments before making contact with the enemy chariots and tanks alike *might* increase their speed for the purpose of delivering shock; but they would do so only rarely, when shock might prove beneficial: which is to say, when the enemy force was already showing signs of weakness

---
[123] Lichtheim 2006: 66–67.

leading to collapse. In the Poem we are told that Ramesses counterattacked the besieging Hittite chariotry at the gallop.[124] But charging at speed in this instance would have been a temporary expedient, for short distances only, in order to reach and establish a favourable position on the battlefield vis–a–vie that of the Hittite chariots. The objective was to strike the first blow in the resulting encounter rather than trading blows at the encounter's outset. The advantage he enjoyed thereby would have lasted only seconds, but in that short time the pharaoh and his Sherden swordsmen might conceivably have engaged and defeated several Hittite chariots before turning about and galloping/sprinting back to the refuge of the shield wall – before, that is, the Hittites could respond, gathering at the point of contact to engage the Egyptian king with their superior numbers. In the event that Ramesses remained to battle these chariots the clash would have assumed the characteristics of a melee, with all the variations in speed – swift bursts at the gallop, interspersed with sudden starts and stops and sharp turns – that melees entailed (Figure 18.28).

The arrival of the Nearin changed the entire complexion of the battle. Where victory had seemed assured for the Hittites catastrophe now loomed. This happened within the space of a few minutes. The prospects for Muwatalli's chariotry soon worsened precipitously when Ramesses, heartened by the turn of events, rallied his troops for a counterstroke from the camp to coincide with the Nearin attack. As well, it seems that around this same time the leading elements of the Ptah battlegroup began arriving from the south. The Hittites thus found themselves hemmed in on three sides, fighting outnumbered with chariotry only against three combined arms battlegroups, of which two (the Nearin and Ptah) comprised troops and horses fresh to the fighting and one (Amun) had troops brimming with new–found confidence and thirsting for revenge against their erstwhile tormentors.

The Hittites' position was untenable. Unable to withstand the Egyptian onslaught they exited the battlefield in the only direction open to them, east across the Mukadiyeh stream. The stream was broader at this location than it was a short distance to the south, where the Hittites had forded it, and a number of the Hittite charioteers, along with their horses, met their death in the water, felled by the arrows and feathered javelins of their pursuers, causing them to 'plunge into the water as crocodiles plunge [and fall] on their faces one on the other' (Figure 18.29).[125]

Those Hittite chariots that managed to reach the east bank found refuge there among the Hittite infantry groupings, by now fully arrayed for battle. Elements of

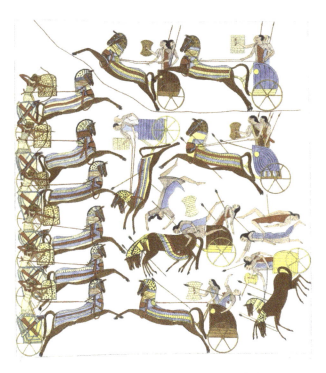

Figure 18.28. Nearin chariotry (left) engages Hittite chariotry. Note the two types of Hittite chariots, 'square' (or 'box') and 'D–shaped' models (public domain; NYPL digital collections).

the Kadesh garrison had also turned out to receive them. The mystery of why Muwatalli did not commit his infantry brigades to the battle is really no mystery at all. Arriving late to the scene, the infantry required yet more time to deploy from column of route to line of battle of formation, a complex and time-consuming undertaking. Rather than sending his infantry units across the river piecemeal to assemble on the battlefield, in the midst of the fighting, Muwatalli had decided, correctly, to have them form up on

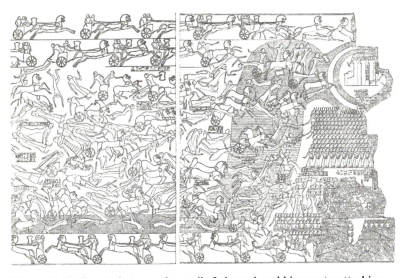

Figure 18.29. Caught between the anvil of pharaoh and his counterattacking forces, and the hammer of the Nearin battlegroup, and with the Ptah and Seth battlegroups approaching from the battlefield from the south, the Hittite chariotry was routed and driven into the Mukadiyeh stream toward the refuge of the City of Kadesh. But the Hittites were by no means beaten. On the right bank of the stream, within the shadow of the city walls (bottom right), the full might of two large Hittite infantry groupings were arrayed, fresh and ready for battle (public domain; https://en.wikipedia.org/wiki/File:Battle_scene_from_the_Great_Kadesh_reliefs_of_Ramses_II_on_the_Walls_of_the_Ramesseum.jpg.

---

[124] Lichtheim 2006: 69: 'His majesty then rushed forward / At a gallop he charged the midst of the foe'.
[125] Lichtheim 2006: 66.

the east bank. But events had moved too swiftly to accommodate the delay this entailed. By the time the infantry brigades had fully assembled the battle for the camp had been decided. Recognizing that this was the case, the Hittite king realised that committing the infantry would be tantamount to reinforcing defeat, and that he would not do. He held them back and waited on developments. If the Egyptians attempted to cross over to the east bank he would meet them head–on with 37,000 fresh troops supported by the uncommitted chariotry still available to him. The confidence Muwatalli must have felt in the ability of his forces to smash an Egyptian cross–stream assault was surely justified, and the king might be forgiven for hoping that Ramesses would be so reckless as to attempt such a foolish undertaking.

But Ramesses would not oblige him. He held his army, and himself, in check. His army was too badly mauled, and the Hittites were still too strong for him to do otherwise. Thus, as the day waned and evening came on the two armies sat glaring at each other from opposite sides of the Orontes River and the Mukadiyah stream, a curiously anticlimactic denouement to the prolonged kinetic violence of the battle preceding it.

The next day would see minor skirmishing between Egyptian and Hittite chariotry units, but it all came to nothing. If these small combats represented an attempt by Muwatalli to draw the Egyptians out and provoke them into initiating another round of fighting, it failed. Again, Ramesses would not be baited. Instead, he occupied himself with beheading a number of his charioteers who had deserted him in the hour of his, and his army's, crisis. These unfortunates had come slinking back to the camp begging his majesty for forgiveness and praising his glory. Ramesses was unmoved by their pleadings. Indeed, he was incensed and had determined to make an example of them, *pour encourager les autres*. He had them executed on the plain between the camp and the Orontes, in full view of the Hittites, who must have found the spectacle vastly entertaining. We may well imagine the cacophony of jeers, whistles, and catcalls emanating from the Hittite host as Egyptian heads rolled. By contrast the Egyptian troops, assembled, and ranked to bear witness to the proceedings, must have watched in horrified silence. It is probably safe to assume that they grasped the point made so emphatically by their king.

Shortly thereafter the Egyptians packed up and decamped for home. Ramesses would later claim, famously and ceaselessly, that he had won the battle. The validity of his claim rested on the fact that he held the battlefield at the end of the fighting. But the Hittites still held Kadesh, and Ramesses' abandonment shortly thereafter of both the battlefield and the region that encompassed it constituted a certain if tacit admission of defeat. His battered army limped back to Egypt with the Hittite army, also much depleted, following at distance, conducting a cautious but nonetheless steady pursuit, signalling thereby a different interpretation of the battle's outcome: one more in keeping with reality. Subsequently the strategic objective of the Hittites, the Kingdom of Amurru (located south of Kadesh), passed firmly into Hittite control: a clear victory for Muwatalli. The Egyptians had won merely a phase of the battle at the tactical level of war, but the Hittites held dominion over them at the strategic level. Ramesses' claim of battlefield victory notwithstanding, Muwatalli had won the war decisively.

Summary and Conclusion

It is in the nature of battle to put the devices and designs of the combatants to the ultimate test and in so doing to reveal the strengths and deficiencies of both. The mighty passage of arms that took place outside Kadesh on a summer's day in 1274 BCE was an early known occurrence of this phenomenon, serving as a proving ground for two competing concepts of mobility at the tactical level.

As evidenced by the chariot technologies respectively employed by the Hittites and the Egyptians, both accepted that tactical mobility occupied primacy of place in the Iron Triangle hierarchy and that it generally served 'as a bill–payer for virtually everything else in a vehicle's design.'[126] It was in their understanding of what constitutes tactical mobility that major differences arose. For the Egyptians tactical mobility was synonymous with *vehicle agility*; for the Hittites, tactical mobility meant *total force mobility*.

Egyptian Chariot Design: Emphasis on Vehicle Mobility

The Egyptian emphasis on vehicle mobility/agility necessarily relegated the attributes of protection and firepower to subordinate positions in the Iron Triangle hierarchy. This trade–off was unavoidable, the only way to resolve what Joshua Keena described as 'the real competing demands between principal attributes.'[127] Protection in its conventional form – 'passive protection' – was limited to that which was provided across the frontal arc of the vehicle by the horses. This was not insubstantial, but it was effective only for so long as the chariot was head–on to the enemy, an infrequent occurrence in chariotry melees. The Egyptian chariot's 'fenestrated' (open) sides, a feature of the vehicle's lightweight construction whence its agility was chiefly derived, left the crew totally exposed to missile fire (arrows, darts, javelins, slingstones) and spear thrusts. Vehicle firepower, embodied in the warrior–as–archer, was similarly limited by the requirements of agility. Adding a third man to the crew riding in the chariot would have doubled the vehicle's firepower but this would also have added to vehicle weight which in turn would have diminished its agility.

On the plus side of the capabilities ledger, the Egyptian chariot was quick and nimble, i.e., manoeuvrable in the sense that it could swiftly turn in a small radius circle (turning radius) without losing stability. These characteristics are the hallmarks of agility, correlating positively with the vehicle's lightweight construction.

---
[126] Kelly et al. 2011: 68–69.
[127] Keena 2011: 373.

The Egyptian chariot's lightweight construction might also correlate positively, by virtue of its agility, with survivability on the battlefield. As Goh observed, 'to achieve high mobility, vehicle platforms are commonly designed to be lightweight with limitations on allowable payload.' Admittedly, 'the lower carrying capacity has an adverse impact on the amount of armour that could be carried as add–on armour'; what's more, 'up–armouring of a platform improves crew survivability.' Even so, and notwithstanding the protection offered by extra armour, this impacts the vehicle's weight and degrades its mobility. Hence, instead of vulnerability reduction, a *high–mobility platform leverages its movement to avoid threats and enhance its survivability through susceptibility reduction'* (emphasis added).[128]

Writing in the same vein, Keena points to the positive effect 'greater mobility' has on what he terms 'platform performance,' encouraging (or, more precisely, compelling) operators to embrace 'a faster–paced, harassing fire and attack method.'[129]

But protection through mobility (vehicle agility) was attainable only for so long as the Egyptians adhered to an operating concept and tactical scheme for their chariotry that was centred on vehicle agility based on an active–versus–passive concept of protection. Thus, in a melee the Egyptian chariot's survival was contingent on constant movement. This was essential to its survival and also fundamental to its combat effectiveness, which was actualised through fire–and–movement tactics. In the confusion of chariotry combat, the Egyptian chariots would endeavour to stay in motion, nimbly weaving their way through the swarm and chaos of careering chariots, using their agility to avoid destruction and death even as they visited the same on their enemies.

Hittite Chariot Design:
Emphasis on Force Mobility

The Hittite concept of tactical mobility was based on the mobility of the chariotry force in its entirety rather than the mobility of individual vehicles. In the Hittite scheme, force mobility was enhanced by increasing individual vehicle firepower, and thus overall formation combat power, through the addition of the (formerly) dismounted runner/man–at–arms to the 'riding crew.'

What this amounted to was a tactics–drives–technology design paradigm, whereby the three–man chariot was developed to fulfil a pre–conceived operating concept formulated for the purpose of implementing a specific tactical system predicated on force mobility, which entailed an increase of firepower assets in each individual vehicle. This was achieved by placing the third man in the chariot and arming him with a spear and, probably, a bow as well. The use of a centre axle on a vehicle providing excellent protection via a sturdy wood construction and the possible use of armour – these all worked synergistically to enhance force mobility for the purpose of increasing force combat power, defined as 'the total means of destructive and/or disruptive force which a military unit/formation can apply against the opponent at a given time.'[130]

The Hittites' purpose in this ambitious undertaking of tactical and technological innovation was to achieve concentration of force and to bring maximum firepower to bear on the battlefield at the point of contact with the enemy, thereby breaking the chariotry stalemate that had characterised warfare in the Near East for the most part of four centuries in the second millennium BCE. What they sought was a means of reliably creating the conditions for fighting and winning a decisive battle, a goal that had proved elusive so long as the circumstances of this chariotry stalemate, as played out in slowly unfolding and generally indecisive set–piece battles of tactical attrition, continued to obtain.

Steven Weingartner
Military Historian and Author

---

[128] Goh 2014: 6.
[129] Keena 2011: 380.

[130] DOD Dictionary 2021: 39.

Military Abbreviations

DA	Department of the Army
GCV	Ground Combat Vehicles
METT–TC	Mission, Enemy, Terrain and weather, Troops and support available – Time available, Civilians (see https://metttc.com/)
MMI	Major Military Innovation
SLOC	Sea Lines of Communication (see https://military-history.fandom.com/wiki/Sea_lines_of_communication)

Bibliography

Abbas, Mohamed Raafat. 2017. Survey of the Military Role of the Sherden Warriors in the Egyptian Army during the Ramesside Period. *Égypte Nilotique et Méditerranéenne* 10: 7–73.

de Backer, Fabrice. 2009. Evolution of War Chariot Tactics in the Ancient Near East. *Ugarit-Forschungen* 41: 29–46.

Bagdonas, Raymond. 2014. *The Devil's General. The Life of Hyazinth Strachwitz, Panzer Graf.* Havertown: Casemate Publications.

Barkley, Andrew and Paul W. Barkley. 2013. *Principles of Agricultural Economics*. London and New York: Routledge.

Beal, Richard H. 1992. *The Organization of the Hittite Military*. Heidelberg: Winter.

Beal, Richard H. 1995. Hittite Military Organization. In: *Civilizations of the Ancient Near East*, edited by Jack M. Sasson, vol. 1, 545–554. New York and London: Scribner.

Beckman, Gary. 2006. Hittite Historical Texts I: The Anitta Text. In: *Historical Sources in Translation: The Ancient Near East*, edited by Mark W. Chavalas, 216–219. Malden, MA: Blackwell.

Bell, Lanny. 2007. Conflict and Reconciliation in the Ancient Middle East: The Clash of Egyptian and Hittite Chariots in Syria and the World's First Peace Treaty Between 'Superpowers'. In: *War and Peace in the Ancient World*, edited by Kurt A. Raaflaub and Nathan Rosenstein, 98–120. The Ancient World-Comparative Histories. Malden, MA: Blackwell.

Bessonov, Evgeni. 2017. *Tank Rider. Into the Reich with the Red Army*. New York: Skyhorse.

Blackmore, Tim. 2011. *War X. Human Extensions in Battlespace*. Toronto: University of Toronto Press.

Blair, Halworth W. 1999. *The Bradley and How It Got That Way. Technology, Institutions, and the Problem of Mechanized Infantry in the United States Army*. Westport: Greenwood Press.

Brand, Peter. 2023. *Ramesses II. Egypt's Ultimate Pharaoh*. Columbus, GA: Lockwood Press.

Breasted, James Henry. 1903. The Battle of Kadesh. A Study in the Earliest Known Military Strategy. *The University of Chicago's Decennial Publications* 5: 81–126.

Breasted, James Henry. 1906. *Ancient Records of Egypt, Historical Documents, Vol. 2: The Eighteenth Dynasty*. Chicago: The University of Chicago Press.

Breasted, James Henry. 1909. *A History of Egypt from the Earliest Times to the Persian Conquest*. New York: Scribner's Sons.

Bryce, Trevor. 2005. *The Kingdom of the Hittites*. Oxford: Oxford University Press.

Burgess, Michael and Svetoslav Gaidow. 2015. Conceptual Modelling and Analysis of Protection, Signature Management and Survivability: Considerations for Deployable Protected Land Vehicles. *Journal of Battlefield Technology* 18 (2): 1–6.

Burmeister, Stefan and Peter Raulwing. 2012. Festgefahren. Die Kontroverse um den Ursprung des Streitwagens. Einige Anmerkungen zu Forschung, Quellen und Methodik. In: *Archaeological, Cultural and Linguistic Heritage. Festschrift für Erzsébet Jerem in Honour of her 70th Birthday*, edited by Peter Anreiter et al., 93–113. Archaeolingua 25. Budapest: Archaeolingua Alapítvány.

Burne, A. H. 1921. Some Notes on the Battle of Kadesh: Being a Military Commentary on Professor J. H. Breasted's Book, The Battle of Kadesh (University of Chicago Press, 1903). *The Journal of Egyptian Archaeology* 7: 191–195.

Cantrell, Deborah O. 2011. *The Horsemen of Israel. Horses and Chariotry in Monarchic Israel*. Winona Lake, IN: Eisenbrauns.

Cavillier, Giacomo. 2006. *La Battaglia di Qadesh. Ramesse II alla conquista dell'Asia. fra mito, storia e strategia*. Torino: Tirrenia Stampatori.

Cavillier, Giacomo. 2010, 'Shardana Project': Perspectives and Researches on the Sherden in Egypt and Mediterranean. *Syria* 87: 339–345. DOI: 10.4000/syria.695.

Chandler, David G. 1988. *The Military Maxims of Napoleon*. New York: MacMillan.

Clayton, Hillary M. 2002. The Canter Considered. *USDF Connection* 4 (6): 22–25.

Clausewitz, Carl von. 1989. *On War.* Edited and translated by Michael E. Howard and Peter Paret. Princeton: Princeton University Press.

Cockrell, John T. 1978. *Evaluation of Four Target Identification Training Techniques*. Technical Paper 301. Alexandria, VA: U.S. Army Research Institute for Behavioral and Social Sciences.

Council of the European Union. 2014. *EU Battlegroup Concept*. Press Release by Council of the European Union, European External Action Service (EEAS), 7 July 2014. http://

data.consilium.europa.eu/doc/document/ST-11624-2014-EXT-1/en/pdf.

Creveld, Martin van. 2007. War and Technology. *Foreign Policy Research Institute* 12 (25); http://www.fpri.org/article/2007/10/war-technology-2.

Crouwel, Joost H. 1981. *Chariots and Other Means of Land Transport in Bronze Age Greece*. Allard Pierson Museum Series 3. Amsterdam: Allard Pierson Museum.

Crouwel, Joost H. 2019. Wheeled Vehicles and Their Draught Animals in the Ancient Near East – An Update. In: *Equids and Wheeled Vehicles in the Ancient World. Essays in Memory of Mary A. Littauer*, edited by Peter Raulwing, Katheryn M. Linduff and Joost H. Crouwel, 29–48. BAR International Series 2923. Oxford: BAR Publishing.

Davis, Todd Alexander. 2013. *Archery in Archaic Greece*. New York: PhD thesis, Columbia University. https://academiccommons.columbia.edu/doi/10.7916/D8QF912R.

Department of the Army. 1993. Operations: FM 105. Washington, D.C., Government Printing Office. https://cgsc.contentdm.oclc.org/digital/collection/p4013coll9/id/49.

Department of the Army. 2015. *The US Army Combat Vehicle Modernization Strategy*. Fort Eustis, VA: US Army Training and Doctrine Command. https://ec.militarytimes.com/static/pdfs/Master-CVMS-1300-01-SEP-2015.pdf.

DOD Dictionary. 2021. *DOD Dictionary of Military and Associated Terms*, edited by the Office of the Chairman of the Joint Chiefs of Staff. Washington, DC: The Joint Staff. https://irp.fas.org/doddir/dod/dictionary.pdf.

Downs, Bill. 1943. Red Army Tactics on the Eastern Front: 1943 Soviet Tank Desant. CBS Moscow Radio Broadcast March 5. Transcript at https://www.billdownscbs.com/2015/04/1943-russias-tank-desant-tactic.html

Edel, Elmar. 1949. KBo I 15+ 19, ein Brief Ramses' II mit einer Schilderung der Kadešschlacht. *Zeitschrift für Assyriologie* 15: 195–212.

European Council. 2013. *EU battlegroups*. European Council of the European Union press release, updated April 2013. https://www.consilium.europa.eu/uedocs/cms_data/docs/pressdata/en/esdp/91624.pdf.

Fecht, Gerhard. 1984a. Das 'Poème' über die Qadeš-Schlacht". In: *Festschrift Wolfgang Helck zu seinem 70. Geburtstag*, edited by Hartwig Altenmüller and Dietrich Wildung, 281–333. Hamburg: Buske.

Fecht, Gerhard. 1984b. Ramses II. und die Schlacht bei Qadesch (Qidša). Überlegungen im Anschluß an meinen Aufsatz in der Festschrift Helck (SAK). *Göttinger Miszellen* 80: 23–53.

Freedman, Lawrence. 2013. *Strategy. A History*. Oxford University Press.

Gabriel, Richard S. 2002. *The Great Armies of Antiquity*. Westport, CT: Praeger.

Gabriel, Richard S. 2004. *Empires at War*, vol. 1. *A Chronological Encyclopedia From Sumer to Persia*. Westport, CT: Greenwood Press.

Gabriel, Richard S. 2006. *Soldiers' Lives Through History. The Ancient World*. Westport, CT: Greenwood.

Gabriel, Richard S. 2009. *Thutmose III. The Military Biography of Egypt's Greatest Warrior King*. Washington, DC: Potomac Books.

Gabriel, Richard S. and Karen S. Metz. 1991. *From Sumer to Rome. The Military Capabilities of Ancient Armies*. Westport, CT: Praeger.

Gardiner, Alan H. 1947. *Ancient Egyptian Onomastica*, vol. 1. *Text*. Oxford: Oxford University Press.

Gardiner. Alan H. 1960. *The Kadesh Inscriptions of Ramesses II*. Oxford: Oxford University Press.

Gnirs, Andrea. 1996. *Militär und Gesellschaft. Ein Beitrag zur Geschichte des Neuen Reiches*. Studien zur Archäologie und Geschichte Altägyptens, 17. Heidelberg: Heidelberger Orientverlag.

Gnirs, Andrea. 1999. Ancient Egypt. In: *War and Peace in the Ancient World*, edited by Kurt A. Raaflaub and Nathan Rosenstein, 71–104. The Ancient World-Comparative Histories. Malden, MA: Blackwell.

Gnirs, Andrea. 2000. Militärtechnik, II. Ägypten. In *Der Neue Pauly* 8, 187–188. Stuttgart and Weimar: Metzler.

Gnirs, Andrea M. and J. Hoffmeier. 2001. Military. In: *The Oxford Encyclopedia of Ancient Egypt*, vol. 2, edited by Donald B. Redford et al., 400–412. Oxford: Oxford University Press.

Goedicke, Hans, ed. 1985. *Perspectives on the Battle of Kadesh*. Baltimore, MD: Halgo.

Goh, Wei Jun. 2014. *Survivability Design of Ground Systems for Area Defense Operation in an Urban Scenario*. Monterey, CA: Masters Thesis, Naval Postgraduate School. https://apps.dtic.mil/sti/citations/ADA619504.

Greenhalgh, P. A. L. 1973. *Early Greek Warfare. Horsemen and Chariots in the Homeric and Archaic Ages*. Cambridge: Cambridge University Press.

Greenwood, Ted. 1990. Why Military Technology is Difficult to Restrain. *Science, Technology, & Human Values* 15 (4): 412–429.

Gronow, Rees Howell. 1892. *Reminiscences and Recollections of Captain Gronow*, vol. 2. New York: Charles Scribner's Sons.

Guidotti, Maria Cristina and Franca Pecchioli Daddi, eds. 2002. *La battaglia di Qadesh. Ramesse II contro gli Ittiti per la conquista della Siria*. Livorno: Sillabe.

Healy, Mark. 1993. *The Warrior Pharaoh. Ramesses II and the Battle of Kadesh*. Oxford: Osprey Publishing.

Heidenreich, Susan M and Jonathon P. Roth. 2020. The Neurophysiology of Panic on the Ancient Battlefield. In: *New Approaches to Greek and Roman Warfare*, edited by Lee L. Brice, 127–138. Hoboken, NJ: Wiley Blackwell.

Heinz, Susanna Constanze. 2001. *Die Feldzugsdarstellungen des Neuen Reiches. Eine Bildanalyse*. Österreichisches Archäologisches Institut. Zweigstelle Kairo: Untersuchungen der Zweigstelle Kairo des Österreichischen Archäologischen Institutes 17 / Österreichische Akademie der Wissenschaften: Denkschriften der Gesamtakademie 18. Vienna: Österreichische Akademie der Wissenschaften.

Hickey, James B. 2004. *Surprise, Shock and Daring. The Future of Mobile, All-Arms Warfare*. The Land Warfare Paper 45. Arlington, VA: The Institute of Land Warfare. https://www.ausa.org/sites/default/files/LWP-45-Surprise-Shock-and-Daring-The-Future-of-Mobile-All-Arms-Warfare.pdf.

Hofer, Peter. 2006. Die Schlacht von Qadesh im Lichte eines modernen militärischen Führungsverfahrens. *Göttinger Miszellen* 208: 29–50.

Howarth, David. 1968. *Waterloo. Day of Battle*. New York: Galahad Books.

Jarymowycz, Roman Johann. 2001. *Tank Tactics. From Normandy to Lorraine*. Boulder, CO: Lynne Rienner Publications.

Keena, Monroe Joshua. 2011. Demonstration of Decision Support Tools for Evaluating Ground Combat System Survivability, Lethality, and Mobility at the Tactical, Operational, and Strategic Levels of War. Austin: PhD Thesis, University of Texas. https://repositories.lib.utexas.edu/bitstream/handle/2152/ETD-UT-2011-08-3781/KEENA-DISSERTATION.pdf?sequence=1&isAllowed=y.

Kelly, Terrance, John E. Peters, Eric Landree, Louis R. Moore, Randall Steeb, and Aaron L. Martin. 2011. *The U.S. Combat and Tactical Wheeled Vehicle Fleets: Issues and Suggestions for Congress*. Santa Monica: RAND Corporation.

Kenning, Jürgen. 2014. *Der Feldzug nach Kadesch. Das Ägypten des Neuen Reiches auf der Suche nach seiner Strategie*. Hildesheim: Georg Olms.

Kitchen, Kenneth A. 1994. *Ramesside Inscriptions, Translated and Annotated. Notes and Comments*. Oxford: Blackwell.

Krepinevich, Andrew. 2009. *7 Deadly Scenarios. A Military Futurist Explores War in the 21st Century*. New York: Bantam Books.

Kuschke, Arnulf. 1979. Das Terrain der Schlacht von Qadeš und die Anmarschwege Ramses' II. *Zeitschrift des Deutschen Palästina Vereins* 95: 7–35. [English translation by Donald Keith Mills, Aspley Guise, Sept–Oct 2015, Oct 2017: https://www.academia.edu/34800528/The_Terrain_of_the_Battle_of_Qadesh_and_the_Approach_Route_of_Ramses_II].

Kuschke, Arnulf. 1984. Qadesch–Schlacht. In: *Lexikon der Ägyptologie* 5, 31–37. Wiesbaden: Harrassowitz.

Leprévost, Thierry and Georges Bernage. 2002. *Hastings, 1066. Norman Cavalry and Saxon Infantry*. Bayeux: Heimdal.

Lichtheim, Miriam. 2006. *Ancient Egyptian Literature*, vol. 2: *The New Kingdom*. 2nd ed., Oakland, CA: University of California Press.

Ling, David H. 1993. Combined Arms in the Bradley Infantry Platoon. Fort Leavenworth, KS: Master's Thesis, US Army Command and General Staff College. https://apps.dtic.mil/sti/pdfs/ADA274095.pdf.

Littauer, Mary Aiken and Joost H. Crouwel. 1979a. *Wheeled Vehicles and Ridden Animals in the Ancient Near East*. Leiden: Brill.

Littauer, Mary Aiken and Joost H. Crouwel. 1979b. Military Use of the Chariot in the Aegean in the Late Bronze Age. *American Journal of Archaeology* 76: 145–157. [Reprinted in Littauer and Crouwel 2002: 75–99].

Littauer, Mary A. and Joost H. Crouwel. 1985, *Chariots and Related Equipment from the Tomb of Tutʿankhamūn*. Tutʿankhamūn's Tomb Series 8. Oxford: The Griffith Institute.

Littauer, Mary A. and Joost Crouwel. 1996. The Origin of the True Chariot. *Antiquity* 70 (270), 934–939. [Reprinted in Littauer and Crouwel 2002: 45–52].

Littauer, Mary A. and Joost Crouwel. 2002. *Selected Writings on Chariots and Other Early Vehicles, Riding and Harness*, edited by Peter Raulwing, 45–52. Leiden and Boston: Brill.

Liverani, Mario. 2001. *International Relations in the Ancient Near East, 1600–1100 B.C.* London: Palgrave Macmillan.

Loffler, Jürgen, Karsten Schiller, Manfred Schmitt, and Holger Hlüser. 2001. Cartronic System Architecture for Energy and Powertrain Management. In: *Proceedings of 3rd IFAC Workshop Advances in Automotive Control*, edited by Gerard L. Gissinger and Uwe Kiencke, 173–180. Karlsruhe: Elsevier Science.

Lorenz, Jürgen and Ingo Schrakamp. 2011. Hittite Military and Warfare. In: *Insights to Hittite History and Archaeology*, edited by Hermann Genz and Dirk Paul Mielke, 125–151. Leuven: Peeters.

Mauer, Gerlinde. 1985. Die Schlacht von Kadesch nach den Quellen aus Boghazköy. *Dielheimer Blätter zum Alten Testament und seiner Rezeption in der Alten Kirche* 21: 86–93.

Mayer, Walter. 1982. Eine Schlacht zwischen Ägyptern und Hethitern bei der Syrischen Stadt Qadesch im Jahre 1285 v. Chr. In: *Land des Baal. Syrien. Forum der Völker und Kulturen*, edited by Kay Kohlmeyer, 342–345. Mainz: von Zabern.

Mayer, Walter and Ronald Mayer-Opificius. 1994. Die Schlacht bei Qadeš. Der Versuch einer neuen Rekonstruktion. *Ugarit Forschungen* 29: 321–368.

McCrindle, John Watson. 1896. *The Invasion of India by Alexander the Great as described by Arrian, Q. Curtius, Diodoros, Plutarch and Justin*. New York: Barnes and Noble. [Reprint 1969].

McKeever, K. H. 1997. *Electrolyte and Water Balance in the Exercising Horse. Nutrition Manual for Veterinarians*. St. Louis, MO: AAEP and Purina Mill.

McKeever, K. H. and Robert A. Lehnhard. 2014. Physiology of Acid–Base Balance and Fluid Shifts with Exercise. In: *The Athletic Horse. Principles and Practice of Equine Sports Medicine*, edited by David Hodgson, 69–87. St. Louis: Elsevier.

Milevski, Lukas. 2014. Asymmetry is Strategy, Strategy is Asymmetry. *Joint Forces Quarterly* 75 (4): 77–83.

Military Field Manuals FM3-90. No date. Chapter 14 'Troop Movement'. https://www.nuui.com/Sections/Military/Field_Manuals/FM3-90/ch14.htm#:~:text=During%20movement%2C%20elements%20within%20a,an%20undesirable%20accordion%2Dlike%20effect.

Monash, John. 2020: *The Australian Victories in France in 1918*. Frankfurt am Main: Outlook.

Moorey, P. R. S. 1986. The Emergence of the Light, Horse-Drawn Chariot in the Near-East c. 2000–1500 B.C. *World Archaeology* 18: 196–215.

Murnane, William J. 1990. *The Road to Kadesh: A Historical Interpretation of the Battle Reliefs of King Sety I at Karnak*. Second Edition Revised, Chicago: The Oriental Institute of the University of Chicago.

Neu, Erich. 1974. *Der Anitta-Text*. Studien zu den Boğazköy-Texten. Wiesbaden: Harrassowitz.

Obsomer, Claude. 2016. La bataille de Qadech de Ramsès II. Les n'arin, sekou tepy et questions d'itinéraires. In: *De la Nubie à Qadech/From Nubia to Kadesh. La guerre dans l'Égypte ancienne/War in Ancient Egypt*, edited by Christina Karlshausen and Claude Obsomer, 81–170. Brussels: Safran.

Piggott, Stuart. 1983. *The Earliest Wheeled Transport from the Atlantic Coast to the Caspian Sea*. London: Thames and Hudson.

Piggott, Stuart. 1992. *Wagon, Chariot and Carriage. Symbol the Status in the History of Transport*. London and New York: Thames and Hudson.

Pinheiro, Elias Manuel Morgado. 2010. *The Origin and Spread of the War Chariot*. Lisbon: PhD thesis, Universidade Nova de Lisboa.

Radner, Karen, Nadine Moeller, and Daniel T. Potts, eds. 2022. *The Oxford History of the Ancient Near East*, vol. 3. *From the Hyksos to the Late Second Millennium BC*. Oxford :Oxford University Press.

Raulwing, Peter. 2000. *Horses, Chariots and Indo-Europeans. Foundations and Methods of Chariotry Research from the Viewpoint of Comparative Indo-European Linguistics*. Archaeolingua, Series Minor 9. Budapest: Archaeolingua Alapítvány.

Raulwing, Peter and Juliet Clutton-Brock. 2009. The Buhen Horse: Fifty Years after its Discovery (1958–2008). *Journal of Egyptian History* 2 (1–2): 1–106.

Rovetta, Alberto, Iskander Nasry, and Abeer Helmi. 2000. The Chariot of the Egyptian Pharaoh Tut Ankh Amun in 1337 BC. Kinematics and Dynamics. *Mechanism and Machine Theory* 35 (7): 1013–1031.

Sagona, Antonio and Paul Zimansky. 2009. *Ancient Turkey*. London: Routledge.

Sandor, Bela. 2004a. The Rise and Decline of the Tutankhamun-Class Chariot. *Oxford Journal of Archaeology* 23 (2): 153–175.

Sandor, Bela. 2004b. Tutankhamun's Chariots: Secret Treasures of Engineering Mechanics. *Fatigue & Fracture of Engineering Materials & Structures* 27 (7): 637–646.

Santosuosso, Antonio. 1996. Kadesh Revisited: Reconstructing the Battle Between the Egyptians and the Hittites. *The Journal of Military History* 60 (3): 423–444.

Schivelbusch, Wolfgang. 2014. *The Railway Journey. The Industrialization of Time and Space in the Nineteenth Century*. Berkeley and Los Angeles: University of California Press.

Schmitt, John F. 2002. *A Practical Guide for Developing and Writing Military Concepts*. Red Team. Working Paper #02-4. McLean, VA: Hicks & Associates. https://www.navedu.navy.mi.th/stg/databasestory/data/youttasart/youttasarttalae/bigcity/United%20States/1.dart_paper.pdf.

Schrakamp, Ingo. 2013. Warfare, Ancient Near East. In: *The Encyclopedia of Ancient History*, edited by Roger S. Bagnall, 7046–7048. Chichester: Wiley-Blackwell.

Schulman, Alan R. 1962. The N'rn at the Battle of Kadesh. *Journal of the American Research Center in Egypt* 1: 47–52.

Schulman, Alan R. 1963. The Egyptian Chariotry: A Reexamination. *Journal of the American Research Center in Egypt* 2: 75–98.

Schulman, Alan R. 1964. *Military Rank, Title, and Organization in the Egyptian New Kingdom*. Berlin: Hessling.

Schulman, Alan R. 1981. The N'rn at Kadesh Once Again. *Journal of the Society for the Study of Egyptian Antiquities* 11: 7–19.

Schulman, Alan R. 1995. Military Organization in Pharaonic Egypt. In: *Civilizations of the Ancient Near East*, vol. 1, edited by Jack M. Sasson, 289–391. New York and London: Scribner.

Searles, P. J. 1924. The Tactics of the Battle of Kadesh. *The Military Engineer* 16 (90): 456–457.

Shaw, Ian. 2001. Egyptians, Hyksos and Military Technology: Causes, Effects or Catalysts? In: *The Social Context of Technological Change. Egypt and the Near East, 1650–1550 BC*, edited by Andrew J. Shortland, 59–72. Oxford: Oxbow.

Simpkin, Richard E. and John Erickson. 1987. *Deep Battle. The Brainchild of Marshal Tukhachevskii*. London: Brassey's Defence.

Spalinger, Anthony. 1981. Notes on the Military in Egypt During the XXVth Dynasty. *Journal of the Society for the Study of Egyptian Antiquities* 11: 37–58.

Spalinger, Anthony. 1985. Notes on the Reliefs of the Battle of Kadesh. In Goedicke 1985, 1–42.

Spalinger, Anthony. 2002. *The Transformation of an Ancient Egyptian Narrative. P. Sallier III and the Battle of Kadesh*. Göttinger Orientforschungen 4, Reihe Ägypten 40. Wiesbaden: Harrassowitz.

Spalinger, Anthony. 2003 The Battle of Kadesh: The Chariot Frieze at Abydos. *Ägypten und Levante / Egypt and the Levant* 13: 163–199.

Spalinger, Anthony. 2005. *War in Ancient Egypt. The New Kingdom*. Oxford: Blackwell.

Spalinger, Anthony. 2013. Egyptian Chariots: Departing for War. In Veldmeijer and Ikram 2013, 237–256.

Spalinger, Anthony. 2018a. *Ramesses II. Pharaoh and Warrior. Leadership under Fire. The Pressures of Warfare in Ancient Egypt*. Paris: Éditions Soleb.

Spalinger, Anthony. 2018b. Mathematical Factors of the Battle of Kadesh. In: *Feasts and Fights. Essays on Time in Ancient Egypt*, edited by Anthony J. Spalinger, 89–107. New Haven: Yale Egyptological Institute.

Spruytte, Jean. 1983. *Early Harness Systems. Experimental Studies. A Contribution to the History of the Horse*. London: Allen.

Stillman, Nigel and Nigel Tallis. 1984. *Armies of the Ancient Near East 3000 B.C. to 539 B.C. Organisation, Tactics, Dress and Equipment*. Devizes: Wargames Research Group.

Sturm, Josef. 1996. *La guerre de Ramsès II contre les Hittites. Der Hettiterkrieg Ramses' II*. Translation from German by Claude Vandersleyen. Connaissance de l'Egypte Ancienne 6. Bruxelles: Connaissance de l'Egypte Ancienne.

Trimm, Charlie. 2017. *Fighting for the King and the Gods. Survey of Warfare in the Ancient Near East*. Resources for Biblical Study 88. Atlanta: SBL Press.

Trout, R. S. 1992. Missing the Deep Battle. U.S. Marine Corps Command and Staff College. https://www.globalsecurity.org/military/library/report/1992/TRS.htm.

Turchin, Peter, Thomas E. Currie, Edward A. L. Turner, and Sergey Gavrilets. 2013. War, Space, and the Evolution of Old World Complex Societies. *PNAS* 110 (41): 16384–16389. DOI: 10.1073/pnas.1308825110.

United States War Department. 1944. War Department Field Manual FM 17-40: Armored Infantry Company. Washington, DC: U.S. Government Printing Office.

Veldmeijer, Andre J. and Salima Ikram, eds. 2013. *Chasing Chariots. Proceedings of the First International Chariot Conference*. Leiden: Sidestone.

Veldmeijer, Andre J. and Salima Ikram, eds. 2018. Chariots in Ancient Egypt. The Tano Chariot. A Case Study. *Chariots. Proceedings of the First International Chariot Conference*. Leiden: Sidestone.

Vergauwen, David and Ive De Smet. 2017. From Early Farmers to Norman Borlaug – the Making of Modern Wheat. *Current Biology* 27 (17): R853–R909. DOI: 10.1016/j.cub.2017.06.061.

Wass de Czege, Huba. 2010. Winning the Cyberelectromagnetic Dimension of 'Full Spectrum Operations'. *Military Review* March–April 2010. 20–32. https://www.armyupress.army.mil/Portals/7/militaryreview/Archives/English/MilitaryyReview_20100430_art006.pdf.

von der Way, Thomas. 1984. *Die Textüberlieferung Ramesses' II. zur Qadeš-Schlacht. Analyse und Struktur*. Hildesheimer Ägyptologische Beiträge 22. Hildesheim: Gerstenberg.

Weingartner, Steven. forthcoming. When Chariots Collide: Understanding the Battle of Kadesh as a Clash of Competing Chariot Technologies and Tactical Systems. In: ICH 10: Proceedings of the 10th International Congress of Hittitology at the Institute for the Study of Ancient Cultures of the University of Chicago (formerly The Oriental Institute of the University of Chicago), August 28–September 1, 2017.

Welles, C. Bradford. 1963. *Diodorus of Sicily*, vol. 8, Books XVI, 66–95; XVII. Loeb Classical Library 422. Cambridge, MA: Harvard University Press.

Wernick, Nicholas E. 2013. K(no)w More Spears from the Backs of Chariots: Problems with the Battle of Kadesh's Thrusting Spears. *Journal of Ancient Egyptian Interconnections* 5 (2): 48–51.

Wernick, Nicholas E. 2014. *The Logistics of the New Kingdom Egyptian Military in the Levant*. Liverpool: PhD thesis, University of Liverpool. https://livrepository.liverpool.ac.uk/18573/1/WernickNic_May2014_18573.pdf.

Wiegand, Brian P. 2018. *Ancient Mass Properties Engineering*. https://www.researchgate.net/publication/324279809_ANCIENT_MASS_PROPERTIES_ENGINEERING.

Wiener, Craig J. 2010. *Penetrate, Exploit, Disrupt, Destroy: The Rise of Computer Network Operations as a Major Military Innovation*. Fairfax, VA: PhD thesis, George Mason University. https://mars.gmu.edu/items/0038844a-731b-4175-942e-af22f11aeabf

Wong, Luhai. 2016. *Systems Engineering Approach to Ground Combat Vehicle Survivability in Urban Operations*. Monterey, CA: Master's Thesis, Naval Postgraduate School. https://apps.dtic.mil/sti/pdfs/AD1030159.pdf.

Zaloga, Steven J. 1999. Soviet Tank Operations in the Spanish Civil War. *Journal of Slavic Military Studies* 12 (3): 134–165. http://bobrowen.com/nymas/soviet_tank_operations_in_the_sp.htm.

Index

Pagination in italics indicate that a term is mentioned in the footnotes.

A

Abbott, Henry William Charles (1807–1859), 268
Abu Simbel relief, depicting infantry phalanx, 302
Acemhöyük, *104*, 246
Geraki (South–East Laconia, Greece), 3; acropolis, 11
Adoption of mounted archery of the Hu tribes by King Wuling of Zhao 赵武灵王, 239
Aegean Prehistory, 11
Afghanistan, 33
African savannah, 264
Agate, 231, 233
Agriculture, 226
Aim of the manoeuvre battle: the destruction of the enemy via annihilation, 285
Aim of the set–piece battle: the defeat of the enemy via attrition, 285
Akhal–Teke, 67
Akhenaten, *18*, 73
Alaca Höyük, 92
Alakul archaeological cultures (ca. 2050–1650 BCE), 125, 191
Alakul Cluster cheekpieces, 162, 168–172
Alakul Culture (ca. 1900–1450 BCE), 158, 169, 172, 177
Alakul period, 126, 138, 141 f., 147 f.
Alakul quadrant, 159, 161–164, 172
Alalakh, 105
Alcohol, 227
Aleppo (Halab), 89, 93–97, 288–291
Alexander the Great (356–333 BCE), 278 f.
Algeria, 256 f., 264, 266, 268 f.
Algiers, 264
Altdöbern, *114*
Altynbekov, Kyrym, 50 f.
Amarna, 4, 61, 63, 71, 72, 83; check rowel, 83; grooms, 77; period, 68, 70, 83; princess poking horse with a goad, 75; reliefs with chariot horses, 71; royal family, 73; tablets, 22; tomb of Meryre, 73
Amenemhab (end of the 18th Dynasty), 277
Amenhotep (Amenophis) II (1438–1412 BCE), 74 f., 78, *267*, 279 f.; carnelian plaque, 74; TT 95, Tomb of Meri (reign of Amenhotep II), 249
Amenhotep (Amenophis) III (1386 to 1349 BCE / 1388 to 1351 BCE/1350 BCE), 18, 246 f.; wheel hub, 246–248
American Indians, *116*
AMS radiocarbon dates, 138
Amulet, made from a horse tail vertebra, 144; made from the canine tooth of a wolf, 147
Amun Camp of Ramesses II at Kadesh, 284, 290–292, 294–298, 300–302

Anatolia, 18, 23, 28, *29*, 33, 89, 93, 95, 97, 104, 153, 179 f., 246, *249*, 299
Ancient harnessing, 3, 6, 183, 255, 258, 265
Ancient Near East, 11, 15 ff., 153, 245 f., *273*
Ancient principality of Guo, 188
Andreas, Friedrich Carl (1846–1930), 18
Andrieşescu, Ioan G. (1888–1944), 111
Andronovo culture, 47 f., 182, 201, 208
Andronovo dishes, 189
Andronovo Pictorial Tradition (APT), 190 f.
Animal bones, 112, 114, 133, 139, 145, 149
Animal décor at Majiayuan, 238
Animal products, 61. See also Rawhide and Leather.
Animal representational types decorating gold and silver ornamental plaques, 238
Animal–shaped plaques, 233
Anitta of Kuššara (ca. 1740–1725 BCE), 274
Antechamber, 83. See also Chamber.
Antelope, 64, 182, 191
Antiquities dealer. See Tano, Georges.
Anthony, David W., 31, 48–50, 131
Antler, 151 ff., 203, 207, 210; antler bone carving, 126; cheekpieces, 5, 48, 103, 105, 109, 111, *112*, 114, 116, 128 f., 132, 134, 138–141, 144, 147, 148, 208, 210; elk 168, 109; plaques, 125; tines, 151
Anyang, Henan, 6, 199 ff., 206, 208 f.; horses appearing in great numbers in burial contexts along with chariots, 199; early horse and chariot burial context at Anyang, 200 ff.
Appliquéd decoration, 64
APT code fragments, 190
Arab Syrian Republic, 273
Arabians, 67
Arcalia (Hungarian Arokalja), 115
Archer, 91, 105, 182–187, 191
Archery, 12, 239, 277–282, 286, 295, 297, 304
Arisman, 112
Arkaim, settlement, 49, 126
Armed anthropomorphic figures (archers, opposing club–bearers, charioteers), 182
Armenia, 26, 251, 253
Armouries (ku 庫), 216, 219
Armoury complex, 189
Armoury, of the Qin County of Qianling, 216, 219
Arnapuwa, *16*
Arrapḫa, *16*
Arrow, 105, 183 f., 187, 189, 200, 209, *217*, *221*, 264, 279–283, 293, 295–301, 304
Arrowheads, 127, 138, 144, 186; bone, 141 f., 144; 146 f.; bronze, 189; flint, 139, 143 f., 167; horn, 189; metal, 167; stone, 139, 148
Arslantepe, *98*
Artificer's Record, 215 f.

Arwa, *16*
Aryan/Aryans, self designation of the peoples of Ancient India and Ancient Iran who spoke Aryan languages, 15
Arzhan I burial mound, 188 f.
Ashmolean Museum, Oxford, 74, 83, 247
Asia Minor, 15, 22, 24
Ass. See Donkey.
Assyrian palace reliefs, 252
Assyrian triga, 260
Astralagus, 144
Atshisu, Bestamak, 187
Aunjetitz culture, 114
Auul Kasym Amanzholov, 142
Avesta, 18, 22, 26, 34
Awl, 143 f., 146 f.; bronze, 138; metal, 137
Ax chariots (*fuche* 斧車), 221
Axle, 29–31, 48, 50–52, 62, 64, *97*, 99, 115, 125, 128, 130 f., 141 f., 171, 185–187, 202, 206, 226, 233, 245, 259–261, 264–266, 274–276, 285, 305; rear, 31, 50, 52, 186, 259 f., 264, 266, 276; square–ended, 245
Axle block, 62
Ayat River, 141. See also Karagaily–Ayat River.
Azurite, 138

B

Babino, 113; culture, 166; pottery, 168. See also Srubnaya.
Babylonia, 16, 20, 22, 105, 179
Babylonians, 21 f.
Bactria–Margiana archaeological complex. See BMAC.
Baggage train of battlegroups for transporting camp and field equipage, 286
Baifu burial, 188
Bailiff of the Armoury (*ku sefu* 庫嗇夫), 219
Baked clay, 151
Bækkedal hoard (Late Bronze Age, Denmark), 116
Bakun period, at Tol–e Nurabad, 112
Balanbash, settlement, 166–169, 177
Bands, 209; coloured appliquéd, 64; of rawhide, 268; T–shaped pattern decorative, 209; zigzag decorative, 209
Bangyou, Ding, 226
Banners, 216, 234. See also Flags.
Barb horses, 67 f.
Barbary, 68 f.
Bashkiria, 167, 169, 177, 180
Battle of Gaugamela (331 BCE), 278
Battle of Hastings (1066 AD), 280
Battle of Kadesh (1274 / 1275 BCE), 6 f., 68; 273 ff.; Battle Phase I, Shock: Re Destroyed, 289 ff.; Battle Phase II, Siege: Amun Embattled, 296 ff.; Battle Phase III Melee: Battlegroup Amun Rescued, 302 ff.; may be understood as three distinct battles, 283 f. See also Battlegroup and Ramesses.
Battle of the Little Big Horn, 79
Battle of Megiddo (ca. mid–15th century BCE), 283
Battle of the Hydaspes (326 BCE), 279
Battle of Waterloo (1815), 279
Battle order of an Egyptian chariotry grouping, 281
Battle scenes, 75, 189, 191

Battle wagon, 274
Battlefield, 6, 49, 75, 79, 86, 215, 217, 273, 276, 279, 281 f., 284 f., 287, 291, 294, *296*, 297 ff.
Battlefield command, 297
Battlegroup (or divison) of Ramesses II, 284; 286 f., 290–292, 293 f., 297, 300–302; Amun, 288, 290; Nearin, 284, 288, 297, 301, 303; Ptah, 288–291, *294*, 297, 303; Re, 284, 288, 290–292, 295, *296*, 297; Seth, 288 f.; 297; baggage train, 289
Battlespace, 275, 277, 280, 282 f., 286, 288; movement to contact, 275, 280, 292, 295
Bayesian model, 32
Bayonet, 279
Beads, 142, 144, 149, 232 f.
Beal, Richard, *286*, 288
Beamish Museum Town Livery Stables, United Kingdom, 73
Begazy–Dandybai, 189; Begazy–Dandybai period (14th–10th centuries BCE), 189; Begazy–Dandybai and Sargary–Alekseyevo, ceramics, 184. See also Karasuk.
Behaviour, of horses, 5, 67, 69–71, 74, 77 f., 267, 278, 294, *296*; behavioural problems, 256
Beijing, *188*, 190
Bekaa Valley region, 284
Belt plaques, 232
Bending jig, 248
Bending process of wood used for chariots, 249; timber bending for the V–spoked Egyptian wheels, 248 f.
Bennu bird, 68
Bentwood, elements, 251; parts, *252*, 253
Berber horses, 67
Berel, Altai Mountains, 232, 238 f.
Berettyó settlement (Hungarian Danube region), 171
Berlik Cemeteries (Northern Kazakhstan), 125, 127, 130, 137 f.
Berrard, Jean–Luc, 257
Bestamak Cemetery, 127, 138, 169
Bibby, Miriam, 71
Big carts (*dache* 大車), 224
Birch bark, 238, 246
Bird, 116; bennu bird, 68; bird shaped objects, 95 f.; bronze chariot from Monteleone decorated with images of birds of prey, 189; harnessed birds, 103; protomes, 116; *rekhyt* bird, 77; stylised S–shaped bird–heads, 236; wagon model ending in bird–heads, 109
Bit rings, 75
Bits, *72*, 85, 116 f., 125, 130, 134, 152 f., 173, 185 f., 203–205, 207; bronze, 105; made from various materials, 70; early bits most probably made of organic materials (soft cords or rigid bars of wood, antler), 203
Black–figure neck amphora 600–590 BCE (National Museum, Athens), 261
Blades, 278. See also *ge* blades and Shoulder–Blades.
Blanket, 75; saddle blankets, 112
Blinkers, 73, 276
Blitzkrieg–style thrusts, 287
Blondheitskult (cult of blondness), 18

Blood, 69, 301; blood–stained reins, 97 f.; blood relatives, 189
Bloodshed, 296
BMAC (Bactria–Margiana archaeological complex), 190
Boar tusk, *114*, 144
Boat, *104*, 217, 259; building, 251
Bochkarev, Vadim S., 152
Body garments, 209
Body ornaments, 232, 239
Body trapper, 276
Bodyguard, elite Sherden swordsmen, 288, 297–299; royal, 90
Börker–Klähn, Jutta (1942–2019), 92, *93*, 94, *96*
Boguslav settlement (Ukraine, Dnepropetrovsk region, Pavlograd district), 168
Boguslav, 163; settlement, 168
Bolingbroke, Henry (Henry IV, c. 1367–1430), 67
Bones, animal bones, 133 f., 139, 145; artefacts, 165; awl, 147; and antler cheekpieces, 103 ff., 153 ff.; arrows, 189; arrowheads, 142, 144, 146 f.; bushings, 164; caprid, 140, 147; carving, 126; cone–shaped bone nails, 142; funerary objects, 231; horse bones, 53, 128, 137, 139, 140, 143 ff.; harpoon, 144; human bones, 13, 139, 141, 144 ff.; javeline, 189; jawbone, 143, 146; limb bones, 132, 141, 149; measurements, 129; oracle bones, 190, 200, 211; pegs, 156; pelvic, 143, 146; plaque, 146, 191; of sacrificed domestic horses, 125; bone shaft, 144; sheep/goat, 142; spatula, 144; spearheads, 189; spindle whorl, 139; studs, 164; tubular bones of chariot horses, 137; of large ungulates, 153; wolf, 140, yoke saddle decoration, 233. See also Cheekpieces and Oracle Bones.
Boroffka, Nikolaus, warning against a one–sided Sintashta fascination, 33
Botai, 188
Bovids, 30, 33, 71, 104 f., *114*, 182, 190 f.
Bovine, 97, 140
Bow, 48, *96*, 105, 171, 181, 183 f., 186 f., 191, 209, 264, 276, 278 f., 280, 295, 298 f., 305. See also Arrow, Composite Bow, Cross–Bow, Dagger, Javelin, Spears, Sword, Weapons.
Bow–Cases, 62–64
Bow–Shaped Objects, 200 f., 208
Bowshot, 280–282, 293, 295
Bowstring, 280
Brad, Eastern Romania, 169; special Brad–type cheekpiece, 169
Bradley series (Badley Fighting Vehicle (BFV), 281
Braking element, 259
brand mark, on the right shoulder of a horse, 225
Breast traction, 258 f., 261–264
Breastcollar. See Collar.
Breasted, James Henry (1865–1935), 283, *286*
Breeds, 67 f., *262*
Breuil, Henri (1877–1961), 264
Bridle, 33, 35, 52 f., 70, 74 f., 85, 117, 125, 129 f., 139, 151, 153, 170 f., 173, 199 f., 201–204, 206 f., 208 f.; bridle accessories, 151; bridle bits, 134, 152 f., 162, 173; bridled cattle, *85*; bitless, 72; designed for onagers and donkeys or their hybrids (according to E. E. Kuzmina), 153; driving chariot without bridles, 35; fittings, 199; harness, 32; horse bridles and harness of the 'chariot cultures' (*kolesnichnye kul'tury*), 52; leather, 208; made of metal, 33; made of organic materials, 33; manufacture, 168; ornaments (bronze), 199; soft–bit bridle, 125; straps, 163, 200, 208–210; from Tell Haror as part of a Bronze Age shrine, 33; trapezoidal disc–shaped cheekpieces with inserted sharpened spikes, 113; two bridle systems, 153; wood, *116*
Bronze, accessories, 199; adze, 141; animal decoration, 238; arrows, 189; arrowheads (two–bladed), 189; artefacts, 146; awl, 138; axe, 209; bits, 105, 151, 203 f.; bridle ornaments, 199; bosses, *266*; cast bronze figures, 237; C–shaped object with prongs, 204; chariot from Monteleone, 189; as part of chariot manufacture, 248; cheekpieces, 116, 151 ff., 200; decorative elements, 235; Department of Archaeology of the Bronze Age at the Institute of Archaeology (the Russian Academy of Sciences, Moscow), 54; drawings on Hittite cuneiform tables, 89 ff.; 'fortified' settlements, 49; Harpoon, 144; headstall ornaments, 201, 203; helmets, 280; hook, 138; horsegear, 108; hypothesis of the introduction of chariots into the Ancient Near East, including Asia Minor and Late Bronze Age Greece, 24 ff.; inscriptions, 211; javelins, 189; knife, 138, 144, 146; used for linchpin shafts, *266*; miniature bronze chariots, 216; models of spoked wheels from the Bronze Age from the Carpatho–Danubian region, 114; models found in the mausoleum of Emperor Shihuang, *183*; motive of curved hemlines (*geschwungene Säume*) in the Late Bronze, 95; naves, 115 f.; used for outer nave hoops, *266*; ornaments, 148, 199, 209; small pins used in attaching decorative roundels, *266*; plaque–pendant, 138; plaques, 191, 236 f.; (animal shaped), 233; plaque–like attachments for chariots, 236; production, 126; ring, 144; scale armour, 299; Shang ritual bronzes, 209 f.; (bronze–plated) shoulder strap of Egyptian horse harness, 276; sickles, 138; spikes, 83; spearhead, 138, 146; terminals, *266*; tool, 138; (sickle–shaped), vessels (ritual), 234; wagon model with cauldron from Bujoru with iron axles, 115; weapons, 199, 232; wheels, 115; complete bronze wheels suggested for Saharan chariots, 266; wire (bronze or copper), 143; Zhou bronzes, 209; zoomorphic finials with rings, 188
Bronze Age. Bronze Age Greece, 3; Bronze Age in the Carpatho–Danubian Region, 5, 103; Bronze Age horse–and–chariot complexes, 36; Bronze Age cheekpieces across northern Eurasia (Volga–Urals, Don and Dnieper), the Carpathian–Danube region, Southern Greece, and Western Asia, 5; Bronze Age cemeteries of the Eurasian steppes, 142 f.; Bronze Age Eurasia, 47; Bronze Age cultures: Komarov, 113; Monteoru, 114; Noua Wietenberg, 114; Potapovka and Pokrovskaya, 154 ff.; Sintashta, 154 ff., 258; Srubnaya, 168; metal reinforcements nailed to the felloes, 267; transportation, 182; wheel makers, 246;

Early Bronze Age, 4; Early Bronze Age motive of Storm God mounting his chariot and standing on his chariot, 89 ff.; Early and Middle Bronze Age kurgan graves with wagons, 51; Late Bronze Age Anatolia, 93; Late Bronze Age and the Iron Age Anatolian kilts, 95; Late Bronze Age Bækkedal hoard from Denmark, 116; Late Bronze Age catalogue of chariot burials from the Eurasian Steppes, 137 ff.; Late Bronze Age burials of chariots from Germany, 114; across the steppes, 134; Late Bronze Age of Central Asia, 5; Late Bronze Age cheekpieces, 134, 280; Bronze Age chariot clay models from Dupljaja, Vojvodina, 109; Late Bronze Age chariotry and chariot warfare in the Near East, 6, 273 ff; Late Bronze Age climate of the Trans–Urals, 126; Late Bronze Age cremation and burial in urns, *114*; Late Bronze Age faunal assemblages, 107; Late Bronze Age graves in the Volga–Ural region indicate two–horse chariot, 48; Late Bronze Age Imamkulu relief, 93; Late Bronze Age petroglyphs, 131 f., 184; Late Bronze Age Piliny culture, 108; Late Bronze Age remains of actual chariots in graves in the Trans–Ural region, 47; Late Bronze Age rotating wheel technology, 130; Late Bronze Age rudimentary' representation bird shapes of wheeled vehicles, 96, 125 ff.; Late Bronze Age in the Trans–Ural region, 4; Late Bronze Age (Urnfield Period), 112; Late Bronze Age two-wheeled vehicles from the Eurasian steppes, 5; Middle and Late Bronze Age 'chariot cultures' (*kolesnichnye kul'tury*) in the Eurasian steppe and forest steppe, 53; Middle and Late Bronze Age of Central Asia, 179; Middle Bronze Age connection of Europe and the Caucasus, 52; Middle Bronze Age Kamenka–Liventsovka group, 166; Middle Bronze Age petroglyphs in Central Asia, 191; Middle Bronze Age spoked wheel models, 32; Middle Bronze Age Tumulus culture in Hungary, 197

Brooklyn Museum, New York, 247, 265, 268

Brooklyn wheel, 247 f., 265, 267 f. See also Wheel.

Brotherhood (*Männerbund*), 16, 35

Brownrigg, Gail, 11, *17*, 72, 183, 203, 206

Bryk, Jan, 113

Buckles, 53; metal, *165*, 232

Bujoru (Carpathian Basin), 115 f.

Bukivna (old name Bukówna), 113, 116

Bulgaria, 106, 180

Bulgarian Thrace, 263

Bull, 79, 168

Bull–drawn two–wheeled vehicle, 91 ff. See also Cart, Chariot, Wagon and Vehicle.

Bulletin (Egyptian source of the Battle of Kadesh), 283, *291*. See also Poem of Pentaur,

Bunker, Emma (1930–2021), 201

Bundesarchiv Berlin–Lichterfelde, 23

Bunnens, Guy, 93

Bureau of Chariots (*che cao* 車曹), 219

Burial, from Encs in Hungary – four spoked wheels, 32

Burial grounds, 126, 180, 189, 191

Burial rites, 48 f., 131

Buruktal River, 138

Büyükkale, 97

Byzantium, 258

C

C–shaped mouthpiece, 202, 205, 207; known from a small contemporary tomb M33 in Shang cemetery at Hougang (Anyang), 201

C–shaped object with prongs, 204–206

Cairo, *61*, 245, 248 f.

Calf, 91, 140, 145

Calibrated 14C data, 32; radiocarbon chronology, 106 f., 152, 179

Camel Corps *(Compagnie Méhariste)* of Hoggar, 256 f., 264

Camels, 34, 103, 180, 191, 256, 268, *294*. See also Two–Humped Camel.

Candelora, Danielle, 79

Cândeşti (burial), 111; settlement, 171

Canine tooth, 147

Canopy, 226

Caprid, 10, 147 f.

Caracole, half–turn of chariots, 281 f.

Carcass (calf and dog), 145

Cârlomăneşti, 109

Carnelian plaque Amenhotep II (ca. 1427–1401 BCE), 74

Carpathian Basin, 32 f., 35, 108 f., 112 f., 116 f.

Carpathian region, 5, 32, 34 f., 103 ff., 152, 159, 170

Carpathian–Danube cheekpieces, 158, 162

Carpatho–Danubian Region, 5, 103, 107, 109 ff.

Carpenter, 218

Carpet, 62

Carriage, 6, 71 f., 215 ff.; 222 ff., 235 f., 257, 262, *263*, 279; built in armouries (ku 庫), 219; canopy, 226; carriage horses, 223; with curtains, 218; deployment and management, 219; display of on tomb walls, 224; driving, 257; driver, 255; 'Entertainment carriages', 221; of envoys, 223; horse–drawn, 72, 87; light carriage (*yaoche*); 227; making of, 219 f.; for official communications, 223; for travel of functionaries, *pengche* 輧車 carriages, 217; platform without visible handrails, 187; prices, 226 f.; stored in the armouries, 219; technology, 223; travel by carriage influencing the development of tomb art, 224; used for civilian purposes, 222; women not allowed to ride in official carriages (Qin law), 223

Carrington–Farmer, Charlotte, 76

Cart, 6, 11, 32, 51, 130, 133 f., 181, 187, 208, 215 ff.; esp. 224 ff., 262, 286; 'big carts' (dache 大車), 224; clay models, 51; construction in Roman provinces, 11; definition, 1, 104; Egyptian army's supply carts, 288; fines for building inferior carts, 220; government's carts, 225 f.; greasing the axles of the carts, 225 f.; on the Hüseyindede vase A from the Çorum province, 97, *98*; *ju* carts, 225; loaned carts by the Qin state, 226; lubricartion during repair, 219; 'ox carts' (niuche 牛車), 224; ox–drawn, *98*, 235 f.; prices, 226 f., 286; travel distances for heavy and empty carts, 222, 225. See also Carriage, Chariot, Cart, Wagon.

Carter, Howard (1874–1939), 83, *246*, *267*

Casing, leather, 63 f.; of the Tano chariot, 63; T–shaped, 63
Cast bronze, 236 f.
Castration, of male bovids, 105
Cassin, Elena (1909–2011), 275
Casualties among the foot soldiers in battle, 278
Casualties, 278, 280, 289, 300
Catacomb culture, 32, 51, 130
Catalogue of Late Bronze Age chariot burials
from the Eurasian Steppes, 137 ff.
Catatonia, 301
Categories of cheekpieces dated to the second millennium BCE classified according to their shape, materials used in manufacture, and equid control techniques, 152
Cattle, 32, 49, 84 f., 180; wild, 191, 231 f., 258, 262, 264, 268, 287
Cavesson, 151
Cemeteries, Anyang, 199 f., 201; Baifu, *188*; Berlik, 125, 137 f.; Bestamak, 127, 138, 169; Bolshekaraganskiy, 167; Ilekshar, 162; Kamennyi Ambar 5, 32, 132, 138–140, 160, 167, 187; Kenes, 127; Komarovka, 134, 152; Krivoe Ozero, 125, 134, 140 f.; Maitan, 134; Majiayuan, 231 ff.; Monteoru, 112; Nanshangen, 190; Nikolayevka II, 127, 141 f.; Novoil'inovskiy 2, 129; Ozernoye, 127, 142; Ouren II, 164; Potapovka, 164, 166, 168; Shanshan, 128, 208; Sazagan, 167; Satan, 125, 128; Selezni–1 and –2, 165; Sintashta, 16, 125, 128, 133 f., 142–146, 152, 187; Shang, 209; Solntse II Cemetery, 127, 146 f.; Stepnoye, 127, 147 f.; Tabyldy, 134; Ulubai, 127, 148 f.; Utevka VI, 159, 163 f.; Uvarovskiy II, 164; Vetlyanka IV, *31*, 127, 149; Xibeigang, 201; Yanghai, 190, 208; Yuhuangmiao, 190; Zolotaya Gora, 165, 169. See also List of Cheekpieces Grouped According to Archaeological Cultures and Sites, 176–178
Central Asia, 34 f., 47, 110, 115, 125, 153, 159, 166 ff., 172; rock art (petroglyphs) with depictions of chariots, 179 ff.
Central Sahara, 256, 258, 264, *267*,
Ceramics, 75; Andronovo (Alakul, Fedorovo), 187; Begazy–Dandybai, 184; found in the chariot burials in Sintashta and Petrovka, 182 f.; bi–triangular style of goats as on Near Eastern painted ceramics, 190; Kamennyi Ambar 5, 187; depicting horse running freely wearing bridle/halter with lead rope dangling loose, 75; Sargary–Alekseyevo, 184; semantic connection and a similarity between two–component ornaments on ceramics in burials, 191; typology of the Kamennyi Ambar 5 cemetery, 32; vertical zigzags indicative of ceramic and cheekpiece decoration of Sintashta–Petrovka appearance in the chariot burials, 187; vessels, 127, 137–142, 144–149, *165*. See also Ostraca.
Ceremony, 5 f., 52, 103, 131, 215, 234
Cetra, 151
Chagar Bazar, equids in, 26
Chain, *85*, 151, 248
Chamber, burial, 31 f., 51 f., 83, 126–128, 130–133, 138–148, 180, 188, 232 f., 235, 238, 250, 277; rock cut, 249. See also Antechamber.

Champollion, Jean–François (1790–1832), *265, 267*
Charcoal, 112
Chariot, 14C data and the group of Sintashta and Petrovka chariots, 32; accessories, 64; carrying multiple–bolt arcuballistae, 221; actions taken by the enemy to stymie chariotry's movement and neutralise its mobility, 277; in the Aegean, 32, 103 f.; Akhenaten and Nefertiti kiss in a chariot, 73; Akkadian terminology, *97*; alleged chariots in catacomb burials and the Kurgan Tyagunova Mogila and the Bolshoi Ipatovskiy kurgan in the North Caucasus, 51 f.; archaeological indications for chariots, 108 ff.; in Bronze Age Greece, 3; in Assyria, 17, 20, 247–249; 251, 255, 258–260, 263, *287*; ax chariots (*fuche* 斧車), 221; in a battle scene from Taksai, 180; bell chariots, 221; as a new feature in the burial context in Wu Ding's time, 199; in the Carpathian Region, 103 ff.; in Central Asian Rock Art, 179 ff.; with mounted crossbows, 221; in China, 199 f., 215 ff., 231 ff.; cladding and decorative components, 63 f.; avoiding collisions in battle, 292; crew, 49, 227 f., 281 f., 293, 296 f.; See also Hittite Three–Man–Chariot; critical examination of prehistoric sources for chariots, 30–36; 'chariot cultures' (*kolesnichnye kul'tury*) – or the 'block of chariot cultures' – in the Eurasian steppe and forest steppe during the Middle and Late Bronze Age, 53; chariot desant, 294, 296; descriptions of chariots in the Bible, 15; definition of, 4, *15*, 30, 34, 103, 126; driving characteristics, 31; drum chariots, 221; placed in the earthen pit, 232; Egyptian, 3–6, 11, 15 ff., 30, 33 f., 48, 50, 52, 61 ff., 67 ff., 83 ff., 103–105, 125, 186, 188, 245 ff., 255, 258 f., 263, 265–267, 273 ff.; Greek imagery of chariots, 105; groupings, 189, 273, 275, 278 f., 284 f., 292 f., 303; strike force attacking Ramesses' Amun Camp of Ramesses II at Kadesh, 284, 290–292, 294–298, 300–302; introduction to Egypt, 28; in a relief from Medinet Habu, *28*; from the tomb of Meryre at Amarna, 73; from the Tomb of Tutankhamun, 70, 84; Tutankhamun in his chariot, 76; in the Eurasian Steppes, 48 ff.; elites, 35, 105, 240; in Etruria, 255, 260–262; used in executions, 222; firepower, 285, 304 f.; fittings 105, 199, 216, 232; Florence chariot. See s.v.; gauge and importance for stability and function, 31; general indications for the preconditions of chariot technology and use, 103–105; genesis of chariot technology, 32; heterogeneous Bronze Age horse–and–chariot complexes, 36; Hittite chariot design with emphasis on force mobility, 285, 305; Hittite chariot sources, 97 ff.; Hittite Horse Training Texts, 16; Hittite motive of Storm God mounting his chariot, 89 ff.; horse–chariot–complex, 103; for hunting tigers, 221 f.; image, 5, 68, 71 ff., 80, 103, 105, 237 f., 240, 256; of supposed blond, Nordic, Indo–Germanic chariot warriors with racial ideological content, 18; of camels used to transport both people and goods of chariots, 264; of a chariot or carriage under a roof 庫, 216; of 'entertainment chariots', 221; on Greek vase paintings from the 8th century BCE, 260–262; of storm god riding in vehicle,

97; of war scenes and actual chariots, 52, 54; Indian chariots, drawn by four horses and carrying a crew of six (two archers, two shield–bearers, and two drivers), 279; Indo–Aryan in the ancient Near East, 15 ff.; the so–called Indo–Aryan horse–and–chariot–ideology, 15 ff.; 31, 35; Indo–European *termini technici* for Horses and Chariots, 28 f.; in Inner Eurasia, 125 ff.; issues determining origins of horse and chariot cultures, 53 f.; in Italy before the Roman Empire, 3; leather, 61 ff.; Majiayuan Chariots, 231 ff.; chariot–making, 32, 219, 245; chariot reconstructions, 245 ff., 255 ff.; railing, 50; 62 f., *64*, 95, 129, 131; map of spoked wheel models and images of chariots, 106; in the Minusinsk basin and Mongolia, 208; Eduard Meyer's hypotheses of the introduction of chariots into the ancient Near East, 21 f.; Nubian chariot drawn by bridled cattle, *85*; origin, 15 ff; overturned chariots, 279, 301; *pars pro toto* grave goods representations of chariots, 31; pictorial motif from Egypt as proposed by F. Schachermeyr, 16, *26*, 28, 47; long poles erected, 221; and Proto–Indo–Europeans, 15 ff; research of chariots in the ancient Near East, 15 ff.; reconstruction of the Eurasian war chariot from Sintashta, 50 f.; replica of an Egyptian chariot, 84 f.; research in Slavic studies, 47 ff.; role in daily life, 215 ff.; in the Sahara. See Rock paintings, North Africa and Sahara; Fritz Schachermeyr's hypotheses of the introduction of chariots into the ancient Near East, Egypt and Bronze Age Greece, 24–28; sharp turns, 256, 303; the Sintashta Chariots and the Question of origin of the 'true chariot', 48 ff.; speed, 34 f., 64, 84, 125, 130, 151, 282, 285, 287, 289, 292, *294;295*, 299, 302 f.; charging at speed, 299, 303; experience of speed, 19; concept of sport and speed, 19, 27; manoeuverability and turning ability at high speed, 34, 61, 184, 258, 262, 264, 268, 274, *275*, 278–280; image of a chariot or carriage under a roof 庫(maybe to be interpreted as 'carriage house'), technical and typological interpretation of the Proto–Indo–European *termini technici* for horses and chariots, 29 ff; textual and archaeological source of early Chinese chariots, 215 ff.; the so–called 'true chariot', 34, 48; from the temple at Karnak, 71 f.; in the Ullikummi Myth, 97 f.; as war and prestige items in Shang society, 199; chariot warfare in the Near Eastern Late Bronze Age and the Battle of Kadesh, 273 ff.; Joseph Wiesner's hypotheses of the introduction of chariots into the ancient Near East, 23 f. See also Carriage, Cart, Florence Chariot, Wagon.

Chariot models (ancient and replicas), 109, 247 f., 255 ff. (Jean Spruytte)

Charioteer, 19, 21, 34, 49, 53, 62, 64, 73, 79, 86, 97, 126, 154, 171, 180–188, 191, 259, 264, 266–268, 275, 278 f., 281, 296–299, 301, 303 f.; Ramesses has a number of charioteers beheaded who had deserted him, 304

Chariotry, 4, 6 f., 15, 17, 19 f.; attack methodology, 279

Chariotry research, 30, 36, 49, *61*, 79, 114, 273 ff.; of Eduard Meyer, Joseph Wiesner and Fritz Schachermeyr, 21 ff.

che/ju 車, used for all vehicles, machines, and other apparatuses that used wheels, 216

Chechushkov, Igor V., 49, 208

Check Rowel, 70, 75 f., 83 ff.

Cheek straps, 202 f.

Cheekpieces, 32, 47, 53, 85, 125 f., 131, 183; 187; the Alakul cluster of cheekpieces, 162 f.; ancient Near East, 49; antler, 48; bone cheekpieces, 48, 103 ff.; bone cheekpieces in the Carpathian Region, 103 ff; esp. 109 ff.; of the Danube Region, 169–171; early cheekpiece development in the Late Shang Dynasty, 199 ff. (plaque–shaped, plaque–shaped with animal design, L–shaped, and rod–shaped); early cheekpieces in Eurasia, 125 ff.; the Eurasian group of cheekpieces, 166–169 (with Appendix 137 ff.; 151 ff.); cultural–typological chart of cheekpiece evolution according to chronological diagrams of the European Late Bronze Age, 173; in the Danube region and Mycenae, 170; discussion in the context of horse harnessing, 52 f.; horses and cheekpieces, 128–130; critique towards the hypothesis of cheekpieces being regarded as main indicator of the use of a horse–drawn chariot and as key evidence, 35; list of cheekpieces grouped according to archaeological cultures and sites, 176–178; of Mycenaean Greece, 171 f.; in the Pontic–Caspian steppe, 47; the Petrovka cluster of cheekpieces, 113 f.; the Pokrovskaya cluster of cheekpieces, 164–166; the Potapovka cluster of cheekpieces, 163 f.; the Sintashta cluster of cheekpieces, 159–161; transformation of cheekpieces through the centuries in terms of cultural–typological classification, 172 f.; types of cheekpieces (rod–type, shield–type, flat–type) 151 ff.

Chechushkov, Igor, 49, 208

Chelyabinsk (Southern Urals), 126, 152

Cherednichenko, Nikolay N., 48, 52

Cherlenok, Evgeny, *31*, 49

Chisel, 138 f., 246

Chivalry (*Ritterlichkeit*) and charioteers, chariot drivers, 16, 30

Chivalrous Mariannus (*ritterlicher Mariannus*) as proposed by F. Schachermeyr, 28

Chronology, 5, *26*, 54, 104, 111, 115, 117, 125, 151 f., 172, 188, 207; of the early horse and chariot burial context at Anyang, 200 f.; Eastern European chronology of the Late Bronze Age after Bochkarev, 173; of the Eurasian steppe chariot complex and the related material culture of the Late Bronze Age, 123 ff.; Middle Chronology Babylonia, *26*; calibrated radiocarbon chronology of the the Mad'arovce culture and Transdanubian Encrusted Pottery, 106 f.; Helladic Bronze Age chronology after Furumark, 173; Mesopotamia, 54; long chronology, 179; of the Monteoru culture, *110*; radiocarbon chronology for Transylvania, 106; Reinecke's Middle European chronology, 172; Second Transition Period in the radiocarbon chronology system of Egypt, 179

Chu–style script on slips of bamboo, 216

Ciceu Corabia, 106

Clash of chariotry forces between the Hittites and the Egyptians involving two technologically different types of chariots with different tactical objectives, 273 ff.
Clay models, 51, 105–109
Clay nozzles, 146
Climate, 126, 249, 287
Club, 73, 96, 186 f., 191; club–bearer, 181 f.
Coachbuilder, 218
Codex Ḫammurapi, 20, 22
Collar, 109; modern, *85, 86*, 258 f., 261 f., 265; tensioning collar (*collier de serrage*) 268
Coloured appliquéd bands, 64
Comanche horse, 79
Composite Bow, 280, 282
Controller of Standards, 223
Controlling horse behaviour, 77 ff.
Copper, alloy rivets, 113; copper bronze wire, 143; ore, 147; pins, 64; side panels of chariots with bronze or copper discs, 285; smelting of, 126; shooting at copper targets, 279
Cornelius, Friedrich (1893–1976), *16*, 20
Corselets, made of bronze or leather scales or lamellae, 280
Cranium, horse, 128, 134, 137–140, 143–146, 148 f.
Crete, 22, 37, 251
Crimean Peninsula, 23
Coss–Bar Wheel. See Wheel.
Crossbow, 221
Crossbowmen, 225
Crouwel, Joost H., 1 ff., 11–13, 19, 48, *231*, 246–248, 253, 255, 260, 269, *274*, 275 bibliography, 7–9
Cult of blondness (*Blondheitskult*), 18
Cultural morphology (*Kulturmorphologie*) and chariotry research, 24
Cuneiform script, 89; KUB 20.76, 89 ff.
Cuneiform tablets, 15–18, 22
Curb bit, 151
Cursus clavularius, *258*
Cursus publicus, *258*
Cursus velox, 258
Curtius, see Quintus Curtius Rufus.
Cutting tools, 258
Cylinder seals, 93
Cyprus, 3, 11, 105

D
Dancers (Hittite), 92
Danube region/Carpathian–Danube region, 5, 151–153, 169–173, 177
Darius III, Achaemenid king, 278
De Garis Davies, Nina (1881–1965), 73
de La Broue, Salomon (ca. 1530–ca. 1610), 69
De la Guérinière, François Robichon (1688–1751), 69
Decker, Wolfgang (1941–2020), 19, 75, 78
Decomposition, 127; decomposition process, 145
Deer stones, 191, 208
Deer Stone–Khirigsuur Complex, 208
Delbrück Hans C. (1848–1929), 284

Delpeut, Lonneke, 68, *71*
Dent, Anthony, *67*
Diakonov, Igor M. (1915–1999), 21
Dietz, Albert, *91*
Dietz, Ute, 35
Diocletian (284–305 CE), *258*
Diodorus Siculus, 278
Disc–wheels, see Wheels.
DNA studies, 126, 128, 143
DOM2 line of domesticated horses, 104, 123, 128, 143
Domestication of Horses, 4, 15, 47, 53, 68, 104, 173, 191; of equines, 275
Don–Volga region, 154, 161, 164, 169
Donkey 22, 33, 68, 74, 85, 112, 152 f., 173, 262, 286 f.
Dorsal yoke. See Yoke.
Downs, William Randall 'Bill' (1914–1978), 293
Draught animals. See Bovids, Horses, Donkey.
Draught pole. See Pole.
Draught system, 260, 266
Driving or Riding (*Fahren und Reiten*), 23 f. 210 f.
Dromedary, 256
Duke of Wellington, Field Marshal Arthur Wellesley (1769–1852), 300
Durusha, prince of Kadesh, 277

E
Earrings, 232
Eastern Zhou period (770–256 BCE), 232
Eder, Christian, 20, 31
Three–dimensional animal style objects, 238
Ehelolf, Hans (1881–1939), 5, 89
El Kurru, 75
Elephants, 264
Eleutheros River, 288, 291, 297; valley, 290, 301
Eleutheros Valley, 3
Elizabeth I (1533–1603), *246*
Elm, 249, 251–253
Emmer wheat (*Triticum turgidum dicoccoides*), *291*, 295
Endurance riding, 257
Epimakhov, Andrey V., 49
Equestrian military training of cavalry regiment, 256
Equestrian Neighbours of the Shang, 207–210
Equid control techniques, 152
Equines, 33, 275, 287; equine physiology, 287
Erickson, John, 293
Ermitage Museum, St. Petersburg, 151
Etruria, 11; chariots, 255, 260–262
Etruscan, bronze chariot from Monteleone, 189; chariots, 258; tumuli, 11
Eurasian steppe region, 32
European cavalry of the Early Modern Period (sixteenth and seventeenth centuries), 282
Experimental archaeology, 4, 6, 61, 86, 116, 130, 132, 245 ff., 255 ff.

F
Fabrics, netted, 75
Faience, 231
Fan–bearer, 73

Farmers, of the Carpathian–Danube region, 152
Fatigue, 282
Fatyanovo culture (ca. 2800–1700 BCE), 207
Feathers, ostrich, 295
Feldman, Marian H., 103–105
Felloe, 30, 267
Femur, 141, 143, 146
Feudalistic structures in the Ancient Near East, 19
Fezzan (southern Tunisia), *256*
Fibres, 116, 248 f.
Firewood, 223
Fishhook, 144
Fishing, 126
Flags, 216, 220
Florence chariot, 17, 33, 61, 246–248
Flying gallop, 264, 266
Foal, 75, *78*, *114*
Fodder, 69, 73, 287
Foot–soldier, 221, 278–282, 286, 293 f., 296 f., 299 f., 302
Forelock, 187
Forschungsgemeinschaft Deutsches Ahnenerbe e.V., 21, 23
Forrer, Emil (1894–1986), *91*
Fort Riley (Kansas), 79
Francis, Dick (1920–2010), 76
Franck, David, 255, 263
French Equestrian Federation, 257
French legionaries, 264
French automobile terminology, 35 f.
Frontal traction, 258, 266
Full quadrant of learning, 75
Funerary, chariots, 237; complexes, 169; goods, 76, 238; monument Igel (Austria), 262; myth, 49; objects, 231; offerings, 127; practices, 11, 127; processions, 224; ritual, 105, *114*, 126, 128, 132, 138
Füzesabony culture, 169

G
Gabriel, Richard, 280, 282, 287, 298
Gallo–Roman, harness, 263; vehicles, 262
Gallop, 222, 256, 261 f., 264, 266, 268, 278, 280, 282, 292 f., *294*, 296, 302 f.
Gansu Province, 200, 231, 237, 239
Gardel, Gabriel, 264
Gârla Mare (Žuto Br) culture, 106–109
Gazelle, 63
GCV Ground Combat Vehicles, 6 f., 273–276
ge blades, 199
Genetics, 104, 179
Geraki (Laconia), excavation lead by J. H. Crouwel (retired), 3, 11
Ghat (Libya), 256
Giraffes, 264
Glass, 62, 231, 233
Glue, 219 f., 246, 253
Godunov, Boris (1552–1605), *246*
Goh, Wei Jun, 276, 305
Gold, 223, 231, 233, 236 f.; death mask, 171; figurine of goddess from the Metropolitan Museum, 92; flakes decorating the rotted wooden whip, 209; foil, 62, 238, 246; gold foil tigers, 236; gold and silver over wooden horse model, 239; golden horse image on the hat of the occupant of the tomb of the golden warrior, 238; golden warrior from the Issyk Kurgan, 236, 238; openworks design, 233; ornaments, 232 f., 234 (human–faced–shaped), 234, 238 f.; plaques, 232, 236, 238; ring, 171, 234; sheets, 63; yoke saddle decorated with, 233
Goldsmith, 236
Gonur tepe, 179, 190,
Gonzaga family of Mantua, importing Barbs and breeding them for racing, *67*
Gorelik, Mikhail V., 126
Grain–pounders, 220
Grand Coachman (*taipu* 太僕), 219
Grand Stables, 219
Grassland, 126
Grease, 219 f., 226
Great armoury of the Western Han dynasty, 216
Greco–Persian wars, 188
Greenhalgh, P. A. L., 275
Griffons, 103
Grigoriev, Stanislav, 32, 49, 53 f.
Grinder, 144
Grinding stone, 138 f., 143, 145
Grisone, Federico (16th century Italy), 69
Groom, 67–69, 73, 76–78, 112
Grooming, 76
Ground Combat Vehicles. See GCV.
Günther, Hans Friedrich Karl (1891–1961), 25
Güterbock, Hans Gustav (1908–2000), 89, 91–95
Gustav Adolf of Sweden (1594–1632), 79
Guyuan 固原, 236

H
Haas, Volkert, 98
Halab. See Aleppo.
Half–turn of chariots. See Caracole.
Hallstatt culture, 115, 246, 267
Halters, 75
Hammer, 285; porphyrite, 139; hammered gold and silver foil, 238; gold or silver sheeting, 237
Hammer–and–anvil tactical scheme, 290
Ḥammurapi of Babylon, 26, 168
Han capital of Chang'an, modern Xian, Shaanxi Province, 220, 223
Han Chang'an Armoury Inventory, 220 f.
Han Dynasty (202 BCE–220 CE), 216–218, 220–226, 258, 262
Hančar, Franz (1893–1968), 19, 24, 26
Handler, 69, 71
Ḥanigalbat, *16*
Harappa, 179
Harnessing systems, 11 f., 183, 208, 258 f., 267 f.; Gallo–Roman, China, 262 f.; resembling that of Tassili depictions, 258, 265
Harpoon, 144
Hartebeest, 63
Harvey, Stephen, 245

Hatti, 105, 273, 284, 289, 301
Hatvan culture, 105, 108
Hauer, Jakob Wilhelm (1881–1962), 18
Hawkins, J. David, 96
Head poles, 70, 84
Headstall, 116, 162, 199 f., 201–203, 206 f., 266
Heat bending, wood, 248
Helck, Wolfgang (1914–1993), 19
Hettema, Hylke, 68
Hieroglyphic Luwian inscriptions, 69
Himmler, Heinrich (1900–1945), 21, *23*, 25
Historical Records, 222; (*Shi ji* 史記) of Sima Qian 司馬遷, 215, 239
Historical–Comparative Indo–European Linguistics, 4, 30, 35; methodological boundaries, 29
Hisuwa–festival, 98
Hitler, Adolf (1889–1945), 21, 23
Hittite, army at Kadesh, *285*, 286, 288–290, 304; cuneiform tablet (KUB 20.76), 5, 89 ff.; classification as an Indo–European language, 16, 22, 23, 36; Egyptian artists depiction of Hittite horses, 72; horse training texts, 15 f.; Indo – Aryan and Hittite in the context of horses and chariots, 20; literature, 17; personal name, 20; paleography in dating Hittite texts, *90*; scouts, 290 f., 293 f.; Spearmen, 297, 299 f.; Storm God mounting his two–wheeled vehicle, 89 ff.; sun goddess, 90.
Hittite Three–Man Chariot, 277, 285 f., 289–296, 298, 300; and 'third man' armed with a spear, 285; changing role in chariot warfare, 283; design, 291, 294 f., 305; number of Hittite chariots, 285
Hoard, 115; from Bækkedal, 116; from Cioclovina, 112
Holocene, 104
Homer, stating that chariot spokes are made from vinestocks, 251
Homeric epics, 22, 261
Homs Gap, 290 f.
Homs, 273
Hook, 189, 232; bronze, 138; fishhook, 144
Horse, Amenhotep II feeding his horse, 74, 78; banning the use of horses to 'open up fields' (ploughing), 234; behaviour, 67–71; 74, 77, 77–79 (controlling horse behaviour in the context of Ma'at), 256, 267, 278, 294, *296*; breeding, 16 f., 20, 23, 68, 103–105, 224; bones, 53, 125, 128, 132, 137; 139 ff., 208; skeletons, 31, 48 f., 53, 112–114, 116, 123, 128, 132, 134, 137 ff., 151; care, 67 ff.; colour, *18*, 67, 104; decoration, *18*, 83–87 (Egyptian 'check rowel'), 187, 191, 239; depictions and figurines of horses, 71, 73 (Amarna); 72 (Karnak); 179 ff. (on Central Asian rock art); 181 (Early Sarmatian wooden comb); 180 (horse figurine from the Buzykai river valley in Bashkiria, Russia); 74 (ostraca and ceramics); 74 (from the temple of Taharqa now in the Ashmolean Museum, Oxford); 48 (Tell es–Sweyhat); 75 (on a box from the Tomb of Tutankhamun); 191 (Western Zhou, bronze plaque, Metropolitan Museum of Art, New York); 239 (horse from Berel with wooden recurved horns like ibex); deity, 218; foal, 75, *78*, *114*; gear, 12, 114, 116 f.; discussion of horse harnessing in Slavic studies, 52 f.;

horse–human relationships, 5, 67, 71, 80; horsemen, 280 (Norman); 204 (in the Spanish tradition), 75 (in Nubia); 86, 286 (Jean Spruytte); 279 (Porus dispatched mounted horsemen against the Macedonian army); 257 (in the Sahara); keeper, 75; Icelandic horse, 263; introduction to the ancient Near East, 16, 21 f.; managers, 105; mane, 67, 190, 199, 236; mare, *78*, 79, 224 f., 277, *294*; horse–chariot–complex, 103; horse (–chariot) pits, 210 f.; horse–and–chariot pits in China, 201 f., 206, 209; paired horse burials, 106, 113–117; pierced by one or more spears, 278; pink skin, 74; as an element of personal names, 18, 27; Przewalski's horses, 104, 129, 182, 18; riding, 21–23, 33, 35, 53, 69, 104, 112, 114, 117, 123, 130, 199 f., 206–211; sacrifices, 6, 134, 143, 201, 208, 215; skull, 31 f., *114*, 128, 141, 143, 146 f., 151, 235; terms for horse in ancient languages (Vedic, Avestan, Mycenaean, Greek, Latin, Gallic, Old Irish, Old English), 19 f., 28 f.; trading, 105; horse trainer, (LU*aššuššanni*) from the land of Mittani, *16*, 17, 20; terms for horse in Proto–Indo–European, Indo–Iranian, Indo–Aryan, Ugaritic, Egyptian, 19 f., 28–30; training and treatment of chariot horses in ancient Egypt, 67 ff.; Scythian, 103; winged, 103; young horses, 70 (training system), 78 (scene in the tomb of Ipuya). See also Domestication of Horses.
Horseback riding. See Riding.
Horseflies, 69
Hrozný, Bedřich (1893–1951), 22
Huaiying, Chang, 204, 206
Huan 洹 River, 200
Hub, 125, 185, 231, 233 f., 245–248, 268, 278; 31 (from Krivoe Ozero, Kazakhstan); 29 f. (reconstructed *termini technici* in Proto–Indo–European)
Humidity, 249
Huns, 187
Hunting, 4, 34, 48, 63, 67, 74 f., 103, 105, 107, 126, 180, 182, 184, 186, 188, 189, 191, 216, 221, 234, 264, 267
Hurrian–Aryan symbiosis, of horses and chariots as posulated by Fritz Schachemeyr, 19, 26
Hüseyindede vase A (Çorum province), 97
Hüttel, Hans–Georg, 30, 36, 105, 111–114, 117, 151
Hwang, Ming–chorng, 202 f., 206 f.
Hydaspes (modern Jhelum), 279
Hyksos, 25, 27 f., 30, 86, 104, 274

I

Iberia, 104, 251
Ibex, 74, 103, 236–239
Idea of sport and speed for chariot drivers (*Sport– und Schnelligkeitsgedanke*), *19*, 27
Ikea, 253
Ilek River, 149
Ili River, 238
Imamkulu relief, 89, 93 f.
Imprints, partial wheel in Sintashta, 33, 48 ff., 125, 127 f., 130–133, 137, 140, 143–146
Indo–Aryan, 15 ff.; defined as a Dialect group of Aryan (Indo–Iranian), *15*; esteem of horses and chariots, 20; horse–and–chariot–ideology, 31; numerals for rounds

horses are running, 17; personal names with the element 'horse'; 18, 27; *termini technici*, 15 ff.
Indo–Iranian, *15*, *17*, 20
Indus culture, 104
Infantry, 79, 215 f., 273 ff. (chariot forces vs. infantry and infantry support). See also Red Army Rank Riders (*tankodesantniki*).
Inlays, semi–precious stones, 62; turquoise, 234
Iron, 231–233; axle on bronze wagon model, 115; cast iron ploughshares, 226; mouthpiece, 116; tools, 220; tyre, *246*, 267
Iron Age, 5, 11, 30, 91, 93 ff.; 103, 106, 108, *114*, 115, 237, 278
Iron Curtain, 31
Iron Triangle, 6, 273, 275 f., 304
Iron Trinity, 6, 275
Ishim Basin, northern Kazakhstan, 138
Ishim River, 137, 148
Isserson, Georgii (1898–1976), 294
Issyk–Kul, southeastern Kazakhstan, 237 f.
Issyk Kurgan, 236, 238
Ivory, 151, 171 f., 252
Izbitser, Elena, 32

J

Jade, horses from the tomb of Fu Hao, 199 f.; objects, 204; symbolic offering, 206
Jaimiṇīya-Brāhmaṇa, 19
Jankuhn, Herbert (1905–1990), 23
Jasper grinding stone, 139
Javelin, 48, 187, 189, 278, 280, 285 f., 301, 303 f.
Jawbone, 143, 146
Jensen, Peter (1861–1936), 16
Jerusalem, 249 f.
jing luche (井鹿車), 227
Junger Banner in Inner Mongolia, 239

K

Kadesh, City of, 273, 284, 293, 302 f. See also Battle of Kadesh.
Kakovatos, tholos, 170, 172, 177 f.
Kamenka settlement Eastern Crimea, 166, 177
Kamenka–Liventsovka group, 166
Kamennyi Ambar 5 cemetery, 32, 126 f., 130, 132, 138–140, 187
Kammenhuber, Annelies (1922–1995), *16*, 19, 21, 24
Kappzaum, 33
Karagaily–Ayat River, 138
Karasuk culture (ca. 1400–1000 BCE); graves (Khara Khaya burial grounds in Tyva), 179
Karasuk (Begazy–Dandybai) pictorial traditions, 179, 192
Karkamish, *91*, 93 ff.
Karnak, 71 f.
Kassite period, 22
Keena, Joshua, 304 f.
Keenan, Jeremy, 267
Kemp, Barry, 73
Kendall, Timothy, *16*

Kesselwagen from Bujoru, 115 f.
Khorsabad, 17
Kikkuli (horse trainer from the Land of Mittani), 16 f., 20, 23
Kingdom of Amurru, 284, 304
Kingdom of Yan, 190
Kneeling running (*Knielaufschema*), 91
Knife, with an animal–head pommel, 201; bronze, 138, 141, 144, 146; metal, 139, 143
Knightly nobility (*Ritteradel*) of the Near Eastern and Egyptian chariot drivers and charioteers, 19 f., 23, 28
Köster, August (1873–1935), 26
Koksu River (southern Kazakhstan), 183 f.
Komarov culture, 113
Komarovka, bank; cemetery, 134; kurgan 152, 177
Kosintsev, Pavel A., 129, 168
Krater, in Ugarit imported, 105
Krivoe Ozero (Southern Ural), Cemetery, 31, 34, 48, 50, 125, 127–132, 134, 141 f.
Kültepe, *20*, 22, 33
Kunz, Jürgen, 266–268
Kurgan, 32, 50 f.; 129 f., 132, 137–142, 146–149, 159–168, 184, 187, 232, 236, 238; interpretation of the vehicles from Kurgan Tyagunova Mogila and the Bolshoi Ipatovskiy kurgan in the North Caucasus, 51 f.; List of Cheekpieces Grouped According to Archaeological Cultures and Sites, 176–178
Kurruḫanni, *16*
Kuzmina, Elena E., 153, 203, 207 f.

L

La Tène elite cremation burial, 12
Lacquer, black, 233 f.; lacquering, 235
Lacquerware, *237*
Ladder, 221
Lake Homs, 284, 290 f.
Lake Van, 249
Lance, 264
Lao Ai, Lord Shang in the state of Qin in 338 BCE, 222
Lateral projection (*Zapfen*), 111
Leather, 4, 61–64; bridles, 208 f.; of American Indians, *116*; casings, 64; curtain, *217*; halter (modern), 266; as integral part of chariot technology, 61; leatherwork, 70; masks, 238; nave sleeves, 62; original samples from the New Kingdom, 63; pad, *86*; rope, 116; scales or lamellae, 280; skullcaps, 280; straps, 116; thongs, 83, 209; tyre, 142, 266. See also Rawhide and Tano Chariot.
Leclerc de Hautecloque, Philippe (1902–1947), general, 256
Legrand, Sophie, 208
Leopard, 221, representation of a snow leopard jumping upward in Issyk, 238
Leopard, skin, 62
L'Èperon d'Argent ('Silver Spur'), 257
Levant, 30, 103 f., 105, 172
Lhote, Henri (1903–1991), 264, 266 f.
Libya, 75, 256, *261*, 266, 268

Lidar Höyük, 246, 249
Linchpin, 131, 206, *266*
Linear–B tablets, 104
Linguistic palaeontology, 29
Lion, 79, 89, 236
List of Cheekpieces Grouped According to Archaeological Cultures and Sites, 176–178
Littauer, Mary A. (1912–2005), 3 f., 11 f., *70*, 84, 86 f., 103, 206, 246, 255, 259, 268 f.; papers at the at the Museum of the Horse archives (Kentucky), 255
Lixian 礼县, County in southeastern Gansu, 239
Liye (Qianling County) hoard, 220
Liye archive, 224, 225
Loess Highland, 200, 208, 210
Longshan Mountain, 231
Looters, 143
Louvre, 93
Lubrication, 219
Lucius Columella, 3
Luwian, 89, 98 f.
Luxury objects, 231, 240, 293; royal chariots, 87, 239 f.

M
Mace, 83, 96, 138 f., 186; mace god, 96; heads, 49, 127, 146
Macedonian, army, 279; foot–soldiers, 279; infantry, 278; phalanx, 278 f.
Mahābhārata, 48
Mair, Victor, 209 f.
Majiayuan, 6, 231 ff.; cemetery, 237, 239; chariots, 231 ff.; elite, 231; tombs, 231 f.
Major Military Innovation (MMI), 274, 306
Malatya, relief, 89, 91, 93–97
Man–of–the–Storm–God, 98
Mandibles, 133, 144
Männerbund. See Brotherhood.
Mantua. See Gonzaga Family.
Makarowicz, Przemysław, 113
Malov, Nikolay M., 166
Maoqinggou 毛庆沟 culture, 232
Map, of spoked wheel models, images of chariots, paired horse burials, Middle Bronze Age and Late Bronze Age/Early Iron Age sites, 106
Maran, Joseph, 16, 21
Marble, 210; tile, 147
Mari letters, 26
Marlstone, 146
Marshall, Michael, *263*
Mass panic, 295
Mauretania, 256
Mayer, Walter (1941–2019), 285
Mayrhofer, Manfred (1926–2011), 19, 21
MDA (Multivariate Data Analysis), 157, 159
Medveditsa river, south Saratov region, 168
Megiddo, 188, 283
Méhariste, 256 f., 268
Meissner, Bruno (1968–1947), 26
Melee phase of the battle, 302
Menena, chariot driver of Ramesses II, 297 f.

Mercenaries, 288; '*Reisige*', 16
Metallurgy, 4, 134
Metz, Karen, 280, 282
METT–TC: Mission, Enemy, Terrain and weather, Troops and support available – Time available, Civilians, 287, 306
Meyer, Eduard (1855–1930), 15, 17 f., 21–24, 26 f.
Miniature bronze chariots, 216
Minoan culture, 11, 16, 22, 27, *28*, 89
Mironov, Nikolaj D. (1880–1936), 20
Mitanni. See Mittani.
Mittani, *15*, *16*, 17, *18*, 20, 27, 105, 179, 253
Mizoguchi, Koji, 200
MMI (Major Military Innovation), 274, 306
Mobile force de frappe, 296
Mobility, 7, 36, 209, *256*, 262, 273, 282, 285, 287, 292, 300; Egyptian chariot design: emphasis on vehicle mobility, 304 f.; mobility, the Iron Triangle and tactics, 275–277
Model T (Ford), 274
Modern horsemanship. See Grisone and Pluvinel.
Mongolian and Russian Altai (Kalbak Tash and Tsagan–Salaa), 189
Mongolian Steppes and the Loess Highland, 208
Moorey, Roger (1937–2004), 275
Moortgat–Correns, Ursula (1920–2008), 89, 91–94
Mortuary practice, 235, 238
Mountain sheep, 183 f.
Mouthpiece, 116, 129, 139, 141, 147, 151–156, 162, 167–169, 172, 200, 202 f., 203–210
Mozi (Philosopher of the Warring States period), 218
Mukadiyah stream near Kadesh, 284, 290, 292, 294–296, 300 f., 304
Mule, 85, 144, 147, *258*, 262 f., 286 f., *294*
Multi–Roller Ware Culture (now named Babino), 113
Multivariate Data Analysis (MDA), 157
Mureş–Chernyakhov culture, 113
Musée Saharien, Le Crès, Montpellier, France, 265, 268
Mut–is–Content (name of Ramesses chariot horse), 298. See also Victory–in–Thebes.
Muwatalli II (1295–1272 BCE), during the Battle of Kadesh, 284 ff. See also Battle of Kadesh.
Muzzle, 71, 74, 183, 186
Mycenae/Mycenean, acropolis; chariots, 28, 50; cheekpieces, 25, 151, 158, 170–173, 177 f.; culture, 27; find from Mycenae in Sintashta burials, 125; frescoes of the thirteenth century BCE from Tiryns, 249; 'House of Shields'; alleged Mycenaean–Indo–Aryan contacts, 28; ivory; monuments, 26; pictorial pottery, 3; princes, *28*; Shaft Grave Circle, *27*, 35, 153; word for horse, 29
Mythology, 11, 180

N
Nachod, Hans (1885–1958), 17
Nagel, Wolfram (1923–2019), 19 f., 31, 34
Naharain, 253
Nail, 141 f., 145, 233, 267
National Socialist Ideology (*nationalsozialitische Ideologie*), 23

National Socialist Racial Doctrine (*nationalsozialistische Rassenlehre*), 25
Nave, *29*, 31, 34, 48 f., 52, 64, 105, 115 f., 125, 128, 130 f., 141 f., 144, 245; hoops, 62, *266*; sleeves, 61 f.
Nearin, arrival of the Nearin battlegroup at the Amun camp of Ramesses II., 284, *286*, 288, 297, 300–303
Neck yoke, 183, 258, 260–262, 264, 276
Neckstrap, 84, 86, 224, 258, 260–262
Needham, Joseph (1900–1905), 258
Negative reinforcement (removal something unpleasant) as part of horse training, 68, 75
Nemesnádudvar wagon model, 105
Neša, *274*
Nestor, Ion (1905–1974), 11
Network, 104, 207, 217, 22, 238 f., 245, 268
Ney, Michel, Marchal of the Empire (1769–1815), 279
Nimrud, 17, 249
Nineveh, 17, 249
Nizhniy Toguzak River, 146
Nizhnyaya Krasavka II settlement, 163, 168, 177
Nomadic dress, 239
Nomadic steppe groups, 190
Noncombatant support personnel, 286
Norbert Schimmel Trust, Metropilitan Museum of Art (New York), 92
Nordic Race (*Nordische Rasse*), 23
Norman cavalry, 280 f.
North Africa. See Spruytte, Jean and Sahara.
North Mausoleum at Ghirza Libya, 261
Noseband, 72, 151, 154, 156, 162, 164–166, 168–172, 207
Noua culture, settlement Trușești eastern Romania, 11, 113 f.
NSD–Dozentenbund (*Nationalsozialistischer Deutscher Dozentenbund*, The National Socialist German Lecturers League), 25
Nubia, chariot drawn by bridled cattle, *85*; and Kushites, 75; skilled horsemen, 75; temples, 75
Numerals, Indo–Aryan for 'round', 16, *17*
Nuoffer (*1867), Oskar, 17
Nūrestānī, *15*
Nuzi, *16*, *18*

O

Oarța de Sus (Wietenberg culture phase II, ca. 2000–1750 BCE), 110, 112 f., 114, 116, 169, 177
Oettinger, Norbert, 20
Onager, 153. See also Donkey and Horse.
Operating concept for two–man chariots, 276, 305
Oracle bone inscriptions, 190, 200, 211
Ordinance of the Bureau of Granaries in the Capital Region, 223
Ordinances (ling 令), 219
Ordinances on 'Side' Gold and Cloth of the Governor of the Capital Area, 223
Orontes River, 274, 284, 289, *292*, 293, 295, 300, 304
Osteological collections, 107
Ostraca, 75
Otten, Heinrich (1913–2012), 91
Oued Allarama, 266 f.

Outrigger, 187, 260
Ovicaprids, *114*
Ox, 6; ox carts, 98, 224, 226 f. (niuche 牛車), 224; shoulder–blades (used for oracle bone inscriptions), 190

P

Paheri, 78
Pakistan, 33, 104
Paleographic criteria (Hittite cuneiform texts), 91
Palisade, chariots avoiding driving into palisades, 297; of shields around the Amun camp, 289
Pan Geng, King, Shang dynasty (died 1375 BCE), 200
Papyrus, 78; Papyrus Lansing, 78; referencing the anointing of chariot, 74
Pars pro toto, grave good representing a chariot, 31 f.; principle, 132 f.; for wheeled vehicle, 99; terms, 29
Paso llano (Peruvian), horse gait, *262*
Pastoralists on Chinas Inner Asian Frontier, 232
Patron deity, master carpenter Lu Ban, 218
Pazyryk (Altai Mountains), 180, 232, 235 f.
PCA (Principal Component Analysis), 157
Pearson Correlation Coefficient, 157
Peng, Wang, 207
Penner, Silvia, *27*, 35
Persia/Persians, 20, 179, 187 f., 278
Persson, Axel W. (1888–1951), 27
Pesditschek, Martina, 25
Pestle, 138, 140, 144, 147
Petroglyphs, 5, 47 ff., 131 f., 179 ff.
Petrovka and Alakul' periods, 138, 147
Phalanx, 275, 277 f., 280–282, 286, 299, 301 f.; of marching gods at Yazılıkaya, 92
Physical and psychological strains of battle, exhaustion of both mind and body, 282
Piankhi (Piye), Victory stela, 75
Piggott, Stuart (1910–1996), 19, 79, *274*, 275
Piliny culture, 108
Pit Grave and Catacomb cultures/Afanasievo tradition, 51
Plaque, 111, 125, 129, 138 f., 152 f., 173, *183*, 188 f., 191, 202; carnelian plaque of Amenhotep II, 53; plaque cheekpieces, 202 f., 206–208, 232 f., 236–238, 263
Ploughing, 226, 258, *261*
Plumed headdress of horses, 276, 295 f.
Plumes, 76
Plurale tantum (in Hittite cuneiform text), 98
Pluvinel, Antoine (1552–1620), 69
Podhajsky, Alois (1898–1973), 69, 71, 77
Podoved, Viacheslav A., 53
Poem of Pentaur, Egyptian source of the Battle of Kadesh), 283, 286, 289. See also Bulletin.
Pokrovskaya cluster cheekpieces, 159 f., 163, *164–166*, 168 f., 171
Pole, 29 f, 32, 49 ff., 62, 64, 70, 84–87, 98, 109, 127, 130–132, 134, 141, 143, 182–185, 187, 189, 221, 224, *225*, 233, 235 f., *249*, 258 f., 261, *262*, 264, 266–267, 275
Poliakov, Léon (1910–1997), *15*
Polyany settlement, 168

Ponies, 72, *75*, 78, 84–87
Pontic–Caspian steppes, 51
Pontic Yamnaya and Catacomb Culture, 32
Porsche, 274
Positive punishment (application something unpleasant) as part of horse training, 68, 72 f., 75
Positive reinforcement (reward) as part of horse training, 68, 74, 77
Potapovka, 129, 154, 158 f., 166–168, 172, 176 f.; cluster, 163 f., 203, 206
Pottery, 30, 112–114, 126, 220, 232; Babino and Srubnaya pottery, 168; figurines, 216; Mycenaean pictorial, 3; Transdanubian Encrusted Pottery, 106 f.
Principal Component Analysis (PCA), 157
Proto–chariots, chariots labeled as, 248
Proto–Indo–European(s), 16 f., 19, 21 f.; archaeology, 29; alleged Proto–Indo–European chariots, 35; homeland discussion, 15, 35; reconstructed terms, 29 f.
Protomes, bird–shaped, 116; bovid, 105
Przewalski horse, 104, 129, 182, 188
Przybyła, Marcin M., 113
Psaliy, 151
Ptahhotep, 77
Pulley wheel, 216
Punishment and reward in horse training: historical context (application of something unpleasant), 67, 69 f.

Q
Qin and Han China, 215 ff.
Qin, capital of Xianyang in the northwest, modern Shaanxi Province, 219, 221; control of foreign interaction, invaluable technology and the ability to restrict access to knowledge and exchange with the outside world, 240; road system, 222; statute on Government Service, 222; vehicles, 216
Quadriga, *86*, 112, 183, 187, 190 f., 261
Quintus Curtius Rufus, 279
Quiver, 63 f., 183, 186–188, 296, 301

R
Racial studies and studies of antiquity (*Rassenkunde und Altertumsforschung*), 25
Racially ideological world view (*rassenideologisches Weltbild*), 24 f.
Racing, cars, 61; chariot racing, 4 f., 16, *17*, 23, 34 f., 48, 103, 107, 125 f., 261 f., 264; horse racing, *67*; at speed along the flanks of the fleeing troop mass, 282
Radiocarbon chronology, see Calibrated 14C data.
Raepsaet, Georges, 262
Railings, see Chariot.
Ramesses II (c. 1303–1213 BCE), at the Battle of Kadesh, 283 ff.; counterattacking the besieging Hittite chariotry, 297, 300, 303; executing officers for cowardice, 304; his favourite horses horse 'Victory in Thebes and 'Beloved of Mut', 68, 74, 298; being fed in his presence, 78; number of his chariot forces, *286*; praising his chariot horses after the Battle of Kadesh, 68. See also Amun Camp of Ramesses II at Kadesh and Battle of Kadesh.
Rams, 103, 221

Rassenkunde und Altertumsforschung (racial studies and studies of antiquity), *25*
Ratio of chariots to infantry, 278
Rawhide, 4, 61 ff., 142, 246, 248, *266*; Bands, 268; bindings, 247, 268; strap, 248; strips, 185; tyre, *115*, 246, 266. See also Leather.
Reconstruction of the Eurasian war chariot from Sintashta, 50 f.
Red Army Tank Riders (*tankodesantniki*) during a battle with German forces on the Eastern Front in World War II, 293. See also Tank *desant*.
Reins, 70, 72 f., 84–86; 97 f., 109, 116, 129, 151, 183 ff., 204, 233, 260, 262, 264, 266, 276, 279 f., 298
Auxiliary reining system, 70
Reisige. See Mercenaries.
Rekhyt bird, 77
Relaxation for horses, 76
Relay system, *258*
Remains of chariot boxes from a royal tomb at Xibeigang, Anyang, 201
Remudas (herds), 286
Repair, chariot production and repair in Chinese legal and administrative documents, 218 ff.; cheekpieces, 146, 164, 171
Kazakhstan, 4, 15, 17, 21, 31, 53, 110 f., 126, 128 f., 134, 137 f, 142, 148, 153 f., 156, 159 f., 162 f., 181 f., 183 f., 187 f., 190, 236–239
Restoration laboratory Ostrov Kirim, 182
Rhinoceros, 264
Richard II, 67, 76, 78
Rider, 35, 69–71, 74, 77, 103, 123, 204, 207, 255, 279, 291, 293 f.
Riemschneider, Margarete (1899–1985), 91
Rigveda, 16 f., 18, 26, 48, *50*
Rim, 29, 31, 52, 96, 127, 130, 142, 144, 147, 154, 157–170, 172, 245–247, 266–268, 280
Rings for reins and special devices preventing harness straps, 186
Rites of Zhou or Offices (Zhou guan 周官), 215 f.
Road systems, 104
Rock carvings. See Petroglyphs.
Rock cut channel moulds, 249
Rock paintings, North Africa and Sahara, 255–258, 263–265, 267 f., 269
Rogozhinskiy, Alekei, 182
Roman archaeology, 11
Roman Empire, 11, 152, 258, 260 f.
Roman provinces, 11
Rong (Xirong, Shanrong) and Di groups, 189; Rong pastoralist group, 239; Rong 戎 leadership, 231
Rope, 70, 74 f., 78, 116, 183, 203 f.
Rosellini, Ippolito (1800–1843), *265*, *267*
Roslyakova, N. V., 168
Royal burials, Egypt, 104
Royal hunting, Egypt, 75
Royal Navy, 251
Royal Ontario Museum, 209
Royal propaganda, Egypt, 104
Royalty controlled chariots, 105
Runners, 223; chariot runners 280 f., 285, 298, 300

S

Sabotage, 75
Sacrificed animals, 127, 144; horses, 125 f., 128 f., 131–133, 156, 238
Sahara, petroglyphs depicting chariots. See Rock paintings, North Africa and Sahara.
Saka, 187, 237
Salonen, Armas (1915–1981), 19
Samara River, 168
Samara Volga region, Russia, 152, 159, 166
Samashev, Zenola, 182
Sântana de Mureș–Chernyakhov culture, 113
Santosuosso, Antonio, 288
Sărata Monteoru culture/settlement, 110–112, 171, 177
Saratov Volga region, 166
Sardinia, 299
Sarmatian period in the western part of the Kazakh steppe, 180; early Sarmatian wooden comb with double–sided chariot composition, 181
Sarmatians, 187
Sauvage, Caroline, 103–105
Scale-armour, 295, 299
Scapula, 84, 149, 259 f., 262
Schachermeyr, Fritz (1895–1987), chariotry research, 16 ff., 21, esp. 24–28
Schivelbusch, Wolfgang, 295
Schlerath, Bernfried (1924–2003), 29 f.
Schliemann, Heinrich (1822–1890), 171
Schrader, Otto (1955–1919), 17
Schulman, Alan R. (1930–2000), 281, *286*
Schulz, William, 204
Scribes, China, 223, 225; Hittite, 20
Scythian–Saka animal style, 190
Scythians, 210
Sea Lines of Communication (SLOC), 288, 306
Second Intermediate Period in Egypt, 79
Sedan chair (*jiaoche* 轎車), 218
Segner wheel, 165
Seima–Turbino style, 187 f.
Self-sustaining battlegroups, 287
Seri and Hurri, 97. See also Serisu and Tella.
Serisu and Tella, 98
Services and supply functions in the army, 286
Sewell, Anna (1820–1878), *Black Beauty*, 70
Shabtuna (modern Riblah), 288–291, 302; camp, 289; forest between Shabtuna and Kadesh, *294*; road, 291, 294 f.
Shakespeare, 67 f., *78* 'As You Like It'. See also Richard II.
Shanchengcun, on a possible route by which the Shang elite may have introduced horses, 208
Shang burial contexts, Yinxu phases III and IV, 202
Shang dynasty (also known as the Yin dynasty, 16th–11th centuries BCE), 6, 134, 182, 199 ff.
Shangzunling necropolis, 188
Shaughnessy, Edward, 211
Sheep, 49, 140, 143, 287; big-horned, 238; mountain, 183 f.
Sher, Yakov, 47
Sherden swordsman, cutting off the hand of a Hittite chariot warrior, 299
shi (bushels) of grain, 223
Shield, 181, 278, 280 f., 289, 296 ff.
Shield–Bearer, 279
Shiji 史记 (Historical Records), 239
Shipbuilders, 251
Shosu (Bedouin) tribesmen, 288 f.
Shoulder–Blades, 190
Shoulder strap, 276
Shoulder traction, 258–260, 263 f., 276
Sievers, Wolfram (1902–1948), 23 f.
Silver, 140, 231–233, 239; foil, 236, 238; rings, 234; sheeting, 237; 'Silver Spur'. See l'Èperon d'Argent; silver tigers from Majiayuan, 238
Simpkin, Richard K., 293 f.
Sintashta (southern Russian Urals). See Cemeteries and Chariot.
AMS dating, 179
Situla, 12
Skeleton, animal, 113, *114*; dog, 140; horse, 31, 48 f., 53, 112, 116, 123, 128, 132, 134, 137 f., 143–147, 151, 232; human, 139, 141; wolf, 140
Slingers, 280, 286, 302
SLOC – Sea Lines of Communication, 288, 306
Solar deity in the Andronovo petroglyphs, 190
SS–Sonderkommando Jankuhn (special SS unit Jankuhn), 23
Song dynasty (960–1279 CE), 218
South-pointing chariot (*zhinan che* 指南車), 218
Spanish Riding School, 69
Spearhead, 127, 140, 146
Spiked 'check rowel', 70
Spokes. See Wheel.
Spruytte, Jean (1919–2007), 6, 12, *17*, 70, 72, 84, 85 f., 87, *246*, 248, 255 ff. See also Experimental Archaeology and Chariot Models.
Spurs, 69, 83, 184, 255
Srubnaya culture, 113, 159, 161, 168
SS–Panzer–Division 'Wiking', 23
SS–Standartenführer and General Secretary of the *Forschungsgemeinschaft Deutsches Ahnenerbe e.V.* See Sievers, Wolfram.
SS–Standartenführer, Curator of the AE, Rektor of the *Ludwig–Maximilians–Universität* in Munich. See Wüst, Walther.
Stable, 34, 75 f., 78, 219, 225
Stabsabteilung der Waffen–SS beim Persönlichen Stab Reichsführer–SS, SS–Sturmmann lecturer. See Wiesner, Joseph.
Stag, 103
Stallions, 128, 185
Starčevo–Criș culture, 113
Starke, Frank, 98
Statutes (*lü* 律), 219
Statutes on Checking (Xiao *lü* 效律), 220
Statutes on Hunting of the Major of the Gate Traffic Control Office, 221
Steam bending, of wood, *248*

Steel tension strap, 248
Stephanie, L. E., 151
Steppe, 4, 22, 32, 35 f., 47 ff., 104, 110 f., 117, 126, 128, 152 f., 164, 167, 173, 179 f., 182, 188–190, 199 f., 206–208, 210, 215, 219, 236–238, *274*
Storehouses, 226
Storm God, mounting a vehicle, 89 ff.; on his throne at Alaca Höyük, 92
Studniczka, Franz (1860–1929), 17
Study of chariots/carriages (xueche 學車), 220
Sugar plantations, 76
Sumerian, city–states, 274; pictorial tradition, 190; plural morpheme, 98; terms for chariot/two–wheeler; 16
Surinam, horses, 76
Swarming Egyptian foot soldiers assault Hittite chariots, 300
Swingletree, 261
Swordsmen, 288, 297, 299, 303
Synopsis of the main phases of the Battle of Kadesh, 284

T

Tagar culture (Minusinsk Basin), 189
Taharqa, 74
Taldy River, 142
Tamadjert (Tassili n'Ajjer), 256, 264–268
Tamadjert rock painting, 264 f.
Tank Desant (*tankovyy desant*), 293. See also Red Army Tank Riders (*tankodesantniki*).
Tankodesantniki, Red Army tank riders, 293. See also Red Army Tank Riders.
Tank, *275*, *276*, 287, 293, 296, 302
Tano, Georges, 61
Tano chariot, 61–64
Taohongbala 桃红巴拉 culture, 232
Tarim Basin, 209
Tassili Camel Corps, 256 f.
Tassili n'Ajjer. See Tamadjert.
Taylor, William, 208
Tel Haror, 33, 151–153, 172
Tell es–Sweyhat, 48 f.
Tell Laodiceia, 292
Tell Nebi Mend, 292
Tensioning collar (*collier de serrage*), 265, 268
Tepe Hissar (Tappeh sār, northern Iran), 33, 104
Tepe Sialk (Isfahan Province), 112
Textile, 62, 95, 209, 216, 236, 280
The National Socialist German Lecturers League (*NSD–Dozentenbund, Nationalsozialistischer Deutscher Dozentenbund*), 25
Theban Dynasty, 75
Theban Tombs, TT86 (Valley of the Kings, Tomb of Menkheperraseneb), 245; TT155, Tomb of Intef (reign of Hatshepsut/Thutmoses III), *249*; TT95, Tomb of Meri (reign of Amenhotep II), bending of wood, *249*; Tomb of Ipuja, Saqqara (possibly late 18th Dynasty), bending of pole (?), *249*
Thebes, 17, 33, 68, 75, 78, 170–172, 177, 253, 265, *267*, 276 f., 298
Theodosian Code, 258

Third Man. See Hittite Three–Man–Chariot.
Third Reich, 16, 23 f.
Tholos tomb A at Kakovatos, 172
Three–man vehicle of the Hittites in the Battle of Kadesh. See Hittite Three–Man–Chariot.
Thunderbolts, 96
Thundering, 96, 98
Thutmose III, 277, 279
Thutmose IV, 61, 63
Tianshan 天山 Mountains, 236
Tibia, 143, 146
Tile, 218; marble, 247, quartzite, 147
Timber, 31, 246, 251, 253; fibers, 249; process of bending timber, 248 f.
Timber–Grave cultures (ca. 1800–1200 BCE), *159*, 182, 207
Tin, 231–233
Tjuiu, see Yuya.
Tobol River, 126 138, 140, 142
Tölt (gait), 262
Tomkins, Silvan S., 77
Traction bar, 258, 265–268
Traction, 62, 85, *104*, 107, 114, 152, 208, 216, 256, 258 ff.; frontal, 266
Trade network, 239, 245
Traders, 225
Training, chariot horses, *16*, *17*, 27; Hittite horse training manual, *17*, 20, 67 ff.
Trans–Ural region (Russia), 4, 47 f., 125
Trans–Uralian and North Kazakh chariots, 32
Trans–Uralic steppes, 32 f.
Transcaucasia, 153
Transformation of Cheekpieces Through Centuries in Terms of Cultural–Typological Classification, 172 f.
Travellers, 222, 264
Triandafillov, Vladimir (1894–1931), 294
Trigae, 187, 191
Triumphant advance of the automobile starting in France, 35 f.
Trot (gait), 70, 78, 84, 256, 261 f., *263*, 280, 295
Troy, film, 266
Trzciniec culture, *114*
Tschudi, Yolantha (1925–2011), *267*
Tsimidanov, Vitaliy V., 53
Tukhachevsky, Mikhail (1893–1937), 294
Tumulus culture, 197
Turkomans, 67
Turner, Susan, 72
Turquoise, 231, 234
Tušratta, King of Mittani, 18, 22
Tutankhamun, box with chariot display, 76; chariots, 61–64, 70, 246 f., 253, 266–268; chariot components, 249; check rowel, 83 ff.; wheels, 248 f., 253; Y–shaped objects, 259
TV documentaries, TV6 film about Egyptian chariots (2012), 245
Twelve–Gods relief at Yazılıkaya, 92
Two–Humped camel (Bactrian), 187, 190
Tyre, 62, 115, 142, 246, 266–268

U

Ubagan River, 138
Ugarit, 20, 98, 105
Ui River (Tobol River basin), 126, 140, 147
Ullikummi myth, 97 f.
Ulmus, 251
Ulubai Cemetery (Northern Kazakhstan), 127, 148 f.
Ummān Manda, *16*
Ungnad, Arthur (1879–1945), 26
Untermann, Jürgen (1928–2013), 30
Upper Don region, 165
Upper Xiajiadian type at Nanshan'gen, 190
Ural Mountains, 126
Ural River, 126, 149
Ural steppes, 4, 48
Ural–Kazakhstan steppe, 181, 190
Urartian rock cut moulds, 249
Urhitessub seal impression, 89, *91*, 93–97
Urhitessub/Mursili III (ca. 1274–1267 BCE), 89, 93
Urnfield Period, 106, 112, 115 f.
US cavalry, 79
Usachuk, Anatoliy N., 53, 166, 168
Uzbekistan, 167

V

V–spoked chariot wheel, 246, 248
Valeriu Kavruk (Cavruk), *111*, 114
Valley of the Kings, *267*
Valley of the Nobles on the west bank of the Nile near Luxor, 245
Vărșand, 106, 109
Vatin settlement, 170, 177 f.
Vehicle, agility, 274, 285, 304 f.; architectural hardware, 19, 275 f.; Bull–drawn two–wheeled vehicle, 91, 94 f., 97; design objective hierarchy, 275; firepower, embodied in the warrior–as–archer, 273, 275 f., 278, 285, 304 f.; with scythes attached to the wheel hubs, 278
Veldmeijer, André, 70
Velem Szent Vid, 106, 108
Veľke Raškovce, 106, 108 f.
Velocity, 278, 280
Vertebra, 141, 144, 147 f., 264
Vesely Khuto, 165, 176
Vessels, two–wheeled platform car with spoked wheels depicted on a vessel from eastern Iran, 33
Vetlyanka IV cemetery, 31, 127, 149
Victory stela, 75. See Piankhi (Piye).
Victory–in–Thebes, 298. See also Mut–is–Content.
Vinon sur Verdon (Provence), 257
Vine, 251–253
Vinestocks, 251
Vinogradov, Nikolai B., 31, 48, 50, 131, 134
Viștea, 106
Vocal tone, 70. See Facial expressions.
Volga River, 116, 164, 236
Volga–Don steppe, 104
Volga–Urals, 48, 53, 152 f., 159, 162, 166
Völkischer Beobachter, 25
Von Beckerath, Jürgen (1920–2016), 19
Von Blücher, Gebhard Leberecht (1742–1819), 300
Von Clausewitz, Carl (1780–1831), 277
Von Mercklin, Eugen (1884–1969), 17
Von Soden, Wolfram (1908–1996), 18
Vulnerability to high UV exposure, horses with pink skin, 74

W

Wagon, 4, 11 f., 29–32, 47, 51 f., 97 f., 104–106, 130, 180 f., 187, 258, 263 f., 274
Wagon model, 32 f., 51, 103, 105–109, 114, 116 f., 246; with cauldron from Bujoru with iron axles, 106, 115 f.; from Ciceu Corabia, 105–107; from Dupljaja (attributed to the Gârla Mare culture) 106, 109; from Encs (Hungary), 32; Nemesnádudvar, 105–107
Walled settlement, 126, 142
War goddess, 75
Warfare, 16, 22 f., 28, 30, 48 f., 67, 75, 103, 105, 107, 112, 115, 117, 125 f., 151, 190, 209 f., 216 f., 222, 227, 245, 273, 275, 277, 279 f., 281, 283 f., 287, 291, 294–296, 300–302, 305
Warring States, 6, 180, 188, 210, 215, 217–219, 231, 238
Wass de Czege, Huba, 297
Weaving, 123, 126
Wei River Valley, 231
Weidner, Ernst (1891–1967), 20
Western Han dynasty (202 BCE–9 CE), 216, 226, 262
Western Zhou, 188, 190 f., 202, 210, 215 f., 232
Wheel, 60° V–shape, 250, 252; detached, 301; diameter, 31, 52, 83, 130–133, 137–149, 184 f., 234 f., 238, 245, 248; of large diameter with ten spokes, 185; models, 32 f., 103, 105–108, 114, 117; tracks, 11, 31, 34, 137; wheel–pits/slots, 52, 130, 134, 138–148; spoked wheels, 30–32, 103, 106, 108, 172, 247, 249, 274
Wheelbarrow, carrying a human, 216, 218, 227; known as a "deer cart" (luche 鹿車), 227
Wheelwright, 218 f., 246
Whip, 69, 75, 85, 186 f., 189, 206 f., 209
Whippletree, *261*
Whorl, 83, 139
Wiesner, Joseph (1913–1975), 16–19, 21, 23 f., 26, 112
Wietenberg culture, 106, 108, 110–114
Windpipes, 258
Winged horses, 103
Winckler, Hugo (1853–1914), 17
Withers, 84, 87, 131, 152, 185, 257, 259, 262, 276, 295
Wood/Wooden, decay, 52, 127, 134, 138, 140–144; club, 73, 96, 181 f., 186 f., 191; framework, 61, 64; stirrups, 116; tyre, 267 f.
Woodworking, 126, 199
Wong, Raphael, 236
Written instructions, by Ptahhotep had for young men to ensure their success, 77
Wu, Hsiao–yun, 116, 180
Wu Ding, Late Shang ruler (reign ca. 1258–1200 BCE), 199 f., 202 f., 206–210
Wüst, Walther (1901–1993), 23 f.
Wusun 乌孙 period, 238
Wuzhi Rong 乌氏戎 group, 239

X

Xenophon (ca. 430–355 BCE), 69
Xi Rong 西戎 (Western Rong), 239
Xiaotun, 200–202, 204–206, 209
Xibeigang, 200–202
Xicha, Shanxi, 208
Xinjiang Autonomous Region of the PRC, 179, 190, 200, 203, 208–210, 236 f.

Y

Yamnaya Culture (Pit–Grave), 32, 104, 113, 123, 179
Yan population, 188
Yanghai trousers, 209
Yanglang 杨郎 culture, 232
Yazdepe, 189
Yazılıkaya, 92 f.
Yellow River Valley, 232
Yeshkiolmes ridge, 179, 184–189, 191
Yinxu period, 200, 202 f., 207
Yiqu Rong 义渠戎 (local sub–group of Rong), 239
Yoke, arched, 262; dorsal yoke, 86, 256, 261 f.
Yoke fork, 71, 83–85, 87, *183*, 185, 258–260, 262, 264
Yoke saddle, 3, 30, 185, 187, 233, 236, *259*, 286
Yoke saddle bosses/finials, 105
Yu state at Baoji, Shaanxi, 210
Yuelu hoard, 219, *222* f.
Yuhuangmiao 玉皇庙 culture, *188*, 190, 232
Yuya and Tjuiu chariot, 61, 64

Z

Zardča Khalifa/Zardcha–Khalifa, 35, 167, 177
Zhangjiachuan Hui Autonomous County, Gansu Province, 231, 236, 239
Zhangjiapo (Changan, Shaanxi), 188, 210
Zhangjiashan Tomb no. 247 collection, 220, 223
Zhuangzi, Daoist philosopher, 218
Zhao Zheng shu 趙正書 (Book of Zheng of Zhao), 222
Zheng, King of Qin, 222, 224
Zhou, communities, 187; dynasty (ca. 1045–265 BCE), 6, 180, 187 f., 190 f., 206 f., 209 f., 215 f., 231 f., 234 f., 237–239; ritual system, 239